The
MX Book
of
New
Sherlock
Holmes
Stories

Part LII
The True Sherlock Holmes:
England's Greatest Hero
(1902-1923)

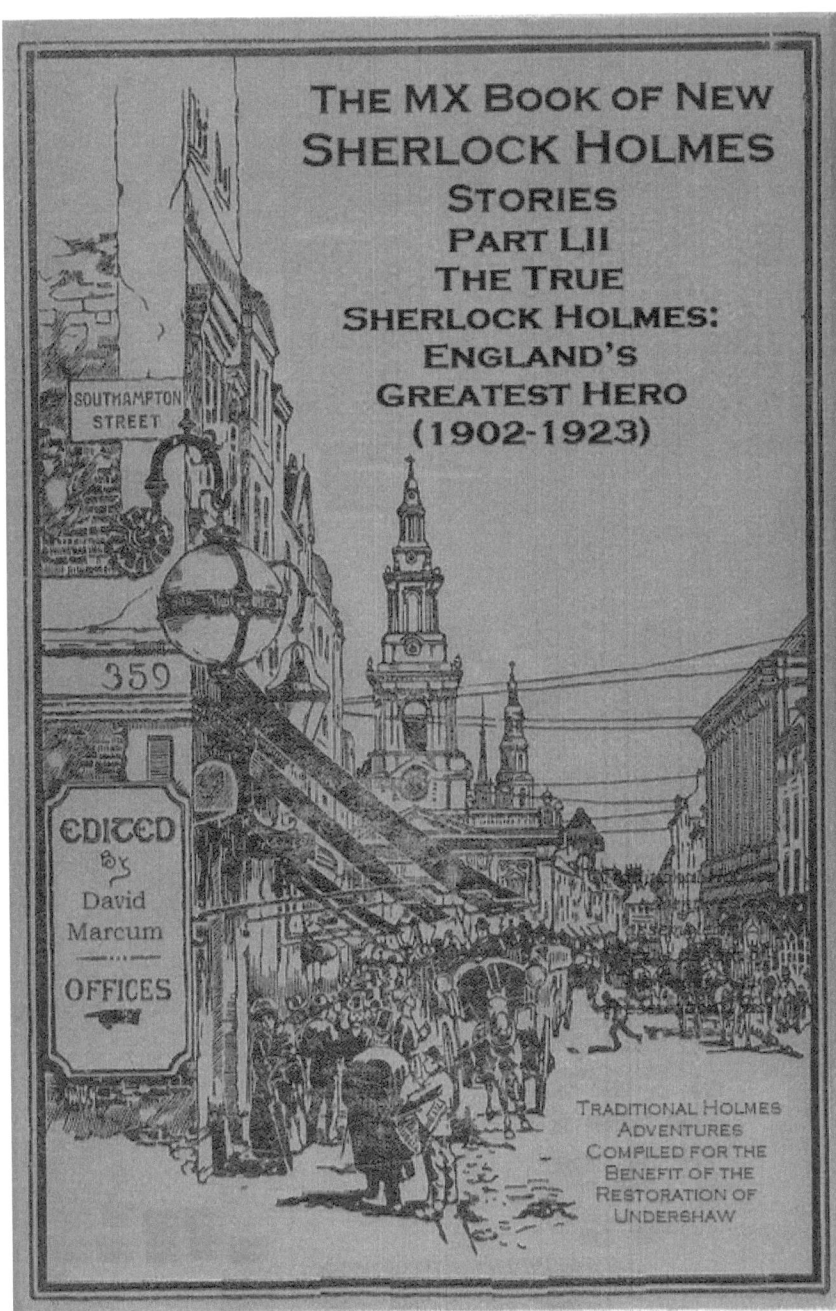

THE MX BOOK OF NEW SHERLOCK HOLMES
STORIES
PART LII
THE TRUE
SHERLOCK HOLMES:
ENGLAND'S
GREATEST HERO
(1902-1923)

SOUTHAMPTON
STREET

359

EDITED
BY
David
Marcum

OFFICES

TRADITIONAL HOLMES
ADVENTURES
COMPILED FOR THE
BENEFIT OF THE
RESTORATION OF
UNDERSHAW

ISBN Hardback 978-1-80424-695-5
ISBN Paperback 978-1-80424-696-2
AUK ePub ISBN 978-1-80424-697-9
AUK PDF ISBN 978-1-80424-698-6

Published in the UK by
MX Publishing
335 Princess Park Manor, Royal Drive,
London, N11 3GX
www.mxpublishing.co.uk

David Marcum can be reached at:
thepapersofsherlockholmes@gmail.com

Cover design by Brian Belanger
www.belangerbooks.com and *www.redbubble.com/people/zhahadun*

Internal Illustrations by Sidney Paget

CONTENTS

Forewords

Adventures

(Continued on the next page . . . .)

(Continued on the next page . . . .)

These additional adventures are contained in

**Part XLIX – The True Mr. Sherlock Holmes:
England's Greatest Hero (1880-1888)**

**Part L – The True Sherlock Holmes:
England's Greatest Hero (1889-1896)**

(Continued on the next page . . . .)

Part LI – The True Sherlock Holmes:
England's Greatest Hero (1897-1901)

(Continued on the next page . . . .)

The MX Book of New Sherlock Holmes Stories
Parts I – LII (2015-2025) contain the following:

(Continued on the next page . . . .)

PART III: 1896-1929

PART IV – 2016 Annual

(Continued on the next page . . . .)

PART V – Christmas Adventures

(Continued on the next page . . . .)

(Continued on the next page . . . .)

PART VII – Eliminate the Impossible: 1880-1891

PART VIII – Eliminate the Impossible: 1892-1905

(Continued on the next page . . . .)

Part IX – 2018 Annual (1879-1895)

(Continued on the next page . . . .)

Part X – 2018 Annual (1896-1916)

Part XI: Some Untold Cases (1880-1891)

(Continued on the next page . . . .)

Part XII: Some Untold Cases (1894-1902)

PART XIII: 2019 Annual (1881-1890)

(Continued on the next page . . . .)

PART XIV: 2019 Annual (1891 -1897)

(Continued on the next page . . . .)

(Continued on the next page . . . .)

Part XVII – Whatever Remains . . . Must Be the Truth (1891-1898)

Part XVIII – Whatever Remains . . . Must Be the Truth (1899-1925)

(Continued on the next page . . . .)

Part XIX: 2020 Annual (1882-1890)

(Continued on the next page . . . .)

(Continued on the next page . . . .)

Part XXII: Some More Untold Cases (1877-1887)

(Continued on the next page . . . .)

(Continued on the next page . . . .)

Part XXV: 2021 Annual (1881-1888)

(Continued on the next page . . . .)

(Continued on the next page . . . .)

Part XXVIII: More Christmas Adventures (1869-1888)

(Continued on the next page . . . .)

Part XXIX: More Christmas Adventures (1889-1896)

Part XXX: More Christmas Adventures (1897-1928)

(Continued on the next page . . . .)

The Adventure of the Chained Phantom – J.S. Rowlinson
Santa's Little Elves – Kevin Thornton
The Case of the Holly-Sprig Pudding – Naching T. Kassa
The Canterbury Manifesto – David Marcum
The Case of the Disappearing Beaune – J. Lawrence Matthews
A Price Above Rubies – Jane Rubino
The Intrigue of the Red Christmas – Shane Simmons
The Bitter Gravestones – Chris Chan
The Midnight Mass Murder – Paul Hiscock

Part XXXI: 2022 Annual (1875-1887)
Foreword – Jeffrey Hatcher
Foreword – Roger Johnson
Foreword – Steve Emecz
Foreword – Emma West
Foreword – David Marcum
The Nemesis of Sherlock Holmes (A Poem) – Kelvin I. Jones
The Unsettling Incident of the History Professor's Wife – Sean M. Wright
The Princess Alice Tragedy – John Lawrence
The Adventure of the Amorous Balloonist – I.A. Watson
The Pilkington Case – Kevin Patrick McCann
The Adventure of the Disappointed Lover – Arthur Hall
The Case of the Impressionist Painting – Tim Symonds
The Adventure of the Old Explorer – Tracy J. Revels
Dr. Watson's Dilemma – Susan Knight
The Colonial Exhibition – Hal Glatzer
The Adventure of the Drunken Teetotaler – Thomas A. Burns, Jr.
The Curse of Hollyhock House – Geri Schear
The Sethian Messiah – David Marcum
Dead Man's Hand – Robert Stapleton
The Case of the Wary Maid – Gordon Linzner
The Adventure of the Alexandrian Scroll – David MacGregor
The Case of the Woman at Margate – Terry Golledge
A Question of Innocence – DJ Tyrer
The Grosvenor Square Furniture Van – Terry Golledge
The Adventure of the Veiled Man – Tracy J. Revels
The Disappearance of Dr. Markey – Stephen Herczeg
The Case of the Irish Demonstration – Dan Rowley

Part XXXII: 2022 Annual (1888-1895)
Foreword – Jeffrey Hatcher
Foreword – Roger Johnson
Foreword – Steve Emecz

(Continued on the next page . . . .)

Part XXXIII: 2022 Annual (1896-1919)

(Continued on the next page . . . .)

(Continued on the next page . . . .)

Part XXXVI: "However Improbable . . . ." (1897-1919)

(Continued on the next page . . . .)

(Continued on the next page . . . .)

Part XXXIX: 2023 Annual (1897-1923)

Part XL: Further Untold Cases (1879-1886)

(Continued on the next page . . . .)

Part XLI: Further Untold Cases (1877-1892)

Part XLII: Further Untold Cases (1894-1922)

(Continued on the next page . . . .)

Part XLIII: 2024 Annual (1874-1888)

(Continued on the next page . . . .)

(Continued on the next page . . . .)

Part XLVI: Occupants of the Canonical Realm (1861-1889)

(Continued on the next page . . . .)

Part XLVII: Occupants of the Canonical Realm (1890-1898)

Part XLVIII: Occupants of the Canonical Realm (1899-1924)

(Continued on the next page . . . .)

Part XLIX: The True Mr. Sherlock Holmes – England's Greatest Hero (1880-1888)

Part L: The True Mr. Sherlock Holmes – England's Greatest Hero (1889-1996)

(Continued on the next page . . . .)

Part LI: The True Mr. Sherlock Holmes –
England's Greatest Hero (1897-1901)

(Continued on the next page . . . .)

Part LII: The True Mr. Sherlock Holmes –
England's Greatest Hero (1902-1923)

The following contributors appear
in the companion volumes:
The True Sherlock Mr. Holmes –
England's Greatest Hero
Part XLIX – (1880-1888)
Part L – (1889-1896)
Part LI – (1897-1901)

A Thousand Cunning Windings
by David Marcum

"*. . . a thousand cunning windings . . . .*" So said Mr. Sherlock Holmes in "The Final Problem" to describe the path he traced when cornering Professor James Moriarty. But that phrase can also apply to over one-thousand brilliant Holmes adventures in *The MX Book of New Sherlock Holmes Stories*, now finishing at fifty-two massive volumes . . . .

Know this from *The Gospel* of The Church of the Traditional Canonical Sherlock Holmes:

> "*In the beginning was The Canon, and it was good.
> But it was not enough.*"

> – *The Book of Holmes*, (Chapter I, Verses 1-2)

And if that isn't clear enough, Verses 3 and 4 continue:

> "*Verily, verily, I say unto thee: There have
> NEVER been enough traditional and
> Canonical Holmes adventures.
> There NEVER will be.*"

And as Dickens wrote, "*This must be distinctly understood, or nothing wonderful can come of the story I am going to relate.*"

The initial original Canonical (and pitifully few) Sixty Tales were just the merest glimpse into the long lives of Sherlock Holmes and Dr. John H. Watson. Those Canonical adventures served as the main structural fibers of *The Great Holmes Tapestry*, but there were so many empty spaces in between that needed filling in order to reveal a full and vivid image. This is accomplished by way of post-Canonical adventures called *pastiches*.

The Canon relates sixty events across a period from 1874 ("The Gloria Scott") to 1914 ("His Last Bow") – from when Sherlock Holmes was twenty years old to when he was sixty. Forty years. But consider that most of those cases just take a day or so, or sometimes only a few hours. Forty years is approximately 14,600 days, and yet the total on-page narrative of most of the Canonical cases, when tallied, equals around six months – three days here, two here, and approximately one month for *The Hound*. (Even the off-stage events of The Great Hiatus, nearly three years in duration, is just a fraction of forty years.) There is so much more between 1874 and 1914 that is left undescribed – not to mention whatever happened in Holmes and Watson's lives before 1874 and after 1914.

And even though The Canon is the core of The Great Holmes Tapestry, the stories that make up this core were chosen by Watson as representative examples of Holmes's skills – they were not necessarily his greatest triumphs or "best" cases. Watson had thousands of recorded adventures from which to choose when selecting for publication, and he had reasons for what he picked . . . and for what he suppressed. *What about all of those other cases that weren't published in Watson's lifetime?*

That's where the Post-Canonical Chroniclers step in . . . .

> *"Apart from what you have told me,*
> *can you give me any further*
> *information about the man?"*
> – Sherlock Holmes
> "The Illustrious Client"

In 2015, we knew less about Mr. Sherlock Holmes than we do now, for back then, there were over one-thousand fewer of his adventures that had been revealed to the curious public. Don't misunderstand – there were still quite a few post-Canonical Holmes narratives in 2015, but they were harder to find, *and there were not enough.*

> *". . . we must hunt for this man's secrets."*
> – Sherlock Holmes
> "The Illustrious Client"

Growing up, I had the very-common experience of discovering and reading The Canon, and re-reading it, and then realizing with crushing disappointment that the ride was seemingly at an end. I was fortunate to discover Holmes in 1975, at age ten, just one year after Nicholas Meyer had ignited the current and still-burning Sherlockian Golden Age with his discovery of the lost manuscript for *The Seven-Per-Cent Solution* (1974). While it was flawed – the implications that Moriarty was not evil, and that the Great Hiatus did not occur, were obviously grafted onto Watson's original manuscript by some later Moriarty heir to posthumously rehabilitate the evil Professor's reputation – this book revealed the basic but staggering truth that Watson's stories *did not have to cross the First Literary Agent's desk to be both accepted and amazing.*

2

The hunt was on to locate Watson's other missing narratives, filling in all the gaps and spaces between what we know from The Canon. Meyer continued by finding an exponentially better second Watsonian manuscript, *The West End Horror* – and the dam holding back the release of these various historic documents was washed away forever.

> *"But that is not enough, Mr. Holmes."*
> – Lord Bellinger, Prime Minister
> "The Second Stain"

In the following years, I tracked down, collected, read, and chronologicized almost every existing traditional Canonical Holmes adventures – *but there were not enough.* And in the early 2000's, I noticed a disturbance in the Holmesian Force: Several media adaptations that incorrectly placed Holmes in Modern Times began popping up. One in particular gained a lot of traction, painting Holmes as a broken sociopathic murderer. That would be fine if it stopped there, for there have been a lot of insulting works over the years that similarly attacked Holmes – the worst up to that point being Michael Dibdin's *The Last Sherlock Holmes Story* (1978), in which Holmes was presented as a gleeful Jack the Ripper, whose death was arranged by Watson.

> *"We must not lose sight of our main inquiry."*
> – Sherlock Holmes
> "The Naval Treaty"

I was dismayed when aspects of this modernized sociopathic Holmes began creeping into what were supposed to be traditional Canonical adventures, as presented by people who should have known better: In these "traditional" adventures, supposedly Canonical Holmes now had a "mind palace". Watson's wound was psychosomatic. Mrs. Hudson was the widow of a drug dealer. Irene Adler was a dominatrix. Mary Watson was a secret agent assassin. And people were adapting to this – accepting this – as if maybe Holmes *had always been a sociopath*, or that Watson *really wasn't wounded*, if one just read The Canon a little more closely. Many said, "It's okay – as long as this attracts new people to Sherlock Holmes, who cares how they get there?" But they were all showing up with the expectation and looking for hints that Irene Adler really was a dominatrix, or that James Moriarty was . . . whatever that was supposed to be.

I became increasingly . . . shall we say *peeved*. And then I became motivated – a fiery motivation that has only increased every day since.

I little dreamed the strange shape
which that campaign was destined to take.
– Dr. John H. Watson
"Charles Augustus Milverton"

One night in early 2015, I had a dream, and it abruptly awakened me. If I'd gone back to sleep, I might have forgotten it, but instead I went ahead and got up, as it was nearly time to arise anyway. And I kept thinking about that very-vivid vision.

I had dreamed that I'd edited a book of new Holmes stories, along the lines of *The Mammoth Book of Sherlock Holmes Stories* (1997), or the many volumes that Martin H. Greenberg co-edited with a number of other people over several decades – new Holmes stories, set in the correct time, indistinguishable from the Canonical tales that originally appeared in *The Strand.*

". . . we must take our own line of action."
– Sherlock Holmes
"The Disappearance of Lady Frances Carfax"

That morning before going to work, I looked around at my Holmes collection – now nearly 5,000 volumes, but somewhat less then – and saw a number of authors represented there that I'd love to invite. Later that morning, I emailed Publisher Extraordinaire Steve Emecz with the idea, and he was willing. (Steve has always been most supportive of various project ideas.) I had no idea that I'd started something that would be a huge part of my life for the next ten years . . . .

That email is on the next page . . . .

David Marcum   Jan 22, 2015, 9:40 AM   ☆ ☺ ↩ ⋮
to Steve ▾

Steve,

This is the idea I had for a future book. I was literally dreaming about it when I woke up this morning.

I would like to contact a specific list of authors (see below) – who I would pick because they write well and who write the kinds of Holmes stories that I would want to read – and have each one of them pen a Holmes short story.

The volume would be along the lines of all of those anthologies that have come before, such as *The Mammoth Book, Holmes for the Holidays, Murder in Baker Street,* etc. Like *The Mammoth Book,* I would arrange the stories by chronological date, and not by a perceived author importance.

I would be the editor, and I would format it. (As you know, I have strict standards.) I would ask that each story be 5,000-8,000 words in length, much like stories from the Canon. The stories would be traditional and Canonical Holmes only, as narrated by Watson. The characters would be in standard settings, and it would be like when authors were writing *Star Trek* novels, and they were told that they could use the characters, but essentially put them back as they found them when they were done. There would be no weird Alternate Universe or present-day stuff, no Holmes-is-the-Ripper, nothing where Watson is at Holmes's funeral or vice-versa. etc. Essentially nothing that shockingly contradicts what is in the Canon.

I would contact each author personally to explain the project and request a submission. That way other authors who didn't get to play wouldn't necessarily get their feelings hurt, since it would go on behind the scenes and the book would simply appear as a finished product.

Each author would retain the rights to his or her story, for use in a future collection of their own. To avoid the question of who gets what, royalties would go to Undershaw, or some other good cause of your choosing.

Also, it would generate some new Holmes stories that I would get to read, and that would be great!

If eight participated, it would be a pretty good nice book. If more played, so much the better. We could even consider doing two versions, the standard paperback, and possibly a collectible hardcover – that would be your call, of course.

So, what do you think? I think I could put this together fairly easily, once the stories arrived. It would be a lot of fun, and it would be something really cool for MX as well.

I await your thoughts....

David

    . . . and if you can't easily read it, I wrote:

January 22, 2015 9:40 a.m.

Steve,

This is the idea I had for a future book. I was literally dreaming about it when I woke up this morning.

I would like to contact a specific list of authors (see below) – who I would pick because they write well and who write the kinds of Holmes stories that I would want to read – and have each one of them pen a Holmes short story.

The volume would be along the lines of all of those anthologies that have come before, such as The Mammoth Book, Holmes for the Holidays, Murder in Baker Street, *etc. Like* The Mammoth Book, *I would arrange the stories by chronological date, and not by a perceived author importance.*

I would be the editor, and I would format it. (As you know, I have strict standards.) I would ask that each story be 5,000-8,000 words in length, much like stories from the Canon. The stories would be traditional and Canonical Holmes only, as narrated by Watson. The characters would be in standard settings, and it would be like when authors were writing Star Trek novels, and they were told that they could use the characters, but essentially put them back as they found them when they were done. There would be no weird Alternate Universe or present-day stuff, no Holmes-is-the-Ripper, nothing where Watson is at Holmes's funeral or vice-versa. etc. Essentially nothing that shockingly contradicts what is in the Canon.

I would contact each author personally to explain the project and request a submission. That way other authors who didn't get to play wouldn't necessarily get their feelings hurt, since it would go on behind the scenes and the book would simply appear as a finished product.

Each author would retain the rights to his or her story, for use in a future collection of their own. To avoid the question of who gets what, royalties would go to Undershaw, or some other good cause of your choosing.

Also, it would generate some new Holmes stories that I would get to read, and that would be great!

If eight participated, it would be a pretty good nice book. If more played, so much the better. We could even consider doing two versions, the standard paperback, and possibly a collectible hardcover – that would be your call, of course.

So, what do you think? I think I could put this together fairly easily, once the stories arrived. It would be a lot of fun, and it would be something really cool for MX as well.

I await your thoughts . . . .

David

"We must define the situation a little more clearly."
– Sherlock Holmes
"The Red Circle"

When Steve approved, I also emailed a couple of Sherlockian friends, and their opinions were positive. So I started sending out invitations – and I was very clear: The books could have no actual supernatural solutions. There might be some element of *"What was that . . . ?"* at the end of the story – perhaps Watson looks back as they drive away and sees a mythical creature after all – but the crime could not have been caused by the creature. No real vampires or wolfmen or actual Jekyll-Hyde transformations. No aliens or Old Gods or intelligent brain-mutating parasites. Although one naysayer who is bored with The Canon and favors pure Holmes-versus-Actual Supernatural Creatures later sneered at these "Scooby Doo solutions", Holmes stated it exactly right: *"No ghosts need apply."*

Likewise, there could be no anachronistic elements. "Mind palaces" and other such incorrect modern references were forbidden. Technology had to agree with the year in which the story took place – with absolutely no Steampunk. The story itself had to fit into the Holmes and Watson chronology. For instance, close reading of The Canon shows that Watson only had a practice during those years when he was married. Watson's residences when living away from Baker Street – Paddington and Kensington and Queen Anne Street – had to be correct for the period in which the story occurred.

Finally, there could be no aspects of parody. People had been calling Our Heroes things like *Hairlock Combs* and *Fetlock Jones* since the late 1800's. It wasn't funny then, and it isn't funny now.

"We must strike while the iron is hot."
– Sherlock Holmes
"The Cardboard Box"

When I started sending invitations, I was afraid that no one would respond, so I kept widening the net. I went through my entire Holmes collection, looking for pasticheurs and finding ways to contact them. Then, to my amazement, I had the first positive reply – from Lyndsay Faye, who wrote back within a few hours of my initial email, stating: *"I'd be happy to – when do you need it by?"*

Wow – this thing might happen after all.

7

> *"Well, I think we must wait*
> *for a little more material."*
> – Sherlock Holmes
> "The Red Circle"

I'd been worried that there would be no interest, and I'd also thought that, at best, the final result might be a one-volume paperback of maybe twelve stories – if I was lucky. So I kept sending more invitations, and getting more replies from people saying that they were in. Then . . . the first story arrived, from Luke Benjamen Kuhns, and I first experienced that brand-new thrill – that *addiction* – of receiving new Holmes stories in my inbox.

> *"Our material is rapidly accumulating."*
> – Sherlock Holmes
> "The Dancing Men"

As 2015 progressed, word spread about this new project, and an increasing number of people wanted to join the party. I began receiving more emails and more stories, and pretty soon it became apparent that this was going to be a really big book. Maybe too big for just one book . . . .

> *"We will confine ourselves for the present*
> *with your permission to this very*
> *interesting document."*
> – Sherlock Holmes
> *The Hound of the Baskervilles*

Over several months, Steve Emecz and I worked out book lengths and sizes, and he was receptive when I shared that I thought it would become a two-volume set. And he was still receptive when that grew to three volumes. By late Summer 2015, the set had grown to 63 stories – more tales than in The Canon.

> *"We need certainly to muster all our resources."*
> – Sherlock Holmes
> "The Five Orange Pips"

From the beginning, the royalties from this project have gone to support the restoration of Undershaw, one of Sir Arthur Conan Doyle's former homes. For a number of years, the site had been in disrepair, and was more recently in danger of being torn down or cut up into private dwellings, disrespecting the historical significance of the place. A movement had helped to save Undershaw, and Steve Emecz and MX

Publishing had been part of that, having published several previous volumes whose royalties had also helped the site.

> *"Now, we must make the best use of our time . . . ."*
> – Sherlock Holmes
> "The Speckled Band"

Now the building was saved, having recently been purchased by the nearby Stepping Stones School for special needs children – and Steve suggested that the royalties from the new books go to the school. This only made the project more popular with the contributors.

The three volumes were published in Autumn 2015, and I was very fortunate to be able to travel to England – my second Holmes Pilgrimage – to attend a launch party high on a festive outdoor deck atop one of London's noted skyscrapers – at the location of Steve's then-employer. And then I returned home, and things settled down for a week or so . . . but it wasn't long before I started receiving emails about when to contribute to the *next book . . . .*

> *"Why should you go further in it?*
> *What have you to gain from it?"*
> – Sherlock Holmes
> "The Red Circle"

Next book? Next book! I'd had no plans for anything past the first three books. But receiving new Holmes stories by email *was* an addiction, and people wanted to contribute – both former and new pasticheurs – and others wanted to read further volumes with stories about the True Holmes, and most of all, *there are never enough traditional Canonical Holmes adventures. Never enough.*

> *"We must begin again."*
> – Sherlock Holmes
> "The Disappearance of Lady Frances Carfax"

So I wrote to Steve and explained, and we decided upon one more book – or maybe we decided on one new book per year. (I can't remember exactly.) In any case, I announced it, and more stories arrived, and Part IV, published in Spring 2016, had twenty-one stories. And then came the questions about the *next* volume . . . .

> *"We must begin from a different angle."*
> – Sherlock Holmes
> "The Illustrious Client"

It became apparent that there were so many contributors anxious to reach into Watson's Tin Dispatch Box, and also so many readers who were *starving* for more traditional Canonical adventures, that we could produce a lot more than one book per year – so it was decided to have a Spring *Annual*, and an Autumn themed volume. And 2016's themed Autumn volume was *Christmas Adventures* – 30 stories, (It's still one of the most popular of the series. We did another three-volume Christmas set in 2021.)

> *"We must hustle and put the thing through."*
> – Sherlock Holmes
> "The Three Garridebs"

By then, the pattern was set. I would announce a "Call for Submissions" about six months before publication of a particular set – the *Annuals* in Spring, and themed books in Autumn – such as Christmas, and Untold Cases, and seemingly-supernatural-but-not-really. More and more stories would arrive, necessitating that we eventually grew to six volumes per year – three for the *Annuals*, and three for the themed sets. I was usually reading new stories for the next set while also finishing final edits for the current set, and by the time the current set was published, fresh to the excited reading public, it was far in my rear-view mirror as I edited the new stories.

> *"We will raise as much as we can in money . . . ."*
> – John Ferrier
> *A Study in Scarlet*

In September 2016, the Stepping Stones School at Undershaw held their grand opening, and my deerstalker and I were invited as special guests (representing Holmes and Pasticheurs) because of the books' connection to the school. It was my own Holmes Pilgrimage No. 3. At that time – and since then as well – I was told that while the money raised for the school was substantial and useful – over $135,000 as I write this foreword – the more important aspect of the books' association was that they raised awareness of the school all over the world.

> *"We will have some indication as to*
> *where the document has gone."*
> – Sherlock Holmes
> "The Second Stain"

There were a number of milestones as the books progressed. A set of six volumes, taken from the early anthologies, were published in India by

Jaico. A single volume was translated and sold in Japan. Phil Growick, an initial contributor, had the brilliant idea of taking Holmes stories and assigning them to different artists – each of whom would produce a painting related to that tale, and all for charity. He published four different volumes of *The Art of Sherlock Holmes*, and almost all of the stories in those books were taken directly from *The MX Book of New Sherlock Holmes Stories*. He even had a gallery showing for one set of paintings, and more were planned before COVID shut things like that down. And contributor Sean Wright – who co-wrote (with Michael Hodel) *Enter the Lion* (1979), one of the best post-Canonical adventures way back in the late 1970's, not long after the current Sherlockian Golden Age commenced – suggested a volume of stories from this series that were contributed by members of the BSI – and thus *An Investee's Anthology* was published in 2022.

"*. . . he has done a considerable amount of writing lately . . .*"
– Sherlock Holmes
"The Red-Headed League"

During his lifetime, the late Philip K. Jones compiled an amazing database of post-Canonical stories – approximately 16,000 of them at the time of his passing, not long after the first MX anthology volumes were published. If one disregards the number of parodies and non-traditional non-Canonical stories that he included, then there are approximately 10,000 traditional and Canonical adventures listed – a fairly complete list up to that time. Since then, *The MX Book of New Sherlock Holmes Stories*, with these final four volumes, has 1,063 stories – or approximately ten percent (10%) of the other traditional and Canonical adventures ever written. Additionally, these books have had over 200 contributors world-wide. Some authors wrote a single story, while others have stepped up and contributed dozens – to my everlasting gratitude.

"*We must each try our own way
and see what comes of it.*"
– Sherlock Holmes
"Wisteria Lodge"

I never cease to be amazed at the directions taken by the different contributors. From the common point of the traditional Canon, stories in these books may be comic or tragic. One might find a cozy murder or a strict police procedural murder investigation – or no murder at all. Holmes might investigate a stolen document or jewel – or something that ends up completely crime-free. The setting might be a British city or the countryside, or another country or continent. Holmes's client might be a businessman or a criminal, or a little old lady or Royalty. He might work for a private interest, or as an agent of the Government. The adventure might be a complicated swindle or a ghost story or a spy mission. The tale may be cerebral, or filled with breakneck action. Holmes might progress steadily from one witness to another, or he may be settled in to unlock a mysterious puzzle or code. Holmes might solve the crime from his armchair, or – as he says in *A Study in Scarlet* –*"Now and again a case turns up which is a little more complex. Then I have to bustle about and see things with my own eyes."*

> *"I should wish to go further into this matter.*
> *It interests me."*
> – Professor Presbury
> "The Creeping Man"

Another wonderful thing to me that occurred along the way was that these books gave some people their first opportunities to be published authors, and they went on to write more stories – about Holmes, and in other areas too. Some authors used these books as a "prompt" – reminders every six months to write more Holmes stories so that, as these accumulated, they would have enough to be collected into their own books. There have been quite a few volumes of these "children" of the MX anthologies.

> *". . . we will go out together and see what we can do."*
> – Sherlock Holmes
> "The Norwood Builder"

One of the best stories of a "child" of these books was the creation and success of Derrick and Brian Belanger's *Belanger Books*. I first "met" Derrick when he reviewed one of my own books, and we became email friends. He was among the very first group of authors that I invited when I had the idea for the anthologies, and his contribution was his first written Holmes adventure. I "met" his brother, Brian, when he took over as MX's cover artist after the untimely passing of the previous artist. (I've since seen them several times on those occasions when I've attended the yearly Sherlock Holmes Birthday Weekend in New York.)

After Derrick had a taste of writing about Holmes, he and Brian had an idea: To form their own publishing company. I had an email from Derrick in August 2015 – a month or so before the first MX anthologies were published – asking me if I'd be involved in their publishing venture, and I've been thrilled to be associated with them ever since. I've edited over two-dozen books for them, and they've published both of my Solar Pons short story collections, with another on the way.

Belanger Books has published many Holmes anthologies since its inception, including several volumes in their anthology series *Sherlock Holmes: A Year of Mystery*. They have themed Holmes collections related to Poe and Lovecraft and H.G. Wells. There are sets devoted to The Early Years and The Denarian Years, and The Great Hiatus and World War I, and the Montague Street days Before Watson. There are Canonical sequels and team-ups with Solar Pons and other Great Detectives and Female Detectives, and stories centered around the Theatre.

I'm thrilled that Belanger Books came into being, and I believe that it was directly because of Derrick's initial involvement in *The MX Book of New Sherlock Holmes Stories*, and the joy he found when writing his first Holmes adventure. More important, I'm also thrilled that Belanger Books has gone on to be one of the two most-respected and important Sherlockian publishers ever – the other being MX Publishing. Both companies work together very closely to support each other's projects and charities, and spread the True Sherlockian Word far and wide. I'm very proud to be associated with both MX Publishing and Belanger Books.

> *"I cannot really see how we can get*
> *much further than our present position."*
> – Sherlock Holmes
> "Silver Blaze

In 2023, one of the MX contributors wrote, asking me what the future plans were for the series. He wanted to keep contributing for as long as the books continued, and he wanted to keep collecting every volume too, but he wondered how many stories that meant he'd need to write over the years, and how much extra bookshelf space he'd require. His email set me to thinking about an end game . . . .

> *"I think that we have gathered all that we can."*
> – Sherlock Holmes
> "The Priory School"

I'd joked before that the books should fittingly go to Part MX – Volume 1,010 for those who don't speak Roman Numeral – but sadly that wasn't realistic. When I started considering, we were then up to forty-two volumes, and I wondered if we could reach fifty – which seemed like a good number upon which to stop. If we had three Spring volumes in 2024, (Parts 43, 44, and 45), and three in the Autumn (Parts 46, 47, and 48), then we could reach fifty with just two volumes in Spring 2025. If the stories kept arriving at the usual rate, we would have over 1,000 of them upon reaching the Spring 2025 volumes. And personally, 2025 would be ten years since the books began in 2015 – a milestone – and personally I would turn sixty – my own milestone.

"We must prepare for the worst."
– Sherlock Holmes
"The Disappearance of Lady Frances Carfax"

The same person who had asked me about the books' future warned me that strictly limiting the final set to two volumes might be a mistake, as a lot of people would certainly want to participate at the end, but I was adamant: Fifty was a solid and pleasing number, and I would close the door. But that person – it was Kevin Thornton – was correct: Enthusiasm was high, and we were going to need extra volumes. I didn't want to increase to fifty-one – there's nothing pleasing about that number – but fifty-two felt good. There are fifty-two cards in a deck, and fifty-two weeks in a year – and an ambitious reader could read one volume of this series per week for an entire year. (I highly recommend this as a self-improvement activity, and would like to hear from whomever completes this Noble Quest.)

"In over a thousand cases I am not aware that
I have ever used my powers upon the wrong side."
– Sherlock Holmes, "The Final Problem"

As I write this foreword to the final volumes, I'm currently finishing the final editing process. As mentioned, I've been thrilled to receive new Holmes stories nearly every day for the last decade, and I'm going to miss that incredibly – although I will now have more free time to read other things, without my spare minutes and hours being devoted to printed-out stories on 8½ x 11-inch paper and with an editing pen in hand. I've also enjoyed being something of a Sherlockian influencer, able to nudge the Sherlockian ship in directions that I wanted it to go . . . .

"Then we must take that as our working hypothesis."
– Sherlock Holmes
"The Bruce-Partington Plans"

Not long after I first discovered Holmes in 1975 – before I'd even read all of The Canon – my parents gifted me with William S. Baring-Gould's incredible *Sherlock Holmes of Baker Street* (1962), the amazing biography of Holmes that establishes so many things – his birth date and background, his *other* older brother Sherrinford, his upbringing and schooling, his travels in America as an actor, his relationship with Irene Adler and his son, and the circumstances of his death. (That's right – as a historical figure, he wasn't immortal.) I don't agree with everything Baring-Gould posited, but I concur with much of it, and it was a great jumping off place when constructing my own 1,200-page (and ever-growing) Holmes Chronology.

> *"Well, we will take it as a working hypothesis*
> *for want of a better."*
> – Sherlock Holmes
> "The Man with the Twisted Lip"

As the editor of these fifty-two volumes – and a few dozen more as well for MX and Belanger Books, I've been able to nudge the ship in the direction I believe to be correct, encouraging certain ideas that I hope will become even more established in the reading consciousness as time goes on, in the same way that Baring-Gould's ideas have found popular footing. For instance, whenever the question came up, I encouraged contributors to reinforce the idea that Holmes lived at No. 24 Montague Street (as first discovered by Sherlockian Michael Harrison) before moving to Baker Street. I arranged the stories of each set in chronological order, and in the order to match what I believe is the correct chronology. I firmly aver that Holmes wore a deerstalker, and that he wore it in town and also the country. (Anyone who would shoot *V.R.* into his wall with a hair-trigger pistol would not be concerned by fashion dictates. He would dress as needed in useful clothing to go to work at a moment's notice.) Thus, he wears a deerstalker in these thousand-plus stories.

> *"We must look for consistency."*
> – Sherlock Holmes
> "The Problem of Thor Bridge"

These books helped to further establish that Holmes retired to Hodcombe Farm at Beachy Head on the Sussex Coast. Study of The Canon reveals that Watson had *three* wives – not two, not seven – and these books strengthen that conclusion. There is now much additional evidence, by way of these books, that Nero Wolfe was Holmes's son, and Solar Pons was his nephew. We know a great deal more about The Great Hiatus than what was revealed in "The Empty House", and we also know why Holmes "retired" in 1903, and more about what he was up to in those years leading to World War I and "His Last Bow".

*"Their cumulative effect is certainly considerable,
and yet each of them is quite possible in itself."*
– Dr. John H. Watson
"The Abbey Grange"

While these books are coming to a close, there are already plans for other similar volumes, although they will not be the size of the MX anthologies, and they will be one-time projects with much-less rigorous editing demands. But one thing will not change: The new books will absolutely stick to what made the original MX volumes so successful: *Firm adherence to the Canonical model.* Holmes will not be substituting for Van Helsing or Doctor Who. He will not be a sociopathic murderer with a "mind palace", and he will not be a joke, or realize halfway through and adventure that he's a character in someone's book, or be covered in tattoos while paying off a prostitute in the doorway of a modern-day Manhattan brownstone. These new books (when they arrive), as well as all fifty-two volumes (and over one-thousand stories) of *The MX Book of New Sherlock Holmes Stories,* hold to a basic premise: They were all generated by a desire for more traditional Canonical adventures – *and there are never enough traditional Canonical Holmes adventures.*

* * * * *

*"Of course, I could only
stammer out my thanks."*
– The Unhappy John Hector McFarlane
"The Norwood Builder"

As always when one of these collections is finished, I want to thank with all my heart my incredible, patient, brilliant, kind, and beautiful wife of almost thirty-seven years, Rebecca – Every single day I'm more stunned at how lucky I am than the day before! – and our amazing, funny, creative, and wonderful son, and my friend, Dan (with whom I was able to share a multi-week Holmes Pilgrimage No. 4 around England and Scotland in Spring 2024). I love you both, and you are everything to me!

With each new set of the MX anthologies, some things got easier, and there were also new challenges. For several years, the stresses of real life have been much greater on all of us than when this series started. Through all of this, the amazing contributors have pulled truly amazing works from the Tin Dispatch Box. I'm more grateful than I can express to every contributor who has donated both time and royalties to this ongoing project. It's amazing what we've accomplished.

Finally, I cannot express how thankful I am to all of those who keep buying these books and making them the largest and most popular Sherlockian anthology ever.

I'm so glad to have gotten to know so many of you through this process. It's an undeniable fact that Sherlock Holmes authors are the *best* people!

I wish especially thank the following:

- ☐ *Steve Emecz* – From my first association with MX in 2013, I saw that MX (under Steve Emecz's leadership) was *the* fast-rising superstar of the Sherlockian publishing world. Connecting with MX and Steve Emecz was personally an amazing life-changing event for me, as it has been for countless other Sherlockian authors. It has led me to write many more stories, and then to edit books, along with unexpected additional Holmes Pilgrimages to England – none of which might have happened otherwise. By way of my first email with Steve, I've had the chance to make some incredible Sherlockian friends and play in the Holmesian Sandbox in ways that I would have never dreamed possible.

  Through it all, Steve has been one of the most positive and supportive people that I have ever known.

  From the beginning, Steve has let me explore various Sherlockian projects and open up my own personal possibilities in ways that otherwise would have never happened. Thank you, Steve, for every opportunity!

- ☐ *Roger Johnson* – From his immediate support at the time of the first volumes in this series to the present, I can't imagine Roger not being part of these books. His Sherlockian knowledge is exceptional, as is the work that he does to further the cause of The Master. But even more than that, both Roger and his wife, Jean Upton, are simply the finest and best of people, and I'm very lucky to know both of them – even though I don't get to see them nearly as often as I'd like. I look forward to getting back over to the Holmesland sooner rather than later and visiting with them again, but in the meantime, many thanks for being part of this.

- ☐ *Brian Belanger* – I initially became acquainted with Brian when he took over the duties of creating the covers for MX Books, and I found him to be a great collaborator, and wonderfully creative too. I've worked with him on many projects with MX and Belanger Books, which he co-founded with his brother Derrick Belanger, also a good friend. Along with MX Publishing, Derrick and Brian have absolutely locked up the Sherlockian publishing field with a vast amount of amazing material. The old dinosaurs must be trembling to see every new and worthy Sherlockian project, one after another after another, that these two companies create. Luckily MX and Belanger Books work closely with one another, and I'm thrilled to be associated with both of them. Many thanks to Brian for all he does for both publishers, and for all he's done for me personally.

☐ *Bonnie MacBird* – I first met Bonnie in 2013, during my Holmes Pilgrimage No. 1, when I was joining Roger Johnson and Jean Upton for lunch at The Sherlock Holmes Pub, and they brought Bonnie along. I didn't know she was famous then – just that she was a very nice lady. After lunch and an extensive exploration of the Holmes exhibit, Roger guided us on the route taken by Holmes and Watson, as described in "The Empty House", from Cavendish Square to Camden House in Baker Street. Later that evening, Bonnie attended my first book signing at the Sherlock Holmes Hotel in Baker Street. I saw her again in 2015 at the launch party of the MX anthologies, and then several times after that at Sherlockian gatherings in Indiana and New York. In the meantime, we've stayed in touch by email.

During our first meeting, along the way of the "Empty House" walk, she rather shyly stated that she was working on writing a pastiche. I hinted that I'd like to read it, but no such luck – until *Art in the Blood* was published in 2015 and I was able to read it as my book-of-choice while in London for Holmes Pilgrimage No. 2 – the first of her very successful Holmes series from HarperCollins. Bonnie has been an incredible supporter of these books from the very beginning, and I'm thrilled and thankful that she is a part of them for the final volumes.

And finally, last but certainly *not* least, thanks to **Sir Arthur Conan Doyle**: Author, doctor, adventurer, and the Founder of the Sherlockian Feast. Honored, and present in spirit.

As I always note when putting together an anthology of Holmes stories, the effort has been a labor of love. Looking back over ten years, this has never wavered. These adventures are just part of the many tiny threads woven into the ongoing Great Holmes Tapestry, continuing to grow and grow, for there can *never* be enough stories about the man whom Watson described as "*the best and wisest . . . whom I have ever known.*"

David Marcum
March 4ᵗʰ, 2025
The 144ᵗʰ Anniversary of
the monumental first day of the
Jefferson Hope Murder Investigation

Questions or comments
may be addressed to David Marcum at
thepapersofsherlockholmes@gmail.com.

Foreword
by Bonnie MacBird

Well, here it is. Bringing it on Holmes, editor and Sherlockian scholar extraordinaire David Marcum presents the final volumes of his magnificent series for MX publishing, which has brought 52 volumes of over 1,000 stories by Holmesian writers from all over the planet – from the famous to the newly fledged, all writing from the heart and from the mind, reflecting our hero: Mr. Sherlock Holmes. This series has taken in more than $134,000 in support of the Undershaw school for special needs children.

You hold in your hands the last of these volumes, representing over ten years of David Marcum's creative life. He's diligently read, edited, championed, and also beautifully added to this astonishing collection of ongoing adventures of our heroes.

All of these works have been traditional, in emulation of that genius storyteller Sir Arthur Conan Doyle, whom we happily acknowledge here as the mastermind. He has enthralled thousands of readers for more than 130 years. His craft seems so effortless (until you try your hand at it), his prose both brisk and evocative, and even "cinematic", although most of it predates cinema. His wit is crisp, his insights subtle, his characters unforgettable.

How wise that he chose as the storytelling "voice" that of the pragmatic, energetic man of action, John Watson, who doesn't waste words on endless scenic detail or overweening innuendo but, by golly, gets cracking on with the story.

And how exquisitely drawn is Sherlock Holmes, with just enough mystery to the man himself to make us insatiably curious! He is acknowledged as the first superhero of popular fiction, but with no supernatural trappings. He seems to work miracles – but its sheer intelligence, knowledge, stamina, reasoning . . . and let's not forget . . . artistry that are his superpowers. He is a scientist, a logician, and an artist who sees what others do not. Of course, there's also a facility with baritsu, boxing, and single stick when needed.

Ah, the aspiration these stories awaken! Could we not be more like Holmes or Watson with practice, with learning? And wouldn't we be a better person if so?

But setting aside inspirational qualities of these stories, we must also acknowledge the absolute crazy fun they provide, and even more so, the comfort. In a world fraught with conflict and violence, with ignorance and prejudice, these stories amuse and entertain as they bring us close to characters who demonstrate what our world needs most – rational, fact-based critical thinking, courage, and friendship. Armed with those, these two men stand side by side to fight evil and win. Always win.

And at the end, we find ourselves fireside, once again at 221b. And so very glad to be there. Thank you, David and MX. And thank you, Sir Arthur.

Bonnie MacBird
Author, *The Sherlock Holmes Adventure Series*
for HarperCollins
February 2025

"Let me recommend this book – one of the most remarkable ever penned."
by Roger Johnson

That, you'll remember, was Sherlock Holmes's opinion of *The Martyrdom of Man* by William Winwood Reade (1838-1875), who was pithily defined by the *Dictionary of National Biography, 1885-1900* as "*traveller, novelist and controversialist*". The *DNB* noted of the book so remarkably endorsed by Holmes: "*in this work the author does not attempt to conceal his atheistical opinions*". S.C. Roberts, in the very first issue of *The Sherlock Holmes Journal*, observed that "*Holmes, with his social moodiness, his artistic temperament and his queer intellectual interests, had no doubt re-acted against the conventional beliefs of his squirearchical family and Winwood Reade's book was exactly the work that would catch him on the rebound.*"

Reade was an extraordinary man, who led an extraordinary life. The same could be said of Sherlock Holmes, of course, though his life was considerably longer. It was fairly early in their partnership that he urged John Watson to read *The Martyrdom of Man*. If the Good Doctor did so, he probably didn't accept Reade's statement that: "*The soul must be sacrificed; the hope in immortality must die.*" And if Holmes's own opinion at the time matched Reade's, we know that it did become more positive. Consider his discourse on the moss rose in the case of "The Naval Treaty":

> "*What a lovely thing a rose is!*"
> *He walked past the couch to the open window, and held up the drooping stalk of a moss-rose, looking down at the dainty blend of crimson and green. It was a new phase of his character to me, for I had never before seen him show any keen interest in natural objects.*
> "*There is nothing in which deduction is so necessary as in religion,*" *said he, leaning with his back against the shutters. "It can be built up as an exact science by the reasoner. Our highest assurance of the goodness of Providence seems to me to rest in the flowers. All other things, our powers our desires, our food, are all really necessary for*

our existence in the first instance. But this rose is an extra. Its smell and its colour are an embellishment of life, not a condition of it. It is only goodness which gives extras, and so I say again that we have much to hope from the flowers."

That has nothing to do with the case in hand – not directly, at any rate. The intention was probably to encourage his client Percy Phelps to a more optimistic attitude, but Holmes's observations are surely sincere, however unexpected. And no one, surely, can doubt the sincerity of his admonition to the tragic Eugenia Ronder:

We had risen to go, but there was something in the woman's voice which arrested Holmes's attention. He turned swiftly upon her.

"Your life is not your own," he said. "Keep your hands off it."

"What use is it to anyone?"

"How can you tell? The example of patient suffering is in itself the most precious of all lessons to an impatient world."

Detective stories didn't begin when Arthur Conan Doyle wrote *A Study in Scarlet*. Among the Baker Street sleuth's predecessors were the Chevalier C. Auguste Dupin, protagonist of three short stories by Edgar Allan Poe, Emile Gaboriau's Monsieur Lecoq of the French Sûreté, Inspector Bucket in *Bleak House* and Sergeant Cuff in *The Moonstone* – creations respectively of Charles Dickens and Wilkie Collins. Their exploits are still read and enjoyed more than a century-and-a-half later. But who now reads, for example, *The Boy Detective, or The Crimes of London* by Edward Ellis, the apparently endless exploits of Deadwood Dick by Edward L. Wheeler, or those of Jack Harkaway by Bracebridge Hemyng?

Even though he ranked the Holmes Saga low among his literary work, Conan Doyle achieved something remarkable: Fifty-six short stories and four novels, of genuine quality. At first, the detective appears to be essentially one-dimensional, but as we and Dr. Watson come to know him better, we realise that this is a character of real depth. It isn't merely the excitement of the crime and the solution that keep us reading and re-reading – there's also the fascination of his personality – and not only his but the admirable Doctor's as well. *

Even before the last remnants of copyright in the Canonical Holmes stories finally expired, there was a considerable output of parody and pastiche. Parody has different aims and different rules, but pastiche requires fidelity to the substance, the style and the spirit of the original, and that fidelity is too often missing – especially since the expiration of the Conan Doyle copyright – and the ability to post pretty much anything online. As they used to say, *"Never mind the quality, feel the width!"*

Fortunately, that does not apply to this book and its predecessors. David Marcum has worked tirelessly with his many authors to ensure that these new tales of Sherlock Holmes and John H. Watson are up to scratch.

And don't forget that none of the contributors will receive any financial reward, as the proceeds from the publication will go to the upkeep of Undershaw, the house that Arthur Conan Doyle had built for himself and his family near Hindhead in Surrey. Since 2016 it has been home to the Undershaw School, providing care and education for children aged eight to nineteen with Autistic Spectrum Disorder and associated learning needs.

Roger Johnson
BSI, ASH
February 2025

---

*   Watson has so often and so unjustly been depicted as an idiot, especially on film! That will probably continue, but eventually, I hope, it will only be for comedic purposes.

An Ongoing Legacy
for Sherlock Holmes
by Steve Emecz

Undershaw
Circa 1900

Fifty two is a wonderful number of volumes to complete the world's largest-ever Sherlock Holmes anthology. It's unlikely we will ever see another collection like this, with over twohundred Holmes authors participating. It has taken ten years and a mammoth amount of editing from David Marcum to gift the world more than one-thousand new, traditional stories.

As many have commented – the fifty-six short stories and four novellas that Sir Arthur penned was painfully few for the dedicated fan, and wading through the myriad of pastiches on offer is difficult for those yearning for more Conan Doyle. *The MX Book of New Sherlock Holmes Stories* is a haven for those wanting an extension to The Canon in a very similar voice to ACD.

Whilst the collection draws to a close, our work continues with multiple resulting projects coming from this huge set of stories. We come together on 17th May, 2025 at Undershaw to celebrate in person with David and many of the participating authors – and hopefully many of you online too. We'll raise a glass to Sir Arthur, who would no doubt be proud with what we all together have been able to achieve.

Steve Emecz
February 2025

The Doyle Room at Undershaw
Partially funded through royalties from
The MX Book of New Sherlock Holmes Stories

A Word from Undershaw
by Emma West

Undershaw
September 9, 2016
Grand Opening of the Stepping Stones School
(Now *Undershaw*)
(Photograph courtesy of Roger Johnson)

It is with immense gratitude that I write the final words from Undershaw for this last publication of *The MX Book of New Sherlock Holmes Stories*, a collection compiled in support of Undershaw's restoration.

These stories have not only entertained us, but have also played a vital role in transforming the lives of our students. Thanks to the generosity of MX Publishing, we have been able to maintain this historic building while developing an inspiring learning environment for 102 students with Special Educational Needs and Disabilities.

Our partnership with MX Publishing has enriched our school community, offering opportunities and experiences that may otherwise have been out of reach for many of our students. Undershaw stands as a beacon of creativity, learning, and success – fitting for a place so closely linked to the literary legacy of Sir Arthur Conan Doyle.

As we mark this milestone – 52 volumes in the series – we also look forward to celebrating with "A Soirée with Sherlock Holmes", a special event dedicated to the great detective and his creator. Led by MX

Publishing, the evening will include a wonderful auction, streamed around the globe, with proceeds directly benefiting our students. These funds will support the creation of a cutting-edge media lab, complete with state-of-the-art computers, cameras, editing software, and a green screen, allowing our budding writers to bring their stories to life in print and on the screen.

Undershaw is more than just a historic site – it is a place where storytelling, imagination, and creativity thrive. The legacy of Sherlock Holmes continues to inspire our students, equipping them with skills for the future while fostering a lifelong love of literature. We are incredibly fortunate to be part of this ongoing journey and deeply grateful for our enduring partnership with MX Publishing. Their unwavering support has helped change the lives of countless young people.

Though the final volumes of this incredible collection, the impact of these stories – and the generosity behind them – will live on. The pages may close on this chapter, but the spirit of Sherlock Holmes, and the difference this series has made, will remain. Thanks to the unwavering support of MX Publishing and their community of authors and readers, Undershaw will continue to inspire generations to come, ensuring that the Great Detective's legacy is not only preserved, but carried forward into the future.

With heartfelt thanks and appreciation,

Emma West
Headteacher
February 2025

"Undershaw," Hindhead. Conan Doyle's House.

Editor's *Caveats*

When these anthologies first began back in 2015, I noted that the authors were from all over the world – and thus, there would be British spelling and American spelling. As I explained then, I didn't want to take the responsibility of changing American spelling to British and vice-versa. I would undoubtedly miss something, leading to inconsistencies, or I'd change something incorrectly.

Some readers are bothered by this, made nervous and irate when encountering American spelling as written by Watson, and in stories set in England. However, here in America, the versions of The Canon that we read have long-ago has their spelling Americanized, so it isn't quite as shocking for us.

Additionally, I offer my apologies up front for any typographical errors that have slipped through. As a print-on-demand publisher, MX does not have squadrons of editors as some readers believe. The business consists of three part-time people who also have busy lives elsewhere – Steve Emecz, Sharon Emecz, and Timi Emecz – so the editing effort largely falls on the contributors. Some readers and consumers out there in the world are unhappy with this – apparently forgetting about all of those self-produced Holmes stories and volumes from decades ago (typed and Xeroxed) with awkward self-published formatting and loads of errors that are now prized as very expensive collector's items.

I'm personally mortified when errors slip through – ironically, there will probably be errors in these *caveats* – and I apologize now, but without a regiment of professional full-time editors looking over my shoulder, this is as good as it gets. Real life is more important than writing and editing – even in such a good cause as promoting the True and Traditional Canonical Holmes – and only so much time can be spent preparing these books before they're released into the wild. I hope that you can look past any errors, small or huge, and simply enjoy these stories, and appreciate the efforts of everyone involved, and the sincere desire to add to The Great Holmes Tapestry.

And in spite of any errors here, there are more Sherlock Holmes stories in the world than there were before, and that's a good thing.

David Marcum
Editor

Sherlock Holmes (1854-1957) was born in Yorkshire, England, on 6 January, 1854. In the mid-1870's, he moved to 24 Montague Street, London, where he established himself as the world's first Consulting Detective. After meeting Dr. John H. Watson in early 1881, he and Watson moved to rooms at 221b Baker Street, where his reputation as the world's greatest detective grew for several decades. He was presumed to have died battling noted criminal Professor James Moriarty on 4 May, 1891, but he returned to London on 5 April, 1894, resuming his consulting practice in Baker Street. Retiring to the Sussex coast near Beachy Head in October 1903, he continued to be associated in various private and government investigations while giving the impression of being a reclusive apiarist. He was very involved in the events encompassing World War I, and to a lesser degree those of World War II. He passed away peacefully upon the cliffs above his Sussex home on his 103rd birthday, 6 January, 1957.

Dr. John Hamish Watson (1852-1929) was born in Stranraer, Scotland on 7 August, 1852. In 1878, he took his Doctor of Medicine Degree from the University of London, and later joined the army as a surgeon. Wounded at the Battle of Maiwand in Afghanistan (27 July, 1880), he returned to London late that same year. On New Year's Day, 1881, he was introduced to Sherlock Holmes in the chemical laboratory at Barts. Agreeing to share rooms with Holmes in Baker Street, Watson became invaluable to Holmes's consulting detective practice. Watson was married and widowed three times, and from the late 1880's onward, in addition to his participation in Holmes's investigations and his medical practice, he chronicled Holmes's adventures, with the assistance of his literary agent, Sir Arthur Conan Doyle, in a series of popular narratives, most of which were first published in *The Strand* magazine. Watson's later years were spent preparing a vast number of his notes of Holmes's cases for future publication. Following a final important investigation with Holmes, Watson contracted pneumonia and passed away on 24 July, 1929.

Photos of Sherlock Holmes and Dr. John H. Watson courtesy of Roger Johnson

The
MX Book
of
New
Sherlock
Holmes
Stories

Part LII
The True Sherlock Holmes:
England's Greatest Hero
(1902-1923)

Sherlock Holmes: The End?
by Joseph W. Svec III

Sherlock sat in contemplation,
silent as can be.
Almost as in mediation,
for it was time, you see.

The end was near, "retirement".
Strange as it may seem.
For many years as by they went
It was just a dream.

He had discovered every clue.
Resolved every case.
Now it's time for something new,
to run a brand-new race.

Demon dogs, and hidden rooms,
cryptic dancing men
are in the past with all their dooms.
This is the time when

he can relax. (Can he really?)
But what will he do?
Something new that he can freely
enjoy through and through.

Should he take up gourmet cooking,
create that perfect dish?
It's almost like searching, looking
for clues as he might wish.

Or should he take up writing riddles
for readers to resolve?
Or just continue playing fiddles?
How might that evolve?

Sherlock pondered more and more
when at last he did see
buzzing through the open door
a solitary bee.

"Fascinating", he did muse,
"Now there is something sweet,
 a whole new subject I can choose,
It will be a treat!

Beekeeping now I shall try.
Thea's so much for to learn.
To crime solving, I say goodbye.
And with that I adjourn."

And so, my dearest reader friend,
that's how it came to be.
His detecting came to an end,
as clearly you can see.

But he is Sherlock! It can't end!
What would readers do?
Their demands they always send
for cases strange and new.

So here we are with this book,
the MX Anthology.
Brand new stories. Take a look.
As clever as can be.

Sherlock lives on in stories new
for your reading pleasure.
Yes, you'll find Watson too.
Their friendship you can treasure.

What is the newest adventure?
(That won't involve a bee?)
Turn the page and do venture,
and surely you will see.

The Adventure of the
Disgraced Baron
by Derrick Belanger

We rode home in silence. I stared out the frosty window, listening to the clopping sound of the horses' hooves and felt the gentle rocking of the carriage jostling back and forth as we made our way back to Baker Street. I couldn't see much through the window, just the occasional glow from a streetlight, or the bright beams from a passing motor coach.

London had changed. The world had changed, I thought to myself on that frigid evening early in 1902. My friend Sherlock Holmes remained quiet, and so my mind continued ruminating on the marvelous changes to the world which had occurred over the last few years. Holmes and I now, on occasions traveled in automobiles rather than in coaches. The detective rarely sent letters or telegrams, preferring to conduct business via the telephone, and I clacked away at a typewriter while drafting my tales instead of writing out by hand.

Holmes and I were returning from an amateur production of *Othello* at a new theatre near the Strand. The theatre, while small in size, did not lack talent. The company was called The Stratford-upon-London Players, and their focus was on the Bard. I was particularly impressed by the fellow who played Othello, an Egyptian named Al-katib, as well as the cast member who played Iago, a Welshman named Evans, who perfectly captured the villain's duplicitous nature. The actress playing Desdemona, while competent, seemed a bit old for the part, but she captured the innocence of the woman at the heart of the tragedy.

My friend and I had remained long after the end of the performance, which was not well attended. Holmes, playing the part of fellow actor, offered his advice to the Company on ways to improve not only their performance, but their business acumen. The troupe listened attentively, as did I, for it was a side of the detective I rarely saw: That of an entrepreneur.

It was close to midnight when we left the show, and despite the cold and lateness of the hour, there were still three cabs next to the kerb outside the theatre. One was motorized. The second, a small hansom, was taken by a gentleman who looked to be in a hurry, and the third, parked right in front of the theatre, was a cart drawn by two hackneys. I couldn't help but navigate toward the driver of the latter horse-powered vehicle and strike up a conversation.

"I kenna sell ma girls," he said in a thick accent, indicating the two mares attached to his carriage, one named Agnes and the other May. "I see more and more of these horseless contraptions cluttering the roadways, but I'd be lonely driving one o' those." I told him I understood that there was a grace and connection to the old ways of life, of farming and the land, by having a connection to these animals. Before we left, the driver let me feed the two beauties carrots.

I thought Holmes might chastise me for caring about the horses, for taking the longer ride back to Baker Street. He didn't say a word though. He just sat quiet, bundled up and staring out the window, the same as I did.

Despite the changes to the world, despite my using the technological advances, I was still in many ways what Holmes referred to as a "fixed point". I still enjoyed long walks, still enjoyed seeing the red lantern lit outside a medical practice, and still enjoyed handwriting letters instead of using the telephone for communication.

I remained in Baker Street, still roomed with my eccentric friend, still enjoyed Mrs. Hudson's cooking and company.

Though he'd be loath to admit it, Holmes was in many ways just as fixed as I was. He still maintained the same routines, often playing the violin to free his mind and help him solve cases, and he still maintained his odd habit of keeping his cigars in the coal-scuttle and his tobacco in the toe end of a Persian slipper. The portrait of *The* Woman remained upon the mantel, and even though we were now ruled by a king, Holmes never painted or papered over the letters *V.R.* he'd shot into the wall of our sitting room. Holmes would always be a Queen's man.

"We have arrived," my friend said as the carriage turned a street corner. I couldn't tell where we were due to the thick ice upon the window. Holmes, like a homing pigeon, seemed to always know his location in London. "I apologize for being poor company," he added.

"No need to apologize," I said, and added, "I enjoyed the quiet."

He nodded.

"Were you thinking of the play?" I asked.

"I was," he said. "I was trying to remember when I'd seen the actor who played Iago. It took me some time to recall, but I now know where and when. It was some time ago, back in my theatre days when I was performing in America. That was decades ago. He must have been only about five years old at the time. He was with his father, the producer of the show. I'll explain more later. We shouldn't dawdle in the dark and cold."

Holmes stepped out to pay the driver, and I marveled at my friend's memory. That was another thing that hadn't changed: His mind was sharp as ever.

When I stepped outside into the frosty night, I noticed a rather nice jalopy parked in front of No. 219. I recognized the car as a Packard, though I hadn't seen this model before. The streetlamp illuminated the vehicle, and I was struck by its cherry-red color and wood-spoke wheels. The automobile was pricey, I knew, and I wondered which of our neighbors owned it.

The sound of the horses pulling the cab down the road caught my attention, and I turned to find Holmes now standing by my side. "Are you ready?" he asked.

"Ready to turn in?" I asked him.

"No," he chuckled. "Ready to get a firm tongue lashing."

I was perplexed and asked, "What do you mean?"

"Look at the windows, my friend. Even with the ice upon them, you can see that the lights in both the ground floor and up in our rooms. It means we have a client waiting for us inside. It also means that Mrs. Hudson has stayed awake with said client, waiting for us to return. Had I known, I wouldn't have stayed so long with the acting troupe."

Holmes was correct. Mrs. Hudson flung the door open at the sound of our approach, her frail body stood in the entryway, her eyes blazing like the Fires of Hell.

"Well, it's about time, Mr. Sherlock Holmes!" she snapped at my companion. "And you, too, Dr. Watson." She turned to face me, so that I might share in the brunt of her fury. "Making me stay up into the early hours of the morning! Having strange men knocking on my door close to the witching hour! What will the neighbors say? I should charge you an extra sitting fee for this!"

The detective made a slight bow. "I apologize, Mrs. Hudson. Had I known a client would arrive at such a late hour, I would have remained at home this evening. Please, by all means, add a surcharge to our rent for this month."

"Don't think I won't," Mrs. Hudson lambasted Holmes, but her tone had softened. The landlady melted a bit at Holmes's humbling. She just couldn't stay angry with him. "Oh, you both get inside out of the cold. Now that you're here, the client's your problem. I'm going to bed."

Good old Mrs. Hudson! I thought as she made her way to her room. Our landlady had dealt with Holmes's insufferable inclinations over the years – firing guns indoors or setting fire to the carpet to determine the length of time it took for its material to be engulfed by flames, yet I knew Mrs. Hudson had a special place for him in her heart. She would be distraught if he finally decided to retire, move away, and become a full time apiarist as he had discussed with me on several occasions.

"Come along now, Watson. Let us see what brings this wealthy client to our door."

I followed Holmes up the steps to our room as we continued in conversation. "How do you know he's wealthy?"

Holmes paused. "Really, Watson – you were eyeing the man's Packard."

"How do you know that belongs to the client?"

"No one living in Baker Street could afford such a vehicle, or if they could," he corrected himself, "they wouldn't want to draw the attention such a vehicle would bring." Holmes was, of course, referring to the two of us.

When we entered our sitting room, we found a young well-dressed man, sipping tea and sitting by the fire. He put the tea down and stood to greet us. He was handsome, with a face that could have been chiseled by Michaelangelo and eyes that could capture many a young lass's heart. His suit was tailored to accentuate his rugged body, and the ring he wore was more valuable than our abode.

"My name is Sully," he said in a melodic, deep voice. He had an accent, but I couldn't place its region. "You must be Mr. Holmes and Dr. Watson."

"Nice to meet you, Mr. Sully," I said. I hesitated and then added, "It is '*Mister*'?" I wondered if I should be addressing him as '*Lord*'.

"Officially, that's right, Doctor," he explained. "I prefer to be called Baron Sully. In my homeland, that is how the locals refer to me, even though no title has been bestowed upon me."

"Then we shall also refer to you as Baron. You own land?" Holmes enquired.

"I do, sir – or I should say that I did. Quite a bit of land. I had many tenants until recently. My family's land acquisition had been rather new, starting only with my grandfather, and the holdings weren't located in England, but in the Crown Jewel."

"India?" I asked. "Is that where you're from?"

"I am, Doctor, but I've been living mostly in London since I turned eight, so for most of my thirty years."

"And what brings you to us at this late hour?" Holmes asked as he took his seat and motioned for us to join him.

We did so. I took to my chair while the Baron leaned back into the couch across from us. Holmes offered the man more tea or something a bit stronger, but he declined, simply wanting to share with us his troubles.

"Gentlemen, have you seen this?" He took a magazine he'd kept on the stand by his empty cup and thrust it at Holmes. The detective took the printed piece and read the title aloud. "*Grace's Gazette*," said Holmes. I noted a touch of humor in his voice. "I can't say that I partake in magazines aimed at the fairer sex."

Sully shook his head, crossed his arms, and muttered, "To know as much as you claim to know, you really should. The magazine should be called *The Gossip Gazette*. All they do is run insinuations and let the readers believe they are stating fact instead of vaguely worded fiction."

"From your manner," Holmes said, politely, "I perceive that this has to do with your case."

"Turn to page fifty-three," muttered Sully. "You'll see exactly what this has to do with me."

Holmes did as he was asked. I knew when my friend landed on the correct page. His face became much sterner and focused. His eyes moved quickly back and forth like the wipers on the windshields of automobiles. Less than a minute later, Holmes handed the open magazine to me.

The page was one of those with a catchy headline and splashy photographs. The title said, *Is This Caged Bird Free?* Below the title were two paired images of a scandalous and salacious nature. The first group showed a man either speaking into the ear of a very attractive young woman or kissing her neck. The woman's eyes and smile were those of a smitten girl next to her beau. The second picture in the pair clearly showed the identity of the man: It was the person sitting across from me, Baron Sully. He and the girl were longingly gazing into each other's eyes. Below these photos were a second set. This one showed a man with his back to the camera helping a different fetching young woman out of a carriage. The woman was quite pleased with the young man. The second image in the pair, showed that the man who aided the woman was, again, Baron Sully. This image showed him embracing the young woman. I couldn't help but wonder what the pair had gotten up to when they were alone in that carriage. Clearly that was the intent of the headline and images.

The subheading explained: "*In last month's issue, we announced the engagement of Mr. Sully with Lady Gordon, daughter of the Right Honorable Lord Gordon, and called them dedicated love birds. Perhaps, one of the birds isn't ready to settle down quite yet.*"

The article continued to make veiled accusations against Sully, hinting at him being unfaithful to his fiancé with both of these women. It continued on to argue that the affair besmirched not only her Ladyship, but Lord Gordon himself, and by extension the entire House of Lords. Perhaps the most indecent accusation was when it said that when the Baron decided to settle down, he might be more comfortable in the American state of Utah – the writer was accusing the Baron of being a polygamist. The article concluded by implying the only way forward was to have the

Lady end the engagement, thus saving her illustrious family name from being dragged through the mud alongside that of Baron Sully.

I closed the magazine, feeling both shock and astonishment which must have shown. I noted that the article was written by "Miss Noble" – a *nom de plume*, I was certain. There was nothing *noble* about her work.

"It is incredulous that they would publish such an article about me," the Baron complained.

"Is it?" asked Holmes, giving both Sully and me pause. Tension thickened the air in the room. "To be perfectly clear," Holmes continued in a stern voice, "I'm asking if there is any truth to what is implied by both the photographs and the written article itself. If there is, I ask you to be forthcoming."

The Baron inhaled deeply, his fists clenched, and I thought he might take a swing at Holmes, but his anger deflated as quickly as it rose. His shoulders slumped, and the man went from a look of fury to one of despair.

"There's no truth to the matter, Mr. Holmes," the Baron muttered in anguish. "I don't know either of those women."

"The photographs?" Holmes pressed.

The Baron kept his head down, looking shameful. "I was being a gentleman," he said softly. "I don't know those women, but I did meet both of them." He held up his head. "The girl in the first two photos simply asked me for directions. She told me she was hard of hearing, and that's why I spoke into her ear. The other woman's carriage had pulled up to the kerb near me. She called out and asked if I could lend her a hand to step down. She claimed to have a weak ankle. I swear to you. Those are the only times I've seen those women in my life, and my actions were those of kindness, nothing more."

Holmes's grey eyes softened at the man's display of emotion. The detective stood up and excused himself for a moment. He returned with his pipe and some of his tobacco, something he indulged in much less frequently than in the past. "Your situation begins to intrigue me," Holmes said. He struck a match and lit his pipe. After a couple of puffs, he said. "Please – start your story at the beginning. Tell me how you ended up in this predicament."

"It starts with Elsie – that is, the Lady Gordon," Sully answered in his low baritone voice. "I am a man who has always been married to my work. My family has been connected to the Indian Continent for three generations. My grandfather worked for The East India Company before the native uprising. He worked hard and used his salary to acquire land. He loved the country, the jungle, and the natives.

"After the rule of law in India was transferred to the Crown, he was able to negotiate a good price for the crops that the natives grew on his land. He used that money to acquire more land and then diversified his investments. My father continued using grandfather's methods, and then he passed on his knowledge in business dealings to me.

"I apologize, gentlemen," Sully frowned and shook his head. "I was supposed to tell you about when I first met Elsie, and here I am telling you my family history - although now that I think of it, my past is important to understanding the complexities of my case."

"No need to apologize, sir," Holmes said with a wave of his hand. "Your history is quite interesting, and I believe it could be of use to me in solving your problem. You were saying that you learned your business sense from your father."

"Yes," Sully continued. "Father taught me much. However, he also knew his limitations, and insisted on sending me to London for my schooling, despite Mother's protests. She didn't like me spending the year half-a-world away from her.

"Father wouldn't hear of me being taught in Bengaluru, and so, at the age of eight, I was sent away to London. I spent the remainder of my childhood with two homes, spending most of my time in Britain, only returning home once, when I was fourteen, to attend a ceremony in my father's honor. but returning to India for my breaks between semesters when possible.

"It was shortly after my eighteenth birthday when tragedy struck. Both of my parents were killed in a flood. An embankment broke after a monsoon rain, and when it burst, waters washed away a small village that my parents were visiting. There were no survivors."

"How awful," I said. "You lost both your parents at such a young age."

"I was young, but not that young. I was an adult, and I returned to Bengaluru and became consumed by work. I knew with my parents' passing, corrupt businessmen and officials, both of Indian and British descent, would try to take advantage of the situation. I was determined not to let that happen.

"My father had trained me well, and I used my youth and inexperience as a tool, a weapon really, in my dealings. I knew they'd underestimate me because of my age, and I used that to my advantage. By the time I was twenty-five, my family's holdings had doubled.

"Then, I surprised my competitors again by turning around and selling off most of my property in India. I could see that change was in the air. Reform was taking root within the Indian National Congress, and it was inevitable that at some point in the future, the natives would reclaim their land. I don't begrudge them in the least. If some outside force took

51

control of Britain, I'd fight 'til my dying breath to keep the Union Jack flying.

"I sold my land to the farmers who were tending it. That won me goodwill among the people. My additional business investments – my shipping companies, hotels, groceries, butcher shops, the list goes on and on – they all prospered even more than they had before.

"With my additional revenue, I invested heavily in British and American businesses. For the last five years, I've been splitting my time between London, New York, and Bengalaru – at least I was until about five months ago when I met Elsie. I was seated by her at a banquet. She is a fetching, delicate woman, and so I was taken in by her beauty. However, I'd been married to my work for so long that I hardly even noticed the ladies anymore. She struck up a conversation with me, and I was immediately smitten. She asked me about my work, and I responded. I didn't talk down to her. I spoke as a businessman and, to my surprise, she spoke right back to me using the same language. She was impressed with the expansion of my operations, thought it noble that I sold my land holdings to the occupants, and sympathized with the loss of my parents. She, too, has known loss. Her mother died when she was just ten years old, taken by tuberculosis. By the end of the banquet, I knew I wanted to spend the rest of my life with this woman. I asked if I could call upon her at her home. She said that I could, but I'd need to speak with her father first.

"That gave me pause, gentlemen. Although I, of course, told her I'd expect no less, and I'd be honored to meet her father, in truth I was nervous."

"You are a wealthy, young, highly successful businessman," Holmes said to him. "Why were you concerned?"

"For one, my age. While I am thirty years old, Elsie is a mere nineteen. But that is minor compared to my true concern. My family's wealth was acquired fairly recently. I am what the aristocrats mockingly call *Nouveau Rich*. I have no titles. My family has no crest."

"No matter how successful a man is, it is always nerve-racking to meet the father of a belle," I explained to Holmes. Unlike the detective, I'd had some experience with these feelings in the past.

"Ah, Watson, I suppose these are matters where you are more the expert than I," Holmes said to me. He then asked the baron, "Tell me sir, were your concerns warranted?"

"I'm pleased to say they were not. Lord Gordon is a respectful and honest fellow. Naturally, he asked me about my background, business dealings, and of my time in India. While he was kind, I could tell he was probing, checking to make sure I was the man I claimed to be. He was quite knowledgeable about Bengalaru and the customs of the Hindus. I gathered this was from his work as a member of the House of Lords."

"I take it you passed the test," I said, almost ribbing him.

"Yes," he replied with a jaunty laugh. "Lord Gordon and I became fast friends. He had no objection when I asked for his permission to wed his daughter. If he wasn't walking Elsie down the aisle, I would have asked him to be my best man. Alas, now I may have lost them both, all because of these scandalous photos," the Baron lamented.

"Keep your chin up, sir," Holmes said, not wanting the man to wallow in his misery and lose focus. "Tell me more about the photos. Which one was taken first?"

"The one inside Paddington Station. I had just returned from Bristol and had paused to check the time. That's when the woman came up to me. She asked if I could tell her where to catch the train to Reading. I pointed out the track, but she shook her head and told me that she was nearly deaf. That's when she motioned for me to speak in her ear. I leaned in and told her the location. She then looked me in the eye and thanked me before wandering off."

"Was there anything suspicious about her?" asked Holmes.

"Not that I can recall. I thought she looked at me a bit intensely, but I assumed that was probably because she was reading my lips."

"Were you aware of a camera – perhaps a clicking noise such?"

"I did not. The station is quite loud. I doubt I would have heard a camera if it was next to me."

Holmes paused for a moment, soaking in this information. He then asked, "The second woman – she, too, was at Paddington Station, but outside of it?"

"You have a keen eye to catch that, Mr. Holmes," replied the Baron. "That's right. This was three days after my encounter with the first woman. I had, again, returned from Bristol. I had just stepped outside of the station to Praed Street and was going to hail a cab when this woman called out to me. She asked me to help her down, and stated that I could use her cab once she was outside of it."

"Just a minute," said Holmes, interrupting the Baron. "Did you end up taking the cab after she left?"

"I did," he replied.

"Describe the cab to me."

"It was a brougham, painted brown with light blue trim, single steed. The driver was a Scotchman, I'd guess, from his thick red beard and his brogue."

"What else do you recall about the driver?" Holmes pressed.

"Not much. I didn't pay attention to him."

"How about the horse?"

The Baron's eyes lit up at this question. "Actually, there was something unusual about the horse. It was a Clydesdale, but the coloring was interesting. He was black in color, and there was a white stripe going down the stallion's back. The driver called him 'Skunkie'." The Baron paused in his description, his face moving to a look of puzzlement. "Say, I don't see how that's important."

Holmes had a look of triumph in his eyes, but he didn't show it to the Baron. "Perhaps it is, and perhaps it isn't," Holmes replied nonchalantly. "Now, tell me about the woman in the carriage. She asked for help?"

"Yes," the Baron replied. "She said she had a weak ankle and needed assistance stepping out of the carriage. As I told you, I obliged. After she stepped down, she thanked me, and then she slipped, almost tumbling to the ground. I caught her and helped her regain her balance. That is the final image you see in the journal. I was holding her to help her regain her balance. However, in the photograph, it looks like we are embracing as though we are lovers." He let out a groan at this acknowledgement. "When Elsie saw those photos . . . Well, I've never heard her so furious."

"Even the Devil himself is afraid of the fury of a woman scorned," I muttered, also thinking of times I'd faced such a wrath myself.

"The pictures are suggestive," Holmes said. "I'm not surprised that her reaction was one of anger."

"It was, Mr. Holmes, but she did still take my telephone call. We spoke and I explained to her just what I explained to you. She said she wants to believe me, but she also isn't naive. She needs proof. I understand her reasoning. That's why I came straight to you after speaking with her. If there is anyone who can clear my name, it is you."

"I shall do my best, Baron. I have just a few more questions for you."

"Go on."

"What was your business in Bristol?" asked Holmes.

"I was inspecting some of the businesses in which I've invested: A sugar refinery, some tin factories, and a foundry."

"Who had knowledge that you'd be in Bristol on those days and would be at Paddington Station at those specific times?"

"It was no secret. My secretary and a number of my business associates knew my schedule, as did Elsie."

"Is there anyone who you believe would want to personally hurt you or your businesses?"

"I have some rivals, but I don't believe any of them would stoop this low."

"Any jilted lovers?"

"Mr. Holmes, really," the Baron said, insulted. "I've already explained that I didn't have time in my life for romance before meeting Elsie."

"Yes, you did," agreed Holmes. "I just wanted you to say it again while I watched you closely. I now know that you are telling the truth.

"What of Lord Gordon? Have you had any contact with him since the article was published?"

"I'm afraid not," the Baron frowned. "I tried to reach out to him first, but his Lordship will not speak with me. Elsie told me that he's rather embarrassed by the ordeal, and he is rather disappointed in me. He has revoked his blessing of our engagement."

"I see," said Holmes, nodding. He stood and handed the Baron a pencil and some paper. "Please write down the names of all you can recall who knew of your schedule when you traveled to Bristol. I'd like to make some inquiries."

The Baron began writing. "So, you do think one of my business rivals may be behind the pictures," he groaned through gritted teeth.

"I'm not suggesting anything," Holmes countered. "I need data before I can begin calculating. Only with facts shall I arrive at the truth."

"Thank you, Mr. Holmes," said the Baron as he finished up. "I wrote the telephone number to my secretary at the bottom of the page. His name's Mr. Jonathan Belleth, and he will provide you with any information you need about these contacts. If you need their addresses, telephone numbers, places of employment – anything at all – just ask good old Mr. Belleth."

The detective, client, and I stood. We said our goodbyes to the Baron and Holmes assured him that he would be in touch within two days' time.

Once the Baron left, I asked Holmes what he thought of the matter. "The Baron's telling the truth, at least what he believes to be the truth."

"Is he too trusting?"

Holmes thought about that for a moment and then shook his head. "No, I don't think he'd have the success he does if he could be easily tricked. It won't be helpful to speculate, Watson. I must make inquiries tomorrow. Speaking of tomorrow, what does your day look like?"

"I have some appointments I must keep in the morning, but I could easily clear my afternoon."

"Splendid," Holmes replied with a clap of his hands. "I shall begin my inquiries then and have news for you when you come home for lunch."

I returned earlier than expected the following day. A late-morning appointment with a medical researcher was cancelled, and so I was back in Baker Street in time for Elevenses. Holmes was delighted to see me.

"I've made much progress on the case," he explained. "The amount of ground I can cover over the telephone is truly marvelous. I would have returned late this evening if I had to visit Bristol myself.

"Now, thanks to the help of the Baron's secretary, Mr. Belleth, I've been able to interview a dozen businessmen, as well as the author of the journal article."

I lowered the cup of Darjeeling from my lips and said, "I'm impressed. And you never set foot outside of our abode?"

"Not quite, Doctor. I gathered a few of the Irregulars, divided them up, and gave them two missions. One group was tasked with finding the cab that brought the second woman to meet with the Baron. The second group was tasked with finding the two women in the photographs.

"The first group had a much easier task. There are less horse-drawn carriages on the road, and the horse had such distinct features I knew that they'd locate the cab before the middle of the morning. They did, and I telephoned his cab company and specifically requested the man. He left about an hour before you arrived."

"My goodness!" I exclaimed. "You'll have the case wrapped up by sundown."

The detective added more water to his tea and then took a bite out of a scone before continuing. "I've identified the man behind the photographs," he said, decisively.

"Really?" I asked, wide-eyed. "Well, I guess you solved the case before it even began."

"I know the man but not the motive," Holmes countered. "You see, I started by calling the secretary, Belleth, and he gave me the telephone numbers for the men on the list. All of them spoke highly of the Baron's character, and added that he is quite a powerful businessman, yet he's known for being fair and even kind in his business practice. One man, Mr. Argensol of the Argensol Umbrella Factory, told me how the Baron invested in his company when it was in trouble and righted the ship. None of the men I spoke with seemed inclined to want to ruin the Baron's reputation. Since they're in business with the man, they could be considered guilty of poor character by being associated with him.

"I then contacted Miss Noble at *The Gazette*. As I'm sure you surmised, Miss Noble was not the real name of the author. It was, in fact, Mr. Gibbor."

"A man?" I asked, surprised.

Holmes gave me a *tsk-tsk*. "Come now, Watson, it's well known that most, if not all, publications angled at women are authored by men using pen names."

I confessed that I was unaware of this information. Honestly, I had been a widower for a number of years and had no knowledge of the world of publications aimed at a female audience.

"Knowing that the author wouldn't easily give up information, I took the role of a police sergeant and told him a story I'd concocted – that the woman in the first two photographs, Mrs. Merryweather was the name I bestowed upon her – had disappeared and there was belief of foul play.

"I correctly surmised that the man didn't know the identities of the women, and that he'd be interested in a story in which the Baron was seen with a married woman who had disappeared. That was all it took for him to tell me everything he knew. He didn't know much, only the identity of the man who brought him the photographs and the story."

"Who was it?"

"Lord Chauncey Abbot is his name. He's a real Baron – that is, by birth title – and for a reason not yet known to us, he is the man who hired the cab and brought the photographs to *The Gazette*."

"Why would he do such a thing?" I asked.

"You know I don't speculate," Holmes chastised. "But we shall have our answer soon enough. We have an appointment with the man at two o'clock this afternoon."

"So what if I did give *The Gazette* those photographs?" growled Lord Chauncey. "I helped the world see what a cad that fake Baron is. That's all."

Holmes and I were seated before his Lordship in his library, overlooking his vast estate. There was something rather comical about the man. His features made him look like a character from a children's book. His body was round and his legs squat, almost like Humpty Dumpty from the Mother Goose rhyme. His face, with a large nose and jutting teeth, reminded me of the Hatter at Alice's tea party.

Even more ridiculous: When we arrived at the gate of the man's estate, he'd had his servant drive us around the grounds in a buggy, giving us a tour, showing off his Lordship's wealth, before allowing us to enter his home. When we were finally presented to the man, he had us take seats before his desk. I noted that they were designed to be low to the ground so that the squat, portly fellow could look down upon anyone who sat before him.

"It seems odd to ruin a man's reputation on suspicion alone," said Holmes to the Lord.

"What do you mean, *suspicion*? You saw who he was with." His eyes softened at the mention of her name. Then he scowled and concluded, "I've made certain that the whole world knows what a louse the man is.

57

He's rotten, and with the public knowing the man's character, there's no way that Lady Elsie will ever take him back."

"I see," said Holmes, his lips curled up ever so slightly in a knowing smile. "So tell me, how long have you been in love with her Ladyship?"

"What?" snapped Lord Chauncey. "I never said."

"You didn't need to," answered Holmes. "Your mannerisms at the mention of her name tell all. Did you propose and she declined your offer of matrimony, or have you loved her from afar?"

This question stung his Lordship. His eyes evaded Holmes's, and his face showed the pain of his situation.

"You had assistance in this plan to disgrace the Baron," Holmes said. Lord Chauncey continued to look downward, overcome by melancholy. Holmes asked a follow-up question. "Was it a servant?"

The question snapped his Lordship back to attention. He glared at Holmes and gave a menacing laugh. "That's enough from you. I shall speak no more of this matter," he concluded decisively. Lord Chauncey then called his servants and had us escorted off the premises.

Fortunately, Holmes had made sure our cab driver waited for us. Holmes opened his billet and gave the man a small stack of bills along with an address. "My good sir, should you need my services in the future," the driver said as he counted the roll of money, "I promise to make you, as my customer, my number one priority."

"I shall consider your offer. Let me first see how quickly you can take me to that address."

"Lightning will move slower," the driver told us. He then cranked the engine, hopped in the automobile, and we were off, barreling through the roads.

"Why aren't we returning to Baker Street?" I asked as we sped back to the city.

"The case isn't concluded," Holmes responded matter-of-factly.

"But we know that Lord Chauncey is responsible for the photographs, and we know his motivation. Even if there are some lingering questions, what more do you need to tell the client?"

"I owe the Baron the full story. Lord Chauncey may have been the puppet who delivered the photographs, but he wasn't the master pulling the strings and orchestrating this charade."

"Ah, yes. You asked him about someone assisting him. You alluded to one of his servants."

"I wanted to see how he'd react. From his dismissive laughter, I knew it wasn't a member of the domestic class. With the servants and businessmen eliminated as partners, there can be only one man remaining who can be identified by the mastermind behind this evil game."

"Who?"

"You shall meet him soon enough. I had the foresight to make two appointments for us this afternoon."

"One was with Lord Chauncey," I answered.

"And the other is with The Right Honorable Lord Gordon."

If I were an artist commissioned to paint the epitome of the British aristocrat, I would undoubtedly be successful if I were to use Lord Gordon as my model. His stiff, rigid form had a perfect posture. His face was hard set, his lips stony, and his eyes conveyed a learned man who wouldn't flinch if he had to kill an enemy to save a countryman.

"Mr. Holmes, Dr. Watson, it is a great honor to have such renowned visitors in my parlor," he told us after we'd been escorted in by his footman. "Please have a seat," he said, motioning us to sit in the leather recliners. "May I offer you a cigar?"

Holmes and I accepted. "Cuban?" I asked, after enjoying the first few puffs.

"Yes. I have them sent directly from Havannah," he explained, enjoying one as well.

"If I may, my Lord – " Holmes started moving the conversation from pleasantries to the point of our visit.

"You are here on behalf of Mr. Sully," said the Lord.

"Yes," Holmes concurred. "As I'm sure you're aware, some rather salacious photographs of the man were recently published, harming his reputation, as well as his relationship with your daughter."

The Lord gave a jaunty little laugh. "Those photos have caused a bit of a stir, haven't they?" he asked.

"They have, sir."

"I know. I'm the one who had them published," the Lord said, his face returning to that of a chiseled statue.

So surprised was I by this admission that I inhaled a good dose of smoke from my cigar and found myself having a coughing fit. Holmes comforted me, but, though I was red in face and short of breath, I managed to speak. "You . . . you . . . admit to this?"

"I do." He turned to Holmes. "Your reputation precedes you. It would serve no purpose to delay you discovering what I've just told you."

"But . . . but why would you do such a thing?" I asked.

The Lord paused for a moment, thinking how to respond, then continued, "Gentlemen, as the Americans like to say, I'll lay my cards on the table. I hate the Baron." He paused again and sneered in absolute disgust. "There are rumors that he and my daughter have prematurely consummated their relationship. I don't know if the rumors are true, but I did what I had to do to prevent them from being wed."

"My Lord," I started, "I understand how much you care for your daughter and her reputation, but you've said that what you've heard is just a rumor. Why not talk to her and the Baron, perhaps have a frank discussion with the two of them together. I wouldn't be surprised if this is all a misunderstanding because of how close they are. Sometimes when couples show even the slightest public display of affection, people jump to farfetched conclusions."

"It doesn't matter," the Lord grumbled. "Her reputation is already stained."

"But is it?" asked Holmes.

"I say so," the Lord rebutted.

Holmes let out a long sigh and extinguished the stub of his cigar in the ashtray beside him. "Let's look at the facts. The Baron is an exceedingly wealthy man, yes?"

"I don't deny it."

"And he is considered one of the more desirable bachelors in London."

"Perhaps."

"And he has a great love for your daughter and she for him."

"That's irrelevant," the Lord said dismissively.

"Ah," said Holmes with a nod. "You are a traditionalist, my Lord." Holmes paused and steepled his fingers for a moment before continuing. "You said that your daughter's reputation is important to you."

"It is," he agreed.

"And I'm sure your own reputation is as well."

The man *harrumphed* in agreement.

"Then it is peculiar to stand in the way of the marriage."

"I don't follow."

"If your daughter marries Baron Sully, then the issue of her losing her maidenhood prematurely, whether or not it is true, would go away. After all, as the doctor here can attest, a good number of newlyweds have their first child a mere six or seven months after they've exchanged their vows. Isn't that right, Watson?"

"It is quite common," I agreed. "Much more common than people would like to admit."

"There you are," Holmes said, appreciating my response. "But if you prevent the marriage, then the question of whether your daughter has prematurely become a woman would continue to be asked and the rumors would spread. When people are left to their imagination, they tend to fill in blanks with the most salacious explanations." Holmes's steel-grey eyes bore into the man. "You are an intelligent man, Lord Gordon. All I've said has already occurred to you. Therefore, there must be another reason for you to prevent the marriage – a reason more important than your daughter's reputation, and yours as well."

Lord Gordon took the cigar from his mouth, tapped off the ash which was dangling on the shaft, and rested it on the tray. He then shifted in his chair to get comfortable before turning to Holmes and me. "Are you both acquainted with the writings of Sir Francis Galton?"

The name sounded familiar to me, but I couldn't place it. I admitted that I wasn't familiar with the man. Holmes frowned deeply.

"I can see you know his work," the Lord said to Holmes. "Let me explain it to the Good Doctor. Sir Francis proposes that we've made a grave error as a society. We've taken care of the sick and the weak, and we've allowed the lesser humans to flourish upon the Earth. Sir Francis says that in order for natural selection to work, we've got to let the sick and the weak die, and we have to remove the sub-humans from the face of the Earth. Once the primordial masses are removed, then humanity can grow, flourish, evolve to return to the race that we were before being cast out of Eden. It is much like your patients. They can't get to a proper health if they are carrying around sickness and disease."

"I understand," I said coldly to this ridiculous theory. "You don't follow the Biblical view that the meek shall inherit the Earth."

"No, the meek and the huddled masses shall destroy the Earth."

"What the devil does this have to do with your daughter's wedding?" I practically shouted. I was frustrated by the man's ignoble beliefs. How could a man of supposed intelligence be so unwise, even stupid.

"It is Baron Sully's ancestry, isn't it?" asked Holmes, after I raised my question. "Is it one of his parents?"

"His grandmother, on his father's side," said the Lord in disgust. "His grandfather wasn't just seduced by the beauty of India. He betrayed his own race and married a native. Can you imagine, Mr. Holmes – my own flesh and blood marrying a *mongrel*? Can you imagine my bloodline being *tainted*? Only a purebred should have my family's name."

"So you ruined the Baron's reputation simply because his grandmother was Indian?" Holmes asked. I seldom saw such a look of absolute disgust on my friend's face.

"That I did, Detective. I will not have a drop of tainted blood flow through the veins of my descendants. I made certain that my daughter shall never marry the Baron, and there's nothing you can do about it."

"Perhaps the Baron and your daughter will disagree with you when they hear the truth, and how you've deceived them both."

The Lord gave a dark sadistic laugh. "Oh, I made sure that even the truth can't save the Baron. His reputation is as tainted as his blood, and there's nothing you or anyone else can do about it. Nothing at all."

I spent the next day in that odd space of being with patients and consulting with doctors, attempting to conduct my own research for an article I was writing for a medical journal, yet having the conversation with Lord Gordon constantly repeating in my mind. While I understood the man being protective of his daughter, particularly her reputation and all that entailed, I couldn't fathom why a man would cast stones at another because of his ancestry. I thought of how my own family, particularly my brother, was an embarrassment to me. I loathed the thought of being judged by his behavior.

In the Baron's case, he shouldn't feel any shame. His grandfather was extremely successful with his wife, Sully's Indian grandmother, by his side. That alone meant that she was someone to admire. I know of no successful, married man who didn't owe at least some of his success to his wife. I was a widower, and yet I don't think I could have survived the dark times after I thought Holmes had died alongside Professor Moriarty if it weren't for Mary's dutiful nursing of me. I couldn't fathom how Lord Gordon could judge a person simply because he or she came from a different part of the world and had a different skin tone than his own.

I concluded that Lord Gordon was a truly wicked man. He'd tricked his own daughter into doubting her fiancé, possibly even hating him. I thought of how different I would be if I was to ever have a child of my own. Then, I was overcome with melancholy, realizing that my days of romance had passed along with the life of my dear wife. *Will I ever be able to love again?* I wondered.

My sorrow was interrupted by a librarian bringing me a message from Holmes. He said he'd have a driver pick me up at three that afternoon. He believed he'd found a way to bring the Baron's case to a satisfying conclusion.

After reading the message several times, I found myself in a much brighter mood. Indeed, I'd say I was rather chattier than normal with my fellow researchers using the library that afternoon. We had fine conversations about the latest medicines and technological breakthroughs. By midafternoon, all the medical men I spoke with had a smile upon their faces. My optimism was contagious.

I stepped outside at exactly three o'clock after saying goodbye to my fellow researchers. I was most pleasantly surprised to find the Baron standing next to his Packard.

"Baron," I said. "How nice to see you."

"It's good to see you as well, Doctor," he said with a firm handshake. He gave me a brotherly slap on the back. "Holmes tells me you're to fill me in on the case while I drive us to Baker Street."

We both hopped into the vehicle. Before heading out into the traffic, I asked the Baron, "Has Holmes told you anything?"

"He told me you met with Lord Gordon, so I'm assuming you both have some information to share on the matter."

"I'm afraid that we do," I said sadly and told the Baron everything.

When the Baron finally parked his jalopy at my doorstep, I breathed a sigh of relief and wiped some sweat from my brow. As I explained the actions of the man who would've been his future father-in-law, the Baron's anger grew and grew, and his driving became more and more erratic. We'd had a few close calls, one where we almost nicked an omnibus, that I thought might be the end of our lives. Fortunately, we arrived safely.

On the way up the steps, the Baron started telling me his plan. "I'll explain everything to Elsie, and she'll take me back. She must! I can't give up," he lamented. "To think, there are rumors about our relationship." The Baron had paused and turned round to complain directly to me. "Her Ladyship and I have never strayed from proper behavior. We've never committed any acts of sin!" The look of utter anguish on the man's face showed the severity of his emotional pain. I thought he might say more, but he turned back and stomped his feet as he ascended the stairs.

We were almost at the last step when we heard a sound which struck us as odd. It was the sound of laughter, of giggling female laughter. The Baron walked forward, grabbed the door handle, and threw it open. I followed him into the room.

There was Holmes, pretending to look puzzled. He took two giant steps forward then purposely tripped and fell to the ground. Sitting on the couch were three well-dressed women who whooped and laughed joyfully. I recognized two of them from the photos in the magazine. I didn't know the third woman who was sitting in the middle. Her identity was revealed to me when the Baron shouted, "Elsie! What is going on here?"

"Oh, darling," the young woman said as she stood and came to her fiancé. "Mr. Holmes has been entertaining us with a one-man version of the play, *Charlie's Aunt*. He is hilarious! Did you know he used to be an actor?"

"I . . . I . . . No . . . I . . . ." He stumbled, then with a quick shake of his head, he pulled himself together and said, "Wait – just what are you doing here?"

Lady Gordon gave an alluring smile to her man. "Mr. Holmes invited me to meet here with Miss Ashley and Miss Fitzgerald. They told me everything – how you were an absolute gentleman." She paused, and her expression became forlorn. "I know everything. The ladies and Mr. Holmes explained it to me. I know about Lord Chauncey. I know about Father." There was heaviness in the air at these words. We all felt her pain.

Then, the Lady sprang to her beau, embraced him, and kissed him on the cheek. "Oh, my dear, I was such a fool for ever doubting you! Let's run away together. I want to spend my life with you!"

"And I with you," the Baron responded, and despite us being in the room, the two lovers kissed on the lips.

The Baron and her Ladyship heaped praise upon Holmes. They thanked him, and the ladies, and me. "We best be off," the Baron concluded with one of his jaunty laughs after they'd concluded their pleasantries. "I have a wedding to plan! My own!" The two then flew down the steps. We heard the Baron's jalopy zoom out into the street, and they headed we knew not where – only that it would be together.

After all of the guests had left, Holmes told me all about what had transpired that day. "When the Irregulars returned to Baker Street this morning, I had already surmised what they had to say about the women in the photographs."

"They struck me as fine ladies who I'm sure will also soon be married to a promising young man one day."

Holmes gave one of his odd silent laughs. "Don't be too sure of that. Those ladies are enjoying their independence. They may live a life of luxury all on their own."

"What do you mean?" I asked, truly perplexed by his little game of implying but not directly stating.

"I mean those two ladies are what we call *courtesans*."

"You mean they're *prostitutes*," I nearly shouted. "Holmes, you brought prostitutes into . . . Good God, man! What would Mrs. Hudson say if she found out?"

Holmes was chuckling again. "Now, now, Watson. You saw the ladies. The average person couldn't discern their business, and if they were seen with a client – well, these women only work with members of the House of Lords. That's how Lord Sully knew of them."

"Wait . . ." I started. "That's why he said the Baron could never save his reputation."

"Yes, Watson. The Lord thought that if the truth was revealed to the Baron, he'd still never be able to restore his good name. If he tried to tell the truth, *The Gazette* would publish a story showing a different truth, that the Baron was photographed in the company of two illicit women. He'd never be able to recover from that."

"So, Lord Gordon has won," I said sadly. "No matter what, the poor man will always have a stain on his name, even if he marries the Lady."

"That's where you're wrong. You see, while all of this is true, Lord Gordon still can't harm the Baron any further. He was bluffing."

"Bluffing?" I asked, confused. "But he has the evidence to tarnish Sully's good name."

"He has the evidence, but he can't use it. He could never reveal to the press that the women were courtesans. A number of the members of the House of Lords have been seen in the company of these same women – seen by the public and seen by their respective wives. If the truth came out, their reputations would be just as stained as the Baron's. A much larger scandal would ensue. No, the other Lords wouldn't allow Lord Gordon to go that far. They'd destroy his reputation along with theirs, whether they had some truly diabolical information on him or made it up. Lord Gordon would never take that risk."

Holmes was correct. *Grace's Gazette* never published another story questioning Sully's reputation – though they did have a follow-up story.

Like Desdemona betraying her father and marrying Othello, so too did Lady Elsie. After leaving Baker Street, the two drove to Southampton, where they were married by the captain of one of the Baron's ships. The two then spent their honeymoon at sea and arrived in America where, as far as I know, they've lived to this very day. *The Gazette*'s story was about how romantic it was that the two lovebirds eloped and escaped to the New World, symbolizing the modern love embraced by the youth of the Twentieth Century.

65

Holmes the Hunter
by Susan Knight

"I have been thinking, Watson." Holmes was adding something unspeakably rank to the concoction brewing in the flask suspended over his Bunsen burner. "A few days in the countryside, enjoying the fine spring weather, would do us both a power of good."

I had been absorbed in the latest intelligence from South Africa, where the Boers were continuing to wage war against our boys, but I now gazed at Holmes over the top of my newspaper in no little astonishment. When had Holmes ever expressed delight at the prospect of uprooting himself from Baker Street, unless it be in pursuit of a criminal?

"The countryside?" I queried. "Where?"

He turned to me then.

"An old acquaintance in Sussex has been invited for the weekend, and is hoping we might accompany him. I thought it would make a pleasant break."

I was even more astonished.

"A weekend in Sussex!" I exclaimed. "What old acquaintance is this?"

"Someone from years ago. The invitation is to a house party."

I threw down my paper. A house party, indeed! The prospect of which would usually make my friend run twenty miles in the opposite direction.

"Come now, Holmes," I said. "There's must be more to this than a social engagement."

He grinned merrily at me. "Ah, Watson, there is no fooling you. In fact, I barely know the fellow. It's a chap my brother went to school with. Mycroft has kept in touch with him over the years."

I began to see the light. There was certainly something afoot if Holmes's brother, who held a powerful but mysterious role in the government of the country, was involved.

"The invitation," Holmes continued, "was, in point of fact, initially made to Mycroft, but, as you know, he is exceedingly loath to venture beyond the isosceles triangle that comprises his apartment, his place of work, and the Diogenes Club. He suggested to our friend that you and I might attend the party in his place, to which the gentleman was most agreeable."

"So what is it all about?"

"For many years, this Frederick Jansson worked abroad, in various embassies . . . ." Holmes paused, and gave me a significant look. I understood this to mean that the man was a spy. "He has connections, let us say. And certain of these have led him to intelligence of a plot by a group of people opposed to our current government's activities abroad to assassinate a number of key individuals."

"Good Lord!"

"Suspicion points to the hosts of this party, neighbours of his, as being involved."

"So is this not rather a matter for the police?"

Holmes sighed. "Would it were so simple. No, Jansson has no firm evidence to lead to a prosecution. He fears an attempt will be made over this weekend to eliminate at least one of the men on the list."

"So we would be walking into a lion's den?"

"Not for the first time, Watson. Come, now, man, things have been desperately quiet since we returned from Constantinople with Mrs. Hudson. * What do you say?"

"I shall pack my revolver."

Thus it was that the following Friday afternoon saw us on the Brighton train, our destination Coombe Hall, a country house on the banks of the River Ouse. We alighted at Haywards Heath, where Frederick Jansson was awaiting us with a carriage. He was a jolly, chubby man in his late forties, of small stature, and with a baby face that spoke of an innocence, which I suspected from the little I had heard of him, hid a shrewd, if not devious, mind.

"Holmes!" he said in a high-tenor voice, grasping my friend's hand the while and shaking it heartily. "I am delighted to see you again after so many years. And to meet you too, Dr. Watson. I have followed your accounts of this rogue's exploits most avidly."

As he drove us from the station, he explained how he considered it wise for us not to reveal our true identities to our hosts, something we had already decided upon.

"I told them that you are my house guests for the weekend, whereupon Metcalfe insisted I bring you along as well."

To my amusement and Holmes's dismay, Jansson had already taken it upon himself to assign us new names. I was to be Dr. John Willoughby, while Holmes was newly styled Stanley Hunter.

"Stanley!" Holmes expostulated (the only verb to describe his outburst). "I abhor the name."

"Then blame your parents," Jansson replied drily. "If anyone tries to check you out, they are the names of two most respectable gentlemen of my acquaintance, buried alive in the backwaters of Norfolk."

He then described our hosts. Vernon Metcalfe was a man who had made his fortune in the diamond mines of South Africa. His wife Helene was of Dutch descent.

"A Boer?" I asked.

Jansson nodded his head. "It's probable. Metcalfe is British, but his sympathies, though concealed, certainly lie, I understand, with the Boers, particularly their notions of the right to keep slaves from among the indigenous population. He is deeply religious, but someone who believes in the God-given superiority of the white man."

"Surely," I said, "a man like that wouldn't wish to shed the blood of others – would not be involved in any assassination plot."

Jansson laughed. "You might think so, Doctor, but in my experience, it is common for people who claim the highest principles to be able to condone, for whatever reason, the most unspeakable acts. In fact, the very notion that they are chosen of God seems to them to justify anything they want to do – in His name, of course. Their enemies are God's enemies."

It was a depressing thought, but one with which, from my own experience in Afghanistan and elsewhere, I had to agree. If this Metcalfe was to be our host for the weekend, I rather dreaded the experience.

After about forty minutes of a drive, we found ourselves skirting high stone walls – the estate, as Jansson told us, that was Coombe Hall.

"It seems," Holmes said, "that they value their privacy."

At last, we arrived at the heavy metal gates that marked the entrance to the property. These were padlocked shut, so it proved necessary to ring a bell to summon the gatekeeper from his lodge to open for us. This the humpy-backed old fellow did willingly enough, recognising Jansson, though squinting rather suspiciously at Holmes and me. With some effort, he caused the gates to swing open with a loud squeal, like an animal in pain. I wondered aloud that no oil had been employed to ease the hinges and lessen the noise.

"But you see, Watson," Holmes replied, "no one can come and go through these gates without being heard."

That explanation did nothing to relieve my anxieties.

A long driveway led up through an avenue of lime trees, opening out eventually to the manor house, in front of which a circular pool sported a three-tiered fountain. The house itself, of pale brick, was handsome in the formal way of a Georgian mansion, stone steps leading up to an exterior landing surmounted with high pillars and a mansard roof. The many windows glinted in the afternoon sun. If anyone was watching us from behind them, they could not be seen.

As we approached, a young groom appeared from the side of the house. The three of us having descended from the carriage with our travelling cases, the lad sprang into the driver's seat and caused the horse to trot away, presumably to the stables. I watched it go reluctantly, as if our last hope of escape had gone.

My fears, however, were soon dissipated by the emergence from the house of a tall, well-built, genial man in, I surmised, his late sixties, along with a truly beautiful blonde woman, many years younger than himself. They welcomed us effusively with what seemed sincere warmth. If this was Vernon Metcalfe and his wife, Helene, then, I felt sure, Jansson's suspicions were misplaced.

"Delighted to meet you, Dr. Willoughby, Mr. Hunter," Metcalfe said. "Any friend of Freddie's is a friend of ours. By the way," he added, addressing Holmes, "are you one?

"I beg your pardon?" Holmes replied.

"A hunter . . . We are rather given to the pleasures of the chase – here, d'you see?" The man rubbed plump hands together. "Only sadly, it isn't the season just now. However, you would be very welcome to return in the autumn, if your tastes are in that direction."

Holmes smiled. "A very generous offer, sir. I shall certainly consider it."

Holmes the hunter? Perhaps. But never of game. I hadn't discussed it with him, but I imagined his opinion concurred with that of mine and Mr. Oscar Wilde, who described hunting as *"the unspeakable in pursuit of the uneatable"*.

"Now Vernon, don't keep our guests on the steps." Helene Metcalfe spoke with a very slight, attractive accent, which I assumed must be Dutch. "Please follow me, gentlemen."

She led the way into the house, into an airy hallway with a pale marble floor and ionic pillars, painted white. Servants divested us of our outer garments and we proceeded through to a reception room, where several people sat or stood, conversing. The older seated couple were introduced to us as Lord and Lady Tonbridge, unimpeachably respectable, evidently, and rather conscious, I felt, of their own superiority. Or perhaps I simply received that impression because of the way Lady Tonbridge viewed us through the lorgnette she held up to her long aristocratic nose, as if afflicted by a bad smell.

Gretta, the Metcalfe's daughter – But surely Helene was far too young to have a daughter in her forties! – was bony, pallid, and too thin for good health. She immediately apologised for the unavoidable absence of her husband, of whom we knew nothing until that moment, so were unlikely to care one way or the other.

"Darby would have so much liked to meet you both," she twittered.

"Perhaps another time," Holmes replied.

I noticed that Vernon Metcalfe was frowning slightly.

"Your husband, Gretta," he remarked, "might have made an effort to turn up for once."

"Oh, Dad's the absolute limit, Grandfather!" a lively young girl of about seventeen piped up. "Always too busy to enjoy himself."

This was Veronica, or Ronnie as everyone apparently called her, the Metcalfe's bubbly granddaughter. A solemn boy stood beside her – her brother Aubrey.

Lounging on a couch was a somewhat flash-looking man who turned out to be Gretta's younger brother, Philip. He didn't bother to get up, just nodded at us in an off-hand manner.

"Is Sybil ever coming down, Nunc?" Ronnie asked him. "She's been an absolute age."

Philip laughed with something of a sneer. "Oh, she's probably getting herself all dressed up to meet our venerable guests."

Was that us? Venerable? He wasn't much younger than we were.

"And what about Bertie?" Ronnie turned to the Tonbridges. "And his friend, Winnie? Where are they?"

"Oh, you know Bertie," Lady Tonbridge replied. "Always late."

"Bertie," Lord Tonbridge explained, for our benefit, "is our scamp of a son."

"Well, they'd better be here in time for tennis tomorrow," Ronnie said. "I've been looking forward to a return match for an absolute age. I quite intend to give Bertie a good thrashing."

A merry smile accompanied these rather violent words.

"I sincerely hope they'll be here by dinner time," Helene Metcalfe said. "Cook will be really put out otherwise. She's preparing Bertie's favourite mess."

I was beginning to feel distinctly uncomfortable, as if we had intruded on a family get-together, and a rather dull one at that. However, here we were, with a job to do, even if the present company appeared to be the least-likely nest of conspirators that we were ever likely to come across. At least the sherry we were served was excellent, and I was happy to sit myself down and quietly take in more of my surroundings.

The drawing room where we found ourselves was decorated in luxurious good taste, walls hung with pale green silk, and surmounted here and there by unremarkable paintings of country scenes in heavy gilt frames. A handsome white marble chimney-piece in the style, if not the work of, Robert Adam, stood below a ceiling festooned with moulded plasterwork. The chairs and couches were upholstered in shades of green slightly darker than the wall hangings, and a pale rug covered the parquet floor, the whole lending the room a charmingly light atmosphere, enhanced by the view through French windows, and out over the back lawn of the estate, where the setting sun was turning the distant River Ouse to a ribbon of molten gold. Again, I doubted that sinister goings-on were likely in such a setting.

After a decent interval of polite conversation, Holmes and I excused ourselves to go to our rooms and change for dinner. On the stairs, we met a young lady hurrying down. This had to be Sybil, all decked out in snowy frills and unseasonal puffs of white fur.

"Oh Lordy!" she exclaimed. "Am I too late?"

I couldn't help but be reminded of the white rabbit from Mr. Carroll's charming tale of Alice in Wonderland. There was certainly something of the bunny about the girl, who was petite but prettily plump, with big scared eyes, a twitching snub nose, and a prominent overbite.

We assured her that the company was still assembled below, so she gave us a quick smile and scampered on down.

"'*Curiouser and curiouser,*'" I remarked, but I am afraid Holmes missed the literary reference.

Dinner was a dreary-enough affair. The company was wrapped up in their own interests, which involved extensive discussions of local people Holmes and I didn't know – and showed no curiosity concerning us, which I suppose was quite useful for our *incognito*, if rather discourteous. Perhaps Jansson had spun a confection which told them all they wished to know. At least the food was delicious, if very rich: Mulligatawny soup, stewed eels, saddle of mutton with redcurrant jelly. A Nesselrode pudding for dessert, followed by Stilton cheese. All washed down with excellent burgundies and port.

Of the two young people yet to arrive there was no sign, so whatever Cook's mess consisted of – and I couldn't hazard a guess – was wasted.

After dinner, we gentlemen withdrew, in the traditional way, to what Vernon Metcalfe called "the smoking room". There we were expected to smoke, drink more port, but also to sit down to a game of poker.

"I trust, gentlemen," our host remarked to us, "you have no objection to a little wager."

The smile that accompanied his words was, I have to say, somewhat wolfish. For the first time, I suspected a ruthless side to the man.

I had no great liking for the game which I had only played once or twice before, and tried to beg off. Metcalfe wasn't having it.

"Come now, Willoughby," he insisted. "Only a little fun among friends."

I sat down with the others, Holmes giving me a wink. I rather dreaded what would happen next. At first, however, all went well. Our host had the upper hand, as he no doubt expected, greedily pulling the heap of coins towards himself each time.

"I fear, gentlemen," he said happily, "that I am quite cleaning you out of your small change. What say we up the stakes just a little? It might sharpen the competitive spirit."

"Count me out, Metcalfe," Lord Tonbridge remarked. "Your fine port has my competitive spirit quite blunted."

I, too, made my excuses, hoping Holmes would do the same. He, however, agreed to play, as did Jansson and Philip – the latter, I am afraid, looking rather the worse for the drink which he had all too freely imbibed.

The new game having started, it soon became clear that the tables had turned. Holmes, unable or unwilling to restrain himself, started to win. Philip soon dropped out, followed by Jansson, leaving Metcalfe facing Holmes (or Hunter, as I had to remember to call him) across the green baize. The stakes rose each time, and our host, while still smiling fixedly, was clearly infuriated at losing. I glanced across at Jansson, who raised his eyebrows and pursed his lips. Antagonising our host was the last thing we should be doing.

It was the last turn of the cards. A sudden grin of triumph lit up Metcalfe's face. His hand beat Holmes's. I knew, of course, that Holmes could have won, that he had lost deliberately.

Metcalfe, suspecting nothing, was become generous in victory.

"My dear fellow," he said gathering his spoils, "you are a worthy antagonist."

"I sincerely hope so," Holmes replied drily.

Preparatory to retiring, Holmes and I, along with Jansson, briefly discussed our impressions so far in the privacy of the latter's bedroom. Our new friend had perhaps over-indulged in fine wines as well, for I noticed that his words were become slurred and his reactions seemed sluggish.

"I wonder," he remarked, sinking into a chair, "if I have brought you here on a wild goose chase, gentlemen. My information came from a seemingly impeccable source, and yet so far nothing has occurred to bear out our fears."

I said that I had been wondering the same thing.

"Let us wait and see," Holmes replied. "This evening, Metcalfe displayed another side to his character. A man who plays poker as relentlessly as that is capable of anything."

"Rather like yourself," I added.

"I am capable of many things, Watson, including winning or losing at poker, but for me, it is incidental how a game like that turns out, while for him to win is everything."

"Hmm." I couldn't remember Holmes ever being resigned to losing in any situation, but didn't voice this aloud.

"There's a certain document I must show you," Jansson said. "I need your help with it. I should have explained to you before, but we are all tired just now, and it can surely wait until tomorrow."

I could tell that Holmes was avid to see it at once, but he rather reluctantly acceded to Jansson suggestion, since the man was clearly on his last legs.

The next morning, I awoke early. Distant, strange noises had roused me, along with a bright sun shining on my face through a crack in the curtains. I resolved to break my fast and then venture out to explore the parkland surrounding the house.

Down in the breakfast room I helped myself to a fine dish of eggs and devilled kidneys with fresh rolls, my only companion there being young Aubrey, who viewed me shyly. I smiled to encourage him, and asked how old he was (nine) and if he attended school. He named a small public establishment, grimacing somewhat.

"You don't like it?" I asked.

"It's all right," he replied. "Only the other fellows make fun of me."

Oh dear. "Why's that?" I asked.

He shrugged. "I don't know, sir. Maybe because I am good at my lessons and like to do well. They say I am stuck up, and regularly give me a pasting for it." He paused. "I have asked Mama if I can come home and have Miss Everdale teach me again."

"She was your governess?"

"Yes. I love Miss Everdale and will marry her when I grow up." His earnest face lit up briefly. "But grandfather says I should stop behaving like a spoilt cry-baby, and that school will make a man of me . . . Mama always does what Grandfather says."

"What about your father? What does he say?"

The boy just shook his head, which spoke volumes.

"Well," I said, "stick it out, old chap. It isn't forever, you know."

He looked back it me doubtfully, then said, "Have a crumpet, sir. They're jolly good. We don't get a spread like this at Highfields."

I obligingly took a crumpet, smothered in melting butter, and agreed that they were delicious.

"Hello," Aubrey said, after polishing off another. "Would you like to see the Imaginary, sir?"

"The what?"

"The Imaginary. It's jolly good."

"Where is it?"

Aubrey waved at the window. Since I had been planning a walk anyway, I agreed, much to his delight.

What had I expected? Some childish haunt, I had reckoned, but the reality, as I now discovered, was quite different. Aubrey had led me to a walled enclosure in a distant part of the estate containing a quantity of animals in cages. A *Menagerie*! Now I realised whence emanated the strange sounds I had heard in the night, whether it was monkeys chattering, wolves howling, foxes barking, parrots squawking owls hooting, or the sawing call of an angry leopard, prowling restlessly in his tiny enclosure.

This was clearly Aubrey's favourite place. He excitedly described each creature to me.

"Do you know what that is?" he asked, pointing to a large black bird, with a viciously curved beak, and what looked to be a horn on its head.

I replied that I did not.

"That," he replied importantly, "is a cassowary . . . It's very wary." He laughed at his own joke. "But do you know something peculiar, sir? It can't fly. What kind of a bird is that, sir, that can't fly?"

I told him about ostriches, which can't fly either. "But they can run very fast."

"So can I run fast," he boasted.

Back at the house, we found four young people heading off to the tennis courts. Ronnie and Sybil were accompanied by two young men, one I supposed being Bertie. But where was Winnie? I had assumed by the name that Bertie's friend was another young lady.

"That's him." Aubrey assured me.

"Winnie? Or Willie?"

"I don't know. Winnie, I think. He writes for the newspapers and escaped from prison." Aubrey obviously considered this very impressive.

"Goodness gracious!" I exclaimed.

"Yes, he had to run like a . . . like an Austrian to get away."

"A what?"

"That bird you said."

We drifted over to the tennis courts to watch the play. I have to say that the new young man, whatever his name was, looked to be a most unlikely jailbird. Slicked-back fair hair, a smoothly polished complexion, a healthy tan: He was for all the world like every other young man of a certain class that I had come across. Aubrey must have got it wrong.

Also watching the play, with a somewhat jaundiced eye, was Philip Metcalfe.

"I say, you're a doctor, aren't you?" he exclaimed. "What can you give me for a splitting headache?

Advice not to drink so much, I could have said. However, I recommended plenty of water.

"Or a tea made of feverfew might prove helpful," I added. "It's a well-tried herbal medicine. Perhaps Cook . . . ."

"Feverfew be hanged!" Philip exclaimed. "I need the hair of the dog."

And before I could reply that another drink was the last thing he needed, he stomped off.

"He's just cross because Winnie is paying attention to his girl," Aubrey opined wisely. "And she likes him, too."

Truly, the young people seemed to be enjoying themselves immensely, and I enjoyed watching them. Suddenly, however, Holmes was at my side. He drew me away from the boy.

"Jansson is gone," he said in low tones.

"Gone where?"

"I was told he was called away early this morning by an urgent message. I don't believe a word of it, Watson. He would have informed me first."

"Good Heavens!" This was disturbing news indeed.

"Did you notice how confused he seemed last night? I put it down to the late hour and the heavy drinking. However, I am now wondering if he was drugged."

"Well, yes," I replied. "That would fit the symptoms."

"In addition, I didn't hear the gates squeaking open, which would have happened if he left that way."

"As to that," I replied, "you might have slept through the noise. We are far enough distant from the gates, after all."

Holmes turned a cold gaze upon me.

"I was awake with the dawn, Watson. And, as you should know by now, I am a light sleeper and possess preternaturally acute hearing."

I decided to let that pass. God forbid I should attribute any physical weakness to the man.

"But surely," I said, "him being gone, for whatever reason, leaves us in a most invidious position."

"Metcalfe has assured me that we are most welcome to stay on, remarking that it is a long way back to Norfolk."

"Norfolk?"

"Which is where we are supposed to be from, in case you have forgotten."

"Oh yes, of course."

"However, I fear friend Jansson may have met with some mischief. If he didn't leave through the gates, there is only one other way. Let us take a stroll down to the river."

"You think . . . ? Oh, God!"

"I think nothing, Watson. I look for evidence."

Aubrey regarded us somewhat sorrowfully as we left him. While I am no great companion for a small boy, I felt for his obvious loneliness. Maybe, among the new people due to arrive in the afternoon for tea, there would be some children of his own age.

The Ouse wound past the lower edge of the estate. Under other circumstances, I should have appreciated the gentle beauty of the scene, willows dipping their new leaves into the slow flow. However, I was conscious of Holmes's attentive examination of the area, and tried to emulate it.

"Look, Watson," he said, pointing down at the ground.

I could see nothing but grass. Holmes shook his head and sighed.

"Look again."

Now I discerned a deeper imprint, and saw that it had created a faint furrow.

"Something has been wheeled down here recently, possibly in a barrow," Holmes said, and started following the trail.

"A boat house!" I exclaimed, indicating a wooden structure ahead of us. Of course, Holmes had noticed it already, and was pacing towards it.

Within, I could see nothing to arouse my suspicions. Just two boats in a boat house. No sign of a body or evidence of a struggle.

Holmes however made an exclamation of satisfaction.

"Ha!" he said, pointing to one of the craft. "Someone has taken this boat out very recently, and bearing some sort of a heavy weight, at that."

"How can you tell?" I asked.

"The oars are wet." He indicated those same implements, hung up on the wall of the hut. "They are still dripping. And look at the side of the boat. Now it floats high, but the waterline reveals that it was recently very low."

I could see that: A darker area very near the gunwale.

"It doesn't mean – "

"No, Watson. It doesn't. But admit it is suggestive."

He climbed into the boat and examined it with the forensic thoroughness so characteristic of him.

76

"Ha!" he exclaimed again, picking up something from one of the seats. He put it on the palm of his hand and held it out to me. "What do you make of that?" It was a thread of some sort that had caught on a splinter.

"It looks rather like the blanket on my bed," I replied, dismayed.

"Exactly . . . Come, Watson. Let's get out of here before we arouse suspicion."

"If it isn't too late for that."

Holmes decided he now needed to gain access to Jansson's bedroom in the hope that the chambermaid hadn't already tidied everything up. The company being occupied outside, either watching the tennis or strolling in the grounds in the late May sunshine, left, we hoped, the coast clear. I was to stand guard on the landing, should anyone happen along. Unluckily for me, it was Helene Metcalfe herself who made an appearance. She was hurrying as if on a mission, but stopped short at the sight of me.

"Dr. Willoughby!" she exclaimed. "Whatever are you doing here? Why aren't you out enjoying yourself with the others?"

"I was just on my way down, Madam," I said in a loud voice, "when my eye was caught by these striking pictures." I indicated the very mediocre set of hunting prints hanging there.

She regarded them, and me, dubiously, and made to pass me. I feared her destination was Jansson's room.

"No news of our friend?" I asked, my voice still raised. "I was most astonished to learn he had gone away without a word to us. Nothing serious, I hope."

She smiled as if to reassure. Really, she had the most charming smile. And dimples.

"Some domestic issue, I understand, that required his immediate attention."

"Well, I hope he will be able to return soon."

She regarded me steadily. "As to that," she said, "I cannot say. Now I must check on the state of his room. In case he left anything behind, you understand . . . Excuse me, please." And, before I could delay her further, she slipped past me quickly and entered Jansson's room.

I waited on tenterhooks, expecting another exclamation of surprise or even anger from her. But nothing of the sort. I slipped into my own room, to await her departure, agonising as to Holmes's whereabouts. After ten minutes or more, I heard the adjacent bedroom door open and shut, and light footsteps hurry down the passage. I waited a little longer to make sure the coast was clear. Finally stepping out of my room, I found Holmes just quitting Jansson's. He placed a finger on his lips and indicated we should go back into my room.

Once there, I asked, "What happened? She didn't see you?"

Holmes was dusting himself down.

"Luckily – and thank you for that – I heard you talking to her, and had time to hide under the bed, where, it seems the maid has long neglected to sweep."

I chuckled at the image of Holmes's long frame in that confined space, trying not to sneeze.

"Could you see what she was doing there?"

"Not exactly, but Helene Metcalfe wasn't engaged in housework. She was clearly searching for something. This perhaps." He held up an envelope. "Jansson had hidden it under the bedframe. Had I not had occasion to hide there, it would have taken me longer to find it."

"Thank goodness she didn't think to look there. But what is it?"

"Let us see."

He opened the envelope and took out several sheets of paper, scanned them briefly, then tossed them to me with a short laugh.

"It's in code," I said.

"Of course it is. Good old Jansson! This must be the document he mentioned last night. Well, it will take me a while to decipher it, but that's for later, I'm afraid. We mustn't stay absent from the party any longer or questions will surely be asked."

As we headed down the stairs together, he added, "And, Watson, I regret to say there was a blanket missing from the bed."

Under the circumstances, it was hard to play the part of the carefree weekend guest, but the arrival on the lawn of a picnic lunch was a good distraction, especially as the fare was excellent: Juicy joints of beef and lamb, roast fowl, crusty pies of pigeon and veal, plenty of ale and cider, or lemonade for younger people. Heaps of sandwiches packed with Cheddar cheese or cress or slices of meat. As for the desserts, young Aubrey's eyes were out on stalks at the sight of so many apple turnovers, cheesecakes, blancmanges, sugared buns, and iced biscuits.

"It's difficult to know where to start," I said to him.

For Aubrey, that posed no problem at all.

"Jolly smashing!" he said, through a full mouth.

My eyes drifted to the river where our quartet of merry young people had taken to the canoes. But what if they found something unspeakable in the river?

"Nunc won't like that," Aubrey remarked, following my gaze.

"What?"

"His girl off with the others again. Ronnie says Sybil has a bit of a pash for Bertie. Still – " He thoughtfully bit into a jam puff. " – Nunc has loads of girlfriends. Don't suppose he'll be too bothered."

I peered across to where Philip Metcalfe was standing by the drinks table. He also was gazing down at the boat people, a fierce glower on his face. He didn't seem exactly unbothered to me.

"And I reckon," Aubrey continued, still chewing, "Ronnie has a bit of a pash for Winnie. I like him, too. I hope they get married."

"Was Winnie really in prison?" I asked.

"Yes." The boy's voice thrilled. "He escaped with his life. I expect they're still after him."

"The police, you mean."

"Yes, but not the bobbies here. In South Africa, you know."

"South Africa . . . Ah . . . ."

Now that was very interesting. So was this Winnie, who seemed to be such a pleasant and unobjectionable young man, a Boer supporter, in fact, and part of the plot? I needed to talk to Holmes as soon as possible. Once again, I abandoned young Aubrey, only to be waylaid a moment later by his mother, whom I only knew as Gretta.

"Dr. Willoughby," she said, "thank you so much for taking time to talk to my son."

"He's a charming young lad," I replied. "You must be very proud of him."

"Yes," she replied uncertainly. "I am of course. But . . . but . . . I worry about him . . . Can I confide in you?"

"Now?"

"If you don't mind."

How could I refuse? She led me away from the throng, many of them still eating and chatting, some making their way to the Menagerie to gape at the caged animals, some wandering down to the river. Seclusion was to be found at last at the side of the house in a formal garden of tightly clipped box hedges that enclosed flower beds in a geometric design beloved of the Italians. It is a style that I, who prefer the abundance of the English cottage garden, can admire but not love. A sundial stood in the midst of all. Gretta was leaning on this, as if needing support.

"I feel," she said, "that I can talk frankly to you . . . as a doctor."

"Of course."

What poured out was typical of the neurasthenic personality I suspected her to be: All manner of anxieties, more related to herself than to her son. I gathered from hints she dropped that her absent husband wasn't only uninterested in his offspring, but also in her.

"How I wish," she sighed, "that I had a mother to confide in."

"But you have . . . don't you?"

She laughed a little wildly.

"Oh, really, Doctor! Helene isn't my mother. Mine died years ago, when Philip was small. Papa only married that woman a few years ago."

"My apologies."

That woman! I could tell from Gretta's tone that Helene Metcalfe wasn't her favourite person. "Did he meet her in South Africa?" I continued. "I only ask because I assumed she was from there."

"Yes . . . ." She turned a plain anxious face up to me. "She has changed my father dreadfully, Dr. Willoughby."

But before I could find out how, the very subject of our discourse swept into view. I wondered if she was keeping an eye on me.

"There you are at last, Gretta," she exclaimed. "Now, charming as the company of Dr. Willoughby must surely be, you are neglecting your duties as a mother . . . Aubrey has just been violently sick."

Oh dear. I felt quite guilty. I should have stopped the child from stuffing himself so much, although it was hardly my place to do so. Gretta rushed off with cries of alarm, while Helene Metcalfe remained, studying me quizzically.

"I suppose she was pouring out her silly little heart to you, Doctor." She chuckled. "I am afraid Gretta tends to behave that way in the company of gentlemen. Her wretched husband isn't a very satisfactory spouse, you see. And then, of course, she has reached that certain age."

Laughing merrily, dimples and all, she tripped away from me.

Well, beautiful she might be, elegant she might be, while, let it be admitted, of a certain age herself – though she bore it well – but the woman was cruel and quite likely dangerous. I made my way back to find Holmes, and briefed him on what Aubrey had told me.

"Escaped from prison in South Africa! You don't think the boy was making it up?"

"I'm not sure. He seemed definite about it. It would be an odd thing, wouldn't it, for a child to say unless it was true?"

"That depends on what he has been reading . . . or hearing. Still, let us bear it in mind."

Aubrey himself had evidently recovered well, and was even having to be restrained from further indulgence in sweetmeats. The party otherwise was still in full flow. I suggested to Holmes that we might take a turn in the Menagerie, but he replied that it gave him no pleasure to see wild creatures caged up. So sometime later, we managed, without offending our hosts, to return to our rooms – Holmes to try and decipher the code left by Jansson, and me to take a nap, since all the food I had consumed lay heavy upon me.

Perhaps I was overly suspicious, but it seemed to me that my room had been searched. Of course, the chambermaid had visited, had made up the bed and tidied, but things that need not have been moved were in a slightly different place than before. I had concealed my revolver, but not so thoroughly that a search among my belongings might not have discovered it. Now I wondered, and decided to find out if Holmes had received the same impression.

"Yes, someone has been here," he said. "I was very careful to leave everything in a certain way and, although the searchers tried to put it all back in place, they didn't quite manage. However, good luck if they hoped to find anything. I kept the papers on me."

I explained about my revolver. Holmes frowned slightly, and I was expecting him to chastise me for my negligence. However, he just remarked that it wouldn't be unusual for a gentleman visiting the countryside to bring with him a gun for sporting purposes, whether it was hunting season or not.

"The very fact that it was not well-hidden actually stands in your favour."

I hoped he wasn't just being kind.

"Now, leave me to my labours," he continued. "And take some rest. If anything is to happen, it may well be tonight, and we need to be alert."

He turned back to the sheets of paper left by Jansson. I was dismissed.

Although afflicted with fatigue, the moment I laid myself down, I couldn't sleep for the thoughts and concerns buzzing around in my head. Where was Jansson? Was he alive or had he – *Horrible thought!* – been removed? Was there a simple explanation for the condition of the boat? Had Jansson taken it himself for some reason? Had Aubrey been fantasising? Was young Winnie involved? And what was the role of the Metcalfes in the business?

Dinner that evening resolved nothing in my mind. The experience was as normal and almost as dreary as before, though lightened somewhat by the presence of the two young men, Bertie and Winnie, and by the continuing excellence of the fare. No mention was made of Winnie's incarceration or escape, so I was inclined to think that, after all, Aubrey's imagination had run away with him. Everyone expressed pleasure at the way the afternoon had gone, although at one point Vernon Metcalfe remarked, "A pity Freddie missed it."

"Have you had any word from him?" Holmes asked in innocent tones. "Any notion of if or when he might return?"

"No," Metcalfe replied. "I was as astonished as you were, Hunter, to find he had done a moonlight flit." He sounded genuine. "But I suppose," he added, "a man in his line of work has always to be prepared to drop everything and obey instructions."

In his line of work, indeed. Now what, I wondered, did Metcalfe assume that to be? I also knew, because Holmes told me that he had made very discreet inquiries, that no telegram or other message had been received the night before that might have summoned our friend away.

We gentlemen withdrew as before to the smoking room, although poker was not offered this time. I rather felt that Vernon Metcalfe had no wish to face Holmes again across the baize. For myself, I had been hoping to engage young Winnie in conversation, to try and assess what sort of a man he was. However, both he and Bertie slipped away before I had to chance to speak to them, whispering about some secret scheme they had. The rest of us seemed destined for an early night, especially since Metcalfe was most insistent that we attend chapel before breakfast, the next day being a Sunday.

"Chapel?" I asked.

"We have our own here, situated in the east wing," Metcalfe replied, looking at us sharply from under sun-bleached eyebrows. "A simple place of worship, with no graven images to distract. No priests here, either. I myself lead the service, and trust that is acceptable."

We all murmured that it was, although I distinctly heard a sigh from Lord Tonbridge, who perhaps perforce had attended such ceremonies before.

I would never consider myself a fanciful sort of man, but since that frightful business in Devon regarding Sir Henry Baskerville and the legend of the hound, I had on occasion been afflicted by nightmares in which I was pursued by a giant beast. Now, drifting into slumber, I found myself once again on that boggy moor, following Holmes and running for my life, except that this time I was suddenly dodging between the box hedges of a formal garden, the creature gaining on me with every step, a creature with the body of a gigantic cat and the face . . . the face of Helene Metcalfe.

Did I cry out? I woke with a start. Someone was bending over me. I was about to cry out again, when I heard familiar tones.

"Hush, Watson." It was Holmes.

I endeavoured to pull myself out of sleep. It had to be the middle of the night.

"What is it?"

"There isn't a moment to lose. Come quickly and bring your revolver. There's evil work afoot here."

I threw my overcoat on over my nightwear, since Holmes wouldn't even let me pause to get dressed.

"And take care."

We made our way out into the grounds. The bright curve of a gibbous moon illuminated what to me looked to be a quiet enough scene. Holmes stealthily led the way down towards the river, under the cover of a line of trees, pausing occasionally to listen. I paused too, but could hear nothing except a light breeze rustling the leaves.

Then a terrible scream rent the air.

"Too late!" Holmes exclaimed, and started running towards the sound.

I followed after, my pistol cocked at the ready.

Had my dream mysteriously and horribly foreshadowed what was to happen? For here was Holmes again, rushing back towards me this time, while behind him, a great beast charged – the body of a big cat, and the head . . . *the head* . . . *Oh God, no!*

I shot it. What else could I do? Two shots, and it gave a great howl and rolled to the ground, panting in its death throes. Now, by the pure light of the moon, I could see it was no supernatural creature woven of dreams, but the leopard from the menagerie. And tumbling from its mouth . . . a head.

Later, huddled together in the green salon, the occupants of the house were trying to make sense of what had happened. Vernon Metcalfe sat cradling a large glass of brandy, Gretta nearby, watching him. Philip had a protective arm around Sybil, while Ronnie sat apart, white with shock. Lord and Lady Tonbridge, wearing their nightclothes like suits of armour, held themselves upright, fearsome expressions on their faces.

"How ever could this have happened, Vernon?" her Ladyship asked. "To think of that great beast roaming free. I have never been more shocked in my life. It could have been any one of us. It could have been me!"

She gathered her robe tighter round her large frame.

"No, Madam, that it could not."

She looked askance at Holmes. Had this man really dared contradict her?

"No, Madam. It was a carefully planned scheme, even though it has so frightfully backfired."

"My wife loved the leopard, Hunter." Vernon Metcalfe spoke up. "She raised Lola from a cub, you know." He turned to me. "Did you really have to kill the poor creature, Dr. Willoughby?"

"I had no choice, sir," I replied. "It was coming for us."

He nodded sadly.

I closed my eyes, the horrid vision of that head held between the drooling jaws of the maddened beast would, I was sure, never leave me.

"You speak of some sinister scheme or other, Hunter," Lord Tonbridge remarked. "What is the evidence, I ask you, for this preposterous claim? Clearly it was just a terrible accident. When the police arrive, I suggest we get them to arrest Briggs for negligence." Briggs being the gatekeeper, who clearly had other duties as well.

"Yes, yes. The senile old fool must have left the cage door unlatched when he last fed the animal," his wife added.

Holmes smiled. "That won't do, Lady Tonbridge, as you very well know . . . ."

Before he had a chance to explain, the French windows opened, and Bertie came in, looking distraught.

"The damned leopard has escaped and is on the prowl." he said. "And now I can't find him."

"The leopard?" asked Gretta.

"No, of course not."

"Winnie?" This was Ronnie. "You can't find Winnie?"

"Yes." He looked around the room. "Why are you all up? Has something dreadful happened?"

Holmes stood up. "I am afraid, Bertie, I have bad news for you."

"He's dead, isn't he? I heard the scream, although . . . ." He frowned.

"Although it didn't exactly sound like your friend."

"Well, no . . . ."

"That's because," Holmes said, "it wasn't."

Everyone stared at him. I suddenly realised that they didn't know. They hadn't seen what we had seen.

"I have to inform you that things haven't worked quite how some of you intended," Holmes said. "Has it, Winnie?"

On cue, that same young man entered in the room, having, as it turned out, remained waiting outside the door until Holmes summoned him in. All eyes now turned to him, surprise and – yes, shock – written on several faces. Not on Ronnie's, however. She looked genuinely happy.

"Oh, Winnie, you're all right!" she cried. "You're alive! Lady Tonbridge said – "

"Yes, I most certainly am alive, and I'm not sure I understand what's been going on here. Please someone tell me."

He looked around the room, expectantly.

"But if not Winnie . . . then who?" Bertie asked.

"Shut up, Bertie." That was Philip.

"Vernon, where's your wife?" Lady Tonbridge spoke again, in urgent tones. "Where's Helene?"

"She's asleep . . . isn't she?" Metcalfe replied. "I didn't want to wake her . . . ."

Holmes shook his head.

"I'm afraid not, sir. Helene went outside to let loose the leopard. It has attacked her."

Metcalfe shook his head. "No, no, you're wrong. It can't be. Lola loved my wife. Helene raised her from a cub, after I . . . after the mother was shot."

"A wild creature has no love, especially one confined like that for years to a small cage." Holmes softened his tone. "She's dead sir. Your wife is dead."

"No!" A terrible wail of despair. "No!"

Before our eyes, Metcalfe aged into an old man. His trembling hand reached for his glass of brandy and he swallowed the lot in one gulp. Then he started muttering what might have been a prayer . . . or a curse. Gretta hurried to his side, showing herself of sterner stuff than I might have imagined, ministering to him, whispering consoling words and holding his hand. My evil thought was that she was even a little pleased.

Winnie was evidently confused.

"I still don't understand what's happened. Mrs. Metcalfe dead . . . and you all thought it was me?"

At first no one replied. Then Ronnie burst out, "That's what . . . what they said."

"I suppose it very well might have been," Winnie replied thoughtfully, "had Mr. Holmes not warned me earlier not to go out."

"Mr. Holmes?" exclaimed Lord Tonbridge. "You mean Mr. Hunter."

"No, sir. This is Mr. Sherlock Holmes, and that's Dr. Watson."

Someone gasped. Lady Tonbridge gripped the arm of her chair so hard that the knuckles showed white.

"Sherlock Holmes!" Lord Tonbridge had turned dangerously red with fury. "This is preposterous, sir, coming here under false pretences! How dare you, sir?"

"I dared, in order to save a life. Or rather, more than one. I regret that Mrs. Metcalfe has died, but she is hardly the innocent victim, is she?" Holmes turned back to Winnie. "Please continue."

"Very well." Winnie looked shaken, but complied with Holmes's request. "I explained to Mr. Holmes how Bertie had suggested we go out late and do a bit of star-gazing: There's supposed to be some sort of a meteor shower tonight. *Why not?* I thought, I'd like to see that, and there's a lovely clear sky for it." He paused, then continued. "Bertie told me to meet him near the Menagerie. However, Mr. Holmes later instructed me under no circumstances to venture out, and not to say a word about it to Bertie – which, I must say, I thought strange and a bit mean. But Mr.

Holmes said it was very important I do as he told me, and even made me promise."

"I actually stood guard outside your room." Holmes smiled at him. "To make sure."

"Did you, indeed?" Winnie looked somewhat offended. "Quite unnecessary. My word is my bond, Mr. Holmes . . . Anyway, I stayed in as you said, and now it seems all hell has broken loose out there. Poor Mrs. Metcalfe." He looked around. "Bloody Hell, what are you doing?"

His supposed friend had drawn a pistol and was pointing it, with a shaking hand, at Winnie.

"Bertie, no!" This was Ronnie again.

"Don't be so stupid, Bertie." This from his mother.

"Come now, young man." Holmes said. "That isn't going to work, is it?"

Meanwhile, I leapt forward, knocking the gun from Bertie's hand, and grabbing it before anyone else could. I have to say I was utterly confused, but trusted that all would become clear in due course.

It did, but not until after the police had arrived in the welcome and familiar shape of Inspector Lestrade, whom Holmes had alerted by telephone earlier in the evening. A couple of burly constables were delegated to guard the occupants of the salon, while we, including young Winnie, decamped to the smoking room.

"I am afraid," Holmes remarked after we had settled ourselves down, "that it took me an unconscionable time to decipher the incriminating code. It didn't help that it was in Dutch, a language I know, but inadequately." He shook his head. "It proved to be the outline of a plot against a list of targets, including young Winnie here."

"Me! Why?"

"I understand you were captured and imprisoned by the Boers in South Africa while working there as a journalist. You managed to escape – quite ingeniously – and made your way to Portuguese East Africa. But later, you returned to South Africa as an army lieutenant, and were present at the Siege of Ladysmith. You ruffled Boer feathers, young man, making them something of a laughing stock, to the extent that a group of them decided to get rid of you."

"But Mr. Holmes, that doesn't make sense. I admire the Boers. I have spoken out against British prejudice against them, and called for them to be treated with generosity and tolerance."

"Sadly, these people here weren't inclined to extend the same generosity to you."

Winnie put his head in his hands. "I thought they were friends. My God, I thought Bertie . . . Oh, how could he?"

The conspirators, as it turned out from the incriminating papers Holmes had deciphered, consisted of Helene Metcalfe (though not Vernon, surprisingly), Lord and Lady Tonbridge, and their son Bertie. Helene was of Afrikaner stock and nurtured a deep hatred of the British in South Africa, while the Tonbridges owned a gold mine in Transvaal and bitterly resented the restrictions imposed on them regarding the treatment of their black "slaves" by the colonial administration. Bertie was simply besotted with Helene and would do anything she asked him to. They had lured Winnie to Coombe Hall, with the express intention of getting him killed in a way that would look like a tragic accident. Apparently, Lord Tonbridge had joked how appropriate it would be to use a South African leopard to do the deed.

As for Frederick Jansson, he too had fallen victim to their deadly plot.

Helene Metcalfe knew full well that he was on to them. It was she who had cut his throat as he lay in a drugged sleep, and who, with Bertie, had taken his body, wrapped in a blanket, down to the boathouse in a wheelbarrow (the signs of which Holmes had noticed). From there, with Jansson tied up and his body weighed down with stones, Bertie had rowed a good distance before tipping the unfortunate man into the river. This we only found out fully when the corpse surfaced a week later, and Bertie confessed all.

"How did you manage, Mr. Holmes, to evade suspicion?" Lestrade now asked. "I mean, with you on the case, they were mad to go ahead with it."

Holmes explained about our pseudonyms.

"They suspected us, of course," he said, "as associates of Jansson, but checked our credentials as Hunter and Willoughby, and found, as they supposed, that we were harmless friends of his from Norfolk. In addition, were we the country bumpkins they took us for, we would have been invaluable as witnesses to the 'accident'." He gave a grim smile. "Once I had deciphered the code, I knew there was no time to be lost. The attempt on Winnie here had to be tonight, for he would be leaving early on the morrow. So when I overheard – " (*Presumably,* I thought, *with those preternaturally sharp ears!*) " – the young men planning their nocturnal excursion, I had to make sure that Winnie wouldn't venture out. Subsequently, a sudden burst of noise from the direction of the menagerie indicated to me that something had disturbed the animals. That's when I woke you, Watson, to go and investigate."

"So, Mr. Holmes," Lestrade remarked, "you can't even enjoy a nice few days away in the countryside without getting into trouble. Still, you've saved this young man's life, and those of the others you found on the list. A good weekend's work, I'd say."

All well and good, and Mycroft would be pleased enough, despite the loss of his old friend. I knew, nonetheless, that it would be impossible to erase from my memory the image of the leopard charging towards us, the head of Helene Metcalfe in its mouth, an expression of sheer terror frozen on to the dead woman's face. Indeed, I still occasionally have those recurrent nightmares.

The conspirators having been arrested, Holmes and I were packing up to leave Coombe Hall. Outside, I found Aubrey tossing pebbles into the fountain in front of the house.

"They say it brings good luck," he told me.

"Who does?"

He shrugged his shoulders.

How much did the child know of what had happened?

"Poor leopard," he said after a while.

Not "Poor grandmother".

"We're going to stay here now," he went on. "Mama will be looking after grandfather."

What she always wanted, I thought.

"And will you go back to school?" I asked.

"Yes, but not to Highfields. Somewhere local, Mama says," adding proudly, "Grandfather wants me here."

"A new start," I told him. "Always a good thing."

"Yes, jolly good." And he threw in another pebble.

Later that day, back in the reassuring comfort of Baker Street, I ruminated on recent events.

"I was quite wrong about Winnie," I said to Holmes. "I thought he was the rotten egg,"

"Mmm," Holmes replied.

He was intent on another of his evil-smelling experiments, and, I could tell, was hardly listening to me.

Nevertheless, I continued my train of thought. "He seems to be an excellent young man with a lot of promise," I went on, reaching for another of Mrs. Hudson's delicious drop scones. "You know something, Holmes: I can't help wondering if Great Britain's future history would be much different, had that plot to kill Mr. Winston Churchill succeeded."

"Mmm," said Holmes, turning up the flame on his Bunsen burner.

NOTE

*   See *Death in the Harem: A Mrs. Hudson and Sherlock Holmes Mystery*, MX Publishing, 2024.

The Adventure of the
Live Burial
by Shane Simmons

"Wiggins who?"

"Wiggins *me*!" I told that clueless guttersnipe who claimed to be an agent of Sherlock Holmes, Consulting Detective.

"Never 'eard of 'im!" was the response I got.

"Former captain, commander, and one true leader of The Baker Street Irregulars," I reminded him, to no avail. No bloody avail at all, if you can imagine that!

True, it had been years since I held my position as lead lookout and street Arab for the Irregulars, but I thought my name might have at least echoed down through the lines as a celebrated Founding Father of the organisation that had served Mr. Holmes so well for so long. No such respect was offered up that day as I made the rounds, reconnecting with the network of deprived child spies and informants who ran wild in the streets of London at the start of a new century.

I didn't recognise nobody no more. Times had moved on, new Irregulars had joined and come up in the ranks, and there weren't no sense of history with any of them.

"What's this geezer want?" asked another filthy mongrel, joining our unproductive conversation.

"Geezer, am I?"

Childhood was an increasingly distant memory, but it hadn't been all that long since I'd been just as filthy a mongrel as any of the current Irregulars. I was a man now, but a young man by any measure. My time working for the Brothers Holmes had whipped some civilisation into me. I couldn't claim to be a learned man of books, but learning I was, more and more each day. Give me a few more centuries, and I might make it all the way up to sophisticated – Just you watch!

The disappearance of the Lady Frances Carfax had become an all-hands affair for a whole week as Sherlock Holmes prevailed upon his entire network to find where in London she had landed. The Irregulars had their eyes peeled and their ears to the ground for any hint of her or the villains who had spirited her away. Even I, now employed as dogsbody to Mycroft Holmes, had been loaned back for the occasion in order to help discover where Lady Carfax got kidnapped to. Coordinating with the up-and-coming generation of Irregulars had not been the happy reunion I'd hoped for, and I found myself in the humiliating position of having to explain my credentials to a bunch of ankle-biters half my age.

Trying to run a spy network of children wasn't as easy as it had been when I was actually a child, and our efforts to lend a hand to the hunt proved futile. It was entirely another source that gave Mr. Holmes the lead he needed to move the case along. Pieces of the woman's jewellery had been pawned, and they, in turn, led to where she was being held captive.

You might have read Dr. Watson's account of the case. Suffice to say, Mr. Holmes was able to save Lady Carfax at the last moment before she was buried alive in a double-deep coffin that previously had held only one corpse. The perpetrators of this nasty attempted murder were a pair of confidence tricksters named Henry Peters and Annie Fraser, who were looking to cover up their crimes, and weren't even honest enough to do their own killing. They thought a combination of chloroform, suffocation, and six feet of dirt would do the job for them. Sherlock Holmes saved a life that day, but the sinister couple had escaped out the back of their hideout with their loot.

Some mysteries have their loose ends, but such a heinous crime couldn't be permitted to pass unpunished. No more than a day after Lady Carfax's miraculous recovery, I was summoned to Baker Street, much as I had been throughout my youth. Mrs. Hudson, for once, wasn't concerned about my tracking dirt through her property. Maturity and gainful employment had cleaned me up to her satisfaction, and the shoes I wore were new and free of holes.

"I'm sorry I couldn't have been more use to you, Mr. Holmes," I began as soon as I was let in. "The Irregulars covered as much ground as they could in the time they had."

"Don't concern yourself, Wiggins," said the detective. "All leads were pursued, and thankfully one paid off. Lady Carfax has her salvation, though I wonder if she will ever be the same after her ordeal."

"With your leave, I'll report back for duty to your brother."

"I have already been in touch with Mycroft about extending your assignment."

"Do you have some other business you want to set me to?" I asked.

"Not at all!" said Mr. Holmes. "I expect you to take the lead in this ongoing investigation and bring it to a successful conclusion."

"It isn't over?"

"Not so long as Peters and Fraser remain at large. Kidnapping, extortion, attempted murder! These crimes aren't so uncommon, but the depravity they brought to their efforts is unique in my experience. They are a husband-and-wife team who have formed a most unholy union. Death by live burial belongs in penny dreadfuls and gothic horror novels, and yet they very nearly dragged the stuff of pulp nightmares into reality."

"The two of them could be anywhere by now."

"They could well be," agreed Mr. Holmes. "Which makes it all the more vital we pick up their trail at once before they attempt to ply their trade again. My chief concern is that they might resort to the same scheme. It very nearly worked. If not for a last-minute intervention, all trace of their crime would have been lost. Having made off with their freedom and their blood money, I expect they will decide it is a formula for success, and will inevitably try it again when they believe they are safe."

With that, I was set upon the road. The degenerate duo were on the loose – somewhere, anywhere. London was too hot for them, but there were plenty of other towns, cities, and villages where they might set up shop again. Wanted as they were, their success and escape would have emboldened them enough to keep at it without the need to retreat all the way back to the Continent. Mr. Holmes suspected they were close, and for what it was worth, I agreed.

I kept in touch about my activities, reporting my movements back to the wire network at the Diogenes Club. An exchange had been set up in the cellar a few years earlier, despite objections by some of the founders. Mostly it was there to keep certain unnamed members in direct and immediate contact with their brokers and bookies, but it also served men like Mycroft Holmes when they needed to send and receive information over distances and at speeds no mere courier could match. No response came back to any of the telegraph offices I visited, and I remained blind as to how Sherlock Holmes was conducting the hunt on his end.

My end involved reading every obituary page I could get my hands on and visiting more funeral parlours than I could have ever imagined existed. Death, it seemed, was a booming industry. I was set to searching far and wide for coffin makers that were open to making a casket of unusual proportions, well off their standard model. Whenever I got a bite from one willing to customise their wares for me, I asked, innocently enough, if they had done any similar jobs of late.

"We keep half-a-dozen models in stock," I was told by one funeral director in Manchester. "But something made-to-order can be arranged."

The mortician was unusually plump and jovial. Most of them where about as grim and gaunt as you would expect, with the sour attitude to go with it. But this one was chatty. He was certainly eager to talk shop with me once I got to asking him about his craft. I suppose it's a lonely business, and you take your company where you can get it if it isn't stiff as a plank and lying in a box.

"Do you do that here, yourself?" I asked.

"We make arrangements with a local carpenter who will customise for us when he isn't otherwise occupied with the business of making furniture. Is there some . . . urgency?" he added, delicately.

"Urgency?"

"Your uncle, is it?" he asked, reminding me of the lie I had started the conversation with. "How long has he been lying in mortal repose?"

"Ah, yes," I said, realising what he was on about. "It's been a couple of days, so . . . you know."

"Ripe, but not yet rank," he nodded knowingly.

"The sooner we get him in the ground, the better. Problem is, we can dig a hole as big as need be, but we'll have a spot of bother squeezing him into any of the coffins I've seen."

"Large man, was he?"

"Still is," I said. "Though the family isn't inclined to wait for him to deflate to a more manageable size."

"No, of course not," said the mortician with a bright smile what wasn't the usual sort of gallows humour I'd come to expect from his line of work. Such a pleasant fellow. "We can put in a rush order, though I'm afraid it might take another day or two. Have you considered a shroud?"

"The family has their heart set on a proper casket," I said. "Tell me, have you had any other such requests lately? You know, for extra-large coffins. Especially deep ones."

"Not wide?"

"My uncle was a man of peculiar proportions."

"We've only put in one order for an extra-large custom coffin in recent weeks," he said.

"Have you now?" I asked, leaping at the lead. "And who might this have been for?"

"Why, myself!" he chuckled, taking a grasp of his substantial belly with both his hands. "Not that I'm planning to shuffle off this mortal coil anytime soon, but one never knows when the Lord will call us home. I wouldn't want my family left short of options when the time comes, as I'm sure you'll appreciate considering your own family's current woes."

Another dead end. The undertaker must have read the disappointment in my face, and assumed there was profit to be had in it.

"Of course, I might be convinced to sell my own grand sarcophagus to accommodate your uncle if the need is so pressing. For an additional charge – which I'm sure your family will find quite reasonable in their moment of grief, of course. We also offer payment plans at a low rate of interest."

I told him I would consult with my loved ones and see if they were keen to still be paying off a funeral long after an overpriced box was buried six feet under and had gone as rotten as its occupant. Booming industry indeed! If Peters and Fraser knew how much money they could swindle in the funeral business, they might have gone all in on it, rather than merely employing it as a component of their kidnapping, murder, and body-disposal scheme. There was more money to be made – half as dishonest and twice as legal.

I spent three weeks in total attending funerals as I crisscrossed England by train, filling seats at wakes for strangers. My attendance was based not on the lives lived, but the weight they'd gained before snuffing it. In each case, I put myself in the awkward position of confirming that the body in the big casket filled it out enough to leave no room for someone else to be tucked in there with them. Easy enough when it was an open-coffin affair. One quick look, due respects paid, and I could nip out before the ceremony even started. Closed caskets were trickier, and I had to pick my moment to have a peek inside without anyone noticing. I often found it was easiest to slip the hearse driver a few coins to have a gander at the goods in back before he made delivery to the local boneyard. It ran up my expense account, but it saved me buying a shovel.

Tragedy and horror as we were trying to prevent, I couldn't help but think Mr. Holmes had me chasing my tail. I'd been at it for the better part of a month without so much as a single update or word of encouragement from Baker Street. Peters and Fraser had left the country or invented a whole new criminal enterprise – I was sure of it. It was only after a five-day gap, with not a single report of a custom coffin measuring an inch off of industry standards, that I caught a break on my third run through Birmingham. A funeral director I had interviewed twice earlier spotted me by chance at a pub down the street from his parlour. I'd been reluctant to bother him yet again, but this time he approached me, remembering my face and odd line of questioning.

"Are you still on the prowl for caskets of unusual sizes and proportions?" he asked me over a round of drinks I was happy to pay for in exchange for a promising tip. "I have one for you. A customer ordered it a few days ago. Deep rather than wide. I never had a request for one with measurements quite like it, and it was only after it was put together that I recognised it was just what you said you were looking for. Fancy I should see you again so soon, but you seem stubborn in your resolve to find what you're after."

"Do you know when the funeral is?" I asked, hoping I hadn't already missed it.

"I'm not sure if there's a funeral scheduled at all," he said. "The order was made and the casket delivered to a flophouse off Bradford Street. I would have thought anyone living there would be too scant to pay a premium on a custom coffin, but their money was good."

"You say 'their money' – as in more than one of them?"

"A man and a woman."

"Married?"

"Husband and wife, brother and sister, I couldn't say. They gave no details, other than the measurements of the casket, and offered no names. Only the fee charged for material, labour, and delivery passed between us."

"You didn't happen to notice if the man had a mangled left ear?" I asked, describing Henry Peters's most notable feature.

"I couldn't say for sure," was the answer. "My attention was otherwise occupied counting his money."

"Do you still have the address the coffin was delivered to?"

It cost me another pint, but he had it for me in his ledger back at the parlour.

That same night, I positioned myself outside the flophouse I had been directed to. My eye was on a second-floor flat in the back that had accepted the coffin delivery, despite there being no indication of occupants living or dead, in mourning or otherwise.

It was about one o'clock in the morning when I saw the gaslight in the rear window flare up and illuminate a single room. Someone was inside, rummaging about. I could see his silhouette upon the ratty curtain that blocked my view through the glass.

I had no real evidence to go on, no proof worth a damn. But the coincidences kept lining up, and I thought if I could just get a look at that man's ear and see if it looked chewed up from an old barroom brawl, it would be enough to report back to Mr. Holmes that I'd found Henry Peters. Probably his wife, too. And if we acted quick enough, more harm could be prevented.

Breaking into a flophouse wasn't much of a crime as crimes go. The door out back looked like it had been kicked in or jimmied more than once in the past, and it was no great feat to crack it open one more time. Silent as I could, I let myself in and crept up the stairs, careful to go slow so the old floorboards underfoot wouldn't creak. Light flickered from within one of the rooms above, and I was able to peek through the door that had been left ajar.

There was a man with a lamp picking through the dank chamber. He didn't appear to be hunting for anything in particular, but rather taking measure of what there was to see by the dim illumination. All I wanted was to catch a glimpse of his left ear and confirm if this was the illusive Henry Peters or not.

"Shall I turn my head so you can have a better look?" the man asked without bothering to face me.

I froze in place, like all my secrets had been exposed at once, including my inner-most thoughts.

"No," he said, "you haven't discovered the whereabouts of Henry Peters. Nor, unfortunately, have I as yet."

If the voice hadn't been instantly familiar to me, the features were once he raised his lamp so I could better see him.

"Mr. Holmes!" I declared.

"I see, Wiggins, that your line of investigation has led you to the same spot as mine. I was expecting you, and your attempt at masking your footsteps announced your arrival at last."

"What if I had been Peters?" I asked. "Or Annie Fraser sneaking up behind you?"

"Quite impossible," said Mr. Holmes. "They were here, of course. Many times, in fact. But they shall not return. I am afraid their crime spree has escalated, and they will seek to put distance between themselves and their first official murder."

"It's come to that?" I asked, disappointed we were too late after weeks of effort.

"While you were following the trail of unusual made-to-order coffins, I was tracking any and all reports of wealthy women gone missing."

"Are there as many of those in the world as there are odd caskets, I wonder?"

"More than you would guess," he said. "Restless women abound, and the thing about wealthy women is that they can afford to go missing. Most of them turn up again after a day or two, once they've had their fling, liaison, or impromptu holiday. Police reports are withdrawn, family concerns are alleviated, and all is forgiven and forgotten about in short order."

"Who was the missing lady you tracked here?"

"Mrs. Bethany Meiser, widow of the famed brass-making magnate. She was seduced away from many a dull day settling her husband's estate by the usual Peters-and-Fraser promise of comfort and spiritual guidance. She was held in this room for the last two weeks of her life. You'll find this door and its lock sturdier than either of the ones we picked to get in."

"Where is she now?" I asked.

"That would be her behind you."

So focused was I on identifying the mysterious man in the room, I had passed right by the coffin I had been after. It was up on blocks, flush against the inner wall, and matched the measurements I had been given at the funeral parlour.

"The worst has already been confirmed," Mr. Holmes said. "I shut it again when I heard your arrival."

"You know I have a stronger stomach than that."

"It isn't your stomach that concerns me so much as your lungs."

Mr. Holmes approached the coffin and took hold of the edges of the lid.

"Hold your breath, Wiggins," he said. "The effects are still quite potent."

Given such an introduction, I expected the late Bethany Meiser to be in an advanced state of decomposition, but as the cover came free, I saw the body inside was fresh. It was, instead, the stink of chloroform that met us as Mr. Holmes unsealed the casket. Linen soaked in the stuff was still draped over her face, and even the smallest taste of the air wafting from the coffin nearly overcame me. I felt woozy at once and had to make an effort to gather my senses and remain upright.

Mr. Holmes threw open the window and fanned the air to better dissipate the fumes.

"There's only one body," I observed.

"Peters and Fraser weren't so precise in their timing this time," said Mr. Holmes. "Their plan went amiss, and the parts didn't come together to make the desired whole."

"What went wrong?"

"They had the custom coffin order in place before a suitable decoy body presented itself. In the meantime, the unfortunate Mrs. Meiser had succumbed to the effects of the chloroform. Sedating their kidnapping victim too many times in order to control her movements has set her still forever. As the coffin had already been delivered, it made for a suitable place to store her body."

"Surely they'll still want to lay claim to another corpse they can set on top of her. Hiding their crime in the wrong grave seems to have been their plan once more."

"With Mrs. Meiser already dead a day or two, the window of opportunity has run short. Finding a suitably slight decedent was challenge enough, but it also had to be someone uncollected by family or friends. Someone they could credibly claim as their own, either by manufactured connection, or by false virtue of charity and compassion. It is an easier thing to do when not pressed for time by an inconvenient body in need of quick disposal."

"Then they've ditched the whole mess and are on the run," I concluded.

"On the run, yes," agreed Mr. Holmes. "But straight to their objective. The late Mrs. Meiser has left a bounty for them to claim, if they can get to it before her death is widely known."

"More jewellery for them to pawn?" I asked.

"I cannot say what Mrs. Meiser may have told them under duress. This prize could be anything. We may, however, deduce where it is to be found."

"How?"

"The walls themselves suggest it. Hundreds of times over, in fact."

Mr. Holmes held up his lamp so I could see what was written in plain sight. It was a signature, repeated so many times, up and down the walls, I had assumed it was the pattern of the wallpaper in the low light.

Bethany Louise Meiser was what the repeating cursive squiggle told us.

"It's the same thing, over and over and over again," I said of the signature that repeated itself, from ceiling to floor, across all four walls of the room. "What does it mean?"

"It means," said Mr. Holmes, "that practise makes perfect."

He showed me to a spot in one corner.

"These must be originals," he said. "Notice how subsequent signatures are rough, hesitant, and poor matches."

"They improve as they go along," I said, as I walked the length of the room.

"The forgeries become more natural with repetition. Every few feet, you can tell when Mrs. Meiser was compelled to provide new examples to be followed. Those look smooth and correct, until we arrive here."

Mr. Holmes slapped his hand against the opposite wall.

"By this point no difference can be perceived. Even an expert in forgery might be fooled. Hundreds of matches were attempted until the signature became as natural as that of its originator."

"So they mean for Annie Fraser to impersonate Bethany Meiser and sign some documents in her name," I said.

"Such is my supposition."

"Like a property deed? Henry Peters could be named as the beneficiary."

"The deception would inevitably be discovered," said Mr. Holmes. "Knowledge of Mrs. Meiser having gone missing will spread. News of her death will spread even faster. No, Wiggins, the forgery must be done to free up some sort of capital that can be made to swiftly disappear along with the kidnappers – before the body is discovered or the missing woman becomes a matter of police investigation."

"That capital could be anything," I said.

"Mrs. Meiser told her abductors where to seek out their loot. She may yet tell us."

Mr. Holmes returned to the body of the dead woman. The air around the coffin was still foul, but the chemical stink had dissipated enough to conduct a proper examination. I left the detective to it. There wasn't anything I was likely to spot that he wouldn't, and it didn't take long for him to pick out a detail I never would have noticed.

"See something?" I asked when Mr. Holmes fixated on a single point of interest.

"The chain around her neck is most remarkable."

"Really?" I said, peering into the box. "It seems awfully plain to me."

The necklace was so ordinary, Mrs. Meiser's kidnappers hadn't even bothered to pilfer it on their way out.

"That is what makes it remarkable," said Mr. Holmes. "No pendant hangs from it, no locket. Nothing at all."

"Was something removed?"

"Most certainly," said Mr. Holmes. "Something important to her."

He reached into the coffin and turned over the woman's right hand.

"She held it tightly throughout her incarceration," he said. "You can see the impression it has left."

There was a discoloured spot in the center of her palm where the skin had become rough. A callus might have formed had she continued to squeeze this trinket like a worry bead. An outline of it had scored her flesh enough for me to tell that one side was flat, while the other had an irregular jagged surface.

"It looks like a bite mark from a tiny animal," I observed.

"The impression is of teeth," agreed Mr. Holmes. "Not those of a rodent, but a key."

"A key to what?"

"Where are portable valuables kept that requires both a key and a signature?" Mr. Holmes asked me. Quizzed me more like, because he already knew the answer. It took me quite a bit longer to get there.

"A safe deposit box!"

"Spot on, Wiggins. But I fear it is a bit of knowledge that helps us not at all. We find ourselves pointed in too many directions."

Once again, we were a step behind Peters and Fraser. In their haste to put the cart before the horse, or rather the coffin before the hearse, they had stumbled but not fallen. They had left a sloppy murder in their wake, but had come away with everything they needed to access the late Bethany Meiser's valuables. In all likelihood, they had already raided the bank vault and were now in possession of the contents of the deposit box. Mrs. Meiser had been dead for at least a day. With nothing more to gain from the unfortunate woman, her kidnappers would have seized the opportunity to visit the bank before it closed. Which bank was the question.

We were out in the street again only a few minutes later, filling our lungs with the comparatively fresh city air of Birmingham. There was a murder to report, and many banks to scout if we were going to pick up the trail again. The whole thing seemed a daunting, impossible task. Who was to say the bank we were after was even local? Mrs. Meiser's safe deposit box might have been anywhere across the whole kingdom as far as we knew.

"We'll be chasing after those two villains into the next century at this rate," I complained.

"They have proved most elusive," agreed Mr. Holmes, "but they have made many mistakes. They will most certainly make more, and one of them will be their downfall."

"I can hardly wrap my head around where this takes us next," I said, "and that bloody racket isn't helping me think."

Several streets away, there was a sudden tedious drone of a bell ringing. It would have been loud in broad daylight on a busy street, but in the middle of the night, with no one around, it was deafening. This wasn't the steady chime of huge church bells, but that of an annoying little one being struck by its clapper so many times in quick succession it created a constant assaulting buzz.

"Quickly, Wiggins!" Mr. Holmes called to me. He was already running down the street and rounding the corner.

I did as I was told and was soon keeping pace with him. The ringing grew closer, or rather we were getting nearer to its source. Something about the sound had set the detective off.

"You know what that noise is?" I panted.

"A burglar alarm!" he shouted back at me.

I wondered what had just put us in the burglary business.

"So?"

"It is a standard model installed in many banks!"

I didn't doubt him. Someone in Mr. Holmes's line of work was likely to know what one burglar alarm sounded like compared to the next. He was, after all, the man who could name every variety of tobacco ash, or tell you exactly where in London any spot of mud had come from.

Four streets and three turns later, we found ourselves outside the building where all the noise was coming from. It was a small bank branch called *Wesser, Leeds, and Company*. The door had been smashed in and a night watchman was laid out on the floor, dazed but not dead.

Mr. Holmes hurried to the guard's side to lend assistance. His head was bleeding, and it looked like he'd had a good crack on the skull. Much harder, and we might have been looking at our second murder of the night.

I took up Mr. Holmes's lamp to see if there was anyone else about. The gates to the teller booths were still closed, as was the vault door, and I could see no evidence that anyone had tried to force either.

"Doesn't look like there's been a robbery," I said.

"Yet an attempt has been made just the same," replied Mr. Holmes, pulling the electric power line that fed the alarm and silencing the damnable thing.

"This can't be related to our case, can it? Peters and Fraser would have been about their bank business earlier than this, and they had no reason do go kicking in doors and knocking watchmen over the head."

"Not unless their first attempt to sign in under false pretences had been thwarted somehow. Their eagerness to get at the safe deposit box may have inspired desperate measures."

I went over to have a look at the vault to make sure it was secure. The heavy iron door was shut tight and didn't look like anyone had been at it. There were no tell-tale scratches from a crowbar, no dents from a sledgehammer, no hint that the hinges had been worked on in any way. I gave the combination dial a quick turn left and right and the movement was too smooth for it to have been molested. Likewise, the spindle handle on the door was firm and fixed in place when I tried it next.

"The alarm must have scared them off," I concluded.

Mr. Holmes was just on his way over to the vault to examine it for himself when we were interrupted by a command from the shattered doorway.

"Step away from there, you two!"

We turned and saw a uniformed bobby. He had his night stick out and looked committed to using it if we gave him any trouble.

"Caught you in the act, did I?" he said.

"You caught us in the middle of an investigation," replied Mr. Holmes.

"You don't look like police."

"My name is Sherlock Holmes. I am a consulting detective."

"*The* Sherlock Holmes?" he wondered.

"None other."

The introduction wasn't winning him over, and the bobby looked suspicious.

"You don't look much like the Sherlock Holmes I seen in *The Strand Magazine*."

"An illustrator must be free to exercise his artistic licence," said Mr. Holmes.

"And he looks awfully young to be Dr. Watson," said the bobby, pointing his night stick at me.

"That's because I'm a Wiggins, not a Watson," I said.

"Wiggins, eh?" the copper said like it rang a bell. One considerably smaller and softer than the alarm bell that had summoned him. "He was a character in the first couple of books, wasn't he?"

"Right. That was me."

"He was just a boy."

"Boys grow up. Those books came out years ago."

Explaining ourselves to a lone helmet on the beat promised to be a long affair, but luckily for us an attempted bank robbery draws the attention of higher-ups sooner rather than later.

"Stand down, Constable," said the next man to arrive. "I hardly think Sherlock Holmes would be the one holding up a bank at this hour."

"Superintendent Humphries," said Mr. Holmes, offering his hand to the latest uniform to arrive on the scene. "A pleasure to make your acquaintance again."

"It's been a few years since you've graced our boys in Birmingham with a visit," said Humphries. "I don't think we would have ever sorted out that nasty business with the sunken narrowboat under the Tivoli without you."

"The Tivoli isn't anywhere near a canal," I recalled, having passed the theatre several times on my recent trips through Birmingham.

"Thus our problem sorting it out," said Humphries.

"It is an entirely different problem that brings me back to Birmingham," said Mr. Holmes. "Some solutions have presented themselves, but the primary mystery that remains is the location of my suspects."

"You think they were here, trying to rob this bank?"

"I think they had pressing business at a bank. Likely one in Birmingham. That an alarm should be tripped and a night watchman attacked in such proximity of time and location is too unlikely to be coincidence."

"What in the blazes is going on here, Superintendent?" demanded a new voice at the scene.

The last arrival was an older man, well dressed but hastily so. His dress shirt was misbuttoned, the laces of his expensive shoes were undone, and he had failed to knot his tie.

"This is Mr. Nathaniel Leeds," the superintendent told us of the interested party.

"You would be the '*Leeds*' over the door, in the middle of this branch's name," said Mr. Holmes.

"Quite right, sir. And you are – ?"

"This is Sherlock Holmes," said the superintendent, "the famed detective, who has been kind enough to offer his services."

"The offer comes at a swift pace, I see," said Leeds. "He beat me here before I was even able to get dressed."

"My associate and I were already in pursuit of two thieves who may be responsible for the break-in," Mr. Holmes told the banker. "Your arrival is most fortuitous."

"I live only one street away and know the sound of my own alarm system."

"Like you, we were drawn by the alarm. We have reason to believe the suspects we seek visited your bank prior to this incident. Tell me, Mr. Leeds, were you at work yesterday?"

"I am not a man known to take time off, Mr. Holmes."

"Then perhaps you could tell us if you saw a man with a mangled ear lurking about, or a tall, pale woman with narrow eyes seeking entry to the vault to check her deposit box."

"As a matter of fact," said Leeds, "there was an odd incident along those lines reported to me in my office late yesterday."

"Any details you can share would be of great importance."

"Then it would be best for you to hear it from the witness himself. Terrance Bogan was the bank clerk who dealt with a most unusual client. I didn't hear all the specifics, but I'm sure he can tell you about it in detail. One phone call can have him down here within the hour."

"Please extend my apologies for arousing him at such an hour," said Mr. Holmes, "but time is of the essence. Our quarry is a slippery pair, and they are likely putting more distance between themselves and their eventual apprehension every moment we delay."

Our witness had to come from clear across town after being roused in the middle of the night. "Within the hour" proved to be an optimistic estimate, and it was closer to two hours before he could make his way to us.

As we waited in the bank, Sherlock Holmes fired up a pipe and paced impatiently, concerned that Peters and Fraser were squirming away through his fingers once more. His frustration was infectious.

"You might want a refill of tobacco, Mr. Holmes," I said. "You've been through two already and it smells like you're smoking the pipe itself."

"I refuse to permit this conundrum to become a three-pipe problem!" he declared, taking another dry puff. "We know all the core facts, and yet we stand helpless to put an end to this crime spree until we can lay our hands upon the deadly couple. Our only hope now is that this clerk saw or heard something that will point us in the right direction before they are out of reach."

At last, Bogan arrived with the first hint of sunrise. He was most apologetic for the delay, having already been told of the dire circumstances that had summoned him. Additional police had been dispatched to the Peters and Fraser lair to attend to the body of Mrs. Meiser. The night watchman had been taken away for proper medical attention, and was too injured to tell us anything of significance. All our bets were on the lone clerk and the usefulness of what he had seen the previous day.

"There was a woman who came in to inquire after her safe deposit box," Bogan reported. "Nothing unusual in that. We get several such requests each day."

"Did she seem to be of a nervous disposition?"

"Perhaps a touch flushed, but it's hard to say."

"If it was Annie Fraser," I commented to Mr. Holmes, "you'd think she'd be out of sorts after being an accessory to murder so recently."

"Her blood is starting to run as cold as that of her husband," he replied to me. "They are increasingly comfortable with their crimes. Killing comes more naturally with practice."

"Who was this client?" Leeds asked his clerk. "Did you recognise her?"

"As you recall, sir, I only started here last month. I don't yet know all the clients by sight, but her name was Bethany Meiser."

"There we have it, Wiggins," said Mr. Holmes. "It was them, only hours ago. Tell me, Mr. Bogan, was there a man with her?"

"I didn't see anybody with Mrs. Meiser," he replied. "But, as it turns out, it wasn't Mrs. Meiser – only a woman claiming to be her. She had the right key for one of our deposit boxes, and her signature was a match for the samples we had in our ledger from previous visits. She might have been let into the vault if not for one of our tellers overhearing me call her by name. Right over my shoulder she was, as I spun the dial and cracked open the door. It was just then the teller came to inform me that this woman wasn't who she said she was. He'd dealt with Mrs. Meiser a number of times, and even escorted her to her deposit box on several occasions, but he'd never seen this woman before. He tried to be discreet about telling me, but the lady must have overheard, and before I could ask her a single question, she bolted like a startled deer. Last I saw her, she had the hem of her dress hitched up and was dashing down the street like runner at a track meet. Not so ladylike, if you ask me."

"You didn't see her again?" asked Mr. Holmes. "Or perhaps a man with a badly scarred ear?"

"Nothing of the sort," said Bogan. "We locked away all our notes at the end of business hours as per usual and closed shop. I said good evening to the watchman and went home. I never knew anything was amiss until I got the call."

"Did you not see fit to report this incident to police?" asked Superintendent Humphries.

"The decision to not involve you was mine," said Leeds. "What I heard of the incident sounded harmless enough. Likely a simple misunderstanding. There was no indication that things would escalate as they have."

"Sounds like your suspects have made two attempts to get whatever it is they're after in the vault, Mr. Holmes," said the superintendent. "Maybe they'll try again, and you can catch them at it."

"We shan't be so fortunate," said Mr. Holmes. "Peters and Fraser are too clever to push their luck as far as that. They know they have exposed themselves and will go into hiding."

The clerk's story had only confirmed what we already thought we knew. If there had been some helpful clue in his tale, I had missed it. Instead, it seemed we had wasted two hours waiting to hear a mildly amusing anecdote. Time we could have spent chasing our kidnapping murderers, if only we knew which way they had gone.

Mr. Holmes had a last look at the impenetrable iron door that had twice thwarted the would-be bank robbers.

"They had the key and number for a safe deposit box," he said, "but what made them think they could get into that vault, I wonder?"

"Maybe they thought the watchman had a way to open it for them," I suggested, "but the alarm was already going, and they'd hit him in the head too hard for him to be of any use. Running away was the only choice left at that point."

Mr. Holmes looked unconvinced, but we'd already seen and heard all the bank had to offer us.

"Thank you for your assistance, Mr. Leeds," he said to the manager. "We won't detain you any further. There is much tidying up to do before your first clients of the day arrive."

"No need to rush, Mr. Holmes. Today is a bank holiday. Time enough to replace the broken glass and repair the lock."

"I shall leave you to it. Come along, Wiggins," said Mr. Holmes. "We may yet be able to perceive some indication of their escape route by the first rays of sunlight."

Outside, Sherlock Holmes stuffed his pipe with a fresh wad of tobacco. It seemed Peters and Fraser had earned themselves the honorarium of becoming a three-pipe problem after all. He was just about to touch a lit match to it when he stopped abruptly, shook the match to extinguish it, and stuffed his pipe back in his pocket.

"Once again, their folly has made a fool of me!" he shouted, spinning around. "Hurry now, Wiggins! There are lives to save, albeit ones that have forfeited any right to life."

Nathaniel Leeds was sweeping up the shards of broken glass on the floor himself when the detective burst back into his bank. He ignored the manager, instead seeking out his junior employee.

"Bogan!" Mr. Holmes cried out, summoning the clerk again.

"Sir?" responded the clerk.

"Get this vault door open at once!"

The order only confused the young man.

"No one's broken in, you can see that clearly."

"They didn't have to," said Mr. Holmes. "You said it yourself: Annie Fraser was poised over your shoulder as you dialled the combination. Even with easy access at hand, her criminal mind would have been quick to remember the numbers."

My heart sank. If I was following Mr. Holmes's thinking, the nefarious pair had already robbed the place and made off with the goods.

"Do you think they had enough time to open the vault, find the right deposit box, empty it, and flee before we got here?" I wondered. "It's an awful lot to do in so short a time. We arrived less than two minutes after the alarm went off."

"Peters and Fraser never went anywhere," Mr. Holmes said. "They've been right under our noses the whole time."

Bogan completed the combination and spun the spindle so he could pull open the door. We were met with a burning smell and plenty of smoke. As soon as the air cleared, we saw a man and a woman lying on the floor of the vault, stone cold dead. I counted twenty-two spent matches lying next to them, along with an open box full of letters, some of them also burnt.

Mr. Holmes had made the odious acquaintance of Henry Peters and Annie Fraser before and recognised the bodies at once. It was my first time laying eyes on them, but there was no need for him to confirm who we had discovered. The torn ear on the man told me all I needed to know.

"Why would they lock themselves in?" I said.

"They didn't," Mr. Holmes told me. "They merely closed the door behind them so they could hide and wait for everyone to leave. With a bank holiday upon us and no business to conduct, they expected to find a moment when they could emerge and slip away. That is when terrible ironic fate struck. Peters and Fraser weren't buried alive, as they intended for their victims, but *entombed*. I'm afraid you're toying with the combination dial sealed their fate as firmly as it sealed the vault."

I was sickened when I realised what I had inadvertently done.

"Do not blame yourself, Wiggins," said Mr. Holmes. "They had every opportunity to surrender and spare themselves such an awful end. Trapped in total darkness, afraid to call out and expose themselves, they lit match after match to keep fear at bay."

Mr. Holmes bent down and retrieved one of the half-burned letters on the floor, still in its envelope. He pulled out the scorched sheet of paper from within and read a few passages before putting it away again respectfully.

"Eventually they started burning these to maintain some light," he continued, "failing to realise even such a modest flame was quickly consuming their oxygen in so tight a space. You mentioned how it smelled like I was burning my own pipe. In fact, it was the scent of burnt paper you detected, seeping out of the seal of the vault door that was too narrow to sufficiently replenish the supply of air within."

"What are these letters anyways?" I asked.

"They are what Mrs. Meiser held so dear in the palm of her hand throughout her final days," said Sherlock Holmes. "It wasn't the key to a safe deposit box but rather the key to her heart. They are love letters from her late husband. A treasure most precious to her, but worthless to the likes of Peters and Fraser. It seems they have served to reunite one husband and wife, and damn another."

Phantom of the Operetta
by Tim Newton Anderson

I had called on Holmes on a frosty January morning in 1903 and was almost knocked over as I ascended the stairs to his rooms by a tall man with a shock of red hair who was leaving. When he mumbled an apology, I detected an Irish accent, but I had little chance to observe more as he charged out of the door and rushed off down the street.

"Who was that extremely rude fellow?" I asked Holmes as I entered his sitting room. My friend was thumbing briskly through a pile of papers and books upon his desk and uttered an "A-ha!" as he obviously found what he had been looking at.

"Sit, and I will tell you about my latest client," he said. "A very interesting fellow, if a little brusque. When I have explained, we are off to the theatre."

I moved more papers from my usual armchair and placed them on the floor by my side. Alongside the documents on his desk, I could see the remains of the breakfast Mrs. Hudson had prepared and a still steaming mug of coffee.

"The theatre? Surely too early for a performance?"

"The case, Watson, the case," he replied. "The gentleman you met on the stairs is Mr. Bram Stoker, who is the manager of the Lyceum Theatre. We went there last year to see the great Irving perform Hamlet. A tad overblown for my taste, but a fitting tribute to the Bard."

"You are to work for Henry Irving?" I asked.

"Not directly," he replied. "Our leading thespian is away on tour and Mr. Stoker is in charge of the theatre. He is our client in what may be a most interesting case. It seems the theatre is cursed."

"Surely you cannot be interested in such superstitious nonsense?"

"Rest assured, there is a human hand behind the mystery and not a supernatural one," he said. "But as you are aware, theatre folk are prey to all kinds of fancies. During my brief period treading the boards in my youth, I discovered the naming of the Scottish Play was the least of their irrational beliefs. There was scarcely a member of the cast or stage crew who didn't have some ritual concerned with their performance which he or she felt forced to re-enact before taking the stage. In this case, the strange occurrences at the Lyceum have the company in such a state of agitation they are threatening to quit the latest production before it reaches opening night."

"Perhaps they have simply lost faith in the play?".

"Not a play, but an operetta," Holmes said. "As Gilbert and Sullivan are no longer writing together, Stoker has a fancy to create a new piece which will attract their enormous audiences: A musical offering based on Chinese legends he hopes will rival *The Mikado*."

"I confess I'm intrigued," I said. "As you know, I'm an admirer of comic opera, and none of the pieces D'Oyly Carte has produced recently come anywhere close to the genius of Gilbert and Sullivan."

"It seems that is the least of his worries," said my friend. "According to Stoker, there have been a series of seeming accidents. The footlights suddenly flaring and threatening to start a blaze. A backdrop collapsing and enveloping the actors. An outbreak of food poisoning, even though none of those affected had eaten the same meal. Even a chandelier plummeting from its place in the auditorium. So far, three members of the cast have had falls and broken their legs, and replacements had to be found.

"The production has acquired a bad name throughout the London acting community, and recruiting more is proving impossible. Doubtless we will discover more when we visit the scene and I'm able to examine the evidence and cross-examine the company. I am glad you haven't had time to take off your greatcoat and scarf, as we must hasten there before any more unfortunate mishaps occur, as I'm convinced they will. There have been no fatalities, but if someone is determined to disrupt the production, then his actions may become more drastic."

I insisted we take a cab, as snow had started to gently fall, hiding the patches of ice on the pavements and making them even more treacherous than they had been when I had walked to Baker Street. It hadn't prevented other pedestrians braving the biting cold, and they bravely negotiated the slippery streets bundled in thick clothes and protected by their umbrellas. Nothing stops the thrum of commerce in London – not snow, not rain, not the blinding fog of a London Particular. Regents Street was particularly busy with shoppers hoping to find bargains in the sales.

The Strand was also busy with sightseers, as well as shoppers and theatre folk going to rehearsals. The cab turned into Wellington Street and dropped us off before the splendour of the Lyceum, and we entered via the side stage door. I was familiar with the plush interior of the theatre, but not the frankly down-at-heel corridors that existed backstage. No gilt or satin here – just utilitarian wood and plaster and props and equipment leaned against the walls, ready to be brought into use as the productions demanded. It was poorly illuminated by a few sparsely placed gas mantles, and there were no windows to let in the thin sunlight from outside, giving it the feel of a set of underground tunnels. After a few turns, I had no concept of where we were in relation to the world outside and became quite disoriented. Holmes, however, seemed completely at home in this environment and strode confidently forward, reaching the backstage area after a few twists and turns.

We met Stoker standing in the wings, waving his arms and shouting instructions to the stage-hands, and the actor who stood alone on the stage in front of a backdrop depicting an ancient Chinese palace. There were no props in sight, and I imagined these were being saved until the dress rehearsal. Standing with Stoker was a Chinese man who fully matched the manager's six-foot-two height. He was dressed in an expensive black suit with a silk collarless shirt underneath, and his hair was carefully brilliantined into place.

"You are here then, Holmes," said Stoker. The Irish accent was more easily discernible now that he wasn't rushing away. "This is Mr. Long – Wayland Long – who is advising me on the correct details of the period. He has been invaluable in helping us get everything right. This production is an important one for me. I have been assured the Prince of Wales and several other dignitaries have expressed an interest in attending the opening night."

The Chinaman gave a slight bow and smiled broadly.

"A pleasure to meet the famous Sherlock Holmes," he said in a rich baritone with no trace of an accent. "And your companion is Dr. John Watson, I presume. I have followed his chronicles of your exploits in *The Strand*. You display a skill at deduction that would rival that of the great Judge Dee."

"How do you come to be assisting Mr. Stoker?" asked Holmes.

"I have an importing business with a base in London, as well as Peking," he said. "Mr. Stoker came to me to purchase some Chinese artefacts for the production, and I was happy to assist in making the show a success. The English have a very mistaken impression of my fellow countrymen, assuming they are barbarians, and I wished to take this opportunity to correct that impression with a show that celebrates our venerable culture – one that has existed far longer than your own, if I may say so."

"I'm aware that it suits politicians and the press to portray your nation in a less-than-flattering light," said Holmes. "There are many interests in downplaying your nation to make our commercial and military adventures there seem more honourable. I saw a little of your country when visiting Tibet, despite your isolationist policies and suspicion of foreigners, and was impressed by the culture."

"I thank you for your kind words," said Long. That smile was still on his face, but I could discern a cold intellect behind it that hid its steel behind a façade of friendliness.

"There was another accident this morning while I was visiting you," said Stoker. "One of the floorboards on stage left gave way while our leading man was making his entrance, and had he not been so nimble, he would suffered serious injury."

"I need to see all the sites of these so-called accidents," said Holmes. "Starting with the most recent, if you please."

The man on stage, who I recognised as the music hall star George Lashwood, had just started signing, accompanied by a piano from the orchestra pit.

"*I really must have the Ring. It will be just the thing. My reign is long, just like my song, but one thing you must bring . . . .*"

The piano cut off as Stoker strode onto the stage and signalled to the pianist and Lashwood to stop.

"I have Mr. Sherlock Holmes here," he said. "He will put an end to all of this superstitious nonsense about a curse."

I wasn't sure Stoker was as convinced his problems weren't supernatural. After all, he was known for his stories of ancient curses and mythical beings. The still face of Long could easily have belonged to his Count Dracula.

"I really must continue rehearsing," said Lashwood. "This song is dashed difficult. So many words once it gets going."

"I have explained we need a good comic song to rival Gilbert and Sullivans pieces for George Grossmith," Stoker said. "They are one of the highpoints of their comic operas. That's what the audience go out humming. I'm sure Mr. Holmes will interrupt rehearsals for no longer than necessary."

Holmes had already strode confidently across the stage past the protesting star towards the far wings. He knelt down and looked closely at the broken floorboard.

"Unless your phantom is handy with a saw, this was sabotage rather than a haunting," he said. "This board has been cleanly cut through half its width so that it would give way as soon as it was trodden on. I suspect your other mishaps will have a similarly human explanation."

Stoker didn't look any less miserable at this news. A human saboteur was no less deadly than a supernatural curse.

"I need to closely examine all of the sites," said Holmes. "Kindly take me to them."

"It isn't a curse, then," said a soft voice by my side. I turned to see a young lady standing by me. I hadn't heard her approach. She possessed considerable beauty, and her face was framed with straight black hair that fell to her shoulders, although I suspected this had been dyed, as her brows and lashes were considerably lighter. I surmised she was an actress by the way she held herself, as if ready to step onto the stage, but her clothing was modest, if fashionable. She wore a long one-piece dress with a high neck cut just below her throat, and her shoulders were shrouded in a green felt wrap that would have helped keep out the chill of the theatre. I had retained my coat, as it was evident Stoker wasted no money on heating when there was no audience to benefit from it.

"My friend never looks for the supernatural when there is a more-human explanation behind any set of puzzles," I said. "If anyone can solve the riddle of the theatre's troubles, it is Holmes."

"I hope so," she said. "This is my first major role, and all of my friends and family are eager to see my debut. I would be devastated if anything spoiled it."

The young actress introduced herself as Sophie Williams. She told me she had grown up in Yorkshire, the daughter of a prosperous farmer who had initially been sceptical and protective when she announced she would like to take the skills she had developed in local theatrical performances and try her luck on the West End stage. She had no trace of a Yorkshire accent, but I attributed that to her skills as an actress and the need to perform in the Queen's English. Her talents had been discovered by Stoker when he saw her in an amateur performance in Whitby while he was in the area researching his novel. His credentials as a theatre manager and his imposing presence had persuaded the Williams family to allow Sophie to try out for Irving's company – at least once his partner Ellen Terry contacted them and reassured them that Sophie would be suitably chaperoned and protected from the questionable life of the theatre's *demi monde*.

"I am to play the part of Koong-se, the daughter of a Mandarin, who falls in love with her father's accountant, Chang. Her father forbids the marriage and promises her hand to a powerful Duke, but the two lovers steal the magical ring that was to be a wedding gift, and the Duke's ship. In the original legend of the Willow Pattern, they are killed and transformed by the gods into two doves, but Mr. Bramah, who Mr. Stoker has commissioned to write the story, has provided a happy ending where Chang invests the stolen money, becomes a duke himself under a false name, and they are then reconciled with Kong-se's father."

"I can see the appeal of basing the operetta on the popular Willow Pattern crockery," I said, "but surely Mr. Stoker is aware both the pattern and the legend were created in the Potteries in the last century."

She smiled and gave a small laugh, and her face became even more delightful.

"That is a point of some contention between Mr. Stoker and Mr. Long," she said. "The businessman believes we should use a more authentic Chinese tale, but everything was already written when he came onto the scene. Our manager has been happy to bow to our sponsor on points of clothing and culture, but refuses to alter our script, claiming preparations are too far advanced to allow it. And doubtless he is reluctant to pay out for a new book and extra rehearsal time."

From what I knew of the man, I could well believe that Stoker was reluctant to spend more money. I had seen a couple of Shakespeare performances by Irving as the Prince of Denmark, and the sorcerer Prospero wore the same costume with some minor alterations.

"Are you not scared by the accidents?" I asked. "I'm sure your parents would be concerned if they knew."

"That is precisely why I haven't told them, Dr. Watson." she said. "I couldn't bear to return to Yorkshire without having something to show for the money they have invested in my lodgings and keep. They insisted on paying for something more respectable than the normal actors 'digs'."

"Do you have any suspicions as to the person behind these 'accidents'?" I asked.

"I can see no reason why any of the cast or crew would be behind them," she said. "They depend on the success of the theatre as much as Mr. Stoker. However, I don't trust Mr. Long. He comes and goes as he wishes throughout the theatre, yet has only the flimsiest of reasons for taking an interest in the production. Perhaps he would prefer it to fail, rather than casting his culture in a poor light."

"Surely that is no reason to suspect him," I stated

"These accidents only started after he became involved," she said. "And then there is the ring."

"The ring?"

"Mr. Long supplied the ring that is at the centre of the plot," she said. "It is the one thing that he persuaded Mr. Stoker to change. In the original plot, the young couple steal jewels, but Mr. Long said it would be better to use the Chinese legend of the ring that changes fortunes. He said he had one that had been handed down in his family that he believed was the origin of the legend. It is a beautiful thing – two intertwined Chinese dragons of gold and silver. It is certainly valuable, for it has been locked in the office safe since Mr. Long brought it to the theatre. The legend is that whoever wears it has his or her fortune changed – good to bad and vice versa. Mr. Stoker tried it on, and since then the accidents have started. No one else in the cast will wear it, and many have begged our manager to get a copy made to use in case even worse things happen. Mr. Long laughed and said it is merely a legend, but I noticed he hasn't worn it himself."

At that moment Holmes returned, striding briskly across the stage with a glint in his eye that betrayed his joy in whatever he had discovered.

"As I suspected," he said. "There is the clear hand of a miscreant behind these events."

I turned to Miss Williams, but she had slipped away without my noticing. Perhaps she was in awe of Holmes, as many people were.

"How so?" I asked.

"There were signs that some kind of accelerant had been added to the gas feed to the footlights, the ropes on the backdrop had been untied and knotted loosely, and the retaining bolt to the chandelier in the false roof below the central dome was shiny from recent use. Definitely the work of human, not phantom."

I told Holmes about my conversation with Miss Williams and a thoughtful look passed across his face.

"That is most interesting," he said. "I believe I have a job for you, if you are free this evening."

"Of course," I responded.

"You have proved quite adept in the skills of disguise and following a trail which I have taught you," he said. "I would like you to follow Mr. Long when he leaves the theatre and tell me what he does. I believe it would be prudent to take your service revolver. Even though he seems to have the manners of an English gentleman, we cannot know if his associates share the same mores. Stoker tells me his import and export business is based in the docks, and that can be a dangerous area."

"What will you be doing?" I asked. "Should we not both go?"

"I have some other inquiries to pursue," he said. "I have the utmost confidence in your ability to track Long. I must return to Baker Street to carry out some research, but if you would like to continue talking to the actors and stage hands, that could be of benefit."

It was several hours later that I also returned to Baker Street. While the details of backstage life and some interesting, if malicious, gossip about some of my favourite actors and actresses were fascinating, I learned little that seemed germane to the case. It seemed that everyone had an alibi for at least one of the incidents, so unless several were working together, they didn't seem to be implicated. The exception, as Miss Williams had said, was Long. He came and went like a ghost, and while he was always there in the immediate aftermath of each accident, no one could remember where he was when they took place.

"Has your gossiping proved fruitful?" asked Holmes. He sat in his chair beside the fire, smoking a pipe of that vile tobacco he favoured. Papers were scattered at his feet and more covered the dining table.

"If you had been carrying out the conversations yourself, you would call it investigating."

"A touch, Watson," he replied with a smile. "While your discussions were probably less focussed than those I would have had myself, I'm sure they still uncovered some interesting facts pertinent to the case. Tell me all. And help yourself to the excellent game pie that is somewhere under the documents on the table. Mrs. Hudson has excelled herself."

I moved aside the papers to find a plate with two slices of pie. I looked with suspicion at the discolouration of the papers, as there was no telling what had caused it. However, I was hungry and pushed aside thoughts of Holmes chemical experiments and took a bite. As my friend had said, it was delicious.

"The other cast and staff confirmed what Miss Williams told me," I said. "The accidents started after Mr. Long became involved, and since the Dragon Ring was introduced to the theatre."

"I don't believe in Chinese magic rings," said Holmes. "But Mr. Long's appearance is certainly the match that lit the fuse on this affair. Why that should be may be something you will discover tonight. I hope your quarry hasn't already left the scene?"

"He had arranged meetings with other backers," I said. "'Angels', I believe they call them in the theatre. He will not leave until after six p.m. I'll return there after finishing this excellent pie."

"If you remove the papers on the seat by the window, you'll find a dock worker's clothing. That should suffice to make you unobtrusive when you follow Long."

"What of your own researches?" I asked. "Have you uncovered the key to the mystery?"

"Not yet, although I had an interesting discussion with my brother at his club on the way back to Baker Street," he said. "As you know, he is not an aficionado of the theatre. He rarely leaves the comfort of his club. However, his network of informants believe there are things afoot in London concerned with Mr. Long's homeland. This ring, for example, is supposed to have been looted from the Summer Palace in Peking during the Opium Wars, and the great powers are still circling China in the hope of acquiring more territory from which to trade. The Chinese, as you may imagine, are less-than-happy with the situation."

"Surely events thousands of miles away can have little to do with the happenings in a London theatre?"

"So you may suppose," he said. "But perhaps your nocturnal wanderings may uncover more."

It was after eight when Long finally finished his meetings and left the theatre. I was waiting in a cab a short distance from the Lyceum and instructed the driver to follow at a discreet distance when he mounted his own vehicle and set off for the Wapping Docks. If he noticed a dock worker alighting from a cab a hundred yards behind him, he gave no sign of it. The docks were busy with workers loading and unloading vessels, and my heavy boots, thick coat, and woollen hat blended in with the other men busy on the quays. Still, I held my service revolver in my pocket for comfort. The gas lamps cast eerie shadows amongst the cranes and crates, and I was aware some of the cargoes were less-than-innocent, and some of the figures that bustled around me were criminals who would brook no interference in their business. A dozen different nations made up the crowd, and the loud conversations and some of those were Long's countrymen.

Long arrived at a large and dark warehouse set aside from the main structures. A ship was moored alongside it, and Chinese dock workers were unloading crates and dragging them inside. My disguise was adequate for most of the docks, but I was in greater risk of being unmasked here and kept to the shadows. I couldn't understand what words passed between the workers, but there was evident haste in their business.

I moved quietly along the side of the building to find a vantage point and saw a side door which had been left ajar. Moving cautiously, I looked inside to see Long directing operations in the centre of the warehouse, shouting instructions in his own language. Unlike Long in his Western clothes, the workers were dressed in more traditional Chinese garb with their partially shaved heads and cues hanging behind. It could have been a scene from a dock in Hong Kong rather than London.

Most of the crates were being stacked at the side of the warehouse, but Long gestured for one to be brought to him. The two men who carried what was evidently a heavy burden placed it before him, and one jemmied it open. Long bent forward and lifted an object from it. It was a rifle, a Lee Enfield of the type the British Army had recently adopted. It certainly had no place in a warehouse in Wapping.

I was about to retreat to tell Holmes when I felt a hand on my shoulder. I drew my pistol and spun round to confront the person.

"There is no need for firearms," he said quietly. "It wouldn't do to be discovered before Inspector Gregson's men are fully in position."

I was about to protest, but Holmes held a finger to his lips to indicate silence.

"We are about to witness the denouement of an operation that has been in place for some time," he whispered. "Mr. Long, under his many aliases, has been bringing arms into the country as part of a plot to disrupt our activities in China. He is a prominent member of The Society of Righteous and Harmonious Fists who oppose foreign interference in their country. Mycroft has been monitoring their plans on behalf of the British and other governments, as he believes they are planning a major uprising both in China and here."

As Holmes spoke, I heard shots at the front of the building, and two-dozen armed police burst through the doors to the dock. Many of the Chinese held up their hands, but Long lifted the rifle to his shoulder and was about to fire. I didn't hesitate and shot at him with my revolver, hitting him in his right arm. The rifle dropped to the stone floor with a clatter and discharged harmlessly, with its bullet hitting one of the crates. I had a moment of fear in case it hit some ammunition, but these proved groundless, and Gregson's men raced across the floor to arrest the Chinaman. Holmes and I stepped into the warehouse as the conspirators had all been subdued. Gregson himself strode across the warehouse to greet us

"Your assistance wasn't required, as you have seen," he said. "Our operation was already planned before you contacted us."

"A fact of which I was fully aware," said Holmes. "However, as it touched on my own investigations, I felt duty bound to be present."

"I hope you realise that Dr. Watson and yourself could have been killed if you had charged in here without my men to tackle Long's gang," said Gregson.

"I was cognisant of the risk," said Holmes, "but confident of your abilities to control the situation. Before you take Mr. Long to the cells, I would welcome a word with him."

"If you think you can persuade him to talk, be my guest," said Gregson. "I doubt he will be too chatty in the circumstances. His kind tend to keep close lipped."

"I think I'll be able to open those lips," said Holmes. "I believe you will find Mycroft has plans for Mr. Long which will remove him from your custody to a place where he can be interrogated quietly. My brother has authorised me to broker a deal which will avoid him facing prosecution in return for his co-operation. He will never, of course, be allowed to return to China or regain his full liberty, but he will also avoid the hangman's noose."

Gregson grunted and waved Holmes across to where Long stood.

"Kindly wait here," he said to me. "Mycroft's instructions with regard to secrecy unfortunately include you."

"But surely I can be allowed to know the details of the affair at the Lyceum?" I asked.

"Rest assured that will all be revealed to you in due course," said Holmes, "although for reasons of national security, this will be a case you will never be able to turn into one of your stories for *The Strand*."

Holmes walked over to where Long was held by two burly policemen and, after a few brief words, Long nodded and the officers withdrew out of earshot. Long continued to look around as Holmes talked, in all probability seeking an opportunity to escape, but after a few minutes his demeanour changed, and he stood still as Holmes spoke to the officers who grasped him once more.

"If you will instruct your men to take Long to The Tower of London," he said to Gregson. "Mycroft's men will take charge. You can congratulate yourself in breaking a deadly conspiracy which would have had catastrophic consequences if it had come to fruition, but there are more secrets which my brother hopes to prise from Long which you cannot be party to."

"I cannot say I'm happy," said Gregson. "It's galling to allow the big fish to be taken away while I must content myself with the sprats."

"If it's of any consolation, I'm also unhappy to be sidelined from this," said Holmes. "However, Mycroft's word is law in this, and many other instances, and we have to be satisfied with the knowledge we played a part in stopping a threat to national security."

Holmes grasped my arm, and we walked out of the building through the front doors where we saw Long's men being bundled into several Black Marias. A carriage with blackened windows stood beside the police vehicles, doubtless to convey Long in secrecy.

"So it was Long who was behind the supposed accidents at the theatre?" I asked.

"Patience, Watson," said Holmes. "I'm not quite ready to reveal the full solution to the mystery. I can, however, tell you that Long's activities are only a part of the puzzle. I believe he planned to assassinate the Prince of Wales and perhaps others at the opening night as a signal to begin the uprising, but that would mean the show had to go ahead. Stopping it by frightening the cast would have been counterproductive to the plot. I will reveal the other pieces at the Lyceum tomorrow. Until then, I would suggest you get a good night's rest to be fresh for further revelations in the morning. I'll meet you at the Theatre at ten a.m. As you know, theatre folk are late risers, and I want them all to be fully alert for the conversation."

I was informed that Holmes had already arrived at the theatre when I presented myself at the stage door. I was escorted onto the stage, where Holmes was seated on the Mandarin's elaborate throne, a part of the production's props. Like most of the items, it looked considerably more impressive when viewed from the audience, rather than when standing close to it. Gathered around him were Stoker and the members of the cast and stage crew.

"Thank you for joining us," said Holmes. "I have explained to Mr. Stoker and the others that Mr. Long will no longer be involved in the production for reasons which I'm not at liberty to divulge."

"But surely you can tell us why Long caused all of the accidents in the theatre?" boomed Stoker. The large Irishman was clearly incensed that his principal backer was no longer available. I guessed that this would cause issues for the production. "Why would he disrupt a show that he was backing with money and other assistance? It doesn't make sense."

"It doesn't make sense because that isn't what happened," said Holmes. "For reasons I cannot reveal, Long was determined that the show should go ahead, and therefore wasn't the person behind the accidents."

"Then who was?" I asked. There are times when my friend could be infuriating in his refusal to reveal his thought processes, and this was one of them. While I would happily risk my life to assist him, I was often frustrated by his habit of only revealing part of a puzzle before he was completely sure of his deductions.

"Come now," he said. "You are aware of much of the background to this affair, and your common sense will tell you who wouldn't benefit from this production being stopped. Mr. Stoker, for instance, has invested his time and reputation in creating this performance, and would hardly want it disrupted. Similarly the others on this stage have put considerable effort into making the show a success."

"Are you saying the accidents are down to some rival impresario?" I asked. "It has nothing to do with Long's schemes?"

"On the contrary, it has everything to do with the mysterious Mr. Long and his plans," said Holmes. He was smiling broadly, as he does when he knows the solution to a mystery and others, myself included, are in the dark. "Remember that all actors play parts and seldom reveal their real face to the world, just as Mr. Long was pretending to be a businessman. How much do you know about your employees, Mr. Stoker?"

"Most of them have been with us for some years, and I know and trust them completely," the Irishman said. "Mr. Lashwood is new to us, of course, but he is well known for his work in the music hall where I've seen him many times. He is no imposter."

I was struck with a realisation.

"Miss Williams is new to your company," I noted. "But surely it cannot be her?"

The lovely young actress looked startled.

"I am who I seem," she said. "Mr. Stoker has talked to my parents."

"Anyone can acquire parents if they have sufficient resources," said Holmes. "I believe the person you really work for has a considerable network to draw on."

"This is ridiculous," she said. She tried to turn to leave the stage, but the stage-hands behind her closed ranks to prevent it.

"I'm sure Mr. Stoker will be happy to allow you to leave when I have finished," said Holmes in a tone that commanded obedience. "Until then, I hope you will be polite enough to stay silent."

"But – " she protested

"But nothing," said Holmes. "I have no idea of your real name, but I know the name of your employer: A certain Rachkovsky of the Russian Secret Police. A person who in this instance shares the interests of the British Government in stopping Long's plot from succeeding. His government may be our rival in capturing a foothold on the Chinese mainland from which to trade, but stands with us and the other Western powers in wanting a weak Chinese government. One that wouldn't be emboldened by Long's scheme."

Stoker and his performers and workers were clearly dumbfounded by Holmes words, but the expression on Miss Williams face told me she knew exactly what he was talking about.

"Watson, and probably the others here, assumed the sabotage was the work of a man," said Holmes "An all too obvious prejudice. The incidents were all, however, ones that required no great physical strength. You were also very careful not to cause serious injury. The broken legs were probably accident rather than design. You wanted to stop the production, and therefore Long's plans, but not hurt anyone. A death would bring in the police and might expose you, and I'm sure you were dismayed when I was commissioned. That is why you invented that story about Stoker seeing you in Whitby."

"I had never seen her act!" said Stoker. "She was recommended to me by a theatrical agent."

"You may wish to exercise caution in using that agent in future," said Holmes. "He was undoubtedly bribed by the Russian government. The conversation with her so-called 'parents' was no doubt set up to give the impression that here was an up-and-coming actress of good reputation – the sort of person in whom you would take a protective fatherly interest. That in turn would discourage others from asking any awkward questions."

"You realise that Rachkovsky will never allow your police to prosecute me," said Miss Williams. Her demeanour had changed to one of defiance.

"Which is why I said Mr. Stoker would allow you to leave," said Holmes. "I'm sure your employer will now send you back to Russia, or wherever you come from. You are now of no use to him in this country, as our government will make sure you cannot engage in any other espionage."

"But what about my operetta?" protested Stoker.

"I'm afraid you will have to abandon that," said Holmes. "Its reputation will hardly inspire another actress to take over as leading lady. I believe Mr. Bramah has written some tales which could be adapted for the stage and make use of the props Mr. Long provided – one that wouldn't have a supposed curse hanging over it. I'm genuinely sorry. From what I saw, I thought this had promise as a performance. Some of the tunes were quite memorable, and I would be happy to forgo my fee in return for a copy of the score. I could entertain Watson by performing them on the violin."

The stage crew who had been hemming Miss Williams in moved aside and she turned and walked out.

"Rest assured," she said as she left, "my employer will remember this disruption of his plans."

"Send him my regards," said Holmes, "and remind him that I played a part in Long's downfall without his help. I'm sure our paths will cross again."*

True to his word, when I joined Holmes for supper that evening, he had opened his violin case and was practising one of the tunes from the operetta – the comic song that George Dashwood was to have performed.

"Feel free to sing along, Watson," he said. "The words are printed on the score."

"Are you sure you wouldn't prefer me to play second fiddle, as usual?" I asked.

"I may be the leader of the orchestra," said Holmes. "However, you are my star performer. I couldn't achieve much of my success without you at my side."

I smiled and took up my usual chair and looked forward to witnessing another performance by my friend.

NOTE

* Holmes also encountered Rachkovsky in "The Unlikely Assassin" *The MX Book of New Sherlock Holmes Stories – Part XLII – Further Untold Cases (1894-1922)* and "Death at the Diogenes Club" *The MX Book of New Sherlock Holmes Stories – Part XLV: 2024 Annual (1898-1917)*

The Ambassador's Dilemma
by Peter Coe Verbica

Chapter I
A Breach of Secrecy

London fog can be coldest at dawn. But with the passing of hours, and a bit of forbearance, even the dreariest day often unfolds to where it is tolerable. For those days when the weather worsens precipitously, there is comfort in one's lowered expectations and a decent mackintosh.

The particular morning when I learned of the Ambassador's dilemma was foggy, much like many others. The sun, initially cloaked and inscrutable, demonstrated a stolid persistence against the haze as it began to illuminate Baker Street and its residents.

Inside Holmes's flat, Mrs. Hudson had arranged morning tea and, I surmised, given her tenant's habits, had brought some order to the bachelor's parlor, including laying out the morning papers before disappearing down the stairs. The hearth, stoked with coal, radiated heat. I was visiting and enjoying the simple pleasure of reading *The Times*.

Holmes cleared his throat from across the small, inlaid table. On that cue, I set the paper upon my lap to observe the detective, who, when in thought, was bereft of normal civilities. He refrained from looking up initially, and I began to speculate what intrigue had attracted his deliberations.

He peered down his long, thin nose and studied an object which looked like a bread dough roller comprised of a series of discs, each inscribed with letters. The cylinder had a brass knob at each end, and he spun each disc with his fingers, as if he were working a combination.

"I will spare you a monograph regarding the ink compound and bleach intensity of the newspaper before you, but it leaves a distinctive residue on the reader's hands, including yours."

"Thank you," I replied, knowing he could alight upon any detail and begin an encyclopedic explication.

"What do you make of this?" he asked, waving the object before me.

I paused, then responded.

"Initially, one might imagine it to be a printer's roller, perhaps inked and subsequently applied to a flat surface. But I would speculate it to be a code device of some sort."

"Splendid. You learned more than surgery while in the Royal Army, I see."

I gave him an informal and reflexive salute.

"Known to some as a *Bazeries* cylinder, the device creates or decodes a cipher to use for confidential communications. It has twenty-six rotating rings, each imprinted with twenty-six letters. The product has an impressive number of combinations – "

"I see," I replied.

"The original inventor envisioned thirty-six wheels on the cylinder. If each ring were imprinted with thirty-six characters, a fifty-seven-digit number of permutations would result."

"Astounding," I replied.

"Thanks to Archimedes and Descartes, we could express the total more efficiently using a smaller number multiplied by units of ten."

"What has you considering coding devices?"

"Since Caesar's reign, sovereigns have attempted to keep their most important communiqués secret. His Majesty's Government has been asked by a friendly country's ambassador to determine how its secrets are being breached, despite the greatest of caution. Mycroft has enlisted my help."

"Are you at liberty to disclose the country?"

"They speak Portuguese."

"Well, that limits the number of nations considerably."

"They use secret methods of communication, and the Ambassador is stumped as to how certain messages are being breached."

"Has someone broken the code system?"

"That's the conundrum. That was the original supposition, but some of the most sensitive information unveiled wasn't committed to print. It was communicated orally to a very small, trusted circle of individuals. And yet, somehow, it's being disclosed."

"Clearly, then, someone within that circle is divulging the information."

"It appears so. The list of who could do so can be counted on one hand. We must examine each of the suspects. According to the Ambassador, all have been impeccably trustworthy – up until now. Most troubling to him is that the nephew of the Prime Minister is the leading suspect. He is from one of the country's oldest and most established families, and, unfortunately for him, the consequences for treason are most grave."

"Death?"

"Indeed."

"Perhaps the man has been compromised?"

"That's one possibility, but let us be like impartial bloodhounds and allow the facts to be our master, rather than our suppositions, no matter where the trail leads us."

"Such is your talent," I responded.

"We all have our aptitudes. Diplomacy isn't always one of mine. I could use your assistance. I have a meeting with Mycroft at the Diogenes Club at three p.m. to discuss the matter."

"I'll be there," I answered.

Holmes returned to spinning the rings of the cylinder, and I resumed reading the morning paper, but my thoughts kept returning to the confidential matter which Holmes had shared with me.

Chapter II
Mycroft at the Diogenes Club

By afternoon, despite the sunlight, winter was still frosting the edges of felt brims and woolen cuffs with its moisture. My overcoat helped fend off the chill as I waited with Holmes for a hansom. Most hansoms are anonymous due to their ubiquity, weaving through London like schools of dark fish, but ours arrived gleaming with its brass trimmings and well-polished harness, as if it had just emerged from its carriage house. The driver checked his reins, and his stout bay horse bowed its head and squared into a full stop.

The horsehair-stuffed carriage cushions were dimpled, quilted, and unfortunately comfortless. They were cold as ice blocks. Holmes instructed the driver through a speaking tube, while I shut the half-door to protect our legs from the wind. Once underway, the rhythm of hoof-beats upon the cobblestones lulled me into contemplation. I reflected on how most Londoners went about their business, giving little attention to international intrigue. The price of codfish was a very real concern. The fate of a foreign dignitary, in contrast, might seem to most abstract and remote.

I was jolted from my distractions upon our arrival at the Diogenes Club. Two Corinthian columns flanked the entrance. A spider-web window topped the doors. I clambered from the cabriolet, one hand on the rail and one on my hat. Holmes reached up to pay our driver and the man gave him an appreciative tip of his hat. With a flick of his buggy whip, the cabbie headed off to his next fare.

"Shall we?" Holmes asked, looking up to the taupe-colored brick building in front of us. He rubbed his hands and revealed a nearly imperceptible smile.

We trotted up the step and stood on the portico. To our right was a small rose-gold colored sign announcing the building's Pall Mall address, etched into the metal in plain script. A muffled bell relayed our arrival. My eyes adjusted to the gas-lit entrance, and I was struck yet again by a full-length oil painting hanging above a stone bench – Diogenes, the club's namesake. The artist, to his credit, had captured the Greek philosopher with life-like detail. With his long beard, the stoic appeared ready to begin a lecture.

Past the anteroom and in the warmth of a narrow hall, we shed our long coats, gloves, and hats. The articles were whisked away by our greeter, who left via an adjacent exit. The small servant's door closed and disappeared into the wall's paneling.

Another attendant, arrayed in a black coat and starched white shirt, led us slowly to the Stranger's Room, the only area where talking was permitted. Elsewhere, breaking the silence was forbidden. Violate the rule three times, and a member risked permanent expulsion. The Diogenes' constituents were illustrious but reportedly unclubbable. Each relished his privacy. Ministers and magistrates had their offices, pedestal desks, and anterooms. In contrast, for Mycroft the Diogenes Club was an unofficial headquarters of sorts. It was here, in the quietude, that he mulled statecraft, espionage, world affairs, and complex stratagems, all for the benefit of His Majesty.

A hearty fire cheered the oval room, lined floor-to-ceiling with bookcases. Mycroft Holmes sat at a green-velvet table, nursing a glass of Scotch. He waved us over perfunctorily and we joined him. But for his heavy frame and slower movements, Mycroft bore a striking resemblance to his younger brother. Their approaches differed. Each had its advantages. The younger brother, a believer in *a priori*, actively pursued and tested his assumptions firsthand. Though intensely deliberative while solving a case, the younger Holmes would pursue, grapple, and pummel his adversaries when such physicality was required.

In contrast, Mycroft shared, and at times exceeded, his brother's powers of observation, logic, and immense intellect. But Mycroft lacked the commitment to complete what was started. Mycroft stood by his initial impressions, more often correct than erring, but his aptitude caused him to quickly lose interest. He reminded me of a prodigy who scores so highly in class that the incentive to pursue a subject wanes and ultimately vanishes. Mycroft had perfected a finesse which most find elusive – that of exerting minimal effort, yet achieving maximum results. His extraordinary power to observe, to concentrate, and to fuse was a true testament to mind over matter.

The large man set his drink upon the table and pulled his mass forward with some effort. We shook hands.

"Dr. Watson, how is your patient with otalgia?" Mycroft began.

"Insufferable, I confess," I answered, startled.

"I take it you don't agree with the remedy?"

"I complied with the patient's wishes, but I find it dubious. How on earth would you know that I'm treating someone for an earache?"

"The small, triangular mark on your finger when you extended your hand. Only one creature leaves such a mark."

"A leech," I said.

"Precisely," Mycroft replied. "But such is the obvious."

"True," the younger Holmes responded before agilely settling into a chair across from his brother.

As Holmes and I poured drinks, Mycroft shifted his weight, and his watery grey eyes seemed to search for something ineffable before him.

"Gentlemen, it should go without saying that what I am about to share is to be kept in absolute confidence," he began.

I looked at Holmes, realizing that I had underestimated the full gravity of events which had been disclosed to me previously.

"As my brother knows, the Ambassador of a certain nation has sought our help. While the currency of politics often involves hollow promises instead of tangible action, in this instance, I can attest otherwise."

"A positive impression based upon experience, no doubt?" the younger brother offered.

"Indeed, Sherlock. To be blunt: The Crown's relationship with the Ambassador's country has been particularly strained over the past number of years – in part because of matters in Mashonaland and Matabeleland."

"And the British South Africa Company . . . settled by the Anglo-Portuguese Treaty of 1891, which resolved the dispute principally in His Majesty's favor," said Holmes, placing the tips of his fingers to his chin.

"Yes, of course," Mycroft replied. "More of an ultimatum by the Queen, who was advised by Lord Salisbury."

"And Rhodes," Sherlock Holmes interjected quietly.

Mycroft waved his plump hand in front of him, seeking to set such specifics aside.

"We have done our best to mend the sting of the resolution which favors The Crown. Let us say, gentlemen, that we are, despite certain differences, enjoying an improving alliance with the country in question. But there are undercurrents forming in certain parts of Europe which concern us greatly."

"Alliances are shifting," Holmes said, his sharp eyes narrowing.

126

"Indeed they are, Sherlock. We are now in a race in which our naval power will be contested. Germany has outpaced us in pig iron and soon will overtake us in steel. They have become the preeminent industrial force on the Continent, thanks to Bismarck, Caprivi, Eulenburg, and, of course, the Krupps."

I took a sip from my glass and did my best to follow the conversation.

"And thus," I offered, "the importance of strong cooperation to counter the rising threat."

"Quite right, Doctor. Such is the backdrop of this current intrigue. Lives are directly at stake, as treason is a capital offense in the sovereign to which we refer. Several innocent men could face the firing squad upon returning to their home country. We have an opportunity to demonstrate our good intentions, with indelible and enduring benefits, should we succeed in demonstrating the innocence of those suspected."

Mycroft cleared his throat and lowered his voice. "To give you a sense of the import, a first cousin of Dom Carlos himself, a duke by the name of Corel do Campo, is a principal suspect. Another man, the Prime Minister's nephew, Luis Homero Falabello, carries a cloud of suspicion over him as well. This is truly a family affair."

"Essentially," I stated, "these men are being accused of divulging state secrets relayed to them verbally. Out of earshot presumably?"

"Correct," Mycroft responded.

"Well, should Watson's schedule permit, the both of us will avail ourselves to determining who is the source of the compromising information on behalf of His Majesty's long-standing ally. What say you, Herr Doctor?" Holmes asked.

"It sounds like we are being drawn into quite a conundrum," I responded. "Of course, I'm at your service."

His brother patted the tabletop and nodded slowly. His eyes then turned to the room's door. Our time with him had ended.

"Any additional facts, Mycroft?" Holmes asked.

"That's the added challenge. Aside from what I have disclosed, we have very few details, other than brief biographies of each of the suspects. I'll make sure that they are provided at your doorstep before day's end."

"Let us set sail among the rocks and crags, as it were, before the sky darkens further," Holmes said.

Mycroft finished his glass.

"Sherlock, I've provided you a favorable introduction to our ally's *interim chargé d'affaires*. Frankly, his initial response was tepid. He has little interest in allowing a foreigner solve this internal matter, but he's willing to accept a meeting with you at his embassy. Your reputation as a private detective precedes you. It is a first step."

"Albeit a small one," Holmes offered.

"Admittedly," Mycroft confessed, taking a pinch of snuff from a tortoise-shell box and sniffing sententiously.

As we stood to take our leave, Mycroft brushed the stray grains of the fine tobacco powder off his waistcoat. He refrained from rising out of his chair.

"Exercise the greatest caution," Mycroft advised, frowning. "Once you enter the embassy in Belgrave Square, by treaty, it's as if you're on alien soil. Thereafter, my ability to assist you diminishes – significantly."

"Mycroft, given the circumstances, I'll enlist the help of eight of most our reliable confederates."

"Who might they be?" his brother asked with a jolt. "We have a *very* small circle of trust on this matter and would like to keep it so."

"You've already met them, Mycroft."

"Have I now?" he asked.

"Why, our feet and hands," Holmes said somberly, morphing briefly into a middle-weight boxer, before quickly returning to his normal persona.

We turned and headed out the door, and Holmes raised an eyebrow in my direction.

I dutifully followed my colleague, mulling over the subtle competition between the two exceptional brothers.

Chapter III
The Embassy

With a few days' passing, I found myself preoccupied with medical appointments. I had just set a West India Port dockworker's leg, sent him along with a pair of crutches, and was engrossed in my notes. A succession of sharp raps at my door interrupted me – two knocks, followed by two knocks, and then a single knock, or numerically, "*2-2-1*".

Opening the door, I perceived a diminutive messenger with coal-black eyes. He displayed a partial array of teeth when he asked if I was Dr. Watson. The young lad, undoubtedly wizened beyond his years, appeared to be one of Holmes's "Baker Street Irregulars", street orphans he engaged for a variety of errands and espionage. Generally ignored by adults, they provided Holmes with an unnoticed network of eyes and ears throughout the city. I traded a coin for the envelope and wished him well.

After closing the door, I examined a red seal on the back of the correspondence. It featured an "*X*", a single dot and the image of a bee. I had seen it before. It was Holmes's sense of humor, and, of course, he had to explain the pun when he had first used the signet. "*X*" was the twenty-second letter ("*Chi*") of the Greek alphabet. The dot signified the number one. I quickly understood the image of the bee. Together, the markings spelled out the familiar address on Baker Street.

I broke the seal, removed the contents, and read the following written upon a yellowed card: "*Should time permit, please join me at 2:15 p.m. for a glass of* Aguardente de Vinho." Pausing for a moment, I realized this was a reference to Portugal's equivalent to our brandy.

Despite Mycroft's warning, my attraction to this intrigue exceeded any concerns of looming risk. While I wasn't naïvely imagining that civility and goodwill would eliminate any upcoming danger, I did have difficulty imagining that I would be at the mercy of a foreign government while still on British soil.

I dressed, hailed a cab, and within minutes was listening to the familiar and somewhat comfortable sounds of the horse's hooves as I sped toward Belgrave Square. I stepped down from the hansom, paid the driver, and proceeded to the address provided by Mycroft.

Holmes stood straight and lean in front of the three-story building's doorway. Flags flew above a small, decorative balustrade. I recognized the seven castle and four shield images topped by a crown in a sea of blue and white – the flag of Portugal. A wrought-iron fence composed of stylized, blunt spears provided a barrier around the building's perimeter.

A straight-faced, wiry manservant wearing a dark coat with an embroidered emblem let us into the foyer. Well into his forties, he moved with athleticism. His trousers were neatly pressed but wrinkled around the knees. He wore a high-collared, starched shirt. We were subsequently greeted and announced by a bespectacled, egg-shaped clerk with an owlish face. He wore a round-edged coat with oversize pockets and pin-striped edges.

While we stood waiting, I took a brief stock of the surroundings. An oval floral painting set in dark tones graced one of the walls. The heraldry of the monarch hung with an ornate border above an arched doorway. In a niche, I observed a large Continental vase on a pedestal. A maid with long braided hair, bright eyes, and shapely bearing was sweeping the mirrored floor in front of it. She smiled fleetingly and returned to her work.

The Ambassador gave the impression of a regal bird of prey as he made his way crisply down the interior stairway. One of his hands skimmed the baluster. The other held a formal cane which he kept elevated to his side as he descended. I recognized his upturned mustache and brushstroke of a beard, so well characterized by newspaper artist Lewis Ward (in an article on the Ambassador that Holmes had given me as a primer). His carriage and mannerism were aristocratic and gracious. I could understand how he fit in well with the Marlborough House set — such was his ease, despite the duress of the present situation.

At the landing, the Ambassador carefully switched his silver-topped cane to his left hand, self-consciously smoothed an uneven pant crease, and walked towards us with a vigorous but slightly asymmetrical gate.

"Ambassador Andador," Holmes said, shaking the man's hand firmly. "Sherlock Holmes and Dr. John Watson. Pleased to be of service."

"Thank you, Mr. Holmes," the man said, touching the detective's elbow. "Your brother assures me of your discretion, and from the local newspapers, I'm acquainted with many of your successes."

"Thank you, Ambassador, but be assured most of what we do, especially for matters of this nature, goes unseen by the public's eye."

"Gentleman, please. Forgive us for the skeleton crew. Most have been sent to Lisbon to attend to a crisis of sorts."

He sighed palpably, the way a father might over an errant child.

"Follow me if you would," and he gestured towards a narrow, less-obvious stairway. We climbed two floors and emerged into a dimly lit hallway with a burgundy rug and cherry-wood paneling. We followed him to an oversized, locked door which he opened with a key affixed to a gold watch-chain. He replaced it within his waistcoat pocket and led us to an interior dominated by a large tapestry on one of the walls: Portuguese Man-o'-war ships at sea animated the scene with their double-masts, layers of gunports, and figurehead bows.

Three cushioned maroon chairs were set about a serving table. Yellow, brown, and blue Portuguese tiles lined the room in lieu of wainscoting. In them, I discerned carefully rendered vignettes of castles. Above us, the unusually tall, concave cathedral-like ceiling was circumscribed by a wide ring which swept around the molding of the entire chamber. One of the interior walls stopped halfway up to the ceiling. Beneath us, a carpet comprised of gold medallions outlined with bluish black were arrayed in a background of cream. Against an opposing wall, a couple of high-back chairs and a small globe on a secretary completed the interior.

We took our seats, and the podgy assistant returned with a tray, carafe, and three short glasses.

"Thank you, Afonso," the Ambassador said.

The man poured our beverages and left the room, shutting the door. The door's mechanism clicked, somehow amplified by the room's acoustics. We were now sequestered from any additional interruptions.

"This is my sanctuary," the Ambassador said, uncrossing his legs and maintaining a steady gaze upon us. "It is perhaps the only place in the world where I can speak freely, though I can't guarantee you that I will."

As we sipped, the Ambassador and Holmes discussed architectural styles in Sintra. Which grapes are most suitable for Douro Valley vineyards. The importance of a caravel's ability to sail windward. Orta's pioneering with respect to tropical diseases (steering clear of heresies and inquisitors). Painters Pinheiro and Malhoa. Violinist and composer Noronha, and other esoterica which I did my best to follow. Their conversation was like a gull trying to land while buffeted by gusts of wind. The diplomat was clearly testing Holmes. I had no doubt that my friend's encyclopedic knowledge would favorably impress Portugal's preeminent envoy.

The statesman finally turned to us with an unconscious tapping of his cane on the floor.

"Clearly, gentlemen, we need answers as to how this confidential information is being divulged. Consider yourselves conscripted, but I'm already prepared to identify two individuals of high station as traitors to our country. It is a difficult decision which draws a shadow over our realm. I'm planning to have them seized within a matter of days. The repercussions for me are dark, but the consequences for the accused will be dire.

"Despite my convictions of both individuals' guilt, I am granting you license to determine if I'm incorrect. But my time and patience for resolving this matter are exceedingly limited."

"We recognize your difficult position, Ambassador," Holmes responded.

The host stroked his neat beard and looked at the painting of a young, blue-eyed duke on the opposing wall. The boy was dressed in military regalia more befitting someone thirty years his elder. The young royal sat with checked reins atop a white stallion. The Ambassador seemed to draw strength from the image which depicted glory and resolution. He leaned closer to us.

"Very well," the diplomat said *sotto voce*, his eyes absent their initial hospitality. "Let us move ahead. What questions have you for me?"

"It's my understanding that verbal intelligence, and not just written, has been appropriated."

"That's correct."

"Did you test each recipient individually?"

"Yes," our host responded. "I gave each a ration of distinct falsehoods to see if these would be disclosed elsewhere."

"What was the result?"

"Damning," the Ambassador responded. "I won't reveal the contents of what was disseminated. I manufactured each ruse to appear believable. I shared that information orally, in this room, and just as we are seated. I emphasized that it shouldn't be written down or shared with anyone else. And I spoke quietly, at a volume discernable only within a few feet."

"Are we to assume the lines of apparent guilt draw back to Luis Falabello, the nephew of the Prime Minister, as well as Duke Corel do Campo, a first cousin of Your Majesty – both of whom work for you at the embassy?" Holmes asked.

"I'm afraid so," the man responded with drawn brows.

"If I may, Ambassador, there's one other primary suspect that you aren't mentioning . . ." Holmes said, letting his statement drift. He looked up at the curved ceiling, further collecting his thoughts.

"If you mean me, of course: I am the hub of the wheel, and these two suspects are the spokes."

"There will be those who may argue that the axle itself is rotten," Holmes said. "You are at the center of all of this."

"Of that I'm well aware," the dignitary sighed. "Of that I am aware," he repeated. "Such inevitable speculation is the reason you're here."

The Ambassador stood and we followed suit. He walked us back to the embassy's main entrance, left us in the attendance of a slim steward, and bade us good day.

Holmes dropped his hat at the step, and the manservant picked it up promptly. After receiving it, Holmes looked the man in the eye, thanked him, and shook his hand. The man was devoid of any flamboyance and stood at ramrod attention.

"How goes your day, sir?" Holmes asked the attendant.

"It depends on," the man responded flatly.

As we walked away, Holmes leaned over to me.

"Good eye contact, minimal gestures, and an iron handshake. If only that would be taught more widely, eh?"

Chapter IV
An Alarm at the Door

The following day, Holmes could be found puffing on his oily briar pipe in front of a well-tended fire. He sat crossed-legged with his fingers steepled against his chin. Layers of smoke revealed he had been engrossed in thought for well over an hour.

"Well, what do you deduce about this current affair?" he asked, his gray eyes assessing me.

"To have prime suspects of such repute must be quite a shock to the Ambassador," I offered.

"One traitor of such prominence is unusual but a reasonable probability. However, two individuals risking death by breaching secrets is most peculiar. What theories might you suggest under these circumstances?"

"I am truly confounded. Perhaps they are being blackmailed?"

"Always a rational possibility. Reasonable, but to risk their very lives in exchange for an unsullied reputation is a high cost, wouldn't you agree?"

"It sounds like a bad bargain," I replied. "However, to be shunned by one's peers is for some aristocrats akin to a death sentence. Perhaps looming gambling debts had to be honored?"

"What else."

"I find it difficult to believe that the Ambassador is a reasonable suspect. He seemed sincere and most collegial. I can't imagine him betraying his country unless he was subjected to a powerful manipulation of the mind – hypnotism, perhaps?"

"I appreciate your ingenuity. You may be onto something. You didn't find him guarded or defensive?"

"Not offhand," I declared. "He showed tact and polish."

I realized that I was about to be re-educated in the powers of observation.

"Did you notice that he carried a cane, but didn't use it when he descended the stairs?"

"Now that you mention it, yes," I replied. "He did have an odd gait, however."

"His gait and cane are both easily explained and give us a window into the seriousness of the man's concerns."

"How so?"

"The cane clearly concealed a hidden sword. I recognized the manufacturer as soon as I spied its sterling top, and I estimated its weight by how it was handled."

"And the gait?"

"The gait is telling. The man carries a concealed pocket pistol. Based on the slight outline, I would venture it is a pepperbox type with revolving barrels."

"Odd items to carry on your person inside the security of one's embassy," I responded.

"Unless you're anticipating trouble."

Holmes stood suddenly, walked diagonally over to the door, and flung it open. To my surprise, a man with enormous teeth tumbled forward into the room. He wore a bowler and was dressed in a dark brown suit. His fist was clenched and his arm comically outstretched. Holmes shut the door behind him.

"Pardon me, gentlemen," he said. "The ground floor door was unlocked, and I came upstairs on my own. I was just preparing to knock at your door." His voice had a sing-song accent of a foreigner.

I determined him to be in his early thirties, of medium build, and dark hair matched the color of his suit. He wore a cream-colored bow tie and a pastel shirt. His face flushed, and he quickly took off his hat. His hair was creased by its brim. The man's face was dotted with perspiration. He looked about quizzically, taking in the room.

"*Bom dia, Senhor Duke*," Holmes welcomed him. "You were at the door for some time, I see."

"How did you know?" he asked, laughing nervously and holding his hat in front of chest, working the felt brim with his fingers. "I thought I had approached quite quietly."

"Your eyes have already adjusted to the dim light," Holmes explained perfunctorily.

"Well, Mr. Holmes, in truth, I was making up my mind as to whether to approach you."

"You appear to have walked here briskly, so something serious must be troubling you. May I introduce my associate, Dr. Watson?"

"Thank you," the man answered, shook my hand once, and quickly released it.

"Would you care for some brandy?" I offered.

"Normally, I refrain from such indulgences," he replied, "but today I'll make an exception."

Holmes gestured to an open seat and the man took it, setting his hat off to the side on the rug.

I poured him a glass of golden-brown liquor and handed it to him. He took a sip, reminding me of a horse nibbling on a fence. He looked at us and set down his glass on an octagonal side table.

"A friend confided to me recently that I am in a bit of a quandary."

"Who might this person be?" Holmes asked, reloading his pipe with black shag tobacco, pressing it firmly into the bowl with his thumb.

"One of the staff at my embassy. An *empregada doméstica*."

Clearing his throat, he continued. "A maid. Her mother's home was threatened with seizure by a hard-hearted lender. My wife suggested that I provide them with funds which enabled them to stay. The gesture might sound kinder than it really was. I assumed title, thereby picking up a good asset at a very reasonable price. They, being simple souls, feel indebted. That said, and again, at my wife's bidding, I provide them tenancy. Both live at the premises rent-free."

The gentleman removed a handkerchief from his pocket, patted his brow, and placed the linen back into his pocket.

"You married a saint," I commented.

"Please continue," Holmes encouraged.

"Afonso, the Ambassador's cleric, is friendly with the maid, as well as the steward who's always repairing something or other about the embassy. Afonso mentioned to the maid a rumor going about that I've been spending time with an actress. He asked her if she knew anything about it, and she replied that she had heard nothing of the sort. She came straight to me."

"Not the sort of thing that helps spousal relations, I imagine," I stated.

The man shifted in his chair, as if experiencing inner discomfort of one kind or another.

"It's worse, of course," Holmes interjected. "The actress he's referring to happens to be a famous German." He mentioned her name.

"None other," the Portuguese aristocrat acquiesced, nodding slowly. "She has been associated with a number of scandals over the past decade. It would be the ruin of me should it be made public."

"This inspired you to visit us?" Holmes asked.

"I chanced to peruse the Ambassador's schedule and saw that you and he had met. He's been treating me with the strangest of caution of late, so I felt it best that I should visit you directly. I've been seeing the actress, but not for reasons which Afonso is insinuating."

"Pray tell," the detective urged.

"I can't go into detail, but I can assure you that my involvement isn't amorous. Rather, it's a sensitive matter of state."

"I would surmise that you are being accused of what you are judiciously seeking to blunt," Holmes said.

"I'm not following," I confessed.

"The actress is a long-time friend of one of the royal family's alleged mistresses. Portugal is undergoing fiscal and civic stresses. The long and the short of it: Dalliances by royalty incite quiet contempt when times are fair. Indiscretions cause outright ire when times are bad."

The Duke looked somberly at Holmes and then took a quick sip of brandy. The gentleman's face no longer glistened, and he calmly returned the glass to the table.

"Though it's been over eight decades, I suppose that we've never recovered from the *Guerra Peninsular*, Brazil's subsequent independence, and the Napoleonic Wars," he said, looking at the plaster bust of Bonaparte on the mantle.

"Presently, of course, we endeavor to recover from our government's insolvency of 1892. So, I do my best. As we say, *"Quem não tem cão, caça com gato."*

Holmes responded, *"'He who doesn't have a dog, hunts with a cat.'"*

135

"You are the Ambassador's cat, Mr. Holmes. And I sincerely hope you understand that I am not the mouse which you and he are seeking."

Chapter V
Scuffle at the Burlesque Theater

"Any further deliberations?" the detective began as he slowly paced the floor, absent-mindedly holding his violin in one hand, bow in the other.

From the chair, I leaned forward and extinguished what was left of a cigar.

"To me," I responded, "the options here are quite clear."

"I agree with you. How so?"

"Candidly, I'm confident that sending Corel do Campo and Luis Falabello, the two main suspects, back to their homeland would be the simplest course. The Ambassador gave his counterfeit bait to two individuals only – practically in a whisper, in a locked room with no others present. It seems as if there are only two alternatives: Either the Ambassador is a liar, or his two employees, both members of the royal family, are traitors."

"It does appear that way, doesn't it."

I crossed my arms over my chest and leaned back. I then offered the rest of my thinking on the subject.

"I do find it a peculiar coincidence that we were visited by Corel do Campo, one of the main suspects. His behavior struck me as odd. Despite the man's insistence to the contrary, he's clearly worried that his jig is up."

"He was perspiring and agitated," Holmes accepted.

"It seems like an interrogation with Falabello, the Prime Minister's nephew, will allow you to reaffirm the obvious if he confesses. The evidence these two men are guilty is overwhelming. This may be the most rudimentary of cases you've encountered, I imagine."

"Mycroft will be disappointed if your conjecture of their guilt proves accurate," Holmes said. "First, this will be a major embarrassment to an ally already saddled with civil strife. And second: His Majesty's relationship with this ally will miss an opportunity for enhancement."

"You advise to always follow the facts," I concluded.

In reply, he drew the bow over his violin and played a brief cadenza from Mendelsohn which showcased his technical abilities. Then, he set the instrument and its bow with care onto his desk.

After a pause, he turned and spoke.

"Falabello will be at the Gaiety Theater this evening for the first run of the burlesque farce, *Peaches and Breeches*. I plan to visit the embassy, so I need you, as my emissary, to observe and question him. His three favorite pastimes are betting on horses, wearing ridiculous regalia, and being a 'Stage Door Johnny'.

"Falabello will be waiting at a theater exit, hoping to escort a singer to dinner, I take it."

"Such is his folly."

"To watch women cavort about in bathing costumes," I replied, somewhat chafed. "Could I meet him at a more civil setting?"

"Time is of the essence. Study this man in his element. Use your powers of observation and report to me anything unusual." He handed me a picture card of the embassy official, which I accepted with some reluctance. The errand's purpose escaped my understanding, but I knew Holmes had his reasons.

Upon arriving at the burlesque, I was struck by its garish banners and tinsel in contrast to its attendees who were chiefly dressed in genteel and fashionable attire. Bankers milled with merchants, and barristers with lords and moneyed heirs. A holiday atmosphere and high spirits encouraged loud voices, the consumption of sherry, and expectation of the upcoming spectacle. Highbrow was here to enjoy lowbrow.

Seated into a velveted chair, I watched a ruddy-faced, portly Master of Ceremonies wearing a tall hat, formal coat, and red waistcoat take the stage. He dragged his long coattails from one end of the platform to the other before he settled at center stage. He challenged the crowd with a theatrical stare. A black-garbed underling whisked out a three-legged stool, placed it before him, and retreated. The showman rested a boot upon it and turned up his chin at us. He doffed his hat with flourish, and the attendant re-emerged, took it from him, and exited stage left. From his coat pocket, the figure removed a cigar, and a rouge-faced woman in a form-fitting outfit and large wig darted out and held a match for him. He puffed until he was satisfied, and his helper flashed us a smile, slowly waltzing out of view.

Despite the theater's dim lighting, I spotted Falabello in the front row, narrow-shouldered, open-faced, and entranced. He sported a waxed mustache and was dressed in high-waisted pants, collared shirt, and a jacket pinned with an array of medals. He giggled like a child at a circus, awaiting the elephants and clowns.

Falabello was spellbound, as if under the influence of an illusionist. He aped the entertainer's facial gestures as if in a trance. He appeared highly impressionable. Such gullibility might be the fodder of penny novelists, but it occurred to me: *Could he be unwittingly manipulated to spill his country's secrets?* Holmes would no doubt criticize me for such speculations, but there is something to be said for intuition. I began to suspect Holmes knew more about this man's preconditions and predilections than he had revealed to me.

After the production's skits, music, and frolic, I followed the man and noted he carried a small bouquet. With a singular mind, he made his way, as Holmes had predicted, to the stage door. He angled through several well-dressed men and waited for the well-formed and attractive female performers to emerge.

After ten minutes or so, the door opened and the lead female singer, a stunningly beautiful woman, emerged. Her brunette hair was arranged in a whimsical twist. Her complexion was hauntingly translucent. She carried an enormous bouquet of colorful flowers, and her soulful eyes audited each of the admirers who surrounded her.

"Dr. Watson?" she called in a loud voice, to my overwhelming astonishment. "Is there a Dr. Watson here?"

My surprise must have been evident. I was speechless for a moment. How in the world could she have known I would be present?

After a pause, I responded, "I am."

She looked at me with relief. "Well, Doctor, you aren't one of my usual suitors, are you? Thank you for the exquisite bouquet. I am simply famished. Let's dine, shall we?"

An agitated Falabello stepped forward.

"Who are you, sir?" he demanded in a threatening voice, stepping toward me. "What nerve you have!"

"Why, Luis, you have no exclusive right to my company!" the actress declared. "Some nights I may prefer mutton, and others steak," she said with a lilting laugh.

The man came at me with a cocked and ready fist, but I too was at the ready and clapped him hard with an open hand. He stumbled back and viewed me with a fiery stare. The other gentlemen stepped back, forming a small circle.

He sprung at me once again, but I stepped aside, sweeping him to the ground. Though tempted to deliver a kick to his ribs, I put a hand out instead and pulled him up to his feet. Combat wasn't my evening's mission.

"You've mistaken me, sir," I said in a calm tone. "Miss, clearly this man is smitten by your beauty," I placated. "It's absolutely justified. I'll take my leave and ask that you direct your attention and appetite at him. No harm done, sir?" I said, patting him on his back.

"Don't look so sheepish," the entertainer chided her admirer. "Very well, Doctor. As you wish. But please consider enjoying an upcoming show."

Chapter VI
An Alibi

The following day, I planned to have words with Holmes. It was clear that he had bought the singer her grandiose bouquet, giving me unwanted credit. I wasn't one to waste time on such evening escapades. More to the point, under different circumstances, I might well have found myself called to a duel with Falabello.

Holmes was engrossed with a set of architectural drawings, and I interrupted his reverie.

"Could you explain what business you intended to get me into yesterday evening?" I asked. "My interaction with Falabello wasn't limited to simple observation. In fact, it nearly became pugilistic."

"Jealousy is a trait which does have dramatic outcomes at times. It's a condition which is largely absent my temperament, but it can be an instructive when observing the emotion in others."

"Why subject me to such antics, may I ask?"

"Your question is reasonable. The answer is quite simple: Confidential information was exchanged at the embassy yesterday evening. *Senhor* Falabello was present elsewhere. Your lively interaction with him provides him an irrefutable alibi."

"But couldn't his prospective dinner companion provided the envoy an alibi as well?"

"True, but your presence is more reputable. Additionally, the scene is indelible to the additional witnesses at the theater."

"I see," I responded curtly.

"Now, let us move along to a different topic, shall we? Have you ever familiarized yourself with the work of Sir Christopher Wren and baroque architecture?"

"I can't say that I have in detail. I seem to remember his being a founder of The Royal Society, and being instrumental in helping rebuild London after The Great Fire of 1666."

"Indeed. Wren was knowledgeable in astronomy, physics, math, politics, and architecture. These – " Holmes pointed to the drawings in front of him. " – are renderings of Saint Paul's Cathedral. Here are the inner and outer domes with their supporting iron chains."

"Why are you looking at his work, may I ask?"

"Wren's stature has waned, but he was part of the Republic of Letters, the Invisible College, and that far-flung collective of scientists which propelled enlightenment. It's always helpful to understand interconnections."

"I fail to see how this is relevant to the Ambassador's dilemma."

"Understandably. At first blush, there is an absence of a nexus, until you undo each strand which, when bound together, together compose the knot."

"I'll take your word for it, as the only knot I can perceive is the one which involves the breach of confidential information. But I do have a premise."

"Please share it with me."

"It occurred to me while I was observing Falabello at the Gaiety Theatre. He was completely enthralled, and I watched him mimic the production as if a mirror. I realized the man is tremendously impressionable."

"Impressionable," Holmes repeated.

"Yes. I was thinking of the Scottish surgeon, James Braid."

"The hypnotist?"

"Yes. It's an explanation that occurred to me. These men are either being hypnotized or drugged. And, while under some type of spell, confidences are being extracted from them."

"You've returned to your previous theory. In the meantime, I've done additional homework. Neither Falabello nor Corcel do Campo have undue debts or compromising friendships. So our possibilities for a solution narrow."

"I see. And I believe that's why you had me observe Falabello's interaction with the actress from the theatre. Who better to imperil a vulnerable subject than during a secluded *tête-à-tête* with an actress who may be conversant with the black arts? Who could mesmerize her victim?"

"A *femme fatale* of sorts, eh Watson? Please continue."

"Again, back to our simple set of facts: Only the Ambassador, Falebello, and Corel do Campo have direct, oral knowledge of what was said in secret – and beyond earshot. These distinct secrets were breached. Either the Ambassador is lying, and Falabello and the Duke are innocent, or the two are guilty of treason."

Holmes lit his pipe using tongs to pluck an ember from the hearth. Puffing, he placed an elbow on the mantelpiece.

"If the two suspects are above board," I continued, "the only remaining explanation is that they had to have been drugged or hypnotized and coaxed into revealing these confidences. Hypnosis is part of a public spectacle. Tickets are sold where skeptics or believers may ratify or debunk such these theatrics. Knowing that such skills have been developed by men of medicine, I am in the camp which ascribes that this phenomenon is very much real. And who better to become versed in such a skill than an actress?"

140

"Or, following your other line of thinking, we need to determine who is drugging these men and questioning them while they are under a state of semi-consciousness . . . ."

"Precisely!" I responded.

"You've taken a long journey only to return back to the beginning. Homer and Odysseus?"

"Or Dante and Virgil," I responded.

"I commend you for your dogged quest, but not all lines are straight. Sometimes, we are presented with curves. Tomorrow, we shall return to the embassy and I'll bring this puzzle to a close."

Chapter VII
Spectacular Reflections

When a bloodhound is on a scent, sometimes a fox jumps a river. Losing the trail, a bloodhound will stop, circle, and then begin to work the bank to see if it can be picked up again. The animal will lift its head and sniff at the air – testing, detecting with innate persistence and a determination unique to its breed. Holmes had these qualities, but his methods, unlike the bloodhound's, were internalized and more difficult to interpret. While I had my theories and conclusions, Holmes might have drawn another.

My bead on the Ambassador was limited, and, as if I were turned around, traipsing through a bog, I began to doubt my conclusions. By way of example, how might the Ambassador benefit if his underlings were successfully convicted of the crimes of which they were suspected? Was the maid grateful her mother's home had been purchased for a pittance by the Duke – or was she instead secretly resentful? Perhaps she realized that she had been hoodwinked. Had she, being in the close quarters of the Ambassador, come across something compromising which allowed her to leverage her position? Why was the Ambassador covertly carrying weapons about his own embassy?

And what of Afonso, the dutiful attaché? Other than his odd, rounded coat with its large pockets, what did I know of this man? Why would he confide the Duke's perceived indiscretions with an actress to the embassy maid?

My other observation was that the embassy, given its stature, appeared lightly staffed, abnormally so. Had members really been called to Lisbon to deal with a diplomatic emergency? Or was it instead good evidence that the home country was under severe budget constraints, despite the spendthrift reputation of its prince?

141

Lost in such thoughts, I traveled with Holmes back to Belgrave Square, and once again found myself standing in the embassy's foyer with its heraldry, reflective floor, and long staircase.

"When we find ourselves in the room to discuss the outcome of this case," Holmes whispered, "I need you to do me a particular favor."

"Of course. What might that be?"

"I want you to block the door against anyone trying to exit. You are the fullback for Blackheath once again, and our last line of defense."

"Very well."

The Ambassador greeted us warmly, but his dark-circled eyes appeared weary. His lids drooped faintly, revealing a lack of proper sleep.

Holmes asked if we might gather upstairs on the third floor, as in our previous meeting with the Ambassador, and include the entire staff. The diplomat agreed. We walked single-file up the stairs and again found ourselves before the large tapestry and the small table flanked by a trio of chairs.

The Ambassador sat, placing his sword-concealing walking cane next to his chair. Holmes and I remained standing, with me to the immediate right of the door and Holmes next to our host. The egg-shaped Afonso arrived with the horse-toothed Duke. The gullible *Senhor* Luis Falabello with his waxed mustache followed next. He jumped at the sight of me, but continued into the room. Afonso then went to close the door, but was interrupted by Holmes.

"House servants as well, if you please, Afonso."

The attaché looked at the Ambassador who nodded his head briefly.

The uniformed maid with twisted tresses and glimmering eyes stepped into the room, curtsying before moving to one of the walls. She kept her hands folded in front of her and looked down at the carpet. I wondered if she was averting eyes to hide her guilt, or simply exhibiting deference.

The sinewy manservant with the impassive face and slightly rumpled pants followed her. The man's motions were eerily cat-like. He set his jaw into his collar and gazed across at the opposing wall.

Afonso followed them in and waited like an alert nightbird to the right of the Ambassador.

I squared my feet, remaining alert and at the ready.

Holmes took command of the room, bracing his shoulders, taking a moment to eye everyone present: Falabello, Corcel do Campo, Afonso, the maid, the steward, Holmes, and myself, radiating around the Ambassador like points of a star. Holmes's voice lowered and he began by acknowledging and thanking his host.

"The Ambassador asked Dr. Watson and myself to take stock of his embassy and its occupants due to a matter of tremendous importance. I'm pleased to report the problem has been pinpointed and will be solved this very evening. Scotland Yard has been absent from this investigation due to the Ambassador's express desire for confidentiality, but you may expect that swift justice is certain to follow."

Holmes paused. The room's occupants exchanged looks. I perceived apprehension.

The detective continued. "I would ask Afonso and the maid to exit the room immediately. Their presence is not required at this time."

After the two left and I'd closed the door behind them, Holmes turned his attention to Duke Corcel do Campo and *Senhor* Luis Homero Falabello. "Gentlemen, you've sworn unwavering fealty to your country, correct?"

"Yes," both men responded, standing perceptively taller.

"Very well. I ask that both of you protect your Ambassador by remaining at his immediate right and left sides. Steel yourselves! Your very lives may be at stake."

The men, looking uncertain, complied with Holmes. Across from the Ambassador and separated by the space of approximately eight feet, the lean manservant narrowed his eyes and he crouched slightly, tightening his body in readiness to move quickly. The room itself seemed to darken with the rogue's diabolical resolve.

He pulled a twelve-inch dirk from the back of his trousers. I grabbed one of the chairs abutting the wall, pointing the legs toward this threat.

Holmes calmly spoke to servant. "*Das Spiel ist definitiv zu Ende, du Schurke!*"

"*Ich bin absolut anderer Meinung!*" the steward shouted back, lunging towards the door.

Stepping between the Duke who was at the Ambassador's shoulder, Holmes grabbed the Ambassador's cane, unsheathed the sword, and stepped into the man's path. Raising his sword high, standing at a right angle, Holmes was poised for a lethal strike. The villain came at Holmes with his dirk outstretched before him, weaving and viciously jabbing at the air between them. With a quick turn, Holmes swung the cane's sheath with a whipping motion, striking a stunning blow to the man's temple. He dropped the dirk, his eyes rolling and crossing, and fell to a knee. I lunged forward, trapped the ruffian between the chair legs, driving him to the carpet.

Holmes placed a foot on the man's neck and handed me a pair of handcuffs. "You'll find these handy."

I clasped them around the man's wrists while Holmes kicked the dirk from the ruffian's reach.

"Thank you," Holmes said matter-of-factly. He returned the cane sword to its sheath and handed the weapon butt-end first back to the Ambassador. I kept the manservant trapped in the chair legs and awaited Holmes's instructions.

Holmes then handed the dirk to the Duke.

"It's a German naval dirk, more commonly referred to as a '*Kriegsmarine dagger*'. This one has been sharpened – *honed* – and is anything but ceremonial."

The diplomats were dumbfounded. The Ambassador rose to his feet.

"How did you winkle out this man as a traitor, Mr. Holmes?"

"My first clue was the unique ceiling of this room, Ambassador. It is filled with curves and bounded by a ringed shape. I thought that perhaps it may produce spectacular reflections."

"Reflections?" the Ambassador asked.

"Certain surfaces can reflect sounds, a hundred feet or more, to another location. Even whispers can be completely audible. A good example of this is at Saint Paul's Cathedral in London."

"The Whispering Gallery!" I blurted.

"Indeed. This phenomenon, while not common, can be found in various structures, including Saint Albert's Hall, Ely Cathedral, Gloucester Cathedral, and the Chapter House at Westminster Abbey. I could name several others."

"I am still disoriented," the Ambassador stated, "but grateful."

"This embassy," Holmes continued, "being manned by a small staff, gave the culprit a multitude of responsibilities. He served as a butler and doorman, but also helped maintain this building. Seeing the rumples in his well-creased pants, I began to suspect that he was using a service ladder to access a hidden part of the embassy where he could listen to conversations occurring in this room at a significant distance."

"Amazing," *Senhor* Falabello blurted. "I never would have thought of such a thing."

"It is an unusual feature. My guess is that he discovered it by accident, while crawling about the building's recesses, but he was lying in wait for any opportunity such as this."

"What focused you on him being the culprit, rather than someone else?" the Ambassador asked.

"Small clues which stacked atop each other. Certain mannerisms are Teutonic by nature: Terseness in speech, a direct gaze, a firm handshake. And though the man was devoid of an accent, he replied to me curtly and ended his response with a preposition – '*It depends on,*' he said. This isn't

144

necessarily unique, but it was similar to Germanic grammar. All these things fit together."

From the floor, the man exclaimed, "*Ihr seid alle Hunde!*"

"Loyal? Protective? Brave? Perhaps being called a dog isn't such a bad thing, eh, Watson?"

"I suppose not," I answered.

"Ambassador, may I ask you a favor?" Holmes inquired.

"Of course!" he responded.

"Remove your pocket pistol and train it upon this criminal, won't you? It would be a shame if he escaped after this effort."

"Yes, yes, I shall," he replied.

"And may I suggest that one of you remove your belt and bind the man's legs?"

"Certainly," the duke responded.

I waited until the man was secured and took my weight off the chair.

Holmes turned to the Ambassador. "We'll have Afonso see us out. Perhaps when normality returns, you can invite us for a glass of *Moscatel de Setúbal*?"

"If you wish, we will send over a wagon full of barrels!" the Ambassador said happily. The other two men were smiling, pleased with the outcome.

Once down the stairs and outside the embassy, Holmes turned to me.

"What do you think will become of the villainous steward?"

"A large trunk and ship's journey to a Portuguese prison, no doubt."

"Mycroft owes us a dinner, wouldn't you say?" as he waved down a hansom.

"I should think so," I replied. "I should think so."

The Adventure of the
Dreaming Dragon
by Josh Reynolds

It was an unpleasantly damp afternoon in the doldrums of winter when I closed my practice for the day and called upon my friend, Sherlock Holmes. I arrived to find him playing host to a familiar face, one I had not seen in nearly a month. "Leverton, as I live and breathe!" I greeted our visitor, and with no small amount of good cheer. "It's been an age."

The American rose from his chair and practically bounded to meet me. Leverton, as might be recalled, was, as Holmes liked to put it, an *agentes in rebus* of the Pinkerton Detective Agency. We'd had our share of dealings with that august organisation, and while Holmes was largely dismissive of their efforts in private, he often spoke highly of Leverton, whom he considered a rare mind.

"Doctor, you're looking fit as the proverbial fiddle," Leverton said, as we shook hands. "Life must be treating you well." Leverton, as always, reminded me of a bantam rooster: Fierce and quick, but compact. I caught the flash of steel beneath his open suit jacket. He never travelled unarmed, whatever decorum – or local authorities – might prefer.

"For the moment," I said. I glanced past him to see Holmes, seated in his customary chair near the fire, watching our reacquaintance with a slight smile. "You didn't tell me you were expecting a visitor, Holmes. Should I leave you to it?"

"Watson, why ask such a ridiculous question?" He gestured toward my old familiar chair near the fire. "If Fate has seen fit to bring you here today, at this time, we must acquiesce to her design."

I snorted. "Since when do you believe in Fate?" I asked. It was Holmes, in fact, who had invited me 'round, but I refrained from pointing this out.

Holmes waved my comment aside and turned his attentions to Leverton, who had returned to his own seat. "In any event, you are here at the right time. Mr. Leverton has brought me a pretty puzzle and I would be most curious to hear what you make of it."

"Not another missing heir, I hope," I said, glancing at Leverton.

"Not this time, Doctor. Nor am I on the trail of a murderer."

"I am glad to hear it," I said, and meant it. While Leverton was a welcome face, he did have the unfortunate tendency to bring trouble with him wherever he went. "Tell me, then, what brings you back to Baker Street?"

Leverton looked at Holmes, who said, "Repeat what you told me, if you please. Word for word. Let us see what Watson can prise from the muck."

"That's one word for it," Leverton said, with grim amusement. He settled himself back. "Doctor, have you heard tell of a fellow named J.T. Cadwaller?"

I paused. "The name is vaguely familiar, though I cannot recall where I might have heard it. American, I take it?"

Leverton nodded. "He's a steel magnate, one of the biggest now that Carnegie has ceded the field. He has employed the agency to see to the return of a certain item of, shall we say, sentimental value."

"Item?"

Holmes spoke up. "A painting, Watson. Of Mr. Cadwaller's fiancé."

I looked at Leverton. "Someone stole it?"

Leverton scratched his chin. "A four-flusher named Moon-Eye Swales, out of Appalachia, by way of San Francisco. A swindler and confidence man."

I frowned. "'Moon-Eye'?"

Leverton tapped his temple. "On account of being born with a cataract over one of his eyes. Makes it look as white as the moon."

"And how did this . . . Moon-Eye come to acquire the painting?"

Holmes gave a bark of laughter. "Therein lies the muck."

Leverton chuckled. "That it does. See, Cadwaller's fiancé has something of a reputation. Rumour has it she was a Toledo Beach dance hall girl when he met her, and she ain't changed much since they got engaged. She made a living as an artist's model for a time – not shameful in itself, but some of her clients were – well . . . ."

I looked at Holmes for embellishment. He smiled. "August Wynn Ostanes, Watson. Ostanes of '*infamous memory*', as *The Times* referred to him. Though I found him to be a most charming young chap when first we met."

I sat back. "Ah. That is unfortunate." Ostanes took his inspiration from the darker side of things – pagan temples, occult practices, that sort of rot. Many of his more-famous pieces were banned from public display, and his career was largely sustained by private showings and discreet patrons.

He'd made something of a sensation in London for the brief time he was here, before thankfully departing for the more welcoming atmospheres of Paris and Vienna. I recalled, too, that he and Holmes shared a lively correspondence, though I couldn't imagine what it was that they discussed. "Is Ostanes involved in this, then?"

"Only in that he is responsible for the whole mess, if inadvertently," Leverton said. "See, the soon-to-be Mrs. Cadwaller was one of his regular models for a brief period, when he was in the States. I'm told she isn't recognisable in most of the pieces he painted during this time, but there is one in particular where her identity is clear and no mistaking the lady."

"'*Young Witch Astride Black Serpent,*'" Holmes murmured, helpfully. "A potent piece, though the style isn't to my taste. Young Ostanes employs a strong use of colour and light to highlight certain aspects of his model to great effect."

Leverton grunted. "If you say so. But in any event, the piece was in a private collection that recently came up for auction. Moon-Eye happened to be there, saw the painting, recognised the lady in question, and managed to legally acquire it." He sat back and spread his hands. "So, being the sort of man he is, Moon-Eye decides to inform Mr. Cadwaller of the painting's existence and demand compensation – or else."

"Or else what?"

"He will sell it to someone else, of course," Holmes said.

"I assume Cadwaller chose not to pay," I said.

"That's the thing – he did," Leverton said. "Only Moon-Eye decided to take that money and abscond with both it and the painting. By the time Cadwaller realised that he'd been had, Moon-Eye was on a ship bound for Liverpool, and Cadwaller was left with nothing more than an empty frame."

Holmes gave him a sharp look. "He left the frame behind? How interesting." He didn't elaborate, but instead gestured for Leverton to continue.

"Like I was saying, Moon-Eye arrived in Liverpool a few days ago."

"But why come here at all?" I asked, bewildered.

"That's a question that I don't have an answer for, sadly," Leverton replied. "I was hoping Holmes here might be able to shed a bit of light on things, as well as help me corral old Moon-Eye." He paused. "There is a significant reward, of course."

Holmes dismissed this detail with a flick of his fingers. "The answer to the first question is obvious: Swales is a swindler and is likely looking to double his investment. That means there is someone in London to whom he wishes to sell the painting." He tapped his lips with a forefinger, eyes narrowed in concentration. "As to the second, Watson, the reason you might have heard Cadwaller's name is because he has recently shown in interest in investing in, or outright purchasing, certain mining operations in Wales."

I snapped my fingers in sudden realisation. "That's it! He wants to buy out Fyfe and Sons. I knew I had heard his name somewhere." The firm was based in Tondu, in Wales, and supplied much of the iron for the railways. When his interest had become public, there had been some small outcry regarding an American industrialist profiting on British iron. Politicians were still fencing with one another in the papers, exchanging open letters.

Holmes nodded. "Yes. He's currently engaged in what I understand to be a complex cross-Atlantic negotiation. Nor is he the only one interested in purchasing the firm. We have our own magnates, after all."

"I still don't see what this has to do with a missing painting," I said, glancing at Leverton. The American had a speculative look on his face.

"Negotiations are funny," Leverton said, slowly. "The littlest thing can make a solid deal collapse. A nasty look, an unthinking comment . . . or maybe the threat of embarrassment and a public scandal."

Holmes nodded, clearly pleased by Leverton's deduction. "Exactly."

I caught the thread a moment later. "You mean Moon-Eye – Swales – has come to sell the painting to one of Cadwaller's rivals?" I sat forward. "You said he purchased the painting legally. Surely it's his to do with as he wishes."

"Ah, Watson, you forget the money Cadwaller paid our Mr. Swales. It could be argued that he has unlawfully reneged on a transaction. Isn't that so, Leverton?"

Leverton smiled. "It's a thin pretext, I admit, but it's all according to Hoyle."

"So, you've come to retrieve the painting and arrest Swales?" I asked. Leverton gave a slight shake of his head.

"I got no interest in Swales, other than that the painting is currently in his possession. To find it, I must find him. Once I've acquired it, he can swim or swing for all it matters to me. All I want is the painting."

I frowned at this display of pragmatism. Surely a man like Swales would be better off incarcerated. But Leverton understood the vagaries of American justice better than I did. "Do you have any idea where Swales is, then?"

"Not a blessed clue, other than he's here in London," Leverton said, giving Holmes a knowing glance. "But I figure if there's one fellow who can find him, it's Holmes here."

Holmes was silent for some moments. Then, with a slight exhalation, he said, "Tell me about Swales. Leave out no fact, however minor."

"Well, I already mentioned his most visible characteristic. He is also of a somewhat pretentious nature, given his proclivities. Carries a walking stick and wears fine clothes. He fancies himself an aesthete, and is an

Orientalist by inclination. There isn't an old curio shop in San Francisco's Chinatown that hasn't sold him some bit of junk on the assurance that it holds celestial wisdom . . . ."

Holmes held up a finger, interrupting Leverton. "Do his vices extend to the poppy?"

Leverton nodded. "That they do."

"And does he know that he is being pursued?"

"I'd guess so. These sorts of men often have an instinct in that regard."

Again, Holmes fell silent, but I could tell that his mind was working. "Swales is – no, not wealthy, but . . . *well off?*"

"How'd you guess that?" Leverton asked, clearly startled.

"Earlier, you mentioned that he purchased the painting at private auction. That implies some level of income, as well as a reputation as a buyer. Your mention of his aesthetic pursuits further lends credence to the notion that he isn't solely in the game for money."

"That is my supposition, yes," Leverton said. "Swales is one of those clever men who gets bored easy. Swindling is how he takes his exercise, and chasing the dragon or gambling is how he takes his pleasure. He's good at the former, so he's never shy of money. But he always needs more, on account of the latter two."

I nodded solemnly. I had treated several patients for addictions to opium and laudanum among other substances. And degenerate gamblers were a common species in the clubs of Pall Mall. As their appetite grew, their finances dwindled until all that they had was spent on getting the next taste of their drug of choice. Even the most disciplined of addicts was still an addict, as both Holmes and I knew all too well.

"Why do you believe he is in London?" Holmes asked. Leverton scratched his chin.

"I nearly caught him in Liverpool. I was two steps behind him when he boarded a train bound for London. I caught the next one, and here we are." Leverton paused. "I can only imagine he's here to meet with whoever he's planning to sell the painting to."

"A fine theory," Holmes said. "Have you made a possible identification, yet?"

Leverton shook his head. "Not as such. I don't believe Swales has contacted anyone as yet, though it wouldn't surprise me if he had a buyer in mind before he started for Liverpool."

"Most of the competing interests will have offices in London," Holmes said. "It would be a simple matter for Swales to write to them, and see which fish takes the bait. But what is he doing in the meantime?" Holmes stood abruptly and went the bookshelf in the corner, where he kept a good number of his enormous collection of files. "Swales isn't the sort of man to stay at an ordinary hotel, I expect."

"Why do you say that?" I asked.

Holmes's attentions were fixed on his files, and he spoke without turning. "Swales strikes me as a man with particular tastes, ones that cannot be satisfied in a legitimate establishment. Leverton, you are a bloodhound. Was there any particular pattern to his previous residences that you can recall?"

"He has a liking for low places, you might say. Brothels and opium dens and such. Places where he can have a smoke and get in a game or two. He pays well and the proprietors take pains to keep him happy. Sometimes they even provide him with a few fellows to watch his back while he's in town." Leverton rubbed the back of his neck. "I had a run-in with some bully boys like that in Liverpool. It's why I missed him."

"And did they survive?" I asked. Leverton snorted.

"I gave them a few bruises to remember me by, but left them otherwise unharmed. Despite what you may think, Doctor, I try not to shuck iron without good reason."

"Ha!" Holmes spun about before I could apologise and proffered a battered notebook, stuffed full of news-clippings and other loose papers. "Low places, is it? Yes, the lower the better, I expect. And there are few places in London lower than Limehouse." He tossed the notebook into Leverton's lap with a flourish. "There – my gazetteer of illicit businesses the city. One of them at least. Though Limehouse's reputation as an opium-drenched pit of mystery and danger is somewhat overblown thanks to the efforts of Grub Street, there are still a number of sites of interest."

Leverton flipped through the notebook. "You think he's holed up in an opium den?"

"Or near one, yes. You yourself said he is a slave to the poppy. It stands to reason that he would want to have it close to hand. But most such places in Limehouse are unfit for habitation. As Watson can attest, they are barely more than dank bunkhouses, where hash-eaters are crammed shoulder-to-knee, to slumber in fitful imaginings. Certainly no place to stash a valuable painting. If he has, indeed, brought it with him."

I nodded. I had visited my share of such places over the years, often in service to a patient. Vile alleys and low rooms, clinging to the curve of the river like barnacles to a ship's hull. Men lost themselves in those places, drowning in darksome dreams. From Leverton's expression, he was no stranger to it himself.

"I still don't see –" he began, looking at the notebook.

Holmes deftly plucked it from his grip. "That is because you aren't in possession of all the facts," he said, as he flipped through the notebook.

"Swales requires a safe lair. There are less than a dozen opium dens in London that provide the necessary privacy for a man of Swales' pretensions. Of those, only seven are frequented by gamblers of any stripe. Four of these provide quick access to the river, and thus an easy escape route, but only two offer private rooms. One, near Limehouse Reach, was recently the scene of a rather nasty killing and is therefore known to the police. Swales is unlikely to risk that. But the other, in Shadwell . . . ah. That is a different story."

With that, he thrust an open page towards Leverton, tapping what was written there with a finger. Leverton frowned and said, "'The Dreaming Dragon'. Sounds like a saloon."

"It could be considered such," Holmes said, "Among other things. The proprietor, Miss Sally Zhou, is known to me. She has provided me with information on a number of occasions – for the right price, of course." He glanced at me. "You'll recall that she was instrumental in the Halliwell case last year. Without the piece she provided, I might never have completed that grisly little puzzle, and the Halliwell girl would have been lost forever."

I grimaced, recalling the incident. It is one of those cases I am reluctant to elaborate on, such as the last performance of the demented puppeteer Lazare or the eerie events surrounding the Clerkenwell Tontine, due both the sensitive nature of the events in question as well as the identities of those involved – both perpetrator and victim. "You think she will turn over Swales, if he is there?" I asked, doubtfully. From what I recalled of Zhou, she was a formidable woman – not one to be bluffed or shrink from confrontation.

Holmes shrugged. "I wasn't planning to ask her to do so."

"I can, if you like," Leverton said, pointedly. I had a brief flash of what that might entail, and couldn't help but wince. Holmes obviously shared my opinion, for he quickly shook his head.

"No need. I have a plan in mind already. First, we must determine that Swales is there. There are myriad ways one could go about this, but the direct approach is often best."

"Kicking down the door is just going to send him out the window," Leverton said, dubiously. Holmes smiled.

"Leave it with me, Leverton. My bag of tricks is deep, and I have a few you haven't yet seen, I think." He quickly scratched out the address on a slip of paper. "I will meet you both here this afternoon, around teatime. Position yourselves at the rear of the building, nearest the river, as we did during the Halliwell case. I suspect Swales will be lost to his dreams then, and we will have the opportunity to put the question to him." He tossed the paper to Leverton and bounced to his feet, fairly a-quiver with eagerness. "Now, I must go. I have certain items to procure before I set things in motion."

And with that, he was out the door. Leverton looked at me, bewildered. "Sometimes I forget what he's like," he said, in some amusement. "What do we do now?"

I rose. "Well, I don't know about you, but I don't fancy a trip to Limehouse on an empty stomach. Shall we fortify ourselves for the adversities to come?"

Leverton slapped the armrests of his chair and rose. "I like the way you think."

We passed the afternoon in amiable conversation at a pub I was fond of, just off Wigmore Street. Leverton had no lack of amusing, if sometimes grisly, anecdotes about his profession, and I, in turn, caught him up on Holmes's recent investigations. As I have noted before, Leverton is a charming man, and several degrees more sociable than Holmes.

Soon enough, we had all but lost track of time, discussing the latest events of interest, including certain rumblings in Europe and the recent Moro uprisings in the Southern Philippines. Leverton's view of the matter was more nuanced than I had expected, and he expressed great consternation at the behavior of both his country and the government.

But our conversation was interrupted by the arrival of one of the innumerable urchins whom Holmes insists on calling "The Baker Street Irregulars". The girl, Piven by name, was a sprightly if somewhat undernourished imp whom I knew to be employed as a mudlark. She wove through the crowded tables until she reached us and snatched Leverton's pint out from under his nose. After gulping down a third of it, she said, "Mr. Holmes 'as wishes your immediate attendance at the aforementioned site, *post-haste*."

"Does he now?" I said, somewhat amused. It wasn't yet teatime, which meant something had occurred to alert Holmes. "Any other instructions?"

Piven gave a gap-toothed grin. "End window, second storey." She sniffed and held out her hand. "Also, payment on delivery, innit?"

"Sounds like he caught the scent," Leverton said, as I grudgingly passed a few coins to Piven. The girl vanished as quickly as she'd come, almost certainly through the pub's kitchen, if the hullabaloo I heard was anything to go by. I wished her well.

"Indeed. We'd best hurry."

Outside, the afternoon fog had turned dull and thick and yellow. It wasn't a fit hour for man nor beast, but acceptable enough for whatever skulduggery Holmes had planned. I caught the attentions of a cab and soon enough we were on our way.

We reached the East End, and the area of Shadwell, in good time. Shadwell hunkered ambivalently on the northern bank of the Thames, between the docklands of Wapping and Limehouse. It had been shaped by the maritime trade, and was home to an ever-increasing number of Lascar seamen. Smaller communities of Chinese and Greek seamen existed here and there, creating a hodgepodge of culture almost in the heart of London.

Dickens had described Shadwell as a place of stale streets and miserable courts, but my view was somewhat more charitable. There was hardship here, and privation, but also life and love and joy. The East End wasn't some termite mound of impossible misery, but a place like any other, with all that entailed.

"Reminds me of parts of San Francisco," Leverton said, as we climbed down out of the cab. He studied a nearby group of Lascars warily. "Too many people, not enough work to go around." He adjusted his shoulder holster somewhat conspicuously, as if warning off any unseen observers. "Where's this place at, then?"

"Near the river," I said, leading him in the direction of the Thames. Soon enough, we had navigated the labyrinth of streets and found ourselves standing opposite a ramshackle structure, perched precariously over a muddy inlet. It had once been a warehouse, or so Holmes had informed me. Now it was something else entirely: A house of vice, of which London had far too many for my liking.

As Holmes had requested, we encamped ourselves in the narrow brick lane that ran parallel to the river's course, and looked up at the rear of The Dreaming Dragon. Though the lane was full of people, mostly Chinese, coming in and out, we were largely ignored. Almost noticeably so. "They've got us pegged for bulls and no mistake," Leverton noted, watching as duo of sailors gave us a wide berth, muttering to one another in Greek. He tipped his hat to them, which only made them walk all the faster, until they'd vanished into the evening fog.

"Most likely," I said. I'd taken the precaution of bringing my Webley, as I'd long ago learned from my association with Holmes that it was always best to have it to hand, though I hoped I wouldn't have to use it. "Perhaps that will make things easier."

"Never does, in my experience," Leverton mused. His eyes strayed to the water where rowboats and skiffs littered the muddy bank, and an irregular grove of mooring posts dotted the murky shallows. Seabirds tumbled raucously through the air, viciously warring with the pigeons and stray cats that prowled the back alleys. He turned his attentions back to the building. "Big for an opium den."

"Miss Zhou has an expansive clientele," I explained. "If I understand it correctly, The Dreaming Dragon is legally a boarding house. Or a chop house. Or both. She provides private rooms for individuals or small parties interested in partaking of the drug, or . . . other pursuits." I gestured to a window was at the far end of the building, overlooking a bend in the inlet. There was a set of rickety wooden steps descending from it, right to the water's edge. "There – that room, I think."

"You sure?"

"As sure as I can be," I said, with a slight smile. While much of Holmes's methodology remained opaque to me, I had picked up the odd trick or two over the years. "I can see no other reason why Holmes might ask us to position ourselves here. It's the only room with easy access to the river. Perfect, if you're the sort of fellow looking to make a quick exit."

Leverton accepted this with a grunt. We settled in and must have watched the window for what felt like an hour until, suddenly, there was a shout, and the window was abruptly jerked open. As we hurried towards the steps, I heard a man cursing loudly and heard a crash. I knew at once that it could only be Holmes. "Quick!" I said, "Up the stairs!"

We ascended as quickly as we could, and I was first through the window. It was no easy fit, but I managed, as did Leverton. The sight that greeted us was almost a comical one. The room was small, but well-appointed. There was a single bed, a writing table covered in the accoutrements of the opium smoker, a chair, and a tallboy wedged in the far corner. A lantern flickered on the table, casting a soft orange glow over the proceedings.

A man I took to be our quarry sat on the low bed, looking discombobulated in the extreme. He was dressed in a heavy overcoat, pattered in oriental fashion – or, at least, an attempt to replicate such. His clothes were dark but of fine cut, and he was handsome enough, if somewhat haggard. I put this down to the opium. In my experience, it often had a debilitating effect on one's appearance.

A walking stick sat propped against the wall, just out of reach, and his gaze strayed towards it more than once. The stick was topped with an ornately carved dragon, coiled as if in slumber, and I couldn't help but admire the craftsmanship.

Holmes, attired in the worn and shiny clothing of a docklands tramp, stood in front of the door, and wiped stage makeup from his lean features with a stained handkerchief. "Ah, Watson," he greeted me. "So kind of you to join us. You'll have to forgive Mr. Swales. My appearance came as something of a surprise to him, and he reacted poorly."

"You aren't hurt, I trust?" I asked.

Holmes finished cleaning his face and smiled thinly. "No. I lounged downstairs, disguised as a tramp, until Mr. Swales here showed his face. Then I followed him upstairs and braced him, as Leverton might say. He came at me with that walking stick there, but I managed to take it from him with little difficulty. Thereupon, he made an expeditious retreat."

"That's why you had us watching the window, just in case he slipped out," Leverton interjected, his eyes fixed on his quarry. "Smart."

"Yes. Though I couldn't be sure that Swales wouldn't simply flee out the door when I blocked his path to the window. Luckily, he was in a pugnacious mood." Holmes indicated the floor near the window, and I spotted a long jackknife laying near the foot of the bed. A scrap of cloth – most likely torn from Holmes's coat – was snagged on the blade. Holmes must have seen my expression for he smiled again and patted my shoulder. "Have no fear, Watson. Were it not for my need to keep him from the window, he'd never have come close. A knifeman our Mr. Swales is not."

"I could have told you that," Leverton said, as he swung the room's sole chair around to face our prisoner and sat himself down. "He's better with a gun, or so I've heard."

Holmes stuffed his handkerchief back into his pocket. Before he could reply to Leverton's comment, there came a sharp rap at the door. We all froze. Holmes chuckled softly. "Right on schedule. Watson, see to the door, would you? And keep your hand on your Webley, if you would. Just in case."

I hesitated, but only for a brief moment, then I did as he asked. The door swung inwards, and I stepped out into the corridor to find myself confronted by a trio of figures. Two were Lascars of unpleasant demeanour. Both were dressed like sailors, though I doubted they'd walked the deck of ship anytime recently. The third was the proprietress of The Dreaming Dragon herself, Sally Zhou.

Zhou was a small woman, round and tidy in appearance. She wore a green dress of fine manufacture, and her thick, black hair was artfully coifed atop her head. She frowned up at me in recognition. "Dr. Watson. I didn't expect to see you here today."

"I did not expect to be here today," I replied. Zhou chuckled dryly.

"And yet here you are. Might I ask why you are in Mr. Swales' room? I heard a commotion. I trust he is well?"

"Better yet, you could come in and ask him yourself," Holmes called out. Zhou raised an eyebrow and gestured sharply to her companions. The two Lascars stepped back and leaned against the far wall of the corridor, their eyes never leaving me. I suspected that both were armed, and knew how to use whatever they carried. I retreated into the room, and Zhou followed warily. She took in the scene at a glance, and then fixed her dark gaze on Holmes.

"Well?" she asked.

"You tell me, Sally," Holmes said. "How do you wish to play this?"

"You get them to leave me be, Miss Sally, and I'll make it worth your while," Swales said, quickly. He made to rise, but Leverton caught his shoulder and shoved him back down. "You know I'm good for it!"

"Is he?" Holmes asked, in a genial tone. Zhou frowned.

"I couldn't say. But let us suppose he was. Do you have a counter-offer? One word from me, and you gentlemen will be out on your ear."

"You could certainly try, ma'am," Leverton murmured.

Zhou ignored him, her eyes on Holmes. "I will not have any trouble, you understand me? But he owes me money. He ran up a tab, and I will not lose my investment."

"Cutting one's losses is often the surest way to ensure that trouble is avoided," Holmes said. "I should warn you that Mr. Leverton there is an American, and Americans can be quite pugnacious in these matters."

"I got money coming, Sally," Swales pleaded. "I swear it! That thing I told you about – I've almost got it clinched. I just need a few more days . . . ."

"Ah," Holmes said, sharply. "So you haven't sold it yet, then. That is good to know. Thank you, Mr. Swales. You are proving quite helpful in this matter."

Zhou glared at Swale. "Fool. You might as well give it to him now and save yourself the trouble." She inhaled sharply and, for a moment, I feared she was planning to call out to the men in the corridor. Then, abruptly she relaxed and smoothed her dress. From her expression, I judged that she had considered the matter and decided against intervention. "I will give you ten minutes, Holmes. That is the limit of my patience. And I expect to be compensated accordingly, eh?"

"I believe that can be arranged," Holmes said, with a glance at Leverton. The Pinkerton frowned, but nodded.

"I expect so. The Agency allows for expenses."

Zhou smiled mirthlessly. "I will hold you to that, Mr. Leverton." Her gaze flicked to Swales. "I shall hate to lose your business, Mr. Swales, but I have my own skin to consider. Do look me up, should you ever come back to London."

He grimaced and said a few things that do not bear repeating. Zhou didn't seem altogether concerned. She departed, tossing a last look of admonishment in Holmes's direction as she went. I closed the door behind her and looked at Holmes.

"Ten minutes," I said. I knew Zhou would be punctual. Her reputation depended on it.

"Ample time," Holmes replied. "It was a wise move on her part."

"Maybe it's catching, and old Moon-Eye here will do the smart thing as well," Leverton said. He peered at our captive. "How do, Moon-Eye?"

"Well, if it ain't the Pink," Swale drawled, doing his best to seem at ease, despite his earlier pleading. "I thought them boys did for you in Liverpool. Guess you got the drop on them, huh?"

"You could say that," Leverton replied.

"You kill them?"

"Nope." Leverton looked at Holmes. "I don't suppose you found it."

"No. Then, I didn't expect to. At least not immediately." Holmes removed his shabby hat and coat. "In fact, I wasn't certain until a few moments ago that he hadn't already sold it. I take it your bait elicited no nibbles, Mr. Swales?"

"I just need a bit of time is all," Swales said. Then, slyly, he added, "Why I could cut all three of you in, if you were of a mind to generous about it . . . ."

"No, thank you," Holmes said. He glanced at Leverton. "I believe Mr. Swales is too clever to have hidden such a valuable item in the room. Why, there's no telling who might come in unannounced. Am I right, Mr. Swales? Or should I call you Moon-Eye?"

"Swales will do, thank you kindly," Swales said, grudgingly. "Moon-Eye isn't a moniker that engenders affability, sir."

"Blame your momma," Leverton said, bluntly. "She's the one who gave it to you, as I recall." He grinned fiercely as Swales lurched up off the bed. The Pinkerton gave the swindler a stiff clout on the ear. Swales collapsed back with a yelp of pain. Leverton rose and leaned over our captive, grabbing two handfuls of his shirtfront. He easily hauled the other man up. "Now, where's that pretty picture you been toting around?"

"What picture that might be?" Swales asked, his white eye glowing eerily in the gloom. He grinned, suddenly, like a man with a winning hand. Leverton tensed and I feared he might hit Swales again, but instead he simply flung the other man back onto the bed and looked at Holmes.

"It's got to be here somewhere, ain't it?" he asked. "Unless he's stuck it in a deposit box somewhere. But that ain't exactly your style, is it, Moon-Eye?" He looked back at Swales. "You don't trust banks nor bankers, do you?"

"I know a scam when I see one," Swales said, with a cruel smile. "Might as well go home, Pink. I ain't got what you're looking for."

"Do you not?" Holmes interjected. Swales glanced at him.

"Do you see it anywhere? And who are you, anyway?"

"Sherlock Holmes, at your service," Holmes said, as he turned in place, studying the room one corner at a time. "Though I do not expect you have heard of me, Watson's literary efforts notwithstanding."

"I know you," Swales said, darkly. He rolled his good eye towards Leverton. "Had to get a real detective to help you, eh?"

"You know us Pinks, Moon-Eye – shoot first, ask no questions," Leverton said as he adjusted the hang of his shoulder-holster. Swales spotted the weapon and licked his lips nervously. I didn't blame him. While I considered Leverton a friend, I knew that the Pinkertons in general had something an infamous reputation. For all their claims of being a detective agency, they seemed to prefer violence to deduction.

Swales produced a handkerchief and mopped at his face. "So Cadwaller hired you to get it back, did he? Well, as I said, I might be as willing to part with it . . . for a fee, of course."

"I believe you have already been paid a substantial amount for the painting," Holmes noted, not looking at him. "Though, perhaps that was simply in the way of a finder's fee?"

Swales snapped his fingers and gave us a sly smile. "That's it exactly, sir! You have the right of it, and I do declare." He spread his arms like a showman. "Why, am I not owed some compensation for my discovery, acquisition and – yes! – protection of said piece?"

"You're lucky Cadwaller didn't have your cheating keister weighed down with stones and thrown in the Mississippi," Leverton said, though he seemed more amused by Swales' spiel than anything. That amusement faded at the next words out of Swales' mouth.

"And you're lucky I don't have the law down on you, Pink. Or you, Holmes. I've done nothing illegal, and you're threatening me in a most ignoble manner!" He pushed himself to his feet and smoothed down the edges of his coat, giving us his best imperious glare. "I am not a man to be bullied, gentlemen, whatever you think. And unless you wish to discuss these matters in a civilised fashion, I'll ask you to leave and thank you kindly." He grinned. "Besides, by my count, you got less than six minutes left. I wouldn't want to get on the wrong side of Sally. Something tells me she ain't a forgiving woman."

In response, Leverton drew his pistol and ejected the cylinder. He gave it a slow spin and a more nerve-wracking sound I cannot recall. Swales watched the cylinder rotate and went white around the temples. I could tell that he wished to bolt for the door, and indeed might have, had Holmes not said, "As much as it pains me, Mr. Swales, you are correct. We are not agents of the law, as such. Rather, we are, like yourself, agents of fortune."

Swales' discoloured eye narrowed. "Oh?" He sounded at once suspicious and, I thought, interested. Or at least curious.

Holmes smiled. "Yes. And I propose a wager . . . If we can locate the prize without your assistance, you will relinquish all claim to it and be on your way. If we require your aid, we would, of course, see to delivering you fair payment for your efforts." He glanced at Leverton, as if for confirmation, and the Pinkerton nodded hesitantly. For myself, I knew Holmes well enough to guess that he had something up his sleeve.

"Five minutes," I said, consulting my pocket watch.

Holmes nodded. "As I said, ample time. Well, Mr. Swales?"

Swales gave a gloating smile. "Well now, I must say that sounds like my idea of a bet. Either way, I win. Fine, then. Have yourself a look, sir. But I assure you, you will not find what you are looking for."

Holmes turned in place, studying the room. "The problem is, of course, three-fold. First, the painting must be transported – a tedious, not to mention risky, chore. However, Ostanes' work is almost exclusively confined to smaller-than-average canvases, especially his more lurid pieces. Cutting it from its frame and rolling it up would allow for ease of movement." He glanced at Leverton. "You said a frame was left behind, did you not?"

Leverton nodded. "I did indeed."

"I thought so. Next, the painting must be hidden. You knew you were being pursued, Swales, and so you would need to conceal your prize somewhere safe but – and this is the third element – close by. You couldn't leave it in a bank or with someone. No, you would want it close to hand, especially as you might be required to show proof to a potential buyer."

Leverton frowned as if something had occurred to him, rose from his chair, and went to the tallboy. He plucked a carpet bag from within and tossed it on the bed. Swales glared at him. "You go no right to go through my private belongings!"

Leverton ignored him and upended the bag, dumping its contents on the bed. Besides clothing and a deck of cards, there wasn't much. Not satisfied, Leverton began to feel around inside the bag. "Saw an old fellow in Natchez pull a trick with a bag like this. He sewed false compartments into the sides and bottom, so he could safely transport his valuables."

Holmes frowned. "I don't think Mr. Swales is so careless, Leverton. A bag can be lost, after all, or stolen. Especially in a foreign country. Nor is that bag fit for purpose. No, he would need something else."

"Three minutes, Holmes," I said. I wondered what would happen, should we run out of time. Would Zhou send her Lascars in? If so, I had no doubt that Leverton, at least, would make it a costly operation. Either way, I wasn't looking forward to finding out.

Holmes turned away from the bed, his gaze raking the room and its contents. I glanced at Swales and saw him looking distinctly ill-at-ease. "Something close to hand," Holmes continued. His eyes widened slightly as they fell onto the walking stick. "Ah. That would do, I believe."

Swales bit back a snarl as Holmes plucked the walking stick up and began to examine it. He peered down its length and ran his fingers along it, until he reached the dragon-shaped topper, gave it a quick twist, and pulled it free. I was surprised to see that the stick was hollow inside. Holmes gave it a shake and a slim, rolled up section of canvas slid out into his waiting hand. He tossed the stick aside and unrolled the canvas.

The painting which covered it was – Well, discretion bids me say only that it was the piece in question, and Leverton later attested as to its strong resemblance to Cadwaller's fiancé. Swales cursed loudly as the painting was revealed and dove for his walking stick. I wasn't certain what he intended to do, and thus I was slow to react as he snatched up the stick from the bed and swung it like an axe. Holmes flung himself back, colliding with the tallboy in his haste to avoid what could have been a cracked skull, and inadvertently putting himself between Leverton and Swales.

As Leverton blistered the air with obscenities, Swales turned his attentions to me. He moved so quickly, and with such desperation that I was unprepared when the stick struck my forearm most painfully and sent me sprawling. My Webley, for which I had been fumbling, clattered from my coat, and slid across the floor. Swales spied it and leapt upon it with a wild yell. I cried out as well and flailed for the weapon.

Swales battered at me with his stick, as well as his fists and feet, forcing me to cover my head and roll away. An instant later, he'd scooped up my revolver and turned it on Holmes. His white eye bulged horribly as he made to squeeze the trigger – only to pitch backwards onto the bed, accompanied by the crashing echo of a revolver's bark.

Leverton lowered his smoking weapon and sighed. "Poor old Moon-Eye. Never met a bad hand he didn't try to bluff his way through." He turned to help me up as Holmes checked Swales for signs of life. I could have told him not to bother, for Leverton's shot had caught the swindler dead in his namesake, and turned the moon a most awful shade of red.

There was an uproar, of course. Sally Zhou was quite upset, and the police as well, when they learned that Leverton had been prowling across their patch without so much as a by-your-leave. But matters were soon settled to almost everyone's satisfaction. Zhou was reimbursed handsomely for the disturbance, courtesy of the Pinkerton Agency, and the police were happy enough to call it self-defence upon hearing Holmes's statement.

I myself was somewhat less pleased, in the aftermath, suffering as I did from a number of bruises and some embarrassment. Holmes and I saw Leverton off the next day, but I chose to stay awhile longer at Baker Street, staring into the fire and trying to come to terms with what had happened. While Swales' death in itself didn't weigh heavy on my conscience, I couldn't shake the feeling that I had been its instigator.

"You seem unusually sour," Holmes said after he had returned. He sat down across from me and gave me a penetrating look. "Especially for a man who has no doubt found inspiration for his latest story." He held Swales' walking stick in his hands and fiddled with the removable topper. "It really is quite the clever contrivance, don't you think?"

I sat back. "Admit it, Holmes – You knew the painting was inside before you made your wager with Swales, didn't you?"

"I had a theory, nothing more." Holmes reattached the topper and thumped the floor with the base of the stick. "When Leverton mentioned the affectation – one shared by many men, I might add – I thought nothing of it, at first. It was only when he mentioned the discarded frame that I began to suspect how Swales was transporting his prize." He leaned back, the walking stick dangling loosely from his grip. "Given that there was no sign of it elsewhere, and accounting for Swales' distrust of banks, I could only guess that he had some means of keeping it on his person."

"And how did you know he hadn't already sold it?"

Holmes chuckled. "Elementary, Watson . . . His mood upon his return was foul, and his need for opium was obvious. Yet he didn't partake. That implied to me that he wished to maintain his wits. And of course, he confirmed it himself." He lifted the stick and peered at the dragon coiled about the top. "In truth, we were fortunate that events transpired as they did. Had Leverton come to us a day, or even a few hours later . . . ."

"I don't think Swales would agree," I said, grimly. "If I hadn't stumbled – if he hadn't obtained my revolver . . . ." I trailed off, irritated with myself.

Holmes was silent for long moments. "He was going for the knife." My puzzlement must have shown on my face, for he continued. "On the floor, Watson. Remember? He was going for it. Likely he intended to take one of us hostage and bargain for the return of the painting as well as a clear path of escape." He pointed the stick at me. "I expect that his hostage's life would have been measured in hours, if not minutes. Once he had no further need, it'd have been into the Thames with them."

I sighed. I knew that Holmes was correct, of course. Swales had been a hardened criminal of a sort we had encountered all-too-often in our time together. Still, it irked me and Holmes could tell. He tapped my knee with the walking stick.

"Think on it this way, Watson: Swales could have fled the moment you fell. His way to the window was clear. Instead, he decided to murder us. He gambled and lost, as Leverton said. That is all there is to it." He smiled and sat back.

"Let us hope that neither of us ever makes such a poor wager, eh?"

The Disappearing Detective
by J. Lawrence Matthews

A Caller at the Door

It was the morning before Easter Sunday of 1903 and I was seated at the breakfast table reading a fascinating account in *The Times* of preparations for the King's impending diplomatic visit to Paris when there came a tremendous ring at the bell. As my surgery wouldn't open for another hour, and our servant girl was in the kitchen, I waited for the caller to give up.

But the ringing persisted, so I set down the newspaper, rose from the table, and answered the door.

To my great surprise, the unwelcome caller turned out to be very welcome indeed: Mrs. Hudson, Sherlock Holmes's landlady.

"It's Mr. Holmes," she said without preamble. "He's been away on a case for two days and hasn't returned. Hasn't telegraphed. Hasn't *any*thing."

"That's hardly unusual," said I, inviting her inside.

"But I'm to leave by the morning express to visit family for Easter, and he had *assured* me he would return in time to escort me to King's Cross."

"Then he'll be back," said I soothingly. "Come in. Have tea – "

"Thank you, Doctor, but this is not like him. Mr. Holmes always keeps me informed when he is detained on a case. Why, he was stranded in the Shetlands last Michelmas, but still got a message through to Baker Street!"

"Where has he gone this time? The Continent?"

She shook her head. "East Dean. In the South Downs, near Eastbourne."

"I've never heard of it."

163

"He was there once on a case and rather liked the area. Well, Wednesday evening a gentleman called and next thing I knew Mr. Holmes was catching the train to Eastbourne. Said he had a case in East Dean, and I believe he was planning to visit an estate agent as well."

"An estate agent! He is *moving* there?"

"I can't say – I don't know. Please, Doctor." She wrung her hands. "My train leaves in an hour. Mr. Holmes should have contacted me by now."

"Perhaps the telegraph lines are down? The weather has been harsh. Please – "

"The lines are up," she said impatiently. "I inquired at the district office."

My wife now appeared on the stairs. She could see at once that something was troubling our old friend.

"John! Why is Mrs. Hudson standing at the door? Take her coat! Offer tea!"

"I did!"

"Thank you, Mrs. Watson, but I haven't come to call on you. It's Mr. Holmes . . . ."

And with that, the story of the disappearing detective tumbled forth from her lips once more.

When she had finished, my wife stared at me, her eyebrows arched.

"What?" I exclaimed, "I've invited her in three times!"

"No, John. I mean, why are you still here?"

In less than an hour I was at Victoria Station, in a train bound for Eastbourne. I placed my umbrella, valise, and medical kit on the rack and took my seat. As the carriage slowly moved out, I opened the morning edition of *The Eastbourne Chronicle* procured at the station and began reading the criminal news.

I was looking for whatever might have brought Sherlock Holmes to the South Downs.

There were the usual horse thefts and house break-ins, of course. More promising was a spate of vandalism at a new lighthouse going up at Beachy Head, between Eastbourne and East Dean. It seemed that lamp-oil had been dumped on the granite blocks, making them dangerous to lift into place, and a local species of poisonous jellyfish had been found in the carpenter's shed, scaring off the men.

But the police had put it all down to lads from the Eastbourne estates "having a laugh" and, seeing nothing else that might have required my friend's great powers of deduction, I set the paper aside and let the gentle rocking of the carriage lull me to sleep.

I awoke when we arrived at Eastbourne Station, found a hansom cab to take me to East Dean, and after a half-hour ride up the coast road in a driving rain, was deposited on a corner of the village green outside The Tiger Inn.

The Tiger is an ancient pub, its low-ceilings held up by thick oak beams, and it proved a most welcome sanctuary, with a roaring fire in the grate, a noisy game of darts going in the snug, and a friendly-looking landlord behind the taps.

Yes, he said, lunch was being served (he recommended the fish and chips), and certainly, he did have a spare room for the night (although I would find it a bit noisy until they stopped serving dinner at nine o'clock).

When I asked if a man from London had recently taken a room, however, he ignored my question, turned his attention to the counter – which looked clean enough already – and began wiping it with a cloth.

"Now, see here, my good man. This fellow is a friend of mine and I'm worried." I spoke quietly, avoiding the use of Sherlock Holmes's name in such a public place. "He came down from London Wednesday evening and hasn't been heard from since. I'm here to find him."

The landlord stopped and met my gaze.

"And how did you say you know him?"

"We worked together for many years."

"And your name is – ?"

"Watson. John H. Watson." I lifted my medical kit and showed him my name stenciled on the leather. A broad smile crossed his face and he put down the rag.

"The genuine article! Delighted to meet you. Name's Jack." He glanced around the pub, busy with a lunchtime crowd. "We try to give Mr. *Gibson* his privacy."

That Holmes was calling himself "Gibson" did not surprise me in the least – he often used an alias when his work took him to small villages such as this, for it allowed him to conduct his inquiries undisturbed.

"I understand completely. Can you tell me where he is?"

"He never tells me anything, Guv. Bit of a lone wolf, you know. Always takes the room over the stables out back. Comes and goes as he pleases."

"So, he's been here before?"

"Couple of times over the years."

"Any idea what brought him this time?"

"Well, I expect it had to do with that business out at Beachy Head."

"But the police said it was lads from the estates having a laugh."

"That's not a job to have a laugh with, Guv. Those men could get hurt."

"Well, when did you last see 'Mr. Gibson'?"

"Yesterday at breakfast." He nodded at one of the tables. "He met up there with old Ingalls."

"Old *Who*?"

"Ingalls. George Ingalls. Runs the telegraph station out at Birling Gap, where the lines come in from France."

The mystery deepened. Why had Holmes sent no telegram to London if he had met with the telegraph operator?

"Do you know what they were discussing?"

"Property. Ingalls looks after the parish land records. Has time on his hands. Wife died a few years back, you see. Lives alone at the telegraph station and helps the estate agents from Eastbourne when they're hunting up a property here. Brought some papers for your friend about some cottage or other."

"Did you happen to overhear where it is?"

"No, and they didn't talk about it long." He leaned in. "Ingalls recognized 'Mr. Gibson' from your books. He was so excited he jumped up, banged his head on a beam. Had to get him a sticking plaster! Then he started asking your friend questions. Wouldn't let him finish his fish and chips." He touched the side of his nose. "Calls himself a '*Sherlockian*', you see."

I have never mentioned them before, but I'm aware that some of my readers have developed a kind of obsession with Sherlock Holmes. A few even formed a 'society' in London devoted to the study of my stories. I was told its members even go so far as to take the names of individuals from the narratives for their own! We had encountered them occasionally, Holmes and I, lingering outside 221b at all hours, hoping for a glimpse or an autograph.

But never in the countryside.

"Did they leave together?"

"No. Ingalls went runnin' off to the church for more papers, his head still bleeding, while your friend wrapped his lunch in a newspaper and went off somewhere with his walking stick."

"Where will I find this Ingalls now?"

"Telegraph station." The landlord waved his rag at the door. "Out the pub, across the green, you'll find yourself on Went Way. Follow it to the last house – that's old widow Dunbar's place, she died last year – and you'll see a footpath just after. That'll take you across the Downs. Make for the old lighthouse, Belle Tout. It's about a mile away, can't miss it. Sits up on the bluff – "

"That's the one being replaced when the new lighthouse goes in at Beachy Head?" I had read about it in the paper. There was some controversy about the plan, as I recalled.

"Right. Head for Belle Tout but just before you get there, when you reach the cliff path, you'll see the telegraph house at Birling Gap to your right. Ingalls should be there, beavering away."

"Thank you. One more thing. Does anyone else in the village know who 'Mr. Gibson' really is?"

"Only a few. We leave him alone. He's a good man, your friend."

"Thank you – and if you see him, please tell him I'm looking for him."

I had departed The Tiger and crossed the green when I saw a butcher's window next to the old bakehouse.

And I recalled something Holmes once remarked upon: When he traveled to a new village on a case, he said, he often stopped in at the local butcher's.

"After all, Watson, the butcher knows *everyone* in a small village."

And East Dean was a very small village.

I went inside.

"Morning." The butcher wore a straw hat and a white apron stained with blood, and he was twisting sausage links from a long tube of encased meat before cutting each link and slapping it onto a growing pile on the scale, his eyes on the needle. "How can I help, sir?"

After my experience with Jack at The Tiger, I had decided the direct way was the best, so instead of asking discreetly about Sherlock Holmes, I simply lifted my medical kit onto the counter and pointed at my name.

"I'll be. Dr. Watson!" He put down the links, wiped his hands with his apron and extended his right to me. "Honored to have you in our village, sir!"

"Thank you." I shook his sticky palm somewhat ruefully and he offered me a wet towel.

"Sorry, I forget myself. Looking for Mr. Gibson?"

"Yes, I take it he's been in, then?"

He nodded. "Came 'round yesterday morning asking about that business at Beachy Head. Then rushed out and I haven't seen him since."

This was progress, anyway: Holmes *had* come to East Dean to investigate the lighthouse vandals.

"Any idea where he might be now?"

"Find George Ingalls. I hear they had a natter yesterday at The Tiger."

"Yes, Jack told me. What does he look like, this Ingalls?"

"Tall, wears thick black spectacles. And one of those hats." He slapped the last of the sausages on the pile and began wrapping the mass in wax paper.

"What kind of hat?"

"You know. A Sherlock Holmes hat." He began tying up the bundle with string. "'*Deerstalker*', he calls it."

I chuckled.

"He'll be at the telegraph station now?"

"Expect so. If he's not at the lighthouse helping Otto."

"Otto?"

"The lightkeeper at Belle Tout – Well, not for long. Poor old fellow's getting the sack when that new light goes up at Beachy Head, if they ever get it built."

He shook his head.

"Gone a bit doolally, has Otto. Won't let anybody near Belle Tout except Ingalls. Chased the postman away with a harpoon, I heard – "

He looked up from his work, an odd expression upon his face.

"What is it?"

"This order. These bangers." He pointed to the scale. "That's five pounds worth of meat."

"What of it?"

"This is the second order from Otto in two days."

"So?"

"So, who's eating all these sausages?"

I left the butcher's at once, umbrella in one hand, medical kit in the other.

And a heavy packet of sausages tucked inside my cloak.

I Am Interrogated

It was a bracing walk across the Downs, for although the rain had stopped, the wind gusted strong, and the path was still quite slick.

But the views were extraordinary.

Windswept trees bent like stooped old washerwomen atop the rolling hills. In the swales were nestled stone cottages, their varied barns and outbuildings testifying to the specialty of each farmer who lived within. And in every pasture were skittish sheep that scattered when I approached, or placid cows that followed me with their eyes as they chewed their cud, or swarms of boisterous grackles swooping up seeds from the newly planted fields.

I understood what had attracted Sherlock Holmes to the area.

It was quite lonely and desolate, but it was also quite beautiful.

168

And it was presided over by a grand sentinel that stood barely one hundred yards from the great chalk cliffs stand tall against the roiling waters of the English Channel.

Belle Tout.

Seen up close, the lighthouse consisted of a granite tower perhaps fifty feet high, with a two-story house attached rather like a barnacle to the landward side.

I made my way around the tower to a walled courtyard protecting the house from passersby, entered through the unlocked gate, and walked quietly past a past a henhouse, a rabbit hutch, and several stacks of firewood to an unlit entryway.

A window above the door showed lights on in the upper floor, but no one was keeping watch. As I wasn't certain what danger lurked within, I decided to use the packet of sausages as a kind of Trojan Horse.

"Bangers!" I yelled in a business-like voice, pounding my fist on the door. "I come from the butcher!" Receiving no response, I pounded once more. "Sausages! Butcher sent me!"

The face of a man appeared in the window above. He wore thick spectacles and a fore-and-aft cap.

It was George Ingalls, no doubt, in his deerstalker.

And he was studying me carefully.

I held up the packet and motioned for him to come down.

He turned away briefly, then reappeared in the window. I was about to bang again when I heard the sliding of a bolt. The door opened a crack and a pair of suspicious watery eyes fixed upon me from beneath a shock of grey hair held down by a woolen sailor's cap.

The old lightkeeper, I presumed.

"Wha'd'ya want?" said he, in a gruff, suspicious voice.

"I bring sausages from the butcher."

"But you ain't the butcher!"

"I've come in his place."

"You from Trinity House, eh?"

"Trinity House? No, I'm a friend of Sherlock Holmes. Is he here?"

The suspicious eye blinked.

"He *is* here, isn't he?"

"Leave the bangers and go 'way!"

"I have come to see my friend and I won't leave until I do. I am Dr. John H. Watson – "

"Don't care who y'are! Go 'way!" The door slammed shut.

"I will *not* go away! I've come for Sherlock Holmes!" I could hear the heavy bolt being thrown. "*I am Dr. John Watson! Open up!*"

Stepping back, I saw the face had gone from the window, and soon heard rapid footfalls clanging on metallic stairs, followed by raised voices. I was about to put my shoulder to the door when the bolt was thrown back and a different face appeared in the doorway.

The face from the window, eyes bulging behind thick spectacles.

"Are you really Dr. Watson? *The* Dr. Watson?"

"Yes, of course. Why? Do you think I go around impersonating the man?"

"One can't be too careful! Come in, Doctor, come in!"

The door swung open, and I found myself inside a drafty, low-ceilinged basement smelling of kerosene and lit by a single oil lamp hanging from an overhead beam. Beside the door, a fishing pole was leaned up against the wall, and next to this, an old yellow mac hung on a peg. Next to the mac were the source of the strong kerosene odor: Three large casks of lamp-oil.

"Mind the rafters," said Ingalls, slamming the door shut behind me and bolting it.

"I will, but mind *you* bring me to Sherlock Holmes. Where is he?"

"Upstairs."

"Unharmed?"

Ingalls appeared taken aback. "Of course! He's only sleeping! Didn't get much rest last night, is all."

I was much relieved to hear this. Glancing at my surroundings, I could see piles of coiled rope, buoys, rescue flares, and life preservers. Also an irregular mass of flotsam evidently scavenged from the shore – the physical manifestations of a lightkeeper's lonely travels.

And that lightkeeper stood rooted to the bottom of a circular metal staircase, holding what appeared to be a kind of shepherd's staff. My heart almost stopped when I realized the staff was in fact an old harpoon, and the ancient mariner was eying me distrustfully.

George Ingalls, too, seemed suddenly wary.

He had removed his cap and was studying me intently. I could see the sticking plaster on the wound where he had banged his forehead. It was raw and ugly.

"You really should have that looked at," I said kindly. "I'm a doctor, I could – "

"Hmm! You don't *look* much like Dr. Watson."

"For goodness' sake, man. What should Dr. Watson look like?"

"Paget's drawings. From the stories."

I snorted. "Did you think we had time to pose for every story?"

"Well, Sherlock Holmes certainly looked like *his* drawings."

"Yes, and I want to see him!" I snapped. "Tell the lightkeeper to stand down and take me to my friend."

Ingalls eyed me distrustfully. "First, answer my question, if you really are Dr. Watson – "

"What do you mean '*if*'?"

"Tell me, where, exactly, were you wounded?"

"I beg your pardon?"

His eyes grew large behind the thick lenses. "You served in Afghanistan, and you were wounded. *Where* were you wounded?"

"At the battle of Maiwand – "

"No, no. *Where on your body?* Leg or shoulder?"

He was growing agitated. I spoke soothingly, as Sherlock Holmes had always done when confronted by unbalanced witnesses during our grislier cases.

"I'm sorry, I don't understand – "

"*A Study in Scarlet*! Afghanistan!" he abruptly shouted. "The Jezail bullet that struck you on the shoulder! You say it '*shattered the bone and grazed the subclavian artery*'. Yet in *The Sign of the Four* – The very next book! – you sit nursing a wounded *leg!* Which is it, Doctor? Leg or shoulder? The *real* Dr. Watson would know!"

He spoke quickly, nervously, hands clasping and unclasping. I was taken aback at his passionate recitation of details from old stories so little remembered by me.

"It was both places, if you must know," I said with an effort at self-composure. "I took a bullet to my shoulder and a second to the leg while being carried away on a packhorse by my orderly."

He snorted in disbelief. "Then how is it you account yourself a fast runner?"

"A fast what?"

"'*The Hound of the Baskervilles!* Dartmoor! You and Holmes are in pursuit of the deadly hound! '*Never have I seen a man run as Holmes ran that night*,' you write!" Ingalls spoke the *words as if from a sacred text*. "'*I am reckoned fleet of foot, but he outpaced me*.'" His eyes blazed. "How could you be '*fleet of foot*' if you'd taken a bullet to your leg in Afghanistan?"

Again, his agitation was severe, and again I tried to sooth him.

"Well, I suppose I exaggerated my physical attributes somewhat, for the sake of the story. Does it really matter?"

"Of course it matters!" he shouted, glittery eyes popping. "A Sherlock Holmes story must be *rational*! *Precise*! Like Sherlock *Holmes*!"

It was *me* who was becoming agitated now.

Who on earth did he think *wrote* those stories?

"Well, it wouldn't have been very exciting if I said, '*Thanks to smoking his wretched pipe all those years, Sherlock Holmes could barely outrun a wounded doctor like me,*' would it?"

I held out the packet.

"Now see here. I've answered your questions. I'm obviously *the* Dr. Watson, so take these cursed sausages off my hands and lead me to Sherlock Holmes!"

George Ingalls seemed on the verge of another outburst when a very familiar, and very welcome, voice came from the stairwell.

"No need for that, Doctor. *I* am coming to *you*."

"Holmes!" I cried, "Is it really – ?"

"Oh, Watson, don't *you* start with that.

The familiar figure of Sherlock Holmes soon descended the stairs, but he stopped midway when the lightkeeper brandished his harpoon.

"Easy now, Otto. I merely wanted to greet my friend." Then, to me: "What brings you here, Watson?"

"Mrs. Hudson paid us a visit. She was worried. Said she hadn't heard from you."

Holmes fixed a severe expression upon George Ingalls. "It seems that my telegram to Mrs. Hudson went astray. Did you never send it?"

Ingalls, shamefaced, gave a slight shake of the head. "My equipment was down. The generator failed. It does that when the rains blow, you see, and – "

"And you didn't think to tell me?"

"I didn't want to disappoint you."

"Well, you *have*, Professor. Such prevarication is hardly the mark of a true Sherlockian."

I shot Holmes a look.

So, George Ingalls was one of the *Sherlockians*. He had even taken the name of Holmes's most fearsome criminal opponent, the late Professor Moriarty!

I couldn't help but smile at the man.

"Call yourself 'Professor Moriarty' after my stories, do you? Really, I can't imagine anyone less like the dear departed Professor Moriarty – "

"That's my name in the London Society, and I suppose I've earned it!" Ingalls snapped, grabbing the packet from my hands. "I know as much about Sherlock Holmes as any man alive!"

Holmes shook his head at me and spoke quietly to Ingalls.

"Yes, I rather think you do, Professor. May we all go upstairs together? This basement is somewhat drafty and reeks of lamp-oil."

I took a step to the staircase, but the lightkeeper now brandished his harpoon at *me*. As my eyes had adjusted to the light, however, I could see it was so rusted and corroded its victims would die of tetanus before the blade could inflict any harm.

Still, I followed Holmes's example and played along.

"May I go?" I asked Ingalls.

"Yes. Let the doctor upstairs, Otto. He is our friend." Ingalls checked his watch. "Meantime, I must leave for the telegraph house. The late wires will be coming in from the Continent and I must pass them on to London. I'll return after Calais signs off."

"I don't suppose you could send a telegram to Mrs. Hudson while you're at it?" Holmes asked nicely.

"Of course!"

"Just say: '*Dr. Watson arrived. I am alive and well, and by all means go north for Easter.*' And sign it '*S.H.*'"

"I will! I will!" Ingalls appeared positively giddy at being made something of an intimate of Sherlock Holmes. He thrust the packet of sausages into the lightkeeper's hand. "Our guests will be hungry. Cook up these bangers, Otto!" Then, placing his cap upon his head, carefully, for the wound appeared quite sensitive, he exited with a final, disbelieving smile upon his face.

I was stuck with a deranged lightkeeper wielding a rusty old harpoon and a packet of fresh sausages.

But I had found Sherlock Holmes.

The Secret in the Boots

The circular staircase brought me up into a large, well-lighted apartment with windows offering spectacular views of the Downs and the village of East Dean in the distance.

Against one wall stood a large fireplace confronted by a pair of old but comfortable looking armchairs. Opposite this was a small kitchen with stove and sink, a pair of simple wooden berths, and a doorway evidently leading to the lighthouse tower.

And upon every available wall were hung huge nautical charts marked in wax pen.

As the lightkeeper shuffled off to the stove with the sausages, Sherlock Holmes gripped my hand tightly.

"Watson, so good of you to come."

I studied my friend's face. It looked pale from lack of sleep, and an alarming tic was causing his right eye to blink rapidly. "You haven't been injured?"

"No, it's the lamps," he said, releasing my hand to retrieve a pipe and a thin packet of tobacco from his pocket. "Those accursed lamps."

173

"The lamps?"

"I was given the lightkeeper's bunk in the tower last night. Through there." He nodded at the doorway. "The bunk sits right beneath the lamphouse. It takes thirty lamps with thirty mirrors to make the beam, you see, and the beam bounces every which way off the glass windows of the lamphouse . . . ." He shook his head at the memory, spilling tobacco as he filled his pipe. "And that platform creaks all night!"

"What platform is this?"

"The platform! To spin the beam!" He emptied the last of the tobacco into the bowl, muttering. Then, looking up, he apologized. "I'm sorry, Watson. You haven't been given the tour yet. The lamps are mounted on a wooden platform that turns the beam, you see, and it's driven by weights on chains – thick chains that run straight down through the bunk room. It's like living inside a giant grandfather clock!" His voice rose again as he tamped the tobacco into the bowl with undue violence. "*Chunk, chunk, chunk* all night long! I haven't had a moment's peace in twenty-four hours!"

After several attempts at striking a match, he succeeded and began to inhale long, soothing puffs. Then he bade me to sit down at a wooden dining table that stood near the central staircase.

"But why are you even *here*?"

"To inspect Belle Tout, and perhaps to buy it."

"Why on earth would you buy a lighthouse? And one that's going to fall into the sea, no less!"

"I didn't know it was so near the cliffs. Ingalls thought it might be a unique place to raise bees and conduct my chemical experiments. And the views from the lamphouse are not to be missed."

He puffed more sedately and shrugged his shoulders.

"So, as I was coming down from London on a case – "

"That vandalism at Beachy Head?"

"Precisely. You heard about it, then?"

"Only what I read in the newspaper. Didn't think there was much in it for you, to be honest."

"There wasn't." Holmes blew a reflective cloud of smoke at the ceiling. "I solved it before Sir Thomas of Trinity House left my rooms in Baker Street. But I needed to confirm my deductions, so I came down Wednesday evening, got my favorite room at The Tiger, and went out yesterday morning to investigate."

He nodded at the lightkeeper, now stirring a pan of hissing, snapping sausages while muttering to himself.

"Otto was up in his catwalk atop Belle Tout, saw me combing the rocks at Beachy Head, and reckoned I was from Trinity House. He decided

I had something to do with the demise of his lighthouse, and flew into a rage when Ingalls brought me after lunch. Started waving his ancient harpoon about."

"But surely that couldn't stop you from leaving?"

Holmes chuckled. "It didn't. I wanted to spend the night here. Thought I might learn something."

"And what did you learn?"

"That I wouldn't have lasted a week!" He blew precise rings of blue smoke at the ceiling. "And it's no place to raise bees. The winds blow fierce off these chalk cliffs."

"Then I don't see the point of spending another minute here." I started to rise but my friend shook his head.

"I have unfinished business with the lightkeeper."

"Such as?"

Holmes lifted an eyebrow towards the kitchen. "Otto is our vandal."

"What? But the papers said it was the lads from the Eastbourne estates having a laugh!"

Sherlock Holmes puffed languidly on his pipe and shrugged his shoulders.

"That is what I instructed them to say."

His old assuredness was back, the tic in his eye had vanished and his voice was strong.

"So, it was the lightkeeper being made redundant – he wanted to stop the project in its tracks," I stated.

"Precisely. He – ah, and here he comes!"

The object of our conversation shuffled over and set down before us a plate piled high with grilled sausages.

"Excellent, Otto, thank you! Tuck in, Watson."

Otto returned to his stove and Holmes watched me eat, puffing thoughtfully.

"You traced me here by the butcher? I thought as much."

"But why all these sausages?" I asked between mouthfuls of the rather tasty banger. "The butcher told me it was the second package he sent 'round here."

"It was that blasted 'Naval Treaty' story of yours! You proclaimed to the world that I turned my *'attention to the eggs'*, and Ingalls has served me nothing else." Holmes shook his head. "With any luck, the hens will have gone on strike – "

The lightkeeper began cracking eggs into the pan.

"I spoke too soon."

"How do you stand it?"

"I don't." After a quick glance towards the kitchen, Holmes emptied his plate into one of a pair of worn rubber boots beneath the table. "I'm afraid whoever sticks his foot into these is going to find a rather unpleasant sensation awaits them."

"What about Otto, then? That business at Beachy Head was rather serious. Are you going to have him arrested?"

"On the contrary, Watson!" He smiled and pushed back his chair. "I am going to save him. But first, I must replenish my pipe."

The Timeline of a Life

While Otto cooked up the eggs and Holmes searched for fresh tobacco, I took the opportunity to study the old nautical charts that covered the walls. They had been marked, as I said, with wax pencil notations of water depth, tides, shoals, and shipwrecks, evidently by the various Belle Tout lightkeepers over the years.

But next to the fireplace there stood a telltale square of whitewashed wood paneling not yellowed by time where a chart had recently been removed, and the space filled with writing – not in wax pencil but in black pen.

I was attempting to make something of this curious tableau when Sherlock Holmes – his tobacco quest unsuccessful – joined me.

"What's this?" I asked.

"See for yourself," he said, an inscrutable smile upon his face.

And I did.

The text comprised a dozen lines of various lengths, each written in a feverish, intense hand, the words interrupted in many places by arrows, dashes, insertions, exclamation points, and question marks.

Many question marks.

Two stood out in particular: One at the beginning of the first line, and the other at the very end of the twelfth and final line.

It took me some few moments of study to realize what the twelve lines of writing was about: The occurrences from a life.

The Life of Sherlock Holmes.

I was staggered.

"Who did this?"

"George Ingalls. He wrote it all out last night while I was trying to sleep."

"It is a timeline of your life!"

Holmes thoughtfully chewed the stem of the unlit pipe. "Yes. Remarkable, is it not?"

"Where did he get all this from?"

"Where else – your stories!"

"And you told him nothing?"

"Nothing."

"But this is so utterly correct. How did he divine you were born on January 6th? In North Riding? In Yorkshire?"

Holmes shook his head. "Work, I imagine. Observation and deduction."

"I never said a thing about North Riding or January 6th in the stories, Holmes. Honestly. In twenty-seven stories, I have never purposely divulged a true biographical detail – "

"I know, Watson, I know. I've read them all myself. Approved every sentence . . . ." He looked at me with a wry smile. "But brother Mycroft is going to have something to say when he hears about this."

"I can only imagine."

Mycroft Holmes had never liked the idea of me writing up our cases. He thought it could only lead to a bad end for his brother. But we had put it to him that these stories could bring cases that might prove of inestimable benefit to the most exalted superiors in his government, and he had agreed – on the condition that I present any necessary biographical details in a way that confused, rather than enlightened, his enemies.

By the look of this timeline, I failed quite miserably.

But Holmes clapped me on the shoulder and chuckled. "Well, at least Mycroft can't say it wasn't worthwhile. I daresay that business with the Naval Treaty proves the point. Your stories did bring us some of the most abstruse and absorbing cases any man could claim."

"They also brought out obsessives like George Ingalls," I said ruefully. "You overheard his interrogation of me when I first arrived?"

"I think that was the bump on his head talking, Watson, not the man. In fact, I'd like you to look at that injury when he returns."

"But this is dangerous, Holmes!" I read aloud the first entry: "'*Born to parents named Siger and Violet Holmes*.' Where on earth could he find a '*Siger*' in my stories? How could he have divined that?"

Holmes smiled.

"It's not quite so abstruse as you think, Watson. He somehow learned that I traveled *incognito* as a Norwegian explorer named Sigerson. Well, '*Sigerson*' could mean '*Siger's son*', could it not?"

"Oh, my! I never thought of that. But how would he have deduced '*Violet*' for your mother?"

"Because you bestowed that name upon no fewer than three women in your stories, as I recall. No doubt Ingalls reasoned it was a clue to my mother's true name."

I threw up my hands. "Your brother is going to string me up. We must put an end to this speculation. We have to convince Ingalls he's entirely wrong."

"I suppose you're right." Holmes glanced at the lightkeeper sliding a huge pan of scrambled eggs onto a platter. "But I see the eggs are ready, and we must return to the vicinity of those rubber boots before they are served."

As we departed, he cocked an eyebrow at the wall.

"I'll have a little chat with George Ingalls about all this before we leave."

"I should hope so. It must stop."

"It will, Watson. It will."

Otto set the giant plate of eggs before us, but instead of turning back to the kitchen, he stood there, twisting his wool cap anxiously in his hands.

"What is it?" Holmes asked in a kindly voice.

"Half-hour 'til sunset. Time to light the lamps. But I can't do it alone."

"Oh?"

"Aye. Takes two men, you see. The Professor usually helps, but he ain't here, so . . . ."

Holmes shot a glance my way, then smiled at the lightkeeper.

"Tell me Otto. Would *three* men suffice?"

"Oh, more than suffice!"

"Well, Watson, what do you say?"

"I say we help light the lamps."

"How about it, Otto?

"I thank ye both!"

The old man placed his cap on his head and waved us to follow him.

"Thank goodness," Holmes said under his breath as we left the eggs behind, dumped in the boots. "I couldn't have eaten another mouthful."

The Lightkeeper's Reprieve

A winding stone staircase took us to the top of the tower and into the lamphouse, a large, octagonal, glass-enclosed room smelling strongly of kerosene.

In the center stood the reason for Belle Tout's existence: A giant tubular brass structure, looking not unlike an enormous three-sided Christmas tree, with ten lamps arrayed on all three sides of the "tree". Each lamp was backed by a highly polished mirror and fed kerosene – as Otto proudly explained – through the brass tubing, from a cask one level below us.

The entire structure stood on a round wooden platform that would rotate exactly every two minutes once the giant weights were set in motion – but first the lamps had to be lit, and Otto now came alive before our eyes. Gone was the muttering lightkeeper with the quivering harpoon. In his place was a vigorous taskmaster who knew what he required of us and had no hesitation to make certain we got it right.

After handing us very long, thin tapers, Otto demonstrated how to light the lamps just so, making certain to drip no wax onto the reflective mirrors. When we had gotten the hang of that, he set to work performing the more intricate task of adjusting the mirrors behind each lamp so the accumulated light of each bank of lamps could be focused into a most powerful, and surprisingly hot, three-part beam.

It took some doing, but when the beam finally shone to Otto's satisfaction, he released a metal lever beside the platform, setting the giant weights in motion on their slow descent through the floor, causing the platform to begin its slow rotation.

Finally, Otto motioned us to follow him out of the lamphouse so he could judge how the light was performing.

Stepping onto the catwalk, Holmes and I found ourselves occupying the best viewing platform in the South Downs, with unimpeded views in every direction – so long as we maintained our grip on the iron railings, for a biting wind blew so fiercely it seemed to be trying to lift the entire structure and send it crashing into the sea!

But our lightkeeper was paying no attention to nature's impressive works.

He was studying man's own creation – the Belle Tout beam – as it swept across the waters far out to sea.

And by the proud look upon his face, he was satisfied.

"Tell me, Otto," Holmes shouted against the wind as the lightkeeper peered into the gathering gloom, "how far does that light shine?"

"Twenty-three miles! See there?" He pointed to a freighter suddenly illuminated in the light. "That there's the *Cantlemere*. She's twenty miles out. Bound for Rotterdam."

"Remarkable!"

"Just wait, though!" Otto's eyes stayed fixed as the beam swept past the ship and she was once more encased in darkness.

He seemed to be listening for something.

I was about to speak – I had noticed the shadowy form of a tower being constructed about a mile to the east, down on the beach, which I expected was the new light going up at Beachy Head – but Holmes touched a finger to his lips, and we waited.

Suddenly, a long, deep, ship's blast, reached us, sounding like a distant, eternal thunderclap.

"That's her!" Otto exclaimed. "Always thanks me as she passes!"

He touched his cap in tribute to the invisible vessel, and I saw in his eyes a gleam I shall never forget, evincing pride and satisfaction for a job well done.

But his pleased countenance did not last long.

And I regret to say I was the cause of its dissipation.

I wanted to ask about that tower at Beachy Head and I recalled something I had read about the reasons for replacing Belle Tout.

"Apparently the fog pushes up the cliffs here and obscures the beam?" I remarked to Otto, gesturing at the fog now rolling in over the shingled beach and up the cliffside towards the base of Belle Tout.

It was a statement I instantly regretted.

"You tellin' me they get no fog at Beachy Head?" Otto pointed an accusatory finger east towards the unfinished tower of the lighthouse that was going to replace his own. "Somethin' stops it from blowin' in there, too?"

"No, but they say the fog comes into the cliffs a certain way here – "

"They say? *They* say? Who says?"

"Well, I read it in the newspaper."

"Does the paper say the fog don't go to Beachy Head too? Fog only comes in *here?*"

"Of course not. I only meant – "

Holmes cut me off with a glance, and at that moment the Beachy Head site was suddenly lit up by the Belle Tout light. "See, Watson?" he exclaimed. "See there! The very same fog is finding its way to Beachy Head!"

Tendrils of fog could be seen creeping over the large granite blocks and circling the carpenter's shed where the vandalism had taken place.

A smile crept to Otto's lips, and he nodded. "Tha's right, Mr. Holmes. Tha's exackly right."

I knew – as did Holmes, I was sure – that it wasn't "exackly right". The erosion of the cliffs here at Belle Tout was making her vulnerable to fog in a way its builders had not foreseen. And the Beachy Head light was being built down on a point near the water where the fog would lay below the light.

But by the glare in Holmes's eyes, I dared not argue the point.

"I'm sorry," I said. "It's been some years since I've experienced fog like this. Not since my return from Afghanistan . . . ."

"Oh, eh?" Otto's expression changed. "What regiment?"

"66th Berkshire. Battle of Maiwand. And you served . . . where?"

"*HMS Cordelia*, sir. Under Hume, that was."

"Ah! The New Zealand wars. You had a rough journey home, I know."

"Aye, that we did." Otto turned his eyes upon a second freighter exposed by the light beam as it cut through the waters far offshore. "Typhoon come up before we could blink. But we all pulled together and made it through. That we did. Not like today, when nobody pulls together . . . ."

He fell silent, and after a few moments, Holmes gripped my arm and winked. Then he cleared his throat and began speaking to me in a conversational tone – but loud enough to be overheard by the lightkeeper.

"I say, Watson, did you happen to hear about the vandalism there at Beachy Head?"

"Why, yes," said I, catching something of my friend's intent by the glint in his eye. "Read it in the papers. Bad business, it sounded like."

"Indeed! Lamp-oil dumped on the blocks so they couldn't be lifted! Dead jelly fish – a very poisonous species, too – left in the carpenter's hut! The men couldn't work."

"I read the police put it down to some toughs from the Eastbourne estates."

"They did, Watson, they did. But Sir Thomas of Trinity House wasn't satisfied. Thought there must be more to it. I spent yesterday morning combing those rocks, looking for clues."

The lightkeeper stiffened beside me.

"And did you find any?"

"I did. An empty cask was smashed on the rocks. And do you know, it looked very much like those casks of lamp-oil in the basement here."

The lightkeeper had begun his muttering ways, his hands seeming to grope for the harpoon he had left behind.

"What about the jellyfish?" I asked.

"Ah, yes., that was a puzzle . . . but did you happen to notice the fishing rod by the door when you came in?"

"Yes, what about it?"

"A piece of squid was still baited to the hook. And I'm told the jellyfish in these parts do enjoy their squid."

The lightkeeper was now trembling, his mutterings intense.

"What do you make of it, Holmes? What are you going to tell Sir Thomas?"

The lightkeeper had stopped breathing, and I thought he might faint. I braced myself to support him.

"I'm going to tell Sir Thomas," Holmes said, placing a gentle hand on the shoulder of the trembling figure in the wool cap, "that lads from the estate pinched that cask of oil and the fishing rod from Belle Tout and ran riot at the new lighthouse."

Otto let out a long breath, and I now expected he might faint from relief!

"And that's the end of it?"

"Not entirely. Tomorrow morning I'll be dropping a line to Trinity House that the only acceptable payment for my services will be the appointment of our friend Otto here as the *locum* for the new lightkeeper at Beachy Head. That is, as long as Otto wishes it."

Holmes looked questioningly at the lightkeeper, who stared at him open-mouthed.

"But do you think Sir Thomas will agree?" I asked.

Holmes smiled. "He'll have no choice."

With that, Otto hugged my friend.

And began to cry.

Deerstalkers on the Downs

Holmes and I had circled the catwalk to the landward side, leaving the much-relieved lightkeeper to his scrutiny of the Channel for passing ships.

The Downs now spread out before us like a three-dimensional map enshrouded in darkness, its farmhouses and the cottages of East Dean distinguished from the landscape only by the flickering of yellow lamps in their windows.

"That was very kind of you," I said. "And a very wise solution, I might add."

My friend dismissed my compliment – as he had always dismissed such encomiums – with a wave of his hand.

"You can't replace thirty years' knowledge of these waters with just anybody. Sir Thomas should have known that already – " He abruptly stopped speaking.

Something had caught his eye.

Then I saw it too: Several flickering lights had emerged from the shadows of East Dean. They appeared to be moving.

Towards us.

"Do you see that?" I asked.

"I do."

"Searching for a lost dog, perhaps?"

The several lights multiplied into half-a-dozen distinct lights.

"That would be a very large search party for a lost dog."

The number doubled again.

"Sheep, then?"

Holmes chuckled and shook his head. "That is no search party."

"What is it?"

"He's bringing them here."

"Who's bringing who here?"

"George Ingalls. He's bringing the Sherlockians. They've come all the way from London . . . ."

"I don't believe it."

But at that moment the Belle Tout light swept across the Downs, lighting up their figures like a noonday sun. Each held a torch and wore a deerstalker cap.

I counted twelve in all.

"Do you believe it now, Watson?"

For half-an-hour we observed them from the catwalk, their progress exposed several times every two minutes by the three-part beam: Bunched together waiting to pass through a turnstile. Marching single file across a pasture, passing through the next turnstile, crossing the next pasture . . . .

With George Ingalls always in front.

When they reached the cliff walk for the final dash up the bluff to Belle Tout, however, Holmes said goodbye to Otto, and we entered the lamphouse to make our way down the winding tower staircase.

"You're going to tell them," I said as the excited voices of a dozen Sherlockians reached. "Remember: You're going to set them straight."

"I will, Watson. I will."

The ecstatic figure of George Ingalls greeted us as we entered the living quarters.

"They all came!" he cried. "Every member of the London Society came!"

"Yes," Holmes said dryly. "It seems they did."

Ingalls appeared crestfallen. "I thought you would be honored."

Holmes smiled politely. "Did you at least send the telegram to Mrs. Hudson?"

Ingalls nodded and handed over a confirmation receipt from the District Office in London. Holmes glanced at the paper and stuffed it in his pocket.

"Very well, then. Lead on."

It had come to this: Sherlock Holmes stood before a crowd of expectant Sherlockians in deerstalker caps, his back to George Ingalls' handwritten sentences on the wall beside the fireplace, prepared to rebuke the life these enthusiasts had created for him.

They were middle-aged men for the most part, although one or two younger faces peered out beneath their caps, and three were women, hair piled up beneath their deerstalkers.

In place of the torches that had shown them the way across the Downs, they now held pencils or pens, and either a book – one of *my* books – or a dog-eared edition of one of the magazines in which the stories had been serialized.

They were ready to take notes of everything that their *beau idéal* said.

Needless to say, the presence of so many people crammed together had warmed up the living quarters considerably, and the heavy scent of old sausages and cold scrambled eggs only added to the stuffy atmosphere.

But it did nothing to dampen the excitement and expectations of these men and women, and I couldn't help but dread the outcome.

How would this collection of devotees react when Sherlock Holmes refused to discuss the biography of his life?

Would they turn on us as the poor lightkeeper had done to Holmes the previous day, when he thought my friend had come from Trinity House to shut down Belle Tout?

As Ingalls had turned on *me?*

I couldn't make out his wound now – it was hidden by his cap – but I expected it had only gotten worse since my arrival. I recalled his bulging eyes and barking voice when I had made fun of my own stories and couldn't help but wonder how he would feel when Sherlock Holmes turned his considerable intellect against this collection of names and dates and places derived from those same stories so that such precise details never fall into the hands of his enemies.

I began to consider how we might extricate ourselves from that confined space if things went very wrong.

Seated at the wooden dining table, I quickly realized it could be a natural barricade, turned on its side. That would help me keep an escape route to the staircase open for my friend, if need be.

But I needed a weapon to use in self-defense. The plate of cold eggs was no help, and I briefly considered the rubber boots near my feet. Being full of old sausages and eggs, they might weigh enough to serve as a kind of truncheon, if necessary. But they wouldn't look like weapons, and I needed something that would cause an angry crowd to have second thoughts.

Then, I remembered.

And while all eyes were on Sherlock Holmes, I surreptitiously made my way to the kitchen, as if to fetch a glass of water – but instead retrieved the only thing I could think of. Then I sat back down at the table and rested the artifact across my knees, easy to grasp but hidden from view.

Just in case.

It was the lightkeeper's ridiculous harpoon.

The encounter got underway.

Ingalls, speaking as "Professor Moriarty", introduced each member of the London Society by their chosen sobriquet.

They included "Wiggins" of The Baker Street Irregulars, Holmes's brother "Mycroft", Scotland Yard's "Inspector Lestrade", the villainous "John Clay" and "Jonathan Small" – even "Arthur Charpentier" and "Major Sholto" among the men, and of course, Holmes's favorite of women: "Irene Adler".

Then Sherlock Holmes was asked to say a few words before the questioning would begin.

I held my breath as my old companion surveyed the assembly – I knew what disdain that grim countenance could hold – and for a moment the only sound in the room was the low rumble of the wooden platform and the *chunk, chunk, chunk* of the metal weights slowly descending through the tower.

"Thank you, Professor," he finally said. "I have a confession to make."

The smiles under the deerstalkers turned to confused looks, and there was a sudden alertness in their posture, a craning of their ears as they seemed to ask themselves: *Confession? What confession could Sherlock Holmes possibly make?*

"I must confess," said he, "I simply don't enjoy sausage and eggs quite as much as you think I do, thanks to that blasted story by my friend over there!"

And as his frown turned into a smile, I realized he wasn't going to disappoint them.

He was going to give them exactly what they hoped for.

Striding briskly through the parting crowd to the table where I sat, Holmes caught my eye with a sly wink and picked up the rubber boots from the floor. Then he held them over the plate of eggs and turned the pair upside down, causing two gelatinous masses of uneaten sausages and eggs to begin oozing out of each boot and slopping onto the plate of eggs.

"And you can see where I've been hiding the evidence!"

George Ingalls looked momentarily surprised and a bit embarrassed, but as smiles and laughter broke out among the other Deerstalkers, he smiled, too.

And when one last sausage plopped onto the plate, the laughs became a roar.

"The truth is," Holmes shouted above the merriment, "I *do* enjoy a good steak now and then. Eh, Watson?"

"Yes," I said, letting the harpoon drop to the floor while all eyes were on my companion. Then I rose to stand with him. "We both do!"

"Now, your questions?" said Sherlock Holmes.

We stood together before the wall beside the fireplace, facing a dozen cheerful Sherlockians, their pens and pencils at the ready.

Hands shot up, and Holmes called one man forward.

"You say you enjoy steak, Mr. Holmes, but there's no record in The Canon of that. Beef, certainly – "

"In the *what?*"

"'The Canon'. The Canon of Sherlock Holmes."

Holmes looked perplexed. "Your name is Wiggins, isn't it?"

"Yes, sir."

"Tell me, Wiggins, do you mean to refer to those books and stories of my friend Dr. Watson as a Biblical *Canon?*"

"Yes. We all do." Deerstalkers nodded all around.

Something in their manner – in their polite earnestness – caused my friend to be overcome. I don't ever recall him being speechless before, but at that moment, he appeared to be just that.

He recovered, as only Sherlock Holmes could: By an improvisation that fooled everyone but me. Taking his pipe from his pocket and holding it up before the crowd, he said, "Before we answer Mr. Wiggin's most excellent question, does anyone have spare tobacco of which I might partake?"

There was a scramble as coat pockets were searched. Finally, a pouch was offered, its owner saying proudly, "It's shag tobacco, of course!"

"My favorite! How did you know?" Holmes asked happily.

"'A Scandal in Bohemia'!" was shouted in unison.

"Very good!" Holmes took his time charging the pipe and lighting it, exhaling great puffs of smoke towards the ceiling while eying the crowd. Then, when he was once more composed, he asked Wiggins, "And what is your question, sir?"

"It's just that there's no record of you eating steak in the Canon. Beef, more than once – "

"*Cold* beef!" exclaimed another voice.

"Yes, cold beef."

"Cold beef?" Holmes said smoothly. "But why only *cold* beef?"

"'A Scandal in Bohemia'!" cried someone.

"Yes, you ate cold beef in "'A Scandal in Bohemia'," Wiggins explained. "'*Some cold beef and a glass of beer.*'"

"But don't forget 'The Beryl Coronet'," came another voice.

"Yes, well, in 'The Beryl Coronet', you and Dr. Watson kept a joint of beef on the sideboard."

"Made a sandwich out of it '*between two rounds of bread*'!" someone else shouted, waving a copy of *The Adventures of Sherlock Holmes* opened to that page.

And as speaker after speaker shouted references from "The Canon" enumerating Sherlock Holmes's taste in foods, and as those references grew ever more arcane, Sherlock Holmes finally held up his hands and motioned for quiet.

"I *am* here, you know," he said in mock exasperation.

This drew laughs from the Deerstalkers, and what came next positively thrilled them.

"And so is the author of nearly every word of The Canon!" Holmes clapped me on the shoulder "We're both here, and that means you won't have to guess anymore. And I don't have to tell you that I *never* guess . . . and why?" He looked expectantly as they finished the line straight from my very first book:

"'*It is a shocking habit*'!"

"Well done," said Sherlock Holmes when the cheers had subsided. "Well done!"

Rolling Away the Stone

It was nearly midnight when Holmes and I stepped outside into a wind that felt even colder and sharper than it had up on the catwalk at sunset. My companion took his time buttoning his cloak and readying his walking stick for the footpath back to The Tiger. He was waiting to see the Belle Tout beam sweep the countryside before us.

As it did, he looked up and gave a wave to Otis, who saluted back from the catwalk.

I studied my companion with no little admiration.

The questions had come at us for two hours, and Holmes, for the Deerstalkers really wanted to hear from him, not me. He had answered them all in his most precise and didactic manner.

And entirely in accordance with the timeline on the wall.

"Why did you do it?" I asked.

"Do what?"

"Give your approval to that timeline?"

187

"I didn't give them my birth year! I thought you might want to work that another story one of these days – "

"I'm serious, Holmes. What did you change your mind?"

"I saw their faces, Doctor. They put so much into it. I couldn't deny them."

"But what about your enemies? They'll only have to see this timeline to know your true biography?"

"They can have it, Watson. I'm finished."

"Is there something behind this retirement business? Something about your health you haven't told me?"

"Not a bit. I feel as healthy as the day we met at Barts. And that's rather the point. To retire from the detective field while I can, not when I must."

"I've tried to leave the medical profession behind several times, you know, but I find nothing can replace the mental stimulation it provides."

"I have no apprehension about finding stimulation here, Watson. There will be beekeeping to master, and my chemical experiments . . . and just look at those stars and that moon. Look how bright it shines! How close it appears!"

At that moment, the great yellow beam of Belle Tout suddenly caught us in its brilliance and the stars and moon disappeared from our sight.

Holmes chuckled. "And, of course, Otto reminds us that there is beauty in our own creation, too."

I was sitting down to breakfast at The Tiger the next morning when Sherlock Holmes burst in from a walk and joined me. He was in high spirits.

"You seem rather jolly this morning," said I.

"I've found it!"

And with that, he described the cottage George Ingalls had found for him.

"Perfect for raising bees, an easy walk to The Tiger, and with a telegraph office at hand if ever the odd case comes in and I have to dust off my deerstalker."

"Are you going to show me?"

"There isn't time." He pointed out the window of the snug.

At that moment, the bells of the parish church of St. Simon and St. Jude came to our ears.

"Eat up, my friend. The church bell tolls . . . and it tolls for thee and me. Our London guests will be arriving at The Tiger any minute."

It was only then that I remembered it was Easter Sunday.

The Detective and the Dalai Lama

The pews in the sanctuary overflowed with the country folk of East Dean, and a surfeit of Londoners.

There were Holmes and myself, my wife of course, Mycroft Holmes, and Inspector Lestrade. There was, too, the loyal Mrs. Hudson, who had brought the case of the disappearing detective to Mycroft Holmes after leaving my doorstep and had chosen to accompany Mycroft and Inspector Lestrade to East Dean in search of her missing lodger rather than visit her family in the North, because, as she told us, "I thought it would be the last Easter I could ever spend with Mr. Holmes."

There were also a dozen Sherlockians, led by George Ingalls, whose split forehead I had cleaned and bandaged before we had departed from Belle Tout the night before. Despite all twelve spending spent the night in the lighthouse, they appeared entirely unfazed by the lights and noise that had so disturbed Sherlock Holmes.

The vicar's homily was a good one, its theme being that we should all be prepared to "Roll Away the Stone" at times in our lives, and the closing hymn was a rousing *Eternal Father, Strong to Save*", one of Holmes's favorites.

Afterwards, we made our way to The Tiger – Sherlockians as well – in excellent spirits, sharing a good French Beaune while Holmes sat in the snug with George Ingalls and signed the necessary papers to purchase the Dunbar cottage.

Then we all sat down to enjoy a hearty Easter meal prepared by Jack the landlord, who grilled the lambs, and Grace, his wife, who made the pies.

George Ingalls sat at our table, for although brother Mycroft had protested his presence, Sherlock had argued it would be churlish not to let the man who had aided Holmes in buying his new house to help them celebrate.

Mycroft had agreed, but with the stipulation that Ingalls not so much as breathe a question of him or his brother that might tread upon affairs of state.

So awestruck was Ingalls in the company of individuals about whom he had only read, however, he spent most of the meal shifting his gaze from the dialogue between Mycroft and Sherlock Holmes, who spoke in a kind of brotherly shorthand, to that of Mrs. Hudson and Inspector Lestrade, who to his evident surprise got on quite famously.

Nevertheless, as the meal progressed and wine flowed, Ingalls grew more relaxed, and when the discussion between Mycroft and Sherlock turned from the Christian Easter story to Tibetan Buddhist views of life and the afterlife, Ingalls could restrain himself no more.

"'The Great Hiatus'!" he blurted out, causing all heads to turn to his end of the table.

"What was that?" asked Mycroft Holmes, thoroughly confused.

"The years Dr. Watson thought Sherlock Holmes was dead – but it turned out he was in Tibet! We call that 'The Great Hiatus'!"

"There was nothing 'great' about it," said Mrs. Hudson sharply. "We were shattered. Weren't we, Doctor?"

I nodded, but so excited was Ingalls he turned his bulging eyes to Holmes.

"We heard that you met the Head Lama in Lhasa? What was he like? Can he *really* fly in the air?"

Holmes looked at Mycroft, who, seeing the excitement in the face of the dedicated Sherlockian – and in the faces of the other Sherlockians now gathered around to hear the answer – cleared his throat and, with a wink at his brother, said, "What say we 'roll away the stone' on your time in Tibet, eh Sherlock? Tell them everything that happened when you met the head lama of Tibet."

Epilogue

Gazing south from a tidy apple orchard just outside the village green of East Dean, one can see perched on crumbling chalk cliffs overlooking the English Channel in the distance a lighthouse that once kept watch, as the old hymn says, "*for those in peril on the sea*".

Long since decommissioned – the barrels of kerosene that once fed its lamps removed – the lamps themselves dismantled and given away, the heavy clocklike mechanism that turned the beam melted down for guns during the Great War – Belle Tout is now just a place that offers unmatched views of the English Channel to the south and the Sussex Downs to the north.

But the views are not its only attraction.

For written in black ink upon the bare wall beside the fireplace at Belle Tout there appear a dozen lines, some quite long, others shorter, of feverish writing that purport to tell the life story of a man – a man whose career brought him fame across several continents at time when those continents were connected only by sailing ships and the telegraph wire.

To this day, many who book a stay at Belle Tout do so strictly to study those lines of writing in detail.

190

And should one of those enthusiasts venture forth of a summer afternoon and follow the coastal footpath from Belle Tout across the Downs to the village of East Dean, they might just see a sheltered yard with an elderly gentleman keeping watch on his beehives and his apple orchard.

And they may mistake him for the gardener.

But if they were to stop and take the time to watch the man and listen carefully as he went about his work in the garden, they might discern that he brought to his winged charges the keen perception of one who once made a life out of the precise and rational observation and deduction of human behavior, much like the man whose timeline is written upon the wall of the apartment they have been occupying.

And if they could bring themselves to interrupt that diligent and determined beekeeper to ask if he is indeed the same person as that whose life they have been studying, he will, it has been reported, look past the beehives and the apple trees and the greening pastures with their white sheep to the distant figure of Belle Tout, and he will shake his head and say, "No, I'm not. Not anymore."

And he will smile and politely excuse himself and return to the garden.

The Adventure of the
Unfinished Case
by John McNabb

A little over a week had passed since our return from the varsity town of Camford. I have written of that case elsewhere (see "The Adventure of the Creeping Man" in *The Strand Magazine*). Here it is sufficient to remark only that in the autumn of 1903, my friend Mr. Sherlock Holmes had been summoned to Camford to investigate the increasingly aberrant behaviour of Professor Presbury. His investigations revealed that the foolish professor had been injecting himself with a serum extracted from a climbing species of monkey native to the Himalayas. Rather than instill in him the vigour of youth, ahead of his impending nuptials to a much younger woman, Professor Presbury had taken up the behaviour of that primate. A tragedy was narrowly averted when the professor's greyhound, Roy, had launched a deadly attack on the professor while he was under the baleful influence of the serum. The matter had been hushed up to avoid a scandal. Holmes, I knew, was dissatisfied with the resolution of the case. The drug itself had been procured from Bohemia, from Professor Lowenstein of Prague, via his agent in Britian, A. Dorak, who maintained premises in the Commercial Road, London.

"It's no good," said my friend as I visited Holmes's Baker Street study. "No good at all. I shall have to take the case up again."

"Whatever do you mean?"

"This Lowenstein business."

He tossed the morning edition of *The Times* across the table. An inch of column on the fourth page announced that Professor Presbury was taking a leave of absence from the varsity to pursue research in the Sorbonne, Paris. He would be accompanied by his daughter, Miss Edith Presbury, and his assistant and future son-in-law, Mr. Trevor Bennett. It was anticipated the young couple would marry in Paris.

"You don't think the professor is on the track of Lowenstein do you?" I asked, alarmed, but Holmes shook his head.

"No, I do not. He has had a close call and a bad scare. As his normal more temperate personality reasserts itself, I feel confident he will follow the straight and narrow. Trevor Bennet and Edith Presbury will see to that.

"No, my worry is more to the link with Prague. We know the eminent physician had a second client here in England. It is to that line of enquiry that we must apply ourselves." He waved his hand airily at the breakfast table. "Break your fast, Watson, and after some of Mrs. Hudson's inestimable scrambled eggs, we are away to the Commercial Road."

Within the hour we were seated in the back of a motorised taxicab en route for the lower end of the Commercial Road, with the chill of the coming fall in the air. Motorised vehicles were becoming more common on the streets of the metropolis, and although I missed the elegance of a hansom, motorised taxi cabs were roomier and a great deal warmer. On our right we passed a warren of dreary residential streets opening onto the Commercial Road. As we passed Berner Street I gave a start. One of Jack the Ripper's victims had been discovered in the entrance to a yard part way down that street. Holmes stared ahead and paid no attention.

Commercial Road became Commercial Road East. As we approached the docklands, Holmes ordered the cabby to slow down. We passed St. Michael's church and rumbled over the bridge under which Regent's Canal flowed into Limehouse Basin and the Regent's Canal Docks. All the premises hereabouts were associated with trade and commerce and linked in one way or another to the docks.

"Pull up, cabby," Holmes rapped smartly into the speaking tube. In short order we stood on the busy pavement. I could smell the docks and the great river beyond. With his stick, Holmes pointed out a premises sandwiched between an engineering works and a flour mill. "*A. Dorak. Live Animal Importers and Exporters*" announced a sign. The entrance was down a dingy ally.

"What do we know of this Dorak?" I asked.

"Little, I am afraid. As you can see, he runs a live animal emporium. He procures specimens for zoos and private collections. He specialises in rare and exotic plants and animals – birds too. I had Gregson look into him. He is known to the Yard as a possible smuggler, but they have never succeeded in turning rumour into a conviction."

A sign fixed to a door with dirty glass panes – "*Closed. By Appointment Only*" – suggested an end to our adventure, but Holmes wasn't so easily deterred. He rapped sharply with his stick on the metal finger-plate. Peering in through the filthy glass he muttered, "Looks as if no one is home."

Cupping his palm theatrically to his ear he said, "I say, did you hear a cry for help?"

"No, I didn't hear – "

But before I could finish, Holmes had put his elbow through a glass pane and reached through to unbolt the door.

The inside was as dingy as the outside. Over everything lay the pungent aroma of livestock.

"Be careful, Watson. I fear something is amiss."

We stood in a largish shop front. Cages with all manner of animals, large and small, were everywhere. As we entered, we set off such a cacophony of chattering and alarm that we were quite deafened. If our entry had passed notice before, it certainly wouldn't now. Still, no one appeared from the depth of the shop to challenge us.

We moved through the shop quicky, heading for a counter at the back, beyond which was a doorway.

"Observe," said Holmes quietly. "Beside a number of cages are various piles of leave or nuts, and over there some diced meat. Someone has been here recently and prepared the daily meal for the inmates."

We moved on cautiously. An opossum hissed at us from behind its cage bars. Further along a tortoise watched us with an antediluvian impassivity.

"We seek any correspondence or invoicing that may lead us to the name of Dorak's second contact."

However, the sales counter appeared devoid of any record keeping or paperwork. The door behind it into the back of the shop was a stout one, faced with metal sheeting.

"Perhaps the more dangerous creatures are kept in the back?" I ventured. Holmes nodded. By unspoken agreement we both drew our pistols. Using his stick, Holmes pushed the door open. I shall never forget the sight that greeted us. A man lay on his back. He wore a thick apron and long thick leather gloves. He was dead. His neck was swollen, and his face had contorted into a rictus of such horror that a chill ran down my spine. I'd seen such a death before. As Holmes began to move forward to examine the body, I called to him urgently.

"Holmes – on your life, do not move." As he froze to the spot I heard him gasp. From the opposite side of the body a long sinuous and hooded shape rose up. A cobra, and by the size of it a king cobra. Utterly deadly.

"Shoot on the count of three," he said. Two loud reports rang out and the snake, its head weaving soporifically, was flung backwards.

Lying on the floor not far from Dorak's body, for it must have been him, was a large glass tank. Its glass lid lay broken nearby. To one side lay a long pole with a retractable catching loop at one end.

"He must have had an accident while moving the tank?" I noted.

"You look, Watson, but you do not see. Roll down his gloves."

I did so and immediately saw there was bruising on both forearms. It was fresh and still swelling up an angry purple. "Holmes, he has been held down, by at least two people, both with very strong grips."

He nodded. "I suspected as much. The snake-catching device was used to deliver the death bite."

"That's monstrous." I had seen a man in Afghanistan die of a cobra's bite. It was a particularly unpleasant death.

The room in which we stood was large, more like a smallish warehouse. Cages and tanks lined both walls. An iron circular staircase led up to an upper level, and I could see more cages. All the creatures in here were bigger than those in the front of the shop. Here there were more snakes, and even a crocodile. Their eyes followed us with hungry anticipation. Following Holmes's gaze, I saw in one corner a series of record drawers and storage cabinets. They had been ransacked and their contents tossed to the floor.

"Someone came looking for the same thing we did – " He stared down at Dorak's body. " – and then made sure there were no clues for us to follow."

We walked to the end of the warehouse. A single door was set in the wall and it was ajar. Holmes cautiously peeped through into the daylight beyond. There was a narrow cobbled thoroughfare evidently designed to allow access and deliveries to the back of the commercial premises. It disappeared around a corner. On the opposite side of the roadway was a high brick wall with a gate set into it, wide enough for a horse and waggon to pass through. Given our location, it wasn't difficult to deduce that the Regent's Canal Docks lay just behind the wall.

Holmes nodded. "And that gateway will be how Dorak smuggled some of his less-than-legal pets out of the docks – but only after a suitable amount of money had exchanged hands. Hullo, what do we have here?"

Holmes was staring down at the roadway. There was a little valley where the camber of the road met the curb. It was filled with mud. A tyre track was clearly visible. A little further on, the track became rather confused.

"Here is our assassin's escape route, unless I'm much mistaken," he said, peering down at the jumble of imprints. "The track stops here at the warehouse door. The driver then turned the wheels in toward the curb. What does that suggest?"

I thought for a moment. "The hand brake was unreliable?"

"Capital, Watson. Now here you see the tyre has been turned away from the curb again."

"The miscreants were leaving?" I ventured.

Holmes nodded. "But what do you notice about the track over here?"

I looked carefully. "The track is deeper."

"You scintillate today. Yes. I will venture this is a delivery waggon, and a number of men got into the back before it drove away. And see how fresh the tyre impressions are."

"You think they were here when we arrived."

"I fear so. A few minutes earlier and we might have prevented this ugly murder. This has all the hallmarks of organisation. But to send a group of men to eradicate any clues – Now that is instructive."

He tapped his lip with a forefinger, lost in thought. "I wonder," he murmured to himself. "I wonder."

We made our way back through the warehouse and into the shop. As we did so, there was a disturbance toward the front door. Conscious of the murderer's return, Holmes and I froze in our tracks, pistols at the ready. I was a step or two ahead of my friend and could cover the doorway. A man stood outside, though the filthy glass prevented me from seeing him properly. He was searching for something. I raised my pistol in readiness. Then an avalanche of envelopes fell into the shop. It was the postman with the late morning delivery.

With an animal-like cry, Holmes was at the door in a moment. "Is it possible?" he cried with feverish excitement. He tossed envelope after envelope aside, and then suddenly held one up in triumph.

"A veritable hit, Watson. Postmarked Camford!"

He visibly had to restrain himself from tearing open the communique. "Good quality envelope, but otherwise unremarkable. Easily purchased in any quality stationers, of which there are many in a varsity town. The handwriting is clear – a man's, I think – and notice the forcefulness of both the down and upstrokes. A man of some confidence, and perhaps position in life."

"A Don then?" I suggested.

"Possibly so. Postmarked early this morning, so destined for the early mail train." Carefully he peeled back the gummed flap. "Notepaper matches the envelope, so likely bought as a set." He held it up to the light, looking for a watermark, but huffed with disappointment. "Otherwise unmarked."

Eagerly I leaned over his shoulder and read:

My Dear Sir,

I have heard nothing from you for over a week. Presbury is abroad, recuperating, and the detectives have left the town. There is no further danger to ourselves. Presbury had no knowledge of me. In any case, we have breached no law – none of man's at least.

Send as soon as you have news. I am feverish with anticipation.

R

Holmes and I stared at each other for a moment. I wasn't sure whether this brought us any closer to our quarry.

"Watson, our first call must be to Gregson. Then to Baker Street to pack our valises, and a train to Camford." He clapped me on the shoulder. "If my suspicions are right, and I pray they are not, there may be some danger ahead. Are you game?"

"I have never funked at the wicket," I replied a little truculently. "No intention of starting now!"

Holmes gave me one of his rare smiles. "There's my Watson."

We were as good as our word. Not long after lunch time we were on the train for Camford and our old rooms in The Chequers. I noted in my diary that the quality of both the port and the linen were still above reproach.

Before boarding the train, Holmes had dashed off a telegram to *The Times* personals and to *The Camford Herald*:

> *Lowenstein of Prague: If you have dealings, make contact with Sherlock Holmes at The Chequers, Camford. Urgent.*

"Are we not exposing ourselves to danger here?" I asked. "At the very least, are we not announcing to the enemy we have re-entered the game."

Holmes nodded. "Yes, but I see little way forward, and I deeply suspect our every move is already watched."

"Do we not then put '*R*' in danger?" I asked.

My friend nodded solemnly once more. "Yes, we do, but it cannot be helped. I'm afraid this this time, the quarry must come to the guns."

We settled into our rooms. Almost immediately, Holmes was away, leaving me to hold the fort in case anyone made contact. As I later learned, he had scoured the university and college libraries for lists of faculty staff and Fellows whose initials were "*R*".

"I have to report," he said upon returning, throwing himself into an armchair, "that *Richard, Robert*, and *Roderick* are confoundedly popular Christian names amongst the academic community. As are the surnames *Richards, Roberts, Robertson*, and *Richardson, etcetera*." He waved his hand dismissively. "We are no closer to knowing who *R* is, and not a whiff of Lowenstein or his agent."

He made an unhappy growling sound at the back of his throat and stared defiantly into the empty grate. "There is nothing for it. We shall just have to wait it out."

And that is what we did. I found it prudent to excuse myself for long walks. A stroll up the river was most pleasant, and watching the rowers practice reminded me of my own varsity days, though rugby was my sport. In addition to the quality of the port and the linen, The Chequers public bar served a pint of best bitter that was equally above reproof.

It was on the afternoon of the third day that the game finally began, though at the time I thought it an unlikely start. I was reading the afternoon edition, with Holmes's message repeated in the personals. There was a footfall on the stair, and Holmes's head shot up like a dog scenting the quarry.

"A woman, unless I am very much mistaken," he said. "And by the speed at which she ascends, a much-agitated one."

There was a short urgent rapping on our door and a young woman entered. I took her to be young, in her middle-twenties. She wore a bonnet and a long dark overcoat. Her rosy cheeks had an anxious blush, and her eyes darted uncertainly from Holmes to myself.

"Is one of you gentlemen Mr. Sherlock Holmes, the famous London detective?"

It was my friend's turn to blush slightly.

"I am he, but please sit and tell us what is the matter. I appreciate you have little time before you have to return to your situation." Holmes paused thoughtfully. "And you don't wish to find the shop has run out of eggs."

"Oh," said the young woman, looking startled.

"It is an easy deduction to make," replied Holmes with a depreciating smile. "It is early in the afternoon, a common time for younger household staff to be sent out on errands. I see your bonnet is slightly to one side, and you have mis-buttoned your coat, indicating haste and concern – an urgent errand, therefore, and with little time. You have flour on your cuff, so you aren't a lady's maid, and you are rather young to be a cook. A junior position in service isn't an illogical deduction."

"How did you know I was sent out for eggs?"

Holmes sat back down in his chair. "Kitchens are usually well provisioned, and early afternoon is a time when many cooks like to get their baking done – hence the flour. A hasty mission to the shop suggests a shortage. Perhaps some item was unexpectedly popular at breakfast?"

The young woman nodded. "Eggs, sir!"

"But I presume you are not here about the eggs?"

"Oh no, sir, I wouldn't dream of wasting your time about the eggs. No, sir. This is about the bananas."

It was rare to see Holmes nonplussed, but his eyebrows shot up and he stared at the young woman with surprise.

"Perhaps you might want to start at the beginning, my dear," I interjected suppressing my amusement.

The young woman collected herself and began her story. "My name is Masie Anne Cooper, and I am a serving maid in Professor Lloyd Owen's household. We are a small house, so I double-up as kitchen maid and upstairs maid as well. My father, Mr. Cooper, is butler, and my mother is cook. There is a boy, Jimmy, who also helps with chores around the house, but he's no relation.

"The master works in the University's Natural History Museum, and lectures on, umm, animals and things. My mother thinks it's a bit godless, but we don't say nothing, and His Nibs – umm, I mean the master – he's a decent employer, if a bit scatty like."

As she spoke, Holmes leaned across to consult a sheaf of papers. "Professor Owen is the Regius Professor of Evolutionary History at Wenban College. Now, there was something about the bananas?"

"Well, sir, it's like this: My mother has bowls of fruit around the house and in the professor's study. He's always grumbling about that one, and tells her to take it away. She says it's good for him and leaves it there. They have a sort-of joke about it. Anyway, it was Tuesday last and I put a new fruit bowl in the study and there was three nice bananas on the top. Wednesday morning when I went into the study to do my dusting, the bananas was gone. I was quite taken aback. We'd been expecting the master home Tuesday night, but he decided to stay over in his rooms in college. I went and told my mother about the bananas and she comes up to see for herself. So I wasn't day-dreaming."

Holmes looked across at me. I could sense his frustration mounting.

"But then the next day, they was back, only now they was back, but rotten." I noticed Holmes brow furrow slightly. "Not an hour later, the professor had a telegram delivered to him in college, and then he's back at the house all of a bustle like. He has to go to London, right there and then. So we pack his bag and he's away in a cab for the station."

"Was that normal for Professor Owen?" asked Holmes.

"He will sometimes stay in college and forget to tell us, sir, but going to London at the drop of a hat? No, sir. Even for him that was unusual. So we settled back into our routine. I went into the study to clean out the grate, before my father locked up for the night, and blow me if the replacement bananas wasn't gone again!" She looked at each of us, her dark brown eyes wide and serious. "And that's when I heard it – *the ghost!*"

"Ghost!" I exclaimed.

"Yes, sir. I heard it in the study. It started with a faint sound, like a wailing, but then it got louder, coming nearer." Maisie's cheeks had lost their flush and were now pale. Her hands had begun to shake. "It was like a voice – no words. Just a moan, like what Mr. Evans the rector says – a soul in torment. I don't mind telling you gentlemen, I screamed and ran right out of the house. You would 'ave and all if you'd heard it."

That her distress was genuine was only too evident. I prepared her a very weak tonic while she recovered, and she drank it gratefully.

"My dear," said Holmes in a gentle tone, "I think you misunderstand the nature of our work. Dr. Watson and I investigate crimes in the real world. We apprehend criminals who are very much alive. Matters of a supernatural character are well out of our sphere," he smiled. "More in the field of Watson's literary friend, Sir Arthur Conan Doyle."

"Oh, I wrote to him first, sir, but he wrote back and said it wasn't important enough and that I should engage you."

Holmes *harummphed*.

"Then I saw in the newspaper you was in Camford. I have told my parents that I'm not going back in that house until that ghost is removed. I turned in my notice and I am staying with friends of my parents." She rung her hands in anxiety. "They are my mum and dad, and I am frightened for them. I know something terrible is going to happen, I just do." She fished around in her handbag and drew out an envelope. I could see money inside. "I have taken my savings out so I can pay you. Please, I am ever so worried for my parents."

She put the envelope on the table in front of her, but Holmes pushed it gently back. "I am sorry, Miss Cooper, but this case lies beyond the limit of my expertise. We cannot help you. If you think there is real danger toward your parents, you should go to the local police, though I don't know what they could do to help."

The young woman nodded. I could see tears forming at the corner of her eyes.

"There, there, my dear," I said, patting her shoulder reassuringly. "I'm sure that there is a rational explanation for all of this, and that no one in your household is in any real peril. In any event, a ghost with a taste for bananas is unlikely to pose much of a problem for anyone."

She sniffed and nodded, still holding back the tears. She reached out for her envelope, but as she did so caught sight of the letter underneath it. It was *R*'s missive to Dorak.

"Oh, you know the professor then?"

Holmes head whipped round. "What do you mean? This letter is signed '*R*'."

"Yes, sir, but that's the professor's handwriting. I'd know it anywhere. He's a Regis Professor. They're always addressed by the first letter of their title. It's like an old varsity tradition. *R* is Professor Owen."

The look on Holmes face was a picture. "Well, Watson, that serves me right for ignoring centuries of scholastic tradition. *Omnia causa Fiunt*," he muttered under his breath.

"Miss Cooper we are taking your case."

It was only with great reluctance that Mr. Cooper the butler allowed us entry into Professor Owen's household. My friend's reputation and a mention of the police were forceful arguments, but at the last it was the earnestness of Holmes's entreaty that made the difference.

"Mr. Cooper, let me assure you that I do not say this lightly: I firmly believe that the life of your master is in imminent danger."

And so we gained entrance.

Still clearly uncertain, Mr. Cooper followed us round as Holmes inspected every room in the large mansion, from garret to cellar. In fact, the whole family, and even Jimmy the handyman, accompanied him. The cellar was situated well below ground, a voluminous storage space, albeit smelling of damp. Holmes examined every inch with a magnifying glass and looked carefully into every dark corner.

"The foundation and walls here are stone, yet the house itself is brick," commented Holmes. "However, I noted evidence of an older structure in some of the pillars and ceiling supports on the ground floor."

"Indeed, sir," replied the taciturn butler. He swept a thin raft of hair back across his otherwise-bald head. "The building was an old priory, closed by the eighth Henry. It was left to fall into wrack and ruin, but then bought up. What was left standing was incorporated into a new building. There have been any number of improvements over the centuries, Professor Owen being the latest to add extensions to the house, and only recently."

The beam from Holmes's pocket torch picked out the shiny copper of new gas pipes running along the junction between ceiling and wall, another of the professor's additions.

"Is it possible to trace the lines of the old priory?" Holmes asked, but the butler shook his head.

We made our way up to the professor's study once more. Here Holmes shooed everyone out, but they clustered at the door peering in as he again explored the ground with his magnifier. The study was a reasonably sized room. A large desk opposite a fireplace and bookshelves lined all four walls. Holmes tapped here and there with the head of his cane, evidently sounding out the shelves and wood-panelled walls for hidden doors and secret passages, but there was nothing. A pair of French windows looked out onto the lawn beyond. Holmes tested them, but they were securely fastened. He scraped up dust from the sill and scrutinised it on his forefinger.

"I take it these are locked at night?" he asked.

Mr. Cooper nodded. "I do the rounds each evening before retiring. I check that all windows and door are fastened tight."

In the centre of the room, a circular table held stacks of books and sheafs of handwritten notes. In the middle was the fruit bowl that had so disturbed Masie.

"That's where the bananas were, sir," she said, peeping over her mother's shoulder. Holmes examined the fruit bowl carefully from every side before picking it up to inspect the base.

"A fruit bowl," he said matter-of-factly. "Just a fruit bowl. Miss Cooper, you say you heard your ghost from in here? Will you show me where you were standing?"

With great reluctance, Masie came up to the table. "I had been cleaning out the grate, and laying the fire for the morning. Then I'd come over to the table and I noticed the bananas was gone again." She looked around, her eyes widening in apprehension. "Then I started to hear it – the voice – getting louder and louder. I was proper terrified, sir, so I screamed and scarpered."

"Did any of you hear this ghost?"

The knot of people at the door shook their heads. "I'm afraid my daughter is a little overly sensitive," said Mr. Cooper, with a stern but not unkindly look.

"She was always so, sir," Mrs. Cooper interjected. "Always seeing things or hearing things as really wasn't there."

Mr. Cooper hesitated a moment, but then informed us. "There is long tradition of the house being haunted, sir. Not surprising really, given the age and history of the property, but we deliberately did not inform Maisie of this in order not to over-excite her."

"And this spirit has never troubled you?" asked my friend again.

"No, sir, and we have been here some ten years or more. Not so much as a rattled chain."

"But there is a ghost though," young Jimmy suddenly piped up. "I seen it!"

The Coopers looked at him in astonishment. "Don't be so foolish lad," said Mr. Cooper reprovingly.

"But it's true, sir, I did! I come in here Tuesday night to refill the coal scuttle, an' I looks out at the French windows, and the ghost is there. An old monk in a grey habit, and its cowl pulled up close. I could see its face, pale and deathlike. It looked straight at me."

With her hand raised to her mouth, Maisie asked in a quiet voice, "Whatever did you do?"

"I did what you did, Miss Masie. I scarpered quick-like."

"Why did you not say anything?" asked Cooper.

"What? And seem like a fool? Not me, sir." Then, realising what he'd said, he looked sheepishly down at his feet. "Sorry Miss Maisie, begging you pardon."

Further enquiry was forestalled by a ringing from the front door. Cooper excused himself and went to deal with it. Holmes now turned his attention to the table on which the fruit bowl stood. On his hands and knees he examined the carpet around the table legs. As Cooper re-entered the room, he had turned his attention to the chandelier above the table.

"It would seem, gentlemen, that your fears are now irrelevent," the butler said loudly. He held up a telegram. "It is from the professor. He has successfully conducted his business in London and will be home on the evening train. Consequently, gentlemen, I must ask you to leave. We have much to prepare before the master's return, and no further time for ghosts, poorly behaved fruit, or any other nonsense. I am sure you gentlemen will forgive us."

With that, our tenuous welcome in Professor Owen's establishment was very definitely at an end.

Leaving Maisie to make her tearful way to her temporary lodgings, Holmes and I walked back slowly in the direction of The Chequers.

"The return of the professor would seem to prove that there is no real concern for his life. Perhaps the events at Dorak's were just a series of unfortunate coincidences," I opined.

"Not a bit of it," said Holmes with unusual vehemence. "The telegram is a fraud."

"How can you know that?"

"Because I caused it to be sent."

At my look of astonishment, Holmes took my elbow and steered me towards a side road. "Are you up for a little breaking and entering? Tonight we must be in Professor Owen's study before darkness falls. We must give the impression that he is at home and at work behind closed doors and drawn blinds."

"But why?"

"Because Watson, if my theory is correct, an attempt will be made on his life – tonight. We will return to the hotel, partake of a light early supper, and arm ourselves appropriately."

"But what of the professor?" I asked. "What if he returns suddenly?"

"I very much doubt that he will return. I'm certain the professor is no longer in the country."

So it was at dusk that Holmes and I clambered over the wall at the bottom of Professor Owen's garden and made our way cautiously to the French windows. Back at The Chequers, our curtains were drawn and we had to all intents and purposes retired early for the evening. The landlord, a willing ally, went up to our rooms at odd intervals to move around in front of the windows, lending to the impression we were at home.

"Now," Holmes whispered, "if I am correct, we will find these doors have been tampered with. There was the faintest trace of sawdust along the sill." He felt around the edges of the frame and with a grunt of satisfaction took hold of the horizontal slats running along the centre of both doors. He pulled upwards and, to my surprise, both doors swung noiselessly outwards.

"Both French windows open normally," he whispered, "but when locked, they can both be opened as a single door from the garden side. I suspected something as much when I examined the hinges." We pushed through the curtains, closing the door behind us.

The study was brightly lit, a fire burned merrily in the grate, and a cold supper accompanied by a decanter had been left on the desk. Holmes's telegram had in reality contained instructions for Mr. Cooper to prepare the house as if the professor was returning, and then retire in good order for the night. The family were under strict orders not to come downstairs or interfere in any way.

I had been enjoined to strict silence once we were in the study, but I could barely supress a gasp. In the fruit bowl on the centre table were two rather blackened bananas, the skin of one of them had already split, leaving a faint tang on the air. They hadn't been there when we searched the house.

Holmes nodded in evident satisfaction.

I took a comfortable leather chair near the fireplace, helping myself to a peg from the decanter. Holmes sat behind the desk, engrossed in one of Professor Owen's own books taken from his bookshelves. My old service revolver rested in my pocket, and I took comfort from its weight, but when I had heard Holmes describing our main means of defence for the evening, quite frankly I thought he had taken leave of his senses.

On the table beside me lay – a damp towel!

"Not a word more," was all he had said. "All will become clear in due course."

And so we began our dreary vigil.

I must confess I had started to drop off when the chimes at midnight from the hall clock brought me awake with a start. Holmes was staring straight at me, his face expressionless. I steeled myself. At one o'clock the hall clock chimed once more, and again at two o'clock. As the second note faded, the house became silent again, but now there was another sensation. An ethereal expectation seemed to fill the air. I became convinced something was about to happen. Holmes noted my state of heightened alert. As one we took hold of the corners of our damp cloths.

Then I heard it. Just as Maisie had described. A sound, like a wailing soul in torment. It rose in pitch, then fell, then rose again, and all the time it appeared to be getting nearer. My hair stood on end. I think at that moment I could well have abandoned my disbelief in the spirit world, so uncanny yet so immediate was that awful wailing.

"Holmes," I whispered through gritted teeth, "what is that? It is almost upon us."

By way of reply he enjoined me to silence, but pointed at the chandelier. It took me a moment to realise his meaning. One of the *faux* candles, in reality lit by gas, was slowly leaning over to one side, exposing the gas pipe beyond. The awful sound was suddenly magnified, and before I could utter another word something emerged from the pipe.

It was a giant flying insect, a hornet I thought, but larger than any I had ever seen. It flew straight at my head, I ducked swinging the damp towel above me to fend it off. It veered away and made for the ceiling where it did a rapid circle of the room.

"For mercy's sake, Watson, don't let it sting you!" cried Holmes. The enraged hornet made another pass at me and then at Holmes, who tried to use his damp towel like a whip, snapping it as the damnable creature sped past. He missed, but managed to anger the hornet even more. It buzzed around his head, making attempts to strike at his exposed neck and face.

I shouted and waved my towel in an attempt to distract it, but it was no good. It was determined to sting Holmes.

I had a moment of inspiration. As it flew past me, still trying to penetrate Holmes's increasingly wild defences, its wicked looking stinger was facing me. I opened up my damp cloth and tossed it as a sheet at the distracted hornet, now less than a foot away from me. It sensed something and turned towards me, but at the same moment Holmes copied my manoeuvre, throwing his open towel a little higher. As the creature moved away from my towel Holmes's caught it. Struggling and buzzing furiously it was borne down to the tabletop.

"Quick Watson – use the butt of your pistol. Kill it."

I fumbled in my pocket and using the revolver as a hammer I clubbed the writhing creature, once, twice and then a third time. It became still.

Gingerly I pulled the two cloths away. I must say that I felt rather poor about having to kill it that way.

"Don't feel too bad. It was either us or it. Look at its stinger."

I bent to take a closer look. Something was attached to the hornet's sting. It was an artificial extension of some sort, coated in a brown substance.

"A fine example of the Asian giant hornet, *Vespa mandarinia*," said Holmes. "It will give you a very nasty sting, but a healthy adult is unlikely to die from it. However, note the appendage to its stinger. While at Dorak's, I noted that the cages of a number of venomous species were empty, including that of *Dendrobates azureus*, the so called poison-dart frog of South America. Its skin secretes a deadly toxin for which there is no known antidote."

I shuddered. "Who would do such a thing?"

"Who indeed?"

But there was one more surprise in store for us. As I opened the curtains I gave a cry of horror. Staring directly at me from the other side of the French Windows was a cowled monkish figure, its pale face shadowy and indistinct, but looking straight at me. Holmes turned, instantly grasped the situation, and made a leap for the window, but the figure stretched out an arm and touched part of the frame. It turned and disappeared into the darkness beyond. Holmes furiously worked the handles, but it was no use they were fastened shut.

"My God, Holmes, what was that? I don't think I can cope with more horrors tonight."

"There is little point in giving chase now," said Holmes resignedly. "He will be long gone."

"But what was that?"

"Not *what. Who*. Someone was sent to retrieve the hornet after it had done its grisly work. The creatures are partial to fruit, especially rotting bananas. It would be a simple matter to recover the hornet while it gorged itself."

"You suspected something like this?"

"You recall the copper gas piping in the cellar? I noticed a new tap and joint had been added very recently, probably at the time that the professor was extending his property. I suspected the addition was to allow something to be introduced into the piping, but I was unsure as to what. A clear instance of the damp towel being mightier than the sword, eh?

"Pour the both of us a stiff drink, there's a good fellow. I think we have earned it tonight. We have learned one important fact, though: The enemy doesn't have Owen, and they don't know where he is. If he did, he wouldn't have attempted this rather desperate manoeuvre. We are still one step ahead of him."

"How so?" I asked, surprised.

"Because I have a shrewd suspicion that I know where the good professor is." He turned to me. "Watson, we must make our next stop Prague. The race is now on to find Lowenstein, because there we will most assuredly find Professor Lloyd Owen.

It was a few days later that Holmes and I sat in the office of gendarme-police Captain Jan Macek in Prague's police headquarters. Its grandiose and ornate imperial frontage made the London police stations with which we were familiar seem drab by comparison. The captain was an earnest young man in an immaculate dark military-style uniform. He was well built, and had that suppressed energy that I envied in the younger men I met. A small, clipped moustache turned up at the corners with geometric precision finished his professional appearance. Did I detect the faintest hint of a scar on one cheek?

"We were informed of your presence in Bohemia the moment you crossed the border, Herr Holmes," he said in a tonally flat, but otherwise near-perfect, English. "I received a message from the Interior Ministry the following morning." And he passed over a letter with a crest that took up almost half the page. "We are to provide you with any and all assistance you may wish. You will see it is signed by the very highest authority." He gave a small smile. "It seems you have very powerful friends in Bohemia, Herr Holmes. But then, of course your reputation precedes you. We assumed you are working on a case? Following a lead?"

Holmes gave him a full history of the affair, leaving out only the names of the two professors. Captain Macek looked up at the mention of Dorak's name, and a frown of concern creased his brow as Holmes began to explain the significance of Lowenstein. At the end of Holmes's explanation, the captain walked to the door and said something to a subordinate beyond. As he reseated himself, an older uniformed man brought in a thick buff-coloured dossier which he laid on the desk with a crisp salute. I wondered how a man as young as Jan Macek could have risen so quickly through the ranks. Perhaps his family was well connected? Later, we came to realise his rank was won entirely through ability.

"We have been observing Lowenstein carefully for some time now, intercepting his mail and watching those who come and go from his home. You have confirmed my suspicions, Herr Holmes." With that, he passed another document across. I recognised the wording. It was a facsimile of Holmes original letter to Lowenstein, sent at the conclusion of the Presbury case.

"Lowenstein first appeared in Prague perhaps eighteen months ago. It isn't clear. He is very reclusive and has no connections with the German University at Prague, or any of the medical or scientific societies in the city. He doesn't frequent any of the intellectual salons. The few medical people who have met him and whom we have been able to interview speak highly of his knowledge. He doesn't seem to be – How do you English say? – a *duck*?"

"A *quack*!" I responded.

"*Ach, ja*, just so."

"Why have you been watching him?" Holmes asked.

"His so called 'Elixir of Rejuvenation' has caused quite a disturbance among many of the older and more powerful men in the city, even members of the imperial government in Vienna. The Office of Internal Security has to be aware of anything that might be a potential threat to the safety of our civic and national leaders."

"His elixir is widely distrusted by the English medical establishment," I said. "He has refused to release his formula or make clear its source."

Captain Macek nodded. "And from what you have told me about the formula, this distrust is justified. I have heard more than enough to convince me that Professor Lowenstein is a potential threat to the stability of the state. I think it is time we acted."

In short order, Holmes and I found ourselves sitting with Captain Macek and a number of armed gendarmes in the back of a motorised paddy waggon, part of a raid on Lowenstein's home. Their long military greatcoats and spiked steel helmets were imposing, as were the sabres they wore at their sides and the rifles they held rigidly in front of them.

"You gentlemen are armed?" Captain Macek asked and we nodded. "Good, but please only use your weapons in self-defence. This is an internal matter for the Bohemian Police."

Holmes nodded in assent. In fact, as we pulled up, Holmes indicated that he and I should stay in the waggon until the raid was over. This we did. After five minutes, a rather crestfallen young Macek returned to announce. "We are too late. The professor has eluded us."

Lowenstein's house was narrow, baroque in style, four stories tall, and part of a long continuous terrace that curved out of sight down a gentle cobbled slope. From the street, five steps led up to a front door, and another set of steps led down to a sunken basement. We were in the Jewish quarter of the city. Not far away was the Old Jewish Cemetery, and the Staronova Synagogue, which my guidebook told me was the oldest in all of Europe.

"The professor occupied the basement and the first two floors," the Captain informed us. "His reception and consulting rooms are on the ground floor. The upper floor is his dressing room and bathroom, and his bedroom which is at the back of the apartment. The basement is some kind of laboratory. It seems he lived alone, and kept no staff or man-servant."

We climbed to the upper level. A small dressing room with a window looked out onto the main street. A door led off to the bathroom. Holmes inspected both, but found nothing of interest. The bedroom, at the back of the apartment, was reached by a darkened corridor. I didn't need to be a detective to recognise all the signs of a hasty departure. Clothes were scattered everywhere, strewn across floor and bed. On the bed was an open suitcase containing clothing, but it had evidently been abandoned only half-full.

Captain Macek waved his hand in encouragement to Holmes, who needed no second invitation. With his glass in hand, he moved around the room, scrutinising every inch of the chaotic apartment. In between the wardrobe and the window, he dropped to his knees, examining the floorboards carefully and giving a grunt of satisfaction. From the top of the wardrobe, we were greeted with a sigh of approval, and from the bed and suitcase a nod of appreciation.

"Yes," he muttered more to himself than to us. "I think I have the gist of it. Lowenstein was certainly preparing to leave, but he was in no rush. Then his preparations were unexpectedly interrupted. After which, he made haste to depart. He wasn't alone, so I will surmise that he received a visitor who precipitated his disordered retreat."

Captain Macek and I exchanged a look. Holmes caught it and chuckled. "You see, gentlemen, but you do not observe. It is a fault I've never cured in my friend, Watson."

Charmingly, the gendarme captain stared at his boots, embarrassed on my behalf.

"The evidence is before you," continued Holmes. "And to the trained eye it tells a clear story."

I smiled reassuringly at our Bohemian colleague, knowing my friend too well to rise to the bait. Captain Macek looked on, bemused.

Holmes began his exposition, as I knew full well he was going to. "Professor Lowenstein is much in need of a cleaning lady, but fortunately for us, he doesn't have one. The dust in the room is an open book.

"The suitcase has been taken down from atop the wardrobe. Its lid has a liberal coating of dust, so it has been up there some time. It was placed here on the bed and the professor began to pack his clothes into it. You see how those garments at the bottom of the case are neatly folded? At this point, he isn't unduly hurried in his packing. But then something occurs. Now do you see how these remaining shirts are draped over the side of the case? Their creases have been disturbed and show they were hastily removed in a larger pile, of which these few remain abandoned. And look here – a partly crumpled shirt on the floor.

"Now I draw your attention to the space between the wardrobe and the window. Again, the dust comes to our aid. A valise has rested here. You can still see its marks. Since the valise isn't in the room, nor are the missing clothes from the suitcase, I suggest that suddenly he began to hastily re-pack his garments into the smaller bag."

"But why?" I asked.

"Easier to carry," was Holmes's reply, "if one is being hunted."

"I surmise," he continued, "that someone came to warn him. Here – do you see the boot marks in the dust? Wherever we look, we find the impression of a narrow and square-toed boot, which I take to be the professor. However, in one place, here, a wider and more-rounded imprint."

"A second man!" exclaimed Captain Macek.

Holmes nodded. "Yes. He stands here companionly close to Lowenstein. I surmise this new arrival precipitated a more hasty departure. There is nothing more to learn here, and the day rooms will tell us little. Let us examine the basement."

The basement rooms were less elegant than those above. The ceiling rosettes and gasoliers lacked the floral elaborations I had noted in the floors above. Coving and cornices were much plainer, or absent, and the floors were flagged with stone rather than wooden floorboards and carpets. I quickly surmised that these had been the kitchens and utility rooms for a much-larger household, before it had been broken up into separate apartments.

We stood in Lowenstein's laboratory.

That he had converted this to his workplace was clear. A large table stood in the centre of the room, while the walls were entirely taken up with shelving or smaller tables. Two large ceramic sinks stood below a window looking up toward the street level. A brass microscope was stationed on a table nearby so its mirror could catch the light. Every available surface was littered with scientific equipment, and every imaginable variety of glass jar, bottle, and beaker. Most were filled with coloured liquids and powders. A Liebig condenser stood on a shelf connected by a hose to some coloured liquid in a vessel on the shelf above. Another hose, connected to its base, emptied an entirely different coloured liquid into a jar on the shelf below.

Holmes's face resembled a child in a sweet shop. He rushed around examining everything.

As I looked around, something struck me as odd, but before I could bring it clearly to mind, Holmes was speaking.

"Note gentlemen: No dust in here. The professor kept the true focus of his life scrupulously clean."

It was true – not a speck of dust anywhere, except chalk dust. Over in one corner three blackboards had been arranged next to each other, a larger one in the middle and two smaller ones on each side, all standing on easels. Holmes pounced, dropping to his knees, magnifying glass in hand.

"Capital, capital," he announced. "Watson, is there a paper block and a pencil on the table?"

I looked around. "Yes."

"Is the top sheet a blank one?"

"Yes."

"Good. Now rub the pencil lightly over the top sheet."

Recognising his intention immediately, I gently ran the pencil backwards and forwards over the page. The impression of what had been written on the previous sheet was visible in places, but the whole text was not.

"I can make out a few chemical symbols. I'd say it's part of a formula." Then I realised what had been nagging at me when we first entered. Not a single jar or bottle had a label to identify its contents. There were none of the copious notes lying about that scientists normally take to record their experiments. It would be impossible to reconstruct anything from Lowenstein's laboratory. I said as much to Holmes who, still on his knees, nodded.

"Quite deliberate. Now look here." He pointed at the chalk dust in front of the central blackboard. "Many jumbled impressions of the professor's square toed boot, all pressed into each other. This is Lowenstein working normally in front of the blackboard. But see here: Square toe and round toe stand together in front of the board, and do you see how they are picked out in sharp silhouette? Chalk dust falls either side of their boots as they stand side by side.

"They were wiping the blackboard clean," ventured Captain Macek.

Holmes nodded. "I suspect Lowenstein had been working on his formula, refining it. He and his visitor transferred the formula to paper and then wiped the boards clean."

"Now then – " Still on his hands and knees, he crawled 'round the edges of the room, examining the flagstones in front of each cupboard or table. "Yes, I thought so. A faint trace of chalk dust here. Captain, would you please have your men move this cabinet to one side?"

It proved surprisingly easy to move, as it had been cleverly hinged to the wall. Beyond it a tunnel.

"Not a foolproof escape route," said Holmes, "but enough to buy Lowenstein and his friend a few precious minutes. When we arrived, I noted there was nowhere in the front of these houses for domestic deliveries to be made. I suspected that all the houses would have to share a basement tunnel connecting their kitchens to a common entrance somewhere further down the street."

The captain barked orders at his men and electric pocket torches appeared. With two of the armed gendarmes taking the lead, we followed the tunnel. It sloped downwards. In a few moments, we stood in the basement of the next house. Here the tunnel was open, and both the passageway and the basement itself were obviously used for storage. Boxes and bails were piled up, neglected in every nook and cranny. It was the same for the next five or six houses. In places, a narrow squared boot and a wider round one had left faint impressions in the dust. The tunnel turned a corner. A barred metal gate opened into a small enclosed and cobbled courtyard. I noticed a series of metal rings set into the walls where the horses that pulled the delivery drays could be tied.

The courtyard opened onto a street, downhill and around the corner from that of Lowenstein's. The sudden appearance of armed gendarmes caused a slight panic amongst the passers-by.

"Hmm," said Holmes. "Our birds are well and truly flown."

As we made our way back to Lowenstein's laboratory, I ventured the question that had been uppermost in my mind.

"This visitor who so disturbed Lowenstein: It was Professor Lloyd Owen, wasn't it?"

"We have no evidence of who it was," Holmes replied, perhaps more sharply than he intended, "and you know my views on speculating without sufficient facts," I took no hurt, as I knew full well his words were born of frustration.

Back in Lowenstein's laboratory, Holmes looked around once more. On the table, a small leather case attracted his attention. He moved over to the window to examine in the light, and then arranged one side of it on the microscope stage.

"Have you found something?" I asked.

He pointedly ignored my question. "Perhaps we should approach the problem from a different direction. We know that one use of Lowenstein's formula involves substances from the body of a Himalayan Langur monkey. We also know that the formula can be adapted to other primates.

"So then, from where is he getting his raw materials? Where is the source of these poor creatures?" He looked over to Captain Macek. "Is there an animal emporium in the city? Is there a Prague equivalent of Dorak?" But Captain Macek shook his head.

"Well then a zoo, or zoological gardens? An ape or monkey house?"

Again the good captain shook his head. "There are plans to build one. However . . . ." He trailed off with a shrug.

"But Lowenstein may have had agents in other cities?" I ventured. "Most of the capitals of Europe have zoos. Perhaps he has recruited unscrupulous animal keepers to send him his supplies."

"A good thought, Watson, but think of the difficulties. The keepers would need to be trained in extracting whatever it is the formula requires. Everything would have to be done in the utmost secrecy. The animals would have to show no ill effects. No, too impractical."

Captain Macek nodded. "Lowenstein certainly has a network of agents in all the major European cities, but our investigation shows he isn't receiving a stream of parcels from abroad. Rather, it is he who was despatching his serum out to his agents."

"So the ingredients are coming to him somehow. I fear I have underestimated the professor." Holmes invited us over to look at the leather case.

"Notice the thumb print," he directed.

On one of the sides was the oval impression of a thumb. The ridges and whorls clearly discernible.

"Of what use is Lowenstein's thumb print now?" asked Captain Macek.

"It is not Lowenstein's print, "Holmes replied. "In fact, it is not even human. The thumb is too short, and the whorl patterns less dense than that of a human. This is the print of a chimpanzee."

Captain Macek and I looked on perplexed for a moment, but then the lightning of inspiration struck us simultaneously, and in unison we said, "*A circus!*"

On our return to Captain Macek's office, he began enquiring as to what circuses were in the habit of visiting Prague on a regular basis. There were a few, but only one of them boasted anthropoid apes: *Doctor Liu's Travelling Extravaganza* had both gorillas and chimpanzees. Holmes forestalled any further research by handing us a gaudily coloured handbill that he picked up of the street.

"As I expected," he asserted. "They are in town."

The handbill showed a ferocious gorilla rattling the bars of its cage, while a scantily clad circus damsel cowered before it, one hand thrown up to her face and her mouth open in a scream. Behind, a dashing young man in a pith helmet looked on helplessly. To one side, a smaller image showed several chimpanzees in waiter's uniforms serving at table. A banner next to the image announced something in Bohemian Czech. Captain Macek translated: "*Darwin's Tea Party*", and in a smaller font below it "*Nothing to fear in the Darwin idea*".

Captain Macek insisted on a change of clothing. Even our day-to-day tweeds apparently announced us as foreigners and tourists. Suitably attired in Bohemian attire, we travelled to a large open park surrounded by forest to the southeast of the city. Here we found the circus in full swing. I was accustomed to English travelling circuses, but they didn't prepare me for Liu's Extravaganza. It was vast, spread over acres, with every kind of act that one could imagine. It boasted at least five big-top tents, each in its own compound, and each highlighting a different style of entertainment. I can no longer recall all of them, but I seem to remember a rather daring high-wire act was in one, and an animal act with lions and tigers in another.

The circus was also packed. Huge crowds wandered in and out of each compound. Clowns worked the hubbub, bringing excited gasps from adults and children alike as they performed magic tricks or terrified their audiences with fire-eating displays. Everywhere there was noise, colour, and movement. It was a veritable assault on all of the senses – so much so that I almost walked under the trunk of a passing elephant. Holmes pulled me back by my collar and I saw an Indian face in a howdah look down anxiously.

"Really, Watson, be more careful," announced Holmes tersely. Then, pointing with his stick, he directed my attention to the elephant's side. Suspended from the howdah was an advertising board. The gorilla was once more menacing the young lady.

"It seems the main event of the afternoon is about to start in the anthropoid enclosure," said Captain Macek. "We have just time to secure a seat."

As he spoke, a young man in a long coat and hat brushed past him and said something quietly in Czech. "Ah, excellent," announced the captain. "Our men have identified Lowenstein entering the anthropoid marquee with another man." He smiled at Holmes. "The game is afoot, Herr Holmes?"

"Quite so captain, quite so," Holmes replied with a terse smile. We pushed our way through the crowds and, at the turnstile, the captain showed his identification and secured us immediate entry. I noticed a number of young men standing nearby, gendarmes in plain clothes, to whom Captain Macek issued terse instructions. They disappeared to various positions inside and outside the big-top.

Inside the tent, a circular central ring was surrounded by tiers of bench seating. A curtained-off exit led from the sandy ring to whatever hidden treasures were secreted backstage. Inside the tent, it was as noisy as it had been outside. Excited children squealed and shouted at one another while admonishing parents called after them anxiously. Pervading it all was that distinctive odour of animals. It reminded me of the aroma filling Dorak's establishment.

"Lowenstein and his companion are down there on the front row," said Captain Macek, directing our gaze. I recognised Lloyd Owen immediately from photographs in his Camford study. Lowenstein was taller, bigger than I had expected for a scientist, more like a rugger prop. He had a broad open face with a substantial moustache. His thinning hair was combed across his head to emphasise a wide scholarly looking forehead.

Lowenstein was constantly looking about, peering over his shoulder, for what I did not know, but he had the demeanour of a hunted man. Owen said something, but the professor just brushed his words aside with a curt shake of the head.

"Careful, Watson – don't make eye contact," said Holmes, and I looked away quickly. Rather cleverly, the good captain had positioned us behind two large families on a joint outing. A casual observer would assume that we belonged to their party.

I was about to ask Holmes what our next move was when the crowd became quiet. The ringmaster had emerged from the curtained-off area. He began a short welcome in Czech, French, German, and – to my surprise – in English.

"My Lords, Ladies, gentlemen, boys, and girls: Welcome to Doctor Liu's Travelling Extravaganza! This afternoon we have a special treat for you! Let us transport you to the wilds of darkest Africa and a lonely hunter's camp in the heart of the jungle . . . ."

As he spoke, the lights went out, and there was some movement in the ring. I felt Holmes grow tense, but as the lights came up Lowenstein and Owen were still in their seats. The three of us let out a collective sigh of relief.

In the ring, a small scenario had been assembled. An empty cage on wheels stood next to an untended fire. All around were trees and bushes. The audience gasped as a huge snake slithered across the camp site and out of sight.

It was a scene out of Du Chaillu. With no warning, a huge gorilla seemed to materialise out of nowhere inside the cage. The audience gasped. It roared and beat its savage breast with its mighty fists. The audience recoiled, and one or two children began to wail in fright. The gorilla charged the bars and shook them with all its strength. The audience were mesmerised and terrified in equal measure.

Then the mighty anthropoid attacked the bars of the cage door, and in an instant it had shaken them open and was free! The audience let out a howl, and I must admit that I too was taken up in sympathy with their alarm.

Those in the front row benches began to push back against those behind. Then, without warning, the giant creature leapt over the low wall of the ring and was amongst the crowd. There was a shrieking of fear, and to my horror the beast pulled a woman out from her seat and flung her over its shoulder. I felt myself reaching for my pistol when Holmes pulled me down.

"Not so hasty, old friend. Observe."

The beast was back at the campfire and unceremoniously dropped the hapless woman onto the ground. It turned its back on her, and in a trice she was up and making her escape, straight toward Lowenstein and Owen. She flung herself into Lowenstein's lap and wrapped her arms around him.

"Oh, sir, I beg you, save me, save me!" she cried out, loud enough for the whole audience to hear.

Before Lowenstein could do anything, the enormous brute had recaptured her. Owen was standing looking on, horrified – but Lowenstein sat unruffled, with a slight smile on his face. Just then there was a rifle shot, and a tall young man with a very square jaw wearing a pith helmet and flared jodhpurs appeared from the foliage. The gorilla beat its chest and then fled off into the audience while the hunter gave chase. There was of course pandemonium. Finally, the hunter cornered the brute and, producing a bull whip, began to manoeuvre the creature back toward the cage. The audience cheered when the beast was secured once again.

As if on cue, the ringmaster appeared, and once he had restored order he invited the man and the woman to the centre of the ring, and to the audience's horror, unlocked the cage and helped a now very docile gorilla to stand next to the hunter and the woman. With a sweep of its hand, the gorilla reached up and pulled off what was clearly a mask – it was a human in a suit. All three bowed to thunderous applause.

"Holmes, you knew?" I asked.

He nodded. "Nevertheless, it was very well done. I presume payment was made – either when the lights went out, or when the woman threw herself at Lowenstein. The latter I think more likely."

I was about to question Holmes when the ringmaster was calling for attention. It seemed our tickets gave us exclusive entrance to their authentic and traditional African *Biergarten*, with lemonade available for the young ones. Holmes's eyebrows shot up at the mention of "traditional", but we nonetheless followed Lowenstein and Owen into an adjacent tent. Making ourselves inconspicuous, we three sat at one end of a long table while Lowenstein and Owen took up a small, reserved table for two.

To my surprise, a chimpanzee in a waiter's costume appeared at our table, holding a menu card and a pencil. I made to pinch its nose and force the human within to remove the mask, but Holmes stopped me."

"I wouldn't if I were you, Watson. These apes are real."

I was flabbergasted. Holmes marked three beers on the card and returned it to the ape, who made for the bar where human barmen poured out the drinks.

"I read in Professor Owen's book that Mr. Darwin considers chimpanzees to be our nearest evolutionary cousins," said Holmes. "It is degrading to see them so shamefully used." I could only nod in agreement.

Elsewhere, other chimps were taking orders or delivering glasses of beer, or plates of food and lemonade.

"Look at Lowenstein and Owen's order," said Holmes in a hushed whisper. As their glasses of beer arrived, I could see what looked like a small leather case on the tray. It was identical to that in the laboratory. "Payment has been received, and now delivery is being made."

"The mystery component for the serum?" I queried.

He nodded, and turning to me added in a low whisper. "These poor brutes are likely to be providing the 'serum of anthropoid' that Lowenstein could not at that time provide for Presbury."

Holmes was right. Presbury had been given a serum containing some essence of the Himalayan Langur monkey. Lowenstein had bemoaned the lack of the more appropriate anthropoid essence.

"I presume the circus was not then in town," muttered Holmes.

Captain Macek was not listening. His attention was wholly focused on Lowenstein and Owen, who were standing and making as if to leave. In the busy tent, no one took any notice. Captain Macek was in the act of raising his police whistle to his lips when Holmes put out a hand to stop him. Three rather unsavoury looking toughs blocked the exit and were pointedly staring at Lowenstein and Owen. They were short and powerfully built Oriental men. I looked over toward the tent's entrance. Three more fellows were stationed there.

"The enemy is showing his hand," said Holmes. "Now, Captain: Summon your men".

Macek's whistle let out a single shrill note. In a heartbeat, the tent was silent and all eyes were now on the standing Captain who, pointing at the two scientists, said loudly in Czech, "Hold! You are both under arrest!"

Then mayhem broke out. Plainclothed gendarmes were barrelling into the tent, straight into the fists of the waiting toughs. Tables and benches were overturned. Women were screaming and trying to gather their children to safety while their husbands did their best to fend off the rolling fist-fights. Although the gendarmes outnumbered their opponents, they did not have the upper hand. The Oriental men were trained in some form of martial fighting technique and, by the number of policemen lying on the ground, it seemed the gendarmes were outmatched.

"Where is Lowenstein?" cried Holmes.

"Over there!" I said. Someone had opened one of the side walls of the tent to form an impromptu exit. Families were being evacuated through the opening, and I could see Lowenstein's tall frame just ducking under the canvas flap.

"They are getting away!" shouted Captain Macek. We forced our way through the struggling crowds. Outside, there was no sign of our quarry.

"There!" cried Holmes, arm upraised.

Perhaps fifty yards away, I could just make out Lowenstein being bundled into the back of a horse-drawn waggon by more of the rogues. Owen was nowhere to be seen. Captain Macek drew his revolver and fired two shots rapidly in the air. The intervening crowd froze.

"Everybody down!" he yelled, taking a bead on the rapidly disappearing waggon, but it was no use. The distance already too great for a revolver.

He swore with vehemence.

"And you have no idea who this mysterious opposition force is?" asked Captain Macek.

We sat once more in the good captain's office. Holmes was pacing up and down, much to the irritation of the Bohemian policeman, but he was too much in awe of his famous visitor to express his displeasure. Holmes had that effect on people.

"None whatsoever. I have become aware of them only recently, though their presence behind affairs is longer than that. They are everywhere and they are nowhere. They recruit from all walks of life. They pay no heed to class, culture, creed, or colour of skin. Unlike Professor Moriarty and his organisation, this is not a coming together of criminals for the sake of crime. This is different. I sense criminality is a means to an end, one weapon in a much larger arsenal."

"But to what end?" I interjected. "And who are their leaders?"

Holmes shrugged. "No one is prepared to talk. I suspect a single authority sitting at the centre of the web – whoever killed Lowenstein in Whitechapel – but it is useless to speculate."

We fell into an embarrassed silence. Truth be told, there was little we could do. Captain Macek's gendarmes were scouring the city, and police informers were being pressed to learn what they could of the shadowy group that had so effortlessly abducted Lowenstein and Owen. The few captures we had made at the circus had resolutely refused to talk, and no inducement or threat appeared to impress them. Holmes felt the frustration keenly, as did we all.

The silence was broken by the entry of a subordinate who placed a newspaper on the captain's desk. He looked over the headline and his lip curled in distaste.

"A development?" enquired Holmes.

"No," the captain exclaimed. "A distraction. A step backward. Are you familiar with the legend of the Golem?"

I shook my head, but Holmes nodded. "A Jewish legend from Old Prague. The Golem is a creature fashioned of clay and made in the image of a man. It is lifeless until a Rabbi with knowledge of secret kabbalistic rituals writes one of the sacred names of God on a piece of paper and inserts it into the Golem's mouth. Then it comes to life. It then serves its master, though it does not have the power of speech."

"Bravo, Herr Holmes," the captain replied. "The most famous version of the tale is that Rabbi Judah Loew created a Golem here in Prague in the sixteenth century to defend the Jews against attacks from Christians. In some versions of the story it was a benign protector, while in others a monster unable to be controlled."

"What has this Golem to do with us?" I asked.

"Nothing, but every now and again the story resurfaces. Usually a drunk, or perhaps someone of a nervous disposition, will jump at a shadow. Suddenly the Golem has returned. Last night, a woman passing the Old Jewish Cemetery claims to have been attacked by a Golem."

Our host dropped the newspaper on the desk in front of us. "The woman claims it leapt over the cemetery wall and confronted her. She is neither an imbiber, nor does she have a delicate constitution. Quite the contrary, she is a respected member of the Jewish community and appears very level-headed.

"If you are interested, you could interview her if you like. She is here now, giving her statement. It might prove an amusing distraction, and her English is very good."

Holmes nodded in assent, but I could tell he was holding something back. Holmes and I were escorted to another part of the building while Captain Macek continued with his duties.

Frau Hana Breznicky was a tall elderly woman. She wore a long dark coat and an old-fashioned hat with a very wide brim. She did indeed speak English well. She had worked as a lady's maid for an English family for eleven years. As we entered the interview room, I detected a slight tremor in her hands, but the eyes that retuned our gaze were steady and full of resolve. A bandage was wrapped around one side of her head. She had certainly had a bad fright, but it had not bested her.

"Oh, sir," she said in answer to a question from Holmes, "I was that afraid. I thought that the Good God had at last called me to his work. My thoughts were with my boy, his wife, and little Truda." At Holmes's prompting, she told her story one more time.

"I was walking up the lane past the cemetery. My boy, he lives in the next street on from the Old New Synagogue. It's an easy short-cut from my home. The wall in the lane is a high one, and I heard some commotion on the other side, but I thought it was just an animal.

"There are trees that grow in the cemetery, but their branches hang over the lane. One of them started shaking. I stopped and looked up. I screamed at what I saw there. Then the Golem swung down from the branch. It stood in front of me – no further away than you are. I say 'stood', but it was hunched over more like a monkey." At this, Holmes gave me a significant glance while Frau Breznicky threw up her hands, reliving the terrible moment.

"I thought it was going to kill me! I prayed out loud to the Good God to preserve me." And here she leaned forward, as if she was about to impart a secret. "Then I knew it was a Golem, and it was the Good God's own creature. It heard my words and it tried to speak to me, but it couldn't. It could not make the same sounds that God gave to men to praise His glory aloud."

I understood then that the strength I had detected in her came from an unshakeable faith.

"Then the officers came. I heard them coming around the corner. The Golem made a sound like a monkey makes and fled up the alleyway. I am afraid I passed out and struck my head on the cobbles."

"You say it tried to speak, but couldn't?" asked Holmes. "Are you sure?"

The old woman nodded. "Yes, it is so. It shaped its mouth to make the words, but they would not form. I could tell the frustration in its eyes. It was getting angry."

Holmes thanked her, and a gendarme led the courageous old soul out.

I turned to Holmes. "Are you thinking what I am thinking?

He nodded. "I suspected the timing was more than mere coincidence. Monstrous though it is, somehow Owen escaped capture and has recreated the serum of anthropoid from the supply he received at the circus. In the absence of a genuine Golem, there is no other explanation."

I agreed, although there was still the nagging memory of the ghostly prior I had seen in Camford.

"But why? Why would Owen experiment on himself? Surely what happened to Presbury was warning enough?"

"A zeal bordering almost on obsession," was Holmes's reply. "It isn't unusual with academics. Do you recall the book I was reading while we waited for the phantom monk in the professor's study?"

"Yes. It was one of Owen's own works."

"Quite so. It was most enlightening. While most scientists accept Darwinian evolution as a fact, there is heated debate about how it happens. Natural selection, Mr. Darwin's explanation, is no longer popular. Its detractors argue there isn't enough time for new species to evolve in many short jumps. They believe that new species can arise in one or two rapid leaps."

"They are called 'Saltationists'," I interrupted. I had kept up with some of the literature, as it occasionally appeared in *The British Medical Journal*.

"Indeed. They have the authority of a Dutch botanist called de Vries at their back. He has proven such leaps – 'mutations' he calls them – are clear in experiments with the evening primrose. It was all in Owen's book. I suspect the professor is trying to show that these mutations are real, and that they apply to human evolution as well as plants and animals. He is making himself into a human test subject."

I was astonished, and said as much to Holmes,

"Yes," he continued. "It does beggar belief, but there you have it. Academic obsession can be a dangerous path in many ways."

"But how does he intend to prove it?" I asked.

Holmes steepled his fingers in front of him. "You know how I loathe conjecture in the absence of facts. Well, let me break my own rule for once, since we will almost certainly never know the truth.

"From certain passages in Owen's book, I surmise that he believes Lowenstein and Presbury to have been wrong in their interpretation of the serum's effects. They believed it imparted the energetic character of the animal from which the elixir was drawn. I conjecture Owen believes the serum returns someone to an earlier state of evolutionary history – in this case, what Professor Haeckel of Jena has termed *Pithecanthropus alalus*, the ape-man without speech. I take the professor's book as my authority.

"He has turned himself into a living laboratory of proof for the mutation theory of evolution."

I sat quiet for a moment, trying to take in Holmes's words. It was quite fantastic. Eventually I was able to mumble, "The arrogance! The hubris of it!"

Holmes nodded. "As I have already remarked, 'When one tries to rise above nature, one is liable to fall below it'. There is an interesting juxtaposition here. On the one hand, the Golem needs a fragment of divinity to induce the spark of life, whereas *Pithecanthropus* is a creature of nature. Yet neither have the power of speech."

"What are we to do?" I asked.

"There is little we can do. We must join the gendarmes tonight as they patrol the streets of Prague."

Our watch began just before midnight. We patrolled the narrow lanes of the Jewish quarter. Always at the centre of our search was the Old Jewish Cemetery, where we knew Professor Owen had been hiding. A search of the cemetery itself had revealed little. Some of the gendarmes reported a nest-like collection of twigs leaves and branches, but there was nothing to say it had been the professor, or whatever he had now become.

To the east and north of us, the Vltava river flowed sedately, criss-crossed by many bridges. Gendarmes patrolled these in order to prevent our quarry from escaping to the woods and parks surrounding the higher ground on which stood the great cathedral named after St. Vitus. Holmes had muttered something about "already having Hyde, and not wanting to add Victor Hugo".

Captain Macek's plan was to sweep across the Jewish quarter toward the river and hopefully bring Owen into the open along its banks. We were woefully undermanned, and no one had much faith that the plan would work. However, no one had a better one.

Earlier in the day, we had returned to Lowenstein's house. The street door and the entrance to the small square had been carefully watched by Captain Macek's men, but they had nothing to report. However, once inside, it was clear that Owen had been there. Equipment and many of the jars and bottles had been moved. Evidently the professor had returned to Lowenstein's laboratory to make up the serum. How he had gained entrance or avoided detection we could only conjecture. Holmes examined every inch of the laboratory and the apartments above, but there was nothing new to learn. The bed had not been slept in.

So it was with a heavy heart that we began our cold and dreary patrolling of the streets, waiting for the whistle to blow to announce the beginning of the sweep. A cold mist had risen off the Vltava and invaded the narrow lanes and alleys of the Jewish Quarter. Denser patches hung wraith like in the air.

"Remind you of somewhere?" Holmes had asked with irony, and I nodded in agreement. We could have been walking through the fog-girt streets of Whitechapel or Limehouse.

I looked at my pocket watch under a street lantern. It was twenty minutes to the hour before the sweep was due to begin.

But then the sharp *skreel* of a police whistle cut the night.

"It's too soon!" I cried.

"Come, Watson – it was in this direction!"

Hot on his heels, we approached the end of the street. We heard several more blasts on the whistle. Answering calls from either side told of other gendarmes converging on our position. We rounded a corner and almost crashed into Professor Owen, or at least what had become of him. With an angry cry, he leapt backwards and raised what appeared to be a crude wooden spear. Later examination showed he had chewed it into a point. He firstly menaced Holmes, then myself, while wildly looking around for an escape route.

I will never forget that moment when we confronted each other. I think it will stand shoulder-by-shoulder with the sight of Presbury in the grip of the Langur serum, on all fours, baiting his wolfhound into a murderous frenzy. At first, the figure before us seemed neither simian nor was it human, resembling instead some atavistic form that embodied something of both. Its clothes were shredded and hung like rags from a powerful but hunched frame. I could plainly recognise Lloyd Owen's features, but his face seemed strangely distorted. He had thrust his jaw forward, while his eyes brows were contracted together, giving him a beetling-browed look. Yet the eyes that stared at us were bright with intelligence. It was as though the outer body no longer fitted the inner man. Lowenstein's damnable elixir had done its foul work, stripping away the civilised man to reveal the primitive beneath. I would swear that it tried to speak, but all that came from its mouth was a strangled cry, more pathetic than frightening.

Holmes held up his open palms to show he was unarmed. "Professor, if you can hear me, if you can understand me, then know I mean you no harm. We can help you. The effect wore off Presbury in time. It may well do so with you."

He would have said more, and I do believe that his words were beginning to take root, but at that moment a gendarme came round the corner, pistol in hand and his whistle between his teeth. Answering whistles told us that other gendarmes were but seconds away.

With a guttural roar, Owen leapt up onto a low balcony and, swinging himself up, he leapt to the next one up. Before Holmes could stop him, the gendarme had fired a shot. It missed the still-climbing figure, but elicited a hideous chattering from the *faux* ape-man. A leap to the balcony of the next house, and the figure was gone from sight.

We gave chase, following the sound of grunts and that strange chattering noise. I recall little of the chase now, but we were headed in the direction of the river. We came out onto the wide ornamental promenade which paralleled the riverbank. Before us was the Charles Bridge. Alerted by the whistles and the pistol shot, the guard on the bridge raised his rifle and took aim. However, Holmes waved him, reluctantly, to stand back.

"We must try to save him if we can," cried my friend. Like myself, he was winded from the chase. So too was the creature. It panted as it walked over to the bridge, wary and exhausted by its exertions. The bridge guard, now mindful of his orders, raised his rifle once more and fired, this time hitting the professor, although it was only a glancing shot in the arm. With a cry, the creature leapt into the middle of the bridge.

Immediately, Holmes put himself directly in the line of fire with his hands held high, pleading with the guard not to shoot. I did the same. Blocking the *gendarmes'* line of fire, we two walked onto the bridge. The professor was spent. He lay up against the plinth of one of the statues that lined the bridge.

"Professor Owen!" I cried. "Professor Owen, please, let us help you." I took a step forward, arm stretched out in appeal, but this seemed only to enrage him. He tossed his wooden staff into the air and caught it with his uninjured arm, making to throw it as a spear.

"Have a care, Watson. I'm afraid you will not find the professor in there. He is a Palaeolithic hunter now, cornered by men of an enemy tribe. For him, there is only fight or flight. He is beyond our reason."

"My God, this is too fantastic. What are we to do? How are we to save him?"

Any answer was curtailed when the professor jumped up and onto the stone balustrade, looking over the side of the bridge to the river below. He chattered at it aggressively, as if it too was an enemy to be faced and fought.

"He's going to jump!" I called out in horror, but the bent and brutish figure merely ran along the balustrade with a simian agility and dropped down back to the roadway at the next statue. There he took a two handed grip on his spear and gibbered at us once more. It set my nerves on edge. It was primal, and yet in some way vaguely familiar, as if it spoke to a forgotten part of me.

"He means to make a fight of it then," said Holmes.

As we spoke, there was a sound from the opposite end of the bridge. My first thought as I looked up was that more gendarmes had arrived. In the thickening fog, I could just make out the chiselled roofs of the bridge's guard tower. As I peered, a coach-and-four emerged from the swirling mist, followed by a square waggon drawn by a pair. The hoofs of the horses clattered on the cobbles as the coach and waggon pulled up opposite the professor. A marked change had come over him. The primal aggression had vanished. Now it looked as if he was trying to push himself into the very stonework of the bridge. He whimpered in fear, his makeshift spear forgotten beside him.

The door of the coach opened and a slender figure emerged wrapped in a long grey opera cloak. A cloud of lustrous black hair was caught momentarily by the breeze. The new arrival was a woman. She took a few steps forward and looked at the professor as he cowered on the cobbled surface. She said something to someone in the coach and then a man emerged, but such a man as I had never seen before, or since. Even at that distance, I felt the force of his personality. He radiated a power, an energy that told me I was in the presence of someone quite extraordinary.

He was tall and skeletally thin. He wore what seemed to be a long yellow robe beneath a coat with an astrakhan collar, and a soft astrakhan hat on his head. The man was evidently Chinese, but he looked like no Chinese man I had ever seen before. His skull was large, with a high domed forehead that bespoke a towering intellect. It seemed almost too large for his body. But it was his face that drew and held my gaze. I have not the power to properly describe it. Was he daemon or angel? Or perhaps some ancient Egyptian mummy returned to life by dark sorcery?

Beside me, Holmes drew in a sibilant breath, and I thought he whispered, "At last."

The figure stared at us for but a moment and then, as if dismissing us he turned away, but not before his eyes flashed a vivid green.

He turned toward the professor, who howled in terror before the power of this man's presence. He buried his head in his hands. The man uttered one word, evidently a command, and the professor immediately fell silent. The girl walked over to him and knelt fearlessly beside him. She said something soothing and stroked his hair. She took his hand and he followed her meekly to the back of the square waggon. The girl opened the back gate, and Owen went in quietly.

As the tall Chinese man re-entered the carriage, the girl walked over towards us. As she did, I became aware of a faint musical tinkling. She wore tiny bells affixed to soft Persian slippers. I could see that under the cloak she wore some form of gauzy pantaloons. For some reason, the image of the Ottoman harem came to mind, but I dismissed it as nonsense in this modern day and age.

She stopped a few paces in front of us. I hadn't thought that night could hold more surprises. Yet when I looked at her face, clearly visible through a gossamer thin veil, I could not, but help gasping out loud. She was beautiful, perhaps the most beautiful woman I will ever meet, but her beauty possessed a transcendent quality. It seemed to set her apart from the tawdriness of this world, as if she belonged to some more ethereal realm. If she but summoned me, I wondered whether I would have the strength to resist.

Even Holmes, I think, was affected.

"Mr. Sherlock Holmes and the excellent Dr. Watson – it is a pleasure to meet you! My master esteems you both greatly. He apologises that a trifling domestic problem should have so inconvenienced you."

"Domestic problem?" queried Holmes.

"Yes. A companion of our sacred order stole a portion of a formula that he didn't understand. He changed his name and went into hiding, hoping to profit from it. It is regrettable that he managed to elude us for so long. But he has now been recovered, and the incident will not reoccur."

"You speak of Lowenstein," said Holmes.

The girl nodded. "That is the name he chose to hide under."

"And what of Professor Lloyd Owen?" asked Holmes.

"My master regrets what has happened, though both men were in no small measure responsible for their own misfortunes. Professor Owen was a guest of ours briefly, but he managed to win his freedom. We will do what we can to restore him, but it may be a long time before he recovers. He may be beyond even the skills of my master."

She bowed in a rustling of silk and began to turn away. Surprising myself, I suddenly blurted out, "My dear, if you are held against your will, come over to us now. We are armed. We can protect you."

She smiled, bewitching me for all time. She took a pace forward, laying a bejewelled arm on my chest. "You English and your gentlemen. You have always fascinated me." She stepped back. "The chains that bind me are finer than silk yet stronger than the steel of your dreadnoughts."

She turned on her heel and began to walk away, drawing up the cowl of her grey opera cloak to complete the monkish appearance.

As she did so, Holmes called out. "Tell me – what is your master's name?"

She paused and without turning back said, "The world is not yet ready for *that* name. Fare you well. The work goes on." And with that she disappeared enveloped by the thickening mist.

Postscript

Many readers may remember the stir some years ago which was occasioned by the sudden appearance of Professor Lloyd Owen on his own doorstep in Camford after an absence of nearly eleven years. His mind was intact, as was his memory up to the moment he departed for Prague. But from that moment on, and of the intervening decade, he had no recollection whatsoever, nor indeed does he have to this day. He resumed his post at

226

the university and still lectures there, though his research is now on a different topic.

On one thing all parties are agreed: On his return, he had not aged a day.

The Interrupted Retirements
by Dan Rowley

"Gentlemen, I shall now summarize what we have seen and heard, with respect to the body, the scene, and the various witnesses. But first I shall remind you of our remit. We are not here to place an accusation against any person. Rather, we are to ascertain the cause of death. Given that the deceased perished from multiple stab wounds in the back, I believe we can fairly rule out such things as natural causes, accident, misadventure, suicide, industrial disease, and neglect. That means you should consider whether the cause was lawful killing – for example a case of self-defense – or unlawful killing. If you cannot make that determination, you may return an open verdict. Whatever your verdict, I shall pass on your ruling and the evidence we have gathered to Scotland Yard."

The coroner, Mark Comstock, paused and scrutinized the faces of the jurors. He was approximately seventy years of age, with a kindly face and once-reddish hair turning white. He had a solid reputation and was well-known for fairness and impartiality. My companion stirred, but I motioned her to remain still so that I could focus on Comstock's factual summary.

"You will recall, Gentlemen, that the deceased, Vittorio Pasquano, was the conductor of the Camden Symphony Orchestra. He had decided to retire and return to his native land, so the management of Camden Theatre, where the Orchestra regularly performs, decided to hold a farewell party for him at the theatre, attended by many patrons and their friends. During the party, three members of the orchestra and the current guest artist performed several pieces for piano and strings. Those three members are the principal or first chairs for their respective sections of the Orchestra." Comstock took a moment to glance at his notes. "They are Richard Chambers, violin, Frederick Harris, viola, and William Nugent, cello. The guest artist was the renowned pianist, Lucille Armstrong.

"After the guests departed, Pasquano retired to his dressing room. The impresario of the theatre, Giovanni Sabbatini, informed the four musicians that he wished to speak to each of them separately about certain upcoming performances. Sabbatini's office is on the right side of the building next to that of the manager, who was not present, having already left the theatre. Pasquano's dressing room is at the end of the hallway from Sabbatini's office. The musicians stayed in the theatre proper and went one by one to Sabbatini's office. The last to do so was Chambers, the violinist. He and Sabbatini discussed a solo that Chambers was going to play. Chambers inquired whether Sabbatini still planned on appointing him conductor, but Sabbatini said that Pasquano had asked to speak to him about that before he finalized the decision.

"Shortly after Chambers left, Sabbatini heard a noise down the hall. He went to Pasquano's dressing room, where he found Chambers kneeling next to Pasquano, who was lying face down on the floor. There was a large pool of blood around the body, and Chambers was holding a dagger with blood on it in his hand. Sabbatini rushed to the stage and asked one of the men to summon a constable. When he returned to the dressing room, Chambers was sitting in a chair away from the body.

"You have heard the testimony of the doctor who examined the body. The multiple wounds in the back of the deceased were the same size and shape as the dagger that Chambers had been holding. We heard testimony that the dagger had been hanging on the wall, along with other memorabilia from operas that Pasquano had conducted. It was the doctor's opinion that death was due to exsanguination, meaning the loss of an excessive amount of blood, which is understandable given the number of wounds. The doctor also assumed that the first blow knocked the decedent to the floor face down, and the remainder of the wounds were inflicted while he was in that position. We also saw the rather large blood stain on the carpet in the room where the deceased was found.

"Does anyone have any questions? No, good. You may retire now to deliberate. I shall remain here if you do have any questions."

The jury was out only a short while. When they came back, Comstock asked, "Gentleman, have you reached a verdict?"

A tall, lean man in the front row stood up. "We have, Your Worship. We find unlawful killing by person or persons unknown. If I may, we believe it was murder."

Comstock thanked the jurors and dismissed them. My companion and I filed out with the other spectators. Once we were alone, she turned to me, imploring, "Uncle John, you must convince Mister Holmes to help us, even though he has announced his retirement. I just know the authorities will arrest Father. But he did not do this horrible thing. He is kind and gentle."

So spoke Meredith Chambers, a young, comely woman in her twenties, with auburn hair, delicate features, and piercing blue eyes that now stared at me. My beloved Mary had been her godmother, and despite Mary's untimely demise, Meredith still called me "Uncle".

"There, there, my dear. I believe Holmes is packing and planning to leave for the Sussex Downs. We shall go now to see him, though I cannot promise the outcome." I obtained a cab, and we proceeded to the address I knew so well. When I rang the bell and received no answer, I let myself in. I could hear my dear friend and Mrs. Hudson upstairs, and I decided it might be best if I initially ventured forth alone so that Holmes wouldn't feel I was pressuring him with Meredith's presence. I indicated she should remain in the entry hall, and I went up to the rooms which held so many fond memories for me.

Our old common sitting room was filled with boxes of all shapes and sizes, in the midst of which Holmes and Mrs. Hudson were intensely discussing the best way to pack his various chemical apparatuses. I stood quietly, and he finally looked up. "Ah, Watson. Come to bid me farewell?"

"Well, not quite. I have just come from the Coroner's Inquest into the death of Pasquano, the conductor."

"Oh, what a terrible situation!" Mrs. Hudson exclaimed. "One of my friends is an acquaintance of the cook for Pasquano. The cook and the other domestics knew that, with his departure, they would need to be seeking new employment. But not this suddenly. My friend was visiting me just yesterday and she mentioned the inquest."

Holmes gave me a wry look. "Do not tell me you have come here in an attempt to interrupt my retirement. I plan on leaving in several days and, as you can see, there is much packing still to be done. My bees await."

I then began to explain my involvement in the case, and mentioned that Meredith had come with me but we didn't want to impose on Holmes. At this, Mrs. Hudson scolded me. "Good Heavens, Doctor. You left that poor young thing in the chilly hallway? Mary loved her so much and wouldn't have allowed this. We'll have none of that. Mister Holmes, I know you are anxious to leave, but what could it hurt to listen for a bit to her and the Doctor. I'll send her up, and then be along with some nice tea and freshly baked shortbread."

Mrs. Hudson bustled from the room, and Meredith soon appeared at the door. "Uncle John, are you sure it's acceptable for me to come in?"

Holmes gave a gallant bow, greeted her warmly, and escorted her to a chair by the fire. "Miss Meredith, I don't believe I've seen you since Mary passed away. I'll take a break from packing, and we can discuss the events involving your father. But I should caution you that I'm scheduled to leave London soon, and cannot commit to anything at this point."

"Oh, Mister Holmes, I'll try not to abuse your hospitality. I wouldn't have prevailed on Uncle John to come here, but the inquest was so horrid. Why did they have to drag all that out into the public?"

"An astute question. While the inquest technically is concerned only with the cause of death, the authorities often use it to engage in finding facts and creating a record. Unfortunately, people don't always tell the police the entire story. The solemnity of being under oath sometimes makes witnesses more conscious of the need to be truthful. Also, the police like to catch people out in inconsistencies, and the inquest, so to speak, sets certain things in stone. From what I read in the newspapers, it is no surprise that the authorities decided to hold an inquest."

Meredith didn't seem comforted by this explanation, as analytical and rational as it was. I spoke up. "Perhaps it might be helpful if I summarized what came out at the inquest. There were some facts that haven't appeared in the newspaper accounts." When Holmes nodded and leaned back to close his eyes, I repeated most of the summation of Coroner Comstock. When I finished, Meredith seemed ready to speak but I shook my head, knowing that Holmes was digesting and applying his great intellect to what I had recounted. While he was in that posture, Mrs. Hudson quietly entered with the promised refreshments, poured three cups, smiled warmly at Meredith, and then left.

After a few more minutes, Holmes sat upright. "I'm not yet persuaded that this matter warrants changing my plans. Miss Meredith, did your father have a motive to wish for Pasquano's demise? Please don't become upset. I must have all the facts if I'm to postpone my departure."

Meredith blushed a bright red, looked at her lap where her hands were fidgeting, and replied in barely audible voice. "Father wanted to become conductor of the orchestra. He felt that Sabbatini, the impresario, had all but promised it to him. But he suspected Pasquano was against the appointment for some reason. Although being a conductor was his life's dream, he never would have committed murder to achieve it."

"So, we have a man who had a motive found with the body, the bloody weapon in his hand. The police will decide that motive, means, and opportunity all point to one suspect."

Meredith was on the verge of tears. "Mister Holmes, my mother was the closest friend of Uncle John's Mary. You knew Mary well. Does that count for nothing?"

"Miss, I only referred to what the police would think. The case does have some items of potential interest, given the facts and rather unusual circumstances. I am familiar with your father. I once heard him play a piece by Paganini, who, as Watson knows, I consider to be an extraordinary man. Your father's performance was profound, and his attack and bowing almost the equal of Wilhelmina Norman-Neruda, whom I once had the pleasure to hear. But I warn you, that would not influence my investigation. My search would be for the truth, wherever that may lead."

"I understand, Mister Holmes. I will accept your conclusions. But I am confident they will show my Father's innocence."

"Very well then. I suspect a day or so more here in London will not hurt. I'll send off a note to the man who has been caring for the bees that his services will be required a bit longer." He rose and went to one of the boxes, from which he withdrew one of the books in which he kept clippings about various criminal activities. I assumed he was rereading one or more accounts of the case.

I patted Meredith's hand. While I knew my friend was intrigued by the challenges the facts presented, and was sure his own musical ability played a part, I wanted to believe that his relationship with Mary and me had some weight.

Holmes looked up from his reading. "Miss Meredith, I think that will be all for now. Is there a convenient way I could interview the witnesses and examine the scene?"

"Yes, they'll be rehearsing tomorrow morning at the theatre. I can have a word with Father so that he can speak to Sabbatini. I'm sure they can accommodate you."

"Excellent. Was someone from the Yard at the inquest?"

"Yes. Inspector Gregson was there."

"I'll send him a telegram. I want him to know we're involved, and I'm going to ask him for the file, particularly any photographs." He went to the desk, wrote a few lines, sealed them, and handed it to me. "Ask Mrs. Hudson to have one of the Irregulars take this to the telegram office. Watson, why not come tomorrow for breakfast – say at nine?" Meredith and I thanked him. When we left he was filling his pipe with shag that he procured from one of the boxes.

When I arrived the next morning, Holmes was already sitting down to a breakfast of poached eggs, sausage, and freshly baked bread with homemade jam. I joined him, and he already was studying the file from Gregson, which apparently had arrived by messenger earlier that morning. The grisly photographs had no impact on his eating, which he absentmindedly continued while studying them and the rest of the materials in the file.

"Very interesting. I've been considering preparing a monograph on the impact of photography on detection, and these pictures support my thesis. Not only are there photographs of the victim, showing the large quantity of blood, but they took some of Chambers as well, with the blood still on his hands and the knees of his trousers." He got up and obtained a magnifying glass from one of the boxes and used it to continue scrutinizing all the photographs. I had looked at them as well, but was at a loss as to what seemed to interest him so much.

At length, he rose from the table, picked up his stick, and donned his hat. "Well, shall we go to the theatre?"

We went down the stairs and flagged a passing cab. It was a short ride from Baker Street, past Regent's Park, to Camden High Street, where the

232

theatre was located. We alighted in front of a building with arched windows framed by pillars and a rather austere entablature, crowned by a triangular pediment, all in all giving the effect of a Roman temple. The entrance was covered with a semicircular red awning with electric lights. We entered the lobby. To the left were the ticket windows. On the right in the far corner was a door marked "*Private*".

"Presumably that is where we will find Sabbatini." We went through into a long hall that ran the length of the building. Along the right side were a series of doors. The second door was marked "*Señor Sabbatini*", so Holmes knocked and we heard a voice behind the door asking us to enter. Inside, the walls were covered by programs from recent and upcoming performances. There was a large desk by the opposite wall, behind which were shelves overflowing with papers and what I took to be scores and scripts. To the right was a sofa and two chairs with a small, low table between them.

A corpulent man was walking toward us from behind the desk. He was in his fifties, with a red face and luxuriant mustache, which compensated for the complete lack of hair on the top of his head. "Welcome, welcome. You must be Mister Holmes and Doctor Watson. Chambers told me Meredith had asked you to look into this terrible business. Please, let us sit over there. May I offer you refreshments? No? Very well. How may I be of assistance?"

Holmes commenced. "Thank you for your time. May I say that your English is excellent. Did you pick that up when you studied at Harrow and Oxford, which has all but eliminated the Lombard undertones?"

"Ha ha! I have read the Good Doctor's stories, and know that you possess a number of acute faculties. You are correct. My family was originally from Milan. We moved here when I was four because my Father was in banking and obtained a position in the City. And I was educated where you indicate. Do you have questions for me before you see the others?"

"Can you tell us about the character of the deceased."

"Well, you know, say nothing ill . . . ."

"In a case of murder, let us dispense with that, please."

Sabbatini sighed. "I must admit, I regret having brought him here. He was from Napoli, and was, not to be too stereotypical, rather hot tempered and mean spirited."

"In what way?"

"Well, he took pleasure out of collecting unpleasant facts about people and then holding them over their heads. He also could be cruel and thoughtless, even to those who may have cared for him."

"Can you give me an example."

233

"I have heard that he put one of his maids, Alyson Morley, 'in the family way', as the saying goes. He was also somewhat romantically involved with Miss Armstrong, our guest pianist. Her dressing room is next to my office, and one day I was leaving and overheard them shouting at one another. She apparently had confronted him about the maid, and he said words to the effect that the maid meant no more to him than Miss Armstrong. She stormed out, but was in such a fury that I doubt she noticed me."

"I understand that, after the guests left, it was only the four musicians and yourself that were here."

"Not at first. I had a brief conversation with the manager, and then he left. My butler, Dawson, was here for a while overseeing the caterers and the rental people who were packing up things. I don't believe any of them were here for long. Pasquano came in to tell me the noise was bothering him, so he went to his dressing room to lie down. Shortly, I went into the theatre proper, and saw that the clean up was almost done. I told them and Dawson to leave as soon as the work was finished. I invited the four musicians to have a drink. I told them to come see me individually after giving me some time to look over the upcoming schedule."

"What did you want to talk to them about?"

"Miss Armstrong is on contract for another month, so I wanted to discuss with her what music she would like to play. The other three are all scheduled to be soloists in the next two months, so we needed to decide what and when each of them would perform. I need to know that so I can schedule the appropriate rehearsals around the various plays we will be performing over the same time period. As you can see from these programs on the wall, we like to provide the public with a varied menu of drama, comedy, and music. I pride myself that this keeps the theatre going."

"Did Chambers also inquire about becoming the conductor?"

"Yes, he was my first choice. However, that rascal Pasquano had asked me to delay the announcement. In his usual secretive way, he wouldn't tell me why, but I suspect he had someone else in mind. It wouldn't surprise me if he took a bribe in that connection."

"Does everyone have a dressing room?"

"Not all of them. As I mentioned, Miss Armstrong is next door. The other rooms in this hallway are reserved for actors and actresses, but are unoccupied right now. Pasquano's was at the end of the corridor. When you go left, along the back of the theatre there are storage rooms for equipment, a scene room, and a costume room. Along the other side, parallel to this one, are larger rooms where musicians and actors can prepare, often many to a single room."

"I see. Who is conducting today?"

"Given the circumstances, I didn't feel it appropriate to allow Chambers to conduct, so I temporarily asked Nugent, the cellist, to fill in. He has no aspirations for the job, which makes him a somewhat neutral choice."

"One last question: After the discovery of the body, I know you went out to the other three musicians. Did you notice whether any of them had blood on their clothing?"

"I don't believe so, although I was somewhat in shock and may not have noticed."

"I understand. Could we impose on you further? I wish to speak to the four musicians. Is there somewhere we could do that?"

"Certainly. You're welcome to use this office. I must run to my bank and see to some other errands. Do you have a preference for the order in which you see them?"

"Thank you so much. I'll commence with Chambers, then the others in any order that won't inconvenience your rehearsal schedule."

"I'll go speak to them now. Please make yourself comfortable. If you need anything, just ask the manager, who is in the first office as you enter the hallway. "

After he left, Holmes walked around the room, looking at the papers on the shelves and carefully studying the various programs on the wall. I knew that, earlier in life, he had some experience in acting, even to touring in America. That experience was well manifested in his uncanny ability to masquerade as various characters during his investigations. I was amused to see that his old interests still could be kindled by these theatrical programs.

There was a timid knock on the door, and a slight man in his late forties entered. He squinted at us through thick lenses, which made his eyes seem to bulge. His brown hair was trimmed rather short, and his clean-shaven countenance was almost boyish in appearance. "Mister Holmes, how do you do? Doctor. It is always a pleasure, even after so long a time. Meredith explained to me your agreement to look into this. I assure you I'm an innocent man."

"Please have a seat, sir. Although we haven't met before, I have had the pleasure of hearing you play. I believe it was on a Guarneri, although I myself prefer a Stradivarius."

Chambers gave a wan smile. "Perhaps under better conditions we can discuss the relative merits of each. What would you like to ask me."

Before Holmes could reply, the door opened and a voice said, "Oh, I am so sorry, sir. I didn't realize anyone was in here."

Chambers turned. "What is it, Dawson?"

"Master Sabbatini forgot to bring his evening clothes, and as he has an appointment this evening that requires him to go straight there, I thought I should bring them along." The speaker was in his early forties, tall, thin, with sharp features, and the deferential manner of a long-time servant.

Holmes gestured for him to come in. "No problem. Please put them over there. How long have you been with Sabbatini?"

"My father, now retired, worked for his father. I started out as a footman when I was barely ten. In fact, my entire family – father, mother, stepmother, and siblings – all have lived a life of service."

"Given that you're here, I might as well ask if you saw anything unusual the night of the murder."

"As I testified at the inquest, I spent all my time with the people providing the food, drink, service, and rental items. When they had finished cleaning up, I also left."

"How did you exit the building."

"The backstage door that lets out onto the alley on the left side of the building."

"Could you see the door to Pasquano's dressing room from there?"

"No, sir. The corridor along the back is rather dim, and the door to his dressing room isn't aligned with the corridor."

"Are those the same clothes Sabbatini was wearing that evening."

"Yes, sir. I always clean and press them after each outing."

"Thank you, Dawson."

"I apologize again for the interruption."

Once he had left, Holmes resumed with Chambers. "Tell us what happened after the guests left that evening."

"Sabbatini told the four of us that he wished to speak to each of us individually, and he invited us to have claret left over from the reception while we waited. We sat chatting in the orchestra pit."

"Do you recall the order in which each of you entered?"

"I believe Miss Armstrong was first, then Harris, and Nugent. As each was finished, they returned and indicated who Sabbatini wanted to see next."

"How long was each person gone?"

"Perhaps ten to fifteen minutes – possibly more or less."

"And you were last. I understand you asked Sabbatini about the conductor position. How did you feel about his response?"

"I would be lying if I didn't say I was disappointed and a bit angry. In fact, when I left I decided to go and ask Pasquano what he was up to. Frankly, the man, while a brilliant musician and conductor, was quite unpleasant. Always ferreting out others' secrets and having those of his own."

"What happened when you went to his dressing room."

"I knocked, but there was no response. In my mood, I decided to confront him, so I opened the door. He was lying on the floor in a pool of blood. I rushed over to look at him, and was so startled, I jumped back. That is when I must have bumped the coat rack, which fell onto his dressing table, knocking it over with a loud crash. I went over and knelt by the body, started to turn him over, then realized I should leave him alone. In my shock, I picked up the dagger lying on the floor. That's when Sabbatini came in, I suppose because he heard the noise the coat rack and table made.

"I know how this looks, Mister Holmes, but I didn't do it. I have never been in a situation like this. I see now I was foolish, and didn't realize what I was doing. I've caused Meredith such pain. I don't know how I can live with myself. Please help me for her sake."

"We will see what we can do, Chambers. For now, calm yourself. Watson, please go with him and render whatever assistance you deem necessary so that he can return to the rehearsal in as normal a condition as possible."

I took Chambers outside to smoke a cigarette and tried to be as reassuring as possible. Any dose of medication seemed unwise given Holmes's instructions. When he had calmed down, we went back inside, he into the theatre and me to Sabbatini's office. When I came in, Holmes was inspecting the evening clothes brought by Dawson. He finished and looked at me.

"I spoke to the manager, who has asked the steward to run errands for us. I told him to bring Miss Armstrong when you returned. She should be here shortly. I went down to look at the dressing room, but the police have trampled any evidence that might have been there. The blood stain is as it appears in the photographs."

As if on cue, the door opened and in swept a striking woman in her early thirties, with auburn hair, green eyes, well-proportioned features, and a demeanor that indicated she was accustomed to being the center of attention.

"Mister Holmes, I presume. And you must be his Boswell. I don't quite understand why we need to go over what I've already told the police and the coroner. But Giovanni asked, so how could I refuse?" She settled herself in the most comfortable chair and nodded to Holmes to start.

"Thank you for your time. I had hoped to hear you play during your tour here, but my schedule hasn't permitted it. I take it that on the night of the murder, you were the first to see Sabbatini."

"Yes. It was tiresome. He wants more Beethoven. I wanted to do Tchaikovsky's *First*. It is unending. I adore him, but he seems to live in a German-Italian world. What can one do? It is the price of being an artiste."

"After you left Sabbatini, did you go see Pasquano?"

"Ha, the cur! I suppose someone has been feeding you gossip that we were involved. It was a bagatelle – a diversion. He meant nothing to me."

"And it didn't bother you that he was also involved with one of his maids?"

"Pah! It merely shows his peasant nature. I'm a woman of the world. Why should I care?"

"So you never had an argument with him about it."

"Vicious rumours. I wouldn't waste my energy, which I must conserve for my public."

"We have been told that Pasquano had a habit of collecting other's secrets. Can you shed any light on that?"

"I do not, of course, engage in common gossip."

"I wasn't suggesting that. I thought perhaps Pasquano might have mentioned something in passing while you were out socially."

"The cad was always implying he knew something about everyone. For instance, I seem to recall he once gloated that Nugent's manuscripts weren't all they appeared to be."

"Could you elaborate, please."

"I find business matters so mundane and dreary. I have heard Nugent prattle on about collecting manuscript scores. I think he was talking to some count or other about selling some of them."

"Thank you, Miss. That will be all for now."

Her exit was as dramatic as her entrance. Holmes, who always has believed I'm an expert when it comes to women, looked at me. "Well, what do you think of that, er . . . ?"

"I believe 'performance' is the word for it. I tend to believe Sabbatini, and that she is attempting to hide her true emotions. She would likely do that in any event, but the circumstances of that evening give her all the more reason."

"I felt the same. Shall we take a short break before seeing Harris and Nugent? I would like to have the steward deliver a message, and then walk around the premises for a bit. If you like, I can ask him to bring you some tea." He then went over to Sabbatini's desk, extracted a piece of paper, wrote several lines on it, and then left me. Shortly, the steward came in with a pot of strong tea, which I enjoyed while pondering what we had learned so far.

After a few minutes, Holmes returned with a man about forty, very mousy and nondescript, with pale skin, fingers almost as slender as my friend's, and a seeming inability to meet one's gaze. Holmes introduced him as Frederick Harris, the violist. Harris nodded with a painful shyness and meekly took the chair Holmes indicated.

"Now, Harris, no need to worry. We just have a few simple questions." Holmes quickly ascertained what Sabbatini and Harris had discussed (apparently an obscure, at least to me, discussion about Telemann versus Hummel), and that Harris said he immediately returned to the others without seeing Pasquano or anyone else.

"Very good. Now what was your impression of Pasquano."

We could barely hear him. "A fine conductor. "

"Come now, my good man. I mean his character."

"He could be unpleasant."

"Was he that way with you?"

"Well, he often sneered at me and belittled my experience. He never went into detail, but he was like that with nearly everyone else."

"Was he the same with the impresario, for example?"

"Hmm. I have heard him say that Señor Sabbatini seemed to make quite a few trips to visit his bank and conduct unspecified errands. One time they were talking, and Sabbatini turned rather red in the face."

"Could you hear anything?"

"Just something about Lady Luck. I was embarrassed and moved away from them."

"I see. That is all I have. Could you ask Nugent to come in?"

He left, and Holmes closed his eyes for a few minutes. He opened them when there was a knock on the door. "Enter." A young man in his early thirties came in. He was rather handsome, with wavy blond hair, blue eyes, and an athletic build. He introduced himself as William Nugent, the cellist, and took a chair next to Holmes, who began his questioning.

"You saw Sabbatini next to last. Correct?"

"Yes, he and I had agreed I would perform the first sonata by Brahms. He wanted to know if I was ready. We talked about the piece, and I told him I needed another month to ensure an excellent performance."

"When you were done, did you return directly to the stage."

"As I believe the Doctor heard me testify, I went straight back, saw no one, and certainly didn't see Pasquano."

"What is your opinion of him?"

"A nasty specimen if there ever was one. Always making sly insinuations, especially if there was someone there to hear him."

"Can you give me an example."

"A few days before he died, he and I were comparing our training and background. He feigned interest purportedly because I'm relatively young. I believe it was actually because Harris was standing nearby. I recall

Pasquano looking at Harris and saying something about it being a shame that not everyone had such opportunities for excellent training. I don't know what he was insinuating, but Harris blushed and hurried away."

"Although not germane, it has been mentioned that you collect manuscript musical scores. Doctor Watson has a similar passion and might be willing to purchase them." I was startled by this statement, but kept silent because I suspected what Holmes was after.

"Yes, I have been doing that for several years. I hope to sell them to generate sufficient funds to hire someone to care for my parents, who are becoming rather frail. They had me later in life and, as their only child, I feel an obligation to care for them."

"Where did you obtain the manuscripts?"

"Ah, here and there."

"Well, thank you for your time. Could you ask Chambers to come in?"

"Certainly."

He left, and Chambers soon came in.

"Yes, Mister Holmes. Do you have a solution?"

"I have one more matter to confirm, but, yes, I believe I know what happened. Can you and your daughter come by my residence later today – say at three o'clock?"

"Of course. We will be there."

We decided to walk back to Baker Street. Holmes produced two cigars, and we had a pleasant smoke as we walked through the park. He asked me my thoughts, and, while admitting that I didn't know who committed the crime, I went over my interpretation of the facts, especially those that hadn't come out at the inquest due to the scope of that proceeding being limited to cause of death.

When we returned to Baker Street, I went upstairs to our old sitting room while Holmes turned toward the kitchen to talk to Mrs. Hudson about the guests who were coming. A bit later, she brought up a cold collation of meat, cheese, and bread, which we had with a white Bordeaux. As we were finishing, Mrs. Hudson escorted Chambers and Meredith into the room. Both appeared to be anxious, but waited for Holmes to begin. I served everyone sherry and we settled in by the fire. Meredith spoke first.

"Oh, Mister Holmes, I do hope you have exonerated Father."

"I think it would be best if we first go over the complexities of the case The account in the newspapers and at the inquest is woefully incomplete. Watson and I have discussed means, motives, and opportunity, so I'll ask him to go over those for you now."

I was a bit taken aback, given that he had given me no warning that he wished to proceed in this fashion. I took a sip of sherry, cleared my throat, and began. "Through my long association with my friend, he has taught me to observe, rather than merely see or hear. Let us begin with motive.

"Please forgive me, Chambers, but both you and Meredith admitted you wanted to be Pasquano's replacement. You and Sabbatini both said that Pasquano had asked Sabbatini to wait. It seems probable Pasquano had an alternative in mind – possibly someone who was paying him to obtain the position.

"However, there are ample other motives as well. Beside the fact that Pasquano was cruel and conniving, it would seem that the four other people we've questioned had more specific motives beyond mere dislike of the man. Miss Armstrong was jilted by Pasquano, and she learned he was romantically involved with one of his maids at the same time he was seeing her. She tried to dissemble with us, but clearly she is a proud and haughty woman who was deeply hurt and humiliated."

"The other two musicians had motives as well. The police would need to do further investigation, but Pasquano seems to have implied that at least some of the manuscripts possessed by Nugent are forgeries. Nugent was quite vague about the provenance of those manuscripts with us, even though he thought I had an interest and the money to acquire them. That was decidedly odd, given that he feels a very strong filial obligation to his parents and wants the money to care for them. At a minimum, Pasquano's disclosure would ruin any chance he had of fulfilling that obligation.

"Although the implication was more vague, it sounded as if Pasquano believed Harris didn't have the musical qualifications or background everyone believed he had. Perhaps he lied when hired by Sabbatini. Possibly it was something more nefarious. In any event, revealing it would likely end his career, based on the reaction he had when hearing Pasquano mention it."

Chambers interjected. "You just now mentioned four other people with motive. Who is the fourth?"

"Sabbatini. When he left Holmes and me, he said he was going to the bank and then carrying out other errands. Apparently that is a frequent pattern of his. Pasquano implied at least once that Sabbatini has a gambling issue. Examination of the books at the theatre could reveal some unpleasant facts. Even if Sabbatini isn't using theatre funds, the type of people who invest in his productions are unlikely to hand their money over to an inveterate gambler, thereby ruining him.

"Opportunity and means are the same for everyone. The murder weapon was on the wall in the dressing room, based on the evidence at the inquest. And all five people could have slipped down the hall and killed

Pasquano — the four musicians before or after seeing, Sabbatini, and Sabbatini himself, at virtually any time before the interviews.

"Holmes, would you care to continue?" I knew he would, but I had a moment of anxiety because I didn't yet know the identity of the murderer.

"Thank you for an excellent summary. Let us begin with the evidence concerning the blood. The police kindly provided me with photographs taken the night of the murder. There clearly was a large amount of blood from the multiple wounds. The number of wounds itself suggested the murderer was in a rage and continued stabbing Pasquano while kneeling over him. That would mean the blood would splash onto the murderer's upper body. Yet when I examined your photograph closely, Chambers, you only had blood on your hands and the knees of your trousers. Your face, shirt front, and shirt cuffs hadn't a speck of blood on them.

"I also asked Sabbatini if any of the other musicians had blood on them, and he thought not. The police, who at times can be careless, surely would have noticed blood on the clothing of Sabbatini or the other musicians, yet there is no mention of it in their report.

"I deduced from this that the murderer may have changed clothing. During a break in our questioning, I went to the wardrobe room, which Sabbatini had mentioned to us. I located a hamper for dirty clothing, and found what I was looking for at the bottom of the hamper. I hid it it where no one could find it, but I was fairly certain there are traces of blood.

"One other observation I made early on: Everyone agreed that Pasquano was an unpleasant human being, and that was often accompanied by a suspicious nature. How, then, did Pasquano come to turn his back on the murderer, which clearly must have happened?

"The answer again comes from the police photographs. The dead man was wearing a lounging jacket, not an evening dress jacket. So here is what I believe happened: The culprit changed into the clothing I found, went to Pasquano's room, offered to help him into the jacket, stabbed him with the dagger from the wall (which the murderer likely obtained during the party), went back to the wardrobe room, and hid the bloody clothes. Presumably the murderer reasoned that the clothes would be bundled off to a cleaning establishment, which would assume the blood was part of a dramatic performance and not report it."

Meredith was wide eyed, never having been present at such a recitation. "Mister Holmes, I still don't understand how a change of clothing could induce Pasquano to turn his back."

"Ah, Miss Meredith, to a man of Pasquano's temperament, most servants are, so to speak, invisible. It was a *butler's* uniform. I knew it couldn't have become dirty from a performance, because the programs on

Sabbatini's wall demonstrated that not a single play in the last several months had a butler as a character."

Chambers stared at Holmes. "Do you mean to say – "

"Yes, Dawson was the murderer. He didn't leave with the people cleaning up, but rather slipped down the hallway. He changed out of his normal uniform into the one in the wardrobe room, then went to Pasquano's dressing room, probably to ask if he could provide any service. He may even have suggested Pasquano change his jacket to be more comfortable. He likely ascertained the lounging jacket was there when he earlier obtained the dagger. He then washed his face and hands in the lavatory, changed back into his normal clothes, thrust the costume to the bottom of the hamper, and left."

"Why on earth would he murder Pasquano?"

"He provided the vital clue when he said his entire family had been in service. He also mentioned a stepmother and siblings. I sent a note to Mrs. Hudson asking her to go visit friend, who knew Pasquano's cook. Mrs. Hudson arranged to have her friend invite the cook over for tea, and the three of them had a quite convivial time. Mrs, Hudson thus had the opportunity to ask the questions I outlined for her, which she cleverly did using feigned gossiping to allay any suspicions. I spoke to Mrs. Hudson when we returned earlier. As I had surmised, Alyson Morley is the daughter of Dawson's stepmother from a previous marriage. Miss Morley is the maid Pasquano disgraced. Dawson clearly has a sense of family pride, and the murder was to avenge his stepsister."

Meredith jumped up and ran to hug Holmes, which he bore with grace. He assured them he would lay all this out for Inspector Gregson, and that the police would have no trouble confirming additional facts, such as that Dawson did not leave with the other people.

After they again thanked us and had left, we settled in front of the fire with brandy and cigars. Holmes lifted his glass to me with a smile. "Well, this can certainly be fodder for another of your tales. I can envision it now: '*The butler did it!*'"

"Holmes, when you say it like that, it sounds like a cliché."

The Adventure of the
Longest Case
by I.A. Watson

"Dr. Watson, he's done it again!" Mrs. Hudson greeted me as I let myself through the door of 221 Baker Street. "Again! There's no telling him. There's no reasoning. I had it all packed lovely, ready for the drays tomorrow, all labelled, all wrapped in newspapers or rags as required – and now he's pulled it all out again and spread it everywhere over the floors!"

It seemed as though I would be required to smooth over one more domestic misstep before I turned in my key to the flat that Holmes and I had occupied for so long. "I shall go up and speak to him," I promised. "All shall be made well."

"I don't know how he expects to get on in Fulworth," our outraged landlady declared, referring to the white-cliffed farm cottage on the Southern Downs that Sherlock Holmes had selected for his rustication. "What will he do when he wants a bit of paper that he filed away in Isandlwana Year?" [1]

"I expect he will have to cope. You have not yet wavered on your decision whether to accompany him on his retirement?"

Mrs. Hudson snorted. "Landlady to mere housekeeper?" [2]

"It might be your retirement also."

"It is true that I am not so spry on stairs as I used to be. Seventeen steps up and down at all hours of the day, and so many odd visitors – it can be wearing on a woman. And staff today need so much more supervision in service than they did when I was a girl."

I wasn't clear whether that was an argument for or against our former landlady accompanying her longest resident into his retirement. Nor was I foolish enough to get between the ongoing debate between two resolute and irrepressible antagonists. "I shall see what he is up to, shall I, Mrs. Hudson?"

"I suppose you had better. He won't be doing his trousers any good, crawling about on the floors like that. All the carpets have already been taken up."

I navigated around the stack of trunks and boxes that were piled in the hallway in readiness for the removers tomorrow. It was strange to recognise items of furniture to which I had become accustomed over so many years now sheet-swathed and piled ready for Fulworth. My own

244

chair, in which I had sat to hear so many of Holmes's plaintiffs' stories, was already in my home and my thriving practice, despite my dear wife's teasing about my sentimentality. [3]

"Tell him that he may repack it by himself," Mrs. Hudson's remonstration followed me up to the first floor.

Odder than to see our many well-remembered tokens piled for transportation was to find our Baker Street chambers quite stripped out, bookshelves bare, furniture absent or swathed in dust-covers. There were still signs of our occupation: The patriotic pattern of bullets in the wall plaster where Holmes had decided to write out *V.R.* in tribute to Her late Majesty, the unfaded patches where our photographs and pictures had protected wallpaper from sunlight, the charred floorboards under where Holmes's chemical bench had stood, the splintered wood where Colonel Moran's assassin shot had ricocheted.

Most obvious sign of all, though, was the Great Detective himself, sprawled out upon the floor surrounded by a hundred documents that he had pulled out of once-packed file boxes. The whole centre of the room was now re-carpeted with papers. Holmes sat like an unruly child making a fort of cardboard boxes within a chaotic circle of reopened chests and sundered luggage.

"Ah, Watson!" he greeted me. "Be so good as to break open the tea-trunk labelled '*1882-1883 Blackmails and Forgeries*', would you? It is the one with the Scotland Yard seal still affixed to the flap, under that shipping-case of memorabilia from our journey on the Orient Express."

"Before I commit myself to such an act," I responded, "which will make me complicit in compounding your infuriation of the estimable Mrs. Hudson, may I enquire as to the reason for my search?"

Holmes waved one slender long-fingered hand at the chemistry set he had unearthed from the boxes awaiting removal, as if that explained everything. I saw test tube racks, acid bottles, a portable Bunsen burner, stained filter papers, a Zeiss microscope, a Pocket Kodak camera, [4] and a good deal of scattered graphite powder, but none of that immediately enlightened me upon Holmes's project.

"Assume, Holmes, that even in over twenty-two years of acquaintance with you I do not always immediately follow your chain of thinking," I suggested.

Holmes snorted, slumped, and set down the file through which he was rifling. "I have perhaps become a trifle too focussed upon my enquiry at hand," he recognised. He looked around the disordered room as if seeing the mess for the first time.

"You haven't advanced your campaign to transport Mrs. Hudson to Sussex in any positive way," I advised him. [5]

Now that the folder had been set down, I could see its faded yellow label. Written in Holmes's distinctive script were the words "*Sasanoff Tour, November 1879 – August 1880*". I was at a loss as to why Holmes might be consulting a file about his long-ago days as part of a travelling Shakespearian acting company in the United States of America.

Roused from his obsession, Holmes was now allowing himself a moment of wider reflection. "I have perhaps suppressed a sentimental response *in re* moving from our chambers," he admitted.

I could have told Holmes that, had he been ready to listen. Our recent extraordinary investigation of Professor Presbury had been a sudden and spontaneous affair, preceded by Holmes's peremptory summons of "*Come at once if convenient—if inconvenient come all the same. – S. H.*" The affair of "the Creeping Man" had demonstrated my friend's secret reluctance to let go of that life and profession which had sustained him these many years. [6]

"Perhaps you might indulge me one more time?" I appealed. "Explain to your old dear friend what it is that you are doing. What has set you onto this unwarranted disruption of Mrs. Hudson's packing?"

Sherlock Holmes sighed. He rubbed his charcoal-grubbed hands absently on his smoking jacket and, satisfied that his fingers were clean if not his robe, passed me a calling card, upon the reverse of which were scrawled some numbers in faded blue ink.

He was careful to hold the card by its edges and cautioned me to do the same. I noticed that the pasteboard had been dusted with clinging black powder, and that by that coating the whirls of partial fingerprints could be discerned.

I read the printing on the card out loud:

"'*Mr. Sherlock Holmes, Consulting Detective, 24 Montague Street, London*' [7] – Holmes, this is your own business card! Or at least it was."

Before Holmes and I had agreed to share expenses on a better set of rooms at Baker Street, he had lodged for several years in inferior digs beside the British Museum, eking out on a tiny allowance from his father, and attempting to establish himself in a profession that didn't exist until he created it.

It was during that period that he had encountered the theatrical impresario Michael Sasanoff, and had dabbled in acting as a means of training himself in disguises and performances under the stage name "William Escott". Holmes's familiarity with the United States came from a tour he undertook with Sasanoff's Shakespeare Company that swept around much of that country in the winter of '79. He is mentioned several times in Sasanoff's memoirs, *Seventy Years a Showman*, [8] which spends some detail on the tour's one-hundred-and-twenty-eight performances in New York and the principal cities of America.

I was still at a loss regarding the scribbled numbers or the grubby fingerprints, however. The hand-penned digits read:

$$1.I.1.98.9$$
$$10.II.3.25.5$$
$$27.II.1.53.8$$
$$8.I.2.150.15$$
$$9.III.2.231.7$$
$$2.II.7.43.4$$
$$27.I.1.180.5$$

Holmes took pity upon me and explained. "I was finishing the classification of my earliest files. There are some folders from my old Montague Street days that I have had no reason to consult since I received them back from Scotland Yard on the occasion of my return after Reichenbach. [9] Some of the contents are quite shuffled. I should have known better than to trust police detectives to respect orderly filing."

I reviewed the scattered piles of papers that now decorated the bare boards of 221b.

Holmes recognised the censure. "It was necessary to pursue an enquiry," he defended himself. "You see, I came across that card you hold between your fingers. It is a sad souvenir of one of my earliest investigations – one of my earliest failures."

I settled cross-legged across from him in a rare remaining clear patch on our boards. "You haven't mentioned this case to me before?"

"I have had no reason to. Nothing came of it, except that I learned there were limits to my capacity to uncover information that simply wasn't there. Except that now I have a means of following the case that wasn't available to me in 1879."

I looked at the card again. "Fingerprinting."

"Indeed. The technique was undreamed of back then. Well, actually the Babylonians were taking fingerprints of criminals during Hammurabi's reign seventeen-hundred years before Christ and were still signing contracts with fingerprints in 200 B.C. In the ninth century *Anno Domini*, the Chinese were using handprints to authenticate loans. In 1788, German anatomist Johann Mayer first told Western science that fingerprints were unique to each person. But the technique was neither trusted nor developed until recently."

"It is recognised now," I prompted, but Holmes had more to say about the development of the method.

"Provincial doctor Robert Blake Overton contacted Scotland Yard in 1840 following the murder of Lord William Russell, proposing fingerprint checks. [10] In India in 1858, Sir William James Herschel was utilising fingerprinting to prevent relatives from fraudulently collecting the pensions of deceased relatives. Just one year after my failure in the case regarding that card, Scottish surgeon Henry Faulds produced his first paper on the uniqueness of human fingerprints. His offer to introduce the technique to Scotland Yard in '86 was declined. Francis Galton's *Finger Prints* in 1892 offered a detailed statistical model for analysis and identification and calculated that the chance of two persons having the same fingerprints was about sixty-four-billion to one – but of course, I was presumed dead and was preoccupied with surviving Moriarty's remaining minions at the time, so perhaps I might be excused being behind on my reading."

"Indeed," I responded. To nudge Holmes from his lecture and to remind him of his previous historical enumerations I added, "It was the Argentinean Inspector Álvarez who, in 1892, based upon work pioneered by his Chief of Police Juan Vucetich, solved the throat-cutting of two children by means of a bloody thumb-print, proving their mother to be the perpetrator of that appalling crime. That was the first occasion when fingerprints were utilised to solve a police case." [11]

Holmes looked abashed. "I have droned at you upon this subject before," he apologised.

"Your conversation is seldom boring," I assured my friend. "I hope you recognise, however, that I do attend to what you are telling me. For my essays on you, if nothing else."

I felt another twinge. I would miss Holmes's lectures when he was no longer in London.

Holmes continued, unaware of my precocious nostalgia. "My point is that since the recognition of Paul-Jean Coulier's iodine fuming method to transfer latent fingerprints from surfaces to paper, Scotland Yard has these last two years begun fingerprinting criminals. And of course, last year Alphonse Bertillon was able to secure the identification, arrest, and conviction of the murderer Scheffer based upon fingerprint evidence alone, by matching prints on a broken glass case to those kept on police file." [12]

"And therefore, though you couldn't draw imprints from your old card back when you were investigating something to do with it, you might now revisit the case and apply new techniques to its solution."

Holmes nodded, gesturing to the array of bottles and jars, litmus paper, Petrie dishes, and scientific instrumentation which he had unpacked around himself.

He received the card back from me and folded it in a preserving sheet of waxed paper. "You have been most patient, Doctor," he assured me. "I shall now discipline myself to a cogent account of my endeavours."

"I shall be most interested to hear them."

The detective chuckled. I saw him stiffen a little as he automatically reached for a brandy and his tobacco pouch, only to realise that they were packed away for the haul down to Sussex.

"On Friday, 12th September of 1879, I was approached by one Miss Gladys Orpington, whom I had recently encountered under her stage name '*Delia Fount*'. We had played together in *Twelfth Night*, in which I had understudied the role of Orsino and Miss Fount portrayed the role of Countess Olivia's maid, Maria. I cannot accord her performance any distinction. [13] But the cast and crew were naturally aware of my deductive acuity and detective ambitions, and so she brought her problem to me.

"The girl's situation was a delicate one. She had been walking out with a theatrical music hall performer by the name of Joseph Fletcher, although onstage he used the soubriquet '*The Remarkable Odin von Morden*', where he performed conjuring tricks and memory feats with middling success."

"When you say a delicate situation . . ." I ventured.

"She had contracted a pregnancy, yes. And the remarkable Odin von Morden had performed a remarkable vanishing trick."

"That trick is all too common," I commented.

"Fletcher had vanished from his rooms on the ninth of September. He had abandoned his suitcase and personal belongings, including his conjuring impedimenta, but he had also left behind two weeks' rent arrears and an irate landlord. None of his friends could say – or at least would say – where he might have gone. Miss Fount prevailed upon Fletcher's landlord, Mr. Eric Ladner, to allow her to search her fiancée's things, though Ladner had already ransacked his defaulting lodger's possessions to seek any items he might distrain towards his costs. Fletcher's wallet was the first thing to be raided. Miss Fount found it emptied – save for a small tintype of herself and that card of mine that I have just showed you."

"Why should the fellow have your card?" I wondered. "And what are those numbers on the back for?"

"That was in part why Miss Fount sought my services. She wished to know the nature of my business with her fiancée – which was none. I had only met the fellow once, at the Criterion Bar after a matinee performance of *Twelfth Night* as the cast refreshed themselves for the evening show. We had not spoken."

"What did the numbers mean?"

"I don't know," Holmes confessed plainly. "At the time, I reviewed all kinds of possibilities: Map co-ordinates, train timetables, horse race annotations, stock prices, various cyphers, mnemonic signifiers . . . Without further data it was impossible to discern."

"How did the 'Remarkable von Morden' come to have your card?"

"It was one that I had lodged with the ticket office at the theatre where Sasanoff's troupe were playing in London. As I mentioned, I began as a humble understudy, unwanted unless called for. The card was so that they could wire me or send a runner if I was urgently required to step in at quick notice. I verified with the porter that Fletcher had seen it on the corkboard and begged for it, probably on the night of the eighth, right before his disappearance. In fact, that porter was one of the last people to see him. The very last were two vaudeville pals from who he cadged five shillings at ten a.m. on the day he disappeared."

"Money to fund his escape," I supposed.

"Or to meet my consultation fee and expenses," Holmes speculated.

I hadn't considered that possibility. "He may have inscribed the numbers on your card to show them to you?"

"It occurred to me at the time as one explanation. For whatever reason, no consultation took place."

"Did you accept Miss Fount's – that is Miss *Orpington's* – request to locate her missing swain?"

"I didn't believe that the case accorded much material of interest. The only unique feature was the possibility that Fletcher might have wanted to contact me for some reason, but that was hardly enough to attract my attention. I was keen to develop techniques and methodologies suitable to my chosen career. Then, as since, I was picky in my investigation-load."

Holmes looked reflective. "Besides," he reminisced, "It was shortly thereafter that Reginald Musgrave brought me the nice problem of his family's Ritual. [14] By the time I had resolved that historical puzzle it was time to pack up my things for an Atlantic voyage."

"Miss Fount didn't remain with the company," I supposed.

Holmes fished out from his Sasanoff folder an albumen print [15] of a thespian troupe lined in three rows beside a proud-looking chap with bulging waistcoat and prominent side-whiskers. Scratched onto a corner was the legend, "*Sasanoff Players, Oct '79*". Centre-back was a thin-faced beaky-nosed fellow who was only a couple of years off the Sherlock Holmes whom I had first met in Barts laboratory rooms in 1881.

Holmes indicated a dark-haired young woman seated to the left on the front row and identified her as Delia Fount.

"I did spend some effort in verifying the departure of her betrothed," Holmes admitted. "Such was her distress, and indeed her circumstance, that though I wouldn't take her case or her money, I bent some small attention to her situation."

Holmes is never quite so severe as he seems in these matters. "You couldn't find the fellow?"

"I could find no account of him after his scrounging visit to his two friends at the Lambeth Palais de Variety. He *may* have shown himself at his fiancée's theatre, but it being late morning and there only being one clerk at the booking box, it was impossible to verify. Someone came to ask if I was inside, but the harried attendant didn't know and took little note of him who asked. 'Some fellow,' was his best description. Thereafter Fletcher, if Fletcher it was, completely vanished."

Not wishing to be thought indifferent in my estimation, Holmes added, "I canvassed the cabbies, of course, for at that time I had just completed the training in the Knowledge of London required by all hackney drivers, [16] and knew them well. I checked the morgues and police registers. I kept an eye out in the theatrical trade papers for reviews of any new player who debuted a memory and conjuring act, in case it was Fletcher with a new alias. I don't think I neglected any standard recourse, but in the end, I had to put the enquiry aside without resolution."

I asked what had become of Miss Orpington.

"She retired from the stage and married Fletcher's landlord," Holmes told me.

All of that explained a minor incident from twenty-four years before, at I time I had been serving as a medical officer with the Fifth Northumberland in Afghanistan, but didn't explain Holmes's need to disarray our landlady's fastidious packing today.

"I found the card," my friend explained. "It occurred to me that a method I might have used had I pursued the matter today wasn't available to me back then. Hence, I applied the dusting powder and identified what prints I could off the item."

"You could lift images from so long ago?" I enquired.

"The card has been folded in grease-proof paper, enclosed in an envelope, since 1879," Holmes replied. "There are six distinct print sets or partial sets that I can discern. I have been taking photographic plates of them."

The developing agents and dishes and a small serge "blackout box" were also amongst Holmes's bench equipment scattered over the floorboards.

"Even if you have the prints, how could you match them to people?" I challenged.

"One set, the oldest and most smudged, is my own, from when I presented the card at the front office," Holmes supplied. "Another set matches that old programme there, from the *Hamlet* production, and on those cancelled ticket stubs, from which I infer that it belongs to one of the box office staff. A third set is juvenile, most likely one of the theatre runners set to pin the card on the board."

"That seems common sense," I allowed. "The others?"

"This smaller single fingerprint and a matching thumb on the reverse is the same as those left by Miss Fount on a note of hand in the file, which she sent round to ask about my progress in finding Fletcher. That was four of six I could easily place."

"Surely there must also be the marks of the bilked landlord who went through the absconder's things?"

"It might well be so. There isn't enough of the pad to read any clue to the fifth man's occupation. This last set, though, there the index finger betrays a most interesting callosity – one that sent me this lunchtime to say my farewells to Stanley Hopkins at Scotland Yard."

I hadn't thought Holmes so sentimental as to take special leave of the Detective Branch, even of such an admirer of his work as Inspector Hopkins.

"I required sight of the fingerprint books which the Yard now keeps on hand," Holmes explained to me. "There isn't yet any comprehensive database for criminals convicted before 1901, or those outside London, but one felon in particular was sure to have his prints on file. I cross-referenced those whorls and arches with the ones on this card and – the mystery intensifies!"

"Who is it?" I appealed. "What odd circumstance placed that card in the hands of a known criminal, over two decades ago? And what criminal?"

Holmes paused for effect and then revealed, "This callus is typically found on the index finger-pad of men who regularly fire heavy ordinance, heavy-gauge hunting rifles and elephant guns. On the trigger finger. The print taken in 1902 matches the second-most dangerous man in England: Colonel Sebastian Moran."

It was our last night as comrades in Baker Street, we told ourselves. We had twelve hours before the drays would arrive to begin Holmes's removal to a retirement from the solution of crimes. Surely there was time to plumb one more mystery, to tie off one final thread, before morning came?

Hence, as evening drew on, Holmes and I found ourselves in The Curtain, one of the many drinking holes that proliferate behind Drury Street, clinging to the shadows of the great theatres, catering to the eccentric and eclectic members of the acting profession.

We walked down a half-dozen steps into a smoky half-filled cellar bar. A long counter lined one side with a mirror behind it. A painted brick wall was covered with photographs and newspaper reviews, framed and unframed, depicting stars of the boards and old notices of long-forgotten plays. Many of the pictures were scrawled with autographs.

Some of the more famous portraits were of giants of the stage: Alfred Vance, Edward Craig, Sir Johnson Forbes-Robertson, Dan Leo (as Mother Goose), Basil Gill, Charles Blondin, Wilson Barrett, and in pride of place Sir Henry Irving, who must have drunk in every public house in the West End.

Amongst the actresses so galleried I recognised Ellen Terry and Lily Langtry (inevitable in any collection), Mable Love, Lennox Grey, Maude Branscombe, and a long row of other languid ladies portraying Guinevere, Juliet, Ophelia, or Little Nell, or else wearing bathing suits, trapeze slips, or Columbine costumes.

There were posters for Harry Lauder in *When I Get Back Again Tae Bonny Scotland*, for Dan Leno in *The Merry Widower*, Marie Lloyd in *Madame Duvan*, George Robey in *The Simple Pimple*, and a great many more productions I had never heard of. There were company photographs for productions of many Shakespeare plays, Gilbert and Sullivan, and light operettas, alongside old shows I couldn't remember such as *The Golden Ladder*, *A Lesson for Life*, *A Comedy of Sighs*, *How London Lives*, and *Oh Look At Her Crinoline*.

Holmes paid no heed to the newly framed photograph of the cast of the Lyceum Theatre's *Sherlock Holmes* production, recently and successfully transplanted from Mr. William Gillette's Broadway version, or to the flyer for its burlesque rival *Sheerluck Jones, or Why D'Gillette Him Off* at Terry's Theatre. [17]

Such a wall of fame might be found in twoscore such venues within a stone's throw of the theatres. The Curtain was hardly the most salubrious, with its poor lighting, smoky rafters, faded upholstery, and leaky gas lamps. Accordingly, its patrons weren't usually the glittering stars of Drury Lane, but rather the bit-players, the out-of-work choruses and terpsichores, and a good number of older professionals for whom the stage was a receding memory.

"I still gets a bit of work in character parts," assured the grizzled old thespian to whom Holmes and I resorted in the lee of the taproom. "It's experience as tells, you see. These youngsters don't know upstage from down! When I think the drilling we had to go through in the old days, the good old days – Why, these modern pups don't know as they're born!"

"Dr. Watson, this is Charlie Ladner," Holmes introduced me to the seedy old actor, "or rather I should say Mr. Charles Ladner-Green, as he was known in his salad days. How are you getting along, Charlie?"

"Oh, you knows," the old man replied, accepting his drink with a grim smile and a small flash of the stage presence he must once have possessed. "I gets by. And sometimes an old comrade treats me to a toothful of gin." He hoisted the glass and toasted our health, downing the contents in one gulp.

Holmes provided a replacement measure. "I want to pick your memory about a fellow from rather a long time back – the seventies."

"I remembers *you* all right, Mr. Holmes!" the veteran actor insisted. "How you strode them boards. 'I saw Sherlock Holmes murder Julius Caesar!' I tells 'em. 'And watched 'im play the Jew, and the Devil, and in the Scottish Play!'" [18]

"Yes, yes," Holmes responded a trifle impatiently, "but that isn't what I require you to recall. Do you remember a vaudeville man who went under the stage name of 'The Remarkable Odin von Morden'? His actual name was Fletcher."

"Odin von Morden?" Ladner sipped at his gin this time, grizzled brows furrowing in effort to stir up recollection. "Yes . . . yes, I knows him. Or knew him. Saw him about, I mean, back in the day."

"What can you tell me of him?"

Another sip. "Memory man and slight-of-hand fellow. He had an act where he would ask the audience to name any classical work and he would quote from it, as well as list from memory all the Derby winners, cricket matches, boxing champions, and suchlike. 'Name me a year!', he'd ask the audience, and then he'd reel off runners and riders and odds and all! Not the best of the memory acts, but he had a second string."

Holmes enquired what that might be, and supplied another tithe of alcohol.

"He was a dipper, see? A hand-in-pocket conjurer, meaning he would have your watch and wallet off you with no more than a brush of the hand – and you were watching the other hand! And then he'd have a quick look through the wallet, see? Nothing criminal, but to learn about the fellow he's dipped it off. Then he can make amazing mental predictions about who this fellow is, about where he lives, about his profession and family. All from what a quick look at the chap's calling card or wallet photographs can betray. Even a bus ticket or a train stub could offer 'amazing revelations', you know? And at the end, when everyone is stunned by von Morden's abilities, he tops it by handing back the punter's pocketbook and taking his bow. Well, that's what his act used to be, quarter-century ago."

"What became of him, do you know?"

Ladner shrugged. "He faded away, I reckon. A lot of 'em do. One empty belly too much, one more bad review, too many useless auditions – it can break a heart! So they drop out and they're gone from the Profession. The handsome lads and the pretty lasses sometimes find a score to batten on, a soft cushion from an indulgent patron or sponsor. The others . . . Well, they put their dummies away or pawn their tap shoes or sell their joke book, and they're just . . . *gone*."

I enquired whether Ladner could name the last time he heard of von Morden.

He knuckled his forehead as if that would stimulate recollection. "There was a young woman . . ." he said, then hesitated, then pressed on. "She was an actress. Did bit parts and walk-ons and got second-*ingénue* parts: The heroine's sister, the young housemaid, that kind of thing. What was her name? Delia something . . . *Fount*! That's it, Delia Fount. Married out of the Profession, to a theatrical landlord – Sleeping with the enemy! Still runs his boarding house now, for all I know. But back then she was going about with von Morden – his fiancée, I think. And Morden did a runner on her."

"Why might von Morden have disappeared?" Holmes pressed.

"Well, the usual," Ladner judged. "I heard as the girl was in the family way, so there's that. I'd have said debts, maybe, except that evidently he had quite a windfall due before he disappeared, a big win with the bookies that he seemingly never collected. But that was a long time ago now. No, sorry, don't recall who the wager was laid with, or even who told me about it. It might all be rubbish."

Ladner would have been quite content soaking up Holmes's gin and talking about the old days all night, but Holmes and I were on a clock. Once my friend had gleaned everything the old thespian knew about Fletcher and his betrothed, we made our farewells and continued on our hunt.

"Could we not go and ask Moran how his fingerprints came to be on your card?" I asked Holmes as we passed through a narrow ginnel into another shadowed courtyard off Old Kent Road.

Nine years after his attempted murder of Sherlock Holmes by air rifle, former Colonel John Sebastian 'Tiger Jack' Moran [19] was still a prisoner at His Majesty's pleasure, convicted of many minor crimes that would incarcerate him for life but by his master's cunning precautions insulated from such charges as would warrant a sentence of death. [20] Moriarty's right hand man – and, I confess, his only true friend – was kept under constant watch by a vigilant guard, and the precautions against him still felt insufficient. [21]

"We have pacted to have one last night of detecting before we part, Watson," Holmes reminded me. "It would take days to gain permission to see the old *shikari* [22] again. And were we to possess our souls in patience [23] and await an interview, he might well refuse to see us, or to tell us what we wish to know."

"Especially if he had anything to do with Fletcher's disappearance," I considered.

"We shall follow the trail by another route," Holmes told me. "Perhaps Moran would appreciate the strategy." [24]

"If there was gambling involved, considering what Ladner said about von Morden's windfall, we know that Moran wasn't above cheating at cards. He resorted to murder at least once because of it."

Holmes shook his head. "What I must fathom is how those prints came to be on my Montague Street card. It will come to me. I had those cards printed in July of '77, upon establishing myself in my elected occupation. At that point Sebastian Moran was already in the 1st Bangalore Pioneers, on a different continent. That year and into the next he was part of the punitive Jowaki expedition, [25] and then fought in the same Second Afghan conflict that ended your military service. He was at Cherasiab and Sherpur." [26]

"In other words, all the time that you were in Montague Street, Moran was in India or Afghanistan. Had he even met Moriarty at that time? Surely that was later, after scandal required him to quit the army."

Further discussion of that mystery had to be postponed. Holmes led me to a shuttered rear door on a gloomy tenement. At his coded knock and spoken password, we were admitted into another cellar, this time set up as a cock-pit.

It was still early for the gamblers to arrive. The men who would fight their fowls were still setting up. In a further corner, a number of terriers were locked in cages, ready for the ratting contests later.

A balding fellow in his shirt-sleeves was stood on a stool chalking names and odds on a long wall-blackboard. Holmes strode over to him and called out, "Lofty Soaper!"

"Mr. 'Olmes!" the bookmaker recognised, trying to keep the look of horror from his face. "We'd 'eard as you'd retired!"

"Not yet, I'm afraid. I've come to task you one last time."

Lofty gestured around the gambling hell. "It's just a bit of fun amongst friends, all this," he promised.

"Not to the creatures in the ring," I disapproved. [27]

Holmes kept to the point. "Believe it or not, my interest is in a wager you accepted a great many years ago. Do you recall an accumulator bet that you took from Joseph Fletcher, the remarkable Odin von Morden?"

Lofty's jowly face dropped. He went ashen and climbed down from his perch to speak to us more privately. "That's a name I 'aven't 'eard in a donkey's age, Mr. 'Olmes. 'E . . . 'e's not back, is 'e? Because I don't 'ave that sort of money for a payout. Not after this long. And anyways, it was a cheat."

"Calm yourself, Lofty, and tell me the circumstances of it. What was the wager, and how was it crooked?"

The bookmaker swallowed hard. "Well, you remembers 'ow it was in them days, sir. Big 'Arry Stormer ran the gambling 'round the West End, and you *knows* 'oo he reported to. And I was a very small fry back then, working for Big 'Arry. So when Fletcher comes and wants ten shillings on a long string of no-'opers, I took his money and gave 'im his receipt an' counted it a fool parted from his cash."

"Except the no-hopers won," I supposed.

"Right on! String of five, 'undred-and-fifty-to one, that was. And it came in for the win! I thought Big 'Arry was going to rip me in two right there. I mean, it was clear it was a fix, and Big 'Arry wanted to know what part I'd 'ad in it, taking the bet. I still limps a bit in damp weather."

"The chances of Joseph Fletcher randomly picking five winners on the same day and linking them in an accumulator are somewhat scant," I estimated.

"Just a bit!" Lofty snorted. "But Fletcher never came back to collect 'is winnings – just vanished. And my skin was saved."

"How long before the meets did Fletcher lay the bets?" Holmes wished to know.

"Might 'ave been best part of a week," the bookmaker estimated. "It was all a long time ago to remember – but he laid his wager early doors. Right keen he was, with a shiny 'alf-sov."

"A ten-shilling coin," Sherlock Holmes noted. "Not change? One gold coin? That was a rare enough sight in those days. How might the impecunious Fletcher have come by one?"

"Dunno," Lucky replied. "But it was genuine. I checked. A proper *mazda pooner*, as we used to call 'em back then." [28]

"So Fletcher won seventy-five pounds [29] – but he never claimed it. Might Stormer have done away with him?" I wondered.

"Big 'Arry could 'ave if 'e'd wanted to," admitted Lofty, "but I never 'eard as 'e did. But yes, the fix was in on them races. 'Ooever had set that up wouldn't be so stupid as to try an accumulator – that's for amateurs. But they wouldn't 'e 'appy about someone else queering the pitch and drawing attention with stunt gambling, neither. So maybe that was what became of Fletcher?"

Holmes allowed that was a reasonable supposition.

"That was the bad old days," Lofty proclaimed with some nostalgia. "Real characters we 'ad back then. Not faceless nobodies like today – cartels and companies with their ledger sheets and quotas. You should never 'ave done for the Professor, Mr. 'Olmes. 'E was a right old monster, 'e was, but it was all better back then all the same."

"Crime is not the same," Holmes admitted, bleakly. "There is no challenge anymore. The spark of criminal imagination has gone out. It is all mundane, routine, repetitive, and derivative. Dreary." He turned away sourly. "Come, Watson – we should be elsewhere."

"Close this den down tonight," I advised Lofty Soaper. "It's likely to be raided."

Mrs. Gladys Ladner was plump and florid-faced, but I could still discern in her the shade of the ingénue Delia Fount that I had seen in Holmes's cast photograph. The theatrical landlady stared at Holmes in slow recognition as if she had encountered a spectre from the grave.

"I am continuing the investigation you requested some time back," Holmes conveyed to her. "I am returned to the trail of your once-fiancée. This is my friend and colleague, Dr. Watson. May we come in?"

The landlady's sheer surprise got us through the door. It was now past dinner-time. The common meal-table had been cleared away, though the odour of boiled cabbage and beets still lingered. The residents of the house were dispersed to their own pursuits or to early bed.

"The . . . the investigation," Mrs. Ladner said hesitantly as she supplied us with the cups of tea that basic hospitality required by rote. "Mr. Holmes, that was twenty-four years ago!"

"Sherlock Holmes is nothing if not persistent," I assured her.

"I prefer to find solutions," Holmes agreed. "It makes my files tidier. And I like to know the truth of things."

"I am settled now," Mrs. Ladner protested, "a respectable married woman. My husband will be home from the pub for his supper shortly."

"Good," Holmes approved. "I should like to interview him also."

The landlady perched on a kitchen chair opposite her unexpected guests. "What can you do now, so many years later?" she demanded. "Joe Fletcher is long gone. So are Gladys Orpington and Delia Fount, for that matter."

"I didn't have certain critical information then, Mrs. Ladner. With such intelligence, I may be able to fathom this puzzle at last."

I wondered if Holmes meant the fingerprinting that implicated Moran in the case, but his questions went in a different direction.

"When did you begin your relationship with your fiancée's landlord?" Holmes began.

The matron frowned. "You mean my husband! I don't see how that is any of your business, Mr. Holmes!" she replied sharply.

"Was it before or after you consulted me regarding the writing on my business card?"

"I don't rightly remember."

"It makes a difference," I reviewed. "You told Holmes that you were looking for your missing suitor . . . but the problem you brought before him was one of interpreting some cypher on the obverse of his card."

"As my way of finding Joe," Mrs. Ladner protested. "By knowing what he'd been up to!"

"The card was unwritten on at the time it was handed over to Fletcher," I supposed. "The box office clerk would have noticed odd scribblings on it."

"The handwriting is Fletcher's," Holmes supplied, "using the same leaky fountain pen with which he signed for his box office receipts at the Lambeth Alhambra, his final billed venue."

"This is all old news, Mr. Holmes," Mrs. Ladner insisted. She made an attempt to rise and bustle us out of her kitchen.

"Sit down!" Holmes commanded her. "We shall have the facts at last!"

It took more cajoling and Holmes's wit to convince the proper story out of the landlady, but when it came it filled many blanks in the narrative we were assembling.

"Joe's act as Odin von Morden," the former actress began, "it started with picking the pocket of some distinguished-looking punter that was waiting at the box office. Joe needed to check the fellow's wallet, see, and use the clues he found in there to supposedly mind-read the punter he called up on stage. It wasn't stooge-work. The audience member wasn't in on the act, as so many are. It was borrowing his pocket-book and working out from there who he was, his family and profession and so on. Then, while the mug was up on stage, Joe would slip the wallet back where it had been before, without his 'audience guest' ever knowing – unless he wanted to present the fellow with his belongings back in a grand flourish at the end."

"Fletcher therefore picked distinguished-looking vaudeville-goers from the lobby queue," Holmes deduced. "They were more likely to have fat wallets that betrayed identity and profession, and might even be figures known to the general public and therefore assuredly not 'plants' in the crowd."

"That's just it. Then one night, just before he vanished, Joe picked out a sporting-looking cove and did the usual, lifting his pocketbook and getting the squint on him. Except, in *that* bill-fold, along with his calling card and some tickets and suchlike, there was a folded list of racehorses, with dates and times they were running – and whether they would come first, second, or third!"

"This was not in the account you gave me originally," Holmes mentioned.

Mrs. Ladner sniffed. "Well, information like that, five horses and their places, it was worth a fortune, wasn't it?"

"Fletcher was a memory man," I realised. "He could read that list and commit it to his mind, return the papers to the wallet and the wallet to his 'volunteer', and still know how to place the accumulator he took with Lofty Soaper."

Holmes nodded at my proposition. "On the performance with this particular 'mug', did your fiancée sneak the wallet to its place or hand it over in finale?" he enquired of Mrs. Ladner.

"He handed it back, to applause from the house. The fellow was quite discontented."

"Because he knew what notation had been folded in with his banknotes," I guessed.

"Joe told me about what he'd found, and that he was going to risk a flutter. There were five nags listed on the paper he saw, all for the next Saturday's fixtures, and those were what he was going to back. It'd be a proper nest-egg for us to get married, he told me – before he disappeared!"

"But that isn't all that was in the notes," Holmes went on in that stating-deduction-as-fact style of his. "There were also other lines in a code he couldn't crack."

"Why . . . yes," the landlady admitted, disconcerted. "A second sheet. We thought they must be more horses for the next week, because there was a date on top of them that said '*W.S. 14-10*', which we took as '*week starting 14th October*'."

"The ciphered lines were those that Fletcher memorised and then later wrote out on the back of my card. He intended to seek me out to decode their meaning."

"I told him . . . I said you were this queer cove who was hanging about Sasanoff, playing about with make-up and suchlike, poking your nose in. But you were smart as a whip and good with puzzles, and you called yourself some kind of detective. So Joe got your card and he was going to look you up – or said he was."

"He disappeared the day before the races on which he had bet," I reckoned up.

"Disappeared off without me!" Mrs. Ladner answered bitterly. "Left me in a right pickle, and all!"

"And you brought the card to Holmes, hoping that he might interpret its contents, as well as locate the missing father of your child."

"And no good it did me," the landlady responded, more sour than before. "You might be a famous detective now, Mr. Holmes, but you never answered my case, did you?"

I defended my friend. "As you can see, Mrs. Ladner, Holmes is still on it."

"I was missing the key item of information!" Holmes answered her severely. "You have just given it to me now, after all this time!"

"The story of how the cypher was discovered," I supposed.

"The top line of the original message!" Holmes responded passionately. "Oh, with that I might have decoded the thing in an instant. It is the key to the cypher! Without that, translation is impossible. With it, all is known."

"You know what it says now?" Mrs. Ladner asked, incredulous.

"Of course I do. Might I borrow your notepad and pencil, Watson? Let us decipher this at once."

"'*W.S. 14-10*'," I reviewed. "What *does* that import?"

"Not what Joseph Fletcher imputed. Though the fourteenth would have been the first day when shops, banks, and book-makers would have been open for business, the week in question would have commenced on Sunday, 13th October. The remarkable Odin von Morden was a vaudeville man, so perhaps he can be excused for thinking of 'week starting' rather than 'William Shakespeare.'"

"Shakespeare?" Mrs. Ladner repeated, blankly.

Holmes stared at the code for a long time, performing such mental calculations as few men might have done. "Not in the order of the Arden Folio . . ." he muttered to himself. "Can it be so simple as to be alphabetical? Yes, let us see . . . ."

He wracked that mighty brain and coaxed out the material he required. I once believed that Holmes gathered and retained little information beyond that necessary for his studies – although those studies were wide and diverse indeed – but he has always had a passion for Shakespeare and often resorts to quoting the Bard.

And now he proved his ability. "1.I.1.98.9 . . . That would be *All's Well That Ends Well*, alphabetically the first play, Act One, Scene One, line 98 . . . which is the second line of a sentence from Helena: '*It were all one that I should love a bright particular star, and think to wed it, he is so above me.*' The ninth word of line 98 is '*above*'."

Holmes inscribed '*above*' and carried on.

"The code uses words from Shakespeare's plays, as listed *A* to *Z*, with act, scene, line number, and word in line," I understood.

"10.II.3.25.5 . . . *Henry V*, describing the dying Falstaff, '*As cold as any stone*.'" Holmes wrote the word '*stone*'.

"27.II.1.53.8 is part of Gaunt's famous '*Sceptered Isle*' speech in *Richard II*, '*Or is a moat defensive to a house*.' House. And 8.I.2.150.15 would be Falstaff himself in *Henry IV Part 1*. Let me see, yes – '*By the Lord, thou sayest true, lad. And isn't my hostess of the tavern a most sweet wench?*'"

"'*Tavern*'," I counted. "Above '*Stone House Tavern*'."

"I played Doll Tearsheet in that one," Mrs. Ladner reminisced nostalgically.

Holmes continued his translation. "9.III.2.231.7, '*We have heard the chimes at midnight*.'" My friend cast a glance at me that almost betrayed affection. "Have we not, Watson!"

And then he passed on to, "2.II.7.43.4, from the '*All the World's a Stage*' speech in *As You Like It*. This would be . . . '*His acts being seven ages . . .*' And then we are back in *Richard II*, Act One, Scene One, line 180: '*A jewel in a ten-times-barred up chest*.' Might we interpret '*seven-ten*' as the *seventeenth of the month*, the Thursday after the horses would have run, by which time winnings might have been collected and assembled for delivery?"

"'*Above the Stone House tavern, midnight, the seventeenth*.' The second message wasn't more gambling tips, but rather where and when to take the money?" I asked.

"'If this were played upon a stage now, I would condemn it as an improbable fiction,'" Holmes declaimed. [30] A Shakespearian cypher had amused him, fixing together as it did two of his enthusiasms.

"There wasn't any other horses?" Mrs. Ladner asked, dismayed.

"Only directions to meet with whichever unscrupulous race-fixer had organised the races," Holmes replied. "Someone with a literary education and in a position to make such arrangements. Moneyed and landed, I would expect, and not someone who would take exposure lightly – or be forgiving regarding his agent fumbling the list of bets and ruining his plot."

I understood. "Once Fletcher placed his massive accumulators, then the odds would plummet. It would be clear to any seasoned gambler that the races were compromised. The racing swindlers would shy away, losing their profits."

Mrs. Ladner looked concerned. "You mean . . . Big Harry might have done for Jim?"

"The fellow overseeing the gambling for the West End in Moriarty's day?" I considered.

"I would have heard about such a murder," Holmes insisted. "Indeed, it might well have been bruited around the demi-monde as a lesson in

262

keeping out of Stormer's business. I was closely following such rumours for my developing understanding of the criminal class at that time, and there was no such whisper."

"What became of 'Big Harry'?" I asked him.

"He tried to become too big," Holmes told me. "He died of a long shot from a rifle in '88."

"An air rifle?"

"No, Watson, not by Von Herder's remarkable weapon, constructed at James Moriarty's special order for Colonel Moran. Though Stormer's assassin was a crack shot with a gun, Moran was hardly the Professor's only enforcer."

"Have you ever met Sebastian Moran?" I asked Mrs. Ladner. Miss Delia Fount had been an attractive ingénue, and 'Tiger Jack' had once had an eye for the ladies.

The matron denied all knowledge of the Colonel, though she recognised his name from the papers around the time of the murder of the Honourable Ronald Adair. [31]

"I would need to consult my case-books and clippings files to be certain of suspicious deaths in London in October 1879," Holmes reflected. "There *was* the demise of Trevor Crawley, a sporting gentleman with an interest in track and turf about that time. His body was fished out of the Thames a couple of days after I had departed for New York. He may well have been the theatre-going volunteer who unfortunately allowed Fletcher to see the list he carried. If so, then his sponsors weren't pleased at his failure."

Holmes's feats of recollection on his subjects of interest – crime and Shakespeare – rivalled those of any vaudeville memory man, but Mrs. Ladner had another old resentment to gnaw at. "*I* should have been on the *Empress Queen* with the rest of the troupe, crossing to America," she complained. "Except that I was beginning to show."

"Instead, you wedded Fletcher's landlord, Mr. Eric Ladner," Holmes noted. "Ladner was quite accommodating to you when you wished to look through those abandoned possessions of your former fiancée's to retrieve the card that Fletcher had written on and had intended to bring to me."

Mrs. Ladner flushed. "Well, I knew what it was worth – or I thought I did. So I convinced Eric." She hesitated a moment before blurting out, "It isn't as if I could have got any *more* pregnant."

"Did Ladner know what the card signified?"

"I told him. That is, he got it out of me. He already knew about the wager that Joe had placed."

"How?" I wondered.

263

"Come, Watson," Holmes chided me in that familiar tone. "Fletcher owed two weeks' rent arrears. He was flat broke. Where do you think he got the half-sovereign coin to lay on his accumulator?"

"He borrowed a crown [32] from his two friends before he vanished," I replied. "But . . . he laid his wager with a ten shilling coin, and had probably already done that before his disappearing act."

"He took Eric on as a partner," Mrs. Ladner confirmed. "And then bilked Eric as well as me when he did a runner."

"Perhaps he squeezed his vaudeville pals for a little extra for another bet with a different firm to maximise his hoped-for win," I suspected. "Unless it was just to fund his flight from London."

"Or to cover my consultation fee," suggested Holmes with more acuity.

"I don't know what Joe was up to, those last days," admitted Mrs. Ladner. "I thought he was going to marry me, that we might have a future together with . . . with a family. But it wasn't so. He jilted me."

Holmes was unmoved by such personal tragedy. He continued his interview. "And that is when you agreed with Ladner to follow Fletcher's plan of laying the code before me, to see if I might decipher more information that could be used for further wagers. But at the same time, you hobbled me by rendering me an incomplete account of matters."

"I could hardly go telling you that Joe was cheating the bookies about a race-fixing game," the landlady pointed out.

"And after I was unable to trace Fletcher or solve the code on the card?"

Mrs. Ladner looked sullen and unhappy. "Well, I was in a different kind of fix, wasn't I? No career-making American tour. No fiancée. I tried to convince Eric that the babe was his but he . . . he arranged for me to see the Old Woman of Kitchener's Yard . . . ."

"The abominable abortionist, Merridew!" I snarled, from previous ill acquaintance. [33]

"The complication was taken care of, and Eric married me. It was the best future I could make."

Holmes frowned at the landlady's protestation, but his next query was interrupted by the abrupt arrival of Eric Ladner.

The burly fellow bustled in through the kitchen door. I could smell the drink on his breath from across the room. "What's this?" he demanded. "Who's these two, then, Gladys? We're full up. We don't need no more broken-down actors!"

"Then you will be pleased to learn that we are no such thing!" I replied hotly. "You are in the presence of Mr. Sherlock Holmes, the renowned detective."

Holmes laid a restraining hand on me too late. Ladner blanched as if he had encountered Banquo's ghost at the feast.

"You perhaps remember me, Mr. Ladner?" my friend enquired. "We spoke many years since, on the subject of this lady's then-betrothed. If you cannot recall that, you will at least know my reputation for unearthing the truth."

Ladner abruptly and unaccountably lunged at Holmes.

"Eric!" Mrs. Ladner shrilled. "What has got into you?"

Holmes avoided the jab that the landlord aimed at his jaw. Old pugilistic instincts from my friend's boxing days welled up inside him. He balanced his weight on his forward leg and delivered as splendid an uppercut as I have ever seen.

Ladner crumpled on the linoleum.

"Eric!" his wife screeched. She hastened over to tend to her red-faced, half-stunned spouse.

"Get out!" the fellow roared at Holmes, clutching his face. "Get out of my house!"

"Certainly we shall go," the detective agreed. "We must summon a constable."

"Holmes, what do you mean?" I asked, baffled as of old.

"Mr. Ladner has a confession to make, to us or to Scotland Yard. And also to his wife."

The former Delia Fount looked upon her husband with suspicion. "What does he mean, Eric?"

Ladner shuffled backwards on the seat of his trousers until his back was propped against the sink cupboard. He rubbed his swelling jaw, wiped blood from his chin, and glared at Holmes with loathing.

"I had only a hypothesis," Holmes instructed the landlord, "until your ill-conceived and poorly executed assault offered more reason for my suspicion."

"I don't know what you're talking about," Ladner spat.

Holmes turned to speak to me – an old trick of ours when cracking an intransigent interviewee. "We might need to call Inspector Hopkins or one of his colleagues, Watson. The whole house will need to be thoroughly searched, with an especial attention paid to the floor or the cellar. A scent-hound would be useful, but it may not be necessary."

I followed Holmes's thinking. "All those years ago, the only person other than Miss Orpington who knew what Fletcher had come upon, the whole story, was Ladner. Fletcher had to let him in on it for the funds he needed to place the accumulator bet. And it would have made both men a lot of money. Or one man alone twice as much money."

"What are you saying?" Mrs. Ladner demanded. "Eric, what's he saying?"

Ladner stared at Holmes with hatred. He clamped his rattled jaw tight shut.

"Fletcher departed from his lodgings on Tuesday, 9th September, 1879 with the intention of borrowing five shillings from friends at the Alhambra," Holmes addressed the room. "He succeeded in wheedling the loan, promising his impecunious fellow vaudevillians a quick payback at the weekend. That was possibly the last time he was seen alive – except by his murderer."

"Murder?" echoed Mrs. Ladner.

"He had almost certainly laid his wager days before that. Might we surmise that he didn't entirely trust his landlord and financier, and thus concealed the betting slips from Mr. Ladner as insurance against being cheated? If it was me, I would have hidden them somewhere inconspicuous at the theatre. Amongst an old props box perhaps, or amongst a dusty pile of sheet music."

"He went to both Miss Fount's theatre and his own that day," I remembered.

"At the theatre?" Ladner muttered, almost to himself.

Holmes continued his exposition, as he was wont to do. "Let us presume that Mr. Ladner decided that he would prefer the entire windfall for himself. He had the keys to search Fletcher's chamber, but the receipts weren't there. He therefore waited for Fletcher to return from his visit to his friends and accosted him for the stubs he expected to find upon Fletcher's person. But they weren't there either."

Ladner looked at Holmes aghast, as if wondering how the detective was reading his mind. Holmes's act put the remarkable Odin von Morden's to shame.

"I might have deduced this back then," Holmes reviewed, "had I been aware of the wager that was made. Nor did I apprehend Ladner's attraction to Miss Orpington, a desire that eventually led to matrimony – once Fletcher was out of the picture. I was on a different continent when that scene of the story played out."

I saw it clear now. "Fletcher objected to being searched by Ladner. Things became violent."

"It was an accident!" Eric Ladner exclaimed. His resistance and denial crumbled all at once. "I only wanted the tickets. I only wanted Gladys. I didn't mean . . . He hit his head as he fell . . . ."

"Fletcher's death might have been accidental," Holmes replied. "Your concealing his body under your cellar floor was a choice. Your conspiring with Fletcher's fiancée to have me decode the card's numbers was quite calculated. But in causing Fletcher's death, you silenced forever the one voice that could tell you where the betting slips were hidden. And in obscuring key information from my investigation, you and your wife made the code's solution impossible."

Mrs. Ladner gasped. "Joe . . . buried in the cellar? *My cellar?*"

"Be quiet, Gladys!" Ladner barked at his spouse. "A wife can't be forced to give testimony against her husband!"

"Forced?" Mrs. Ladner shouted back. "You murdered Joe Fletcher! *My* Joe! To steal 'is money and the steal me from 'im! You stole 'im from me. *You stole my life!*"

The rest of our evening was concerned with the too-familiar consequences of a Sherlock Holmes investigation. Ladner had lost his nerve and helped Holmes to verify his conclusions. Scotland Yard appeared in its detective majesty to verify statements, take down accusations and confessions, and to begin lifting the floor of the landlord's cellar.

I was still unclear on one key point, though. "You have accounted for the memory man's discovery, the wager that was laid but never collected, the movements and misadventure of Odin von Morden, and the long-delayed arrest of Mr. Eric Ladner, Holmes. But what of the point that set you onto these revelations? Where does Colonel Moran come into this? How were his fingerprints upon your calling card?"

Holmes viewed the battered old card with some nostalgic affection. "I have worked it out now. Trust Moriarty to complicate matters even at such a remove! This card, Watson, with its mysterious code, has remained in my files all those years since, indexed under '*F*' for *Fletcher* and '*M*' for *von Morden*, consigned to a box of inconclusive investigations from my Montague Street days. Until the night of 24th April, 1891 – "

"The night before we fled Moriarty for the Continent." I remembered well that desperate journey and the match of wits between two great and implacable intelligences who could no longer mutually survive. [34]

"The night when our rooms at Baker Street were subject to arson. The damage was negligible, calculated only to keep me off-balance and running, flushed from my lair. But it follows that someone had to have been to 221b, despite my precautions. Presumably that someone would have made a thorough search for any clues I might have been careless enough to leave behind as to my intended movements or about the case I had assembled to bring down Moriarty's empire."

"A man skilled enough to enter Baker Street unnoticed like that – " I pondered, " – surely it was most likely the tiger-stalker Moran. And he searched your files."

"He couldn't have had the time to finger every page. However, might we posit that he saw '*M*' for '*von Morden*', recognised the name from some similar index of his employer from the time when that a racing syndicate was taken down by mischance, and paused a moment to examine that card?"

"Then Moran never had anything to do with the case. His principal might have."

"It is impossible to be certain at this remove. Nothing about Professor Moriarty would surprise me now. Certainly not the implication that the Shakespearian code might be part of one of his early schemes or consultations." Holmes broke into a broad smile. "It is rather refreshing to brush wits against the old spider again, one last time!"

Our long night was coming to a close. By the time we had satisfied Hopkins and seen Ladner off in a police wagon, and I had passed Mrs. Ladner into the supporting arms of her sister, the first smudges of a grey dawn were showing in the foggy sky over wet and chilly London.

"I shall miss these odd excursions, Holmes," I told my friend.

"As shall I," he replied.

We shook hands and Holmes departed through the fog to complete his packing and retire from his consultations.

NOTES

1. That would be 1879, during which the Battle of Isandlwana on January 2nd proved to be a memorable tragedy and decisive British defeat, with a column of 1,800 British, colonial, and native soldiers and 350 civilians overwhelmed by approximately 20,000 Zulus. British and Zulu fatalities were around 1,300, and 1,000 to 3,000 respectively. News of the battle sent waves of dismay through the British public and remained a memorable event in Victorian memory around which to pin other chronologies. The Zulu War effectively ended with British victory at the Battle of Ulindi on July 4th.

2. This significant social distinction might be lost on modern readers. Mrs. Hudson *owned* the property at 221 Baker Street (221b being the upstairs flat), or at least she owned the leasehold on the house, since all the land in that part of London was ground-owned since 1532 by the Portman Estate, let on hundred-year leases or longer. Although Mrs. Hudson *might* offer the same domestic duties as a housekeeper (though not all landlords did or do), she was not an employee of her tenants. They were purchasers of her services. For this reason, Holmes and Watson always address her respectfully as "Mrs. Hudson", while staff that she employs are usually called by their first names.

    None of this helps with "A Scandal in Bohemia" (1891, collected in *The Adventures of Sherlock Holmes*, 1892), wherein Holmes promises Watson, "When Mrs. Turner has brought in the tray I will make it clear to you."

3. Watson's probably-third marriage is generally accounted to have begun on 4th October 1902, which sets our present story just past Watson's first wedding anniversary. He had already vacated Baker Street for chambers in Queen Anne Street in July of 1902. In "The Adventure of the Creeping Man" (1923, collected in *The Case-Book of Sherlock Holmes*, 1927) he recorded that by September 1903 his new medical practice was "not inconsiderable".

4. By the late nineteenth century, German-made Zeiss microscopes had become the scientific optical tool of choice, based upon physics and mathematics professor Ernst Abbe's pioneering work on compound and stereoscopic instruments.

    The Pocket Kodak camera, first sold in 1895 with the slogan "*One button does it*", used front-roll design and daylight film spools, with a number-window showing how many exposures remained on the film. It popularised the term "snap-shot".

5. Holmes's Sussex housekeeper, Martha, "a dear old ruddy-faced woman in a country cap", plays a significant role in "His Last Bow" (1917, collected in *His Last Bow: Some Reminiscences of Sherlock Holmes*, 1917). Many Sherlockian historians have been tempted to assume that Mrs. Hudson, landlady of 221 Baker Street, accompanied Holmes on his retirement to Sussex, and that therefore her otherwise-unrevealed Christian name was Martha. Others rebut the idea, since a housekeeper is a significantly humbler role than landlady or landlady/housekeeper, as Footnote No. 2 discusses.

Our present manuscript adds little to our understanding of this Holmesian marginalia.

6. "The Adventure of the Creeping Man" (1923, collected in *The Case-Book of Sherlock Holmes*, 1927) is one of the stranger stories in the Canon, featuring as it does the odd Hyde-like transformation of Professor Presbury after an experimental rejuvenation injection of langur monkey essence prior to his marriage to a much younger wife. The narrative is controversial amongst Holmes commentators and has led to various theories about what Watson might have concealed about the "true" events.

7. The Canon does not offer a house number for Holmes's former lodgings *"around the corner from the British Museum"*. Michael Harrison in *The London of Sherlock Holmes* (1972) offers evidence for number 26, but had previously espoused No. 24 in an earlier edition, based up on the old lease records of a "Mrs. Holmes" renting that property in the 1870's. Several pastiche writers have standardised No. 24 as Holmes's initial practice address, and *sans* any material in contradiction, the assertion is honoured herein.

8. At least according to W.S. Baring-Gould in his biography *Sherlock Holmes of Baker Street* (1962). *Seventy Years a Showman* (apparently published by Hodder & Stoughton, 1923) is a very elusive book to find these days, leading many Sherlockians to question whether this might be another "Watsonian misdirection".

9. Holmes is referencing "The Great Hiatus", the the years after his final encounter with Professor Moriarty near Meiringen, Switzerland during which he was assumed dead, wherein it appears that many of his files were bequeathed to the Detective Branch of the London Metropolitan Police Force for reference purposes.

10. Lord William's Swiss valet, François Benjamin Courvoisier, committed this murder on 6th May, 1840. It is an early example of a crime being solved by forensic investigation.

11. Francisca Rojas is cited as the first criminal in the world to be convicted through fingerprint evidence. Her motive was believed to have been to rid herself of her "encumbering" six- and four-year-old children, since her boyfriend had been overheard saying that he would marry her "except for those two brats."

12. In *The Hound of the Baskervilles*, Holmes is ranked as the *"second highest expert in Europe"* after Paris police officer and biometrics researcher Alphonse Bertillon (1853-1914). Holmes *"expressed his enthusiastic admiration of the French savant"* in "The Adventure of the Naval Treaty" (1893, collected in *The Memoirs of Sherlock Holmes* that same year but dated 1894).

13. Baring-Gould quotes Sasanoff commenting in *Seventy Years a Showman*: *"So much absorbed was Sherlock Holmes in his own achievements that he was unable or unwilling to appreciate the achievements of others. At that time, at least, it was never any great pleasure to him to see the acting of others."*

Baring Gould's biography records Holmes's debut performance as being in the role of Horatio in *Hamlet* on 13th October, 1879, less than six weeks before Holmes took off for his eight-month theatrical tour of America. If this is accurate, then Holmes was never actually required to stand in as Duke Orsino in *Twelfth Night*. The play is suggested to be Holmes's favourite, as evidenced by it being the only Shakespeare work that Watson mentions his friend quoting from twice.

14. A reference to "The Musgrave Ritual" which Holmes decoded in the 1893 story of that name, collected in *The Memoirs of Sherlock Holmes*.

15. That is, an early method of printing a photograph on paper, the most popular form of photographic positives from 1855-1900.

16. The "Knowledge of London" is a test for the coveted Green Cab Driver Badge. It was first instituted in 1865 for hackney cabmen with horse-drawn carriages and is still required today to drive a taxi in the City of London. Candidate Knowledge Boys (and now Girls) are expected to do 320 preparatory "runs" or trips outlined in *The Blue Book* that are designed to instil a comprehensive understanding of "the patch", before attending twelve "appearances" for oral examination over an average thirty-four months. It requires intimate and detailed memory of 25,000 miles of city road routes, sites of interest, schools, hospitals, civic buildings, public houses, statues, and plaques.

It is often held to be the most difficult and rigorous examination process in the world. Passing "The Knowledge" can take as long as earning a degree and takes thousands of hours of study. There are ten schools presently dedicated to tutoring Knowledge Boys and Girls for their subsequent test, with tuition costs of up to £200,000.

One can see why Sherlock Holmes might find such training valuable, and how he might pass such a test with distinction.

17 Gillette's adaptation of *Sherlock Holmes* (starring himself in the title role) premiered at the Star Theatre in Buffalo on October 23rd, 1899, opened on November 6th at the Garrick Theatre in New York City for more than 240 performances, then commenced a long tour across America. It arrived with Gillette at the Lyceum Theatre in London in September 1901 for more than 200 performances, before commencing a British tour with H.A. Sainsbury in the title role. Gillette played Holmes on stage in this and other plays over a thousand times. His portrayal of Holmes fixed in the public's mind the signature images of meerschaum pipe, deerstalker hat, and Inverness cape which are now often assumed to have been established in the original Canonical adventures.

The comedy *Sheerluck Jones* was also successful, parodying Gillette's play in 138 performances as a *"dramatic criticism in four burlesque paragraphs and as many headlines."*

18. According to Baring-Gould, Holmes's London theatrical debut was as Horatio in *Hamlet* in 1879. His first major role was Cassius in *Julius Caesar*. On tour across the U.S. with the Sasanoff Shakespearian Company, Holmes's Malvolio "offered the most adequate presentation of that character

that America had ever seen until that time." His other notable performances were as *The Merchant of Venice* Shylock, *Faust*'s Mephistopheles, and *Macbeth*.

19. Thanks for Moran's full name and army nickname are due to George MacDonald Frasier, who includes him as a boy in *Flash for Freedom!* (1971) and chronicles his adult adventures from Isandlwana to Rorke's Drift in *Flashman and the Tiger* (1999). Holmes and Watson also cameo in the latter book, but the unreliable narrator, Flashman himself, does not portray them generously.

20. Holmes himself offers confirmation of Moran's survival until at least September 1902 in "The Adventure of the Illustrious Client" (1924, collected in *The Case-Book of Sherlock Holmes*, 1927).

21. And proved to be insufficient in I.A. Watson's novel *Holmes and Houdini* (2017), which took place over a year before our present story.

22. Big game hunter, especially in India.

23. The answer to the trivia question "What phrase does Sherlock Holmes use the most?" is not, as many might guess, "*Elementary*" (three occasions) or "*Whatever remains, however improbable, must be the truth,*" (also three occasions), but actually "*Possess our souls in patience,*" (four occasions) quoting Luke 21:19 – unless one admits the words "*And yet – and yet – *" which Holmes utters no less than six times in the Canon.

24. Colonel Moran authored *Heavy Game of the Western Himalayas* in 1881.

25. In retaliation for the British government intending to reduce payments for protecting the Kohat Pass in the Northeastern Frontier of India, the Jowaki tribe staged raids upon British territory, including the killing of over a dozen Sepoy guards. The British expedition of 1877-1878 sortied 1,500 troops of the Punjab Frontier Force, soon augmented by 5,900 others, to push the Jowaki out of their stronghold in Jummu and chase them through the Naru Khula gorge.

26. The Battle of Charasiab, 6th October, 1879, and the siege of the Sherpur Cantonment, 15-23 December, 1879, were key events in the Second Afghan War. Both incurred minor British casualties and major Afghan losses.

27. *The Cruelty to Animals Act* 1835 made cockfighting illegal in England and Wales and in the British Overseas Territories. The prohibition extended to Scotland in 1895. The bloodsport is still practiced in some countries today.

Ratting, or rat-baiting, involved timing how many rats in a pit-ring a dog could kill within an allotted time. Although also prohibited in the 1835 Act, the ban on ratting contests was not enforced until the end of the nineteenth century. The *World Sporting Annual* claimed that a thirteen-pound black-and-tan bull terrier named Jacko held the world record for killing one-hundred rats in five-minutes-twenty-eight seconds and that Jacko also slew a thousand rats in less than one-hundred minutes in 1862.

The use of terrier dogs for pest control of unconfined rats is legal in the UK under *The Hunting Act* 2004, and is generally considered to be environmentally friendly, humane, and efficient.

28. This was a Victorian slang amalgam corruption of the Italian *mezzo*, meaning "half", and of *poona* for "pound". Since there were twenty shillings to the pre-decimal British pound, ten shillings was literally a half-pound. From 1838 to 1887 these coins were "Victoria young head" sovereigns minted in 22-carat gold.

29. This would be around £117,000 or US $152,000 in 2024. An average wage in England in 1879 was around £46/12-per-annum. According to *Cruchley's London in 1865: A Handbook for Strangers* (1865): *"The tariff at the respectable Boarding-Houses in the City appears to bear the following average: Bed and breakfast, 3s; dinner (chop or steak), 2s.; tea, with chop, 1s. 6d., without chop 1s.; private sitting-room, 2s. 6d; attendance, 6d. per day. But at many Eating-Houses and Coffee Houses of good character the traveller may obtain respectable accommodation at still lower rates."*

30. From *Twelfth Night*, III. 4. 192-193.

31. *C.f.* "The Adventure of the Empty House" (1903, collected in *The Return of Sherlock Holmes*, 1905).

32. Five shillings.

33. *"Merridew of abominable memory"* is amongst the criminal characters filed under M in Holmes's case files in "The Adventure of the Empty House." Those Holmesians who care to admit I.A. Watson's additions to the corpus will find his story "The Abominable Merridew" in *Sherlock Holmes, Consulting Detective* Volume 5 (2013) and collected in *Sherlock Holmes Mysteries* Volume 1 (2015, Kindle only).

34. As recounted in "The Adventure of Final Problem" (1893, collected in *The Memoirs of Sherlock Holmes*, 1893).

The Clue of the
Undamaged Stones
by David Marcum

"Many has been the occasion," said Sherlock Holmes when we spoke on the telephone that morning, "when you have recommended rest and a change of scene when I displayed signs of overwork. A short sojourn by the sea, to be alliterative, can only do you some good."

He wasn't incorrect, and I acknowledged that a few days rusticating in Sussex would not be unwelcome. For the last couple of years, there had been rising-and-falling surges of smallpox cases in the capital, and recently I had been heavily involved in getting ahead of the latest wave. Although my help was still needed, I knew that I would be more effective and useful if I returned refreshed.

By that afternoon, the twentieth of June, I arrived in Eastbourne and left the station to find a cab. The resort town was rather crowded at that time of year, and there was a mugginess in the air that forced people to slog along, dragging their feet and considering the possibly they should have picked somewhere else to holiday, or that they should have made arrangements to travel at a different time of year. Having served in much hotter climes a quarter-century earlier and still retaining my acclimation for it, I was indifferent to the temperature, which was no higher than the low eighties. However, but I knew that to the average Britisher, it seemed as if he or she had been unhappily transported to the tropics.

The cab took me to Holmes's small farm, approximately five miles from Eastbourne and not-quite five acres on the Downs, just north of the base of Beachy Head. He had acquired it during the course of an investigation, with the idea of retiring there. I'd always assumed that said retirement would occur at a much older age, but he had surprised me in early October of 1903, not quite two years before, when, at the age of forty-nine-and-three-quarters, he had unexpectedly announced his imminent departure from London.

Of course, "retirement" to Sherlock Holmes wasn't quite what it would mean to other people, as leaving his consulting practice meant taking on more clandestine investigations for the British Government, away from the prying eyes who would have observed his comings and goings from his old London lodgings. Still, since moving 56.69 miles as the crow flies from 221b Baker Street to his farm – he had measured the distance to the hundredth-deimal from a series of sequentially placed

Ordinance Maps, providing explanatory commentary regarding making adjustments in his calculations to take into account the curvature of the earth – he'd settled in easily to country life, as if he'd been down there for years, dividing his time between learning the intricacies of being an apiarist and taking on various investigations – some rather publicly displayed and along the lines of those handed in his former Baker Street practice, while others were of a more discreet nature at the behest of his brother, Mycroft. These latter required that he sometimes slip away unseen, while giving the impression that he was still ensconced as a recluse behind the shoulder-high walls of his enclave, constructed from locally gathered quartz many generations before our time.

I spent the ten or fifteen minute drive between station and farm conversing with a fellow named Hibbert whom I'd met numerous times before since making this part of the world a regular stop. The fellow was in his fifties, and moved down from London nearly a decade earlier, finding a job as a cabbie – first with a horse, and lately with an automobile. As usual, the drive was mostly his lamentations along the theme that he'd never be accepted as a local. The rest was spent expressing interest in Holmes. Hibbert had first become aware of Holmes during the 1880's, when my friend was initially building his reputation, and it always pleased him to be able to drive Holmes or me when given the opportunity.

Hibbert seemed pleased as we approached Holmes's farm, as the retired detective was standing outside, in front of the house at the termination of the short drive that connected to the road.

"Well met, Watson!" he said. "Stow your bag inside, and then Hibbert can drive us up to the village. Tom Keller has something he'd like to discuss."

Keller was the owner and keeper of The Tiger Inn, located a mile-and-a-half to the north if we walked across the Downs, traversing the pastures and their *Ovis aries* denizens, and climbing stiles and passing through gates, or another mile longer than that by way of the winding road that went from Holmes's gate to Birling Gap, and then north toward the village of East Dean. Whenever I visited, we always ended up at The Tiger – but not usually so early.

I had also met Keller when Holmes relocated to Sussex. Holmes had performed several services for him, sometimes with my assistance, and just the previous June, we had been involved in the curious incident of the inn's ghostly "White Lady" – a matter that still generated some friendly disagreement over the interpretation of what I saw that stormy night. [1] But on that particular warm and muggy last day of spring, not long after my arrival from London, Keller wished to consult Holmes about a different manner, and someday I'll record the events concerning the German medal.

It was a short and tidy affair, but it had implications for both an immigrant from the Continent, and Holmes's secret activities in the years leading up to The Great War.

We were back at Holmes's "villa", as he liked to call it, by suppertime, and I was feeling weary as the sun was setting at nearly half-past-eight. With a yawn, I said goodnight and went up to my usual room when visiting there. It seemed as if I'd barely gone to sleep when I was awakened by a knock. Fumbling for my tableside traveling clock, I saw that it was just after midnight. I sighed and bid Holmes to enter.

"Sorry, Watson. We've received an urgent summons. Dress quickly – Hibbert is already waiting for us downstairs."

When I descended five minutes later, Holmes was waiting by the door, holding my coat and hat and wearing his own. "Many apologies," he said with sincerity – which hadn't always been the case in our younger days when a nighttime caller would awaken Mrs. Hudson, who would then retort upon Holmes, and he would then share the experience with me. "We have a bit of quick traveling in front of us." He led me outside and walked to the waiting automobile. "I've received a summons – to Salisbury."

As we settled ourselves for the fast drive back to Eastbourne, I grumbled, "There are no trains running this time of night."

Meanwhile, I tried not to consider how little I could see of the surrounding night from the rear seat of the coach as Hibbert wrestled his rather battered four-seater Wolseley across the dark and narrow road.

"Arrangements have been made," said Holmes. "The client is a man of influence. He indicates that we'll have use of a special train. I have no doubt that he set about arranging it as soon as he sent the wire requesting my presence."

And such was the case. I can only imagine the effort needed to have a locomotive and tender, as well as a couple of coach cars, ready and waiting at the station, but we were able to depart within a minute of exiting Hibbert's cab and being ushered aboard. Only after we were seated on the train did Holmes hand me the telegram, that he'd received just before waking me up.

> *Come at once to Salisbury* [the wire read]. *Murder – Cannot draw attention from imminent important celebration at site. Will have special train immediately ready and waiting for your departure from Eastbourne.*
>
> *Antrobus*

I raised my eyes to meet Holmes's. He wore a slight smile, and his eyes shone with anticipation. Retired he might be to the public, and there was no doubt that he did enjoy his new rustic life, but his reaction to the promise of an intriguing case was no different than the old dog rising and stretching in anticipation upon hearing the call of the hunting horns.

"Antrobus?" I asked. "Sir Edmund Antrobus, the baronet?" Holmes nodded, and I continued. "Hence the connection to Salisbury. His involvement with the restoration of Stonehenge – somewhat controversial – has been in the newspapers." I recalled the date – it was now the next day. "The twenty-first – this is the first day of the Summer Solstice. Sunrise will be in just a few hours – "

"Three-forty-four," interrupted Holmes. "Less than three hours."

" – and the Druids will be gathering at Stonehenge."

"Surely the 'important celebration' referenced in Sir Edmund's wire."

I tried to remember what I'd read a few days before in a small newspaper article. At the time, it had seemed nothing more than a curiosity, scanned quickly, and I wished that I'd paid more attention.

"I recall that Sir Edmund started some work at Stonehenge a few years ago. A restoration to the site – for safety concerns, I believe – and he's received a lot of criticism for closing it to the public. This year, he's allowing the Druids to hold a sunrise ceremony there." A thought occurred to me. "How is it that – even with a murder – Sir Edmund can command your presence so easily? And of greater interest, how can he arrange a special train with such ease?"

Holmes leaned back, his mouth a thin line. After a moment, he said, "As you know, my relocation to Sussex had less to do with a need to actually retire, and more with the necessity of carrying out various tasks for Mycroft as we drift ever closer to war with Germany. You have been of vital assistance in helping me maintain the fiction that I'm now nothing more than a reclusive beekeeper. There are others who are living the same sort of double life, secretly carrying out governmental tasks – and one of those is Sir Edmund.

"He was involved in the Suakin Expedition in Sudan twenty years ago, and his quality was recognized. Since then, he's maintained a rather shadowy connection with the Government – and with my brother, who, as you know, sometimes *is* the Government. And more so with every passing week. Sir Edmund became the fourth baronet upon the death of his father six years ago, and since then his involvement with these surreptitious affairs – and his association with Mycroft – has deepened considerably. I can't say that he has any sort of authority over me – I report only to Mycroft – but he does have influence, and more important, I respect him.

If he felt the need to summon me, then I am willing to respond. And clearly he has the influence to arrange a special train."

We were now speeding along, and with the lines being cleared ahead of us, and I had no doubts that we were making fifty miles an hour or better. At that rate, we'd likely cover the hundred-miles or so of our journey in just a couple of hours. From Eastbourne, the cities, towns, and villages flashed by in the night, and it was only by luck that I was able to read a few of the quickly passing signs that identified small stations, or to judge from context which bigger southern cities we were traversing. Eastbourne to Brighton to Southampton, and then we turned, more sharply curving to the northwest, arriving in Salisbury at five-minutes-to-two — surely not quite a record, but still quite fast nonetheless.

A man in chauffeur's livery met us as we stepped to the platform, briskly chivying us with no nonsense outside to a waiting automobile. I had a chance to look back at the modest red-brick station building, then just two or three years old, pondering with amazement how quickly one could now travel — turned out from a warm bed one moment, and then suddenly walking just a few miles from a mysterious historical site in the time one might take to watch a long play. Just a few hours before, I had been asleep in an entirely different part of England, and now I was relocated by way of modern technology — a fast train and telegraph communication to clear the way – to a different point in space and time in nearly the blink of an eye (in the great scheme of things), where I was climbing into a vehicle that would transport me – I assumed – to one of the notable ancient sites of the British Isles.

As we settled into the rear of the automobile, the man waiting inside, perched on the rear-facing seat, commanded to the chauffeur, who had also just settled himself behind the steering wheel, "Quickly, Clayton. As fast as you can." Then he turned back to face us, leaning forward to shake Holmes's hand, and then offering his grip to me as well, while peering with a look of stern curiosity.

"Watson, I presume?' He looked back at Holmes. "He happened to be in Sussex when my wire arrived?"

Holmes nodded. "Down for a short holiday."

"Pleased so meet you, Sir Edmund," I said.

"Antrobus," he said, settling back in his seat. "Edmund Antrobus. None of that 'Sir' business, please. I still don't like it. And I'm glad that you're here, Watson." He leaned back. He was in his mid-fifties, and appeared to be fit and in good health. He wore a wedding ring, and even in the first moment I met him, I could see that he still carried some of the authority that marks the military man for the rest of his life. Knowing that

Antrobus was involved with Mycroft Holmes and the secret business of protecting the Kingdom didn't surprise me in the least.

"Rum business," said Antrobus, looking back at Holmes with a tight smile. "I suppose you've already deduced everything, and there's nothing for you to do but point the coppers at the guilty party."

He was serious, but there was still a look of warmth in his eyes, and I knew that he was teasing Holmes in his own way. Clearly the two of them knew each other rather well. Holmes shook his head with his own small smile.

"We aren't quite so fortunate to have reached that stage just yet. Perhaps you should provide a few more facts before we arrange the arrest. It often helps to have all the pins lined up *before* the accusation." Holmes's tone turned darker. "Murder, is it?"

Antrobus nodded. "We have ten miles to go – I'll just have time to tell you about it. You'll have heard of Sir Edvard Bilbrey?"

I turned my head in surprise. "He is the victim?"

"That's right. And it couldn't have come at a worse time."

I dimly perceived why, and wished again that I had paid more attention to the press reports. It has now been a number of years since Sir Edvard was regularly mentioned in the newspapers, and if he is recalled now at all now, it is only as a figure of fun. He was quite influential in those years just before and after the turn of the century, if for no other reason than his ability to stir up controversy. As a young man in the seventies, he'd had a rather undistinguished military career, noted only for losing several toes upon one foot when a locker was dropped upon them on his way out to India. Upon his return to England, he'd dabbled around the edges of his father's mining interests.

Upon the elder Bilbrey's death, a victim of his own unsafe mines when he was on a poorly timed site inspection, the younger came into his sizeable fortune, as well as taking over his father's hereditary position in Parliament. It was there that he gave the famous speech that defined him thereafter. When a number of hecklers interrupted him, he was moved to testily reply – quickly rising to anger as was his general response to most situations. He apparently meant to say that he greatly disliked individuals who displayed such rude behavior, or something along those lines, but he shook his fist and cried haltingly, overcome by emotion and in a breaking voice, "I . . . hate . . . *people* . . . !" He later claimed that he meant to add more qualifying information as to what sort of people he hated, but he apparently hated so many different sorts that he couldn't decide which group to specifically identify. By then the crowd was roaring, surprisingly with approval, and the quote became a rallying cry. He even attracted a

279

group of unwanted followers who also espoused the "*I hate people!*" philosophy.

After that, his participation in Parliament waned – he'd never had much interest in it from the start – and he turned in other directions.

"I recall," I said, making a connection, "that a year or so ago, Sir Edvard aligned himself with the Druids."

"That's right," Antrobus agreed. "The Ancient Order of Druids, they call themselves. Not so ancient – they just formed in the 1780's. Rather more like imitation Freemasons than Druids, from what I can determine. I've had dealings with them lately, too – because of Stonehenge. Rather silly, if you ask me – chaps wearing masks, apparently because they're ashamed of themselves, demanding to wander the site in different routes and patterns, chanting and carrying cardboard sickles. Overgrown children," he spat. "And yet, some of these same men are respected members of society – politicians and doctors and lawyers and such – so I have to allow them some leeway.

"The property has been in my family since 1824 or 1825, and every generation, it seems as if the Druids come crawling out of the woodwork with some new kind of request or demand. Until recently, we've never kept much watch on the place, and I expect that they've come and gone in secret over the years much more than we've ever realized. But this 'Ancient Order' has become my particular cross to bear, as they've decided that they want to hold their Solstice ritual this year – today, in a few hours. I think that it's become more of an issue because this year they're vexed since I put up a wire fence around the place – twenty acres or so. And I hired a policeman to stand guard during the day. Blast! If only I'd thought to have someone professional here at night, too. But the daytime seemed sufficient."

"And you felt the need to have a guard because someone could get hurt" said Holmes. "Due to the restoration work,"

Antrobus nodded. "That's right. Back in 1901, I instituted some repairs – nothing major, and all of them working with The Society of Antiquaries, to make sure it's done right. I felt like I had to something after one of the uprights and the lintel resting on it fell down. How much longer before they're all tipped over? So I paid to have the tallest trilithon stood back up – and that's when the Druids started howling. You'd think they'd be thankful, if the place really means that much to them, but no. And the worst of them has turned out to be Sir Edvard – although I think he was just looking for the latest cause with which to associate himself and garner attention."

"And now he's dead," replied Holmes, drawing our attention back to the present events. I glanced out of the window at the passing countryside.

It was less than two hours until dawn, and there was nothing yet to be seen, as all was still in darkness. I thought that we had about five miles remaining before reaching the site. I didn't have a sense of where we were on the road between Salisbury and the famed stone circle, but I was fairly certain we had already passed Old Sarum, the ancient settlement and later Iron Age fort that – so I'm told – was the first known settlement in Salisbury. Holmes and I had many occasions when we visited Stonehenge, Old Sarum, and Salisbury on various cases, and sometimes I wondered if that spot was a focal point of crime, both new and ancient, in the same way that Holmes had once said some jewels are the "the devil's pet baits", seemingly created specifically to attract evil.

"Ever since I fenced off the stones and started the repairs," Antrobus continued, "the Druids have poked up their heads and pestered me about it. They wanted to be here for the Solstice, but I said no. It isn't safe, and I don't want the liability if one of them gets hurt. But Sir Edvard wouldn't be quiet, so I finally compromised and said that he and a few of his 'deputies', as he calls them, could come down and be there for the sunrise. And then he goes and gets killed!"

I thought that Holmes would ask for specifics related to the crime, as we seemed to be skirting the edge of the event, but first he had another question. "Not to negate any man's death," he said, "but why this urgency? The bother and expense of a special train in the middle of the night? It's overcast, but there's no sign of rain that might destroy vital clues. Is there some question that the killer might flee?"

"No, no. Although you may find something to the contrary, I think that we can narrow the killer down to one of three men – Sir Edvard's 'lieutenants'. Those deputies of whom I spoke. They're all prospective sons-in-law as well – interested in the dead man's daughter. No, the urgency is to get the matter settled before sunrise, because despite my wishes, a larger clot of Druids is planning to be there anyway – Who knows how many? – and we need to have answers before things have a chance of getting out of hand." He glanced my way. "No offense, Doctor, but I'm sure you're aware that there are matters of statecraft that cannot be shared with you – just as there are also currently investigations that Holmes here is carrying out at the behest of his brother in strict confidence. I, too, take on such duties, and there is one such event that's coming to fruition in the near future that would be spoiled by an incident this morning. I'm afraid that I cannot explain the details to either one of you.

"But know that this murder couldn't have come at a worse time. I'm being watched, and I don't need the kind of attention just now that an unsolved mystery will generate – or a riot by a bunch of Druids if they get stirred up. By the time the Druids learn of Sir Edvard's death, we need to tell them who is responsible – present them with a *fait accompli*, so to speak."

"Tell us more of these three lieutenants," Holmes said. I knew that in just a few moments, we would be arriving at the prehistoric structure.

"All three are in their early twenties, just a few years older than Sir Edvard's daughter, Rachel. Between us, she's a rather unpleasant girl, spoiled and sour as you might expect, but she has the advantage of being his only child and heir. And now she's an orphan, as her mother died years ago.

"The first suitor is Clifford Estes, the second son of Lord Estes. He's being groomed for some sort of Foreign Office position, but expectations are he'll end up being the primary heir sooner rather than later, as his older brother Gerald is a sot who will likely be dead from drink in just a couple of years."

I was beginning to see that Antrobus didn't believe in sugar-coating hard facts. As I came to know him better, I learned that this was his regular nature, as in his secret work, he was often forced to cut to the quick of the matter in little time, seeing and describing things with honest bluntness.

"The second of Bilbrey's followers is Andrew Garvey, of the Lancaster mill family. Also a second son, but it's no secret that there's so much money in the family that Andrew and his two brothers will all receive substantial fortunes. Still, he'd do well to align himself with Sir Edvard's resources.

"The third is Tyler Gilman. His father is Lord Randolph Gilman – you'll have read of his moral dissolution – and his mother is the American heiress, Wanda Gilman *née* Copeland, of the Boston Copelands. Like Andrew Garvey, Tyler Gilman is set to have a considerable amount of money bestowed on him, by way of his maternal grandfather, in less than a year – but he also wants that connection with Sir Edvard's daughter.

"From what I understand, all three likely joined The Ancient Order and curried Sir Edvard's favor solely as a way to win his endorsement of their interest in his daughter, and not because they have any true interest in Druidism. Wherever Sir Edvard has gone, they've gone, and when he showed up here yesterday, they were here too. And then, when he came up with the ridiculous notion that the stones needed to be guarded through the night, they were designated for the task."

"Guarded?" I asked. "From what?"

"That you'll have to ask them. Right now the local constable has all three in custody, under suspicion, in my local lodgings. But I see that we've arrived, and I've had the body left *in situ* for you to examine, Holmes."

The vehicle had slowed to a stop, and the chauffeur hurriedly exited to pull open the door. Antrobus climbed out, followed by Holmes and me. My eyes were now adjusted to the darkness, but the night was still too black to really see anything clearly. I had the sense that we'd stopped a dozen yards or so from the famed stones, but they were more of a looming presence felt than anything truly discerned.

Antrobus sought his bearings and then turned away from the great monoliths, leading us a hundred yards or so in the opposite direction until there was something of a long arcing ditch in the rough turf. There were two men standing beside it. In the darkness, I could barely make out that one was a constable, while the other fellow seemed to be dressed like a workman. As we approached, both took a few steps to one side, while the constable said to Antrobus, "No one has been here, sir."

As they moved, I could see an irregular shape in the ditch just beyond them, a darker blackness than the surrounding ground. Before anyone could ask, the constable turned on his electric torch, pointing it toward the form. "Pleasure to see you again, Mr. Holmes," he said, handing it to the detective.

Holmes glanced up. He must have recognized the voice, because there was no way to determine features in that gloom. I'd only been able to determine one of the men was a constable by the shape of his helmet. "Ah, Adams. I hope that the family is well. Still the one child?"

"Two more now, sir, thank you for asking. We're all doing very well. Hello to you, too, Doctor."

I recalled the officer from when I'd once set a broken finger after a scuffle with a raging cat's-meat lady, and I also asked a couple of questions about his current situation while Holmes knelt by the shape, which I could now see was a canvas tarpaulin. After giving it an intense examination, he pulled back the wrappings to reveal the body of a man.

I took a step forward, still staying out of the way, and yet still able to make my own observations. Holmes moved the torchlight where he needed so that it never held in one spot for too long, but I was able to determine that it was a man in his fifties, about six feet, and in a suit of some dark wool. He'd still had his hair, even in mid-life, but it was going gray at the temples. He was clean-shaven, and in death, the frown lines which had made Sir Edvard Bilbrey so recognizable were only deepened, engraved there as his final epitaph. His lips were pulled back in a rictus of agony, frozen upon his face, revealing the significant gap between his front teeth – a feature that the newspaper artists had used for quick effect when illustrating him.

Holmes motioned for Adams to help him roll the corpse. As the dead man was turned up in my direction, I couldn't tell what they found

283

underneath him, but I could see more clearly that there was a bullet hole centered on the body's chest. At that moment, Holmes motioned me forward for my own examination.

"Have a look," said softly. "And can you verify my conclusion that the bullet went straight through, likely avoiding hitting bone?"

Knowing what he was getting at, I quickly ascertained for myself that he was correct. "He was shot from the front, and the route taken by the bullet does appear to have gone straight through, as you thought. The exit wound is straightly aligned with the entry wound, and is slightly larger, as one would expect – although I doubt that this was an expanding lead slug, due to the small amount of exit damage. Likely a jacketed slug. And while an autopsy will confirm it, I believe that the heart and pericardial sack were both torn, leading to a great deal of immediate blood loss. You can see that it soaked into the man's coat and vest during the moment after he was shot, before the heart stopped – but neither this tarpaulin nor the ground below him any true staining." I looked over to where Holmes knelt beside me. "He was shot elsewhere and moved here."

Holmes nodded and got to his feet. As he did so, Antrobus spoke.

"This is Grieg, my caretaker. He discovered the body. Tell him, Grieg."

Holmes had left the pocket torch on, but directed it toward the ground so as not to blind us. However, it threw enough light to see better than before, even though our range of perception was limited to small lit circle in the middle of the vast inky night. The workman took a step forward and touched a finger to the bill of his wool cap.

"I walked up to give the site a once-over – normal thing every night, but more tonight, you see. I was told to do so about once an hour, all night long – because of the visitors, and the sunrise ceremony today. Those three lads were taking turns playing at guard duty, but we didn't know but what they weren't up to some mischief. It's just luck that I took the direction that I did – I was staying well back from the Stones, because we were told they were all armed – and came across this poor fellow lying in the ditch – about half-eleven or so. I might just as easily have missed him. Rolled in this tarp, as you see.

"Sunset was about half-after-eight, and the sky was full dark by then. Clouds out, like now – no stars or moon. A black night. Hard to see your hand in front of your face. I don't know which one o' them lads was on guard just then, but I didn't see anyone. Likely whichever lad was out here at that time was over by the stones, or sitting down on one of them. In any event, I decided not to alert him, but instead went back to the house double-quick – " He gestured vaguely in one direction which I was to later know was east, nearly to Amesbury. "It's about a mile. I woke up the master,

284

and he got on the telephone and summoned the constable here, and we all drove back over quickly and found him thus."

"Is there a local inspector?" Holmes asked.

"He's away, sir," replied the constable. "Visiting family, up north in Alton. Won't be back for another week, unless we send word."

"No time for that," added Antrobus. He looked at Holmes. "I immediately saw the gravity of the situation and started making telephone calls – to London, and to you. London took care of the special train, and thank Heavens you got here as quickly as you could."

"Where has Sir Edvard been lodging?" asked Holmes.

"With me," Antrobus explained. "I own the house nearby – just to the east. It's where I stay when I have business down this way. When I decided to allow Sir Edvard access to the site this morning, I let him and his daughter stay there, and the three deputies as well. There's plenty of room, and it was all the better to stay on his good side and attempt to keep this as low-key as possible." He growled. "And then he goes and gets himself killed."

Holmes nodded, frowning and concentrating intently. Then he seemed to have reached a decision. "If I may, Adams, I'll borrow your torch once more and make an examination on my own. I believe that I've seen enough here. The body can be moved – back to the house, I suppose – so that it won't be here when people start to arrive for the sunrise event. Watson – can you join me?"

And with that, he turned and went into the darkness, toward the famed menhirs, the torch directed toward the ground. While Antrobus, Grieg, and the constable discussed the best way to retrieve and relocate the body, I trod after Holmes as his light illuminated the stones, and his investigation carried him into the center of Stonehenge.

I caught up with him. "As you noted," he stated without pause or turn, "based on the lack of blood at both the site and on the tarpaulin, Sir Edvard was killed elsewhere and then placed in the ditch." He gestured forward. "It isn't unreasonable to believe that such a notable site as this, on a night of extra impending importance, might be the location where the death would occur."

"Are you hinting at some sort of ritualistic execution?" I asked.

"Not necessarily. But if one of the three suspects, who were supposed to be on guard duty here, wanted to arrange a secret meeting of some sort, then such a site would certainly intrude itself in the making of the decision."

By then we had entered the stones – not our first time there, and not the first time we had investigated a murder there either, but certainly the first to occur in the middle of the night in those impending hours leading to the Summer Solstice. I thought of all the thousands of other solstices that had come and gone over the millennia since these monuments were raised, and the certainty that Death had been summoned to this spot countless times over the ages – but often it was part of some religious rite carried out with the primitive belief that shed blood was required to ensure fertility for the coming season. But how many other deaths had been accomplished here in secret – not by a priest with life-blood spilled in front of many witnesses, but instead carried out in darkness, the murderer creeping and slinking away with the hopes of eternal anonymity and avoidance of responsibility for the craven deed?

Having worked with Holmes for over two decades, I had good knowledge of his methods, and as he systematically examined the grounds, bent forward to see the ground illuminated by the torch as well as he could, I stayed out of his way. He was quite methodical: No haphazard dashes here and there. Instead, he traveled sequential and overlapping lanes, working one completely from my left to right, and then turning and going back in the other direction so that nothing would be missed.

I saw that he paused several times when passing the Altar Stone, seemingly locating something of interest, but he didn't cease his search until the whole site had been examined. Only then did he call me over to the Altar Stone. "Here, Watson," he said. "He was shot here. Look, there are footprints – this one matches Sir Edvard's size elevens. There was a unique cut on the sole of his right boot. Unfortunately, his killer's prints are much more indistinct. All one can see is that they are of average size. Still, perhaps we'll see something useful when we meet the three lieutenants. Possibly two of them will be eliminated by having unnaturally large or small feet.

"In any case, the killer stood here, his back to the Altar Stone, turned northeast – the direction where the sun will rise in an hour or so. Sir Edvard faced him – and it was there that he was shot. You can see the place on the ground where he fell, straight backward. Those are his heel marks, dug in when he landed on his back. There's a spray of blood beyond in the direction where his head would have fallen – what spurted from his body as the bullet passed through. More has soaked into the grass where his body dropped. Then, there are indistinct footprints as the killer moved around, taking one of the tarpaulins from the repair work over there and bringing it back to wrap the dead man. Then, you can see where it was dragged off in the direction of the ditch in which it was found."

He then led me to the northeast, over to the tall Sarsen stones that form the main ring of the structure. Beyond, and in spite of the overcast conditions, the sky was beginning to lighten with the first hints of false dawn. The great Heel Stone, farther in the direction in which we walked, was now visible to us as a great dark shadow against the brighter background. If we were to finish our investigations before the expected arrival of the Druids, it would need to be soon.

"We may have had a piece of luck," Holmes explained when we reached the Sarsen stones located in line with where the dead man had fallen. "The bullet went straight through Sir Edvard, and then traveled in this direction with impacting any of these stones – neither these here, nor on the Heel Stone beyond them. There is no marking on the stones where a bullet strike would have occurred."

"But how does that help us?" I asked.

"You are aware of some of the advances in ballistic science – specifically, that some identifying rifling marks can be found on fired bullets that can be linked to specific weapons. I myself have contributed some knowledge to the subject, and one or two of my own cases have turned on such a point. In this instance, the deadly bullet apparently wasn't damaged – that we know of – by the body or the stones, and if it can be recovered, then we may have additional evidence toward identifying our killer."

I shook my head. "'If it can be recovered'," I said. I gestured out past the Sarsen stones to the expansive plain beyond. "Quite the long shot. Finding it would truly be like locating a needle in a haystack."

Holmes smiled, a gleam in his eye. "Ah, I have an idea about that."

"And even though we were told that the three guards were armed," I continued, "they might have been sharing the same gun, passing it from one to another as their guard shifts ended and began. So even if you prove that gun was the murder weapon, how do you tie it specifically to one of the three men?"

Holmes raised a hand, as if to fend off my objections. "We'll see what other cards are doing to be dealt. Now, let's find our way to Antrobus's lodgings and meet our suspects."

Holmes set a quick pace, and I did my best to follow and breathe steadily. I would be turning fifty-three in a couple of months, and I found when moving at speed that daily city walking was not as efficacious at as I'd like in terms of retaining youthful vigor. I had let my life become more sedentary than it should have been after Holmes's retirement nearly two years before.

As we approached the well-lit house, we found Antrobus, Grieg, and the constable standing by an outbuilding. The knight thumbed toward it, stating, "The body is in there." He then led us inside, adding, "He'll be safe enough here, until he's removed to the morgue."

After a moment of thought, Holmes indicated that he now wished to interview the dead man's three myrmidons. We left Sir Edvard Bilbrey wrapped in the tarp upon the earthen floor – a humble place to tarry at the start of the last journey that would lead to his rather overblown funeral a few days later.

Holmes succinctly explained the indications we'd found of where Sir Edvard had been shot and died. With Constable Adams' agreement, Antrobus ordered Grieg to get some buckets of water and wash away the blood at the Altar Stone to avoid stirring unnecessary speculation. "And find a lock for the shed door, and stay available." We left the caretaker there and walked toward the main house.

We entered by the front door, where two other constables stood unobtrusively on either side, backs against the walls. From where we stood in the entry hall, we could hear voices coming from an electrically lit parlour just to the left. We went in to find a another constable watching over a seated young lady, dabbing her eyes with a linen handkerchief, and the three grim young men seated along a different wall to her left.

Antrobus stepped forward. "With the absence of the local inspector, Constables Adams and Cable here have authority over the investigation, but with their approval, I've called in Sherlock Holmes." He nodded toward the famed detective. "He has been given authority by the constables to conduct the investigation. Please answer his questions accordingly." Then he stepped back, indicating that Holmes should take his place.

Instead, Holmes remained where he'd stopped upon entering, causing the three men to sit turned slightly in his direction. I knew that this was intentional, causing them to be somewhat uncomfortable while he asked his questions.

Before he could speak, the young woman sat up, a harsh look upon her face. "Where is the inspector? Get him here – or another one. Father was *killed*! That requires more than a pair of *constables*, or some private detective! Father is – *was* – a man of importance, and his murder should be treated accordingly, and not left to some *amateur*!" The last was snapped with particular viciousness. But she didn't save all of her frustration for Holmes. Looking at the three men, she continued. "It was one of *them* – Find out which one! I'll see him hanged, and cursed for the killer he is!"

I had no notion of the relationship between this woman the her three suitors prior to that moment, but it seemed that whatever esteem that might have been held between any of them up to then had vanished, and if the bitterness displayed was indicative, it would not be restored. Rachel Bilbrey's tone was vicious, and it seemed that even if one of the young men were singled out as the killer, the rest were damned by association.

When the lady had settled, Antrobus introduced the three young men. Clifford Estes was a rather squat type with a permanent smirk upon his face. My friend Mortimer would have classified his skull as *brachycephalic*, and it did nothing to make him pleasing to the eye. He had thin sandy hair combed down over a high balding brow, and he seemed amused by Miss Bilbrey's outburst.

Tyler Gilman was a complete contrast – lanky with a permanent frown, and a long thin head that nearly looked like he'd been sat upon as a baby. Whatever he was thinking kept him firmly distracted, as he hadn't glanced up at either us or the lady.

Andrew Garvey looked like his mill-working ancestors. He would have passed for solid peasant stock but for his clothing, which betrayed the fact that, as Antrobus had said, there was much money in the family.

I noted that each of the three men had average-sized feet – no help there.

Holmes seemed to be aware of Antrobus's concerns about solving the crime quickly, because he didn't waste time fencing with the different players, instead jumping immediately to the heart of the matter.

"Sir Edvard was murdered within the last six hours or so by a bullet through the heart, fired at him in the center of Stonehenge, near the Altar Stone. As I understand it, you three were sent out to stand guard, so presumably one or all of you were there when the murder occurred. Were you all together, or working in shifts?"

Garvey and Estes looked at one another, while Gilman didn't react. Then Estes replied, his voice a sneering drawl. "We were separated – in shifts. Sir Edvard thought it better that way."

"Why? What were you guarding against?"

Clifford Estes shrugged. "Who knows? The old fool was paranoid – absolutely certain that someone would try to disrupt the sunrise ceremony, although for the life of me, I can't tell you why. He – "

At the use of the word "fool", the lady once again erupted into shrieks of anger, defending her father most vigorously. She abruptly rose, and likely would have approached and clawed at Estes if Antrobus hadn't signaled for Constable Cable to step forward and have her replaced in her seat.

"You always resented Father!" she snarled. "You weren't fit to wipe his boots! You – "

Andrew Garvey talked over the girl, and she fell silent. "We were sent out alone, in shifts. We were supposed spread out the watch over the course of the night – sunset to sunrise. Gilman was the first, to cover nine o'clock or so to eleven. Then Estes until one o'clock, and then me through to the finish. But we thought it was silly, so we talked it over amongst ourselves and shortened our watches to just an hour apiece."

"And you kept to the one-hour shifts?"

"That's right. Well – I was in bed by eleven-thirty. I'd taken the last shift because we had to be up by sunrise, and since I can usually get by on less sleep than the others, I could be in bed by midnight, and still get back up and be out there by three-thirty or so, when Sir Edvard planned to arrive. That way, he'd think that we'd all done our parts, all night long. But I saw no sense in staying to the last minute, so I walked back early."

"And were you all there as you'd planned? Mr. Gilman? Did Mr. Estes relieve you at the end of your abbreviated shift?"

At this mention of his name, Gilman finally shifted his eyes toward Holmes. Following a pause and a deeper frown, as if seeing his questioner for the first time, he muttered, "Yes. Yes, he did."

"And what time was that?"

"Oh, probably about ten, as we had decided. I got out there sometime after sunset, and didn't stay more than I was supposed to – just until Estes walked over." His voice was low and deep, and had a rough edge, as if he'd damaged it at some earlier time in his life. "It wasn't too unpleasant," he added.

"And Mr. Estes – Did Mr. Garvey arrive at his agreed revised time?"

Estes nodded, his mouth pinched as if enjoying a private and unpleasant joke upon his two comrades. "He did. Before eleven. I wasn't out there much longer than an hour, and I was more than ready to leave when he got there."

"And you," Holmes said to Garvey. "Did you actually stay until eleven-thirty, or did you leave as soon as you were left alone?"

Garvey frowned, shook his head, and said shortly, "As I said, I saw no need to stay the entire time, but I did serve some of my sentence. We'd already agreed that being on guard was ridiculous, so what did it matter if I stayed until eleven-thirty, or if I went back even sooner? But I chose the latter. I enjoyed the idea of being alone at night at Stonehenge. I smoked. I listened to distant sounds. I wished that there were no clouds to block the stars. And then I returned to the house, let myself in – quietly, so that my arrival wouldn't be noticed. As I said, I planned to get some sleep, and then dress and slip back out for the sunset, since I was supposed to still be there for the morning watch. But then, just an hour or so after I went to sleep, one of these officers rousted me, and I've been awake ever since."

I considered that I understood how he felt.

"You were armed for your period of guard duty," Holmes continued. "Did you each have a gun, or did you share one between you?"

"We each had one," replied Estes. "When we became Sir Edvard's 'enforcers', as he liked to call us, he bought three identical Lugers from Westley Richards in New Bond Street."

Holmes looked toward Constable Adams. "Where are the guns?"

"In the next room – tagged when we collected them so we know who had each one."

"Excellent. Have any of them been fired?"

Adams started to answer, but Estes cut him off. "No help for you there, Sherlock. All of them have been fired. When we arrived yesterday, the three of us had a bit of fun shooting at bottles out by the stables."

Holmes frowned and looked toward the constable. Adams nodded. "I'm afraid so. All three fired, none cleaned."

"No matter," Holmes said. "There is still hope." He turned back to the three men. "You realize that all of you, by way of your scheduled presence at the Stones around the time when the murder occurred, are the most-likely suspects." There was no reaction. "Which of you had the most reason to kill Sir Edvard?"

There was still no response, and Holmes pressed further. "Come, gentlemen, this is your chance to undercut your rivals and provide us with damning information. I understand that you were each in competition for the lady's hand – and the fortune that comes with it. Who among you had made the best case? Who was the least effective? Who felt like murdering her father? Which one of you would think that killing Sir Edvard would make the path forward easier rather than more difficult?"

Estes smiled. "I thought you were more clever than that, Sherlock. Of course, none of us will rat out the others. Why should we? Certain of my own innocence, I'll wait and see what happens. I can't speak for the others. Perhaps, when you do find the killer – one of my *friends* here, it sounds like – the lady will finally realize that she and I have been the best-suited for one another the entire time – No offense, fellows. Anyway, you're just trying to pick the low-hanging fruit, holding all of us as suspects. I've heard nothing to indicate that the killer couldn't have been someone from the village, or a stranger here to see the sunrise, or some tramp or gypsy who was wandering across the plains. I suspect that's it – Sir Edvard came out after we'd all abandoned our posts to check on us, and that's when he stumbled into his killer. He likely picked a fight with the fellow and got shot for his trouble."

Rachel Bilbrey growled, but stayed still and otherwise quiet.

"Did any of you see or hear anything suspicious during your watches?" asked Holmes, ignoring Estes' points.

"No," said Garvey, glancing distastefully at Estes, as if in confirmation. "But why would we? I've heard nothing to indicate that Sir Edvard was killed during the time when we were there."

"Don't believe them!" erupted the young lady, now moved to lean forward as if she were about to roll upright and charge at her former beaus. "They all hated him! And they never cared anything for me, except for what they thought they might get by marrying me! I told Father, but they were always trying to win him over, and he wouldn't listen. They – "

"That's enough of that, Ma'am," advised Constable Cable, laying a hand upon her shoulder. She subsided, glaring at the three men. I was uncertain as to what peace had been arranged between this peculiar group during the odd courtship, but it appeared to have irretrievably ended with the death of the girl's father.

Estes shifted in his seat, as if preparing to rise. "Now, if there's nothing else – "

"You aren't going anywhere," advised Antrobus.

"Oh, really!" the young man sneered. "By *your* authority?"

"No," countered Constable Adams. "By mine."

Holmes had been thinking to himself, and seemed to ignore the brief quarrel that had bubbled forth. Instead, he caught Antrobus's eye and said, "Can we speak in the other room?"

Our host nodded and turned to walk out. "You as well, please, Adams," added Holmes, and the constable joined us, leaving Officer Cable in charge of the four detainees. In the hall, Adams paused to have the two constables by the door relocate closer to the parlour.

In Antrobus's study, we four stood and faced one another, not bothering with finding seats or getting comfortable. "That was inconclusive," said Holmes without preamble. He looked at our host. "I'm afraid that I cannot name the killer before sunrise."

Antrobus started to speak – to disagree, or to urge him to try harder in the name of national security – but he held his tongue, and then said, "What do you advise?"

"Without taking time to conduct a much deeper investigation into the backgrounds and relationships of those people, to learn the truth about their convoluted relationships, we're at a standstill in that direction. Likewise, the fact that all three guns were fired means that we can't use that fact to narrow down the killer. But there is one possibility, as we've had a bit of unexpected luck: The bullet that went entirely through Sir Edvard and then between the Stones is likely undamaged, and resting somewhere on the plains beyond the Heel Stone."

Antrobus looked at him with a cocked head and said, "And you consider that to be *lucky*?"

292

"It is. It's a chance, and if we can find that bullet, I can name the murderer. In the meantime, you'll have to go ahead with the sunrise ceremony, and if anyone asks about Sir Edvard's absence, put them off. That should avoid the immediate scandal that you fear might disrupt your greater plan." He looked at the desk, and back to Antrobus. "Might I use a sheet of paper?"

"Of course."

Holmes quickly moved around the desk, pulled over a sheet of stationery and a pen, and made a couple of short notations. Then he blotted the paper and folded it in half. He returned to the three of us and handed the sheet to Constable Adams.

"Please obtain these items as soon as possible. In the meantime, we'll be watching the sunrise and awaiting your return."

For those who have never had the chance to attend the Summer Solstice at Stonehenge, I heartily recommend the experience. There are other megaliths throughout the Isles that are also laid out along similar lines as lunisolar calendars, such as the one at Swinside in Cumbria, where Holmes and I once rescued the kidnapped newborn that had been designated the *Electus Puer* by the sinister *Cultus Tenebris*, but Stonehenge is certainly the most famous. (I expect the Winter Solstice, when viewed there, is just as striking, and perhaps more dramatic with its somber connotations of death and darkness, but I have no desire to stand out upon that unbroken plain in late December, with nothing to stop or deflect the wind except possibly the ineffective Normanton Down Barrows half-a-mile to the south, should the wind be blowing from that direction and no other. The dead who haunt that place no longer feel the cold, but it's all too real for those of us still among the quick.)

Antrobus's fears of being inundated by a crowd of Druids, all somehow scenting the death of Sir Edvard Bilbrey and causing a notable riot, turned out to be the merest moonshine. The Ancient Order of Druids, of which Sir Edward was a part, failed to show. Antrobus muttered to himself, irritated that he'd worried for nothing, but he was also clearly relieved that the incident he'd feared, whatever it was, had been avoided.

"And in any case, I'm glad," he added to me in an undertone, "that Holmes is here. Not disparaging the local Constabulary, but I don't see that they would have been able to make much headway with that unpleasant Cerberus known collectively as Sir Edvard's 'lieutenants'."

As the sunrise approached, there were only a few quiet locals in attendance, and I was sure that some of them were likely true Druids, there to quietly contemplate the event. They stood off to themselves, unobtrusively, but positioned in such as away as they could see the sun through the specific stones placed to line up with its first appearance on the Solstice. The day was cloudy, with a uniform gray dimness all around, making the cool morning breeze seem that much more brisk and more unpleasant. But fortunately, as the specific hour and minute approached, there was a break in the clouds to the east, and the sun triumphantly showed through. At the exact moment of sunrise, I was standing in the right spot to see the light lined up through the stones. After looking and glancing away, I noticed that many of the locals in attendance had closed their eyes and seemed to whisper silently to themselves – prayers, perhaps, related to their ancient and personal beliefs. Then, after the moment passed all too soon, they silently drifted away.

I could only imagine the spectacle if The Ancient Order of Druids – that clownish and costumed amateurish group of fakirs down from London, playing at ancient beliefs that held no meaning for them – had actually decided to make the journey.

When we'd first gone back to the menhirs from Antrobus's house, Holmes had taken up a spot to the east, past the Heel Stone, to keep watch over the area where he felt the bullet had landed. He kept his back to the rising sun to protect his vision while he made sure that no one else wandered in that direction, possibly looking for the missing bullet, or simply exploring, but taking the chance that they would somehow make it more inaccessible, perhaps by treading upon it and driving it into the turf.

I had offered to keep watch with him, but he generously waved me back to the central circle where I could see the sun come up – something that, once the moment had passed, I was profoundly glad to have witnessed for once in my life.

As the day grew brighter and the observers departed for their homes, Holmes came back and we walked over to join Antrobus. Holmes explained that we were now waiting for Constable Adams to return with the items he'd requested. To pass the time, Holmes showed where Sir Edvard had been standing when he was killed, and demonstrated how there was no sign that the bullet had hit any of the stones in that direction.

I knew that, like me, Antrobus wanted to ask what difference the undamaged stones made, but he knew enough to possess himself in patience and wait. And it didn't take long, as the constable quickly arrived and pulled to a stop nearby.

"I have everything you wanted, Mr. Holmes," he said. "In fact, I picked up some extra to make a few more, to help it go faster."

"Excellent initiative, Adams! While we get started with our preparations, would you run over and bring back our suspects? It might be instructive for them to watch our investigation – and for us to watch them."

We began to unload various items from Adams' battered Humber, before the officer drove over to Antrobus' residence. Holmes didn't bother to watch him depart. Instead, he began to sort several rolls of copper wire, half-a-dozen iron pipes, one inch in diameter and two feet in length, and a matching number of bulky lead-acid batteries. I dimly began to perceive Holmes's plan, impressed that his mind would have instantly leapt to such an obscure solution to the problem.

By the time Constables Adams, Cable, and the two others returned with the four "guests", Holmes, Antrobus, and I had had constructed three rather unwieldy electromagnets, one apiece, and we had the pieces ready to assemble three more. Holmes had explained that we might as well make the extras while we had the time and materials, in case one of the others failed. Adams had also brought some straps, which we used to fashion handles for carrying our homemade devices.

Construction was an easy-enough affair. We each cut long lengths of copper wire, and then began to wrap it tightly into a coil around the iron pipes. When finished, we connected each end of the wire to the terminals of the battery, thus magnetizing the pipe.

The policemen shepherded the three men and Sir Edvard's daughter to one side, and Holmes began to explain as he finished up his second magnet. Just as he'd done a few minutes before with Antrobus, he indicated where Sir Edvard had been standing when he was shot. At this, the man's daughter began to softly weep, and as Holmes talked she continued to stare at that lonely spot, dramatically facing the Altar Stone. Estes, Garvey, and Gilman seemed fascinated, with Estes seemingly poised to interrupt with some snide remark, but Holmes continued to steadily explain, and he never got the chance.

"We had two bits of good luck," said Holmes. "It might almost seem to be mystical, if one credits the atmosphere of this place. First, the bullet went straight through the body, and east, out of the circle, without hitting any stones. And second, Sir Edvard chose Lugers to arm his three agents, and he used steel-jacketed bullets – a recent innovation by Luger – which mean that the slug didn't deform – and that the bullets are magnetic. This is further confirmed by the straight clean path of the bullet through the body. When we find the bullet, we can examine it to determine which gun fired the shot."

There were a number of curious faces, and Holmes continued.

"In the last few years, there have been significant advances in the science of ballistics, and especially identifying which gun fired which bullet by way of microscopic examination, but the initial work on the subject is seventy years old. In 1835, Henry Goddard, a Bow Street Runner, linked the marks on a deadly bullet to the mold in which it was formed. In the American Civil War, it was seen that the type of bullet that killed the Confederate traitor, General Stonewall Jackson, came from one of his own men, and not a Union soldier. In the last five years, there have been several other cases in the United States where rifling marks made on the bullet by the gun's barrel have provided important evidence. And I myself was able to clear a man early in my career by comparison of two different bullets." [2]

The three men were watching Holmes carefully as he finished up the construction of the magnet and then picked up the strap to lift it. He walked to the automobile, holding the iron bar pointed in front of him. When he reached the vehicle, the bar pulled his arm forward, attaching its end to the iron fender-work with a metallic *thud*. The magnets were activated.

Leaving the four young people with the other two constables, Antrobus, Adams, Cable, and I also picked up our electromagnets and walked east, past the Heel Stone, and began slowly trying to detect the metal in the ragged plains grass. We made a curious spectacle in the early morning light, bent over like scavenging birds, waving our magnetic wands this way and that inches over the turf in wide sweeps while throwing long shadows back toward the stones from the slowly climbing sun.

We all looked back frequently to make sure we stayed relatively lined up with where the body had fallen and the space between the two relevant Sarsen stones. All the while, there was some discussion, as the sun rose behind the clouds and somewhat brightened the early morning, about how far a jacketed Luger bullet might be expected to travel, particularly after passing through the soft tissues of a body. There was no clear consensus, and the search continued.

I was more than amazed when, after no more than ten minutes, I heard a small metallic *click* at the end of my metal wand. I had wandered a bit farther than the others, knowing from my past experience in Afghanistan that bullets had an uncanny way of going past where one thought they could. I had treated too many men, and seen too many others who were dead, who had all believed themselves safe due to their supposedly adequate distance from the shooter.

I had begun to worry that the bullet wasn't in the line we expected, perhaps having been skipped up or to the sides by a bit of turbulent air along its passage. I almost didn't credit that I'd found it, but there was no mistake: I had the steel-jacketed killer resting in the palm of my hand.

I signaled to the others and hurriedly walked back to them. They crowded around, looking in the dim morning light at my discovery. Antrobus crowed and patted Holmes on the back. "Brilliant!" he repeated, over and over, while Adams looked at my friend with even more awe than he had when Holmes had showed him and Inspector Youghal the recovered Irish Crown Jewels from the lonely middle-aged deviant, Christopher Heydon.

Holmes immediately led us back toward the Stones. In addition to the supplies needed to make the magnets, Adams had obtained a microscope from a local physician, and we now planned to relocate to Antrobus's house where a comparison would be made between the bullet and the guns – but it proved to be unnecessary.

When we walked through the Sarsen stones and rejoined the group, all attention was turned to the foot of the Altar Stone, where Tyler Gilman was lying, curled into a ball on his side. He was muttering to himself. The rest watched him in shocked silence.

"We saw you find something," explained one of the constables who had been guarding the group. "We assumed it was the bullet. It was then that Gilman there collapsed. With a moan, he started to sway, and then made it a few steps to the stone, where he laid down . . . like that."

I stepped closer to examine him and found that he felt feverish. He ignored me when I commanded that he unfold himself so that I could see what else was the matter. Instead, over and over, he simply repeated, "He deserved it. I had to. He left me no choice. He deserved it. You all know it. He deserved it . . . ."

A later examination revealed that Tyler Gilman's gun had indeed fired the bullet. He never recovered enough to provide an explanation, or to answer any questions at all, and he was found "Guilty but Insane" and remanded to Broadmoor, where he would likely remain for the rest of his life.

Holmes's subsequent investigations revealed that the young man's father had brought the family to near ruin, and that the house of cards he'd constructed was just about to collapse. Gilman had been under immense pressure to rescue his family by securing a marriage to the heiress, Rachel Bilbrey. It seemed that the apple didn't fall far from the tree in terms of personal character, as it was easily determined that Gilman himself had a number of detestable habits, not much different than those that brought about the ruination of his father. Although not proven, it was speculated Sir Edvard had either discovered this aspect, or suspected it, and was about the bar Tyler Gilman from pursuing any engagement with his daughter.

A note was found wadded in the pocket of Tyler Gilman's coat – simply written, unsigned, in block script, advising *Meet me at the Stones at midnight*. It was felt that Gilman had arranged an appointment this way with Sir Edvard, luring him there to his death when the last of the guards had departed. Then he'd rolled the body into one of the tarpaulin's that littered the site related to Antrobus's restoration work and moved it to a seemingly out-of-the-way place. He'd retrieved the note and returned to the house, and then to bed. But the matter had preyed on his mind, as reflected in his introverted behavior while being interviewed. Seeing that his guilt was about to be revealed had caused the weak-minded killer to crack before the accusation could be leveled and proof produced.

I later heard that Andrew Garvey left London and returned to the bosom of his Lancashire family. Three months after her father's death, Rachel Bilbrey married the disagreeable Clifford Estes, and their life since, while undeservingly wealthy, has apparently been as unhappy as one might expect.

Antrobus, who hinted that he'd seen Holmes in action before, could not have been more impressed. Curiously, for one so centered and grounded, he soon threw himself in an entirely different direction, allowing The Ancient Order of Druids to hold their first ritualistic meeting at Stonehenge the following August, and for himself to be enthusiastically initiated among their number on that sane memorable day. From the impression I'd formed of Sir Edmund Antrobus upon our initial meeting, I could only think that this new role was simply a performance, a part of some mission that he was undertaking for the Government. Of course, I would never ask him to confirm or deny it, and I watched with curious amusement in the following years as he continued along that path – until he passed away ten years later. As there was no heir – his son having been killed the year before in Belgium – the estate passed to his brother, who sold Stonehenge soon after.

Holmes and I were back on the train by lunchtime – this time in a first-class carriage, but by the usual means and methods: No special trains to return us from where we'd started. It certainly took longer than our outbound journey, but I used the opportunity to catch up on my sleep. It's a good thing, as we were met on the platform at Eastbourne Station by Inspector Bardle of the Sussex Constabulary.

"I'm fairly up against it, and make no mistake," he explained, and then he continued to lay out the events related to a corpse, a wool scarf, a rare book, and three sisters – one blind, one deaf, and one mute.

It was two further days before I made it back to Holmes's villa for his "recommended rest and a change of scene".

NOTES

1. See "The Two Different Women" in *The Collected Papers of Sherlock Holmes – Volume IV: Narratives* and *The MX Book of New Sherlock Holmes Stories: Part VIII – Eliminate the Impossible: 1892-1905*
2. See "The Two Bullets" in *The Collected Papers of Sherlock Holmes – Volume V: Chronicles* and *Sherlock Holmes and Doctor Watson: The Early Adventures – Volume I*

25 August, 1905: Sir Edmund Antrobus (and others)
at Stonehenge, being led blindfolded to be initiated
into The Ancient Order of Druids

Some of Sir Edmund Antrobus's restoration work at Stonehenge.
(Photo: 1914)

Personal Notes

My father, John Marcum, spent most of his adult life in law enforcement. He served as an MP in the United States Army during the Korean War, and then returned home to attend college under the G.I. Bill. In the late 1950's, he became a Tennessee State Trooper, and in the late 1960's, he became a Special Agent for the Tennessee Bureau of Investigation, covering several counties, with his office located in our home.

When I was growing up, he let me read his files, and he taught me about criminal investigation, including how to take a person's fingerprints, and how to lift them at a crime scene. I learned about plaster casts in footprints, and I was able to accompany him on a number of investigations, watching him conduct interviews and work with both witnesses and other law enforcement officers. Once, he even let me accompany him on a murder investigation. He finished his TBI career by becoming the State's first polygraph operator – and he taught me how to do that too.

After he retired, he held a number of other law enforcement related positions. At the time he left the State, he was commended for many of his investigations. In one, his diligence was exemplary when he found a bullet casing in a front yard that proved to be the key piece of evidence – somewhat like what Holmes accomplished on that day in June 1905 as the sun rose over Stonehenge.

David Marcum and his Deerstalker at Stonehenge
Holmes Pilgrimage No. 4
June 9th, 2024
(Photo by Dan Marcum)

The Sound of the Grand's Piano
by Paul Hiscock

In the middle of August 1905, I received a curious invitation from Sherlock Holmes. That he was requesting my presence came as no great surprise. Despite his retirement to Sussex, his services as a consulting detective were still in great demand, and he often invited me to join him in his investigations, as I had in the past. However, on this occasion, he asked me to meet him within the next few days – not at his cottage, but at the Grand Hotel in Eastbourne.

Eager as I was to discover what mystery awaited, I hesitated for a moment before responding. Lately, whenever I mentioned that I would be visiting Holmes, I sensed an air of irritation from my wife. She had never objected vocally, but I was beginning to suspect that she had expected me to spend less time with my friend after he retired.

However, while she had not spoken about Holmes, she had been far less reticent about her desire for me to take some time away from the surgery for a holiday that summer. She would enjoy a few days spent by the seaside, especially staying in the opulent surroundings of the Grand Hotel.

I booked the trip immediately and eagerly prepared to share the news with my wife that evening. However, to my surprise, she didn't seem very enthusiastic.

"You are planning to see Mr. Holmes while we are there?" she asked.

"I had hoped to. He lives quite nearby."

"Indeed."

She fell silent, and I started to wonder if my clever idea had been a mistake.

I was about to apologise and offer to cancel the trip when she said, "Very well. I shall invite Miss Finch to join us. She can serve as my companion while you're occupied with your friend."

I nodded in agreement and, in an instant, her demeanour altered. With a smile on her face, she started to talk about how much good the sea air would do us, and suggesting things we might do while we were there.

The Grand Hotel certainly lived up to its name in appearance. It was a gleaming white palace on the edge of town, set back slightly from the seafront. Inside, the foyer was simply but elegantly appointed, and the staff were welcoming and courteous. The gentle sound of a piano wafted through the building, creating a relaxed and tranquil atmosphere.

I was disappointed to discover that our rooms were at the back of the building and didn't have a sea view, but my wife didn't seem to mind. She was entranced by the beautiful vases of pink hellebores, her favourite flower. I was glad they made her happy, but as we were walking down to the Great Hall for afternoon tea, I did wonder where the hotel had found those winter blooms in the middle of summer.

"I see you opted for strawberry jam with your scones. Next time, might I recommend the lemon curd? It isn't a traditional choice, but I think you will find it tart and refreshing."

I looked up and saw Holmes standing next to my table.

"How long have you been watching?" I asked. "You would have been welcome to join us."

"On the contrary, I have only just arrived. Besides, I think you overestimate the limits of your wife's tolerance. I passed her as I entered and when she looked at me I felt a distinct chill, despite the warmth of the day."

I started to apologise, but he shook his head.

"There is no need for that. I don't expect her to like me. It is enough that we tolerate the existence of one another. Now, clean the cream and jam from your moustache while I summon the manager so we can get down to the business at hand."

I picked up a napkin and wiped the tell-tale traces from around my mouth while he caught the attention of a waiter, to whom he passed a note.

We only had to wait a moment before a tall man approached from the direction of the reception area. His appearance was a study in straight lines, from the crisp creases in his suit to the two sharp triangles of his moustache and his square steel-rimmed glasses. He moved like a well-oiled machine, quickly but efficiently, somehow covering the distance from the doorway in the blink of an eye without looking hurried.

"Mr. Holmes, Dr. Watson, I'm Mr. Naylor, the manager. Thank you for coming. I hope you will not feel that this is a waste of your time."

I stood up and shook his hand. However, Holmes remained seated, his eyes closed and his fingers steepled in front of his mouth.

"Well," I said, "I'm grateful for an excuse to stay in your beautiful hotel."

Mr. Naylor smiled, slightly, in response to my compliment. However, it was clear that he was disconcerted by Holmes's demeanour.

"Holmes told me very little about your problem," I said, once we were seated. "Only that you had asked for his help and didn't want the police involved. You are worried about the hotel's reputation?"

"Of course, it is always preferable to deal with matters discreetly, and the police tend to create a spectacle. However, in this instance, I am dealing with a problem that wouldn't interest them." His voice dropped to a whisper. "The truth is, this is a mystery of the supernatural variety."

I sighed. "In that case, whoever suggested that you engage Mr. Holmes advised you poorly. He has no more time for or interest in ghosts than the police. You would be better off contacting a specialist in the occult."

Mr. Naylor bristled. "The Grand has a reputation to maintain. You may find table-tippers gulling fools in the guesthouses of Eastbourne along the front, but you will not find them here."

"It is a field full of charlatans," I agreed.

"Mr. Naylor doesn't believe in ghosts any more than you or I," said Holmes. "However, his beliefs are irrelevant. He is an intermediary and must act as instructed by his guests, especially the rich and famous ones. They asked for me specifically, yes?"

Mr. Naylor looked nervous. "They know your reputation – everyone does – and somehow they learned that you lived nearby. But Mr. Holmes, we shouldn't be discussing this here, in public. These guests are very insistent upon their privacy."

"I wouldn't worry too much," replied Holmes. "Your other customers have all finished their tea and departed."

I glanced about the room and saw that he was correct. A couple of waiters hovered about, tidying up cups and plates, and the pianist was still playing at the piano in the corner, but otherwise the room was empty.

"Still, I think it might be better if we went to my office," said Mr. Naylor.

"No," said Holmes. "In order to decide whether I will take this case, I need to speak to M. Debussy himself."

I was astonished. Although used to Holmes's feats of deduction, I couldn't see how he could have identified the Grand's mysterious guest from what we had been told. However, Mr. Naylor didn't look surprised. Instead, he seemed despondent.

"I thought we had been so careful. Most of the staff haven't even been told who is staying in Suite 200. However, if someone has spoken to you, it's only a matter of time until he or she sells the story to the newspapers too, if it hasn't been done already. He will be furious. After the way the press hounded him in Paris, his most important stipulation was that they shouldn't discover him here."

"It would have saved me some time if you had told me yourself," said Holmes. "However, it didn't take me long to discover the truth. It was obvious that this was a demanding guest. He could have contacted me directly, but instead he insisted that hotel should arrange everything. It seemed likely that this wasn't the only extraordinary service he had insisted upon.

"I decided to find out what other special instructions you had recently fulfilled, and the first step was to make a request of my own. I must say, you really are a most accommodating host. The flowers you ordered for Watson's room matched my exacting specification precisely."

"I thought that must have been your doing," I said. "How else could the hotel have known my wife's favourite flower? Thank you."

"You are welcome, but pleasing Mrs. Watson was a secondary consideration. By taking the place of the delivery driver, I was able to access the service entrance of the hotel without arousing suspicion and strike up a conversation with the staff there about the other interesting orders they had received recently. One stood out among all the others: A grand piano, delivered to Suite 200 for the exclusive use of the guest staying in that room."

"That damned piano!" said Mr. Naylor. "Getting it upstairs was a nightmare, and I was terrified that the slightest knock might damage it. As a result, I enlisted far more people to help than I would have liked. I suppose one of them told you who it was for?"

"You may relax, Mr. Naylor," said Holmes. "Your staff are a credit to this institution. None of them has whispered his name. However, I did learn that the piano had been supplied by the piano merchants, S. Hermitage and Sons, in town. M. Debussy might have allowed you to handle most matters for him, but it is unthinkable that a maestro such as himself would have delegated the selection of his instrument, and therefore he visited the shop himself. The owner, of course, recognised him, and when I visited, was eager to boast that he had recently leased a piano to a famous musician. Mind you, even he didn't reveal the name immediately. However, after a fascinating discussion about the virtues of the extra aliquot strings in the Blüthner grand piano that vibrate in sympathy with the regular strings, he couldn't resist sharing his secret with a fellow musical connoisseur."

Mr. Naylor sighed with relief. However, I wasn't sure that Debussy would share the sentiment. It seemed to me that if the shop owner had revealed the identity of his customer once, he might do so again. However, in that moment I suppose the hotel manager was simply glad that his staff had proved to be trustworthy and discreet.

"Now," said Holmes, an edge of impatience in his voice, "if you still wish for my assistance, please take me to meet my client, so that we can discuss the case frankly without further prevarication. Otherwise, I shall return home, where there are plenty of other matters that deserve my attention."

Mr. Naylor led us up the stairs to Suite 200. He knocked on the door, and after a moment a woman opened it. She was short and wore her hair in ringlets. However, the most striking thing about her was that she was noticeably pregnant.

"Madame, this is the detective Sherlock Holmes, and his associate, Dr. Watson."

The woman replied in English, but with a pronounced French accent. "Gentlemen, thank you for coming."

"It is our pleasure, Mme. Debussy," I said.

"It is actually Mme. Bardac."

"I am sorry, but then you are – ?

"His mistress? Lover? Whore?" She laughed at the expression of shock on my face. "I see no need to be coy. The newspapers have called me all of those, and worse. You haven't read all the scandalous stories about us in the press? How refreshing. Please do come inside."

She ushered us into a comfortably appointed lounge. Under normal circumstances, I would have described it as spacious. However, the furniture, which would normally have been spread across the room, had all been moved to the left-hand side. In its place on the right was a magnificent, jet-black, grand piano. The keyboard and lid had been left propped open, and Holmes headed straight over to study its internal workings.

Mme. Bardac smiled. "Are you a pianist, M. Holmes?"

"A violinist, but I have heard much about this particular instrument and its unusual arrangement of strings."

"Do not let Claude hear you say that. He will spend the whole day lecturing you on the subject. He leaves it open like that just to show off the instrument."

"Is M. Debussy here?" I asked.

"He is out there, on the balcony," she replied, pointing towards the French windows at the back of the room.

At first I didn't see him, just a white stone balustrade, and beyond it the spectacular sea view that had been missing from my own room. However, then I noticed a figure in black, standing off to one side, staring out at the water.

"We left home to get some privacy," said Mme. Bardac, "but we came here for the sea."

"M. Debussy loves the sea that much?" I asked.

"He likes it, but it is more than that. It is the inspiration for his latest work. He is meant to be completing the proofs for his symphony, *La Mer*. We had hoped the environment would provide him with inspiration."

"You say that you 'had hoped'?" asked Holmes. "Has this not proved to be the case?"

"No. I had thought the composition almost complete, and that he just needed to make the final corrections. However, he began to doubt his work, saying that it lacked *la vie*. That it feels lifeless."

"Do you agree?" I asked.

"No, I think it sounds beautiful. However, when he gets like this, he will not listen to anyone. He just needs to be given space to work through it. We have even sent my daughter, who travelled here with us, to stay with friends for a couple of weeks."

"I am sorry to hear that," I said, "but I don't think that is why you asked us here?"

"No. If anything, your presence is more of a distraction, just as he was starting to make some progress. In fact, I considered telling the manager that your services were no longer required, but Claude insisted that we must have an answer."

"In that case," I asked, "does he not wish to join us?"

"Claude will be pleased to meet you, but I should warn you, he will not say much, and he doesn't speak English."

"That isn't a problem," I replied. "*Nous parlons Français.*"

I watched as she tried to stifle a laugh at my pronunciation, then coughed.

"Forgive me," she said. "That was unkind. However, I doubt he will say much to you."

"Because of my accent?"

"No, because he is preoccupied. When his mind is engrossed in the music, he can think about nothing else, and barely even speaks to me. Nevertheless, we can try."

She went over to the windows and opened the door.

"Claude," she called out. "M. Holmes *est arrivé.*"

Debussy turned his head to look at her and nodded, but didn't move immediately, instead returning his attention to the sea. It was another minute or so before he moved to come inside.

My first impression was that he seemed slightly distracted and dishevelled. His black hair was parted at the side, and clearly meant to be combed across, but had drooped down over his forehead, creating an

306

untidy fringe. Likewise, while his beard was cut in that style favoured by the French where it comes to a sharp point, he hadn't oiled it that morning and so it appeared ragged. He wasn't a tall man, but a slouch made him appear even shorter, and there were heavy black circles under his eyes.

He came over and shook our hands, then sat down on the chaise-longue next to Mme. Bardac. He briefly placed a hand on her stomach, in a display of obvious affection and concern for her well-being. There was a nervous energy about him, and his legs twitched as though he was anxious to leave.

Recognising the truth of Mme. Bardac's warning, that we wouldn't have his attention for long, Holmes didn't waste any time.

"M. Debussy, *vous voulez notre aide?*"

"*Oui, pour exorciser le fantôme. Je ne peux pas dormir pendant qu'il joue sur mon piano.*"

"Did I understand that right?" I asked. "Did he just say a *ghost* was playing the piano?"

"That's right," replied Mme. Bardac. "It began last week, on the Tuesday night, although I knew nothing of it until the morning. When I awoke, I found Claude already sitting at the piano, just staring at the keys. That is when he told me that he had heard someone playing in the night. *Tu étais très perturbé, n'est-ce pas, mon amour?*"

"*Parce qu'il jouait ma musique.*"

"Yes, that was the thing that concerned him most. He said he had heard his own music."

"That doesn't sound too strange," I replied. "Assuming it was some sort of trick, it makes sense that the perpetrator would select one of his famous compositions to play."

"No, you don't understand. It wasn't just any piece composed by him. It was the one he is working on now, *La Mer*. Only it has never been performed in public. Nobody should know it."

"I admit that is more mysterious," I said.

"But you didn't believe him at once," said Holmes.

Mme. Bardac averted her eyes in shame. "No, I didn't. *Pardonne-moi, mon amour, d'avoir douté de toi.*"

Debussy didn't say anything, but smiled and gently patted her on the knee.

"I thought he must have imagined it," she continued. "After all, he is spending all day thinking about that music. It is inevitable that it might occupy his dreams as well. However, the next night, he woke me at around one in the morning and told me to listen. At first, I was just annoyed, but then I heard it – the sound of a piano, coming from the direction of this room. We listened for a few minutes, then I declared that it was silly that we were hiding in our bed, and that we should go and see who was playing. However, the second I said this, the music stopped. We hurried through to the lounge, but there was no one here."

"How did you find the piano?" asked Holmes. "Was it locked?"

"It was as you see it now. We never lock it. Why should we? After all, the door to the suite was locked. Nobody else could get in."

"What about the music M. Debussy is working on? Was that left on the piano?"

"No. Claude is very careful about that. He locks it up in our bedroom whenever he isn't working on it. That is why he was most alarmed to have heard it being played, and came to the conclusion that it must be some type of spirit."

"And this 'haunting' has continued?" asked Holmes.

"Yes, we hear it every night. The first few times, I hurried through, hoping to catch the perpetrator, but after a while gave up and just lay in bed, next to Claude, listening. We have grown so used to it, *n'est pas*, Claude? *Nous nous y somme habitués.*"

"*Je suppose, mais son jeu est different.*"

"It plays different pieces every night?" I asked.

"Different passages," said Mme. Bardac, "but all from his latest symphony."

"What do you think, Holmes?"

"It seems straightforward enough. However, there are a couple of points that interest me enough to spend a little time investigating."

"If you are sure, M. Holmes," replied Mme. Bardac. "We do not want to waste your time."

Like Mr. Naylor, she seemed to appreciate the foolishness of asking us to search for a ghost. However, when she told Debussy that Holmes would help, he seemed enthusiastic. Perhaps he truly believed in such things – ?

"First," said Holmes, "we must rule out the prosaic and the predictable. I see you have a phonograph here. Could it have been used to play a recording?"

"No. We have a number of recordings with us and sometimes like to listen to them in the evening. However, there are none of *La Mer*. It will not be recorded until it is complete."

"Nevertheless, we must check them all. Meanwhile, Watson, I want you and Mr. Naylor to search the suite. Behind every piece of furniture. Inside every nook and cranny. Make sure there are no devices concealed anywhere that might have been used to make a recording.

While Mr. Naylor and I conducted our search, Holmes asked Mme. Bardac to play each of the phonograph cylinders in turn. Soon the suite was filled with the sound of beautiful music.

We had clearly reached the limits of Debussy's attention span as he retreated to the balcony to think about his composition once more, closing the doors behind him.

While Mr. Naylor looked in the bedroom, I focussed my attention on the living area. I must have looked quite a comical sight, crawling around on the floor to look underneath the chairs and tables, and my joints ached when I tried to stand up again. However, if my antics did cause Holmes and Mme. Bardac any amusement, they were kind enough not to mention it.

Aside from under the furniture, the most likely place that something could have been hidden was in the fireplace. With the warm weather, it hadn't been lit for some time so any equipment placed there would have been safe from damage. I was leaning inside, trying to look up the chimney when I heard a man speaking. At first, I assumed that it was Holmes or Mr. Naylor, but then realised that the voice was unfamiliar.

I called the others over and told them to listen.

"Sounds carry around the building," said Mr. Naylor. "It cannot be helped. We sometimes get complaints if a guest is being particularly rowdy, but usually it isn't a problem."

"If the sound of a conversation can be carried around the building, surely a piano might also be heard in such a way?"

Holmes smiled. "An interesting theory, Watson. It could explain something that had been perplexing me."

"There was an instrument in the room where we had tea," I said. "Are there any others?"

"There are three," replied Mr. Naylor. "One in the ballroom, one in the dining room, and another in one of the lounges. However, I don't think they could have heard any of those being played in the night. It would have been reported to me, and I would have put a stop to it."

"Nevertheless, we should test them all," I said. "One of us should go and play each of them in turn and see if they can be heard."

"You can go, Watson," said Holmes. "Mr. Naylor will show you where the pianos can be found. I will stay here, in case there is anything to be heard."

Surprisingly, given his enthusiasm a few moments before, he sounded bored rather than excited by this new line of enquiry.

"How will we know which instrument you hear?" I asked.

"Make a note of the time when you play each instrument. I will do the same if I hear anything."

"Are you sure you shouldn't be the one to play the instruments?" I asked. "I have very little musical ability."

"No, Watson. It is your theory. You should be the one to test it. What you play is immaterial. Besides, of the two of us, my hearing is the more acute."

I couldn't argue with that. Many times during past cases, he had heard some small sound of great importance that I had missed completely.

"Very well," I said. "We'll be back soon."

"And I will be listening," Holmes replied, as he sat back comfortably in an armchair near the fireplace.

Mr. Naylor first took me back to the hall where we had enjoyed afternoon tea. The room had been cleared in our absence and there was no one else there.

The piano was locked, just as Mr. Naylor had told us it would be. He took out a large bunch of keys and selected a tiny one, which he used to unlock the cover over the keyboard.

"You carry keys to the pianos with you all the time?" I asked in surprise.

"I carry keys to everything in the hotel. One never knows what a guest might require."

Now that the gleaming white-and-black keys were in front of me, I realised that I had no idea what I could play. I tapped on a key experimentally and was rewarded by the sound of a clear note. Was that enough, I wondered? Almost certainly not. I needed to give Holmes a fair chance to notice me playing.

I struck the key again and then the one next to it, then another, playing notes at random in a pattern which, to my mind at least, didn't seem too displeasing to the ear. As I played, I frequently found myself looking towards the fireplace and wondering if it was carrying the sound of my playing around the hotel for everyone to hear.

I carried on in that style for about five minutes, judging that long enough for Holmes to have noticed me. When I finished, I made a note of the time, as we had agreed, then closed the keyboard and asked Mr. Naylor to take me to the next piano.

Unlike the first room, the lounge he took me to was occupied. Guests were sitting and reading, conversing with each other, or just sipping a drink while enjoying their surroundings. When I first sat down at the piano, nobody looked at me. A pianist playing tunes in the background was part of the ambiance they expected. However, they looked up in curiosity when I started playing my discordant series of random notes, making me feel rather self-conscious. I wondered if I should try to play a recognisable melody for them, but in that moment, I couldn't remember a single tune. I was relieved when the time came to move on.

It took just under half-an-hour to test all the pianos in the hotel. I was surprised that they had so many, and wondered why they couldn't have loaned one of them to Debussy for the duration of his stay. Perhaps none of them had met his exacting standards. Certainly, even I could tell that there was a great difference in the quality of the sound produced by the different instruments.

Eager to learn the results of our experiment, I hurried back to the suite as soon as we finished testing the last instrument. There I found Holmes sitting where I had left him by the fireplace. Mme. Bardac had joined him, and Debussy had come in from the balcony and was sitting at a small desk, working on his composition.

"I must apologise for the quality of my playing," I said. "However, I did warn you that I am not a musician."

"It was of no consequence to us," replied Holmes, "as I am afraid we didn't hear anything."

"Really, nothing?" I asked, despondently.

"I am sorry that you wasted your time, Watson, but as Mr. Naylor said, it was unlikely that any of those instruments had been played without his knowledge. Besides, M. Debussy discounted your theory as soon as we told him. He is certain that it is *this* piano that he has been hearing. The distinctive tones of the aliquot strings leave no doubt in his mind."

"I should have spoken to him before rushing off."

"It was a minor diversion. We have followed longer blind alleyways in past investigations. Anyway, the time hasn't been wasted. I have had the privilege of observing M. Debussy at work. I was just saying to Mme. Bardac how pleased I am to see that he seems to have pushed through the creative block that she mentioned earlier."

"It's true. He seems to have found his inspiration again in the last few days. I'm very grateful. He's poor company when he is frustrated." For a moment she looked worried. "With no offence intended to either of you gentlemen, I wish you hadn't come, at least for a few more days. I'm worried that we might distract him again, so close to the end."

"I wouldn't worry," I replied. "I am sure that once the mystery is explained, he will find it even easier to work."

Mme. Bardac did not look convinced.

"What should we do next?" I asked my friend.

"Nothing. You should return to your room. If I have judged your wife's walking pace and the length of the promenade correctly, she should be returning to the hotel at any minute. She will be expecting you to take her to dinner, and I have no intention of provoking her ire by keeping you from that engagement. Besides, there is little more we can do here now, and I have a few errands of my own to run. We shall return in the morning, by which time I believe matters will look a lot clearer. M. Debussy, Mme. Bardac, *au revoir à demain*."

Mme. Bardac wished us a pleasant evening in reply, but Debussy didn't acknowledge us, so engrossed he was in his work.

As Holmes had predicted, my wife returned to our room just a few minutes after me. She seemed slightly surprised, but pleased, to see me. We changed, and then went down to the hotel restaurant to enjoy a splendid dinner. She asked about the case just once during the meal, but after I told her that the client was particularly concerned to maintain his anonymity, she didn't mention it again.

After dinner, we took a stroll along the seafront. As we walked, I heard music in the air. For a moment, rational thoughts fled my mind and I wondered if the musical spirit from the hotel was haunting the whole town. However, my wife, being ignorant of my preoccupations, quickly brought me back to reality.

"How delightful. There is a concert in the bandstand. We should stop and listen."

She was correct, of course, and when we reached the small structure, we found the Municipal Orchestra performing a programme of light classical music. I purchased a programme and was amused to note that one of the pieces was Debussy's "Clair de lune". They would never know that the composer was just a short distance away. Indeed, it was possible that he might be able to hear them playing from his balcony.

As we walked back to the hotel, once the concert was over, I felt truly relaxed for the first time in months. My wife had been right: I had been working too hard and needed this break from my practice and the hustle and bustle of London.

When we returned to our room, we found the bed had been turned down for the night. The sea air had made me tired, and I was ready to climb in immediately and settle down for a good night's sleep. However, before I could even change into my nightshirt, there was a knock at the door.

I went to answer it and was surprised to find Holmes standing there. I stepped out into the corridor and pulled the door to behind me so that we could speak privately.

"Excellent," he said. "I had hoped that I would manage to catch you before you retired for the night."

"What is it? I thought we weren't meeting again until the morning. Has something happened?"

"No, but if we're going to reveal this invisible pianist, now is the time that we must act."

I groaned softly. "You planned this all along."

"Indeed. We were never going to catch this nocturnal musician in the middle of the day."

"Then why did you not say anything earlier?"

"Everyone needed to be seen to be acting like normal, and to believe that I had left the hotel for the night."

"Still, you could have told me."

"I am sorry. I didn't know who might be listening. Besides, I assumed you would guess what I had planned."

I considered this for a moment. Perhaps I would have anticipated his intentions in the past. However, it appeared that even in the short time since Holmes's retirement, I had lost some of my investigative instincts.

"Very well. Just give me a moment to tell my wife."

I stepped back inside the room, leaving Holmes outside, and found my wife already sitting up in bed.

"You are going out again," she said.

I nodded. "Just for a little while. Holmes needs me."

She scowled at me.

"I will not be gone all night. I expect that I will be back at around two, maybe three o'clock."

Her expression darkened further.

"Or perhaps I should just meet you downstairs at breakfast?" I suggested.

She did not reply – just picked up a book from her bedside table and pointedly started to read.

I might have been surprised to find Holmes at my door at such a late hour, but at least I was used to his eccentricities. However, when Mme. Bardac answered the door to us, she turned pale and almost fainted with shock. It seemed like an excessive reaction, but I attributed it to her delicate condition.

As I helped her inside, Debussy emerged from the bedroom.

"*Que faites-vous ici?*" he asked.

"*Nous sommes venus attraper ton fantôme,*" said Holmes.

"But you said you would return in the morning," said Mme. Bardac.

"I apologise for the small deception, but I promise you it was necessary. You were about to retire for the night?"

"Yes. We usually turn in at around this time."

"Then we must not delay your routine. I must ask your permission to wait in the bedroom. I realise it will be a little crowded, but we will not disturb you if you wish to sleep while we wait."

Mme. Bardac translated Holmes's request, and I waited for Debussy to angrily eject us from the suite, but instead he replied, "*Fais comme tu veux*," or, "Do as you wish," before leading us into the bedroom.

"Switch off the lights on your way through, Watson," Holmes said.

I did as he said, before joining the others in the bedroom. Debussy had already helped Mme. Bardac into their bed, and Holmes had sat down at the desk. I closed the door behind me and then made my way to an armchair on the far side of the room, near the window.

"From now on, we must be silent," said Holmes, before closing his eyes and entering into a state of hyper-alert meditation.

Debussy and Mme. Bardac watched him in bemusement for a few minutes before deciding to settle down to sleep. Meanwhile, I tried to make myself comfortable in the chair. If past events were any indication, we would have to wait a few hours before we would hear anything.

At some point, I must have drifted off to sleep, because the next thing I knew, Holmes was shaking my shoulder.

"Wake up, Watson," he whispered. "Can you hear it?"

Shaking off the fog of sleep, I heard music coming from nearby. I didn't recognise the tune being played, but I could tell that the player was highly skilled, a stark contrast to my clumsy efforts that afternoon.

I looked around. In the dim light, provided by the light of the moon sneaking through a gap in the curtains, I saw that our clients had also been disturbed and were waking up.

"We must stay as quiet as possible," whispered Holmes. Yet, even as he said those words, there was a crash from next to me. I looked around and saw that Mme. Bardac had accidentally knocked a glass of water off her bedside table, which was now in pieces on the floor. For a moment we all froze, and in that moment of silence, I realised that the piano was no longer playing.

"Quickly!" urged Holmes. "To the lounge!"

I leapt out of my seat and rushed to the bedroom door. Opening it, I saw the short corridor beyond was empty. I hurried past the door to the suite and into the lounge. Yet somehow I was already too late – the room was empty.

Debussy and Mme. Bardac followed me into the room.

"Did you catch her?" asked Mme. Bardac.

I shook my head. "No, but I cannot see how the intruder escaped. There is no way anyone could have made it to the door in time."

I went to the fireplace and looked inside. After my search of the room that afternoon, I knew that it was the only place in the room big enough for a person to hide. However, it was empty.

"*Le balcon!*" cried Debussy, pointing towards the window.

I hurried over and opened the doors. In the still of the night outside, I could hear the waves gently lapping at the beach and see the moon reflected in the sea, but I was alone out there.

"You had the right idea," said Holmes, "but you weren't fast enough."

I turned and saw that he had entered the lounge behind Debussy and Mme. Bardac, and he was not alone.

"I caught your ghost trying to come back in through the bedroom window. Had I not been waiting there, she would have snuck around behind your backs and out of the suite."

The ghost he referred to was a young girl. She was twisting and writhing, trying to get away, but Holmes had a firm grip on her collar and wouldn't allow her to escape.

I found myself feeling strangely disappointed.

"Is that all the mystery amounts to?" I asked. "A girl hiding on a balcony? Why, even Lestrade could have solved a case like this without your help."

Holmes laughed. "I agree we aren't dealing with a criminal mastermind. Yet moments ago, you couldn't fathom how she had disappeared, and otherwise rational men and women have spent days contemplating the possibility that ghosts might exist. Even I didn't see immediately how someone could do what had been described to us."

"Just let me go!" said the girl, in a strong Irish accent. "You can't arrest me. I've done nothing wrong. I ain't taken anything or hurt anyone."

"I will release you," said Holmes, "if you promise to sit down and answer our questions."

The girl squirmed in his grip once more, testing whether there was any chance of escape. Then she went limp.

"Very well," she said.

Holmes guided her over to a chair and sat her down before releasing her. The girl looked back at Holmes, making one final assessment of the odds of getting away, then slumped dejectedly into her seat.

"What do you want to know?"

"Let us start with your name," I said, "and why you have been sneaking into this couple's room?"

"My name is Tess, and I've just been doing my job."

"Your job?" I asked incredulously.

"Look at her," said Holmes. "You can see she is wearing the uniform of a hotel maid, although her apron got torn away when I first tried to seize her."

Of course, Holmes was correct. I rubbed my eyes, still bleary with sleep, and reassured myself that I would have noticed had I not so recently been rudely awakened.

"Very well, she works here – but it still doesn't explain why she is sneaking into the guests' rooms."

"I told you, it's my job. I come and go while the guests are out or sleeping – lighting the fires, refreshing the flowers, and doing whatever else is needed to make the place presentable."

"It takes an invisible army to run this hotel," said Holmes, "moving in and out of locked rooms day and night, virtually unseen. It isn't just this suite that has been 'haunted'. Your room has been too."

I remembered how the bed had been turned down in our room while we had been at dinner. I had thought nothing of it. Just an example of the hotel's exemplary service.

"That explains how you managed to sneak in here," I said to Tess, "but it doesn't explain why you were playing this gentleman's piano in the middle of the night."

The girl's mask of defiance slipped a little, and she looked slightly ashamed.

"It was my only chance." She paused, but I stayed silent, waiting until she continued her explanation. "I used to play the piano all the time. My ma would take me with her when she went to clean the big house, and they would let me play. The lady of the house, she liked it – even encouraged me. Said I had a rare talent, though I don't know about that. I just played whatever I heard.

"When I came to work here, I was excited to see all the pianos. I thought that maybe I could play for the guests, like I had before, but of course that wasn't permitted. I'm only allowed to touch the instruments if I'm dusting them, and even then I would get in trouble if I struck a single note."

"Why did you suddenly decide to break the rules," I asked.

"When they delivered this piano, I thought it was for one of the lounges, where everyone could see and hear. But then I watched as they struggled to carry it upstairs to this room, and realised that I might have an opportunity to play without anyone noticing. All I would have to do was wait for the guests to go out for the day and I would have the chance to play, unobserved, while I went about my work. Only, I watched these people for days and they never went out – at least not all of them."

316

"It's true," said Mme. Bardac. "After the fuss in Paris last year, we didn't want to be spotted in public, so we stayed inside. Our dog, Dolly, found it frustrating, and I would take her out occasionally, but Claude would always stay here, rather than risk being recognised."

"I almost gave up," said Tess, "but I would hear the piano and feel that urge to play."

"So you decided to sneak in here in the night?" I said.

"It seemed like the only way, and that first night it was amazing. Nobody disturbed me as I played all the music that had been swirling around in my head for days."

"How did you know what to play?" I asked. "M. Debussy told us he heard you playing his latest composition, yet he keeps the music locked away."

"I wondered about that at first," said Holmes. "It was the one part of the case that made no sense to me – until you solved it."

"I did?"

"Yes, when you suggested that the intruder might have been hearing someone playing in another room. Of course, all the other pianos are too far away for their sound to carry up to this room, as you proved. However, the servants' rooms are in the attic just above us. After we parted ways this afternoon, I went up there and found that I was able to hear M. Debussy playing quite clearly."

"You were able to copy everything that you had heard?" I asked Tess. "That is a rare gift indeed."

All this time, Mme. Bardac had been translating our conversation for Debussy, but now he interrupted us.

"*Non,*" he said firmly. "*Vous ne m'avez pas copié. Vous l'avez changé!*"

"He says you changed the music," Mme. Bardac explained to Tess.

"M. Debussy tried to tell us earlier," said Holmes. "He knew it wasn't a recording."

"Why did you change it?" I asked.

"I don't know," replied Tess. "It just sounded better."

I couldn't believe the presumptuousness of this young girl, believing that she knew better than this famous composer. Yet, when Mme. Bardac translated Tess's reply, Debussy laughed.

"*Mieux? Oui, c'était mieux.*"

"I think Tess's playing inspired M. Debussy, allowing him to overcome his creative *ennui*. And you thought so too, did you not, Mme. Bardac? That is why you played along with this story about a ghost? Why you tried to hide the truth?"

"You knew about Tess all along?" I asked, recalling that she had been concerned whether we had caught "her".

"Of course she did, Watson. I said it before, we weren't dealing with a criminal mastermind. Tess couldn't hope to keep sneaking in here night after night and not get caught."

"It took a few days," said Mme Bardac. "Any earlier and I would have turned her in to the manager. But by the time I caught her, I had started to notice the change in Claude. He was inspired, excited. I couldn't stop that, so I agreed to turn a blind eye. We stopped looking for the ghost playing the piano and just enjoyed listening instead. It was all fine, until you arrived today. I had almost forgotten we had asked the manager to find a detective."

"You kept trying to put us off," I said.

"Indeed," said Holmes. "It was one of the things that made me suspicious, and convinced me that we needed to lay this little trap."

"I tried to find Tess after you left this afternoon," said Mme. Bardac. "I would have warned her not to come, but I would have tried harder if I had known you were going to come back."

"Which is why I did not tell you," said Holmes. "Still, you did your best. Knocking over that glass of water was no accident."

"I'm sorry. It was all I could think of. I just wanted to give her a chance to get away."

"So what do we do now?" I asked. "Should I send for the manager, or the police?"

The last trace of defiance left Tess's eyes and she started to plead with us. "Please don't, sirs! I will be dismissed on the spot, and never find another position."

"This is not a matter for the police," said Holmes. "She hasn't hurt anyone, and she hasn't stolen anything. However, whether we tell the manager is up to M. Debussy. He is our client."

Debussy sat there for a minute, stroking the point of his beard, then turned to Mme. Bardac. They held a hushed a conversation that I couldn't make out, and then he stood and made his way over to the piano. He sat down, then he turned and ushered towards Tess.

"*Venez ici.*"

The girl looked at him in confusion.

"*Montre-moi à quoi tu jouais.*"

"He wants you to show him what you were playing before," I said.

Reluctantly, Tess made her way over to the piano and started to play, hesitantly at first.

"What did he decide?" I asked Mme. Bardac. "Should we send for the manager?"

"No. She has a rare talent. I would hate to see her punished. Claude wants to sponsor her to the *Conservatoire*, but I have told him it is too soon. No, we will find her a new position for her. One where she can practice and hone her talents."

"That is very generous of you," I said.

"It's the least we can do after how she has helped Claude."

"In that case, there is only one thing that I cannot fathom, Holmes. Why did you take the case? You clearly worked everything out almost as soon as we arrived here."

"I was intrigued. I wanted to meet the pianist talented enough to impress M. Debussy."

I turned back to the piano. They were both playing together now and Debussy was speaking in rapid French that I didn't understand.

"What is he saying?" I asked Mme. Bardac.

"It is complicated," she replied. "About chord progressions and harmonic forms."

"The girl cannot even speak French, yet she seems to understand."

"She doesn't need words. She understands music."

I turned back to Holmes, to ask if he understood, but he was transfixed by the music and the sight of the famous composer and the young maid playing together in perfect harmony. It needed no explanation. It was simply beautiful.

The Adventure of the
Fearless Postman
by Andrew Salmon

The newspapers had been full of the Houndsditch Massacre for more than a fortnight, and we had followed it eagerly prior to a sensitive matter taking Sherlock Holmes and myself to the Continent a day or two before Christmas. The facts of the matter were well known: An attempted robbery of a jewelry store on the night of 16 December by Latvian revolutionaries had gone wrong, resulting in a terrible gun battle when the thieves were confronted by the police. In the end, three policemen had been slain, two more tragically crippled for life, and the death of the gang leader. The remaining gunmen and would-be thieves had lost themselves within the London throng, and the frantic manhunt for them was the topic of much heated debate. Home Secretary Churchill had been in touch in the first days following the massacre to inquire if Holmes might lend his considerable talents to the effort to bring the murderers to heel. But we were for Austria on a case crucial to preserving the peace, which one day I may be at liberty to relate.

Our work kept us on the Continent over the Christmas holiday in the waning days of 1910, and my notes show it was the third of January in 1911 when we returned to London to relate to the appropriate agencies the details of our time abroad, only to find the manhunt was not only still ongoing but had taken a dramatic and deadly turn.

By the time the cab Holmes and I were using became hopelessly mired in the interrupted flow of traffic, more than a thousand policemen endeavoured to contain a milling crowd many times that number which had braved the frigid temperature and bouts of snow and sleet to bear witness to a battle raging in Stepney. We couldn't guess what had caused this turnout on so foul a day, but something substantial was certainly in the offing.

Given the choice of remaining stuck in our cab while the chill crept beneath our lap robe or taking action, Holmes was forthright in his determination while irritated by the disruption of his return journey to Sussex.

"I've bacterial cultures awaiting my attention," complained Holmes. "Let's see if we might speed things along for the police. Left to themselves, we'll freeze to death in the cab and all of London will be shot to pieces."

We climbed down and were faced with the massive crowd. Once we ventured into the throng, we would be swallowed whole and swept wherever it had the will to go. Remaining on the periphery, Holmes questioned the men and women all craning to see over the main body before them. The continuous rattle of gunfire was a sound I hadn't heard since my time in Afghanistan and was jarring to hear on the city streets. Holmes spoke loudly to be heard over the incessant din.

He quickly learned that the Latvian gunmen were holed up in 100 Sidney Street, and the police couldn't root them out despite their best efforts, placing themselves at considerable risk in the process. The men inside the house seemed to possess an unlimited amount of ammunition and fired freely at any law officer who came within range. This was great fun for the crowd, but the shooting of a detective earlier that morning was nothing to take lightly.

Maintaining a course along the edge of the horde, we snaked our way through until we could see the policeman on horseback holding the front line of onlookers surging towards 100 Sidney Street. The gunfire grew louder, and the deafening aspect was tempered by the sporadic frequency of the eruptions. At last we found ourselves in the front rank. The remainder of our journey became suddenly much easier as those pressed close to the police horses were also within range of the anarchists' guns, and were more than ready to allow us to step to the front and into the gunsights as it were.

Holmes had chosen this spot well, as immediately we recognized Superintendent John Mulvaney and Chief Superintendent John Stark huddled close to an open gate and peering around an archway to survey the action – of which there was none presently. Sharpshooters had been summoned from The Tower and lay on newspaper placards to blast away at the windows of No. 100 to no noticeable effect we could see, other than shattered glass strewn about the roadway and the agitation of the expectant crowd. There were sharpshooters on rooftops, and in windows – in an unprecedented move, it appeared the military had been brought into the police action.

No sooner had we arrived when a great motion behind us drew our attention. The mounted police had opened a corridor through the crowd and, to our surprise, Home Secretary Winston Churchill had arrived on the scene. Holmes and I had worked with him on a singular matter a number of years ago and had charted his rise in the government since. Of average height with a slight stoop, we didn't immediately notice him in his black greatcoat and top hat. He joined the police officials who brought him up to date on the proceedings, and us as well, as we were permitted to draw within earshot the instant Holmes was recognized. I was shocked to learn of the employment of nearly one-hundred Scots Guards, thirty-five members of the Royal Horse Artillery, and fifteen Royal Engineers in Sidney Street to blow up the house the anarchists were using.

The police officials were most eager to storm the house as some of their number had been shot down by the rascals, and the Home Secretary didn't appear to be resistant to the suggestion. The crisis was undoubtedly about to escalate, and more blood would be spilled.

Remaining close to the wall, Holmes and I were still almost crushed by a mounted officer dealing with a member of the crowd who had taken considerable offense at the presence of so many armed men. The police weren't generally welcome in the East End as a matter of course, and with so many thousands of potentially disgruntled immigrant men and women in the crowd, we seemed perched atop a time bomb. Added to this was a sense of bored expectation. The crowd had formed just after dawn, and it was almost noon with no change to the situation. Events weren't furnishing the distraction they wished from their dreary day, and one sensed a surliness brewing in the angry shouts of the gathered. I followed on my friend's heels, and we were forced to draw even closer to the Home Secretary the hear the details of the siege.

"Is there a foundry nearby?" asked Churchill of his subordinates as we came to stand behind him.

"I believe so, but can't say for certain," Chief Superintendent Stark replied, his long, bushy mustache bristling from his face drawn gaunt at the matter before him. "Whatever for?"

"Your proposed action," Churchill explained. "I'd not like to see your men charge blindly into gunfire. Metal sheets might be used for shields. The risk would be reduced."

"We'll have them distracted, as I recommend men converging from the rear and through the roof while the sharpshooters pepper the house through every window. They are but two men. Of that we are certain."

"Well armed, I see," observed Churchill. "Webley .45's won't manage it, and those Morris-tube rifles are akin to children's pop guns compared to the Mausers those anarchists are using. No doubt of the weapon, as I recall the distinctive noise from the charge at Omdurman. Not likely to forget that. Fitted with attachable stocks, Mausers can be converted to carbines and are accurate to one-thousand yards. Outgunned as they are, many of your officers would be lost in the effort before they even reached the house."

"The men are up for it!" insisted Stark.

"I've no doubt," Churchill replied. "All the more reason not to waste them needlessly."

"The field gun is here and can be moved up," offered Superintendent Mulvaney, his stout frame set to burst through his greatcoat and the glare in his small, tired eyes promised justice. His beard, wet with the sleet, glistened as his fleshy lips worked with tension.

"Good Lord! You'll have the whole street in ruins if that starts blasting away," Churchill concluded.

"There's nothing else to be done but charge," said Mulvaney. "Those murderers aren't coming out and we must get in after 'em. We cannot maintain this siege indefinitely."

The Home Secretary put the matter to the other men clustered around him, and no one could offer an alternative to an all-out gun battle.

Churchill expressed his frustration in the end. "Five-hundred pounds to the man who can bring this thing to a close!"

"Home Secretary! Hello!" Holmes was forced to shout over the din despite our proximity.

Churchill turned at hearing his title, but didn't immediately recognize us. It was many years since we'd last met.

"Sherlock Holmes! Dr. Watson!" he bellowed at last, a smile stretching his fleshy, youthful face. "Join us if you will, please. Your input is most welcome."

Way was cleared for us amidst the illustrious group. Mr. Churchill shook our hands as did the police officials, though the latter did so more for the watchful eyes of the crowd than any enthusiasm over our presence.

"Here's a man to help put an end to this," said Churchill with a nod a Holmes. "What are your thoughts?"

Holmes didn't reply right away. He cast his gaze over the shops lining the streets while bullets clattered against the cobbles and walls. His attention seemed particularly fixed on an old woman who had come to stand in her doorway, directly in the field of fire, to calmly see how things were going. No shots were aimed her way. She turned and disappeared back into her tenement.

Superintendent Mulvaney caught the interest Holmes displayed towards the woman. "Some of 'em won't leave. We moved as many out of the surrounding buildings as we could, but others don't speak English, or simply can't understand the threat. The bleeding postman, Sparrow, delivered the morning mail while my men exchanged shots with the murderers! Right to the house next door. Doing his job, he said! Milk man said the same, if you can believe that! Well, he'll not be going back until we've got the gunmen out. Same for the post. Should have seen the look on his face when we told him this morning not to return until it's safe. Stringbean of a man that Sparrow, but he fought like the Devil. The faces on the lot of 'em. Unable to understand why the routine of the street need be affected by gunfire. We sent the both of them on their way, but I've charged a constable to keep an eye out for Mr. Sparrow. He'll be back, that one."

The sharpshooters let loose a volley in response to shots from the upper window of No. 100. Of course, the police were under strict orders not to fire unless first fired upon, which accounted for the frequent lulls. As the rattle of this exchange dwindled, angry shouts from the crowd reached our ears. The East End residents' objection to the presence of the Home Secretary and the police officials intensified by the minute. However, seeing them huddle from gunfire and no progress made these last few hours after the street had been cordoned off satisfied them somewhat. The anger always directed at officials generally was fueled exponentially as the disruption to their routine continued without furnishing anything of great interest.

"We shall entertain any intelligent suggestion," prompted Churchill.

"You wish to lead this action?" challenged Mulvaney with a sneer.

"Not at all. This is under police jurisdiction, and I'll not interfere unless asked to do so. Matters here cannot stand. We must take action!"

"Rush the house and it'll be over in a thrice," urged Mulvaney. "What say you, Mr. Stark?"

"I see no other alternative."

"Mr. Holmes?" asked the Home Secretary.

Holmes gazed about once more, but his eyes moved more precisely than before then he spoke more to himself. "It might work."

"We've no time for civilian theories," scoffed Mulvaney. "It falls to the police to solve, and we are experts at it."

"So we've seen," said Holmes, drily.

"Now see here, sir – !" Mulvaney took a step towards Holmes, one fist raised.

"Perhaps they're correct," said Churchill who, under the guise of turning his face from some shards of brick kicked loose by bullet strikes, shot Holmes a wink the police officials couldn't see. "Best be off, sirs. There is much danger here. I thank you for your willingness, but we shall manage on our own."

Holmes took me by the elbow, and we receded back behind the mounted police keeping the crowd at bay.

There was an alley cutting behind the houses and shops running along Sidney Street. Holmes made straight for the rear of a butcher shop. We quickly passed inside the unlocked rear door and entered into the dim confines. The grey weather called for illumination, but the proprietor wisely chose darkness against the threat of drawing a shot or two from outside.

"You no barge in 'ere." The proprietor poked his head up from the counter behind which he attempted to conceal his girth swathed in a stained apron. Eyes large as eggs protruded from his fleshy face. His hairless head slick with sweat despite the dank atmosphere of the place.

"We wish to shop," said Holmes, simply.

"All this goin' on?" He gestured with one beefy arm at the front windows. His German accent prominent either through stress or lack of practice speaking English. "Crazy you! No shop today. Closed!"

"Have you had much custom since the shooting began?"

"Not a bit."

"Then it's hardly in your best interest to turn paying customers away, is it?"

The man considered, then moving in a crouch from the front window looking out on Sidney Street, he met us at the rear of the store.

"What 'ave you, then?"

"A penny's worth of twine and your butcher's wrap," said Holmes.

"You'll 'ave me risk life for little as that? Be off with you!"

"A penny's worth of the items I mentioned and payment of half-a-crown for them. Does that improve the transaction enough for you?"

The butcher beamed a broad smile at us and shook with laughter. "Struck a deal, you!"

With the paper and twine in one pocket, Holmes proceeded to the ironmongery next door. This shop had been abandoned in haste, and we were alone as we prowled before the dark shelves.

"What are we after?"

"A coffee percolator," Holmes replied, simply, as if shopping under the guns of desperate anarchists was the simplest task in the world. "A pot as well. If memory serves, that's a grocer's next door. We'll find dried peppers there, I'm certain."

We did indeed, and our motley assortment of items grew as did my confusion. Matches, vodka, a small glass terrarium – all followed in good order. We found ourselves in the apothecary at the opposite end of the street at last. The owner had rightly fled, as the shop was almost directly across from No. 100, and we would have been tempting targets had we ventured anywhere near the smashed front windows. The tramp of feet overhead and the deafening roar of sporadic volleys aimed at the house from the sharpshooters on the roof were stiff reminders of our precarious position.

Yet Holmes seemed content to bring our shopping spree to a close here, though he had the sense to do so at the rear of the building.

"We must have a clean mortar and pestle," stated Holmes.

A quick, careful search turned up both, but the owner used these in grinding herbs and other medicines and they were stained with much wear.

"They aren't to be had," I concluded. "May I be so bold to ask what this is all about?"

"The mortar and pestle or all is lost," Holmes insisted and he sprang up the aisles casting his gaze this way and that. Then he spied them displayed in the front window and made a dash for them. They were barely in his fists when gunfire shattered the remaining glass, casting razor shards about. Holmes smartly leaped behind a stout column near the entrance while I ducked behind the worktable where we had safely deposited the accumulated items. We dared not move until we could be certain the gunmen's attention was elsewhere. An answering spatter of return fire from the roof ahead discouraged another try at us by the anarchists, and Holmes scurried back to the table, coughing mildly on the smoke blown by the draft through the broken windows.

Undaunted, he dumped the red peppers into the bowl of the mortar and began to crush them with the pestle. I questioned him as to the purpose behind this action but didn't receive a reply.

"May I impose upon you to open the vodka bottle?" he asked instead. "Please measure sixteen ounces into one of the graduated cylinders behind you."

I did as Holmes asked though I had no clue as to what purpose it would serve. Holmes dumped the powdered peppers into the percolator and extended his hand for the vodka I had measured out. This also went into the percolator. Holmes lit the alcohol burner beneath the device to begin heating the fantastic mixture. He found a bottle of sulfuric acid on a nearby shelf and added it and the matches from his pocket to the strange assortment without explanation.

"I shall require thirty minutes," said he, cryptically, as he placed the pot at his elbow and inspected the terrarium. "If you please, Watson, can you return to the Home Secretary and humbly inquire if he can delay any police action for the time being? Also, if he might direct a concentration of fire upon the upper windows of the house after the thirty minutes has elapsed, I expect we shall see a beneficial result."

"Certainly. How will they know you've instigated whatever the devil it is you're planning?"

"Why, the evidence of my action shall be before their very eyes. They are to open fire after thirty minutes regardless. I'll have your bulldog, if I may impose."

This request returned the thought of our proximity to the anarchists' lair to the forefront. I couldn't guess what Holmes was planning but an attack on the stronghold with so small a weapon would be futile and perilous. I expressed my concerns as I hesitated to hand over my pistol. "You'll not attack alone. I am prepared to stand with you."

"I wouldn't dream of it, my friend. There's no time to explain, save to tell you that your revolver is of paramount importance to our success."

Reluctance almost stayed my hand. In the end, I passed over the weapon.

My faith in Sherlock Holmes was unflappable and I instantly exited the apothecary and fought my way through the crowd back to Mr. Churchill, though my thoughts burned with curiosity and anxiety over what my friend had planned. Things were even more poised to come to a head. Insults were hurled Churchill's way, and the faces in the front ranks of the crowd were turning surly. A Maxim gun had arrived in our absence with more soldiers, and the crowd became galvanized at sight of this. Through an opening between two of the horses at the barricade, I could see the Home Secretary listening intently to Superintendent Mulvaney, who gestured emphatically at the newly arrived gun. Churchill shook his head before another volley of shots ended the conversation for the moment. It also froze the crowd for an instant. I used the stillness to shoot the gap and reach the Home Secretary. I didn't make my presence known until the police officials were distracted by demands made on their attention by a detective-inspector with an update on the re-positioning of the sharpshooters.

I caught the Home Secretary's eye and leaned in close. Mr. Churchill did likewise. "Holmes requires thirty minutes before he acts. Can you see that he gets this delay? I don't know why he makes this request. I trust his judgment in most matters."

Churchill's lips stretched in a kind smile. "My good man, the only thing politicians excel at is wasting time. If Mr. Holmes believes he can prevent a deadly police charge and end this affair, he shall have the time he requires. Make no mistake about that."

I shook his hand to seal the bargain. "Thank you, sir. Let us hope this can end without further bloodshed."

"Gentlemen," began Churchill as though commencing a speech. "There is still much to consider before bold action is taken. Surely we must exhaust all other avenues before we proceed in so final an act. In the interest of the public good we must only, under careful consideration of the facts and options before us, decide upon a course of action which will ensure we serve the best interests of the men in your charge as well as London's denizens. It seems evident to me that all due consideration be given to the challenges of the moment and the demands made on our duty."

He went on in this fashion, and it was clear he could continue for the rest of the day if necessary. Well, Holmes needed only a fraction of that time. With no clue what Holmes intended, I was fearful he might put himself in harm's way. It was my intention to return to Holmes after my conversation with the Home Secretary, but a pressing forward by the bloodthirsty throng removed any and all avenues I might have taken to cross the breadth of the crowd packing the street. I was cut off from my friend and experienced the anguish of helplessness that I couldn't assist Holmes in the forthcoming action. I remained close to those leading the siege in the hopes of learning something useful while awaiting a path back to Holmes.

"We've lost that blasted postman," I heard the detective-inspector shout over the crackle of gunfire as Mr. Churchill continued to harangue the officers. "Showed up for the noon delivery sure as you're standing there. Didn't take lightly to the constable barring his way, with an earful for good measure, and lit off before our man got ahold of him. Lost 'im when the roar cut loose at sight of the bloody Maxim. Took his eyes off 'im for only an instant to see what's what, and Sparrow was gone like the ground had opened up and swallowed 'im whole. If he thinks he can do his job without catching a bullet for his trouble, he's got another think coming."

"Damn and blast!" said Mr. Churchill and he thrust an hand out to point. "There he goes now! The fool!"

Indeed it was the postman who had somehow slipped through the barricade and was calmly making his rounds with, perhaps, a touch more haste than he would any other day. He clutched his mail sack before him as a pathetic shield in one fist. There was a small package tucked under his other arm.

"Well, he's asked for it now," Superintendent Mulvaney concluded.

A gasp broke forth from the crowd at seeing the postman in his smart navy blue jacket and cap with scarlet trim striding out into the field of fire. One woman close by screamed when she caught sight of the man striding boldly into danger. As the tense moments ticked by, every eye found the slim figure of the postman, and every heart went out to him that he might navigate quickly back to the safety of the barricade. He risked death with every step under the anarchists' guns, yet he continued steadfast in his course though a bullet might lance toward him at any second. Many in the crowd hoped to see their bloodlust satisfied and eagerly charted his progress with flashing eyes.

"I'll not be put off a moment longer!" a voice sounded behind us amidst the sound of a scuffle. "I shall be heard! Let me through!"

We turned at the commotion to find a coatless man shivering in the cold rain while a burly constable gripped his arm. His pinched features glared hatefully at us and his captor while his impeccable hair and Van

Dyke dripped with moisture. His cold blue lips quivered with his ire as he cast a baleful glare at the policemen.

"Mr. Sparrow!" exclaimed Superintendent Mulvaney in confusion. "What has happened?"

"Robbery! Treason!" Sparrow roared. "Robbed at gunpoint! Me post bag and coat stolen! He's tampering with the Royal Mail! Dragged into an alley like a common gutter snipe! I won't stand for this mistreatment, I say!"

"This was the man you attempted to prevent delivering mail earlier?" asked I.

"It is. George Sparrow." Stark's eyebrows drew together in consternation.

"Then who – ?" I asked.

The man we had been watching prior to Sparrow's arrival dropped a packet of letters through the slot of the house not two doors from No. 100. Standing stock still, he dug into his sack, presenting a most tempting target. Then he moved on to the house concealing the gunmen! We could only watch helplessly as he approached the red brick façade. He turned as he dropped some letters through the slot. My blood froze.

It was Sherlock Holmes!

He adjusted the package under his arm once more.

When I had recovered from the initial shock, I took comfort in my friend's presence of mind at his instant of peril. To gaze down at Holmes, the gunmen would have had to lean out the upper windows. Doing so would invite a bullet from the sharpshooters on the roofs across the street. Unobserved, Holmes lay down the mail bag and pulled his lock picks from a trouser pocket. Holmes was expert in their use and had the door open in an instant. He disappeared inside.

"What the devil does he think he's doing?" asked Chief Superintendent Stark.

The door closed behind him. We could only watch the still front of the house in horror of hearing the roar of guns which would signal the death of my dear friend. Unarmed, I could offer no aid and exact no revenge if the worst were to happen. An eerie silence fell over the crowd, the police and the Home Secretary. The moment stretched interminably.

The door opened slowly at last! A figure emerged.

I almost cried out when I saw Holmes stoop to retrieve the mail bag, adjust the hat and coat he'd stolen from Sparrow, and continue calmly delivering mail to the next houses in the street. Once out of view from the house, he abandoned the pretense of mail delivery and ambled over to join us at the cordon. Sparrow was hauled a short distance away, protesting all the while as Holmes approached.

"Good Lord!" I stammered. "Are you all right?"

"Never better."

"That's bloody cheek," said Churchill, a smile on his face. "What's it all about?"

"I believe thirty minutes have almost elapsed," Holmes continued, calmly. "Are the men prepared to concentrate fire on the upper windows?"

"The instruction has been given," Churchill replied.

Superintendent Mulvaney was incensed. "If you've put my men's lives at risk with your antics, you'll pay a high price. You may be assured of that."

"It's time, gentlemen," Holmes announced. "We'll see action soon."

Once again our attention was riveted to the front of 100 Sidney Street. Gunfire exploded from the rooftops, peppering the house's upper front, back and through the roof. The volley lasted but a moment or two but our ears rang nonetheless. As the smoke cleared, we peered through the misting rain but there was no change to the house.

"Damn you. sir!" hissed Mulvaney. "Civilian meddler!"

"Patience!" countered Holmes just as emphatically.

Suddenly shots rang out from the house. They seemed random, chaotic.

"Have your men advance," urged Holmes. "They will not need their weapons."

"Are you mad?"

"Lose no time. Do it!"

Churchill stepped in to settle the matter. "You heard the man. I will assume authority in this instance. Have the soldiers advance. Your men must lead the way."

With no choice but to obey, Mulvaney barked the order to the policemen around him and, after it was put to them to holster their weapons, they scurried off to collect a sufficient force.

Just in time as it turned out. For the door of 100 Sidney Street burst open and the two bedraggled gunmen staggered out, pawing at their eyes and coughing fiercely. The constables met them as they fled the house and pounced upon them. Blinded by red, raw eyes, unable to draw sufficient breath, they fell under the onslaught. Disarmed and handcuffed, the siege was brought to an end as the men bellowed in pain and defiance. The constables, well reminded of their dead brethren at the hands of these men, weren't as gentle as they might have been in securing the gunmen.

"Good show, Holmes!" said Churchill, clapping him on the shoulder. "And a fine ending. You've earned every penny of that five-hundred pounds, and I'll see you get it."

"I believe the money would be put to better use distributed to the families of the slain officers."

This made even Mulvaney smile and a new respect glinted in his eyes. "Damn fine of you, sir. Damn fine."

Holmes returned the garments to Sparrow, who clearly wanted to make his feelings plain on the theft, but the cheers of the crowd over what had just been brought off held his tongue. He couldn't help presenting to Holmes his worst scowl as he accepted the items.

Holmes seemed aware of the crowd for the first time. "With your permission, Home Secretary, we shall be on our way."

"By all means, sir. And thank you, my good man." We shook hands all around.

After we had taken a side street away from the bulk of the crowd, Holmes suggested that we eat. "Our work has kept us busy this morning and we've missed our luncheon. What say you we rectify that?"

"What of your experiments?"

"They'll keep a little longer. Permit me to retrieve my coat."

With that, we found a public house on the next street over.

"You didn't fire at the postman!" I exclaimed as we awaited our meals. Holmes was relating the events I had missed when we were cut off by the press of the crowd. He had returned my bulldog earlier and two cartridges were missing, which had prompted my query.

"Not at all. I wouldn't have hesitated to do so had it been necessary to prevent the carnage the police officials seemed hell-bent on bringing off. I will confess to being forced to show him the pistol – Mr. Sparrow isn't a man to be put off lightly, as you have seen yourself. What he made of the weapon, only he can say. It certainly brought about his instant, though begrudging cooperation. If he has any imagination at all, he'll claim to have been the man who delivered my concoction, and cement an elevated station in the neighbourhood."

"Or earn their wrath. They were a bloodthirsty lot, and no mistake."

"The point is moot, at any rate," concluded Holmes. "Mr. Sparrow struck me as too forthright to engage in deception. His slapdash attempt to avoid the police upon his return placed him easily within my grasp. He isn't one built for adventure. Although I had hoped to intercept him and don his uniform for reasons you've just seen play out, I couldn't count on his re-appearance. I was prepared to play the role of a resident come to see what all the racket was. Fate played a hand and thrust him in my direction."

"I would hardly call it easy. And so, if you didn't fire at the postman, at whom did you aim two cartridges? I admit I heard no gunfire from your location but, over the general din, I had strained my ears to hear. I am at a loss."

"Ah, the missing shells. It was the gunpowder I needed if I was to touch off my device while I was well clear of it. With so little time in which to act, a crude timing device of acid, matches, and the powder from the bullets was indicated."

"What the devil did you concoct from all those elements?"

"A delivery device. The ground dried peppers were distilled through the alcohol in the percolator until only an oil of reddish hue remained. Distilled further and dried during the process, a fine powder was the result."

"What earthly good is this powder?"

"On its own it makes a fine soup ingredient," Holmes replied. "But that would hardly have helped matters in Stepney Street. No, the powder must be burned off to produce gas. To achieve this, I placed the powder on a bed of the remaining butcher's wrap inside the terrarium, over a spread of matches. Beneath the paper were cotton balls the apothecary provided. Then some acid introduced at one end of the glass container and the slow seeping of the acid through cotton wool beneath the paper eventually reached the matches which would set the powder ablaze and produce the necessary gas while the heat cracked the glass and allowed the gas to billow out. * I deposited the terrarium on the ground floor of 100 Sideny Street – a cramped entryway which served my purpose well – poked holes through the butcher paper I had used to simulate a post office package with the twine, and exited. With the concentrated rifle fire on the upstairs windows, the anarchists inside were driven down to the ground floor to escape the fusillade and ran into the waiting gas which my crude device was spreading across the ground floor. The result of this you witnessed with your own eyes before the men were taken."

"I witnessed it, but don't clearly comprehend what I saw. Was it poison you unleashed upon them."

"Hardly," Holmes explained. "It was a variant of a lachrymator agent the War Department has been experimenting with. Lachrymater from the Latin *lacrima*, meaning 'tear'. My familiarity with chemistry earned me visits from a General Officer or two in search of a discreet professional opinion some months ago on the subject of this experimental tear-inducing gas, and its possible uses on and off the battlefield. Exposure to the chemical compound greatly irritates the eyes and nasal passages, incapacitating the afflicted who can hardly defend themselves or sight a weapon with painful tears from the gas running from their red and swollen eyes. As you just saw, an arrest quickly made and an easy end to the matter with no further loss of life."

"I wouldn't call it easy," said I. "You took a terrible risk."

"It was a calculated one," said Holmes. "Remember, the anarchists hadn't fired at the milk man, the postman on his morning run, nor the woman appearing periodically to see how things were progressing. Thus it was unlikely they would fire at the postman upon his return."

"You couldn't be certain of that."

"Let's not forget that anarchists, for all the havoc the wreak, aim their hatred at governments and representatives of authority, not the people. Most would gladly assassinate royalty, but balk at harming the everyman. It's perverse reasoning, seeing as their assaults on institutions in the form of bomb attacks on buildings often inflict harm on innocent bystanders, which isn't their intent. The two in 100 Stepney Street were anarchists who had no reason to kill a solitary postman merely doing his job, though they wouldn't hesitate to blow up a post office."

"I take your point, though I still maintain you took an awful risk."

"That's neither here nor there. It's postman Sparrow who has a daunting task before him."

"Whatever do you mean?"

"I'm afraid I was indiscriminate in the deliveries I carried out in order to get close to 100 Sidney Street. Our fastidious Mr. Sparrow will have his work cut out for him getting the mail sorted now that I've made a mess of it."

NOTE

* The formula and procedure outlined here was deliberately altered to deter the adventurous reader from attempting to replicate the device Holmes employed.

The Adventure of the Cheapside Secret
by Steven Philip Jones

To my Uncle Gene

Chapter I

When Sherlock Holmes retired to the little farm of his dreams in the spring of 1903, he was determined to live the life of a recluse, and for the most part he succeeded. Or he did until one misty day in June of 1912, which began with an early morning call by Chief Inspector Alec MacDonald of Scotland Yard to my Queen Anne residence. My wife was away in Brighton with family, so I was feeling rather forsaken and therefore grateful for MacDonald's visit. The Home Office had need of Holmes' assistance and MacDonald had been dispatched to ask if I thought my friend could be persuaded to help. My answer was no, of course, but I acquiesced to accompany MacDonald to Sussex and provide what support I could in his mission.

It was nearly afternoon by the time we arrived at Eastbourne Station, where we rented a trap for the five-mile journey to Holmes's farm near the bayside village of Fulworth. Along the way I mentioned that a century ago the farm had been home to a noted gentleman-writer whose repute had lost most of its luster over the years, and as the southern slope of the Downs came into view I pointed out Holmes's plain white cottage with the familiar turret in one corner of its walled garden. MacDonald nodded then pointed to a Crossley parked near the gate and asked, "Has Mr. Holmes taken up auto touring?"

"No, that looks like Collinson's, the postman."

Sure enough, as we parked the trap and trudged up the path to the house, Holmes was engaged in a prickly discussion with Collinson, a heavily-built, bow-backed fellow of middle years with clean-cut features. Both were standing near the garden and were so preoccupied that neither noticed MacDonald or me approach, but we heard Holmes complain, "Never have I heard such a *suggestio falsi* in my life! How can you equate sympathy for Captain Smith with condoning his navigation of the *Titanic*?"

"Read the newspapers! They would hardly write of Nelson the way they write of Smith!"

"More humbug! Show me the work of any responsible journalist where Captain Smith is written of in the same terms as Admiral Nelson, and I will gladly send one-hundred pounds to the Fabian Society."

Here MacDonald made our presence known by positing, "Well, there can be no defense that Captain Smith made a terrible mistake, but he was an old and honorable sailor who gave his life in reparation, and that shouldn't be overlooked."

Holmes pointed at MacDonald. "Quite right, Mr. Mac! Bravo to Scotland Yard!" Then he glanced my way. "I say, is that you, Watson? I fear you've changed since you last came to Sussex."

"I could say the same. I see you've sprouted a goatee since I visited you only a few weeks ago."

"Just a lark to keep my chin warm. I doubt I shall keep it with summer coming on."

I turned to the postman. "Good afternoon, Mr. Collinson. How is your daughter?

"Much better, thanks to that salve you mixed up from some of this mulish man's beeswax. Hallie will have no more to do with hogweed, that's for certain."

"Well, unfortunately, we all must burn our fingers on occasion to learn some lessons." Then I told MacDonald. "This is Gerard Collinson, the Fulworth postmaster."

"And," Holmes injected, "my nemesis in all matters common-sensical."

"This is Chief Inspector MacDonald of Scotland Yard," I told Collinson.

Holmes's eyes sparkled. "*Chief* Inspector? Congratulations, Mr. Mac! Your promotion is long overdue!"

"Thank you, sir," MacDonald said, then added somewhat sheepishly, "but it's going on seven years now."

"Truly?" The sparkle dimmed.

"You know, Holmes," I suggested, and not for the first time, "it wouldn't harm you if you came up to London more often than you do. You're always welcome in our home."

"And I've said again and again that – "

MacDonald cleared his throat and asked Collinson, "Dr. Watson says that's your Crossley by the gate. She's a bonnie motor."

"Thank you, Chief Inspector. Which reminds me, I best be returning to my rounds." To MacDonald and me, "Good afternoon, gentlemen." To the landowner, "Mr. Holmes."

Holmes replied, "Mr. Collinson. Now, Mr. Mac, I assume you are here on official business."

"I am. To deliver a letter, ironically enough." MacDonald reached into a breast pocket to remove an envelope and present it to Holmes. "There's no seal, but it's from the Home Secretary and it's confidential."

An expression of puzzlement darkened Holmes's clear-cut features as he opened the envelope, only to fester into annoyance as his eyes scanned the letter. "Mr. McKenna requests my assistance regarding an urgent matter, however he provides no details. So what is it, Mr. Mac? A stolen treaty? Someone extorting a secretary's wife?"

"No, this time it's a treasure."

Holmes seldom laughs, but at that moment he appeared sorely tempted. "Like the Agra Treasure?"

"No, more along the lines of something equivalent to the Crown of St. Edward. As impressive as its monetary value is, the treasure's historical value is incalculable to England. It has been lost for nearly three-hundred years, but now some American adventurers are on the scent of it."

Holmes measured MacDonald's words for several seconds while he deliberately folded the letter. Handing it back, he said, "Perhaps you and the doctor should come inside where we can discuss this flummery out of the sun."

Chapter II

In many respects, Holmes's cottage was as cozy and cheerfully furnished as was our old digs in Baker Street. It was also nearly as cluttered, despite what I was sure were the best efforts of Holmes's longsuffering housekeeper. MacDonald was delighted to see Holmes's old writing desk again, its desktop buried beneath opened texts and manuscript pages while the floor around its base was littered with notes and documents. "It's almost feels like we're back in Baker Street, if you don't mind my saying so."

"Not at all," Holmes remarked as he brought out a bottle of mead and tumblers for MacDonald and me. He poured us each a glass and after MacDonald took a sip the inspector complimented,

"This honey wine is braw."

"I knew a Scotsman would appreciate it. I'll send a bottle home with you. And for you, Watson – a jar of Sussex honey. Sometimes I think it's the only reason you visit when you do."

"Well, actually, if you have another bottle of this – "

"Tut, tut, Watson. Remember how mead goes to your head. Now Mr. Mac, tell me about this historical treasure and these American adventurers. And why has the detective force been brought in on this article of *virtu*?"

336

"Well, sir, the Home Office contacted Scotland Yard when they learned about our investigation into the assault and robbery of an assistant with Theodore and Mark. The man's name is Julius Mancune, and at the time he was delivering two-thousand pounds of jewels and jewelry on approbation."

"I've never understood why jewelers continue with that foolhardy service." Holmes corked the bottle, put it down upon the mantel-piece, and settled into an armchair. "Theodore and Mark? They're in Hatton Garden, correct?"

"Bond Street. Their specialty is antique and vintage jewelry."

"I see. And this robbery occurred where?"

"Number 17b Regent Street. The delivery was carried out on the orders of Mancune's manager, Justice Byles, who believed the house to be the residence of Mr. and Mrs. Uwe Waltermier."

"Aliases, I suspect."

"They are. The house was hired by the Waltermiers last Friday through Mr. Scott Dolash, a West End agent. When Mancune arrived at the appointed time of two o'clock, the couple received him graciously before chloroforming and binding him and absconding with the swag. He and Dolash gave us excellent descriptions of the couple, who we recognized at once as Hunton and Annelise Dwyer, a prig team from east of Aldgate Pump."

"Westminster sounds a bit outside their province."

"Aye, and so is this caper. Instead of staying in lavender, the dafties lumbered some of the jewels to an East London fence named Kemmy Grizzard before bolting for Waterloo Station to buy tickets to Southampton. Och, we nibbed them before sunset!"

"Such maladroitness suggests they were hirelings, not masterminds."

"They were. And in exchange for us using velvet gloves with Annelise, Hunton told us they were hired by two Americans, a Negro named Augustus Bailey and an Indian named Tom Jeffords. Bailey is tall, clean-shaven, about thirty-five, while Jeffords is as big and brawn as William Wallace. We have no record of any persons with those names matching those descriptions, and neither do the New York Police Bureau or Pinkerton's. Oh, Jeffords might also be mute. Hunton said he never talked, just listened."

I commented, "Hardly a pair you see strolling about London every day."

"So you'd think they'd be as easy to track as the Dwyers, but they're a canny pair."

Holmes asked, "Do you know yet how the jewels were divided?"

"Aye. Bailey and Jeffords kept a gold Jacobean posy ring and passed everything else off to the Dwyers."

"That makes no sense," I had to say.

"No, it doesn't, but it's why the King's Historiographer Royal fears Bailey and Jeffords are hunting for what he calls 'The Poleman Treasure'. It's believed that a posey ring holds some sort of clue to its whereabouts."

Holmes leaned back, stretched out his legs, steepled his fingers, and closed his eyes. "All right, then, tell me about this treasure."

MacDonald placed his tumbler on the floor, leaned forward, and propped his elbows on his knees. "Well, the way the Historiographer told it to me, a Dutch goldsmith named Gerald Poleman was returning from the Indies in 1631 on an East India Company merchant ship called *The Brigadier*. The ship's manifest shows that Poleman's cargo included a chest packed with five-hundred pieces of gold, jewels, and jewelry that Poleman had collected to use as working stock. And according to the ship's carpenter mate, Christopher Adams, the hoard also included several exquisite gemstones, and extremely rare and unique pieces of jewelry from all over the world, including the Orient."

I asked, "How did Adams know that?"

"Because Poleman died before *The Brigadier* reached England, and Adams took possession of his chest after cataloguing its contents."

"Surely Poleman's heirs did not stand for that!"

"They didn't, and neither did the East India Company. Eventually, Adams was forced to surrender the chest to the company's Treasurer, Robert Bertie, 1st Earl of Lindsey, who immediately found himself in litigation with Poleman's heirs. Unfortunately, nothing was decided before Lindsey was killed during the First Civil War at the Battle of Edgehill in 1642 without . . . supposedly . . . telling anyone where he had cached Poleman's working stock."

"Which brings us back to the posey ring?"

"Aye, Doctor. Now Lindsey's death is well documented. He was shot through the thigh bone and surrounded by a Roundhead cavalry. Lindsey's eldest son, Montagu Bertie, Lord Willoughby, surrendered his sword and carried his father to the nearest shed, but he couldn't staunch Lindsey's bleeding. After his father died, Willoughby collected Lindsey's sword and the posey ring, knowing it to be a favor from Lindsey's wife, Elizabeth Montagu. At the time, posey rings were worn as love tokens and wedding bands. Apparently, though, neither Willoughby nor his mother had any inkling that this one might hold a hint to where Lindsey stored the working stock." At this juncture MacDonald reached once more into his breast pocket, but this time he removed a piece of foolscap that he handed to Holmes. "Theodore and Mark provided me with this drawing of the ring."

My friend gazed upon the drawing then tossed it across to me. "I bow to your expertise when it comes to jewelry, Mr. Mac, but I'd say it looks like a rather pedestrian gold ring."

"Do you know anything about this inscription?" I asked. The words "*Loving and Giving*", followed by a Christian ichthys fish, had been etched inside the band.

"I'm afraid not, Doctor."

Holmes remarked, "It is most suitable for a favor or marriage band, but rather bland for a cryptogram."

"Perhaps the posies are the clue? 'Ring a Ring o' Rosies'?"

"Or perhaps this legend is merely the filling of a vacuum in history with conjecture, to paraphrase Bernard Shaw. I'm afraid, Mr. Mac, that I fail to see what is so vital about this matter that the Home Office requests that I interrupt my retirement."

"Well, Mr. Holmes, according to Adams's catalogue, Poleman's working stock contained several pieces of early Stuart jewelry. Very few examples of Stuart jewelry have survived from the Seventeenth Century, which is what makes the Poleman Treasure historically significant, and why Mr. McKenna is appealing to your fidelity at the behest of His Majesty and the Historiographer Royal. If we cannot prevent these Americans from locating the treasure, then England shall be robbed of what has too long been a missing part of her history."

Chapter III

I returned home in time for supper, but I was too frustrated to eat. Holmes not only refused the government's request, but he declined to discuss anything except bee culture until MacDonald and I were forced to beg our leave. The chief inspector said little during our journey back to London and spoke not a word against his mentor, but I could see that he shared my exasperation.

I spent the evening flitting between reading and writing, unable to concentrate upon either for long. Eventually the hour arrived that I could reasonably consider retiring, but at about that moment there came a rapping upon the front door. I answered it, expecting to be called out to a patient, but was astounded to find Sherlock Holmes standing on my step, a portmanteau and walking stick in one hand and a corked jar in the other, which he held out for me.

"Good evening, Watson. You forgot your honey."

"I . . . Well . . . Thank you."

"May I come in?"

"Yes. Please." I placed the honey jar on the hall table. "Let me take your bag and stick. Is your rheumatism flaring up?"

"It is rather chilly and damp for the time of year." Holmes doffed his coat and hung it up.

"I'll carry your things to your room after you've had a chance to rest."

"Thank you." Once in my study his eyes darted straight to my desk. "I've interrupted your writing."

"I was just making some notes. Old habits. Have a seat by the fire. When did you arrive? Have you eaten?"

Holmes allowed himself some seconds to warm himself and rub his knees. Then, with a grin, he said, "I arrived at four and I dined at The Red Lion. May I smoke?"

"Of course. There are matches in that box if you need them." Sitting across from him, I inquired, "The Red Lion? In Parliament Street? Did you happen to visit the Home Office?"

"No, but I did visit the London Library. I've always found its historical catalog superior to the British Museum Library, although I was forced to catch up on my three-pound subscriptions to access it. And to answer your inference: Yes, I am here because of the Poleman Treasure."

I must confess that a tremendous sense of relief lightened my spirits upon hearing this. I also felt some of the old exhilaration whenever the game was afoot. "That's marvelous! But why did tell MacDonald that you've done your duty for King and Country."

"Oh, I don't think I was quite that brash."

"You called the treasure 'flummery' and said that it wouldn't have mattered if the Home Office's request had come from Churchill."

"Oh. Yes. I did say that. Well, you see, so long as the government remains ignorant of my interest, I can operate with a free hand. I believe Mr. Mac will understand."

"So do you have a theory as to the cache's location?"

Holmes took a long draw off his cigarette, savoring the flavor of the smoke, then exhaled. "I am erecting the scaffolding of a theory, for which I think this might be of some benefit." He reached into his vest pocket with thumb and forefinger and withdrew a ring whose gold had turned buff from time.

"Lindsey's posey ring! Where did you find it?"

"This fascinating trinket actually found me. It is rather amazing what you can turn up at the London Library."

"Holmes, seriously now, how did come by that?"

"I am being utterly serious, but for the whole story, I must beg your forbearance. You will recall that the Poleman Treasure only came into Lindsey's possession because he was Treasurer of the East Indian

340

Company. Now Lindsey's earldom was in Lincolnshire, and it's quite unlikely the governor and merchants of the E.I.C. would have permitted him to transport such a trove out of the city. If I am correct, then the inscription could be a hint to where Lindsey cached it in London."

"And if you are correct, then the inscription is probably so general that it likely refers to a place that is easily reached – or at least it was, before the Great Fire."

Holmes's eyes kindled. "Our thoughts are in tandem, Watson! After I arrived in London this afternoon, I went directly to the library to research possible locations. However, I had hardly sat down in the reader's room before an American approached and asked to join me."

"Not Bailey?"

"I fear Augustus Bailey is as much an alias as Uwe Waltermier. In any event, he introduced himself as Dr. Percy Harris."

"'Doctor'?"

"Harris claims to be a graduate of the Harvard Medical School, as well as being well-read in Church and Law. I can attest from our conversation that he is a highly educated individual."

"And he approached you in public, bold as brass? Extraordinary! To what end?"

"To present me with this ring. 'Now that you have this,' he told me, 'I believe all of Theodore and Mark's lost property has been returned. I'm sure you're familiar with it. Why else come straight here from London Bridge Station?'

"'My congratulations,' I said. "I saw no one following me.'

"'That is what you may expect to see when Jeffords – Pardon me, his name is Thunenhyarhen, but I call him Stone – follows you. And to be fair, why should you be expecting anyone to tail you? Or that anyone even knew that Dr. Watson and Chief Inspector MacDonald visited you today in Sussex?'

"'And should I deduce that you now have no further need for this ring because you found the Poleman Treasure?' I asked.

"'What I have found . . . is that Pope said it best: 'Welcome the coming, speed the parting guest.' It has been an honor, Mr. Holmes.' And there he left me. As scoundrels go, I rather liked him."

"How can you say that?"

"Well, remember, the most winning woman I ever knew was hanged for poisoning three children for their insurance money."

"And I've often wondered what Freud might make of that. So where did Harris go after he left the library?"

"I haven't a notion."

"But surely you followed him."

"Harris is too clever to have led me anywhere if I tried. However, now that I know about Stone, I am on the lookout for him, and if I can find Stone, then I can locate Harris when the time is right."

"Why should Stone follow you again if he and Harris have located the treasure?"

"If they had located the treasure, then Stone would have had no reason to follow me. He and Harris could have simply mailed the ring to Theodore and Mark on their way out of the country. No, Watson, the Devil can sometimes do a very gentlemanly thing, but he rarely does anything foolish."

"Then what are they up – Oh! Of course! They failed to find the Poleman Treasure, so they hope you'll do it for them. If that's their game, though, once you locate it, they will have no choice but to prevent you from informing MacDonald."

"If they can. Remember, I would never have taken up my former profession if danger did not attract me."

"I know, but you haven't been in harness for several years. Perhaps you should consider Mark Twain."

Confusion clouded my friend's features. "I'm sorry, Doctor, but are you comparing me to *Tom Sawyer, Detective?*"

"No, I'm comparing you to its author, Samuel Clemens, the former Mississippi riverboat pilot. Late in Twain's life, he returned to the Mississippi and was invited to steer a steamboat, but he couldn't navigate the river. It had changed too much over the years."

"Oh, I see."

"You were unaware of MacDonald's promotion. You were off on the location of Theodore and Mark. You also failed to notice this Stone following you."

"'Pon my word, Watson, you've grown most observant."

"I know you prefer a free hand in this matter, but don't you think you ought to bring MacDonald? He is up on London and has kept in practice. And I know you trust him."

"Yes, that's all true." Holmes drew another long puff, but this time his exhale sounded more like a sigh. "It's no small thing to consider that one's skills may have atrophied, but I shall consider your advice. In the meantime, perhaps I was wise to bring along a bottle of honey wine."

"You did? For the Chief Inspector?"

"For my loyal Boswell. If you would kindly fetch two glasses, I will retrieve the bottle from my bag."

342

Chapter IV

Holmes and I shared the bottle as we talked into the night of many things, and I awoke the following day with the expectation that I would accompany my friend to MacDonald's office. To my dismay, I discovered that the morning was nearly gone and Holmes had departed hours earlier after instructing the maid and the cook that I wanted to sleep in. My temper was hot and my head was fuzzy as I dressed and rushed to Scotland Yard, where I broke into MacDonald's office and asked, "Has Holmes been here?"

"Not yet, Doctor."

"'Not yet'?"

"Come sit down. And please close the door." MacDonald explained how he found a letter from Holmes waiting for him when he arrived that morning. "It outlines everything you two apparently discussed last night regarding the Poleman Treasure. By the way, I appreciate you suggesting that he bring me in. Then it – " A knock on the door interrupted MacDonald. He answered it and stepped into the corridor, only to return after a few moments, frowning. "I was about to tell you that Mr. Holmes wrote that he was certain Stone had followed him to Queen Anne Street last night. He was just as certain that he gave Stone the slip this morning and that the fellow would follow you next. Mr. Holmes was also certain that you'd come here once you discovered he'd lit out, so he instructed me to have men ready so we could pounce on Stone. All that sounded logical, but it didn't sit well with me to leave you on your own. So I dispatched two men to follow you here and they've just reported that they haven't seen Stone all morning."

Of all the stubborn men! I thought, but I was even angrier at allowing myself to be cajoled into imbibing as much as I had the night before. After taking a deep breath I asked, "Does his letter say anything else?"

"Only that he will contact us soon. He added to be patient and remember *Justitia Virtutum Regina.*"

"'*Justice is Queen of Virtues*'? I wonder why he wrote that?"

"Quoting Latin is a pet to Mr. Holmes."

"Yes, but his quotes are always relevant to the matter at hand." I paused and then something dawned on me. "Have you a London atlas?"

MacDonald kept an *A to Z* in his desk and handed it to me. "What are you looking for?"

"I'm not looking, I'm trying to remember something." I flipped through several pages, not precisely sure what I was searching for, until – "Ah! There! *Justitia Virtutum Regina* is the motto of the Worshipful

343

Company of Goldsmiths. That can't be a coincidence. Goldsmith's Hall is on Foster Lane and Gresham Street, but it isn't open to the public."

"I bet that didn't stop Mr. Holmes, and he doesn't have my credentials." MacDonald stood, snatched his hat, and motioned me to follow him.

Chapter V

What happened between the time MacDonald and I struck out for Goldsmith's Hall and when we joined the hunt was told to us later that day by Sherlock Holmes, who had indeed finagled permission to research the hall's library. When Holmes finished, he left a message for the Chief Inspector and me, then took a cab down Foster Lane to Cheapside Street and from there to the corner of Cheapside and Friday Streets. Several minutes later another cab arrived at the corner, whereupon Dr. Harris got out and asked his driver, "Your compatriot is certain he brought his passenger here from Goldsmith's Hall? And the man was alone?"

"Yes, to both. George said your gentleman went straight in there." The driver pointed at the furthest building in a row of dilapidated Jacobean shops. "Don't know why, though. It's been empty for years, like its neighbors. Fact is, all three are to be torn down soon."

"S'that so?" Harris tossed two quid to the cabbie. "There's your fare and extra for your assistance. I'll contact you if I need you again."

The driver tipped his cap and smirked. "Any time. G'up, Cordwainer."

Harris strolled to the shop, where he tried the front door and found it unlocked. Opening the door, he gazed into the dark interior. "Mr. Holmes?" he called, and when there was no answer he murmured, "'*Will you walk into my parlor?' said a spider to a fly.*'"

Entering without invitation, Harris closed the door and scanned the forlorn and filthy floor, walls, windows, and ceiling. "'*Tis the prettiest little parlor that you ever did spy.*'"

His attention was eventually drawn to a hatch door set into the floor. "'*The way into my parlor is . . . down . . . a winding stair.*'"

Opening the hatch, Harris descended, but did not step all the way into the shadowy cellar. "'*And I have many pretty things to show you when you are there.*'"

Stopping, Harris crouched and called, "Mr. Holmes?" There came no answer, so he repeated, "Mr. Holmes?" When there was still no answer, he said, "The shop floor and these stairs are rather grimy, and I only saw your footsteps walking towards the hatch and then down here. Can we talk?"

"I would enjoy nothing better."

The voice came from above and behind Harris, who swiveled to find Holmes coldly smiling at him through the hatchway, a revolver targeted at his heart. Harris squinted with disbelief and stepped up a stair. "How – ?"

"Let me caution you, Doctor, that my eyesight may not be what it once was, but I can fell a sprinting rabbit at twenty paces."

Harris halted. "I believe you." Inhaling then exhaling deeply, the man inquired, "May I ask how you managed this trick? You didn't walk backwards in your footsteps like a dime-novel tracker, did you?"

"We call those yellow-backs in England, and there's many a useful maneuver to be found in them. In this instance, however, this shop is 32 Cheapside Street, and its cellar connects to 31 and 30 Cheapside. I merely walked through to the neighboring shop and from that post I watched you arrive."

"Oh." Harris appeared narked. "I saw, but I did not observe."

"To be fair, the cellar is rather dark. Otherwise, I'm sure you'd have spotted the door leading to the neighboring cellar as well as the chest behind you."

Once again Harris swiveled and squinted. "Is that – ?"

"The Poleman Treasure."

Harris clapped. "Bravo, Mr. Holmes! Bravo!"

"I am certain you would have uncovered it for yourself if you had been permitted in Goldsmith's Hall."

"You do me a kindness. I'm guessing from your sullied cane and clothes that you prodded and dug quite a bit before locating it."

"You are correct."

"That couldn't have done your rheumatism much good."

"Your concern is appreciated, Doctor. Now would come join me up here? Chief Inspector MacDonald and Dr. Watson should be arriving soon."

Harris raised his hands, palms turned forward, and judiciously started up the stairs. "Will Stone be joining them?"

"Won't he be following them? I suppose we shall have to wait to see."

"I suppose you're right."

Holmes retreated a few steps as Harris breached the opening. "I admire you being such a gracious loser about this."

Harris halted. "Oh, I'm not, you know. Not a bit of it." And upon the last word he snatched the hatch, dropped, and pulled the door after him.

Holmes grabbed the hatch's handle but Harris had already wedged what turned out to be a bowie knife between the jamb and the door. He could hear Harris scrabble down the steps and realized he had seconds to cut the man off. Limping as fast as his knees allowed, Holmes hurried from the shop just as MacDonald and I arrived. He yelled to us, "Harris is getting away! We can trap him in the cellar if you each go into one of those two shops! I'll guard this one!"

MacDonald swiftly pointed at the shop furthest from the corner. "I'll take that one. Doctor, you take the middle shop. And be careful."

"You, too." My shop, like its companions, was ill-lit inside, forcing me to focus all my attention on locating the entry to the cellar, but before I did a titanic punch cracked the back of my skull like a Jezail bullet and knocked me senseless.

Chapter VI

Stone had indeed followed the Chief Inspector and me to and from Goldsmith Hall, and when we entered our respective shops he pursued and ambushed me. The Americans then fled to Friday Street, where they flagged a cab which delivered them to the Greenwich foot tunnel. From there they could lose themselves amongst the dockworkers and residents on the Isle of Dogs and arrange passage on a ship out of England.

For the next two days I was regulated to bedrest, although the second day came at the insistence of Holmes, who remained in London to (as he put it) supervise my recuperation. So earnest was he that he all but berated me late that second day when he brought two teacups into my bedroom and found me propped up against my pillows and writing.

"Watson!"

"Old habits. And I only have a mild concussion. Don't you suppose I know what's best for me medically?"

"'He that teaches himself has a fool for a master.' And speaking of fools, I shall never forgive myself for sending you into that shop. You were right to worry about the fitness of my skills."

"And I've told you, that was my decision. I never would have done it if I also weren't attracted to danger, although I may be too old for this sort of sport."

"All I can say is that you do me a kindness. Now drink this." He handed me one of the teacups.

I scowled. "More tea and honey? No honey wine?"

"Didn't you have enough the other night?"

"Only because you plied me with more than – "

"And what's wrong with this tea? If you're feeling well enough to be sitting up, then it must be doing you some good."

"I fail to see any correlation . . . but as you wish." I sipped some to satisfy him. "Who's that second cup for?"

"For me." He sat in a chair, sipped, and sighed.

"Any more news from MacDonald?"

"A trifle. It would appear that our American friends have fled the city and the country. After all, what point is there in their staying?"

"Most annoying," I grumbled as I tenderly rubbed the duck egg at the base of my skull. "Still, it isn't the first time some villain has managed to slip through the net."

"No. There was Latimer and Kemp . . . the captain and mates of the *Lone Star* . . . Fritz and his gang of counterfeiters – "

"And *The* Woman."

A most melancholy sliver of a smile split Holmes's lips. "Yes . . . and Mrs. Norton."

"What do you make of that note Harris left on the treasure chest? '*Wind not the green watch or let slip the dogs of war.*'"

"Most likely a feverish attempt at a Parthian shot. Dr. Harris did say that he is no gracious loser. To be safe, though, the Historiographer Royal is comparing the contents of Poleman's chest against Adams' catalogue to make certain the Americans didn't abscond with any of the treasure, and so far it appears they did not."

"So what is this green watch?"

"An emerald pocket watch from Columbia. Columbian-European relations were nascent in the sixteenth and seventeenth century, so the diplomatic corps cannot think how this watch could set off any catastrophe between ours, much less any other countries."

"Perhaps it conceals some forgotten secret that is better left buried."

"Perhaps, but the government can trouble with that."

"How did it feel being back in harness?"

Holmes sighed once more. "I can take no pleasure knowing that, if not for blind luck, Harris and Stone would now be in possession of The Poleman Treasure."

"I prefer to think that you, MacDonald, and I prevented that. Oh, you may have been a bit too willful acting alone like you did, but you did track down the treasure."

"For that, I give all credit to the ring's inscription and the excellent record keeping of Goldsmith's Hall."

"What was it about the inscription that led you to the shops?"

"Nothing astounding, I assure you. Do you remember the fortune-telling song 'Monday's Child?'"

"Yes, though it has been a while. Doesn't it begin, '*Monday's child is fair of face*'?"

"And '*Friday's child is loving and giving*'. Prior to the Great Fire, Friday Street, as well as Cheapside Street, were part of Goldsmith's Row, the center of London's gold and jewelry trade. Friday Street also had three churches, but I think their presence only partly explains the ichthys. My research at the hall revealed that Friday Street is named after a fish market that was held there every Friday, the traditional day for abstaining from eating meat. The ichthys may have also been a reference to the Great Conduit located on the eastern end of Cheapside Street."

"Or perhaps it referenced all of those things?"

"Perhaps, yes. Lindsey was, after all, clever enough to cache Poleman's hoard amongst another goldsmith's working stock. Unfortunately, Lindsey met his demise, followed by the Great Fire in 1666, and then in 1667 the Goldsmith's Company reconstructed three new shop buildings over the cellars of the previous structures."

I could only shake my head in wonder. "It is simply amazing how things can get lost in the shuffle of time and events."

"Not only things but lives, an age-old lesson I fear our modern world is about to tragically and terribly relearn." A glum shiver cascaded down Holmes's lengthy frame, after which he stood and excused himself.

"Where are you going?"

"I find myself in need of what's left of that bottle of honey wine, unless you happen to have a stock of nepenthe in your medicine cabinet."

The Adventure of the King's Code

by Mike Chinn

Ever since he had abandoned London and taken himself off to the South Downs, where bees had replaced his fascination with all things criminal, I heard less from my old friend Sherlock Holmes. Never one to indulge himself in the niceties of simple correspondence, Holmes's natural reluctance to engage with society had become almost hermit-like. Aside from the rare note mentioning his apian researches, or sketching out some simple case of deductive work that locals would bring to him on occasion, his new life was something of a mystery to me.

It was therefore with some surprise that I received a telegram from him one day in early 1914 (not for the Holmes the convenience of a telephone – even assuming his cottage contained such a device). As ever it was to the point:

Café Royal, 5th April, 3:00 p.m. Be prompt.

Holmes

I confess to being more than a little intrigued. The Café Royal was not the kind of establishment I would normally expect my friend to frequent, even in its heyday, when the great and the good – and frequently notorious – could be found gracing its tables. And now that its glory days were most likely behind it, even as a place where the sharpest-eared might catch morsels of carelessly dropped gossip, I saw even less to attract Holmes. Or perhaps he was in a celebratory mood. Another treatise on the nature and behaviour of honeybees was about to be published and he was in the mood to toast the occasion, or perhaps his insects' soporific hum had worked its way into his soul and gentled his more austere nature.

There was only way I would find out, of course.

I received the telegram on the 4th, so had little time to speculate, and the next day found me entering the restaurant and, at the merest mention of my friend's name, being ushered to a small table in a quiet, far corner. Holmes was already sitting, his expression as distant as I imagined his thoughts to be.

He looked well, although his hair was greyer than I remembered. The gimlet eyes above his thin, aquiline nose still glittered with vitality, and his lips seemed to be ever on the verge of breaking into a smile, as at some private amusement. There was the hint of a sunburn both on his face and the hands resting on the silver handle of an ebony stick. Evidently he was enjoying more fresh air out on the Downs than ever he did back in our Baker Street days. I was glad of it. Holmes had always been careless with his own health.

He fixed me with that familiar stare. "You are, as ever, punctual, Doctor. I observe the groove in the skin running across your right index finger, suggesting you have done a deal of writing of late. As your lurid reimaginings of my past cases are published with greater infrequency than once they were, I must infer you have been heavily involved in other communication. Consultancy, perhaps. The Stratford triple murder case? Scotland Yard have had the unusual good sense to ask a man with the required expertise his opinion?"

I smiled at his perspicacity. "Astute as ever. There are suggestions the murderer may have a high level of medical training and I have been liaising with the Yard's pathologist, reviewing some of the more pertinent evidence. A second opinion, as it were." I shrugged, briefly reliving old memories. "But to the purpose of today's reunion – one that has been too long in the coming, may I say – "

His tentative smile did break free at that moment: Brief, apologetic, perhaps tinged with an uncomfortable sadness. It was gone in a second, and he took one hand away from his stick to reach inside his overcoat. He produced a crumpled telegram and slid it towards me. The wording was identical to the one I had received, but the sender had marked it with a single initial: *A*.

I studied the paper for a short time, then pushed it back towards Holmes. "Am I to infer this rendezvous was not of your doing?"

"Capital, Watson." He picked up the telegram and slipped it back into a coat pocket. "I am sure you wondered at the unusual choice of meeting place." He waved a hand at our surroundings. The restaurant was little more than half-full, and the various conversations seemed muted.

"I admit it did cross my mind," I said. "Then who?"

"Who indeed? The initial is suggestive, as though it should convey to me instantly who its owner is, but the one name it prompts most strongly departed this mortal realm a decade ago. Therefore I conclude it was meant to whet my curiosity – which I concede it has done."

"Do you have no idea?" I was imagining some old adversary, come back for revenge or reprisals – although the Café Royal was a curious venue if that were the case.

"I have several. However since I have no more data upon which to build a hypothesis, they must remain – at this moment – nothing but guesses." He produced his watch and glanced at it briefly. "Whoever this person is, since both the original and my own telegrams requested promptness, is being annoyingly tardy."

As though summoned by my friend's ire, a woman appeared, shepherded to our table by the same member of staff who had led me through. Holmes and I both stood as she approached and I had time to observe her before a chair was brought and she sat.

She was of no more than average height, but she carried herself with such grace and grandeur that she appeared taller. She was young, and uncommonly attractive, her exquisitely proportioned face one that no man could forget. She was dressed fashionably, in a dark blue dress and three-quarter-length coat. A large, wide-brimmed hat sat upon her head. A parasol of the same colour as her attire was held lightly in her right hand, and a small reticule was clutched in her left.

She bowed to us both, the ghost of a smile on her lips as she removed her gloves. "Mr. Holmes, Doctor Watson. So good of you to come." Her voice was soft and refined, but carried easily above the low undercurrent of conversation around us.

Holmes inclined his head a little. "Madam. Allow me to offer my belated condolences on the loss of your mother."

She cast him an appreciative look. "A deduction, Mr. Holmes? I understand you are not in the habit of indulging yourself in unfounded guesswork." Her tone was flirtatious. "You have clearly deduced who my mother was. The single initial, perhaps? Too obvious? However, I do thank you for your words."

He shrugged. "Despite your assertion, I am as much prey to fruitless guesswork as any man. The difference is I choose not to pay heed to such glib reactions of the brain. But yes, the initial was a trifle melodramatic."

It was the woman's turn to shrug.

Holmes turned to me. "I know your thoughts are likely to be tripping over each other, Watson, so permit me to introduce the daughter of Mrs. Irene Norton – *née* Adler." His glance flickered back to her. "In looks, you favour your father rather than your mother, which is most likely to your advantage. However, I regret I do not know by which of your several pseudonyms you are presently recognised . . . ."

She laughed in delight. "I thought my mother exaggerated, Mr. Holmes, but I see she did not. You may address me as Miss Iriana Norton, the name by which I was christened. My mother's surname is, perhaps, a little too provocative."

My friend nodded slowly. "Certainly within the circles that form your orbit, Miss Norton."

I took a moment to look at the woman again, and more critically. There was certainly little of the Irene Adler I remembered about her features. Of Godfrey Norton's I remained ignorant, for I had never met him. However, if Miss Norton took after him to any degree, his masculine features were most likely unrecognisable within her remarkable face.

"Might I enquire as to the reason for this extraordinary meeting?" I asked.

"If I might be permitted further speculation," said Holmes, "I suspect it is pertaining to a certain king of our past acquaintance, Watson, and a case from quarter-of-a-century ago."

"The King of Bohemia?" I said, making the connection.

Miss Norton was nodding slowly, her eyes sardonic. "An excellent guess, Mr. Holmes."

"My deductions are built firmly upon a bedrock of reason, data, and logic." His tone was irritable.

"And yet with nothing more than my presence, coupled with the names of my parents, you infer this meeting must be concerning King Wilhelm Gottsreich Sigismond von Ormstein. That's a guess, sir." Her smile widened. I realised she was attempting to bait my friend.

"A logical conclusion. He is the only thing which can connect all three of us – with yourself at one remove, of course. Why else this mysterious assignation and the single initial? You have inherited your mother's dramatic skills, if not her looks."

She bowed her head. "Very well, your point is taken." She glanced in my direction. "I have, of course, read the fictionalised account of your encounter with my mother and the King, Doctor Watson, and I recognise the necessity of livening dry facts with extra dialogue and possibly fictitious insights. However, I must ask, Mr. Holmes: What is your full assessment of the current ruler of Bohemia? The Good Doctor's narrative leaves much unsaid, while hinting that you found the man . . . less than he should be?"

Holmes leaned his chin upon fingers still resting on the cane handle. "I found His Majesty to be a shallow, cowardly man. Arrogant enough to act as he saw fit, yet terrified of the consequences should he be found out. The product of an indulgent mother and an overbearing father, I shouldn't wonder. To the one, unable to do wrong, while to the other he will always be found wanting."

"Very perceptive, Mr. Holmes."

"And after twenty-five years of enduring a regal position that is worth little, wearing a hollow crown – his kingdom a minor cog in a vast Imperial machine run from Vienna, while he is as much a vassal as his subjects – I imagine his self-esteem is crying out for validation. No doubt he has a spectacularly long line of mistresses – " He glanced at Miss Norton, but she returned his gaze boldly. " – and an equally impressive list of failed political initiatives. The Emperor must consider him a dreadful burden."

"I must wonder if you have been studying the man from afar."

"Bah! It is an elementary extrapolation . . . ."

"Even so, an accurate one." She half turned and made a signal. A distant waiter bowed and hurried away. "The King has grown frustrated and peevish under Austro-Hungarian rule, considering both himself and his kingdom to be more in line with the ambitions of Kaiser Wilhelm's Imperial Germany and its 'place in the sun'. It is my belief that he has allowed himself to be influenced by anarchists from the Balkans and their fight against Austro-Hungarian dominance. You do not need me to tell you that Europe is presently a tinderbox awaiting an incautious spark following the Bosnian Crisis and the Balkan Wars. Cooler heads than the King's and his reckless idealogues are needed."

"Your analysis is faultless."

"To that end, were you aware that the King is even now in London?"

Holmes tensed, his gaze sharpening, although his chin moved by not so much of an inch from where it rested. "I was not."

"He has taken up residence in Elizabeth Street, a discreet house, but sufficient for himself and a retinue large enough to satisfy his vanity. It is a busy little place, almost an unofficial embassy, with much coming and going – sometimes by the most shadowy characters, with unusual accents."

"And how would you know all this?" I asked.

She did not answer directly. "The King is a moody and inconsiderate employer, especially to his female staff, and turnover is high. Among my many talents, I am a skilled typewritist, and such a position became open three weeks ago."

At this Holmes did straighten. "You are working in that man's home?"

"As you observed, Mr. Holmes, I have inherited some of my mother's theatrical skills. Thick eyeglasses, hair drawn back into a severe bun – to which is added a modicum of grey – and plain garments turn me into the kind of mouse no man – even one such as the King – would notice. No more remarkable than the furniture. I have no fear that he might notice a familial resemblance."

At that moment a trio of waiters arrived to deliver tea, sandwiches, and cakes to our table. We fell silent as they placed plates, cups and saucers, stands, teapot, milk, and hot water before us. Only when they had retreated, once again bowing to Miss Norton, did any of us speak.

"You seem to be recognised here," I observed, offering her a plate of thinly-cut egg-and-cress sandwiches. She took one and treated my comment with a sardonic look.

"I have dined here often, frequently in the company of men who enjoy the cellar, and the sounds of their own voices even more – especially when onto their second or third bottle."

"A novel form of interrogation," said Holmes. He was sitting back in his chair now, taking no interest in the food or drink, eyes half-lidded.

"I think neither of us is under any illusion about my profession." She poured tea and handed us each a cup. "You have dipped your toes into similar waters."

He pursed his lips but said nothing. I also kept silent, for it had become all too clear to me that Miss Norton was something of an adventuress, if not an actual spy.

"My task at the King's unofficial embassy is to type up handwritten documents as they are provided," she said. "No carbon copies are ever to be made."

"What are these documents?" asked Holmes.

"As they are all invariably written in German, I imagine my employer believes I have no idea."

"And your German is – ?"

"Excellent, Mr. Holmes."

"Then – ?"

"As a rule, all are simply letters back to his court, occasionally his family – "

"Typed?" I said.

"His Majesty is, as we have discussed, a man of peculiar sentiments. Notes – even to his wife, who is not with him – are formal and lacking in any form of warmth or intimacy."

"Theirs was a political marriage," said Holmes, "not a love match."

"Indeed. Yet the same is true of the correspondence with his children – he has three daughters. Never any hint of fatherly love."

"Perhaps he wished for sons," I said, "and is poor at hiding his disappointment. Perhaps in this he also blames his wife. Hence the coolness."

"It is more likely he is re-enacting his own father's hard and aloof manner," said Holmes. "It is an old pattern. However – " He leaned forward. " – this doesn't bring us to the central purpose of your wishing to see us, Madam. Letters to home and dry reports to ministers are of little interest to me."

"No indeed." She reached inside her reticule and produced a sheet of paper. "But this might be."

354

Holmes picked up the sheet, examining both sides briefly. "Quality paper. No identifying watermark." He handed it to me. "However, I note this is not an original, but a carbon copy. You said no copies were ever to be made."

"And none were – until I was handed this. The original was done in a careful hand, and I was told to type it out exactly as written. After days of stultifyingly dull correspondence, it was clear to me that this was something exceptional."

"You took a fearful chance," I said, taking the sheet and examining it. At the top was a date in German, while the rest was simply a square of nonsensical letters:

Sechster April Neunzehnhundertvierzehn

DOEDFRUMSZGILXNQETBVV
MFVITFVFRIIIZVFJBUJAYTFF
AFMTTDEPDOHRSEMORHINI
GIJVJDOEFFMJRGANKFWEM
EZAYCNGPIKGXVVTICNSYIA
GYNLZMHPFKETMMUCBKW
ORHCNSPITAPMNTAIYSIOEP

"A code?" I said.

"Clearly. And dated for tomorrow." All of Holmes's lassitude had evaporated and his bony fingers now twitched upon the table cover, as though eager to be busy.

"The day it is to be sent?"

"Perhaps, perhaps." He faced Miss Norton. "You evidently believe this to be of some importance."

"I am the only typewritist presently employed by the King, and none of the other documents I have been asked to transcribe were presented in such a manner. That it is considered important enough to be encoded is remarkable in itself. We must know its contents."

Holmes raised an eyebrow. "We?"

"Do not tell me you aren't intrigued, Mr. Holmes."

My friend sat back a little, finally taking up his cup. He took a thoughtful sip. "I fear you are correct in your analysis, Madam. We must return to my cottage on the Downs. There I may more easily find the tools by which this mystery will be undone."

The woman tilted her head. "If you are sure, Mr. Holmes?" It was clear to me that she had received the very answer she craved.

"You are transparent, Miss Norton, but I am too old to take offense. Indeed, if this encrypted note is what I believe it to be – the only such missive you have seen – it may well be of paramount importance." Then, with an abrupt change of tack he took a plate and began to heap it with scones and cream. "Now, let us take advantage of this splendid tea you have provided."

He began to eat with clear relish. Despite his protestations of age, I must admit I had never seen him look younger.

We passed the following hour or so enjoying our food. The conversation was light, although it never sank to trivial – I doubt either Holmes or Miss Norton would have allowed it. Nevertheless, neither alluded to the matter which was most certainly dominating their thoughts: The King of Bohemia and his cryptic message. Both ate heartily, by which I took it that she was confident of events now being well in control, and my friend was equally assured that the puzzle was almost certainly solved – although I couldn't help but think his mind wasn't fully on the conversation. There was a mild air of distraction about him, as though his remarkable brain was engaged on quite another matter, even as he spoke to us in a relaxed and convivial manner. For myself, I confess to being perfectly content to await that moment when Holmes would choose to share his solution with us.

Eventually tea was over and we rose, a member of staff hailing a cab on our behalf, and we were on our way to London Bridge Station and a train to Eastbourne, from where I anticipated a short cab ride to my friend's old farm cottage.

We didn't have long to wait for the Eastbourne train and settled ourselves into a compartment where, as the locomotive steamed out of the station, Holmes lit his pipe and began to emit complementary clouds of his own.

"You have nothing more to add to your account?" he spoke at last, addressing Miss Norton. Now we were alone, he felt safe in once again raising the subject that was foremost in all our minds.

"I know only what I have told you," she replied.

Holmes grunted and fell into thoughtful silence once more. I asked that he pass me the sheet of paper, and I spent a fruitless minute staring at the block of meaningless letters.

"Consider the date, Watson," said Holmes as I lowered the paper, with something of an irritated sigh, I confess. I looked again.

"Aside from it being tomorrow, it tells us nothing."

"On the contrary," said my friend, "it tells us a great deal." He glanced towards Miss Norton. "Is the King in the habit of post-dating his correspondence?"

"He is quite particular in that respect. All correspondence is dated only for the day it is to be posted."

"Then we must conclude that either this message – against all habit and custom – was prepared early and is meant to be sent tomorrow, or the date itself has a significance of its own."

"The sixth of April? I can see no significance to that."

"None that we are presently aware of, Watson." He blew out a noxious cloud of tobacco smoke. "Do you know if this message was posted on the day you typed it, or was it held back?"

"It was mailed on the same day. I also typed the envelope."

"Capital! Then do you remember the address?"

"It was care of a Royal Mail sorting office in Bayswater. No help for us there, Mr. Holmes."

He shrugged noncommittally. "Perhaps. But it is as I might expect. So – " He leaned back against the carriage seat and closed his eyes. " – we have a message – that it is coded need not concern us at this point – dated for the day after it is posted, and sent for collection at a post office so that the recipient may retain some anonymity. What does this suggest?"

I thought a moment. "That the message will be sent on to another party, but at a later date?"

"A reasonable deduction, Watson, although it does rather beg the question: Why post-date it at all in such a case? The sixth of April clearly has significance."

"It refers to something within the encoded message," said Miss Norton. "Or is referred to."

"Indeed – although since we presently cannot understand the message itself, that inference must by necessity await the decryption. It is quite the ouroboros."

"Yet I cannot help but wonder if you are already halfway to a solution," she said, her eyes a-twinkle.

"Ha! Halfway would be granting me too much credit. Although I confess to having an inkling." He opened his eyes and stared at us both, half-lidded. "I fancy that I must admit at this point – Friend Watson would no doubt leave it until the final denouement to escalate the wonder at my achievement. – that for two years I have been working under the aegis of the Foreign Office."

"I suspected as much," said Miss Norton. "On three occasions I have heard your name spoken by the King and his closest aides – with some bitterness by His Majesty, and concern by his staff. I received the impression they believed you to be meddling in affairs which were beyond your purview. Their very agitation was the very reason I sought to contact you with the encrypted message."

Holmes laughed briefly. "Then my researches have cut closer to the quick than I had anticipated. Excellent." He puffed a moment longer at his pipe. "I flatter myself that I have been partly instrumental in laying a few foreign agents by the heels, as well as helping distribute misleading intelligence in several quarters. Until recently, I was making my way – under an alias – through certain quarters of the United States, among those who hold little love for Britain, and who would cheerfully ally themselves with any faction powerful enough to do her harm. I returned but lately to my Sussex home – as I have done periodically, to promote the notion that Sherlock Holmes continues to sequester himself in rural England – not two days before I was in receipt of your telegram. I have been working carefully, planning to bring my schemes to fruition in a few months. If I believed in Fate, Miss Norton, I would say your appearance is more than accidental – if your information, and this cryptic piece of paper, are what they hint at being."

She bridled. "I can assure you Mr. Holmes – "

"You can assure me of only what you believe is the truth, and at this stage nothing more. I don't think you are in any way attempting to mislead me, for your information tallies so closely with my own intelligence. But we must allow that the King – or his closest members of staff – may be playing games of their own."

"You think I have been under suspicion?"

"I imagine every member of staff who has ever been recruited from beyond the King's most intimate retinue is under suspicion. Fear of discovery will always colour the thoughts of the guilty, and we already know how His Majesty's mind tends to assemble events into the worst possible construction. I do not imagine you were regarded as any more untrustworthy – or indeed trustworthy – than every other typewritist who has worked at this unofficial embassy."

"Then I am assured." Her tone was sardonic.

"But to the matter in hand – " He took the sheet of paper from me and stared at it. "It is commonly known that the most frequently occurring letter in the English language is '*E*'. However the most cursory glance at this jumble of letters suggests that fact will be of little help. Indeed, we cannot even be confident that the unencrypted language is English."

"As I said," explained Miss Norton, "most communiqués were in German."

"Quite so. A further barrier to solving the mystery. How is your German, Watson?"

"Quite appalling, I must admit."

Holmes gave a thin smile. "Then you will both be relieved to know I have many dictionaries to hand in my cottage." He glanced out of the window. The countryside beyond was bright with the late afternoon sun. "And Eastbourne isn't so far away." He tapped embers from his pipe into an ashtray under the window. "By morning, we should have our answers."

"I admire your confidence, Mr. Holmes," said Miss Norton.

"Not misplaced, I assure you. The sun will rise on a clearer understanding."

As he placed his pipe into a pocket, the woman and I exchanged glances. I could tell she profoundly hoped that my friend's words weren't an idle boast.

Once in Eastbourne, we stepped from the train onto a location that, for all its bustle, was still nothing like as busy as the smallest London station. Making our way outside, I looked about for a cab of some description but saw none. There was, however, a large motor car standing no more than ten yards from the station exit and, with a soft cry, Miss Norton made her way towards it.

I glanced at Holmes, who had uttered an appreciative laugh. "Back in the café," he said, "there was a couple seated a short distance from our table. Not so close as to be able to overhear anything we said, but close enough to watch us easily and observe any visual cues. A young woman, by her looks and attire so unremarkable that she would barely register on any casual observer, and a man dressed in the drab uniform of a lowly clerk. Both so likely to fade into the background that my interest was instantly aroused." He raised his voice. "Colleagues of yours, I imagine."

Miss Norton paused in the action of opening the motor car's back door. "Of a sort. She is a close confidant of mine, quite reliable, whom I occasionally employ in a minor capacity. The young man is a beau of hers, and I'm sad to report quite as dull as he appears."

"Quite. They left shortly before us – no doubt prompted by a signal from yourself – and telephoned ahead for this vehicle. You never left our table and so had no such opportunity."

She looked quite delighted by his analysis. "You are observant, Mr. Holmes. Perhaps annoyingly so."

He waved the comment aside with a curt gesture. "This machine would have been already in place, somewhere in Eastbourne, ready for us when I took the decision to return to my cottage. Do you have other vehicles secreted in other locations anticipating different routes of action? Each with their own unique signal for your associate?"

She completed opening wide the car door. "You credit me with too much."

"I once credited your mother with too little, Madam. I shall never again make such an error of judgement." My friend stood aside so that she might enter the motor car's spacious rear compartment. Once she was seated, he positioned himself on the luxurious upholstery at her side, while I sat opposite Holmes in a seat which folded down from the metal and glass partition between our compartment and the driver's open cab.

At a rap of Miss Norton's knuckles on the partition window, the motor car drove away from the station in a westerly direction. We soon left the town behind and down a quiet, narrow road, meeting no other traffic, the view outside alternating between tall green hedgerows and almost featureless expanses of rolling grassland, all the while climbing gently. After a few minutes the hedgerow grew sparser, eventually fading altogether, and we turned left onto an exposed lane that headed almost due south. I could clearly see the waters of the English Channel, its restless waves dancing in the light of the lowering sun. They were too distant for me to make out, and I'm sure the angle was too acute, but I knew this coastline was edged with precipitous cliffs such as the notorious Beachy Head towards where we were heading, that had claimed many a life over the centuries, and not a few of them suicides. In the late sunshine I found it hard to conceive of such a beautiful spot being such a draw to the lost and desperate.

After several minutes, the lane turned to run parallel to the coastline, degenerating into an even narrower pathway, its surface rutted by the passing of agricultural vehicles. The large motor car slowed to a careful crawl, but we were still tossed rudely as it was bounced by the crude surface. Now I had a clearer view of the distant chalk cliffs, rearing stark and brilliant above an exposed shoreline of black rock. The contrast between white cliff face and dark, wave-torn beach was quite stark.

Up to this point, Holmes had been silent, content to gaze out of his window at the passing scenery, his thoughts far away. Now he commented: "Your driver is very confident in the direction."

"I'm afraid your solitude isn't so complete as you might hope, Mr. Holmes. It is easy enough for someone, asking the right questions, to narrow down your bolt-hole. You have supplies delivered, produce, the post, material for your beehives . . . ."

"Then it is as well I haven't sought to isolate myself completely from the rest of the world." His tone was waspish.

"The world has grown too small for one of your stature – Ah, I believe we have arrived!"

The car drew to a halt and I was grateful we were no longer being jostled. Outside the crude path continued towards a building which stood in splendid isolation among the gently rolling fields. It had been some time since I had visited Holmes's remote and ageing farmhouse, and if I had expected to witness two years' of neglect because of his regular absences, then I was pleasantly disappointed. Clearly he had engaged the services of locals to maintain the building – to at least preserve it from the elements, if not the illusion that he was still in residence. If ivy grew unrestrained up one corner of the front aspect, threatening to totally engulf one of the upstairs windows, it was only to enhance the rustic aspect. The sun, now approaching the horizon, bathed the western wall in an orange tint, while casting the rest into pale violet shadows. In the near distance was the first of Holmes's many beehives, well-maintained and thriving. A local apiarist, I thought, was apparently more-than-happy to keep my friend's bees safe and happy in absentia – in return for their honey.

Holmes opened the automobile door and slid out. He strode towards the cottage, stick rapping impatiently on the uneven path. I opened my own door, allowing Miss Norton to exit before stepping out. She spoke to the driver.

"I believe we may be needing you again in the morning. Would you care to come in and wait out the night?"

The driver – a squat, square-faced individual – gave a smile. "That's all right, ma'am. My sister lives in East Dean. I'll throw myself on her mercy for the night."

"If you're certain – ?"

"She'll be glad to see me, I'm sure of that, ma'am. Thanks all the same."

Holmes turned, leaning on his cane. "Return by first light," he called. "It is possible an early start will be necessary."

"As you wish, sir." The driver reversed the car, turning the wheel, and drove back along the rutted path.

Miss Norton and I followed Holmes into his home.

If the farmhouse's exterior was still neat and manicured, the same could not be said for the room into which we were led. Although light and airy, it was as untidy as Baker Street at its most chaotic, with newspapers and pamphlets strewn about the four items of furniture – large armchairs, none of which matched. In the short time since Holmes had returned from the United States, he had contrived to fill the room with as much newsprint as it could hold. The neatest corner, facing the entrance, was dominated by a dark bookcase, upon which were ranked document boxes and wallets, all variously labelled in my friend's idiosyncratic hand.

Holmes removed his hat and overcoat and threw them both carelessly onto one of the chairs. They were followed a moment later by his cane. He waved the sheet of paper in the general direction of the low door.

"You may find tea and coffee in the kitchen, should you wish to refresh yourself."

"And you?" I asked.

He glanced at me, although his attention was far away. "I need to consult with some volumes I have stored in my bedroom." He stared once more at the sheet and its perplexing, encoded message, then disappeared through a door which led to the staircase. I heard the creak of footsteps on wooden steps.

"I think we should make ourselves comfortable," I said, looking for somewhere less crowded for my hat. In the end, I settled on a small table below the bookshelf which was generally free of discarded material.

Miss Norton unpinned her own hat. "I guess so," she commented, hanging it on a wall-mounted oil lamp. "Would you care for coffee, Doctor, or tea? Making either is another of my talents." Her smile was mischievous.

"Coffee, thank you," I said, casting my eye over the hand-written labels on the shelf's contents. All seemed to be related in one way or another to the care, study, or upkeep of bees, and the production of honey. Nothing of crime that I could see. "I suspect it will be a long night," I added.

It was indeed many hours before Holmes once again showed himself. The coffee that Miss Norton brewed was quite excellent, and served to keep me alert for part of the evening. We spoke little, for I found I had few things to say to the woman. She in turn kept her own council, leafing through Holmes's various files on apiary, while I sorted through the felled woodland littering the floor and furniture, trying to organise it into some kind of system, but confess any reasonable order eluded me. There were newspaper articles circled in thick pencil, clippings, pages torn from a baffling range of periodicals, with whole paragraphs or just a word or two underlined.

The topics ranged from advances in aircraft design, meteorological data for the Channel dating back months, the breeding cycle of honeybee queens, the murder of a minor businessman in Boston, Massachusetts the year before, and dealings on both the London and New York stock markets since 1912. The last intrigued me, for Holmes had never demonstrated any interest in the sale or purchase of business shares, unless such things were directly involved in a case upon which he was working. I could see nothing to connect them – unless they were the acts of a remarkable brain, starved of the action it craved, seeking fulfilment in the pursuit of any gratuitous pattern or hint of such.

I confess that eventually – and somewhat ungallantly – I fell asleep. I was started from my slumbers by the rattle of footsteps hurrying down the wooden steps, accompanied by a staccato series of loud creaks, sounding sharp and loud in the morning quiet. I blinked and stretched, gazing towards both windows. Outside it was light, with that strange roseate glow which heralded dawn. I fumbled for my watch: It was five-thirty-six.

I came fully awake as Holmes entered the room, his face paler than ever, the shadows indicative of a sleepless night stark under his eyes. Yet his tall frame quivered with energy, and his eyes shone with satisfaction. Miss Norton stirred from a sleep of her own.

"I have it!" cried Holmes, brandishing three sheets of paper. "It was quite elementary in the end, the encryption surprisingly straightforward – although by its very nature transcribing the decrypted message was the very devil. And then it had to be translated, of course."

Miss Norton stood, smoothing down her dress. "I'll put more coffee on. Mind you don't explain it all until I'm back, Mr. Holmes." She made her way into the kitchen.

"Yes, yes." Holmes came around one of the armchairs and dropped himself into it, careless of the items already lying there. After a moment he produced his cigarettes and, offering one to me, lit both. Then he handed me one of the sheets. "I trust I have furnished the language with the requisite number of umlauts."

Upon it was a short, carefully printed message in German:

> *Die zeit ist gekommen, Brüder in Freiheit.*
> *VB ist fast bereit. ND, AO, und RM einigen sich auf die bedingungen.*
> *Die taube erhebt sich um sechs uhr-fünfzig.*
> *Gegan mittag wird Berlin alles wissen.*
> *VO*

"Do you understand any of this?" I asked.

He drew deeply on his cigarette and sighed. "With the help of an appropriate dictionary." He barked a sharp laugh and waved the third paper. "But with all due deference to Miss Norton, I shall await her return before giving you both the details."

And so we waited until she entered carrying a tray upon which stood three cups and a large coffee pot. Finding a table upon which to place the tray, she filled the cups while I handed one to Holmes and took a second for myself. Once again seated, and fortified with the hot, strong brew, we listened as Holmes explained.

"It was as I said: The date was the key to deciphering the message. Not as it stood, of course – the words had no bearing on the affair."

"The date had to be displayed numerically," said Miss Norton.

Holmes nodded. "Which raised another conundrum: Is the year to be one nine one four, or simply one four. The insertion or lack of those extra figures would impact on the decryption. The wrong choice would render the coded message into nonsense."

"And which was it?" I asked.

"Good old Watson," said Holmes. "Ever eager to cut to the quick." He handed me another of the sheets. Upon it was a brief message in English.

> *The time is upon us, Brothers in Freedom.*
> *VB is almost ready. ND, AO, and RM agree to terms.*
> *The dove rises at six-fifty.*
> *By midday Berlin will know all.*
> *VO*

"It was the date displayed in full – The sixth of April, 1914: Zero-six, zero-four, one, nine, one, four – giving a key of eight numbers, so the message could be encrypted in blocks of eight letters. It is a rather florid and dramatic communication, I am sure you will agree, but in keeping with the man involved. The letters *VO* at the end are of course for von Ormstein, our somewhat imprudent Bohemian prince."

"Remarkable," I said, glad my friend had lost none of his needle-sharp reasoning.

"Pah. Deducing the key was perfectly elementary. The devil was in transcribing the coded message back into German and then translating it into English."

"Exactly how did the key work?" asked Miss Norton, peering at the paper in my hands.

"A simple substitution code. The first letter of the original message, *D*, was left unchanged, as it aligns with zero. The next letter, *I*, is moved six letters along from its regular position as the ninth letter of the alphabet to the fifteenth, *O*. *E* is again unchanged, as it aligns with zero. *Z* is moved four places to *D*, *E* is transposed one space, I by nine, *T* by one and *I* by four. Repeat for the next eight letters, and so on. Cumbersome, but effective. To decode the message the reverse arrangement is applied: Moving back the requisite number of spaces in blocks of eight. I confess I had more than one false start before the exact numbers of the key were clear, and whether it was a case of addition or subtraction. It was a moment of some satisfaction when I realised my efforts were finally revealing actual words, even if I didn't at that time understand them."

"But the message is still cryptic," said Miss Norton. "*VO* may refer to Willhelm, but who – or what – are *VB, ND, AO,* and *RM*?"

"All initials refer either to agents of foreign powers, nationalists, or those with no love for Britian and her allies. *ND* is, I believe, Nenad Dragin, a Serbian who is associated with a secret military society calling itself The Black Hand. *AO* is most likely the Bolshevik Russian, Artyom Orlov. While *RM* is almost certainly Rian McCartan, of the Irish Volunteers. An unholy alliance whose various agendas have momentarily united them in a common cause. *VB* . . . ." He leaned back and lit another cigarette "I have no proof, but I think this refers to von Bork of the German government – a man for whom war cannot come soon enough. But before it does, he would see us defenceless and unmanned, our closest military secrets in the hands of our enemies."

"The name is familiar to me," said Miss Norton. "Alas, I think you are correct, Mr. Holmes."

"Are these names familiar to you through your recent investigations for the Foreign Office, Holmes?" I asked.

"In part." His tone was non-committal.

Miss Norton drained her cup and rose to pour herself another. "And what about this dove?"

"The dove of peace?" I suggested. "Some warped allusion to their own designs? It is my experience that political rebels rarely see themselves as villains."

"Quite perceptive of you, Watson. Indeed, they are often self-portrayed as warriors against oppression and freedom fighters. The reality is often bitterly different." He consulted his own watch. "But in this case it is rather more metaphorical, I fancy – although there is also a certain humour in the term. The phrase *sechs uhr fünfzig* implies a time, ten-minutes-to-seven, and the dove refers – in part at least – to that which the King, or his agent, expects to meet. In this instance, I propose an aircraft, launched from the cliffs. Due to rendezvous in a little over an hour, then take flight with a treacherous passenger – and perhaps more of our secrets than we might permit to leave these shores."

"But from where – ?"

"You have read my clippings and reports, Watson. I see there has been an attempt to catalogue and categorise them. Did you perhaps come across today's weather forecast in yesterday's newspapers? Specifically for this area?"

"I admit I did not – "

"A fine and dry morning, with a light southerly breeze, gaining strength later. Ideal for an aeroplane. Combine that with the generally smooth grassy fields of the Downs, and high cliffs from which such a machine might comfortably launch itself. At such an hour, who will be about to observe such a singular occurrence, save for a few labourers?"

Miss Norton place her coffee cup on its saucer. "Well, I can think of three, Mr. Holmes."

We pulled on our coat and hats and quickly exited the house. The morning air was fresh, but with the hint of a warm breeze coming up from the Continent. The sun was already several degrees above the horizon, but the eastern sky was still tinted with a pale orange, the few clouds dotting an otherwise clear sky having a delicate saffron glow along their edges.

The motor car was already waiting, engine idling, the driver standing by his door, smoking a cigarette. He hastily threw it to the ground and crushed it out when he saw our approach. I held the passenger door open for Miss Norton and waited for Holmes to also duck inside, but he had paused by the attendant driver.

"I believe there is a feature known locally as Dove's Rise. Are you familiar with it?"

The driver nodded. "Yes, sir," he said. "Just a few miles to the west, as the crow flies, although by road it's a little less direct." He smiled.

"This amuses you?" said Holmes.

"Sorry, sir. Just the local humour. Dove's Rise, you see, is actually a low point between two large hillocks, and when the wind is funnelled between 'em it's anything but peaceful."

Holmes turned to me, his lips twitching in amusement. "Not just a local joke, eh, Watson. You recall the message as I translated it?"

"'The dove rises'?" I said. "Dove's Rise."

"Precisely. It must follow then that this place – partially screened from inquisitive eyes and with sufficient headwind to guarantee a safe take-off for a flying machine – is our destination."

"It might take over half-an-hour to get there, sir," spoke the driver. "This road is bad enough, Lord knows, but to reach the Rise means following a trail worn into the grass by people walking along the cliff's edge. This automobile isn't made for such land. You'd be better off with a horse and trap."

"And from where do you suggest we conjure such a ride from?" snapped Holmes. "This is our most convenient means of conveyance, so I suggest we had best start immediately!" He stooped and slid himself along the upholstery, once again taking his place next to Miss Norton. I ducked into the compartment, unfolding the backward-facing seat as the driver

366

closed the door firmly behind me. Moments later, the motor car was turning away from Holmes's cottage and picking its way carefully along the gouges in the dry mud.

It was indeed slow progress. While the path leading to Holmes's cottage was in a desperate state, the roads leading to it were little better. I hadn't noticed on arrival how poorly maintained they were: Adequate for horse-drawn traffic, but hard on the suspension of modern motor vehicles, and their pneumatic tyres. After a short journey, the macadam road curved to the right, but the driver drove straight forward, onto a narrow strip that ran parallel to the cliff and which could scarcely be describes as a footpath. The driver slowed further, but even so, we were all jostled unmercifully, while I observed Holmes was visibly exasperated by the delay. Indeed, the rising sun seemed to move more swiftly than did our motor car.

To our left was the Channel, its waves once again sparkling in the daylight, and ahead, where the cliffs curved to the left, I spied a dip, flanked on both sides by higher ground, which rose quite sharply to a height of some twenty or thirty feet. No wheeled vehicle would safely traverse such a slope. Even a man would have to watch his step, least he take a tumble. The driver turned the car inland, climbing the gentle incline which led down to the cliffs. He would have to go around the steep slope before us, approaching Dove's Rise from flatter land.

The car bounced suddenly, almost throwing all three of us from our seats. For a moment, I thought the engine was about to cut out, but the driver kept it going.

"Rabbit hole," said Miss Norton, adjusting her hat with the lightest of touches to its brim. "I imagine this place is quite the warren, as much a risk to horses as car tyres."

Holmes grunted unintelligibly, turning his face to stare through the windows behind the driver. A moment later he cried, "There, Watson! Do you see?"

I turned to look forward to where he was pointing. The motor car had climbed past the lowest point of the first hillock and the driver was already turning it to face the flatter land between the two slopes. In the distance, squarely in the middle of Dove's Rise, was the unmistakable shape of a flying machine, already facing out to sea. Too far to make out details, but it looked to be a large biplane, big enough to be able to seat more than just a pilot.

"And we have company," said Miss Norton.

I turned about in my seat. To our right, and approaching from the Rise's western flank, was another motor car, smaller than our own and travelling more recklessly.

"The King?" I surmised, taking out my watch. It had just gone six-thirty. "And early."

"*L'exactitude est la politesse des rois,*" muttered Holmes. "I doubt he would entrust whatever secrets he deems worthy of this foolhardy action to another. He will wish to claim the glory for himself."

"Seems to me he's more likely to wreck that car of his," said Miss Norton. "We're going half his speed, but that rabbit hole almost finished our limousine."

"He sees us," said Holmes grimly. "He knows that should he be caught, it means disgrace and certain expulsion, and whatever allies he might have in Berlin will disown him and swiftly melt away."

The smaller car gradually pulled ahead of our own, nearing the aeroplane. If our driver didn't speed up – and to do so was more than foolhardy – our prey would reach the biplane and be in the air before we could reach him.

"Ha!" Miss Norton abruptly laughed. "I knew it!"

I craned my neck to see. The smaller car had halted, its nose dipping at a strange angle. I couldn't be certain, but it seemed as though the left-hand front wheel was buckled. Two figures – the driver and passenger – were scrabbling out of the vehicle. One – the driver I guessed – was waving their hands towards the distant aeroplane. After a second's hesitation, the second figure began running in its direction.

"Fortune favour us!" cried Holmes. He opened the compartment's nearest door, leaning his head through the gap. "Driver!" he cried. "Take us straight to that aircraft! We may yet beat him!" He fell back in his seat, slamming the door shut. "If I am any judge, the life of a pampered prince of Europe has left our man poorly equipped to outrace us."

Miss Norton said nothing, but a look of satisfaction settled on her face.

We neared the waiting aeroplane and, as I twisted about to see what was happening in front of our vehicle I noted that the running figure – now so obviously the King – was flagging. As Holmes had surmised, the years had added weight to the man's frame while depriving him of any athletic ability he may have enjoyed in his youth. Even so, desperation gave flight to his heels, and it would be a close run thing.

I saw the flying machine more clearly now. All of its outstretched wings were elegantly shaped so that they mimicked the curvature of a large bird's wings. It was the colour of old linen and bore no obvious markings. The engine was already running, the machine's wheels prevented from rolling forward by large wedges. Another member of the crew stood by them while the pilot sat in a long, open cockpit which certainly appeared large enough to accommodate three men. The standing man was watching our approach, in some alarm if his uncertain movements were any indication. I wondered if he had a gun, praying he did not.

The King, spurred on by the likelihood of imminent capture, found an extra reserve of vitality. His corpulent frame sprinted over the final yards and he reached the lengthy cockpit, throwing what looked like a document case into it before attempting to clamber inside. The pilot turned in his seat, offering a hand, and the King was hauled unceremoniously on board the aeroplane. A moment later the other crewman hauled the wedges from under the wheels and ran around the left wingtip as the machine began to roll forward. He pulled himself into the cockpit as the aircraft moved past him. It gathered speed.

"Quickly!" yelled Holmes. "Before it can take off!"

It is unlikely our driver heard my friend's desperate cry, but even so our car turned, heading directly for the aircraft, accelerating despite the treacherous ground. We were thrown about heedlessly, holding on to anything within reach. For a moment the car was flung airborne by some huge stone or earthen ramp and I accidentally bit my tongue, tasting blood.

I thought our driver intended to crash into the aircraft's left wings, but another sharp dip diverted the car sideways. When the driver had regained control we had somehow passed around the wingtips and were now aiming straight for the aircraft's engine. We were also driving unnervingly close to the clifftop. I braced myself.

The pilot turned his machine to the right to try and avoid the oncoming car. Our driver wouldn't be dodged so easily. He spun his wheel, adjusting our course. A moment later I heard a sharp splintering sound and realised the aircraft's bottom left wing had clipped the rear of our car. We were thrown aside once more as the car struck another obstruction, and this time the engine did cut out.

Holmes was out of our vehicle in an instant, his cane stabbing the turf as he ran at the aircraft, which was now travelling almost parallel to the cliff's edge. I followed at his heels. Splinters of wood and fabric hung from the machine's lower left wing. Half of it was in ruins. I couldn't see imagine the pilot thought he could now take off.

Then one of the wheels struck something and the whole aircraft slewed clockwise. I grabbed Holmes and tackled him to the ground as the tail section swung above us, not a yard clear of the grass. The aircraft slowed, losing momentum, and the tail dropped – hanging directly over the edge of the cliff.

For a moment the machine was suspended there, over half of its fuselage and the tail section hanging above the drop. I heard the panicked voices as the three men on board tried to extricate themselves from the long cockpit. Then the wheels started to roll backwards as the aircraft slipped over the cliff, the engine an insufficient counterweight as the centre of balance rapidly shifted forward.

There were screams, then the large aeroplane's nose swung skywards as the machine tipped backwards over the edge and tumbled towards to the sea. I fancied I heard the impact, but that may just have been the waves.

I helped Holmes to his feet and together we made our way toward the cliff's edge. Below there was little to be seen. A shattered wreckage of wood and fabric strewn across the rocks, plucked at by fretful waves. I could see no bodies, but did not imagine anyone surviving such a dreadful fall.

"And now?" I said.

He stared down at the ruin, his brows drawn. "Now I must inform certain interested parties, advising them of what has happened here, before the local constabulary take it upon themselves to investigate. Luckily they have a bucolic tendency towards leisureliness." Suddenly, he sounded tired. "The wreckage will be cleared, whatever remains of the secrets which were copied and intended for other eyes quietly collected. There will be no reports – other than news of a tragic accident when a brave aviator, attempting to cross the channel in a flying machine, met his end but a few yards short of success."

"Are the men for whom you are working so well placed?"

"That, and higher. And we can be certain there will be no voices raised from Berlin or further east. The late King of Bohemia will be returned home – the victim of another calamity. It will be in no one's interests to investigate further." He turned. "It just remains for me to supply the names of Dragin, Orlov, and McCartan – to be added to an ever-growing list – as well as that of von Bork, who will bear watching ever more closely in the weeks to come."

I paused a moment longer to gaze one last time at the shattered remains so far below. I sighed. "A truly wasteful business. In the end, what did we achieve?"

"Some measure of security for the people of these islands." We began walking back to the car. The driver was already running through its complicated start-up sequence. "A strengthening of the bulwarks against an uncertain future."

"I fear the future is for younger men than we."

He went to speak, but Miss Norton interrupted him. "Are you for London, Mr. Holmes?" she asked. "I can return you to Eastbourne Station."

He seemed to consider the idea, then shook his head. "No, you may take me back to my cottage. I have already been away from my bees for too long. They are creatures of impeccably regular habits, and even the smallest change in routine upsets them."

She gave him a frank look. "As you wish." Turning her gaze on me she raised an eyebrow. "Doctor?"

"Thank you, I would be grateful." Still, a small part of me did not wish to be parted from my old friend. Who knew when our paths would once again cross?

"And you, Miss Norton," said Holmes. "What did you gain from today's work? Revenge for your mother?"

She shook her head. "If either of us had nurtured such base desires, we could have taken petty revenge many times during the past years."

"Then why?"

"You are the famous consulting detective, Mr. Holmes. You tell me."

He laughed and shook his head. Ahead of us, the car's engine purred to life. As the driver inspected the damage to the body, tutting loudly and no doubt wondering which of us would be paying for it, we ducked inside and braced ourselves for the unsettling drive back to Holmes's cottage.

His Longest Case
by Martin Daley

Chapter I

It was the second day of August, 1914, when my narrative begins. I was in my surgery, having just completed my appointments for the morning, and preparing to go into our living quarters to have some lunch. At the rear of our Queen Anne Street home, we have a little courtyard where my wife and I regularly enjoy some afternoon refreshment during the summer months. As I went across to close the window of the surgery, a tiny bird caught my eye. Surrounded by the wonderful colours of my wife's potted flowers, it was sitting on the rear wall singing away merrily. I smiled at the beautiful sight that was completely at odds with a pending gloom that had hung over the capital following weeks of turmoil. Although it was appointed as a Bank Holiday weekend – a happy time when families could participate together in leisure activities at the seaside or in the park – for many, myself included, it was a period of concern.

For a month, any diplomatic engagement entered into by the great Empires of Europe had hitherto vainly attempted to restore affairs that many of us felt could never be revived since the dreadful assassination in Sarajevo. The intricate alliances between the giant powers – hitherto unknown to the ordinary man in the street throughout the Continent – had instead been activated to the point where it was more a question of who would *not* be drawn into armed conflict, rather than who *would*. Germany had already pledged its support to Austria-Hungary who, days earlier, had declared war on Serbia and its ally Russia. The Tsar in turn mobilised his army against the Habsburg Empire.

I heard the sound of our front door closing and assumed the maid had taken delivery of the daily newspapers. With a sense of increasing foreboding, I waited for her to appear. As I sit writing this account, years later, I still find it difficult to believe that this catastrophic sequence of events led to the loss of so many lives.

"Morning edition of *The Times*, Doctor," announced the maid, appearing moments later.

"Thank you, Ester."

I took the newspaper and couldn't stop myself from slumping down into a seat and reading the headlines before I went upstairs. It was being reported that Germany was to send an ultimatum to Russia demanding it demobilize.

London and Paris meanwhile continued to hope that a settlement could be negotiated. Sir Edward Grey was suggesting that Russia should cease its military preparations in exchange for an undertaking from Germany that they would seek a way to give complete satisfaction to Austria without endangering the sovereignty or territorial integrity of Serbia. The French premier apparently agreed with this suggestion.

I couldn't say I felt much optimism as I sat there on that sweltering morning. I looked out at the paradoxical sight of the little bird once more and wondered what the next few months might bring. A call had been made earlier in the month for army veterans to consider making themselves available for service should the need arise. Fully aware that a man of nearly sixty-two wouldn't be much good on the battlefield, I did make representation to my old regiment and offered my services in a medical capacity.

With the paper still on my lap and my mind continuing to wander, the maid knocked and re-entered.

"Telegram for you Doctor."

"Oh, thank you Ester," I said, looking up in surprise. "I didn't hear the front door."

I took the envelope from the tray and ripped it open, expecting it to be from the regiment, informing me of my joining instructions. Instead, I was taken aback by the note and was forced to retake my seat in shock. It read:

> *I need your assistance urgently. Bring car – Harwich Harbour, Sunday, 2ⁿᵈ, 8 p.m.*
>
> *SH*

I re-read his note. "*I need your assistance urgently.*" What could this mean? Why would he need my assistance? And what was he doing in Harwich of all places? I remembered when my wife and I last hosted him, he teased me mercilessly about me driving and my little Ford – now here he was insisting that I bring it, no doubt for his convenience.

Rather than be affronted by Holmes's presumption however, I had known him long enough to understand that once he focused that great mind of his on matters he considered to be important, anything else would be considered irrelevant and inconvenient. For my own part, I found myself intrigued.

I rushed to inform my wife of the telegram. She understood my desire to assist my friend in whatever way I could. It was with an air of tremendous excitement that I packed a razor and a clean collar into a bag – not knowing how long I would be away – and set out. As I was leaving the house a telegram boy approached again with another missive. My heart sank momentarily, as I believed there had been a change of plan and my friend did not need my help after all. I ripped open the note and found that it was an instruction from my old regiment to report to the London Barracks on the following Friday. I was amused when I thought how I expected such a telegram, only to be surprised by Holmes's note, and here I was receiving the telegram I had now completely forgotten about. Such was my excitement at seeing my old friend again. I threw the note onto the dashboard of my car and set off for Harwich.

The journey was long and tedious. After two hours, it occurred to me that I had never driven that far before and after a further two, I realised that I had completely underestimated the length of the trip for my little vehicle. It was after six o'clock when I arrived at the harbour and, as tired as I was after such a long drive, I was relieved that I wouldn't be letting my friend down. As I parked my car on the dockside, I noticed that there was a considerable police presence and wondered if it had anything to do with Holmes's request of me to join him.

After stretching my legs and watching the lamplighter illuminating the gas lights along the harbour front, I wandered back to my car. From a distance, I saw the tall, lean figure that was unmistakable to me. My spirits lifted instantly, and I quickened my pace to greet my friend.

"Holmes!" I called, approaching, hand outstretched. "How wonderful to see you again." He was still wearing the dreadful goatee which he'd grown some time previously as part of his undercover work in preparation for the upcoming German war.

"Watson, it was good of you to come. I apologise for the hasty nature of our reunion, but I've been working against the clock these past weeks, and it was only decided on Thursday last that I should make my move this evening. Therefore, I needed someone I could rely upon at short notice, and I knew of no better man."

I was touched by Holmes's words – to speak so kindly meant much to me and I smiled inwardly as I recalled the rarity of such an expression of appreciation back in our Baker Street days.

"My dear chap, I am full of curiosity. What is so urgent? Why do you need my help?"

"All in good time, but time is now of the essence, and we must make haste if we are to snare the villain who we seek this evening. I will give you the directions," he said, indicating that we get in the car.

Chapter II

It has been recorded elsewhere that our journey took us to the villa of the German spy, Von Bork, in the hills above Harwich, where Holmes once again demonstrated his unique skill in capturing such a treacherous villain. What was not recorded however, were details of my friend's two-year adventure that led him to that point.

Once we had bundled Von Bork into the spare seat of my car and had a moment to pause on the terrace of his villa, Holmes instructed me to drive back down to Harwich, where Inspector Reynolds of Scotland Yard would be waiting for us at the police station there. He explained that it would have been too risky for Reynolds and his men to accompany us to the villa. He wanted to ensure he could trap Von Bork personally and access his safe, without the confusion and interference of the police.

"What is more," he explained, "I have instructed Reynolds and his men to be at the port where, with any luck, they should be able to apprehend Baron Von Herling, the Chief Secretary of the Legation, a conspirator of our friend in the spare seat here, who visited him earlier this evening."

"That explains the number of policemen I observed on the dockside," I said.

"Yes. Can you remember we passed a huge Benz car on the way up?"

"Now you mention it," I replied, "I do. Driving like a damned maniac, he was."

"Well, that car contained Von Herling. Hopefully by the time we reach Reynolds, he'll be little more than another stone in this pyramid of evil that has been removed."

Von Bork remained silent throughout, but glowered an evil stare at my friend.

When we pulled up outside the police station in Harwich, Holmes chuckled with delight, as he saw the Benz motorcar parked outside. "It seems as though our man Reynolds has been equally as successful," he said.

We entered the station to see two uniformed officers wrestling with a man I assumed, judging by his attire and demeanour, to be Baron Von Herling, the man Holmes had referred to a few minutes earlier. When we entered with Von Bork and his papers, the man ceased struggling with his captors and looked up in abject amazement. The look that was exchanged between the two Germans rendered the need for any words completely unnecessary. They knew they had been outmanoeuvred and their treacherous scheme was at an end.

"We can't thank you enough, Mr. Holmes," said a plain clothed official I took to be Reynolds when we handed our prisoner over. "We found this one wriggling his way towards the ferry, as you had said we would." He indicated towards the other man. "I was told by my superiors that this has been a long slog to get us to this point, but we're there now and it's well worth it. Not for the first time, Mr. Holmes, I believe we couldn't have done it without you."

"Not at all, Reynolds," replied my friend, as his vanquished foe stared daggers at him. "I am unsure whether the world will be a safer place without him, but at least it is one less evil fish to concern ourselves with." He then turned to his defeated opponent. "Well, farewell, Von Bork. I would be lying if I said it had been a pleasure working with you, but I shall gain some satisfaction when I read of your trip to the gallows."

"Damn you, Sherlock Holmes!" cried the vanquished spy, much to Holmes's amusement.

"And so, Watson," he said, turning to me, "perhaps you would be so good as to allow me to journey back with you to London?"

"On one condition," I replied, prompting Holme's forehead to crease in surprise. "For the longest time, you'd kept to yourself much of your investigations that led to this night – in the name of security. Won't you tell me all about the events that led us to this point?"

We began our long journey back and Holmes commenced his narrative.

"As you know," he said, "it was over two years ago now that Brother Mycroft brought the Prime Minister, no less, to my humble little Sussex home and asked me to identify a spy who they believed was passing secrets to the Germans. It didn't take me long to deduce our friend of this evening was the culprit."

I nodded, recalling his initial conclusions. "With a name like Von Bork," I replied, "I'm surprised it wasn't obvious to more people sooner."

Holmes laughed. "Yes, you would have thought so, wouldn't you? However, in their defence, he is not the only European aristocrat living off the fat of the English land. Indeed, this man in particular has friends in the highest of places. On occasion, he has been known to hunt, shoot, and go sailing with the King."

"Therefore," I said, with more than a hint of frustration, "he was completely overlooked."

"Indeed," sneered Holmes, who I knew loved his country, and yet detested its system of class that dictated one's position in society.

"In discovering that Von Bork was the spy master, I also found he managed a web of villains, all working to destabilise the government and provide Germany with opportunities to gain a march on us, and ultimate domination of the whole continent. Once I had convinced the Prime Minister that Von Bork was his man, I was then asked to pursue the villain and his gang of spies. After some persuasion, I agreed, and two years later, here we are."

I considered my friend's incredible mission.

"And along the way, you placed your housekeeper, Martha, in Von Bork's house."

Holmes chuckled again" I did."

I recalled the events when we first met Martha, four years before, when Holmes had visited my Queen Anne Street home, and he had been asked to look into an issue regarding the suffragette disturbances. * He discovered that Martha was working at a police station and was passing information to the event organisers. Between them, the women were leading Inspector Reynolds and his men a merry dance. Martha didn't have any family and Holmes was in need of a housekeeper, so he resolved the matter for Reynolds without implicating her and offered her the opportunity to work for him. When the Prime Minister subsequently asked him to go on the trail of Von Bork, he knew that he could rely on Martha to act as the perfect spy. She intermittently supplied him with information that would help him snare each individual of Von Bork's gang.

Then another thought occurred to me. "You have been in America off-and-on for the last two years. How exactly did that connect to Von Bork's work taking place *here*?"

Holmes smiled again. "Like Moriarty and Maupertuis before him, Von Bork has been a master criminal with layers of underlings across many countries that provide him with a buffer between the authorities and himself. It is virtually impossible to expose such villains without first stripping away their protection. In this case, in order to create a distraction to the British authorities, Von Bork, Germany's chief spy, allied himself to the Irish Republican movement and their more radical supporters of Catholic emancipation. If Von Bork could assist the Irish in creating a distraction for the British, it could only aid him in his primary function – that of carrying out his undetected espionage. In an effort to free themselves from British domination, two-million disaffected Catholic Irish have immigrated to America over the past fifty years. It was from there that they and their descendants seek to fund and plot Catholic emancipation at home.

"The other benefit from Von Bork's point of view regarding his garnering favour with the Irish was that when war breaks out, which it almost certainly will, Ireland could well become a German base, especially for submarines, who could operate against the British fleet and guard against American assistance at the same time.

"So it was to America that I first went. You may recall from our Baker Street days that I was already acquainted with both Wilson Hargreaves of the New York Police Bureau and the Pinkerton man, Leverton. I contacted them both prior to my journey, to inform them of my investigation and asked for their assistance if required. I was also keeping in regular contact with Mycroft, informing him of progress. I must say that I felt more comfortable knowing that I had the safety net of the authorities to fall back on, both at home and abroad. I myself was now a spy in enemy territory, a long way from home, playing a very dangerous game. Like the other villains I mentioned earlier, I had to dismantle Von Bork's criminal pyramid from the bottom. I'm so pleased that you've been here this evening to witness the removal of the pyramidion himself, my dear fellow."

"How did you know where to start in America?"

"During my investigation and subsequent confirmation that Von Bork was indeed the man the British Government were seeking, I also discovered his deflection tactic regarding the Irish question. I further learned that two of his agents who acted as conduits between himself in England and the Republican Movement in America were U.S. citizens. Jack James and Daniel Hollis ran operations in Chicago and New York respectively. I couldn't find out much about Hollis at that stage, but discovered that James was little more than a ruffian with virtually nothing between his ears. I was surprised Von Bork even entertained someone of that ilk, but perhaps he thought James was so far on the extremity of his spy ring, he could do little damage to his more pressing issues.

"It was James therefore, who I decided to follow. I trailed him back to Illinois and I presented myself as a similar Irish-American named Michael Altamont, a descendant of a family from Cork, who emigrated during the famine of '52. He and his colleagues welcomed me into their group and my work began, ensuring that I did not make any reference to Germany or spying, instead focussing purely on the question of emancipation.

"The Chicago clan basically focussed on fundraising for the cause 'back home' as they continually called it, despite the fact that none of them had actually *visited* Ireland. I therefore worked with them in raising funds among local businesses and individuals of somewhat questionable ethics. I found that anti-establishment feelings at that time amongst the Irish

378

community had peaked as a result of the *Titanic* tragedy a few months earlier. Many of the five-hundred-plus steerage passengers who were lost were from the homeland, and the feeling amongst their Irish cousins was that they had been sacrificed to save the great and the good of society. I'm not sure if the actual statistics of the tragedy would support such a view, but that didn't stop such rumours spreading through the Irish communities of America like a wildfire."

"So presumably, following your arrival, there was seen to be an increase to the coffers, whether that be coincidence or not?"

"Indeed, there was," agreed Holmes, "and with my awareness of how the stock market operated, some imagination, and a little common sense – something of which James was in short supply – I then showed him how to enhance those coffers still further with a little speculation. It wasn't long before the more perspicacious Hollis started to take note of the success of the Chicago operation. Knowing that James was completely incapable of overseeing such an accomplishment by himself, he came west to see what the true cause was. James introduced me to Hollis, and I immediately convinced him that we shared the same political goal – so much so, in fact, that he asked if I would follow him to New York and help with the operation there. I had no objections and, given that James's gang were enjoying their new-found success, he had no objections either."

I interrupted Holmes's narrative. "I thought you told Von Bork earlier that James was in Portland, '*doing time*' as you put it."

Holmes laughed, heartily. "Ah yes. James, the ruffian imbecile! Within three months of my following Hollis east, James had succeeded in ruining his operation. He instantly forgot the techniques I taught him in speculating to accumulate, and resorted to using the money donated by local – shall we say – *businessmen,* at the racetrack in an effort to boost his coffers. When some of his less-tolerant contributors found out about how James was losing their money, it almost inevitably led to violence. During one such engagement, James knifed a man to death. He and his equally dense lieutenant Brendan Kelly were arrested and moved out of the state to ensure a fair and objective trial, the result of which saw them receive life sentences at the Oregon State Penitentiary."

"Holmes?" I began with a certain amount of discomfort. "Were you not actually aiding and abetting this criminal activity by your actions?"

"Of course, and it isn't something in which I take a great deal of pride. However, I was driven by the knowledge that these small sacrifices were leading to a much bigger prize that would far outweigh any wrongdoing on my part."

"I suppose so," I said, understanding Holmes's point without necessarily agreeing with it.

"Rest assured," he added. "I was always one step ahead of my American colleagues, and I therefore always made sure that no one was hurt as a result of my actions."

"I sense from your tone that things became even more challenging after you left Chicago."

"Indeed, they did," confirmed my friend. "With every move, the stakes were raised. I first went with Hollis to New York City, where I worked with him and a few of his confederates – again, raising funds and championing the cause. He was clearly testing me, wanting to see for himself what I was like and if I could be trusted. I played my part to perfection, never suggesting for a moment, in action or deed, that my intentions were anything other than focussing solely on the question of emancipation in Ireland.

"After three or so months, Hollis took me to one side and asked if I would be interested in getting a little more involved directly in the cause.

"'How d'ya mean?' I asked.

"'There's some friends of mine up in Buffalo who work closer with our brothers in Ireland. I've been keeping an eye on you these past months, and I think you're just the type of fella who they would be attracted to.'"

"'Yeah, sure, I'd be interested.'

"We then travelled up to Buffalo where in a room above a pub in the seediest part of town imaginable, Hollis introduced me to a group of around thirty rogues who went under the name of the 'Saoirse Society'."

"'Saoirse Society'?" I repeated. "What does that mean?"

"It is Gaelic for *Freedom*. Whereas the low-level operatives spent their time raising funds for the cause, this group spent their time planning violence and disruption in Ireland."

"Presumably, that is where Von Bork and the Germans came in?"

"Yes, but they were never mentioned, nor did I ask about them. Hollis told me before we went that *Saoirse* was a most secretive group. They had based their headquarters in Buffalo, as it was roughly the same distance between New York and Chicago. Hollis was the agent who moved between both cities, and then liaised with the so called 'Triskelion Master', a fearsome bear of a man called Sean Baxter, out of Boston, who appeared to rule his colleagues with a rod of iron. I was surprised how quickly I was accepted by the society, clearly a testament to the judgement of Hollis who sponsored my application. But I was left in no doubt that if I was to betray the cause in any way, I would meet with an extremely unpleasant end.

"Two further months passed when Baxter ordered Hollis and me over to Ireland, where we would oversee the receipt of some arms delivered to the tiny harbour of Castlehaven on the west coast. I never asked what the arms were for, or who was supplying them, but it proved to be a pivotal moment in my long investigation."

"How so?" I questioned, as the hour approached midnight, and my little Ford trundled its way towards London.

"I had already noticed how Hollis, much like many of his other *Saoirse* colleagues, was a heavy drinker. But on the voyage over to Ireland, with little else to distract us from the tedium of the journey, it became clear that once he had consumed an excessive amount of alcohol, it almost inevitably led to conflict when he encountered someone of a similar disposition. On more than one occasion, I had to stop him from getting into a confrontation with fellow passengers, while keeping my own act up as a confederate of his – someone he could trust.

"When we finally arrived at Queensferry, we travelled by train to the small town of Skibbereen, around ten miles from Castlehaven, where arrangements had been made for us to stay for two days before the shipment was due to arrive. It was only at this point that Hollis informed me that the arms were to be delivered to two members of the Irish Volunteers, a military group formed the previous year, and with whom Baxter and his *Saoirse* Society had links."

"It sounds as though it was getting extremely dangerous at this point."

"Never more so, but again, the monotony of waiting proved too much for my colleague. On our final night before the shipment was due to arrive, I agreed to accompany him to a nearby public house, but first made an excuse and told him I had something to do beforehand. The truth was, that I had arranged to contact Mycroft via the telephone and update him on the latest position. By the time I arrived at the hostelry, I found Hollis had gotten into a brawl with some local ruffians who objected to the presence of the American in their small community. By the time I returned, the police were present and took Hollis, myself, and his opponents away.

"When we were taken to the station, I protested to the officers that I hadn't been involved in the fight and I wanted to speak with the American Embassy. Knowing that I hadn't directly been involved and probably believing that I was more trouble than it was worth, they let me go and I set about contacting Mycroft for the second time that evening, this time with a view to having Hollis released for the greater good of the mission."

"Did Mycroft know you were in Ireland prior to that night?"

"Yes, I had kept in contact with him discreetly throughout my American sojourn by telegram, and telephone when possible, so he and the government knew our every move."

"Wasn't that dangerous?" I asked. "Surely your messages could have been intercepted or overheard?"

"You are correct. It certainly was a dangerous game I was playing, especially when it came to the use of the telephone. When connecting through an operator, it could never be known who that operator might be, or who she might be connected to. Mycroft and I therefore reverted to using a code we devised as boys, knowing that no one would understand what we were discussing.

"When I managed to get through to him for the second time that evening, we both agreed that, whereas Hollis could be extracted from the Irish cells, he – and probably I – would be ordered out of Ireland. To allow the shipment of arms to proceed would therefore be too risky and, if discovered by the Irish authorities, could jeopardise the whole aim of trapping Von Bork and his operation. Therefore, I contacted Baxter in Buffalo and told him that there had been a major accident in Castlehaven and the place was swarming with army and police. I suggested the delivery would be compromised and recommended that it be postponed. Much to his annoyance, he said he would make the arrangements with the transporters, although he still didn't reveal to me who they were."

"But you knew they were Germans, of course?"

"Of course. All the while, I was playing a dangerous game of bluff and counter-bluff, espionage and counter-espionage."

"So you managed to get Hollis out?"

"Well, you give me too much credit. Mycroft and the British authorities brought their weight down on the local police force and he was released, on the condition that he leave the country."

"What was his reaction?"

"He was initially panic-stricken that he had compromised the receipt of the arms. It was clear he was concerned about his return to America, and potentially facing the wrath of Baxter. I told him not to worry, as I had contacted the society's leader and smoothed the situation over.'

"'Gee, thanks pal,' he said, full of relief. After a pause, he then asked, 'Come to think of it, how did *you* get out anyway?'

"'I'd like to say I held sway with friends in high places, Danny boy,' I replied, 'but in truth, it's probably more accurate to say it was a case of greater luck than judgement after a desperate call to an old friend.'

"'Howd'ya mean?' he asked.

"It was at that point, Watson, when I decided to take my subterfuge to the next level. I told him that I had a contact in the American State Department. We had both studied at Trinity College, Dublin, where we had both developed our sympathy for the emancipation cause. I told Hollis that I had contacted him and asked if he had any sway with the British Government, and if so, could it be arranged for my friend to be released from custody. Not only did he say it was possible, he told me that he knew pro-Irish sympathisers within the government who may be able to aid us in the future."

"Hollis's eyes widened and his face adopted an arrogant smirk.

"'This could be significant, Michael,' he said. 'You've done well, buddy.'

"He thought for a while longer, as if contemplating something. It was though I could read his mind. I knew I had him. His look became furtive as he moved in closer, lowering his voice as he did so.

"'I know a guy in England who is always on the lookout for information.'

"'What kind'a information?'

"He paused before answering, as if assuring himself that I could be trusted, 'He's a German spy,' he said at last. 'He's the guy who's providing arms for our activity in the homeland. He figures that if we can keep the Brits busy, they won't be fully focussed on what the Germans are doing. He mixes in high circles himself, and is always on the lookout for information that might give Berlin the edge. If I tell him we have another avenue to explore regarding London's activity, I know he will be very grateful.'

"It was the first time in over twelve months of being in their company that anyone from the American operation had mentioned Germany. Finally, we had confirmation of the connection.

"'Well, any enemy of the Brits is a friend of ours, eh Danny?" I said, with an equally smug expression.

"'Couldn't have put it better myself, Michael. How about you make a discreet approach to your friend in Washington, who in turn can contact his guys in London and see if they would be willing to help us?'

"'Leave it with me.'

"In order to placate the Irish, we made our way to the mainland, where I waited a few days before bringing the subject back up with Hollis.

"'Hey, Danny, I had a bit of luck with my friend in Washington. He contacted a guy in London, who said he would be willing to help us directly – for a small cut.'

"'I'm sure that can be arranged,' said Hollis, his eyes lighting up, once more. He couldn't disguise his enthusiasm for the news, 'Von Bork will be delighted with this,' he said absentmindedly.

"'Von Bork?' I questioned.

"Hollis realised that he had probably said too much in divulging the name, but then quickly reminded himself that I could be trusted, given my track record with him and previously with James.

"'Yes,' he said, 'That's the name of the German over here I was telling you about. I reckon the more information we can give him, the more help he will give us.

"Making out as though Von Bork's name didn't mean anything to me, I concentrated instead on my fictitious contact. 'Well, *my* guy doesn't want his name given out to every Tom, Dick, and Harry, mind you, so I'll keep it to myself if it's all the same. Neither you, nor this Van Bern guy, need know.'

"'Von Bork,' Hollis corrected. 'Yeah, that makes sense. No matter, I think, instead of you returning with me to the States, I reckon its time you started working independently over here. I'll take you to meet Von Bork.'"

Chapter III

"Ingenious," I said. "So you actually turned the fiasco in Ireland to your advantage and supplied the unwitting Hollis with a hook that would lead directly to Von Bork himself."

Holmes smiled. "I've had to think quickly on my feet Watson, these past two years, knowing my very life could depend on a wrong move."

"But how on earth did the Irish-Americans find out about Von Bork in the first place?" I asked.

"My theory is that like-minded people inevitably gravitate towards one another, regardless of geographical distance or social status. In this case, it was the dangerous world of the secret societies that forged the link. Von Bork has spent the last few years mixing with the great and the good of British society. This inevitably means that he is involved in the Freemasons. The highest-ranking members of such organisations have connections with other similar bodies, and it is thought that an esteemed member of our Royal Family introduced the German to an American acquaintance of his, who in turn had links to the *Saoirse* Society. One thing led to another, and here we are."

"What were your first impressions of Von Bork when you met him?"

"I found him to be the same arrogant creature you witnessed for yourself tonight. Hollis and I travelled, not to Harwich, but to his office in London, where he repeated my concocted story about the major incident in Ireland, which prevented the delivery of the arms shipment.

"'I suppose you were right in aborting the mission,' said Von Bork. 'One never knows if the Irish authorities are more akin to those in Germany, or their more docile neighbours in England, eh?' It was the first of many times I would witness him laughing heartily at his own jokes. Of course, I had to play along, in my role as the anti-British Irish-American activist.

"'So, Mr. Altamont,' he said, turning to me, 'Hollis here and Baxter report good things about you. It is a pity that that idiot James did not take more notice of what you were saying.'

"'Well, you can lead a horse to water, as they say,' was my vague response, although it was clear that the spy didn't suspect me of any wrongdoing in James's apprehension and incarceration, which gave me some reassurance about the risky mission.

"'So why did you come here?' asked Von Bork of Hollis.

"'It turns out Michael here has some very useful contacts in both Washington and London,'

"'Oh, really?' asked Von Bork looking at me.

"'Yes,' I said, 'I have a friend in the State Department with Irish Republican sympathies. In turn, he has a contact in Whitehall with the same political tendencies. I think they can both be very useful in providing information about British and Allied activities.'

"'Excellent! Excellent!' cried Von Bork. 'It is just the kind of engagement my government is looking for.' He thought for a while before concluding, "Hollis, I think you should go back to America, but you, Mr. Altamont – I think you should stay here in England and find out what you can about whatever strategic planning and military manoeuvres are taking place.'

"'What's in it for me?' I asked, feigning reluctance at being away from home.

"'Forgive me, Altamont, old man,' said Von Bork, obsequiously. 'With your permission, of course. I will certainly make it worth your while, as you are away from your home and family.'

"'Very well,' I agreed after some thought. 'I'll stay, but I don't want you to think that you are dealing with another Jack James. I'll make sure me and the homeland will be well-rewarded.'

"'Splendid, splendid!' cried the German. 'Then I suggest, Hollis, that you make your way back to America alone. I will make sure your friend here is taken well care of.'

"'So long, buddy," said Hollis, offering me his hand. 'It's been good working with you. Thanks again for your hard work and you helping me out.'

"His last comment was suitably cryptic that Von Bork wouldn't understand it. He left and headed for Southampton, where he would catch the next available boat for New York. Knowing that he and Baxter would be no further use to me, as I was now working directly for Von Bork, I waited a few months, as to not invite any suspicion before arranging with Wilson Hargreaves, through Mycroft, to arrest them and break up their seditious activities.

"Meanwhile, I was meeting with Von Bork every two-to-three weeks at his '*pied-a-terre*', as he referred to it, in Mayfair."

I exhaled in disgust. "It's a disgrace that such a man should be living such an ostentatious life in the heart of the Empire he was working to bring down."

"Such are the workings of the British establishment, Watson," replied my friend. "Wealth and power are everything, and if one is successful in gaining access to the right social circles, nationality and even background are rendered virtually irrelevant. Perhaps Von Bork's assessment of the foolish British aristocracy was not that wide of the mark after all. They couldn't see the Trojan Horse that was directly in front of them. He even told me at one point that he enjoyed sailing with the King and the Prince of Wales off the southeast coast of England and around the Isle of Wight. What the Royal Family did not know, much to Von Bork's amusement, was that he was using the leisure jaunts to assess the security of the southern ports."

"Damn cheek of the fellow!" I mumbled. "In what activity did you have to get involved once you found your way into his lair?"

"That's where things became even more difficult. I note your use of the word 'lair' – I viewed it more as a lion's den, with me reporting directly to the head of the pride. My every move had to be calculated. The information I was passing on had to be sufficiently robust as to maintain a level of trust with the villain, but it could not endanger the lives of British citizens or risk the security of the country. There is no question however, that my actions contributed to strikes at two shipyards and a disruption at Hampton's Munition Works in Lambeth."

"It's clear that you had some difficult decisions to make."

"Indeed, I did," replied my friend, thoughtfully, "but everything I did was with the approval of the Government, and I can therefore say my conscience is clear. In fact, there is no question that Von Bork's underestimating of the British played into my hands. He was easily convinced that there was very little effort being given to the storage of munitions, and that everyone was just sitting around believing that the Germans were full of bluster. This allowed me valuable time and space in which to manoeuvre, when it came to passing false information to him and gaining vital intelligence for ourselves."

"What did you find out?"

"One of Von Bork's chief agents in England was a man called Leopold Steiner, who you heard me refer to this evening. Steiner masqueraded as a respectable Austrian art dealer based in London. In fact, he was a German spy, shipping naval intelligence in and out of the country across the Channel to France, and particularly to Holland, the latter

386

country having declared its neutrality in any possible forthcoming conflict. Since my discovery of Steiner and his techniques, we ourselves have had spies based in the ports of Rotterdam and Caen, watching the comings and goings. It was only three nights ago that he was observed leaving Portsmouth with an antique bureau he claimed was bound for Paris. Contained within the drawers of the bureau was information and maps that were actually bound for Berlin. What he was unaware of, however, was that the information was bogus, having been supplied by myself. It makes me happy to think that he'll deliver that information to the Germans, and that they'll base their upcoming war strategy upon it.

I laughed. "So, what were the 'signals' Von Bork referred to tonight – the information that you were supposedly to hand over?"

"I had informed him two months ago that the Admiralty suspected enemy spies and had changed all of the naval defence codes, as well as details of possible American support."

"American support?" I exclaimed.

Holmes looked at me earnestly and picked up the telegram I had received earlier that day, that still lay on the top of the dashboard.

"I observed this earlier, Watson. I suspect these are your call-up papers?"

"Well, hardly call-up papers," I replied. "Merely an acknowledgement of my willingness to assist if things escalate."

"And escalate they will, my dear fellow. It is no coincidence that you have received this now, as I believe before the week is out, we will be at war."

"You think it is that imminent? I must confess I was a little pessimistic about the proposed diplomatic channels when I read the newspaper this morning, but after this evening's events, I rather hoped we could demonstrate to the Germans that we were no push-overs, and they would perhaps consider slowing down their bellicose rhetoric."

"If only it were that simple, my old friend. I have been working this case for two years, but things have spiralled out of control in the last month since the assassination of the Archduke. I believe the Government will make a declaration of war within the next days, as I was advised by Mycroft on Wednesday last to instigate Von Bork's capture before he himself had time to flee. I contacted the spy and informed him that I would travel to his villa tonight with the codes he required. Knowing that this was the final piece of information he was waiting for, he instructed his wife to leave immediately for Flushing, where he presumably intended to join her tomorrow. It all pointed towards an imminent conflict."

My friend's tone was philosophical, and I caught myself feeling sorry for him. "Surely no one can say your work has been a waste of time?"

"No, I don't think anyone would go that far. It will certainly help when war is declared, as it will greatly reduce the enemy's espionage capabilities. But if the objective was to prevent the armed struggle itself taking place, then sadly I believe it will prove to be unsuccessful."

"Two years," I mused after some thought. "That must go down as your longest case."

Holmes gave a thin wan smile. "Yes, I do believe you're correct. Although I trailed the late Professor Moriarty for many years, unlike my Anglo-American adventure, I did not devote all my time to his pursuit."

"Speaking of America, you mentioned a few minutes ago about their possible support. What did you mean by that? Surely, they won't become directly involved in a war on the Continent?"

"Perhaps not, but they will almost certainly ship supplies across the Atlantic to their English and French allies. That is why Berlin, through Von Bork, were so keen to establish links with Ireland. From there, they could cut off any American vessels heading east. This would not be without risk for them, of course, as if they were to sink an American ship, it would be considered an act of war and Washington would have little choice but to send troops to Europe."

"That would be unprecedented," I exclaimed. "No doubt troops from the dominions will heed the call from King and Empire. If the Americans also travelled to Europe to get involved, it would be tantamount to almost calling it a war of the whole world."

"Sadly, Watson, man's stupidity knows no bounds. History is viewed as entertainment, not as a tool for learning. As long as there will be fools in power, then there will be the futility of death and destruction."

It was in the early hours of Monday morning when we arrived back in London and I dropped Holmes off at Claridge's, where he had arranged to stay. He thanked me earnestly for my help throughout the evening and we shook hands, agreeing to meet for breakfast the following morning. Of course, Holmes's ominous portent was proved accurate, as war was declared on Germany the following day. Although we had mused over the consequences of such a conflict – and Holmes correctly foretold that America would enter the war with the sinking of trans-Atlantic vessels – we could never have predicted the full extent to which loss from seemingly every country was incurred.

It would go on to be labelled "The Great War" and "The War to End all Wars". I can only hope, as the twentieth century progresses, that the world learns from such folly, and we never witness the like again.

NOTE

* For more about the placement of Holmes's housekeeper in Von Bork's residence, see "The Perfect Spy" in *The MX Book of New Sherlock Holmes Stories Part XLVIII: Occupants of the Canonical Realm (1899-1924)*

The Bohemian Corporal
by Orlando Pearson

Even the powers of my friend, Mr. Sherlock Holmes, and those of his even-abler brother Mycroft, have limits. The matter I relate below gives an example of where they both failed, although here they failed where no one else succeeded. It is worth pointing out that from this failure, no one else went as far as they and, in particular, as far as Mycroft, but that does not of course mitigate the consequences of this failure.

In the years after the end of the Great War, I continued to run my medical practice in Queen Anne Street. The history books will record that London at this time was full of demobilised soldiers, many of whom still showing the after-effects of wounds and gassing, and of civilians suffering from Spanish Flu and its aftermath. With the normal onerous workload of a medical practice, I was thus never at less than full stretch, and in the end I was obliged to employ two other doctors in my practice to take the strain.

At this point of my life, my contact with my friend Mr. Sherlock Holmes had been no more than infrequent for several years although, as I have commented elsewhere, he did use my home for London meetings as his retirement to Sussex meant he no longer had a place for meeting clients in London. As the notice I got of such meetings was often the briefest, I came to regard such impositions as the price of our continued friendship.

It was late on the evening of Sunday, the 15th of February, 1920, that there was a knock on the door and, as it was past the servants' waking hours, I answered it myself, fearing a medical emergency and an all-night patient visit. On the step stood Sherlock Holmes, carrying a large case.

"My dear fellow!" said I. "Pray come in!"

"You look surprised, and no wonder! Relieved that you aren't being called out too, I fancy! Hmm! You still, nearly forty years on, smoke the Arcadia mixture of your bachelor days. It's good that the easing of the restraints of supply now that the war is over means that it is available once more. And there's no mistaking that fluffy ash upon your lapel. It's easy to tell that you have been accustomed to wearing a uniform, Watson. You'll never pass as a pure-bred civilian as long as you keep that habit of carrying your handkerchief in your sleeve. Could you put me up tonight?"

"With pleasure," I replied.

"I see that you have no visitors at present in your spare room. Your hat stand proclaims as much."

"I shall be delighted if you will stay."

"Thank you. I'll fill the vacant peg then. Sorry to observe that you've had the British workman in the house. He's a token of evil. Not the drains, I hope?"

"No, the gas."

"Ah! He has left two nail-marks from his boot upon your linoleum just where the light strikes it. No, thank you, I had some supper at Victoria, but I'll smoke a pipe with you with pleasure."

I handed him my pouch, and he seated himself opposite to me. He took a pinch of tobacco from the pouch, rubbed it meditatively between the tips of his long, thin fingers, filled his pipe, struck a match, and then sat in contentment as the mellow smoke rose from the bowl. A thoughtful look came over his face as he smoked for some time in silence. I was well aware that only business of importance would have brought him to me at such an hour, and so I waited patiently until he should come round to it.

"Would you still rate my knowledge and understanding of politics as feeble?" he asked at length.

"That was a judgement I made nearly forty years ago," I replied cautiously, recalling the list of my friend's limitations which I had compiled soon after I had first met him.

"A man from Munich is visiting us tomorrow," replied my friend in what sounded like a *non sequitur*.

"Visiting us?" I exclaimed. While I was delighted to see Holmes, I was by no means sure I wanted a second person, and a stranger at that, under my roof, especially as the size of Holmes's bag suggested a stay longer than one night. At this point, as I cast an uneasy glance down at it, I wondered what my wife would say about a prolonged visit from my friend, let alone the arrival of a second person requiring overnight accommodation.

"A man called Anton Drexler has written to me. He is the leader of a political party in Munich, and he wants to consult with me about a new member of his party. He plans to arrive in London tomorrow morning and to leave as soon as he has seen me. I think he is hoping I will join him on the way back. That's why my bag, at which you just gave a wary look, is of the size that it is, as I may go straight to Germany with him and need clothing for a week. I cannot see any circumstances under which Herr Drexler would look to stay here."

I smiled at the ease with which Holmes had read my thoughts about his bag, but there was still much I didn't understand.

"And the consultation is about *German* politics?" I asked, for anti-German feeling remained very strong in this country only just over a year after the end of the fighting in Europe, and less than eight months after the signing of the Treaty of Versailles. I would be a liar if I denied regarding anything German with only the deepest suspicion.

"Beyond what I have said, I fear I know nothing, but I can see no harm in listening to what he has to say. His letter was very insistent."

At nine o'clock the next morning, the tall, bespectacled, and moustached Drexler sat before us, looking only slightly wearied from his journey. He had the air of a junior clerk, and I wondered whether a man such as this could really be the leader of a major political party. As my readers will know, Holmes spoke excellent German, and I had some knowledge of the language as well, so discussion that I set out below took place largely in that language.

"I founded the German Workers' Party in January of last year," began Drexler. "Our membership consisted largely of railway workers, and I am myself a fitter on the *Reichsbahn*, or the German Imperial Railways."

"Pray continue."

"We meet weekly in one of Munich's numerous beer halls and discuss how to deal with the disastrous situation in our country following the calamitous decision of our leaders the year-before-last to agree to an Armistice when our army was still undefeated in France, and then to sign the Treaty of Versailles in June last year."

Neither Holmes nor I ventured any comment at this.

Drexler then went on to hold a lengthy and somewhat rambling disquisition on what he and doubtless many other Germans saw as the iniquities of the Treaty. It had resulted in the loss of a seventh of German land to create countries such as Poland and Czechoslovakia – an idea which had the support of the great majority of their citizens, although not of their German-speaking minority populations. There was payment of vast reparations to the countries Germany had invaded, and restrictions on Germany rebuilding its armed forces, as they, with the Central Power allies, sent their armies to conquer Luxembourg, almost all of Belgium, a third of France, and a large part of western Russia.

Drexler referenced all of this in what he said.

I omit any further details for the sake of brevity in what I can only describe as a monologue, as neither Holmes nor I made any response. He concluded as follows:

"Our leaders were at best – at *best*, Mr. Holmes – fools, or at worst – and that is what I fear of some of them, Mr. Holmes – traitors to our nation. What was agreed has resulted in stringencies in Germany which you will not believe in the comfortable world you occupy here. People died of hunger because your blockade of our ports continued for eight months after the fighting stopped."

"There was a long period of food rationing here too because of the activity of your country's U-Boats," I countered, "which engaged in unrestricted warfare and sank neutral shipping."

"Children are growing up malnourished."

"In France and Belgium," I countered again, "children were among the victims of your army. No foreign army was ever on any German soil."

"And yet, our streets are littered with the wounded and the dying."

"If you didn't see similar on your way here from Victoria Station," I responded, "it can only be because you weren't looking."

I think realising he had said as much as he could about his sense of injustice, Drexler fished a dairy out of his pocket and studied it.

"Party member Adolf Hitler first came to a meeting of our party on the 12th of September of last year, and he has been to every meeting since."

"He sounds a very dedicated member of your organization," said Holmes, "but I hardly think that that merits you coming all the way here to tell me about him."

"Mr. Holmes, he seems to be in the process in the shortest space of time of taking us over. My fellow party members seem to hang onto his every word."

"So he seems to have the makings of a future . . . ." Here Holmes broke off, looking for the correct word in German, and I broke in.

"*Führer*?"

"Thank you, Watson. Yes, *Führer*, or *leader* to your organization is the word I was looking for. Is your concern, Herr Drexler, really about your own position in the party you founded?"

"My party's beliefs are bigger than any one individual," said Drexler looking defensive.

"Surely that is the point of any political party. Its core beliefs remain constant, even if its members change. Members who are no longer convinced by the party's objectives leave, and the leader of the party is the person who can best articulate those core beliefs to attract voters."

"What is concerning me is that having started as a small grouping of railway workers, our membership is suddenly growing rapidly, and our principal attraction is Member 555, Adolf Hitler. Yet no one knows anything about him. He never talks about his life or what he has done in the past. It appears he lives only for the party."

"My dear Herr Drexler, have you read the numerous works about me by my colleague here?"

"I was not aware, Mr. Holmes," said Drexler earnestly, and at this point he blinked at us quizzically through the thick lenses of his glasses, "that there were people who had *not* read your colleague's works about you."

393

"Then you will know that in the hundreds of pages of writings he has published about me, I have disclosed to him of myself no more information than that I have a brother, that I studied at a university which I have not named, and that I have produced monographs about a diverse range of subjects such as the tracing of footprints and the ash of different cigarettes. If your only concern about Herr Hitler is that he seems to have sprung from nowhere and that he is boosting the fortunes of your party, I remain unsure why you have made the long journey to London."

"There is something about him, Mr. Holmes," said Drexler suddenly sounding plaintive. "He has an intensity of expression, of argument, and of gaze which is quite unlike anything I have seen in anyone else." He broke off once more and stared into the distance. "It is his staring eyes that disturb me most," he added after a pause.

"How does your colleague support himself? He cannot have a paid position within the party if it is as small as you say."

"I do not know. As I said to you, Mr. Holmes, he appears for our meetings, but otherwise I know nothing further about him."

Holmes thought again.

"Does his accent betray no origin?"

"It is southern German," said Drexler after some thought, "but I could not be more specific."

"Do your party records not have an address for him?"

"We asked him about this, and he mentioned a place called Braunau, but then said he would pick up any party mail for him when he came to our meetings."

"Where is Braunau?"

"A town called Braunau is the German equivalent of a town called Brownfield. There is a Braunau in northern Bohemia, which is now in Czechoslovakia, which was until recently part of the Austro-Hungarian Empire. It is German-speaking. And there is Braunau-am-Inn in the newly constituted Republic of Austria. It is on the south side of the river Inn, where it forms the border between Austria and Germany."

"So, based on his reference to Braunau, which may be the one in Austria or the one in Czechoslovakia, is he even a German citizen?"

"I do not know, Mr. Holmes," said Drexler, a note of defiance coming into his voice. "Austria wants to unite with Germany, but is prohibited from doing so by the treaty of St. Germaine. To our east there is a large German-speaking minority placed against its will in this new country of Czechoslovakia. Self-determination, you will note, is not something allowed to German speakers, although it is granted to everyone else in Europe. You will therefore perhaps understand that I have no idea of which country Herr Hitler is a citizen."

"What does he look like?" pressed Holmes.

"He is about five-feet-nine-inches tall, has what is we call a 'toothbrush' mustache because of its shape, and dark brown hair combed into a parting from the right. He is always dressed very smartly."

"So, he has fought on what you call the Western Front, as he will have trimmed his moustache into that shape to fit it under a gasmask, and there was no use of gas by the Russians in the east." Holmes paused for thought. "But I fear the information you have given me about him doesn't enable me to deduce anything else."

"You already seem already know than I do, Mr. Holmes," said Drexler. "I merely know that he seems to dedicate all his time to the party."

Holmes remained silent and then asked, "If Hitler is Party Member 555, and your party has grown rapidly since he became a member, it cannot be all that small."

Drexler went once more back on the defensive.

"Hitler was in fact the fifty-fifth person who paid to be a member, but we gave out sequentially numbered membership cards starting from five-hundred to make ourselves look bigger to people who might want to join."

"So how many members does it have now?"

"We are anticipating two-thousand people for our meeting at the Hofbräuhaus at the end of this month."

Holmes was, I think, quite startled by this figure.

"Herr Drexler, are you saying that, having had only fifty-five members in September, your colleague, Herr Hitler, has attracted nearly two-thousand new members within five months?"

"They attend our general meetings," said Drexler, again looking a little uneasy, "but they are not necessarily all members, although attendance at our meetings implies they are considering membership. Nevertheless, our numbers are now such that we need never have made use of the subterfuge of starting our membership card numbers at five-hundred to make us look much bigger than we in fact were."

Holmes sat back in his seat.

"I think, Herr Drexler," he said at length, "with the support he has attracted in such a short space of time, and the air of mystery about him, your party member Herr Hitler merits an investigation. I will come with you to Munich."

"I am very pleased to hear it."

"Watson, would you like to join us? I am sure there must come a point when your practice can spare you."

The case Holmes was pursuing had seemed so speculative, and the demands of my practice were at that time so exacting, that I felt inclined to turn down the invitation, but Drexler interjected.

"If Dr. Watson could act as a chronicler of what you find, Mr. Holmes, that would, I am sure, be most valuable for posterity."

Eventually I agreed to put the practice in the hands of my two assistants, while I joined Holmes and Herr Drexler in Munich.

As Holmes had predicted, Herr Drexler returned to Germany on the day that he arrived. I went through the process of handing over my practice to my assistants for an undefined period while Holmes spent the next day reading all that he could find about Germany in the reading room of the British Museum and at the National Newspaper Library.

With the whirl of events, it was evening of the second day, as Holmes and I were sitting at the hearth, before I had the opportunity to challenge him on his decision.

"I am not clear," I said, smoke rising vertically from my pipe, "why you took on a commission which, if successful, can only strengthen the Germans, with whom we were until so recently at war."

"I confess, Watson, the same objections crossed my mind, but I have always found it to be a valuable use of time to investigate what our Continental cousins are up to and, if it is a matter of statecraft, I can always refer it to brother Mycroft."

The next day, Holmes and I, much like old time, crossed the English Channel, and on Thursday morning we were in Munich where we took quarters at the Bahnhofhotel, which was, as the name suggests, a short walk from the main station. Even on that short walk, it was obvious that however many wounded and gassed soldiers there were in London, their numbers were multiplied two or three times in Munich. Many sat in ragged uniforms, begging on the pavement.

Holmes had telegraphed our plans to Drexler, and he joined us for a late breakfast.

"We have a committee meeting at seven o'clock in a private room of the Sterneckerbräu Beerhall on Sterneckerstrasse this evening," he said. "On his past record of attendance, Herr Hitler will be there – indeed I would be astonished if he were not. If you like, Mr. Holmes, you might sit with Dr. Watson in the public area of the Brauerei. Hitler will have to pass through it to come to our meeting and on his way out. I will meet him at the front door of the brewery and walk in with him so you can see who he is. Maybe, Mr. Holmes, you can follow him after the meeting to see where he lives."

So it was that a quarter-to-seven saw Holmes and me sitting on either side of a long table in the Sterneckerbräu.

We had bought tankards of beer which we sipped very slowly, and we avoided talking to one another, as we weren't at all sure how our fellow drinkers might react to the sound of English being spoken. Just before seven, we saw Drexler walk through the hall in the company of a man matching the description of Hitler that we had been given. They disappeared through a door at the back of the hall. I'm sure Drexler must have seen us, but he gave no signs of doing so. Holmes and I carried on sipping slowly at our drinks, and at about a quarter-past-nine, the man I knew to be Hitler came back out through the door, this time on his own. After he'd walked past us, Holmes rose quietly and followed him. I first saw Hitler, and then Holmes, walk through the street door and into the Sterneckerstrasse. I slowly drained my beer and returned to our hotel.

I sat up in our room and at a quarter-past-eleven, Holmes came through the door.

"Well," said he, "that was never going to be all that difficult. Hitler headed eastwards from the Sternecker and I was able to follow him easily. Munich is quite a compact city and to the east of it are barracks, and that was where I saw him go."

"Were you able to follow him in?"

Holmes looked as evasive as Drexler had sometimes done.

"In a country as ruined as this one," he said in the end, "poorly paid sentries are amenable to a bribe, and I was able to persuade the sentry to let me in without any difficulty. Hitler went into a building marked 'Offizierkasino'."

"Hitler is a gambler?"

"'Offizierkasino' is the German for the 'Officers' Mess'. The building was lit on the inside, and there were no curtains. I saw Hitler through the window in conversation with another man in a uniform with insignia on it indicating he is a captain – so a senior person on the site."

"The other person may of course have nothing to do with Hitler activities in the German Workers' Party."

"I think that is unlikely. I saw Hitler leave the Officers' Mess and go to quarters marked 'Gefreiterschlafsaal' or 'Corporals' Dormitory'. Hitler had thus come straight from the meeting of the *Deutsche Arbeiter Partei* committee to the Officers' Mess, and then gone to bed in his own non-commissioned officers' quarters. I find it hard to believe that he wasn't debriefing his senior officer on the proceedings of the meeting when I saw him in the Officers' Mess."

"What will you do next?"

"Tomorrow, I'll have business cards made up for us, and we'll present ourselves at the barracks as two journalists from *The Times* reporting from Munich. We'll see whether we can get an interview with the officer I saw."

Soon after eleven o'clock on the next day saw Holmes and me presenting our false business cards – John Smith and Peter Brown – at the sentry box guarding the barracks. I think the sentry was surprised that anyone with a British background should be at a barracks on the edge of Munich but, once Holmes had greased his palm with silver, he agreed to arrange for us to be taken to the most senior man on site and we were soon presented to Kommandant Karl Mayr, of Sixth Battalion of the Guards Regiment in Munich.

"Not, you'll understand, that I anticipate doing any soldiering work any time soon," he said after introductions. "I've always thought that the more the British understand about us, the easier it will be to sort out an accommodation acceptable to all, so I will speak to your newspaper as long as it is off the record."

Holmes nodded his assent and Mayr continued.

"My main activity here is that I am head of the government's Education and Propaganda Department."

"What does that mean?"

"I suppose if means several things," said Mayr, looking at Holmes and me in turn. "As you are no doubt aware, Mr. Smith, the Armistice and subsequent treaty are rejected by many in Germany, and we have not yet entirely stood down our army, although what we have left has a completely different role from what it had eighteen months ago. We need to keep an eye on the population who are restive after a war which required great sacrifice for no gain, and we need to keep our troops employed – how usefully I am not sure matters. So soldiers here are paid forty Reichsmarks a month, which is a good wage when all their living needs are also found. We will be demobilising our remaining soldiers at the end of March."

"Pray continue."

"I send our troops out anonymously to keep an eye out on what is going on. Since the Armistice – we never refer to it as a 'capitulation', though that is what it was, as we were out of ammunition and out of food – political parties have sprung up like weeds in Germany. Nationalists, Bolsheviks, Socialists, Democrats, Social Democrats. I don't think the members of the parties understand what half the terms mean."

"So your troops watch proceedings at these new parties and report back to you?"

"That is so. I get more reports than I know what to do with – generally one account of events is madder than the last. Blaming all the politicians, the Kaiser, the failure of the people, the mutineering sailors, the British not understanding us, and the allies ratting on us."

"And what is you view?"

"In my present position, my opinion is unimportant. We have the politicians that we have, and the Kaiser is gone. The people are the people and will not put up with starvation rations for ever. The sailors mutinied when they were sent on a suicide mission. The British understood the Kaiser only too well, and our allies surrendered because they were in a worse state then we were."

"Do your soldiers not come to agree with a lot of the opinions they hear expressed at these meetings?"

"I do not know how I can keep track of what they think, even if I saw a purpose to trying to do so. They are not supposed to participate in the workings of the parties they observe, but I cannot in fact stop them. That will not matter either once we reduce our army to one-hundred-thousand men by the end of March. In reality, the observation work that they carry out is to keep them occupied, although obviously I do not tell them this. I would be surprised if none of them agreed with any of the many opinions that they hear at all these political gatherings."

The meeting went on, but Mayr had given us a reason why Hitler might be at meetings of the *Deutsche Arbeiter Partei,* why he might say nothing of himself to other party members, how he might support himself, and why he might take up political activities. Holmes soon brought discussions to an end.

"So he is a spy!" exclaimed Drexler when Holmes set out his findings to him. "That is why he says so little about himself! He is not even a true believer." He paused, "And yet, he is the reason why people come to our gatherings. His oratory has them all spell-bound. I cannot understand how he can have such passion when he is no more than a stooge."

"Might he not have been convinced by the arguments of your party?"

Drexler thought for a minute. "I am not sure that the arguments of our *Deutsche Arbeiter Partei* are so different from those of other parties," he replied in the end.

"He would not come to every single one of your meetings and take an active part in them if he weren't convinced by your party's arguments," said Holmes. "I should like to come to your next meeting and observe him at work. You said you would have two-thousand people there."

"Our next meeting is the one I referred to at our first meeting – so next Tuesday. Two-thousand people is our expectation, based on recent meetings organized by our party, but there may be more people or fewer. Hitler has not said he will attend, but it would be the first time he failed to appear if he did not come. I am sure that you and Dr. Watson could slip into the crowd in Hofbräuhaus unnoticed, Herr Holmes."

Holmes spent the next few days reading every newspaper he could find, while I divided my time between walking the gloomy streets of

Munich and making the best sense of my own studies of the newspapers. So it was that at seven o'clock, on Tuesday the 24th of February, Holmes and I joined what were huge queues outside the brewery.

We eventually got inside and sat down at the end of one of the long tables. The other people in the hall were a mixture of the not-very-well-to-do – men in soldiers' uniforms, factory workers in overalls, and a large number of women. We watched as the crowd kept on arriving. Soon every seat at every table and then every other spare space in the hall was filled.

And yet there was no sign of the objective of our quest.

Speaker after speaker stood up and made speeches which sounded lacklustre, or, perhaps to be more precise, sounded to me as though they were being delivered by Anton Drexler. The material they contained was all the same – the Treaty of Versailles, the traitors in Berlin, the impossible obligations placed upon Germany. But the speakers were all reading from scripts, they repeated themselves, they tripped over their words, and I felt no sense of any of them gripping the audience.

I was beginning to wonder whether Hitler was going to appear at all when the main door to the hall was flung open. A drummer stood in the threshold and then walked in playing a slow, regular, insistent tattoo.

As though transfixed, the hall fell silent.

The drummer continued with the same steady beat.

Following the drummer and flanked by uniformed men came Herr Hitler, who walked with a quiet determined tread through the hall and to the head of the hall where the speakers had been addressing the throng from a podium. But suddenly the podium was empty and, as Hitler mounted it, it was lit by a spotlight just as the hall fell dark, which meant that nothing else could be seen.

I have been asked numerous times what listening to a speech of Hitler was like, and I struggle to find an answer.

My German was capable of understanding what he said, and I set it out in the next paragraphs, but I had to look up in newspapers to find the content was, for it was *how* he said things rather than *what* he said that overwhelmed. The only thing I can compare it to is the speeches of the Apostles after Pentecost. The Apostles, filled with the Holy Spirit, spoke to the crowds assembled in Jerusalem who came from every country known to the writer of the *Acts*. And each member of the crowd seemed to hear the apostles speak in their own tongue. The result was that three-thousand Jews from both inside and outside Jerusalem were baptised on the same day.

"Fellow party members," Hitler began, "we are a people awakening. You may look around and think how few we are. But we in this party are the core of the people. It is but a few short months ago that we had a mere handful of members, and now here we are in the thousands. But we knew then, and we know now, that our ideas are to be the only ones with any following in the land, that we want to be the sole power, and that we are only at the beginning of our journey."

"To reflect this, we must move on from being the Party of German Workers. We must be a party to the *nation*, and a party of the *people*. We must become what we are – the party of *nationalism* and of *socialism*. I propose that we adopt the name the National Socialist German Workers Party."

This reads like a minor change of regulations – that a German Workers party would be nationalistic and socialist seemed to me to be barely worth saying – but, even in the short passage I have quoted above, Hitler had captured the hearts and minds of the crowd and the change passed by acclamation.

Hitler continued.

"At present we live with leadership that passed constantly from one group to another. We must replace it with a fixed pole of people of the best blood. Our goal must be that all loyal Germans become nationalists, but only the best of them – we who are gathered here – become party members. We must be swift as greyhounds, tough as leather, hard as steel."

Again this aspiration, which reads as vague at best, captured the mood of the hall, and the crowd broke out into frenzied cries of *"Vivat!"* and – the first time I heard this – *"Heil!"*

"It is my destiny, so help me God, to lead this party – " Again more acclamations. " – and I will do so. We do not believe in the restraints of democracy, but we are in the best sense of the word a popular movement doing what the people want. There will be those who oppose this – the Socialists, the Bolsheviks, the Communists and the like. But they are all controlled by our enemy – that race-tuberculosis of the people, the Jews, which controls our press."

This sudden shift to blaming the Jews for all Germany's difficulties raised the pitch of crowd from enthusiasm to hysteria. Hitler went on to announce a policy of excluding Jews from German citizenship and banning them from ownership of newspapers. He went onto announce no fewer than twenty-three other policies for the party. I do not believe anyone but an orator with complete mastery of his audience could have set out a list of such length and retained their attention, let alone have each announcement met with cried of frenzied support.

He concluded his speech by declaring himself the sole leader or *Führer* of the party, a proposal which attracted roars of *"Ja!"* and *"Heil!"* – and not a word of opposition from anyone.

By the end, I was deafened by the roars of the crowd, and Holmes had gone white with shock. I am not sure I looked all that different. When we returned to our hotel room, he sat in silence. All I could here was his intake of breath as he drew on his pipe. He did not say another word to me until we had crossed the Channel and were on our way back to Victoria.

"I fear," Holmes said at last, "that I have failed Drexler, whom I believe to be an honest although limited man. And I fear I saw nothing in what Hitler said that wouldn't appeal across Germany. He has a charisma, a forcefulness, and a magnetism that will attract people in huge numbers. Yet his hold over his audiences isn't something that is subject to reason, so I know not what I can do. It is obvious that Mayr has no interest in controlling him, even if he were able to, and Drexler has, after last night, already been sidelined. Hitler has been elected at the head of the party by acclamation, and he will govern it by decree."

"What will you do?"

"When it is a matter of state, I defer to the judgement of Mycroft." Holmes glanced at his watch. "By the time we get back to London, it will be five o'clock in the afternoon, and Mycroft will be at the Diogenes. Let us go there and see what he has to say."

All was as Holmes had stated and we sat before Mycroft (whom I shall normally refer to as Mycroft to avoid confusion with his brother Sherlock) in the Stranger's Room.

Holmes set out what we had seen, and a look of quite unwonted concern came across Mycroft's features. He sat for several minutes in thought before he eventually spoke.

"Sherlock," he said, "you have gone so far as to describe me as sometimes *being* the British Government. It isn't for me to comment on whether this is an accurate description, but you will understand that *being* the British Government means that my ability to interfere in German internal affairs is somewhat circumscribed."

He sat again for a while longer, and then said in a voice almost as though he were speaking to himself. His tone sounded almost like a lament.

"If this were in England, it would all be so much easier. I would send in the tax inspectors to investigate the affairs of Hitler's party, or wait until Hitler committed some infraction, and offer the judge at his trial a place in the House of Lords in exchange for a suitable sentence. Or I would offer Hitler or some of his people some worthless honour or a constituency with a large majority so that they could sit in Parliament and go native. All these options are denied to me here."

He thought again.

"Well," he said at last, "I suppose Ludendorff might be . . . ." He paused again as he sought the right word. "Biddable."

It was just a year since the fighting had come to an end, but I had already forgotten who Ludendorff was.

I think Mycroft saw my look because he explained, "Erich von Ludendorff was, along with Paul von Hindenburg, in charge of the German Army in the war just gone. Immediately after the fighting had stopped, we had a military attaché in Berlin, Neill Malcolm. I got Malcolm to feed Ludendorff the line that the German Army had been undefeated in the field but betrayed by the home front. Malcolm passed on the thought that the Catholics were suspect because their main loyalty was to the Pope, workers were suspect because they wanted a revolution like the Russians had, and that the Jews were suspect because the British had promised them a nation of their own in Palestine."

"Was any of that true?" I asked.

Mycroft considered for a moment.

"I think Ludendorff was rather sold on the argument that everyone apart from him was responsible. Neill sensibly refrained from making the rather obvious point that if all the workers and all the Catholics were against Ludendorff, he could hardly claim to have national support. And we the British haven't delivered on any promise of a Jewish homeland in Palestine, although the promise, caveated as it was by the wholly unrealistic wish for Palestine to also be the homeland for everyone else who lived there, was undoubtedly useful for getting the press in the United States on our side."

Mycroft paused again.

"In the end, Ludendorff formulated it that the army had been stabbed in the back. That was certainly rather easier for him to accept that than that the army which he had led had been defeated in eastern France, that they couldn't supply that army because strikes meant they couldn't bring arms across the Rhine, and that we could bring more troops to the battlefield than they could, even though they had defeated the Russians."

He paused and took a pinch of snuff.

"So Ludendorff was able to absolve himself from blame and we could get on with negotiating a peace without the risk of him claiming that the fight could be continued. He dedicated himself to writing his memoirs in which he valued his own skills very highly. If you read them, you will be surprised, given the views that he expresses in them about his own work, that Germany contrived to lose the war."

"So how can Ludendorff help you?"

"We have done him a favour. People believe his word, and he is thinking of re-entering public life. Arranging some success for him – some relaxation of the terms of the Versailles Treaty which he could claim as being his own doing is the obvious one – would increase his appeal among the people. I think he wants to be German President, and arranging some success for him may well be the way to help him achieve that."

I waited for Mycroft to go on, but he had come to an end of what he had to say, and sat Buddha-like with a glazed expression on his eyes. In the end, Holmes and I left him in his thoughts, and my friend returned to his cottage in Sussex.

If this were a normal account of events involving my friend, I would now write about how Sherlock or Mycroft Holmes, or conceivably both, gave effect to Mycroft's plan. Hitler would in some way be rendered harmless and this country would have some sort of accommodation with Germany that both nations could accept – the Holmes brothers had a unique record of being successful in stratagems such as this. In fact, I can only relate an episode that happened nearly three years later and, although, it bears the hallmarks of a plot, I cannot be sure it was in fact instigated by Mycroft, as he only disclosed his schemes to me when he thought I had a need to know what he was doing. Accordingly, what I write below is what I have read in the newspapers.

On the 8th of November, 1923, Hitler staged what became known as the Beer Hall *Putsch* – a popular uprising against Germany's Berlin government, or the "criminals of November", as he put it. Hitler and Ludendorff and a group of National Socialists marched through Munich, where they were confronted by armed police who opened fire, killing sixteen of Putschists. Ludendorff was unhurt, Göring was wounded in the groin, and Hitler dislocated his shoulder. All three were arrested and put on trial for high treason four months later, but Ludendorff was acquitted, Göring was freed because of the time he had already spent in custody, and Hitler was sentenced to five years, but served only fifteen months. At the trial, the Chief Judge addressed Ludendorff as "Your Excellency", and the observations of journalists who witnessed the trial were that the judge wasn't opposed to the objectives of the *Putsch*.

I cannot but wonder whether Mycroft had tried to organize matters so that Hitler was shot by the police in his *Putsch* attempt, and that Ludendorff should become German leader, but that the difficulties under which Mycroft operated – working in a foreign country with forces over which he had far less control over than he would have had here – simply proved insurmountable for him.

As it was, Ludendorff subsequently stood to be German President but attracted few votes and the man who became President was Paul von Hindenburg. It was Hindenburg who had dubbed Hitler "the Bohemian Corporal" even though, as we subsequently found out, Hitler came from

Braunau in Austria not Braunau in Bohemia. He was an Austrian citizen, and hence the name that Hindenburg devised for him was a misnomer.

NOTE

In 1933 President von Hindenburg had made Hitler Germany's Chancellor or political leader. On the death of Hindenburg, Hitler staged a referendum uniting the posts of president and leader, and by doing so assumed dictatorial powers over Germany, with results that readers will know all too well.

– Henry Durham, historical advisor to *The Redacted Sherlock Holmes*

The Riddle of the Sphinx
by Liz Hedgecock

Chapter I

The train swayed as it rattled through the countryside. London was a smoky memory now, and I surveyed the rolling fields and low buildings with pleasure. In less than half-an-hour we would reach the Sussex Downs, and I would meet my friend Sherlock Holmes at Eastbourne Station.

Was I looking forward to it? If anyone had asked, I would have said I was delighted to visit such an old friend. That was the source of my worry: We were both old men.

As a doctor, I am probably more aware than most of the inevitable decay that comes with old age. I considered myself a healthy man, but I knew I had lost some vigour. This had been particularly apparent during the War, when I had rejoined my old service and done my best for my country. Due to my age, my role was limited, working in a field hospital rather than fighting on the front line. My work was vital, but I never saw the heat of battle. I merely patched men up afterwards.

Now, a year-and-a-half after the Armistice, I felt it was my duty to keep active and enjoy life. However, I had fallen victim to a nasty dose of influenza in January, and only now did I feel that I was regaining my strength. I went to my club, dined with friends, and played billiards with good old Thurston. I practised moderation and made sure to take a walk every day. I kept up with current affairs. And because of these things, I worried about Holmes. I had not seen him in a few months, which felt like a long time.

Holmes had retired around seventeen years before and moved from the bustle of London to a small farm on the coast, five miles from Eastbourne. In a career which had frequently astonished me, this had perhaps surprised me most. *How will a man like Holmes survive in the peace and quiet of the countryside?* I had thought. *How on earth will he bear it?*

As I had suspected, Holmes did not retire completely. I knew of some of his cases – and I was privileged to act as participant and chronicler for several. However, there were others, brought to Holmes by his brother Mycroft on behalf of the British government, about which Holmes remained obstinately silent.

Following the Great War, Holmes finally settled into a more traditional retirement. I had expected to receive a letter, or perhaps even a telegram – Holmes's preferred method of communication – saying that he was desperately bored. When none arrived, I am afraid I assumed pride would not allow him to admit his mistake.

Time wore on, and from what I could tell, Holmes seemed content. He had more-or-less exchanged detection for beekeeping, of all things, and while he still maintained a laboratory in an outbuilding of the farm, and travelled to London for concerts and the opera, I couldn't understand what had made him stay in Sussex more often than not. Sherlock Holmes belonged in London. London belonged to Sherlock Holmes. Yet when I visited him, he showed me round his kingdom with pride and good humour. It made no sense to me.

The train slowed and I looked at my watch. According to the timetable, we would soon arrive at Eastbourne. I stood, put *Bulldog Drummond* in my pocket, and reached into the overhead rack for my bag.

"Here, let me," said the young man sitting opposite, and swung the bag down as if it were empty.

"Thank you very much," I said, feeling slightly aggrieved.

The train eased to a stop. Holmes was on the platform. He was as neat as ever, though in country tweeds instead of town tailoring, and his figure was still as upright. I resisted the urge to knock on the window and wave, and concentrated on getting myself safely onto the platform.

"Watson!" Holmes cried, hurrying forward. "You are exactly on time."

"Well, the train is," I said, smiling.

He had already taken possession of my free hand and was pumping it up and down. "How are you? How was the trip?"

"You speak as if I had made a great expedition, rather than a comparatively short journey."

"A short journey may still be an upheaval. I brought the trap, since I thought you might not welcome such a long walk with your luggage. A useful lad is holding my horse." As the trap trundled along, I had a chance to observe my friend. His hair was considerably greyer than when I had last seen him, and his face more lined.

As we approached the turning for the farm, Holmes pointed at a young man on a bicycle riding ahead of us. "That's the second post," he said. He caught up with the bicycle. "Anything for the farm?" he asked.

"There's a letter for you, sir. From America."

"In that case, I'll pull up." Holmes tugged on the reins and the horse slowed to a walk, then stopped. The postman handed Holmes a thick envelope, touched his cap, and went on his way.

Chapter II

"Aren't you going to open it?" I asked.

"Oh, it can wait until we're inside," said Holmes, pocketing the envelope.

"It may be a case . . . ." The words were out before I realised. I blame my choice of reading.

Holmes laughed. "I shall be surprised if it is. No, it is a missive from a good friend, with an enclosure to stimulate the brain." My confusion must have shown in my face, because Holmes laughed again. "I have bewildered you, Watson! My American acquaintance knows my liking for a particular type of puzzle called a *word-cross*, or sometimes a *crossword*, which appears in *The New York World*. He saves them and sends me a batch every so often. This will be a new consignment."

"Oh." I felt disappointed, and hoped Holmes couldn't detect it. I have always thought word puzzles childish things.

Holmes stopped the trap outside the stables. "Now, once I have handed Pegasus to the stable lad, tea should be ready in the house. Then I have new bees to show you. I experimented with cross breeding over the last year, and my latest bees are producing an impressive yield of honey."

Three hours later, I was contented and rather sleepy. We had undertaken a tour of the farm and the hives, followed by an hour's walk to the excellent Tiger Inn in East Dean. There we had eaten a most satisfying lunch, accompanied by more than one pint of exceptionally good ale. I must admit I wondered how, with such an establishment nearby, Holmes managed to stay as trim as he did. I had to ask him to slow down a little on the return trip.

Holmes slackened his pace. "We shall settle ourselves in front of the fire," he said. "If you take a nap, I shall not be offended in the slightest."

"I fear I may fall asleep," I admitted. "That portion of steak-and-kidney pie was gargantuan."

Holmes opened the door of the farmhouse and led the way to the snug sitting room. He stirred the fire 'til it blazed, then invited me to one of the wing-back armchairs. "If you wish, I can show you the puzzles which arrived this morning. The concept is simple, but the clues are often cryptic."

"Still searching for clues?" I said, with a smile.

408

"In a manner of speaking, I suppose I am." Holmes opened the envelope and extracted a single sheet of notepaper and some newspaper clippings. "As I suspected, a new batch of crossword puzzles. Perhaps the British newspapers will pick up the idea one day."

He passed me a clipping and I stared at it. The puzzle was a grid of blank squares, some with numbers in the corner. A few squares were blacked out. Beside the grid was a numbered list.

"Those are the clues," said Holmes. "Each describes a word, and many of the words in the grid intersect with each other, which is another sort of clue." He skimmed the accompanying note and his brow furrowed slightly. "Apparently, I shall particularly enjoy one of the puzzles. Number 221."

"221? How appropriate!"

Holmes riffled through the puzzles in his hand and pulled one out. "Here it is." He scanned it. "Oh, I see. I'm not sure *enjoy* is the term I would use. My vanity is certainly appeased, however. One-down . . . ." He thrust it under my nose.

"'One down'?"

"Yes. Read the clue." He tapped the paper.

I put on my spectacles: *The greatest detective (8,6)*, I read. "Good Heavens."

I glanced at Holmes, who looked rather pleased. Then he frowned.

"You can't possibly be dissatisfied. To be named as the greatest detective by a puzzle-setter who lives on the other side of the world – that is fame indeed."

"No, it isn't that. May I?" Holmes stretched out his hand for the puzzle. "One moment." He went to the bureau, found a pencil, and wrote rapidly. After a minute, he paused and rubbed his forehead.

"What is it?" I asked. "Has one of the clues stumped you?"

"Far from it." Holmes held up the completed puzzle. "Someone is in danger."

Chapter III

I gaped at him. "What do you mean?"

"Precisely what I say. Look at this." He crouched beside me and pointed to the puzzle. "You see the word *confinement*? The clue relating to it is *A laborious process producing a happy event*, but of course confinement has another, familiar meaning. Then the three letters on the first line of the grid spell *SOS*. A cry for help. The reason for my inclusion in the puzzle, I suspect, is so that someone will call my attention to it. This sounds very much like an abduction."

I peered at the puzzle and pinched the bridge of my nose. "Are you sure about this?"

My brain was whirling. Could Holmes be right? Or was he at the stage of life where he saw potential crimes in the most innocent things? In my medical practice, I had known elderly people become scared almost of their own shadows, growing increasingly suspicious of their closest friends and relatives, to the point where they trusted nobody but themselves. It had made me determined to continue getting out in the world, keeping abreast of modern times, and think the best of my acquaintance. Holmes, shut up in the countryside and alone but for his housekeeper, didn't have the same resources. Was Holmes's assertion merely an attempt, driven by my presence, to recapture former glories?

"Three clues in a crossword puzzle may not seem much upon which to build a hypothesis, but I have conjured more from a great deal less." Holmes's tone was reasonable, patient, though with the note of irritation I remembered from our Baker Street days. "Besides, something about this puzzle feels . . . not quite right. I'm well acquainted with the puzzles Sphinx produces – "

"'Sphinx'?" I began to wonder whether I had fallen asleep and this was a most convoluted dream.

"Sphinx is the pseudonym of this particular puzzle setter. She is my favourite, and while this puzzle is mostly characteristic of her, some of the clues are rather elementary. Normally, she is consistently brilliant. On occasion, she has even stumped me with a clue or two."

I blinked. "Holmes, if this puzzle setter uses a pseudonym, how do you know she is a woman?"

Holmes smiled. "It is a hunch. Sphinx is clearly intelligent, and she has hit on using one of her puzzles to reach me. Presumably, these puzzles are currently her only way to communicate with the outside world."

"That is clever," I said.

"Indeed. The disadvantage – for her and for us – is that presumably her captor will check her puzzles and solutions before she sends them to the newspaper, and so she is forced to be even more cryptic than usual. Another obstacle is that we have no way of telling which clues are significant and which exist to make up the grid, so to speak."

I studied the puzzle. Despite my spectacles, the pencilled letters seemed blurred. I cursed that last pint of ale. "Perhaps when I'm recovered from lunch . . . ."

"There is no time for recovery. Every hour – no, every minute – counts. We have no idea of who Sphinx is, where she is, or who is keeping her captive." He checked the date at the top of the scrap of paper. "Moreover, this puzzle is over two weeks old – and that doesn't take into account the time lapse between its composition and its inclusion in the newspaper." He met my eyes. "Who knows what has befallen Sphinx since she penned these clues?"

Chapter IV

I stared at Holmes. "You mean – it may already be too late?"

"I sincerely hope not. Disregarding for a moment the barriers in our way, one element is in our favour: Sphinx's captor must be planning to keep her for some time, as he is allowing her to produce and send crossword puzzles. Presumably this also means she is in reasonably good health and supplied with food and water. And there is the possibility of more clues. Sphinx cannot make them too obvious or her captor will spot them, so there is every chance she has put some in later puzzles."

Holmes picked up the rest of the scraps of newspaper, waved them at me, then leafed through them. "We have another six puzzles. The one I solved, *221*, is in the middle. I shall examine the three puzzles which follow."

His gaze darted about each puzzle in turn. "I don't see any obvious clues to Sphinx's identity or location, but here is a clue: *He aspired to a jumble. Aspired* is an anagram of *despair*."

I considered this. "Oh yes, so it is."

"That clue is ten-down. Ten-down on the first puzzle was *confinement*. So perhaps if we check ten-down on each puzzle, we shall find other significant clues. But I'm getting ahead of myself."

"You are?" I murmured.

"Yes. A woman is in danger. It is our duty to alert her employer."

"But . . . that's an American newspaper."

"Yes, what of it?" Holmes was already at the door. "We can send a telegram. The post office in the village is open until five and it is now – " He consulted his watch. " – ten to three. It will take us no more than twenty minutes at a decent pace." He smiled. "Time to walk off lunch." Then his expression became solicitous. "Unless you would rather stay here? You look very comfortable."

"No, I shall come too, if you give me a moment." With a Herculean effort, I levered myself out of the chair and pulled down the points of my waistcoat. Despite my disinclination to move, I was not about to let Holmes send who-knew-what across the Atlantic. Someone had to keep him in check.

It took us slightly more than twenty minutes to reach the post office. Holmes had an annoying habit of striding ahead, then waiting for me to

411

catch up. "I am normally a fast walker," I said, in my defence. "Pastry is my downfall."

"We are coming into the village," said Holmes, from some yards ahead. "Do not forget, Watson, we are five hours ahead of the east coast of America. They will have plenty of time to take action."

The post office was a long, low cottage with whitewashed walls and a thatched roof. Inside, it was cluttered with racks of greetings cards, postcards, and trinkets. To be honest, I was surprised it had a telegraph at all.

At the counter, an elderly lady was gathering her belongings and taking her time about it. Holmes cleared his throat, and she turned and glared at him. "What's your hurry, sir?"

"I must send a wire to America," Holmes replied.

She squinted at him. "What do you want to do that for?"

"I have my reasons," said Holmes. "Now, if you wouldn't mind."

Grumbling under her breath, she moved off.

"A wire, eh, Mr. Holmes?" said the clerk. He was a plump man, perhaps in his mid-thirties, with thinning hair and a pointed nose which looked as if it enjoyed poking into people's business. I dreaded to think what he would make of Holmes's wire. He fetched a telegraph form and slid it over the counter.

"Thank you, Mr. Peasgood." Holmes took out his pen and wrote rapidly:

> *Suspect contributor Sphinx kidnapped. Alert police. Will wire more information soonest.*
>
> *Sherlock Holmes*

He handed the form to Peasgood, who scanned it and whistled. "That'll cost you a pretty penny."

"The cost is immaterial," said Holmes. He gave Peasgood a pound note.

"Whatever you say, sir. Will you wait for a reply?"

"Please."

Peasgood gave Holmes his change, then opened a door which creaked abominably and took the form into a back room. Three minutes later, he emerged. "It's on its way, sir."

"Excellent."

Holmes moved away from the counter and examined a rack of postcards. "It is approaching half-past-ten in New York," he murmured. I

412

could tell from the way he barely glanced at a postcard before replacing it that he was full of nervous energy.

It seemed an age until we heard the creak of the door, then Peasgood clearing his throat. "Mr. Holmes? You have a reply."

Holmes strode to the counter and almost snatched it from him. I looked over his shoulder.

Assure you Sphinx safe and well. Regards.

"They are very sure of their facts," I ventured.

"I am very sure of something, too," Holmes said grimly. "It is a certainty that I shall be forced to investigate this case alone."

Chapter V

Suddenly, Holmes's lowering expression was replaced with a delighted smile. "No, I am not alone! My friend Watson is here."

"Um, well, if I can be of service . . ." I replied, and I fear that I blushed.

"You always help, Watson, in your own inimitable way."

"Not the reply you wanted, sir?" said Peasgood, whom I now disliked intensely.

"Not yet," said Holmes.

"Was it about your bees, Mr. Holmes? I believe they have great ranches in America where they raise cattle in their thousands, so they must know a thing or two." I wondered how the clerk could possibly think the message Holmes had sent concerned his bees. Then again, perhaps it was for the best that Peasgood had paid no attention to the wire.

"I'm not sure one can apply the same farming methods to bees as to cows, Mr. Peasgood," Holmes replied. "Good day to you."

"And you, sir." But Holmes was already heading for the door.

"The newspaper is sure Sphinx is safe," he said, as soon as we were clear of the village. "So her puzzles are being sent in a timely manner. But perhaps, like my American acquaintance, she sends her puzzles in batches. In any case, presumably the puzzles are coming from the same place." He mused. "Unless she has been forced to write a note accounting for the change." He huffed out a sigh.

I stomped alongside him, uncertain what to say. Indeed, I wasn't sure what I could contribute, save to act as a sounding board for Holmes's theories, despite his claim that I always helped. "Perhaps you might try your former method?" I asked, somewhat timidly.

Holmes gave me an enquiring look. "What would that be?"

"Why, when you had a case to solve you would often shut yourself in a room, sit on a pile of cushions on the floor, and smoke until you had arrived at the solution."

"Oh yes, so I did." Holmes considered my suggestion as he strode along. "If I tried that now, I would be most uncomfortable. For one thing, getting myself to the floor and up again isn't as easy as it once was, and if I smoke too much these days I become nauseous. I know what I *will* do."

"Oh yes? What is that?"

"I shall go and tell the bees."

I goggled at him. "I beg your pardon?"

"Watson, you must have heard of the old country custom of telling the bees your news. Usually it relates to births, marriages, and deaths, but I wouldn't wish to jeopardise the honey."

I accompanied my friend home feeling rather vexed. Surely I was more use than a hive of bees, however productive.

When we reached the farm, Holmes skirted the farmhouse and made his way to the squat hives that stood at the far end of a field, against the hedge. He knocked on the first one. "I have news," he announced.

I couldn't help rolling my eyes. The great detective – the greatest detective, according to Sphinx – had fallen victim to a foolish country superstition.

"I'm investigating the kidnapping of a crossword setter in America," he said, to the hive. "The only clues I have are within seven crossword puzzles which are at least a fortnight old."

I rubbed my forehead. When Holmes put it like that, the case seemed absolutely impossible.

"I shall do my best to solve the case, with the help of my good friend Watson, but it is perhaps one of the most challenging problems I have faced. I thought you should know." With that, he strode towards the farm.

"Shouldn't you tell all the hives?" I asked.

"There are limits, and I'm not in the habit of repeating myself. I am sure the bees will share the news if they are minded to." He took a few steps in silence. "Strange, how they always keep to the same hive. When I was breeding different strains of bee, I feared they would become hopelessly mingled and thwart my plans, but that hasn't been the case – "

He stopped in the middle of the field. "Watson, I am an idiot. We shall assume Sphinx lives in New York City, since her puzzles appear in a New York paper. People live on top of each other there, sometimes literally. Sphinx cannot be imprisoned at home. Her neighbours would have noticed something – no sign of her despite lights and noises, or someone else going in and out. A companion would report her absence, so she must live alone." Then he sighed, and began walking again. "It is a

414

start, I suppose. Our only recourse is to examine the puzzles further." And he increased his pace until I was left in his wake.

Chapter VI

At the farmhouse, I resumed my seat by the fire while Holmes completed the rest of the puzzles. "Now we possess all the information," he said. "And yet . . . ."

"Is there anything I can do to help?" I asked. "I feel useless just sitting here."

Holmes looked round at me. "As a matter of fact, yes. Could you find Mrs. Doughty and ask her to bring some strong coffee? You may have tea, if you prefer."

Mrs. Doughty was Holmes's cook-housekeeper, a stout, no-nonsense, elderly party very different from Mrs. Hudson at Baker Street. She didn't live in, but arrived sometime after breakfast each day and left as soon as she had washed the dinner things. I wondered how Holmes put up with her. For one thing, he seemed to have to keep her happy, rather than the other way round.

"Of course." I rose and went to do Holmes's bidding.

I eventually tracked Mrs. Doughty down to her sitting room, where she was ensconced in an armchair, knitting a sock. She listened to my request with forbearance. "I'll see what I can do, Dr. Watson."

"Thank you," I said, and left before I said anything which might annoy her and thereby cause the delay of our refreshments.

I returned to the sitting room. "I have ordered – What on earth are you doing?"

In my absence, Holmes had torn some sheets of paper into smaller squares and written a word or two on each. He was now in the process of moving them from a small table to the hearthrug. "I am setting out the clues as best I can. Or what I think are the clues." He knelt, grimacing, to place another piece of paper. I saw no order to them at all.

I watched Holmes scribble and place, and scribble and place, and none of it made any sense to me. I didn't recall him doing anything like this in his cases in Baker Street, so many years ago. Then again, no case had resembled this one.

"This may be significant," he murmured, and put down the word *Hawk*. "I feel it is, though I don't know why."

"Another hunch?" I asked.

"Perhaps."

By the time Mrs. Doughty entered with a laden tea tray, Holmes was kneeling on a hearthrug liberally scattered with scraps of paper. "What is this, Mr. Holmes?" she said, placing the tray on a side table. "Why are you making such a mess?"

"Mrs. Doughty, you are standing on a potential clue," Holmes replied. "Please take a step to the left."

"I'll do no such thing," she replied. "You, a grown man, playing with bits of paper like a child! When I come in here next, I expect this gone." And with a final dismissive snort, she withdrew.

"There is a footprint on '*Dakota*' now," said Holmes, picking up a piece of paper and brushing at it.

"Does it matter?" I asked.

"Of course it matters! I'm trying to solve a crime. I cannot have people casually stepping on the evidence." He closed his eyes for a moment. "Mrs. Doughty is so annoyed with me that she hasn't stayed to do the honours." He got slowly to his feet and poured himself a cup of black coffee. "Tea for you?"

"Please."

"The way you usually take it?"

"If you would."

Holmes handed me a cup of tea. "To an observer, this must seem ridiculous," he muttered. "Moving pieces of paper around a rug in the hope that something will strike a chord. But how else can I proceed, given the nature of the case? Someone has requested my help, and what can I do but try my best?"

"Yes, indeed," I said, in a tone I hoped was soothing. "That is all anyone can do."

Holmes looked sadly at the floor. "I'm afraid this isn't a very entertaining visit for you either."

The clock on the mantelpiece chimed. "Three-quarters-of-the-hour," murmured Holmes, still gazing at the rug. "A quarter-to-five. Even if we hurried, we would be hard pressed to reach the post office by five o'clock, assuming we had anything useful to put in a wire." He closed his eyes and passed his hand over his brow.

Chapter VII

"Holmes, it isn't so bad," I said. "Don't forget, these puzzles are two weeks old. One more night, or even two, may not matter."

"Or it may be vital," Holmes muttered. Then he looked up. "Wait – When we work this out, we can simply travel to Eastbourne and wire from there. We must put ourselves into Sphinx's mind and see if we can crack the code."

"This case reminds me of the adventure of the dancing men," I said. "You know, where little figures were chalked in different places, and each pose corresponded to a letter."

"That was much easier," said Holmes. "A simple matter of substitution, assisted by the normal frequency of the letters of the alphabet. This is far more complicated, and made harder because Sphinx has to conceal her message. And though I broke the code of the dancing men, the case had a tragic ending."

"Yet you have deduced that Sphinx's captor was planning to keep her for some time," I persisted.

"That is so," Holmes said, slowly. "Tell me, Watson: If you were imprisoned and you could only communicate in a way that had to seem innocent, what would you do?"

"To raise the alarm, you mean?"

"Yes, exactly."

I pursed my lips and thought this over. "I suppose . . . I would include something normal, but unusual for me to say."

"Yes!" cried Holmes. "That's it! Now, how can Sphinx do that in a puzzle?" He sprang up and paced in the manner I remembered so well from our days of sharing living quarters. "She would . . . She would set an easy clue, or perhaps – she would make an error!" He wheeled round. "Watson, you have saved the day. At last, we have a way forward." He knelt on the floor and began moving the pieces of paper around.

"Holmes, what are you doing?"

"I'm sorting the wheat from the chaff. Namely, picking out the clues which are odd, or simple, or which may be a hint." As he spoke, he was picking up pieces of paper, glancing at them, and either consigning them to a pile at the side or replacing them. "There, that is considerably tidier."

"I wouldn't go that far," I said, regarding the confetti of clues on the rug.

"Watson, you must trust the process, however strange it appears. We have made room to take advantage of our new insight." He sat in his armchair and looked through the puzzles again. "Hmm . . . I believe we can add one or two more to our collection." He tore another sheet of paper into four and wrote a word on each piece, then put them with the other scraps.

I peered at the arrangement on the floor. "Why have you added these?"

"Some simply because they are in position ten-down, as two helpful words have already occupied that position. I have also added *seventeen*, the clue for which was *the atomic number of chlorine*. A numeral could be significant."

"Of course."

"As for simple clues, we have *hawk*, for which the clue was *bird of prey*, *bans*, where the clue was *forbids*, and *rustle*, for which the clue was *the sound of dry leaves*."

"I see what you mean," I said. "You mentioned errors?"

"One clue fits that category: *A state where the information is the reverse of all right*."

I frowned. "I beg your pardon?"

"*Dakota*. Information is '*data*', and '*O.K.*' is a slang expression broadly meaning *all right*. But there is no state called *Dakota*. There *is* North Dakota and South Dakota."

"Good Heavens." I was beginning to revise my opinion that word games were for children.

"So, an error. Unless . . . ." Holmes smacked the table so hard that I jumped. "I am a fool, Watson, an utter fool. I know where she is!"

"You do?"

"Yes. She is still in New York, in the Dakota apartment building by Central Park. I took tea there once in 1913, when I was engaged by the resident of the penthouse suite. It is well appointed – luxurious, even."

"She isn't locked in a cellar, then."

"Far from it. So, the clues we have are *confinement, despair, Sherlock Holmes* – " He smiled briefly. " – "*SOS, seventeen, Dakota, hawk, bans*, and *rustle*."

"*Bans* . . ." I said, meditatively. "Is she forbidden from doing something?"

"Escaping, presumably," said Holmes, "but that is obvious. *Bans* . . . *bans* . . . *Wedding banns!* Not that calling the banns is usual in America. They use marriage licences . . . ." His voice died away. "A forced marriage?"

"Oh no!" I exclaimed.

"It is coming together now," said Holmes. "Sphinx is a clever, independent woman who lives alone in New York. She has an active social life. She drinks martinis at the Hotel Knickerbocker." He tapped the word *martini* on the puzzle he was holding. "Given the learning she displays, I assume a college education, so her family is presumably well to do. She is being held, possibly at the Dakota building, by a man who wants to force her into marrying him. But we still don't know who she is. I wonder . . . ." He jumped out of his chair. "Watson, we are going for a walk."

"Another one?"

"Yes, to visit the comprehensive library of my friend, Stackhurst. He may have what we seek."

Chapter VIII

I peered at the brass plate beside the front door. "*The Gables*," I read. "Is this the school?"

Holmes nodded. "A coaching establishment for young gentlemen. Stackhurst runs the place, and he won't mind a visit at any time." He rang the bell.

Within two minutes a familiar figure advanced to meet us. "Holmes! What brings you here?"

"Good evening, Stackhurst," Holmes replied. "I shall be blunt: I must use your library. You remember Watson. We're looking for society news – American in particular."

To his credit, Stackhurst took Holmes's barrage of information in his stride. "We take *The Illustrated London News* and *The Sketch*, and *The Times* has society news."

"Excellent. Come on, Watson." And Holmes led the way to the library as if he lived at The Gables.

"Would you like tea?" asked Stackhurst.

"No tea," Holmes said, waving away the idea. "Time is of the essence. I shall tell you all about it later."

"Of course you will," said Stackhurst, chuckling, and left us at the library door.

The library was a busy room, rather than an impressive one. A few young men were working at the long table which ran along the centre. One looked up, and said, "Good evening, Mr. Holmes."

"Good evening, Frith," Holmes replied.

"You are known here," I observed.

"At Stackhurst's request, I occasionally give talks on matters I know something of," said Holmes. He scanned the room. "The periodicals are over there."

He marched to a bookcase which contained leather-bound volumes gilt-stamped with the names of magazines. On the bottom shelf, box files contained the most recent additions. Holmes found the box for *The Sketch*, took it to the table, and tipped out the contents. "Watson, we are seeking promising young ladies and gentlemen in New York." He divided the magazines into two stacks.

The young men had given up any pretence of work and were openly staring. I decided burying myself in my task was the best option.

I have never been much interested in gossip about the upper echelons of society. I turned the pages, searching for couples and groups in evening dress and mentions of American states or cities. Fortunately, there were only one or two such pages in each magazine, usually focusing on overdressed middle-aged women with improbable hairstyles.

I sighed and reached for yet another magazine. I riffled through the pages and –

A young woman looked straight at me, smiling. She was sitting at a table, cocktail glass in hand. Her short hair curled around her face, and she wore a simple sleeveless dress with a long string of pearls. She was dwarfed by the young man sitting beside her, awkward in his suit.

I read the caption: *Sophia Hawke and Leo Russell at the Capricorn Club, January 7.*

"Holmes!" I cried and pointed at the page. "We've found her!"

"We have!" cried Holmes. "*You* have! Come on!"

"Where are we going?"

Holmes was already halfway to the door. "To knock up Peasgood. Frith, tidy that mess for me – there's a good man."

Holmes banged on the door of the post office. "Come on, man," he muttered. "You can't be in bed, it's barely seven o'clock."

"He may be eating his dinner," I said. "Or having a drink in the inn."

"Good point. Would you mind walking over and seeing if he's there?"

But then footsteps approached the door, accompanied by muttering. The door swung open and Peasgood stared at us. His collar and tie had disappeared, and his shirt was unbuttoned at the neck. "What's all the fuss about? We're closed."

"I am aware of that," said Holmes. "However, I must send an urgent telegram to America."

"*Another* one?"

"Yes, another one. I am attempting to prevent a crime."

The word *crime* had an electric effect on Peasgood. "Well!" he said. "You'd best come in." He switched on the electric lights, and then went behind the counter and passed Holmes a telegraph form.

"Who will you wire?" I asked.

"A friend of mine at the New York City Police Headquarters in Manhattan," said Holmes, as he scribbled *240 Centre Street.*

I stared at him. "How do you have a friend there?"

"Buffalo is not so far from New York by train," Holmes remarked with an enigmatic smile. He wrote:

> *Suspected abduction. Sophia Hawke held at Dakota building, possibly apartment seventeen, by Leo Russell. Urgent action required.*
>
> *Holmes*

420

He handed the telegram to Peasgood, who goggled at it. "I'll get this sent right away, sir. Will you wait for a reply?"

"I think I had better."

An hour later, we were still waiting. Mrs. Peasgood had provided us with mugs of tea and bread and cheese, but I did little more than nibble at mine.

We were accommodated with stools in the sacred back room of the post office. Every so often, one of us glanced at the telegraph machine, but I recalled that a watched pot never boils and kept my eyes sternly averted.

"What time is it in New York now?" asked Peasgood.

"Around three in the afternoon," said Holmes. "I hope that no news is good new – "

He was interrupted by the telegraph machine. Peasgood slid off his stool and went to look. "It's for you!" He took a piece of paper and began transcribing the message:

> *Couple found. Apprehended entering St. John's Church. Russell arrested. Will write with particulars. Thanks for tip.*
>
> *Fitzgerald*

Holmes closed his eyes and his shoulders relaxed. "The case is over, Watson," he said. "We have saved her."

Chapter IX

A few weeks after my visit to Holmes, I was surprised to receive a thick envelope addressed in Holmes's handwriting. He was an irregular correspondent at best. I ripped it open eagerly and found a single sheet of notepaper and another envelope.

Dear Watson,

> *I received the enclosed yesterday and thought you might wish to peruse it. Perhaps you can bring it back on your next visit, which I hope will be both less eventful, and much sooner.*
>
> *At last I know why the word "Hawk" perturbed me so in the crossword puzzle. I was returning to the house following an evening walk a few days ago when I saw a moth attracted to the light shining through the kitchen window. That was the*

clue I should have picked up. There is a hawk moth, *you see, but its other name is the* sphinx moth. *We have solved the riddle of the Sphinx at last.*

Sincerely,
Sherlock Holmes

My mind whirring, I opened the second envelope and drew out a few sheets covered in a firm, flowing hand.

Dear Mr. Holmes,

I can never thank you enough for what you did. I hope you don't mind my direct appeal to you via The New York World. *I was at my wits' end, and you were my best shot. I guess I owe you an explanation.*

Ancient history. I grew up in a well-to-do, stuffy family in upstate New York, managed to get away as far as Vassar College, and while I was there, convinced The New York World *to hire me as a puzzle setter. With the money that brought after college, I was able to move to the city and live the life I dreamed of.*

I met Leo Russell just over a year ago, at a bar downtown. I was with a group of friends and he charmed his way into our circle. I admit it now: I fell for him hard. He'd had to make his own way in the world, which I admired. He was generous and fun to be with. I didn't think beyond that.

Then I came across something which made me think twice. I daresay it'll come out at the trial. I told Leo I never wanted to see him again. That was six months ago. I did my best to forget Leo, and I thought I had.

I usually compile my puzzles at the New York Public Library. On evening, I left at my usual time, and I was heading for the subway when someone pulled me into an alley. It was Leo, and two minutes later we were in a taxicab. He said he only wanted to talk, and like a fool I listened.

Leo took me to his apartment at the Dakota. There he told me that he'd crossed a few too many people and his business was on the skids. He asked me to request a loan from my family, pretending the money was for me. I refused, and he said "We'll do this the hard way, then."

422

That was the beginning of my captivity, locked in Leo's suite at the Dakota. He never laid a finger on me – he said that wasn't his intention – but he knew if we were married, I'd give in to his financial demands so that my family wouldn't be shamed. He figured I'd crack eventually. And divorce wouldn't be easy – not without a scandal.

I spent most of the first week cursing my stupidity. For a smart woman, I'd got myself into quite a situation. At first, I refused food and drink, partly to punish myself. Then I realised I had more chance alive than dead, and only my brain would deliver me from this mess.

I convinced Leo I had to keep sending crossword puzzles or the newspaper would come looking for me. When I noticed I was compiling puzzle 221, I thought of you and wondered if somehow I could get a message to you. I sneaked a few clues into that puzzle and the ones following. It allowed me to hope.

I'd assumed Leo would leave the building to post the puzzles, giving me a chance of escape, but he got one of the Dakota's staff to do it. He never left the apartment: He didn't trust me an inch – which was fair, because I didn't trust him either.

I don't remember much of the day when it ended. My tea tasted odd that morning and I felt sleepy, but Leo said we were taking a trip. I tried to reply but the words came out wrong. I stood up and the room spun. There was a taxicab, then Leo pulled me into a church. He had the marriage licence in his hand and I was too weak to resist. We'd just reached the altar rail when someone shouted "Police!" Leo dropped my arm and ran, but two officers took him down before he reached the door.

Thank you so much for your help, Mr. Holmes. I hope I didn't disturb you too much in your retirement, and I also hope you will tell Dr. Watson the story. I would rather not have to appear at the trial, but if I must, I shall. I've enjoyed being Sphinx, and puzzling my fellow Americans over breakfast anonymously, but perhaps it is time to be myself.

Yours sincerely,
Sophia Hawke

I smiled as I refolded the letter. There was no need for Holmes to tell me anything about the case. I had helped to solve it!

423

I reread Holmes's note – *your next visit, which I hope will be both less eventful and much sooenr* – and laughed aloud. I was very much looking forward to my next visit to the Sussex Downs. For one thing, my worries over Holmes growing old had vanished. If anything, I would struggle to keep up with him.

The Case of the
One-Armed Crabbe
by Roger Riccard

Chapter I

It was the end of the *"worst of times"*, if I may borrow a phrase from Charles Dickens. The Great War was over at last. But Europe had been decimated by over twenty-million deaths counting military and civilian personnel. In addition to those killed by the horrible weapons of war, some two-and-a-half-million fell victim to the Spanish Flu Pandemic of 1918. The total figures may never be known, but the last estimate I'd heard was that, all totaled, over five-per-cent of the European population, much of it in the prime of youth, was wiped out in four-and-a-half years.

The "Spanish Flu" is, of course, a misnomer. At the time it occurred, Spain was neutral while most of Europe was at war. Thus it was the only nation reporting deaths caused by the pandemic. None of the warring countries wanted their enemies to know what losses they were taking to this terrible disease. It would all come out eventually, but for Sherlock Holmes and me, it was quite evident. We both knew folk who had succumbed to this blight.

It was now summer in the Year of our Lord 1920. Only two months before, I had joined Holmes on a commission from his brother Mycroft to examine the security measures at Checquers, [1] the new country home of the Prime Minister. I had been visiting him at the time at his Sussex bee farm. Now I was back in London, dividing my time between organising my old case notes on the adventures Holmes and I had shared, and making house calls upon disabled war veterans whom I had helped to treat upon their return from what would hopefully be the War to End all Wars.

One such patient was Sergeant Thomas Crabbe, a member of an army tank crew tasked with capturing the Amiens railway line stretching between Mericourt and Hangest in August 1918. [2] During this intense action, Crabbe's tank became disabled, and his crew had to abandon it. While continuing to fight on foot, he was severely wounded, which resulted in the amputation of his left arm.

Like much of my work with the wounded during the war, my regimen with him had consisted of monitoring his surgical healing and advising him on physical exercises to help him adjust to civilian life with one arm. He had recently advised me he was moving to Eagleton Park near

Ramsgate. The village had suffered severe damage when a zeppelin, as part of a group of airships sent to destroy Ramsgate Marina, was forced off course by British fighter pilots. The Germans dropped their ordinance before they crashed, destroying several homes and killing multiple civilians in the area.

After the war, an enterprising Dutch businessman named Jacob Krane had bought up much of the damaged housing, repaired the homes, and was offering the first choice of purchase to British war veterans at substantially low prices and interest rates. While the Dutch were officially neutral during the war, Krane recognised that the multiple German violations of that neutrality, such as sinking Dutch ships, would have been even worse had not England and her allies intervened. This project was his way of showing gratitude to the brave English soldiers and sailors.

At least this was how Crabbe had explained it to me. He was thrilled that he had been accepted to become one of the new residents, with his army pension able to meet the relatively low payments. He had no family, so moving wasn't an issue.

He had first heard of this project from a fellow wounded veteran, Lieutenant Harvey Masters, who had lost a leg in the war. He shared the news with several of his wounded comrades at a club where they gathered. It was one of the few places where they weren't looked upon with pity by the civilian populace.

At one meeting, Masters introduced Krane, who spoke of his sympathy for their sacrifice and the gratitude he was able to express on behalf of the Dutch people. "I have already relocated three other wounded veterans, and Lt. Masters will be the fourth after he comes out to inspect the properties tomorrow. There is housing for six more if you qualify."

He passed out applications and advised them, "If you are chosen, you will be invited to view the properties. Upon coming to an agreement on which home you can afford, you will need to put down a minimum deposit of one-hundred pounds on the spot to reserve it. Of course, the more you can deposit, the lower your payments will be. The outright purchase prices range from nine-hundred pounds to fifteen-hundred pounds. We are also offering a below-market interest rate of two-point-five or three-per-cent, depending on the amount you need to borrow."

Masters had recently moved to Eagleton Park, and even sent Crabbe a telegram advising him how wonderful a place it was. Soon Crabbe received news that he had qualified and he should come down to Ramsgate, where Krane would take him out to Eagleton Park to pick out a home to his liking. At that point, and not before, he could reserve his choice for a one-hundred-pound deposit.

Chapter II

I was very happy for him. So often our wounded veterans are forgotten and find themselves in dire straits. The suicide rate among these heroic warriors who sacrificed so much was intolerable because they frequently felt abandoned by their families and their country. This windfall would give him a fair chance at a decent life.

Imagine my surprise then, when four days after he had informed me of his move, Sergeant Crabbe suddenly appeared in my surgery. Haggard and hurting with three days' growth of beard upon his face, he staggered in and likely would have fallen, had he not the use of a walking stick.

My nurse, recognising his condition, immediately escorted him into my consulting room where he collapsed onto the couch. He did not appear injured, but his breathing was uneven, and his voice hoarse. The nurse quickly brought water while I checked his pulse and temperature. "What's happened to you, Sergeant?" I asked. "Are you injured?"

He shook his head, unable to speak clearly until he took a drink of water. At last, he caught his breath and gasped out a few words. "I've been on the run, Doctor. No time for food or drink. I needed to get to you. I need your friend, Mr. Holmes."

I ordered my nurse to prepare him some broth and bread and tried to keep him calm as he was suffering from shock and some nervous condition. "Holmes lives down in Sussex now. He rarely comes up to London anymore, and it will take time for him to get here, even if I can convince him. Tell me, Crabbe, what is it? Why do you need him?"

He took another drink of water, some spilling down his straggly-bearded chin with the effort. Then he looked me in the eye and said, "I've killed a man, Doctor, and I need Holmes to prove it was self-defence."

Chapter III

My nurse brought in the food just after he made this statement, so she did not hear it. I helped him to my writing table where he could sit and eat and then dismissed her, telling her all was under control.

As he spooned the beefy broth into his mouth, he spoke between gulps to answer my questions. "Start at the beginning," I said. "Who did you kill?"

"It was Jacob Krane, the lying bastard! And it was him or me! You've got to believe me, Doctor!"

After all my years of working with Holmes, I naturally grabbed pencil and paper and began writing down notes. "Where and when?" I asked.

"Two days ago in Ramsgate. Supposedly it was Eagleton Park – but there is no Eagleton Park, Dr. Watson. It was all a ruse!"

I tried to calm him down and said, "All right, take your time. Think carefully and give me the details. How did this come about? Weren't you supposed to go out to Eagleton Park with him to examine the homes he had available for disabled veterans?"

"Yes. All was going as planned. We rode down on the train together, and he hired a gig so we could drive out to this area where he had supposedly rebuilt homes damaged during the war. We had gone west from the station about five miles. The houses in that area are spread out with lawns and gardens surrounding each, and there is a small copse of trees that runs along the back of the neighbourhood.

"He chose to start the tour with the smallest of these houses since I had no family, and we entered a nice little single-storey home. It was freshly painted and quite roomy, having no furniture as yet. The rooms were of good size and well-situated to each other.

"He then took me to the backyard area, where there was a small outbuilding for a mews and the treeline beyond. I noticed a pile of firewood alongside it. This seemed quite convenient, though I don't know how much I will be able to adapt to chopping wood with one arm. Then I noticed something odd. There was a stick on the stack that was not a branch, but rather looked like a finished piece of wood. I stepped closer to get a good look. Just as I realized what it was, I heard a twig on the ground snap behind me. I turned in alarm at what I had seen and now was confronted with its implications. Krane was advancing quickly upon me with an upraised knife!"

"The devil you say!" I exclaimed.

"The devil indeed, Doctor! Fortunately, my combat training stood me in good stead. I ducked and rolled under the swipe of his knife and came up behind where I charged him as he turned back to face me and kicked him in the groin. I didn't catch him quite right though, and instead of going down breathless, it merely knocked him off balance and he fell to a knee. I took advantage of this though and quickly wrapped my empty sleeve around his neck. He slashed wildly with his knife, as you will note by the slices on my coat sleeves. But I had a decided advantage. Realizing this was going to be a fight to death, I tightened my grip on my chokehold until he breathed no more."

He was breathless from describing the fight, so I encouraged him to drink more water. As he did so, I asked him, "What did you see in the woodpile?"

He took a deep breath after a long draught of water and pointed to the walking stick on the floor by the sofa where it had fallen when he sat and replied, "That."

I retrieved it and brought it back to my seat. It was a finely turned oak walking stick with a brass anchor head handle and scrollwork extending from the top about a foot down its length. I noted the initials "*H.L.M.*" etched into the handle. "Who is *H.L.M.*?" I asked.

"Lt. Henry Louis Masters," replied the sergeant. "I recognised it immediately. The Lieutenant used that to help steady him on his artificial leg. He would never part with it. Krane must have thrown it onto the wood pile to be burned, but didn't get around to it before he brought me along. He must have realized his error by my reaction and that's why he attacked me when he did."

I pondered what my patient was telling me as he ate some more broth, dipping the bread into it. Finally, I leaned back to be less intimidating and recounted what he had said.

"So, it is your contention that Krane was running a plot to get disabled veterans to invest in a phoney property scheme, steal their deposit money, kill them, and then run the same scheme again with someone new."

He swallowed a mouthful of broth and replied, "That's all I can figure, Doctor. He probably sent the telegram in Master's name himself to make us think all was as advertised. He might well have only the one property instead of the several he claimed. He could show it over and over, overpowering the disabled clients and pocketing their money."

I nodded. "What did you do with Krane's body?"

"I dragged it to the mews. There was a bag of quicklime in there, so I shovelled some over him to hide the smell, then covered him with a tarp and closed the door."

"Why not go to the police and tell your story?"

Crabbe dabbed his mouth with a napkin and leaned forward to keep our conversation as quiet as possible, even though the door between us and my nurse was closed. He rubbed the growth of beard on his jaw and finally said, "I've been in trouble with the law before, Dr. Watson. Assault and battery during a bar fight three years ago. Put a fellow into the hospital – but I didn't kill him, I swear! Just laid him up for a while. The judge was not convinced that the witnesses were telling the truth about who started the fight, but he couldn't very well let me go. I got sentenced to three years of military service. You know how it was back then. The war was dragging on and there was a shortage of troops.

"Anyway, that's on my record, and I didn't want some police official using my past against me to try and make this into a murder case instead of the self-defence that it is. I knew Mr. Holmes would come at it with an

429

unprejudiced eye. That's why I snuck out of Ramsgate and came to find you in as roundabout a manner as I could, in case the body was discovered."

Chapter IV

I certainly sympathized with Sergeant Crabbe and had no reason to doubt his story. As it was late afternoon and I had no more patients scheduled for that day, I decided the safest course of action for the sergeant would be to let him stay in my spare room until I could convince Holmes to come up.

Fortunately, Crabbe and I were roughly the same size, so I provided him with a fresh change of clothes after he took a bath and a shave. While he was doing that, I got on the telephone and called my friend at his bee farm.

As these were the days of party lines where strangers could listen in on telephone calls, I used an old code which Holmes and I had developed while working the Millais forgery case several years before. [3]

Our conversation went something to the effect of:

"Holmes? Watson here."

"Watson, dear chap. How are you?"

"Oh, the usual. Just some issues with Doyle."

"I am sorry to hear that. Anything you need from me?"

"No, I can handle him. But I have been invited to partake in a golf tournament and need a partner. Are you up for a match?"

"I could come up for a couple of days. Will tomorrow be convenient?"

"That will be ideal. Could you contact Lestrade to see if he would like to join? Don't worry about a hotel, I can put you both up here."

"Splendid! I should arrive on the late morning train."

"Excellent. I shall see you then. *Au revoir*."

Of course, to anyone listening in, it all sounded innocent enough. But my use of the name "Doyle" meant I had a case for him. The reference to golf indicated it was for a client and not myself, and the invitation to stay with me advised him we would be traveling elsewhere. Including "Lestrade'" meant his Bassett hound, named after the Scotland Yard inspector. "*Au revoir*" was code for him to bring his revolver, just in case.

At 10:10 the next morning, Holmes arrived at my door, carpetbag in one hand and golf bag slung over his other shoulder with Lestrade on his leash. I welcomed him heartily and invited him into my parlour, where I introduced him to Sergeant Crabbe. Lestrade waddled over to the veteran, sniffed him, and then nuzzled his hand.

430

"Well that certainly counts in your favour, Sergeant," said Holmes, offering his own hand in greeting. "Lestrade is an excellent judge of character."

I had advised my nurse at the end of the previous day that she could have the next three days off, so we were quite alone to discuss matters and make our plans. I put down a water bowl for the hound and the three of us took up chairs around my fireplace to give the detective the details of Crabbe's case.

When Crabbe had finished his story, Holmes pursed his lips and slowly nodded. "I understand your reluctance to contact the police. They are often too quick to judge, But are you absolutely sure that Krane didn't have an accomplice? No one who might come looking for him?"

Crabbe tilted his head. "The thought never occurred to me, Mr. Holmes. Krane came alone to all our meetings and he made no mention of anyone else. I don't recall him ever using the word 'we'."

Holmes replied, "I only mention it as it is unlikely he made the repairs to the house himself, even if you are correct and it was only the one. Did you ever happen to notice if his hands were calloused from manual labour?"

Crabbe thought back. "Well, I shook his hand on at least two occasions, and they were more the hands of a clerk, though I did notice a blister under his right little finger."

"Possibly he did the repairs himself or merely paid an unassociated contractor to do so. The blister may have been from digging graves to bury his victims. Did you notice any disturbed earth in the area?"

"There may have been some beyond the mews among the trees, Mr. Holmes, but I never got that far before I saw Master's cane."

"Well, we shall venture out to Ramsgate in the morning and see what evidence we can gather to prove your innocence."

Chapter V

We caught the early train and were in Ramsgate by 10:45 the next morning. The smell of the sea was strong in the air, even though we were over a mile inland from Ramsgate Marina. Holmes had provided Crabbe with a disguise for his face and a cloak to hide his missing arm. We rented a growler, and the sergeant guided us to the location of the incident.

We pulled around to the mews in the back so as not to draw attention to ourselves. Before disembarking, Holmes asked Crabbe to point out the locations of the various stages of the fight that he had with Krane.

He indicated a spot about halfway between the house and the mews. "We were just there. Krane was about a pace behind me as he was describing the boundaries of the property. That's where we were when I spotted Master's cane."

"How is it that you were able to identify it at a glance?" asked Holmes.

Crabbe hung his head in sorrow. "I feel to blame for his injury, Mr. Holmes. When I was wounded after we were forced to abandon our tank, it was the Lieutenant who rushed to my aid to assist me to safety. It was as he helped me toward cover under a barrage of German gunfire that he received the wounds that cost him his leg. I've tried to help him however I could through his ordeal. That cane belonged to my grandfather, a navy captain. I thought it fitting it should go to another officer, and I gave it to Masters."

"Your loyalty does you credit, sir," I commented.

He merely nodded. "It was the least I could do, Doctor. I'm only sorry for his senseless end at the hands of this charlatan, Krane. I cannot say I'm sorry for what I did to him, for it was as much out of vengeance as it was self-defence."

Holmes spoke up. "I suggest you keep that part to yourself when you talk to the police, Sergeant. Self-defence should be quite sufficient. There's no use confusing them with a secondary motive which could affect the measure of your guilt in their eyes. Wait here while I examine the grounds."

Carefully Holmes circled the area where the confrontation had occurred with Lestrade on leash. Then he approached cautiously, so as not to disturb the existing tracks and traces. He made a minute examination of the lawn, mumbling to himself and taking measurements. Encouraging the hound to sniff the area where the body had fallen, he then followed the drag marks to the mews. Upon opening the door he turned and called, "You may now join me gentlemen, but mind your step."

Once inside we left the door open to have daylight to see by. Holmes drew back the tarp to reveal the body of Jacob Krane. The quicklime had done its work in minimizing the smell of decomposition. Holmes performed a cursory examination, but more specifically concentrated on Krane's boots to ensure they matched the tracks he had found outside. He asked me to medically verify the cause of death. When I examined the victim's neck, the ligature marks from Crabbe's sleeve were obvious. The pressure applied dislocated the vertebrae at C5 and appeared to have fractured the hyoid bone.

While I was doing this, Lestrade was sniffing the area, while Holmes was checking the ground, and we soon saw him open the back door and follow the hound into the woods. When I asked him where he was going he called, "Please remain where you are. I'll be back momentarily."

True to his word, he returned in about three minutes. "Sergeant Crabbe," he said, "I see that Krane's knife is next to his body. I presume you picked it up and placed it there?"

"Yes, Mr. Holmes, but I took it by the blade. I didn't want my fingerprints anywhere near the handle, just so I could prove it was him that drew it on me."

Holmes smiled. "A wise precaution, Sergeant. Doctor, you may cover him back up. I believe, gentlemen, that we may now report this matter to the police with all confidence in our case for self-defence."

We drove toward the marina. Having worked cases here before, Holmes recalled the location of the Ramsgate Station of the Kent Police, and we arrived just before one o'clock. Upon presenting his card at the front desk, Holmes advised the officer he wished to report a crime to the highest-ranking officer on duty. At that moment, an official walked in the door, having returned from lunch. It turned out this was our man, and we were given over to the Assistant Chief Constable, Matthew Pritchard. Upon Holmes introducing himself, Pritchard welcomed us and bid us to follow him to his office.

There was a sofa to one side, and Holmes indicated Crabbe should sit there with Lestrade at his feet while he and I took up the guest chairs opposite Pritchard's desk. Once settled, the official asked us what we had to report.

"My client, Sergeant Thomas Crabbe, wishes to turn himself in for an official investigation to find a verdict of self-defence in the death of one Jacob Krane, who attempted to kill the sergeant and has apparently killed four other men prior to the sergeant's putting an end to his spree."

Pritchard, a middle-aged, clean-shaven man with a strongly built stature, square jaw, and penetrating blue eyes, leaned back in his chair to digest this revelation. He gave away no emotion of surprise or dismay, but took in the information dispassionately and professionally.

After a moment to consider, Pritchard leaned forward, folding his hands upon his desktop and stared at our client. "Sergeant Crabbe, I must advise you that anything you say can be used against you. Do you concur that this is the action you wish to take, and that you are confessing to the killing of this man Krane, or do you wish to remain silent?"

Crabbe sat up straight and met the Chief Constable's eyes with a steady gaze of his own. "I killed him, sir. But it was self-defence, and that's why I went to Mr. Holmes so he could prove it."

Pritchard frowned, then took up a pencil and paper. "Just where and when did this incident occur?"

"Eagleton Park – four days ago."

Pritchard squinted at him and, with a trace of anger remonstrated him. "Four days ago! Why did you wait so long if it was self-defence? And where in Blazes is Eagleton Park?"

Holmes stepped in at this point. "If you will allow me, Mr. Pritchard: In the course of your investigation, you will find that Sergeant Crabbe has a previous arrest. He wished to lay out his story to a neutral third party before coming to the official police. As I now live in Sussex, it took some time for us to connect, and I have now examined the location of the crime and concur that it was self-defence. I shall be happy to lend my assistance to your investigation to prove these facts to you. As to Eagleton Park, that name itself was made up by Mr. Krane, and is one of the proofs that he was a dishonest man."

Pritchard tapped the pencil in a quick staccato burst upon his desk and finally said, "I don't like it, Mr. Holmes. If it were anyone other than you, I'd hold you for obstruction of justice. This isn't 1895 anymore, and we aren't the overworked inspectors of old Scotland Yard. The rules are more restrictive now. But as it is, let's get all the facts and see where we go from here."

Crabbe told his story from the beginning, from Krane's offer of low-cost housing to disabled veterans, to his discovery of Master's cane and the attack by Krane. He was a little vague on the timeline as to his getting to me, and me getting to Holmes, and Holmes travelling to London, but all in all, it was accurate to what we had been told.

When finished, Pritchard invited Crabbe to review his notes and sign off on them for the time being until an official report could be typed up. Then he said, "Very well. Since we have a good deal of daylight left, let's go see the scene and determine the facts." As we left the station, Pritchard called out, "Sergeant Ruxton, come with us!"

A burly fellow with a uniform bulging with muscles and a thick blonde moustache grabbed his coat and followed. He drove the Assistant Chief Constable behind our four-wheeler, and we led the way to the scene. Upon arrival, when all had disembarked, Pritchard looked at Holmes and said, "This Krane fellow claimed this was Eagleton Park?"

"Yes. The London Disabled Veterans Club will be able to verify that for you."

"This is still the Newington suburb. There was some bomb damage done here during the war, but that has all been repaired. I know of no foreigners being involved."

Crabbe piped up. "I think Krane bought this place and lied about everything else."

"Well, we'll see," replied Pritchard non-committally. "So, Mr. Holmes, show me your evidence."

Holmes led the way to the area of the lawn showing the footmarks where the struggle had taken place. He explained how the prints of Crabbe's boots were different from Krane's, and demonstrated how Crabbe had been able to use his army training to get the upper hand and get Krane into the chokehold that killed him.

"We also have this evidence," added the detective, moving closer to the mews doorway. "Note that we again have the prints of Mr. Krane. But see these prints here?"

Pritchard looked but shook his head. "I only see another boot-print that could just as easily be Krane's."

Holmes knelt and pointed. "We've been fortunate in that the weather has been so mild as of late. These marks are those which correspond to *those* boot-prints," he indicated, "which are a full two sizes larger than Krane's!"

"What? Those holes in the ground?"

"The holes produced by Lt. Masters peg leg, Chief Constable. See? By the pattern, it was here where Krane stabbed Masters, who fell against the door. Note the scratches sliding downward, likely caused by his sleeve buttons as he tried to keep himself upright.

"From here, Krane threw Masters's walking stick onto the woodpile, dragged the body inside, where he loaded it in a wheelbarrow and took it off for burial.

We followed the drag marks into the mews and uncovered Krane's body for Pritchard to examine.

After his inspection, Pritchard rose and said, "Well, it checks out so far. But how do you know he killed Master's and the others?"

Holmes crooked his finger and, letting Lestrade lead the way, he pointed to the ground as we made our way out the back and some bits of quicklime have fallen as it was transported. The footprints following it are a match to Krane's boots. "

Finally, Lestrade came to a halt. We looked around, but saw towards the woods. "See here – the tracks of a wheelbarrow, and every so often nothing. Pritchard asked the obvious. "Why are we here, Mr. Holmes?"

In reply, Holmes bent down, threw back what seemed to be a patch of weeds, and revealed a hole in a wooden sheet. He lifted it, with a layer of ground cover and soil still lying atop it. In this up-tilted position was an exposed larger hole, roughly six feet square and perhaps eight feet deep. Piled roughly in the bottom were the bodies of four men, covered in quicklime and in varying stages of decay. All were in uniform: The previous clients of Jacob Krane.

Pritchard turned away, sickened by the sight. Ruxton braved a closer look, then turned up his nose and walked away, shaking his head. Sergeant

Crabbe fell to his knees at the side of the hole, having recognized his friend, Lt. Masters, and began to weep. Holmes let the wooden sheet fall back over the mass grave and recovered the handhold with the weed patch again to keep others from finding it before the police could recover the bodies.

When our nerves had settled, Pritchard turned to my friend and said, "You have made your case, Mr. Holmes. I still have to follow protocol and hold your client until we finish the autopsy, and verify the story of the real estate deals with the Veterans Club, but I believe that will all be a formality, and no official arrest will appear against him."

Turning to Crabbe he said, "Sergeant Crabbe, please be kind enough to go with Sergeant Ruxton back to our van. The law says I must hold you, but under the circumstances, we will try to make your stay with us as comfortable as possible. With any luck, we should have all this verified in a very few days and be able to send you on your way."

As the two men left us, Pritchard turned to the detective. "Mr. Holmes, I never thought I'd have the pleasure to work a case with you, but I am right glad you came out of retirement for this one, and assured that we found all the evidence to keep an honourable veteran from being prosecuted. Thank you, sir."

He shook Holmes's hand, and we accompanied him back to the vehicles. Assuring Crabbe we would stay in touch until the case was complete, we left him in Pritchard's hands while we returned to the railway station and caught the evening train back to London. Holmes stayed with me for the few days until Crabbe's case was dismissed, and we spent the time reminiscing about old cases. He gave me some further details of the case I had published under the title "His Last Bow". However, they were governmental secrets which I cannot share with the public.

He did make one comment regarding my publications, however, when he stated this to me:

"Should you choose to publish this case, Watson, you will of course change the names of the sergeant and his victim to avoid future repercussions. May I suggest something along the lines of 'Crab' and 'Crane'? The case is very similar to the old Indian Panchatantra tale of that name." [4]

As the reader will note, I have followed Holmes's advice, It is usually the wisest thing to do.

NOTES

1. See "The Game at Checquers" in *Sherlock Holmes and the Seven Deadly Sins* (Baker Street Studios, 2024)
2. In the Battle of Mericourt and Hangest during World War I, specifically during the Battle of Amiens, the British employed a large number of tanks to attack the German lines along the railway line stretching between these two locations.
3. "Sketches of a Blackmailer" – *Sherlock Holmes – Colourful Cases Volume 2* (Irregular Special Press, 2024)
4. *The Panchatantra Tales* were ancient animal stories by Vishnu Sharma written for children to learn moral lessons, very much like Aesop's Fables of Ancient Greece.

The Mystery of the
Graveyard Angel
by Adrian Middlton

Retirement is a state of mind, which needs must be occupied as much as the body. The former is mostly addressed by perambulations across the Downs. One morning, I recall setting off toward the Seven Sisters to enjoy a brisk and breezy three hours, pushing hard against a westerly winter wind as I walked the chalk along the cliff edge into the nearby town of Seaford. I recall it as a morning of mountainous waves crashing ashore, depositing shingle across the roads. As I approached the town, I observed the waves silting up the entrance to the Buckle, a local hostelry that required its patrons to pick their way over abandoned stones to get inside.

As was a habit of mine, I paid a brief visit to the town's Martello Tower, seventy-fourth in a chain of defences built to protect England's coastline from invasion. The tower had become obsolete after Trafalgar, and subsequently fell into disrepair. It then passed into the hands of excise men on the lookout for smugglers until coastal erosion forced its sale to the War Office. Some thirty years later, it was taken over by a local businessman, Tom Funnell, who converted it into the seafront tea room that I chose to frequent. In an effort to retain my privacy, I had arranged for certain forms of correspondence to be sent there.

On this occasion, Tom was busy with another customer, so a delightful young waitress called Rosemary handed over the small bundle of letters set aside for me, along with copies of *The Sussex Express* and *Seaford Gazette*. Finding my favoured table the furthest corner of the café, I settled down with my pipe until noon, catching up on the local news while drinking several cups of Kenyan drip-coffee. On the second page of *The Gazette*, I found a local story that piqued my interest:

Monday, 24 January, 1921

> *In a move that has set tongues wagging across East Sussex, Miss Maud Beverton, an amateur archaeologist from Canterbury, has announced her intention to lead an excavation into the origins of the historic town of Seaford, challenging the prevailing theories of the Sussex Archaeological Society.*

Miss Beverton, who recently became known for uncovering a horde of early Saxon artifacts in a Tenterden field, believes that Seaford holds secrets that predate the Norman era. "The society's position on Seaford is rooted in outdated assumptions," she declared during a spirited address at County Hall, Lewes. "I intend to uncover evidence that will not only rewrite this chapter of the town's history, but that of Lewes itself."

The Sussex Archaeological Society, founded in 1846 and custodian of significant historical collections, has long maintained that, in spite of the existence of a nearby Roman camp, Seaford itself was established during the early Norman period. However, Miss Beverton argues that Anglo-Saxon and Roman influences may have shaped the town's formation.

Although Miss Beverton is arriving today, the full excavation is expected to commence next month, when a team of volunteers and experts will be joining her. The project has already sparked debate within academic circles, and among local residents eager to learn more about their town's past.

What pet theory, I wondered, had set Miss Beverton against her fellow antiquarians? And how was her excavation to be funded? Was there a sponsor, or was she a woman of means?

Without Watson by my side, I find it necessary to disclose some of my thoughts on the case. No, less a case than an adventure, and at this point it was little more than idle curiosity. From memory, I recalled that Seaford had been a thriving Cinque Port in the early Middle Ages. The plague and intermittent raids by the French had spurred on its decline. By the time it ceased to be a Cinque Port in 1832, the town had fallen foul of the "Seaford Shags", a community of smugglers and wreckers whose activities blighted the area for several decades. Seaford clawed back its reputation in the years that followed, establishing itself as a seaside resort and becoming a genteel place to live, boasting no fewer than five preparatory schools. From my many excursions into the town, I could not think of any pre-Norman sites or buildings except, perhaps, for the ancient St. Leonard's Church, which lay adjacent to a public house of my acquaintance, the Old Plough.

I needed little further encouragement to walk the short half-mile into the centre of the town. As I did so, I noticed some atypical behaviour among the locals, whose usual morning greetings were replaced by anxious looks and hurried steps. Something unusual was occurring.

When I stepped into the old red-roofed tavern, the murmur of conversation paused, and more nervous glances were cast my way. I acknowledged the landlord as I crossed over to the bar. He, at least, remained personable. Ordering a mug of Charringtons, and a plate of bread and cheese with a slice of meat pie, I started to discuss *The Gazette*'s news-story as I waited.

"What do you make of this excavation, Ted?" I asked, pointing to the article. "Do you know of any Saxon buildings hereabouts?"

The landlord glanced at the newspaper, scanning the story with interest, before blowing out a sigh and fixing me with his eyes.

"Nothing to be found here, Mr. Holmes. There's plenty out of town, but not in Seaford proper, unless the Rector knows otherwise. The church is the oldest building in town. I shouldn't wonder if its all politics. Those historians are always trying to one-up each other, and the women have it harder than most. Hang on," he said, pointing across the bar. "William over there is the Sexton. He can tell you more about St. Leonard's."

Thanking Ted, I gathered up my ale and crossed over the William's table. He was a little older than me, dressed in a dusty black jacket, beige waistcoat, and matching trousers, with mittens and a silk scarf. A smudged bowler rested beside a pint and sandwich, while his hands looked like those of a labourer, his nails ingrained with dirt. Ironically, he was puffing on a long and rather old churchwarden's pipe.

"William, isn't it?" I enquired. "Ted told me you work next door. Might I join you?"

"Sherlock Holmes, eh? I've seen you around sir. Might I ask why? No crimes round here that I know of, unless you're after that bicycle we found in the churchyard."

"Well, unless I see the bicycle, I couldn't tell you," I japed as he shuffled across to make room for me. "What I'm really after is an opinion about this newspaper article."

Again, I placed the open newspaper down and pointed at the story for William to read. He huffed and puffed as he did so, in a manner I would describe as irritated.

"Most of the original church is long gone, but St. Leonard's was built around 1100, and it's the oldest building in Seaford – which means that story's rubbish."

"Has Miss Beverton approached the church? I presume that if St. Leonard's is the oldest, it might be where her excavation is taking place?"

"We did get a letter from the bishop, giving her licence to investigate. She's meant to come by any day now and discuss it all with the Rector. I dare say, he will not be happy."

"As happy as yourself?"

"My job is to keep order in the graveyard," he replied, gruffly, "and that's where she wants to look. I have enough trouble keeping wayward schoolboys away without dealing with defilers. The dead should be undisturbed. Our churchyard is full. Has been for twenty years or more. And if she wants to go poking 'round the gravestones, she'll find the oldest have been wiped clean by the salt air. There's literally nothing to see."

"In my work, I found there was always something to see. Even the absence of something to see tells a story."

"Aye, well, stories is all she'll find if she comes here. Everybody has one, and they're all tall tales."

"The best kind," I said, checking my watch before slipping William a coin to buy his next pint.

While we had been talking, the patrons' murmurations had returned for a while, only to become silent again as a new customer entered the bar. Moments later, I could hear a new voice speaking with Ted at the bar. Female, youthful, articulate and Kentish. Just few miles can make the difference between a stranger and a local, and a lady enquiring about a room for the night at just a quarter-after-two in the afternoon came as no surprise to me. Indeed, I had been expecting her appearance, although it had taken longer for her to make the short walk from the railway station. The train from Lewes to Brighton had not long passed through, and the Old Plough provided some of the closest accommodation to the church. A brief glance at her luggage confirmed my expectations.

"Miss Maud Beverton, I presume," I said as she passed over her bags and collected a key. "My name is Sherlock Holmes."

Her mouth formed a startled "*O*" before she could respond to the introduction.

"*The* Sherlock Holmes. The detective?"

"The same, but retired. I now keep bees and enjoy the countryside. Your excavation though, being of local interest, intrigued me. As I understand it, archaeology is much like detective work, except your suspects are long-since buried beneath the earth."

"Perhaps . . ." she began, cutting herself short. "That's a good way of putting it, Mr. Holmes, although things may also be above the earth and in plain view. Might I ask what it is about my work that is of interest? The press said very little about my intentions."

"I am interested in the train of thought that made you want to excavate – both the logical, and the personal."

"Oh." Her eyes narrowed, no doubt wondering how I knew there was a personal aspect to her interest. "I'd be happy to show you, Mr. Holmes, although . . . I must see to my room first. May we meet in, say, ten minutes?"

441

Agreeing to wait, I ordered two ginger beers as she left the bar. As I did so, I noted that William the Sexton had left the building. Taking a window seat adjacent to St. Leonards, I looked across towards the church, which formed the centre-piece of a crowded churchyard whose graves, mostly of Sussex Wealden sandstone, but scattered with other materials such as brick, granite, and limestone, made uneven by the grass and pathways raised by centuries of burial. There were plenty of wood and iron rails and foot stones, but not so well ordered that one could walk in a straight line. Most of the round and batted headstones remained upright, but there were signs of severe erosion on those facing the Plough – a clear sign that the cemetery predated any of the Channel-ward buildings. Among the tombstones, I spied William the Sexton at work, raking one of the paths in a somewhat aggressive fashion. Perhaps he had tarried too long on his work break – or perhaps some blight on his precious graveyard had inflamed his humour.

"Mr. Holmes?"

"Miss Beverton, please join me," I said, indicating her drink. Unlike many, she had made no change to her appearance, other than touching up her hair and the powder on her cheeks. "I trust everything is well?"

"I am a little concerned," she added, taking a sip of ginger beer. "My brother was meant to meet me at the station, "but there was always a chance that his schoolmaster declined his request."

"Perhaps we should make our way back to the station – or to his school if it is nearby. If you have no objection to being accompanied."

"Not at all, Mr. Holmes. I should be grateful, and I can update you as to the nature of my planned excavation at St. Leonard's."

"So it *is* within the church grounds. I suspected as much."

"Yes. My brother told me of an old graveyard angel which seems anachronous to the period."

"Anachronous in what way?"

"Graveyard angels came into vogue at the beginning of the last century. None should be older than, say, a hundred-and-twenty years. Robbie described the angel as formless, so badly eroded it must have been an early feature. We can take a brief look on our way."

"I should like that," said I, finishing up my drink and standing to escort Miss Beverton outside. "Erosion would suggest that it lies to the south of the church, but I spied only tombstones. Nothing taller."

"Oh?" Glancing over my shoulder, she looked out of the window. "How very strange. Perhaps it is obscured by shrubbery. It should be over there, where that side man is working."

"That's William, the Sexton," I informed her. "He should know where it is. Shall we?"

Stepping outside, we crossed the cobbled lane and passed under the lych gate, emerging on the other side to find our view considerably improved. Again, we saw no taller structures. Even the few scattered shrubs were low and well-trimmed. The Sexton, meanwhile, was gone.

Meandering through the narrow paths, we made our way toward the southeastern part of the graveyard, where there were signs of raking, but barely any leaves.

"Here," she said, unfolding a sheet of lined paper containing a simple sketch of the church. "This is where Robbie says it should be."

"Indeed," I noted, focusing on the rake-work, which seemed to have been a hasty attempt to cover up a large number of footprints and a mark made by a bicycle tyre. "It seems to correspond with that raised tomb or plinth. Shall we take a look?"

As I sprang forwards to examine the area in more detail, Miss Beverton was keen to draw my attention to her sheet of paper.

"This sketch," she turned the paper over, showing me a rough drawing on the other side, "shows what the statue looks like. There's nothing like it here."

Taking the paper, I examined the form, or perhaps formlessness, of the "angel". Aside from the pose – that of someone with the head bowed in prayer – there were no discernible features, as if it were a drawing of one of the eroded tombstones. One could not even confirm the sex of the supplicant. The wings, however, were exceptionally detailed.

"A clear mismatch."

"My theory is that the wings were added to an earlier statue, and that the statue is of Saint Lewinna, a virgin martyr said to have died at the hands of the Vikings. Legend has it that her relics were translated from a monastery in Seaford, circa 1058, to an abbey in Flanders. Prevailing thought is that with no Anglo-Saxon abbey, her remains must have been taken from a nearby site, either in Lewes or Bishopstone."

"And you believe a statue of this saint will place her abbey on this site, beneath the Norman church?"

"I do, but opposition to the idea has been – well – vitriolic."

"Of course it has. I want you to look around the church square – at the Plough, the Crown over the road, and any unshuttered windows you may see around us. Tell me what you see."

Doing as bidden, she turned full circle before returning her gaze in my direction.

"*Everyone* is watching us. Even passers-by pause to look our way."

"Indeed. I fear the opposition to your idea is not archaeological, but *communal*. Take a look at the plinth, with an antiquarian's eye, and tell me what you observe. Omit no detail."

443

"It is a stone slab. Granite, but set upon limestone. It has markings of dirt, and chalk dust, and the southward edge is caked in soil and grass. Fresh soil. There is also no sign that anything heavy rested upon it. That can only mean it is a replacement for whatever rested here. There are limestone fragments scattered around the base, suggesting something was chipped or smashed."

"A good observation, Miss Beverton," I said, "but there is more. It is surrounded by a short limestone wall, with four chained posts set at each corner. They are all grooved with marks that show ropes were set in place to hoist something. Not recently, but over many years. Whatever lay on that plinth was regularly lifted up. And here," I pointed to the closest of the posts, "is a fresh set of striations. Your statue was moved very recently, but also hastily, sustaining damage before it disappeared. When did you announce your excavation?"

"On Friday afternoon, at two p.m."

"Three days then, and when I arrived at the Old Plough this afternoon, the Sexton told me no crimes had been committed. Yet the statue probably disappeared when news of your visit was made common knowledge by this morning's newspaper. What I can tell you is that the statue was not removed from the site. There is no feasible way in which it could be lifted and moved away in a few short hours."

"But, why – ?"

"I have an idea, Miss Beverton. When statue was lifted, it fell upon the original limestone slab, smashed it, and now lies some yards beneath our feet. Tell me – would your brother have used a bicycle to get to the train station, and might he have cut through the cemetery?"

"He does, and yes, he would. What are you suggesting?"

"If your brother was crossing the cemetery this morning, then perhaps he stumbled on the moving of the statue, or else came upon the Sexton tidying up . . . No." I stopped myself. "The Sexton would not have mentioned the bicycle if that were the case. Your brother fled, leaving his bicycle behind, pursued by some, or all, of the perpetrators. I suspect he is lying low until it is safe enough, either to seek you out or to return to school. I do not believe the conspiracy here is one that will put him in danger. As you have seen, the entire village would appear to be witnesses."

In that moment I was grateful there was no client. The conclusion of this mystery would be swift, and without victims – other than Miss Beverton.

"Come with me," I said, leading Miss Beverton towards the church, in search of the errant Sexton. As we passed inside, I called his name, which echoed around the great arched nave. Sure enough, he appeared, and the look in his face has shifted from irritable to angered.

"What is it?" He asked.

"Would you show me the bicycle you mentioned? Miss Beverton here might know its owner."

Without another word he walked off, leaving us to look upon the church.

"Most of the families in Seaford have been here for generations," I said. "Descended from the same townsfolk who would stand on the edge of the chalk cliffs, waving their lights out to sea in a manner that would drive ships onto the rocks. Imagine some young antiquarian coming into your village and exposing the full history of your ancestors, finding smugglers tunnels and reminding the world of their criminal history."

"I have no interest in their family histories, Mr. Holmes, only in the ancient history of the county, and their ancestors' ancestors."

"Therein lies the problem. You don't see the impact your work may have on the community.

"Here," said William, wheeling in the bicycle. "An Aero-Special. You know whose this is?"

"It belongs to Robbie, my brother," said Miss Beverton.

"I hope the boy is safe," said I. "I know that you all chased him off. If he was caught, please let him go – or even better, have him brought here."

"Why do you say that?" asked William. "I just found the bicycle. I know nothing about a boy being caught, nor by whom."

"Oh, you know – and I'll trouble you to come outside and help us to raise that wretched slab so we can see what's left of your graveyard angel."

William's face fell. The deceit was exposed, and his anger quickly gave way to resignation.

"It'll do no good. The damage is done," he said, leading us back outside. "We can't afford to have the town dug up."

"Because of the tunnels?" I asked.

"Aye. They're everywhere, leading down to the seashore. All blocked off now, thanks to the customs men. They sealed off the tunnels with explosives back in 1850, and pretty much killed off the smuggling trade overnight."

"Why keep it secret after all these years?" Miss Beverton asked. "None of you are smugglers now?"

"That's true enough, miss, but there's still booty down there. Some of us go down and make a bit of extra coin from what we find."

"I think, Miss Beverton, that what matters are family names. No list of all the shags was ever released, and some families still want to hide the shame of a criminal past. Isn't that right, William?"

Nodding, the Sexton led us back to the plinth. At the walls of the graveyard, a number of witnesses, many of whom I knew, stood – waiting, a forlorn look on their faces as the famous detective and the lady antiquarian were about to expose their folly.

Taking one side of the slab while William took the other, we slid it southwards, tilting it to settle gently, albeit heavily, upon the grass.

"There you go," he said, indicating the shaft that lay beneath the plinth. "Our graveyard angel,"

Miss Beverton and I leaned forward to see the limestone statue at the bottom of a shaft some thirty feet deep, broken into a hundred pieces. Its splintered wooden wings, painted to resemble the stone that they had long since been grafted to, rested on either side.

"There is an irony here," said I. "Miss Beverton, would you explain what your excavation would have involved?

"Just a small team examining the statue and tombstones in search of anything that indicated an Anglo-Saxon origin for the village."

"No digging?"

"None. Had we found our evidence, which I suspect we would have, then I would have passed the information on to the Sussex Archaeological Society. I would write my paper, and any further excavations would be out of my hands."

"So William, was it really worth destroying a precious historical object to protect tunnels that were never in any danger?"

"No." The Sexton's head hung in shame. "What will you do?"

"That's up to Miss Beverton, here. Neither she, nor I, know of any name but your own associated with this charade, and I have no interest in discovering who is, or isn't, descended from smugglers."

"Nor do I," said Maud, with a sigh. "I just want to see Robbie, and to examine the statue. If I can confirm it is an Anglo-Saxon object dedicated to Saint Lewinna, then I can write my paper. As an outsider, I don't have the resources to do more, and I can omit certain details if that will help."

William turned to the onlookers, making a thumbs-up sign before waving them away. As the crowd dispersed, Miss Beverton and I made our way across town, wheeling his bicycle to Robbie's school. There were a few details to clear up, but the boy was safe, and the town's reputation would remain unsullied.

Returning home later in the day, I chose to walk by way of the seafront, passing by the chalk cliffs whose secret tunnels were hidden from the naked eye. I spied one or two silt-filled caves, but nothing that would easily give up the secrets of the shags of Seaford. One day, perhaps, the archaeologists shall return. I suspect we will be long gone by then, and much of the evidence will have been washed away by the encroaching sea.

The Adventure of the
Wonderful Things
by Craig Janacek

Prologue

I have written little of late about the adventures of my great friend, Mr. Sherlock Holmes. Even at the best of times, he had an extreme aversion to publicity, and it is now his express wish to entirely fade from the public limelight. He has made the extraordinary request that my literary agent inform the readers of *The Strand Magazine* that no further cases will be forthcoming. What few stories managed to reach publication of late have been those that transpired many years in the past, often long before his retirement to the Sussex Downs. This prohibition on his part has made it such that the details regarding many remarkable episodes that transpired in the shadows of the Great War – save only the escapades of the ersatz spy Altamont – may never see the light of day.

After the ending of that terrible conflict, I attempted to return to my routines in London. [1] And yet, a deep weariness had settled into my bones and my old war wounds ached constantly. My beloved wife had succumbed to a wasting illness, and the fact that I had never been blessed with a child hung heavy over my thoughts – though I occasionally wondered if it were somehow for the best, given how many bright-eyed youths never returned from the Flanders Fields. One morning in early March, my morose thoughts were interrupted by an unexpected telegram from Holmes. As was typical for him, the message was laconic and enigmatic. It read:

> *Any interest in joining the crowds who have recently descended upon Luxor?*

> *S.H.*

I was much surprised to learn that Holmes, tucked away in his remote country villa, was following the remarkable news coming out of Egypt about Carter's unearthing of the tomb of Tut-Ankh-Amun the prior November. [2] Nevertheless, I felt that perhaps a holiday in the Nile Valley might do wonders for my heart and sinew, and promptly returned his wire with a hearty affirmation.

A week later found us taking the usual route via steamer to Alexandria and train on to Cairo, where we followed the advice of Mrs. Maberley and stopped at Shepheard's. Upon first glance, the hotel's opulence – with its stained glass, Persian carpets, gardens, terraces, and great granite pillars – was quite pleasing. However, the wait at the long bar was interminable and the crowds that immediately manifested when one set foot out into the street soon began to wear upon me. We therefore decamped to a pair of rooms at the recently expanded Mena House, which made up for whatever it lacked in cuisine with the stark grandeur of its views over the pyramids and the vast sand dunes of the Giza plateau.

A few days later, Cook's *PS Sudan* carried us up the Nile River, stopping at various sites along the way. Although the noon-day heat was intense, when we repaired back to the boat and took our places on the deck under the stars, we found the nights were idyllic, as if we had stumbled into some fairy-tale romance of Rider Haggard. Throughout the length of the cruise, Holmes was in an unusually garrulous mood, and he regaled me with the recounting of various adventures in which I did not participate for some reason or another. I learned much about his movements during the time I have come to call his "Great Hiatus", when I – and most of the world save his brother Mycroft – believed him to have perished in the great Falls of Reichenbach. Of especial interest were the details of the months he spent in this particular corner of the world, risking his life retrieving the pilfered Black Stone of the Kaaba and locating the dishonoured remains of Gordon. [3]

"You should let me write about some of these!" I cajoled.

My friend shook his head obstinately. "To what end, Watson? There were a good many errors in that last instalment of yours." [4]

I frowned. "What errors? I found it to be one of the most singular of your career – there is some deep and fundamental truth to that case. Anyhow, do you not see that setting your work down is a form of immortality?"

"Whatever are you going on about, Watson?" said he with a frown.

"Think of it!" I cried. "The greatest glory of our country lies in her literature. Though the Parthenon and the Colosseum are now crumbling masses of ruins, their literature remains intact, and Homer, Virgil, and Horace are as fresh to us as they were to their contemporaries. Is that not a way to live forever?" [5]

But Holmes remained unconvinced, so I let the argument drop rather than spoil the mood of our holiday. At Luxor, we took rooms at the Winter Palace so that we could spend a few days in the area. On our final day, as we travelled towards the temple of Hatchepsout, we passed two colossal statues belonging to the King Memnon. [6] Immediately, Shelley's haunting words sprang into my thoughts, and I became deeply conscious of the ticking of the inexorable clock under which we all toil. [7] Beneath the watchful gaze of the natural pyramid of Al-Qurn, the mountain that looms over the Valley of the Kings, we made our way down the dusty stone steps into the lavishly-decorated tomb of the young king. I took my time descending into that dark place, but Holmes bounded down the steps as if he were a young man again, and I marvelled at the wonders that the Egyptian air had worked upon his rheumatism.

After an exhausting but well-spent day scrambling over and under the stones of the western bank of ancient Thebes, our steamer was ready to depart for Assouan, where we had rooms engaged for a week's stay at the Cataract Hotel, of which I had heard many fine things. However, shortly before our planned departure from our current accommodations, a message arrived for Holmes. He tore this open, read it, and smiled, before handing it to me. It read:

> *Continental-Savoy Hotel,*
> *Cairo, Egypt*
> *6th April*
>
> *Mr. Holmes,*
>
> *It cannot be a coincidence that you should be in Egypt at my hour of need. Providence provides! I implore you to return to Cairo forthwith. Last night, at the very moment that my father, Lord Carnarvon, passed from this earth, the city lights went dark. There are already rumours flying about on swift wings that he was struck down by violating that ancient curse carved into the stone archway of The Tomb. Those of us who entered that dark place with him may be at danger. You must tell us whether there is anything that may be done to prevent us all from sharing his tragic fate.*
>
> *Faithfully yours,*
> *Evelyn Herbert*

I looked up at my friend in some alarm. "Shall we order return tickets?"

Holmes shook his head. "My dear Watson, I fear there is little chance of my being able to do anything."

"What do you mean?" I protested. "Surely you must investigate this! What an opportunity to study a possible power from beyond the grave.

There are many tales about the powers of the old Egyptians," I added darkly. "And I know I wouldn't care to go fooling about their tombs and relics. There are many malevolent spirits." [8]

"Come now, Watson, are we to give serious attention to such things? You just spent the day peering into the tomb yourself."

"But I took great pains not to touch – and certainly not remove – any object belonging to the king!" I exclaimed. "As Shakespeare said, '*there are stranger things*'. [9] Do you not recall the mystery of the unlucky mummy and my dear friend, poor Fletcher Robinson? I warned him against concerning himself with it. He persisted, and his death occurred. I told him he was tempting fate by pursuing his enquiries."

Holmes snorted with amusement. "Robinson was overtaken by illness. The immediate cause of his death, however premature, was attributed to typhoid fever by no less an authority than Sir Jasper Meek."

"But that is the way in which the elementals guarding the mummy might act! As Robinson himself wrote, '*It is certain that the Egyptians had powers which we in the Twentieth Century may laugh at, yet can never understand.*' " [10]

"No, no, Watson, let us not invoke such spirits," said Holmes, with a laugh. "We are here on holiday, not to investigate another natural passing into the great beyond. In Lord Carnarvon's case, human illness was the primary cause of death. The papers have been reporting for a week now of his failing health, brought on by a constitutional weakness from his reckless habits, followed by an infected razor cut of a mosquito bite upon his cheek. [11] I still adhere to my past statement: *No ghosts need apply*."

"But it is impossible to say with absolute certainty if this is true. If you refuse to entertain an occult power, then what of the possibility of the dormant spores of some black fungus, reawakening after being once again exposed to oxygen?"

"I am certain that Mr. Carter would have tested for such a pathogen. And it doesn't take a consulting detective to identify toxins in the air – that is a job for a good germ scientist."

"Then what of murder?"

Holmes's eyebrows rose with interest. "On what grounds do you make such an accusation?"

"I can think of three possible theories."

"Oh? Pray tell."

"Did you not write in *The Whole Art of Detection* that there are four prime motives for murder? [12] Given his age and health, we might perhaps discount lust, but what of jealousy? Surely, those who held the *firman* for the Valley of the Kings before Carnarvon must have bitterly resented his fame."

"I believe Mr. Davis has already died, as have his excavators." [13]

"Well, then, what of fear? I read in the papers about some rift that had developed between Carnarvon and Carter of late. Perhaps Carter, or someone on his team, was found in possession of artifacts not belonging to them? Such a theft, if revealed, would deeply affect Anglo-Egyptian relations at this critical juncture. Egypt just obtained its independence less than two years ago, and tensions remain high. Surely someone might kill to cover up such a crime." [14]

"An interesting speculation, but one sadly bereft of any proof."

"Then what of greed? Surely the local tomb robbers must have been angered at that such a rich find was plucked from under their very noses, and suspect that more such treasures may be forthcoming if they could block additional excavations."

"And how might local thieves accomplish the murder of an English Lord?" asked Holmes.

"They might have poisoned his tea?" I postulated.

Holmes laughed. "No, my stormy petrel. I think you have born witness to an excess of crime while accompanying me on my cases. Sometimes a dead man is just a dead man." He reached into his pocket and took out his *J*-pen, scribbling a reply to Lady Evelyn. I glanced over and read his words:

> *Many thanks for your invitation. So kind of you to think of sending it. I am sorry for your loss, but am afraid that I cannot stop in at this time.*
>
> *Re Curses: I assure you that you have nothing to worry about.*
>
> *S.H.*

Once settled aboard the ship to Assouan, we took our customary place on the deck and watched the sun set beyond the western hills.

"Do you recall, Watson, the case of Vansittart Smith?" asked Holmes suddenly.

"Vaguely," I shrugged. "A rather fantastic tale, if I remember correctly. Not anything that I could use for my submissions to *The Strand* about your investigations. I believe that I gave it to my literary editor, who made something of it, though it is likely now long forgotten. [15] What of it?"

"Your mention of Egyptian curses naturally brought it to mind."

"Would you refresh my memory?"

"Certainly. As you know, Watson . . . ."

When I first came up to London from university, [*Holmes continued*] I had rooms at No. 24 Montague Street. Not only were these just 'round the corner from the British Museum, but a short walk down Great Russell Street would take one to Bloomsbury Street where it soon becomes Gower Street. This great artery feeds the University of London, and word soon began to get round the student body that my methods were both noteworthy, and capable of producing unexpected results.

It was a raw, rainy day toward the end of October, shortly after my return from the manor house of Hurlstone, when an individual wrapped in a greatcoat, the high collar raised to his ears, arrived at my rooms. The appearance of my visitor was a singular one. His high-beaked nose and prominent chin had something of the same acute and incisive character that I soon learned distinguished his intellect. And yet, there was something ostentatious and overdone about his utter disregard of all personal considerations that suggested a large amount of petty vanity.

"My name, Mr. Holmes," said this prospective client, "is John Vansittart Smith, F.R.S., of 147-A Gower Street." [16]

"Not the same Mr. Vansittart Smith who once delivered a paper on the properties of belladonna?" I asked.

"Yes," replied my visitor, pecking his head in a birdlike fashion.

"I heard it said that, with your aptitude for botany, you were once looked upon as a second Darwin. But you later turned your whole attention to chemistry, did you not? I assure you that your research on the spectra of metals – especially arsenic and mercury – were of particularly great interest."

"That was the paper which won me my fellowship in the Royal Society," said Mr. Vansittart Smith, modestly.

"Well, Mr. Vansittart Smith, I would say that you are a man whose energy of purpose and clearness of thought places you in the very first rank of scientific observers. And yet, I have heard little of you of late."

"My attentions have turned to other subjects, Mr. Holmes. You might say that I am a victim of an ambition that prompts me to aim at distinction in many subjects, rather than pre-eminence in one."

"I see," said I. "And what subject has now captured your interests?"

"After a year's absence from the laboratory, I joined the Oriental Society, and recently delivered a paper on the Hieroglyphic and Demotic inscriptions of El Kab."

"A strange pivot, Mr. Vansittart Smith." I remarked.

"Perhaps," said the man, bobbing his head. "And yet, the more I burrowed my way into Egyptology, the more impressed I became by the vast field that it opens to the inquirer, and by the extreme importance of a subject which promises to throw a light upon the first germs of human civilisation and the origin of the greater part of our arts and sciences."

As you can imagine, Watson, the origins of our arts and sciences were of little import to my more practical lines of inquiry, so I attempted to hurry my coquettish visitor along with some prodding as to the purpose for his visit.

"Well," continued Mr. Vansittart Smith, "I was so struck that I straightway married an Egyptological young lady who had written upon the Sixth Dynasty, and having thus secured a sound base of operations, I set myself to collect materials for a work that should unite the research of Lepsius and the ingenuity of Champollion. As you may know, Mr. Holmes, the collections across the street are of some modicum of interest, but until lately, the French have been at the forefront of the field. Therefore, the preparation of my *magnum opus* entailed many hurried visits to the magnificent Egyptian collections of the Louvre. Upon the last of these visits, from which I only returned days ago, I became involved in a most strange and noteworthy adventure."

"Pray continue," said I, now growing interested.

Mr. Vansittart Smith drew a copy of the morning edition of *The Times*, turned to the section by the Paris correspondent, and handed it to me. I located the relevant concise narrative, which I excised with the thought that I might one day paste it into my commonplace book.

"Knowing, Watson, that we were about to embark upon this little voyage," Holmes said, "I brought it along, thinking you might find it of some interest."

Holmes proceeded to hand me a yellowed newspaper clipping, which read:

Curious Occurrence in the Louvre

Yesterday morning a strange discovery was made in the principal Egyptian Chamber. The ouvriers *who are employed to clean out the rooms in the morning found one of the attendants lying dead upon the floor with his arms round one of the mummies. So close was his embrace that it was only with the utmost difficulty that they were separated. One of the cases containing valuable rings had been opened and rifled. The authorities are of opinion that the man was bearing away*

453

*the mummy with some idea of selling it to a private collector,
but that he was struck down in the very act by long-standing
disease of the heart. It is said that he was a man of uncertain
age and eccentric habits, without any living relations to
mourn over his dramatic and untimely end.*

*I glanced up at my friend. "I see the obvious connection between this
peculiar episode and our present holiday, but fail to understand why you
this would seem of much notice."*

*Holmes nodded his head in agreement. "I had the same thought, and
said as much to Mr. Vansittart Smith. However, it is the tale that he
proceeded to relate which fully captured my attention. Shall I continue?"*

*"Of course," I exclaimed, always intrigued by any such details of
Holmes's early cases.*

Holmes smiled and proceeded with his story.

"The problem is, Mr. Holmes," continued Vansittart Smith, "that this
is not at all what transpired in the museum."

"Oh?" I asked, intrigued. "How could possibly you know that?"

"I know because I was there," said Vansittart Smith, his voice
ponderous with implied meaning. "Furthermore, I spoke with this man
moments before his death."

"Indeed!" I exclaimed, my interest now fully piqued. "How did you
come upon such a scene? Surely the man could not have pilfered the cases
during opening hours. It must have been the middle of the night."

"You are correct," said he. "I arrived in Paris in a somewhat befogged
and feverish condition. On reaching the Hotel de France, in the Rue
Laffitte, I threw myself upon a sofa for a couple of hours, but finding that
I was unable to sleep, I determined, in spite of my fatigue, to make my
way to the Louvre, settle the point which I had come to decide, and take
the evening train back home. Having come to this conclusion, I hurried
across the Boulevard des Italiens and down the Avenue de l'Opera. Once
in the Louvre, I was on familiar ground, and I speedily made my way to
the collection of papyri that it was my intention to consult.

"I am well aware," continued Vansittart Smith, "that even my
warmest admirers can hardly claim that I am a handsome man. Yet it came
upon me as a sudden jar when an English voice behind him exclaimed in
very audible tones, "What a queer-looking mortal!" Thinking someone
was talking about me, I straightened my lips and looked rigidly at the roll
of papyrus, while my heart filled with bitterness against the whole race of
travelling Britons.

"'Yes,' said another voice, 'he really is an extraordinary fellow.'

"'Do you know,' said the first speaker, 'one could almost believe that by the continual contemplation of mummies the chap has become half a mummy himself?'

"'He has certainly an Egyptian cast of countenance,' said the other.

"At this, Mr. Holmes," said Vansittart Smith, "I had reached my limit. I spun round upon my heel with the intention of shaming my countrymen by a corrosive remark or two. To my surprise and relief, the two young fellows who had been conversing had their shoulders turned towards me and were gazing at one of the Louvre attendants who was polishing some brass-work at the other side of the room.

My client continued his tale. "One tourist glanced at his watch. 'Carter will be waiting for us at the Palais Royal,' said he to the other, and they clattered away, leaving me to my labours. [17]

"'I wonder what these chatterers call an Egyptian cast of countenance,' I said to myself, and I moved my position slightly in order to catch a glimpse of the man's face. I started as my eyes fell upon it. It was indeed the very face with which my studies had made me familiar. The regular statuesque features, broad brow, well-rounded chin, and dusky complexion were the exact counterpart of the innumerable statues, mummy-cases, and pictures which adorned the walls of the apartment. The thing was beyond all coincidence. The man must be an Egyptian.'

"Surely that isn't so unusual," I interjected at the time. However, Watson, my visitor's description of the man was most peculiar.

"Oh, but he was unlike any modern man, Mr. Holmes," said Vansittart Smith, shaking his head. "I shuffled towards the attendant with some intention of addressing him. I am not light of touch in conversation and found it difficult to strike the happy mean between the brusqueness of the superior and the geniality of the equal. As I came nearer, the man presented his side face to me, but kept his gaze still bent upon his work. Fixing my eyes upon the fellow's skin, I was conscious of a sudden impression that there was something inhuman and preternatural about its appearance. Over the temple and cheek-bone, it was as glazed and as shiny as varnished parchment. One couldn't fancy a drop of moisture upon that arid surface. From brow to chin, however, it was cross-hatched by a million delicate wrinkles, which interlaced as though Nature in some Māori mood had tried how wild and intricate a pattern she could devise. [18]

"'Ou est la collection de Memphis?' I asked, with the awkward air of a person who is devising a question merely for the purpose of opening a conversation.

"'C'est la,' replied the man brusquely, nodding his head at the other side of the room.

"'Vous êtes un Egyptien, n'est-ce pas?' I asked again.

"The attendant looked up and turned his strange dark eyes upon me. They were vitreous, with a misty dry shininess, such as I had never seen in a human head before. As I gazed into them, I saw some strong emotion gather in their depths, which rose and deepened until it broke into a look of something akin both to horror and to hatred.

"'*Non, monsieur,*' said he. '*Je suis Français.*'

"The man turned abruptly and bent low over his polishing," continued Vansittart Smith. "I gazed at him for a moment in astonishment, and then, turning to a chair in a retired corner behind one of the doors, I proceeded to make notes of my research among the papyri. My thoughts, however refused to return into their natural groove. They would run upon the enigmatical attendant with the sphinx-like face and the parchment skin. I thought that there was something more to him. In his strange eyes, there was a sense of power, of wisdom – so I read them – and of weariness, utter weariness, and ineffable despair. It may be all imagination, but I never had so strong an impression. 'By Jove,' I cried to myself, 'I must have another look at them!' I rose and paced round the Egyptian rooms, but the man who had excited my curiosity had disappeared.'

"A peculiar tale," I remarked. "However, you mentioned that you spoke with him moments before his death?"

"That is correct, Mr. Holmes," said Vansittart Smith. "It happened like this: I sat down again in my quiet corner and continued to work at my notes. I had gained the information that I required from the papyri, and it only remained to write it down while it was still fresh in my memory. For a time, my pencil travelled rapidly over the paper, but soon the lines became less level, the words more blurred, and then, with a sudden gasp and an intaking of the breath, I returned to consciousness. For a moment, it flashed upon me that I had dropped asleep in my study chair at home.

"The moon was shining fitfully through the unshuttered window, however, and, as my eye ran along the lines of mummies and the endless array of polished cases, I remembered clearly where I was and how I came there. Stretching out my cramped limbs, I looked at my watch – which read close upon one in the morning – and burst into a chuckle as I observed the hour. I thought to myself, Mr. Holmes, that the episode would make an admirable anecdote to be introduced into my next paper as a relief to the graver and heavier speculations. I was a little cold, but wide awake and much refreshed.'

"You must have been quite tired out by your journey, Mr. Vansittart Smith," I said, "to sleep through the clanking civil guard, the footsteps of sightseers, and even the loud hoarse bell which gives the signal for closing. It doesn't speak well for the security of the museum that they should be so lax to allow such an uninvited overnight guest."

"Yes, well, Mr. Holmes – in their defence, it was no wonder that the guardians had overlooked me, for the door threw its heavy black shadow right across the chair in which I lay. In any case, the complete silence was impressive. Neither outside nor inside was there a creak or a murmur. I was alone with the dead men of a dead civilisation. Though the outer city reeked of the garish nineteenth century, in all this chamber there was scarce an article, from the shrivelled ear of wheat to the pigment-box of the painter, which hadn't held its own against four-thousand years. Here was the flotsam and jetsam washed up by the great ocean of time from that far-off empire. From stately Thebes, from lordly Luxor, from the great temples of Heliopolis, from a hundred rifled tombs, these relics had been brought. I glanced round at the long silent figures who flickered vaguely up through the gloom, at the busy toilers who were now so restful, and I fell into a reverent and thoughtful mood. An unwonted sense of my own youth and insignificance came over me. Leaning back in my chair, I gazed dreamily down the long vista of rooms, all silvery with the moonshine, which extend through the whole wing of the widespread building. Then, my eyes fell upon the yellow glare of a distant lamp.

"I sat up in my chair, Mr. Holmes, with my nerves all on edge. The light was advancing slowly towards me, pausing from time to time, and then coming jerkily onwards. The bearer moved noiselessly. In the utter silence, there was no suspicion of the pat of a footfall. An idea of robbers entered my head. I snuggled up further into the corner. The light was two rooms off. Now it was in the next chamber, and still there was no sound. With something approaching to a thrill of fear I observed a face, floating in the air as it were, behind the flare of the lamp. The figure was wrapped in shadow, but the light fell full upon the strange eager face. There was no mistaking the metallic glistening eyes and the cadaverous skin. It was the attendant with whom I had earlier conversed!

"My first impulse was to come forward and address him. A few words of explanation would set the matter clear and lead doubtless to my being conducted to some side door from which I might make my way to my hotel. As the man entered the chamber, however, there was something so stealthy in his movements, and so furtive in his expression, that I altered my intention. This was clearly no ordinary official walking the rounds. The fellow wore felt-soled slippers, stepped with a rising chest, and glanced quickly from left to right, while his hurried gasping breathing thrilled the flame of his lamp. I crouched silently back into the corner and watched him keenly, convinced that his errand was one of secret and probably sinister import.'

I interjected here, Watson, that he had commended his client on making a wise choice, for some criminals would hardly refrain from violence in such a situation.

"There was no hesitation in the other's movements," continued Vansittart Smith. "He stepped lightly and swiftly across to one of the great cases and, drawing a key from his pocket, he unlocked it. From the upper shelf he pulled down a mummy, which he bore away with him, and laid it with much care and solicitude upon the ground. By it he placed his lamp, and then squatting down beside it in Eastern fashion, he began with long quivering fingers to undo the cerecloths and bandages which girt it round. As the crackling rolls of linen peeled off one after the other, a strong aromatic odour filled the chamber, and fragments of scented wood and of spices pattered down upon the marble floor.

"It was clear to me, Mr. Holmes, that this mummy had never been unswathed before. I will admit that the operation interested me keenly. I thrilled all over with curiosity, and my head protruded further and further from behind the door. When, however, the last roll had been removed from the four-thousand-year-old head, it was all that I could do to stifle an outcry of amazement. First, a cascade of long, black, glossy tresses poured over the workman's hands and arms. A second turn of the bandage revealed a low, white forehead, with a pair of delicately arched eyebrows. A third uncovered a pair of bright, deeply fringed eyes, and a straight, well-cut nose, while a fourth and last showed a sweet, full, sensitive mouth, and a beautifully curved chin. The whole face was one of extraordinary loveliness, save for the one blemish that in the centre of the forehead there was a single irregular, coffee-coloured splotch. It was a triumph of the embalmer's art. My eyes must have grown larger and larger as I gazed upon it, and I chirruped in my throat with satisfaction.

"Its effect upon me was as nothing, however, compared with that which it produced upon the strange attendant. He threw his hands up into the air, burst into a harsh clatter of words, and then, hurling himself down upon the ground beside the mummy, he threw his arms round her, and kissed her repeatedly upon the lips and brow. *"Ma petite!"* he groaned in French. *"Ma pauvre petite!"* His voice broke with emotion, and his innumerable wrinkles quivered and writhed, but I observed in the lamplight that his shining eyes were still as dry and tearless as two beads of steel. For some minutes he lay, with a twitching face, crooning and moaning over the beautiful head. Then he broke into a sudden smile, said some words in an unknown tongue, and sprang to his feet with the vigorous air of one who has braced himself for an effort.

"In the centre of the room there was a large circular case which contained, as I had frequently remarked, a magnificent collection of early

458

Egyptian rings and precious stones. To this the attendant strode and, unlocking it, he threw it open. On the ledge at the side, he placed his lamp, and beside it a small earthenware jar which he had drawn from his pocket. He then took a handful of rings from the case, and with a most serious and anxious face he proceeded to smear each in turn with some liquid substance from the earthen pot, holding them to the light as he did so. He was clearly disappointed with the first lot, for he threw them petulantly back into the case, and drew out some more. One of these, a massive ring with a large crystal set in it, he seized and eagerly tested with the contents of the jar. Instantly he uttered a cry of joy and threw out his arms in a wild gesture which upset the pot and sent the liquid streaming across the floor to my very feet. The attendant drew a red handkerchief from his bosom, and, mopping up the mess, he followed it into the corner, where in a moment he found himself face to face with me.

"'Excuse me,' said I, with all imaginable politeness. 'I have been unfortunate enough to fall asleep behind this door.'

"'And you have been watching me?' the attendant asked in English, with a most venomous look on his corpse-like face.

"I am a truthful man, Mr. Holmes, so a lie never crossed my mind. 'I confess,' said I, 'that I have noticed your movements, and that they have aroused my curiosity and interest in the highest degree.'

"The man drew a long flamboyant-bladed knife from his bosom. 'You have had a very narrow escape,' he said. 'Had I seen you ten minutes ago, I should have driven this through your heart. As it is, if you touch me or interfere with me in any way, you are a dead man.'

"'I have no wish to interfere with you,' I answered, now somewhat alarmed. 'My presence here is entirely accidental. All I ask is that you will have the extreme kindness to show me out through some side door." I spoke with as great a suavity as I am capable, for the man was still pressing the tip of his dagger against the palm of his left hand, as though to assure himself of its sharpness, while his face preserved its malignant expression.

"'If I thought . . .' said the attendant. 'But no, perhaps it is as well. What is your name? Vansittart Smith,' the other repeated, after I gave it. 'Are you the same Vansittart Smith who gave a paper in London upon El Kab? I saw a report of it. Your knowledge of the subject is contemptible.'

"'Sir!' I cried, rather offended.

"'Yet it is superior to that of many who make even greater pretensions. The whole keystone of our old life in Egypt wasn't the inscriptions or monuments of which you make so much, but was our hermetic philosophy and mystic knowledge, of which you say little or nothing.'

"'Our old life!' I repeated. And then something else suddenly grabbed my attention, 'Good God, look at the mummy's face!'

"The strange man turned and flashed his light upon the dead woman, uttering a long doleful cry as he did so. The action of the air had already undone all the art of the embalmer. The skin had fallen away, the eyes had sunk inwards, the discoloured lips had writhed away from the yellow teeth, and the brown mark upon the forehead alone showed that it was indeed the same face that had shown such youth and beauty a few short minutes before. The man flapped his hands together in grief and horror. Then mastering himself by a strong effort he turned his hard eyes once more upon me.

"'It doesn't matter,' he said, in a shaking voice. 'It doesn't really matter. I came here tonight with the fixed determination to do something. It is now done. All else is as nothing. I have found my quest. The old curse is broken. I can rejoin her. What matter about her inanimate shell so long as her spirit is awaiting me at the other side of the veil!'

"'These are wild words,' I thought to myself. I tell you, Mr. Holmes, that I was becoming more and more convinced that I had encountered a madman.

"'Time presses, and I must go,'" continued the attendant. 'The moment is at hand for which I have waited this weary time. But I must show you out first. Come with me.'

"Taking up the lamp, he turned from the disordered chamber and led me swiftly through the long series of the Egyptian, Assyrian, and Persian apartments. At the end of the latter, he pushed open a small door let into the wall and descended a winding stone stair. I felt the cold fresh air of the night upon his brow. There was a door opposite me that appeared to communicate with the street. To the right of this another door stood ajar, throwing a spurt of yellow light across the passage. 'Come in here!' said the attendant shortly.

"I am not afraid to admit, Mr. Holmes, that I hesitated. I had hoped that I had come to the end of my adventure. Yet my curiosity was strong. I could not leave the matter unsolved, so I followed my strange companion into the lighted chamber, where the gnarled heavy-eyed man sat himself down upon the edge of the bed and motioned me into the chair. I glanced round and noted a pile of papers upon the table next to me.

"'There may be design in this,' said the attendant, still speaking excellent English. 'It may be decreed that I should leave some account behind as a warning to all rash mortals who would set their wits up against workings of Nature. I leave it with you. Make such use as you will of it. I speak to you now with my feet upon the threshold of the other world. I am, as you surmised, an Egyptian. It was in the Reign of Tuthmosis that I first saw the light.'

"I must have flinched at this mad statement, Mr. Holmes," said my visitor, "but I held my tongue, and the man continued."

"'You shrink away from me. Wait, and you will see that I am more to be pitied than to be feared. My name was Sosra. My father had been the Chief Priest of Osiris in the Great Temple of Abaris, which stood in those days upon the Bubastic branch of the Nile. I was brought up in the temple and was trained in all those mystic arts. I was an apt pupil. Before I was sixteen, I had learned all which the wisest priest could teach me. From that time on, I studied Nature's secrets for myself and shared my knowledge with no man.

"'Of all the questions which attracted me, there were none over which I laboured so long as over those which concern themselves with the nature of life. I probed deeply into the vital principle. The aim of medicine had been to drive away disease when it appeared. It seemed to me that a method might be devised which should so fortify the body as to prevent weakness or death from ever taking hold of it. It is useless that I should recount my research. You would scarce comprehend them if I did. Suffice it that their result was to furnish me with a substance which, when injected into the blood, would endow the body with strength to resist the effects of time, of violence, or of disease. It would not indeed confer immortality, but its potency would endure for many thousands of years. There was nothing of mystery or magic in the matter. It was simply a chemical discovery, which may well be made again. Love of life runs high in the young. It seemed to me that I had broken away from all human care now that I had abolished pain and driven death to such a distance. With a light heart, I poured the accursed stuff into my veins.'"

Holmes paused. "Here, Watson, Vansittart Smith summarized the man's peculiar delusion.

"The attendant went on," he explained, "to describe how he shared his wondrous elixir with his friend Parmes, a priest of Thoth. Later, he fell in love with the daughter of the Governor, a beauty named Atma. However, his friend also loved her and the two of them fell out. When the white plague came to his city, Atma shrank from Sosra's offer of his elixir. [19] A day later, she was dead. In his delirious grief, Sosra tried to end his life, but failed, for the influence of the elixir was too strong. Then his former friend came to him and told him that he had devised a method to counter the elixir and had already taken it. Parmes refused to tell Sosra his secret. However, before he died, he crowed that the poison could only be found in the Ring of Thoth, a large and weighty circlet made not of gold, but of a rarer and heavier metal called platinum. The ring had a hollow crystal set in it, in which some few drops of liquid might be stored.

"According to his tale, Sosra spent many centuries searching for this ring. Even as the town of Abaris vanished beneath the sands, the man persisted in his quest. "I have travelled in all lands," said the Egyptian, "and I have dwelt with all nations. Every tongue is the same to me. I learned them all to help pass the weary time. I need not tell you how slowly they drifted by, the long dawn of modern civilisation, the dreary middle years, the dark times of barbarism. They are all behind me now, I have never looked with the eyes of love upon another woman. Atma knows that I have been constant to her.

"'It was my custom to read all that the scholars had to say upon Ancient Egypt. I have been in many positions, sometimes affluent, sometimes poor, but I have always found enough to enable me to buy the journals which deal with such matters. Some nine months ago I was in San Francisco, when I read an account of some discoveries made in the neighbourhood of Abaris. My heart leapt into my mouth as I read it. It said that the excavator had busied himself in exploring some tombs recently unearthed. In one, there had been found an unopened mummy with an inscription upon the outer case setting forth that it contained the body of the daughter of the Governor of the city in the days of Tuthmosis. It added that on removing the outer case, there had been exposed a large platinum ring set with a crystal, which had been laid upon the breast of the embalmed woman. This, then, was where Parmes had hid the ring of Thoth! He might well say that it was safe, for no Egyptian would ever stain his soul by removing even the outer case of a buried friend.

"'That very night, I set off from San Francisco, and in a few weeks I found myself once more at Abaris, if a few sand-heaps and crumbling walls may retain the name of the great city. I hurried to the Frenchmen who were digging there and asked them for the ring. They replied that both the ring and the mummy had been sent to the Boulak Museum at Cairo. [20] To Boulak I went, but only to be told that Mariette Bey had claimed them and had shipped them to the Louvre. I followed them, and there at last, in the Egyptian chamber, I came, after close upon four-thousand years, upon the remains of my Atma, and upon the ring for which I had sought so long.

"'But how was I to lay hands upon them? How was I to have them for my very own? It chanced that the office of attendant was vacant. I went to the Director. I convinced him that I knew much about Egypt. In my eagerness I said too much. He remarked that a Professor's chair would suit me better than a seat in the Conciergerie. I knew more, he said, than he did. It was only by blundering and letting him think that he had over-

462

estimated my knowledge that I prevailed upon him to let me move the few effects which I have retained into this chamber. It is my first and my last night here.

"'Such is my story, Mr. Vansittart Smith,' concluded the Egyptian. 'I need not say more to a man of your perception. By a strange chance, you have this night looked upon the face of the woman whom I loved in those far-off days. There were many rings with crystals in the case, and I had to test to be sure of the one which I wanted. A glance at the crystal has shown me that the liquid is indeed within it, and that I shall at last be able to shake off that accursed health which has been worse to me than the foulest disease. I have nothing more to say to you. I have unburdened myself. You may tell my story, or you may withhold it at your pleasure. The choice rests with you. I owe you some amends, for you have had a narrow escape of your life this night. I was a desperate man, and not to be baulked in my purpose. Had I seen you before the thing was done, I might have put it beyond your power to oppose me or to raise an alarm. This is the door. It leads into the Rue de Rivoli. Good night!'

"I glanced back," said my visitor. "For a moment, the lean figure of Sosra the Egyptian stood framed in the narrow doorway. The next, the door had slammed, and the heavy rasping of a bolt broke on the silent night. I tell you, Mr. Holmes, that his words continue to haunt me. Could there possibly be some truth to them?"

Epilogue

After a moment's pause, Holmes continued. "I considered Mr. Vansittart Smith's strange story for several minutes, Watson. I assured him that Mr. Sosra was either a madman or someone under the influence of a strong entheogen and that he should erase the entire episode from his mind.
[21] My visitor seemed reassured by this pronouncement and departed back to his studies. He holds, to this very day, the Richards Chair of Egyptian Archaeology at one of our leading universities."

I peered at Holmes. "But that isn't the truth, is it?"

He shrugged. "It isn't an untruth, Watson. There is no doubt that Mr. Sosra was quite mad by the very end. However, it was, perhaps, not the whole truth. As you have now guessed, I suspected that there was more to the tale."

"Perhaps the man was part of a band of thieves?" I suggested. "They fell out over the division of the loot and one man was poisoned."

Holmes shook his head. "I'm afraid that will not do. First, while bands of thieves do turn upon each other from time to time, they typically delay such actions until they are well away from the location of the crime.

Second, if this were an act done in the heat of the moment, surely they would have simply used a knife and not some poison so subtle as to escape the detection of the police. Finally, having silently done away with their partner, why were no items removed from the museum? No, I was immediately certain that something else was afoot."

"But what could you do about it?" I asked.

"It was immediately clear that a trip to Paris would be required. As my purse wasn't overly filled in those days, I made my way to Victoria to catch the London, Brighton, and South Coast Railway to Newhaven and so over to Dieppe. You may recall, Watson, that we once took the same ferry on our way to Brussels. [22] The trains were slow, and the Channel was rough, but my vigorous constitution quickly shook off such inconveniences. I deposited my small carpet-bag at the Hotel du Louvre before turning my steps to the French detective service. It was here that I first met Francois Le Villard, and that gentleman proved to be much more amenable to my inquiries than our friends at Scotland Yard would have been in his stead. Fortunately, the police hadn't yet consigned the body of the attendant who called himself Sosra to the pauper's grave, and I was permitted to examine it. My first impression confirmed Mr. Vansittart Smith's observations that the man must be an Egyptian. The national angularity of the shoulders and narrowness of the hips were alone sufficient to identify him. [23] The man's skin was quite remarkable, being almost completely devoid of visible pores, despite a close inspection with my glass."

"There are various medical conditions which produce a hypohidrotic dysplasia of the skin," I noted. [24]

"Indeed," said Holmes with a nod. "And the man's face was as wrinkled as Vansittart Smith described. But it was his eyes that really caught my attention. There was something saurian about them, something reptilian. It reminded me of the *membrana nictitans* of the snakes, which gives such a shiny effect." [25]

"I have never heard of such a thing," said I.

"No, it was quite peculiar. However, for my purposes, the thing of greater interest was the slightly sour smell upon the dead man's lips. I concluded that poison had certainly been the method of his demise. But what poison? As you know, I have myself dabbled with poisons a good deal." He smiled and held out his hand, still discoloured in places by the strong acids with which he routinely experimented.

"The police had, of course, already emptied the pockets of the dead man and collected his papers," continued Holmes. "These gave his name as Ibsay Sosra, and his birthplace as Tell-el-Daba in the Khedivate of Egypt. His last position listed him as a Professor of Egyptology at the

University of Bonn, but his passport was most recently stamped in Marseilles, Alexandria, New York, and San Francisco, suggesting that there were some elements of truth to his tale.

"I then asked to see Mr. Sosra's chambers. Le Villard gave me a key and directions. I was interested to learn that his position as attendant at Louvre came with a rare privilege – quarters within the building itself. It was a small room, such as is devoted to a concierge. The ashes of a fire were heaped in a cold grate. At one side stood a truckle bed, and at the other a coarse wooden chair, with a round table in the centre, which bore the remains of a meal. I looked over this a careful eye and remarked that all the small details of the room were of the quaintest design and antique workmanship. The candlesticks, the vases upon the chimney-piece, and the ornaments upon the walls were all antiques of the remote past fully worthy of public display in the halls above. Most significantly, I found the ashes of a considerable number of burned papers in the back of the grate, all of it charred to pieces."

"He must have done so before his final journey into the great beyond?" I suggested.

"Perhaps," said Holmes, with a small nod. "Though he seemed intent upon carrying out his action as soon as Mr. Vansittart Smith was turned out into the street. And yet, there was one thing that told me that there another man in those chambers that night beyond Mr. Sosra and Mr. Vansittart Smith. You see, upon the table was a small porcelain tray, within which there were ashes from two different cigarettes. Even in those days, I already appreciated the importance of being able to distinguish between various brands of tobacco – I had even begun an early draft of my well-received monograph upon the subject. The first set of ashes belonged to an Egyptian blend sweetened with molasses, likely made by one of the famed manufacturers of Alexandria, as might be preferred by an Eastern gentleman such as Mr. Sosra. However, the second was a cheroot."

"A strange choice for Mr. Vansittart Smith," I noted.

"Capital, Watson!" Holmes exclaimed. "I see that you observed some important trifles during your time with the Fifth Northumberland Fusiliers. My visitor neither made no mention of smoking that night, nor was he the sort to enjoy such a rude cigar as favoured by those who have spent time in India."

"But how could you track this other visitor? Even after Plassey, the French have retained an interest in Pondicherry. [26] There must have been hundreds of men in Paris who enjoyed cheroots."

"I had a similar thought. However, from the stamps in his papers, the reclusive Mr. Sosra hadn't been long in Paris. I asked myself where he might meet someone with whom he developed such a rapport that he would invite this individual back to his chambers."

"Could it have been a woman?" I suggested.

"Unlikely. First, if we are to believe any parts of Mr. Sosra's tale, he was obsessed with his lost love, Atma. Second, the number of women in Paris who smoked cheroots was undoubtedly close to nil. No, I was convinced this was a man, but how was I to locate him amongst the multitudes of the City of Lights? My only hope was to be found in the remains of the meal upon his table."

"What do you mean?" I asked.

"There was a meal, but no means to cook it. Therefore, Mr. Sosra purchased the meal and brought it back to his room. I obtained a tourist map of Paris and circled all the dining establishments within a brisk walk of the museum. I discounted some of the more fashionable cafés, for a man like Sosra would stick out like a sore thumb in such an establishment. That narrowed the field to some thirty-two potential locales to investigate. I was less flush with shillings at the time and had no confidence in the local boys, so was forced to personally stop in at each place. However, my fourth stop – a brasserie and watering hole for the workers of the market at Les Halles – proved to be the place where Sosra obtained his meal. My quest was made simpler by the fact that Sosra was a physically remarkable individual, as proved to be his companion. A sharp-eyed waitress recalled them, for they were quite the pair. She described the other man as a middle-aged man, with a thin, projecting nose, a high, bald forehead, and a huge, grizzled moustache. His face was gaunt and swarthy, and scored with deep, savage lines much like those of Mr. Sosra." Holmes paused. "Does that sound like anyone you know, Watson?"

"It sounds a bit like Colonel Moran," said I, diffidently.

"Capital!" cried Holmes. "That is exactly who I now believe it to have been. At that time, Sebastian Moran had recently left Her Majesty's Indian Army under a cloud and retired to Conduit Street to begin work upon his first book. [27] Of course, at the time, I had no further way to identify this individual, and my investigation into the death of Mr. Sosra met a dead end. I returned to London and lost myself in other matters."

"I don't understand," said I, shaking my head. "What possibly connection could Colonel Moran have with an Egyptian professor?"

"Ah, yes, I forgot to mention the one other physical clue that I retrieved from Mr. Sosra's room. It was a scrap of paper that had slipped under the truckle bed, and hence escaped the small bonfire set by Moran. On it were various chemical notes, one word of which stood out to me like a bolt of lightning – *cantarella*."

"What is *cantarella*?" I asked.

"It is no surprise that you haven't heard of it, for it is unknown to most. Fortunately, I've read deeply in the criminal annals, both modern and ancient, as there is little new under the sun. You certainly recall the horrible Marchioness de Brinvilliers, one of history's most famous poisoners. But another was the beautiful and terrible Lucretia, once owner of the famous Black Pearl of the Borgias. Her favoured poison was known as *cantarella*, a white powder with a pleasant taste ideal for sprinkling on food or in wine. The exact nature of this poison has been lost to the mists of time. Some scholars have speculated that it was a form of arsenic, others believe it to be something derived from the blister beetle, or possibly some malign combination of agents. However, all agree that the ancient Greeks originally developed it. Of course, there was much exchange between the Greeks and the Egyptians, especially during the Ptolemaic era, and it isn't unreasonable to hypothesize that they first learned of it from the descendants of the pharaohs."

"But if it has been lost, how can one detect it?"

"Precisely. The idea of using a form of poison that couldn't possibly be discovered by any chemical test would be of great value to many clever and ruthless men. Can you think of one whose path we have crossed?"

"Professor Moriarty!"

"And now, with the clear perspective of hindsight, you begin to understand," said Holmes. "In retrospect, this was my first glimpse through the veil. This is when I first developed some small inkling that there was an organizing principal behind all the forgery cases, robberies, murders, and other misdeeds done throughout our great city. As I slowly tugged on that string, it eventually led me to the Mathematical Chair of one of our smaller universities, and from there to a raging torrent high in the Swiss Alps, where I almost met my end. Of course, that was the work of another decade of investigations."

With the dropping of the sun over the Theban Hills and the end of the muezzin's call to prayer, a deep calm and quiet settled over the mighty river. The night was fine, and the stars were twinkling brightly overhead.

"I can see now why I gave this to my literary editor to publish as a fiction," said I, after several minutes of contemplation. "No one would possibly believe it."

"Perhaps not. But come, Watson," said Holmes, with a smile. "'*tis not too late to seek a newer world, for my purpose holds to sail beyond the sunset, and the baths of all the western stars.*"

I chuckled at his slight misquoting of Tennyson, amazed that Holmes had found room in his brain attic for something so extraneous to his work as a simple poem. Certainly, many of the limits of the Holmes that I had first met at Barts back in '81 – with his "nil" knowledge of literature – had long ago been overcome by the man now standing at my side.

"*We are not now that strength which in old days moved Earth and Heaven,*'" said I, in return.

"*Perhaps we have been made weak by time and fate,*'" said Holmes, "*but we remain strong in will to strive, to seek, to find '.* . . for is that not the motto of the firm?" [28] He patted me on the shoulder, his grey eyes shining like stars. "Good night, my dear Watson. Get some sleep. One never knows what adventures tomorrow shall bring."

I watched as he vanished into the darkness beyond the flickering blue light from the flame of the port lamp and then turned my gaze back up to the vast tableau of the heavens stretched out before me. In the dry mystical night air, my thoughts drifted to a young man, dead some three-thousand years, and yet the long night had spread her wings over him, so that he became as imperishable as the stars. Perhaps – through the strange workings of fate that allowed his tomb to escape the centuries unscathed – the boy-king had obtained a sort of immortality. My mind turned to the lifetime of adventures that I had been fortunately enough to share with Mr. Sherlock Holmes. Written in the night sky, I saw flash before me the myriads of faces belonging to clients, foes, and friends, as well as the remembrances of such experiences that knew no rival upon this earth.

I then sensed a presence at my side, and smelled the familiar bird's-eye tobacco favoured by my friend.

"I decided to take a final stroll upon the deck before turning in," said he, amiably, peering into the darkness of the western hills. "Can you see anything, Watson?"

"Yes, wonderful things," said I, trying to conceal the emotion in my voice, which Holmes typically detested.

He stared at me for a moment, and then gave a brief nod, as if he had come to a weighty decision. "Perhaps Hamlet was correct when he spoke to Horatio, Watson."

"What do you mean, Holmes?"

"Have you forgotten," said Holmes, quietly, "what was perhaps the most remarkable part of Mr. Sosra's story?"

"What was that?"

"The earthenware jar."

I shook my head in confusion. "The one that he dropped, spilling the liquid at Vansittart Smith's feet? I fail to see its importance."

"If we were to take Mr. Sosra at his word, then he was one of history's first alchemists. Of course, from such thinkers come our modern term of chemistry, which you know to be one of my great interests. I asked myself: *What was in that jar?*"

I frowned and considered the possibilities. "He was using it to test whether the substance in the ring of Thoth was the correct one."

"Precisely, Watson!" said Holmes, an unusual agitation present in his voice. "But how did it work? Surely the only way to determine if the liquid were the one that he sought would be to see if it somehow reacted with the original elixir that gave him such prolonged life."

A chill passed through me. "What are you saying? Surely, you of all people don't believe his mad tale."

"No? You are perhaps correct, Watson, when you call Sosra's tale mad. And yet, we have seen some remarkable things in our time, have we not? Is such an entity so different than the serum devised by Lowenstein of Prague?" [29]

"Yes, I suppose so," I concluded. "But we shall never know."

"That is where you are wrong, my friend," said Holmes, reaching into his pocket and removing an earthenware jar. He sat musing for some time with this object in his hand before placing it on the table between us.

I finally could stand it no longer. "Is that it?" I asked, a tremble in my voice.

"It is," said Holmes, simply. "When my investigation was complete, I prevailed on Inspector Le Villard that there was no further use for the jar and begged him to allow me to bring it back to my chemical bench for further analysis."

"But Vansittart Smith said that it had been spilled!" I protested.

"Yes, most of it. But there was still a modicum of the liquid left inside."

"And you analysed it?" I asked breathlessly.

"I have tried to do so, off and on, for over two-score years now."

"And what does it contain?"

Holmes shook his head. "It is one of the most complex solutions that I have ever tested. At first, I thought it to be merely a variation of the *mithridate* as transcribed by Celsus, with a small amount of natron added. [30] However, I then recalled Vansittart Smith's description of Sosra's eyes."

I considered this. "The nictitating membrane!"

"Precisely, Watson," said Holmes, nodding. "There was certainly the moulted skin of some snake in it – for isn't the asklepian the symbol of your profession? Though it took much time to determine the precise species involved. [31] And there was one final ingredient that took the longest for me to identify – this was the royal jelly of the humble *Apis mellifera*." [32]

The implications of Holmes's words washed over me. After so long, I finally understood why a genius of his calibre at the very height of his powers would retire to the Sussex Downs.

Holmes then proceeded to pull from his pocket an item that I hadn't seen in many years. It was a neat morocco case, which I knew contained a delicate needle and hypodermic syringe. He set it on the table between us, smiled, and walked away . . . .

NOTES

1.   Later evidence date this case to April 1923, when Watson was seventy years of age (based on his birthdate of 7 August, 1852) and Holmes was sixty-eight (based on his birthdate of 6 January, 1854).

2.   Howard Carter (1874-1939) discovered the tomb of the pharaoh now known as Tutankhamun on 4 November, 1922. Carter did not open the tomb until his patron, George Herbert, 5th Earl of Carnarvon (1866-1923), arrived from England on 24 November.

3.   In "The Adventure of the Empty House", Holmes tells Watson: "*I then passed through Persia, looked in at Mecca, and paid a short but interesting visit to the Khalifa at Khartoum, the results of which I have communicated to the Foreign Office.*" The full details of his perilous journeys in this area have yet to be reported. Non-Muslims are prohibited from entering Mecca, and the meteorite relic called the Black Stone is not known to have ever been stolen. After the fall of Khartoum, the body of General Charles George Gordon (1833-1885) was reportedly "desecrated" and tossed in a well by the victorious forces of the Mahdi.

4.   The most recent instalment published in *The Strand Magazine* prior to the events in this case was "The Adventure of the Creeping Man" (March 1923).

5.   Watson's thoughts echo those of Conan Doyle during a lecture he gave on 15 November, 1893 at the Albert Hall, Leeds, and reported in *The Leeds Times*.

6.   The Mortuary Temple of the queen, now called Hatshepsut, is part of the Deir el-Bahari complex lying just over the hills from the Valley of the Kings.

7.   Watson's weak grasp of Egyptian pharaohs is evident here, for Ozymandias is an ancient Greek name for Ramses II. Percy Bysshe Shelly's viewed the statue that inspired his famous poem (published 1818) in the British Museum, not *in situ*. Nevertheless, the words remain evocative: "*Look on my works, ye Mighty, and despair! No thing beside remains. Round the decay, of that colossal wreck, boundless and bare, the lone and level sands stretch far away.*"

8.   Watson's thoughts again echo the words of Conan Doyle, who spoke about Lord Carnarvon's death to a reporter from *The Glasgow Herald* on 6 April, 1923.

9.   Watson is misremembering the line from *Hamlet*, Act 1, Scene 5. When discussing the ghost of Hamlet's father, Horatio notes: "*O day and night, but this is wondrous strange.*" Hamlet responds with the famous line "*There are more things in Heaven and Earth, Horatio, than are dreamt of in your philosophy.*"

10.   Bertram Fletcher Robinson (1870-1907) was a respected journalist and writer of detective fiction. In 1904, he authored a front-page article for *The Daily Express* entitled "A Priestess of Death", in which he investigated the purported malign powers of an inner coffin lid, painted with the portrait of an unidentified woman. In the possession of the British Museum since 1889, this lid had been blamed for many personal and national disasters. On 6

April, 1923, Conan Doyle told *The Glasgow Herald* that the son of his friend Sir William Ingram had "*found the mummy while hunting in Somaliland. Inscribed on the mummy's breast were the words 'May the person who unwraps me die rapidly, and may his bones lie unburied.*' This young man was drowned a few days later in a watercourse, and his body was never found."

11. Carnarvon's "constitutional weakness" was the *sequalae* of a serious motor accident in 1903. His doctors advised that he "winter" out of England, leading him to Egypt, where he became an enthusiastic amateur Egyptologist.

12. Sadly, this chapter of Holmes's famous *magnum opus* has never come to light.

13. The American Theodore Davis (1838-1915) held the *firman* – or permission to dig – in the Valley of the Kings prior to Carnarvon. In 1912, Davis famously wrote: "*I fear the Valley of the Tombs is now exhausted.*" He died without realizing how supremely erroneous was this statement.

14. Egyptian "independence" from the United Kingdom had only been established two years earlier on 22 February, 1922, and was incomplete, for the British military still occupied the country to maintain control over the critical Suez Canal. The nature of the rift between Carnarvon and Cater in February 1923 has never been fully explained. Watson's accusation against Carter was perhaps not completely unfounded. A 1934 letter from Alan Gardiner accused Carter of stealing an amulet from the tomb, and Henry Burton identified eighteen other treasures found in Carter's home after his death as being taken from the tomb without authorization.

15. One version of Mr. Vansittart Smith's tale was published anonymously in *The Cornhill Magazine* as "The Ring of Thoth" (1890). There is no mention of Holmes's involvement, and the story was later attributed to Watson's first literary editor, Arthur Conan Doyle. Conan Doyle claimed that the tale was inspired by a trip to Paris and a viewing of the Egyptian mummies in the Louvre, rather than having been told it by Watson.

16. A Fellow of the Royal Society (F.R.S.) is an award established in 1663 and granted to those who have made a "*substantial contribution to the improvement of natural knowledge*". Gower Street is in Bloomsbury and runs through the University College of London. Coincidentally, the Petrie Museum of Egyptian Archaeology was established a block away in 1915.

17. Despite the similarity in names, this cannot be the archaeologist Howard Carter, who would have only been six years of age in 1879.

18. At first glance, this appears to be an unfortunate example of the casual racism ingrained in Victorian society, a link between the Māori of New Zealand and a state of being "*wild*". Upon further examination, however, this is simply a reference to the Māori practice of *Tā moko*, or tattooing – which often includes lines upon the face – as being reminiscent of the man's deep wrinkles.

19. The term "white plague" historically refers to tuberculosis, given this name for the pale, sickly appearance it caused in its victims.

20. In 1858, a museum was established at Boulak, now called Boulaq, in a former warehouse. The building lay on the bank of the Nile River, and in 1878 it suffered considerable damage owing to flooding. In 1891, the collections were moved to a former royal palace, in the Giza district of Cairo, where they remained until 1902, when they were moved again to a building in Tahrir Square.

21. Entheogens are psychoactive substances used as part of ancient religious rituals. Archeological evidence suggests the Egyptians were users of such agents as Syrian rue and blue water lily, the latter famously mentioned as the "*lotuses*" of *The Odyssey*.

22. The London, Brighton, and South Coast Railway (LB&SCR) ran a passenger service from Victoria Station to Newhaven, where it connected to the *Chemins de Fer de l'Ouest* cross-channel ferry. Opening in 1868 and advertised as the "*shortest and cheapest*" route to Paris, it was slower than the rival Dover to Calais route due to a much longer time at sea.

23. This observation demonstrates Holmes's early interest in the anthropometrical technique of Alphonse Bertillon (1853-1914), as mentioned in *The Hound of the Baskervilles*.

24. Hypohidrosis, a reduced ability to sweat due to fewer sweat glands than normal, was first reported in 1848.

25. The *membrana nictitans*, or nictitating membrane, is a translucent "third eyelid" that protects and moistens the eyes of many amphibians and reptiles, but also some mammals, such as camels, polar bears, and seals. Most primates, including humans, do not possess one.

26. The Battle of Plassey (23 June, 1757) was a decisive victory of the British East India Company under Robert Clive over the Nawab of Bengal and his French allies. Although the French continued to control Pondicherry in the Bengal – Until 1954! – historians consider Plassey to mark the end of major French influence in the subcontinent.

27. Colonel Sebastian Moran's first book was *Heavy Game of the Western Himalayas* (1881).

28. Holmes and Watson quote excerpts from the famous 1833 poem *Ulysses* by Alfred, Lord Tennyson (1809-1892). In both the 1900 adventure, "The Problem of Thor Bridge, and in the 1903 case "The Adventure of the Creeping Man", Holmes stated that the motto of the firm was "*We can but try*." However, it seems probable that Holmes was rather nonchalant about this, and willing to change it as he saw fit.

29. As detailed in "The Adventure of the Creeping Man", Lowenstein developed the Serum that Professor Presbury self-administered in a quest for "*rejuvenescence*". The truth behind Presbury's strange transformation is a hotly debated topic amongst Holmesian scholars, leaving some to dismiss the entire case as a fiction.

30. *Mithridate* is a semi-mythical remedy antidote for poisoning said to have been created by Mithridates the Great of Pontus in the first century BCE. In 30 CE, the Roman encyclopaedist Aulus Cornelius Celsus detailed one list of its varied ingredients, though other versions existed. Physicians in

473

London prescribed it as late as 1786, with Oliver Cromwell being known to take it. Natron is a naturally-occurring soda ash that was used as a desiccant during the Egyptian mummification process.

31. The *asklepian*, or Rod of Asclepius, the Greek god of Medicine, was a rod with a single snake wound about it, for the snake's shedding of skin was a symbol of rejuvenation. The snake species utilized in Sosra's elixir was presumably the Egyptian cobra, a symbol of sovereignty incorporated into the crown of the pharaohs.

32. The western honeybee is thought to have first been domesticated in ancient Egypt. Tomb paintings dating to 2600 BCE depict the act of beekeeping.

Epilogue
A Travel-Worn and Battered Tin Dispatch Box
by David Marcum

The cold wind rattled one of the two tall windows overlooking Baker Street. Glancing that way from where I stood at my desk while retrieving some notes, I paused in my task, took a moment to fold a piece of waste paper, walk over, and wedge it between the window and the frame – silencing the distraction, if only for a little while.

Outside, what little sunlight that we'd seen on that bleak autumn day was fading, and the dark shapes hurrying along the pavement beneath the window were huddled as they passed in each direction – some on the way to evening shelter, and others upon errands that would allow for no rest this night. I wondered how many were doing good work, and which others were about on bad business. I liked to think that the majority of them, those shadowed and anonymous figures scurrying below me, faces invisible as their heads were turned down to hide from the wind and cold, tended toward the former, but I had long-ago learned what Sherlock Holmes had been at pains to teach me – about things I might never have suspected otherwise.

"Do you remember," I asked without looking around at him, "when you once told me that life is infinitely stranger than anything which the mind of man could invent?"

Holmes, who had spent the day updating his commonplace books with stacks of butchered newspapers, shears, and a glue pot, grunted something to acknowledge that I'd spoken.

"You said something along the lines of being unable to truly conceive what's going on out there," I continued. "Things that might seem so unusual to us, but to the people passing back and forth, they are mere commonplaces of existence."

I turned then to see that Holmes had paused in his self-imposed labor, his gaze distant as he recalled the conversation. I suspected that, if he truly turned his mind to it, he could tell what specific day it had taken place, and what I'd been wearing.

"I said something along the lines of us flying out of the window and removing the roofs, looking in at all the odd and connected things going on all around us, year after year and generation after generation. Coincidences and connections and accidental assistances and cross-purposes – chains of events that sometimes stretch for decades before culminating in the most curious and *outrè* results."

"You said it would make all fiction stale."

He nodded. "In the years since we had that conversation, have you seen anything to contradict the thought?"

"Not at all. In fact, if I was still somewhat surprised at the notion then – having known you for the better part of a decade when you said it – I've certainly seen and experienced enough by now to recognize that you were correct in every sense."

I returned to my desk, retrieved another bundle of papers, and then settled back in my chair by the fire, my old tin dispatch box open at my feet. It wasn't so different than the tin box that Holmes kept underneath his bed, and it was put to the same purpose: Holding records of past cases.

I recalled those first days of early January 1881, when Holmes and I had taken possession of these comfortable but humble Baker Street rooms. I had relocated on the evening of the very day when we first inspected the place, moving from a small private hotel in the Strand and transporting what little I owned in a single hansom cab. I had returned to London the previous November, a wretched shell of the man who had departed so confidently just a few years before. I had abandoned the British shores with neither kith nor kin left in my homeland, and quite frankly I hadn't expected to return – at least not for many years, if not decades. The Army life for me – or so I thought.

But my road took a sharp and nearly fatal turn at Maiwand. I would have died there but for my orderly, Murray, who threw me across the pack-horse carrying our medical supplies, already loaded for the retreat, and transported me to safety. I awoke in the Peshawar base hospital, destroyed, limp with terrible pain. For a few terrible moments, that was the limit of my awareness. I somehow lurched to my feet, unable to comprehend where I was or how I'd arrived there. If pressed, I could not have even stated my name, so great was my confusion. Then, as the staff rushed to lay me back down, I saw, pushed under the foot of my cot, my old tin dispatch box. Painted across it were the words *John H. Watson, M.D. Late Indian Army.* It had already been tied to the pack-horse when Murray slung me across and fled to relative safety. Somehow, he had contrived to see that it stayed with me at the hospital. Seeing that small piece of my old life was enough to calm me.

I'm not sure why Murray went to the effort. When we'd prepared for the retreat, the box was quickly emptied of all the useless detritus I'd accumulated since my arrival in Bombay some months before – meaningless souvenirs collected across India and Afghanistan – and filled with necessary medical supplies. Now, lying before my cot, it was empty, the supplies long-since having been put to good use elsewhere.

Even as I started to recover, I was soon laid low once again with that deadly scourge, enteric fever, and I was told afterwards that I came as close to death then as I have at any other point in my life. In my feverish dreams, my thoughts returned again and again to that tin dispatch box – as if it were an anchor to pin me to that spot where my body fought so that my soul couldn't not entirely drift away, or a rock to which I clung while the boiling waves tried to rip me away.

One's mind is a funny thing. I have no sense whether the times I leaned up to check and see if the box was still there actually occurred, or if that was all part of the tangled pattern of dreams which assailed me. Those occasions certainly seemed real enough – but then so did the bedside visits from my revered grandfather, who had passed away before I ever joined the army. He stood silently, offering no encouragement or instruction – Nothing at all. I couldn't tell if he meant for me to stay or go on.

When I recovered enough, I was returned to England, setting foot on the Portsmouth dock in November. I had very little with me – the clothes on my back, and a spare set tucked into the dispatch box. And my journals – those records that I'd begun to make during my recovery. I have always been a writer, from my youngest age, and I found that when I could not sleep – or would not, to avoid the terrible nightmares that stalked me in that horrific place of dreams, *la petite mort* – I would write. Daily sketches, or memories of my travels across the frontier, or of little incidents that I'd seen. Writing came easily, and it eased my mind so that eventually, sleep was not always the enemy.

I'd moved into our Baker Street rooms on the second night of January, and Holmes brought 'round his belongings from Montague Street the next morning – and it took far more drayage for him than a simple single hansom cab. We spent several days arranging our possessions to their best display, but in truth, I had very little to present. Holmes, of course, noticed immediately, and considering that we were essentially strangers then, it's a wonder he commented at all.

But he did.

"That is a singularly sad and abused piece of kit," he said, nodding toward the dispatch box – by way of starting a conversation, I think. I found myself defensive.

"It's been with me since – "

I stopped, not wanting to explain, even a little. I didn't know this proud young man, seeming so callow and untested when compared to what I had just been through. Though less than two years older than him, I felt that I'd lived more than a lifetime in the last half-year, and now I was an old and feeble man who wanted nothing better, having found a warm and quite place, than to hide and be left alone. Upon our very first meeting, Holmes had somehow rather rudely read my past as easily as if I'd handed him a sheet with the important highlights of my life recorded upon it. Why be forced into sharing anything further?

If nothing else, he was aware that he'd crossed some line and dropped the subject. And I moved my dispatch upstairs, to my own room.

There it remained for a long time. It was something of an object of simple veneration to me, and at first it stood empty, doing nothing but taking up a spot on the floor where it would regularly catch my gaze. Then, I had an idea. I would use it to store items that were precious to me.

I had very little that would meet such a qualification. A few family documents and photographs. Some papers that marked events or achievements in my life that, by someone's reckoning, might be considered important. (I did not choose to give very much honor to my Afghanistan Medal. It was tossed into a desk drawer, subject to my ambivalence when, after several months of recovery, the Army chose not to continue the association that I had fully expected. I would not, I had been informed, be returning to military service after all. Rather, I was left to reside in Baker Street and continue my convalescence and try to decide what I would do with the rest of my life, as my initial plan was burst asunder.)

What finally went into the tin dispatch box was what mattered to me most – *my writings*. For those recordings of life as I saw it felt to me like my most valuable possessions. I had poured my time and thought into each document, and it was only natural that, as more and more of my writing began to be filled with records of Holmes's cases, the box became, by default, primarily dedicated to that purpose.

After an incident or two where we learned that our lodgings weren't as secure as we'd believed, and attempts were made to get at our papers, I came to the conclusion that I would need to relocate my dispatch box to a more secure site. No better place, I thought, than Cox and Company of Charing Cross, a fine institution in general, with that specific branch (at No. 16) long-devoted to addressing the needs of soldiers.

But I had recently retrieved the box, as I regularly did, to add further records to the tightly packed notebooks and tied bundles already contained therein. Having deposited what I needed to, along with sorting and reminiscing about what was already there, I closed the lid, turned the key, and sat back with a sigh.

"It's filling up," Holmes said quietly, a smile in his tone.

I nodded. "Still plenty of room, though," I countered. "If I continue to pack it carefully – it will hold many more narratives of your investigations." I shifted in my seat. "And what about your tin box?" I asked. "How does it fare?"

He glued another clipping into a commonplace book. "There is still room as well. I'm not quite ready to start sorting it and writing my *Whole Art of Detection*. It continues to reside under my bed. I feel that its more esoteric and unexplained contents – as compared to your notes and narratives which specifically describe certain people and events with scalpel-like precision, despite the occasional changed name or place or date – make it somewhat less dangerous if intruded upon."

"Quite. I expect that, should someone once again burgle these rooms, and locate and open the box, they would simply cast aside much of what resides there in frustration. After all, without the stories associated the peg and the ball of string and the rusty discs, or the oversized dried rat paw, those items are meaningless."

"Exactly." He seemed then to be finished, closing the fat and misshapen book before setting it aside and putting the lid on his glue pot. He glanced at the window, and then sniffed.

"From the lack of appetizing aromas drifting up from the kitchen, I suspect that Mrs. Hudson will be serving what remains of the shepherd's pie. I'm rather flush after Colonel Blevins sent a check for that sordid business in Little Venice. What do you say to dinner at Simpson's?"

I leaned forward in my chair, preparatory to standing as my way of answering the question. It was then that doorbell rang, and in a moment, Mrs. Hudson showed in a young lady in her early twenties. *A governess*, I thought. *Not from London. Near-sighted. Recently engaged.* Holmes had taught me well, but I was still the pupil. I would see if his questioning confirmed my initial assumptions.

The young lady sat in the basket chair and began to tell her story, holding out an ancient brass key and a scooping of ash that was found after the most recent visitation of the ghostly founder of the estate where she had been employed for the past quarter. "He's been dead these four-hundred years," she breathlessly explained, "and yet, he appears at my door every night – since I first found the key. He never speaks, but seems to be begging for my help."

Holmes looked at the ash with great interest, pleased to see something new – a surprise that he had not yet encountered or categorized.

My eyes drifted down to the dispatch box beside my chair. The young lady had ignored it – it was just more of the overall clutter that filled the sitting room. It all must be overwhelming to a new visitor – so much of it unique that nothing stood out.

I considered Holmes to be my oldest friend – "*a brother in bond if not in blood*" as we had once been told – but I realized that perhaps the box was perhaps an older friend still. It had been beside me when I set off upon my military career – first to Netley for training, and then sailing to India. Like me, it had been rescued from Maiwand and then sent home. I was no longer an army surgeon, and it was no longer meant for the military. But both of us had found new purposes, and ways that we could serve. That travel-worn tin dispatch box, my old and faithful friend, continued to be the repository of nearly all my most treasured possessions. As I'd told Holmes, the battered box still had room – quite a bit – to hold many more adventures before filling up.

And I felt the same way about myself . . . .

About the Contributors

The following contributors appear in this volume:
The MX Book of New Sherlock Holmes Stories
Part LII: The True Sherlock Mr. Holmes –
England's Greatest Hero (1902-1923)

Tim Newton Anderson is a former senior daily newspaper journalist and PR manager who has recently started writing fiction. In the past six months, he has placed fourteen stories in publications including *Parsec Magazine*, *Tales of the Shadowmen*, *SF Writers Guild*, *Zoetic Press*, *Dark Lane Books*, *Dark Horses Magazine*, *Emanations*, and *Planet Bizarro*.

Brian Belanger, PSI, is a publisher, narrator, graphic designer, editor, and actor. In 2015 he co-founded Belanger Books publishing company along with his brother, author Derrick Belanger. His illustrations have appeared in *The Essential Sherlock Holmes* series, the *MacDougall Twins with Sherlock Holmes* series, and *Scones and Bones on Baker Street*. Brian has published a number of Sherlock Holmes anthologies and novels through Belanger Books, as well as new editions of August Derleth's classic Solar Pons mysteries. Brian continues to design all of the covers for Belanger Books, and from 2016–2023 he designed the majority of book covers for MX Publishing. In 2019, Brian received his investiture in the PSI as "Sir Ronald Duveen". More recently, he created the logo for the *ACD Society* and designed *The Great Game of Sherlock Holmes* card game. In July 2022, he played Sherlock Holmes onstage in "Yes, Virginia, There is a Sherlock Holmes" and "Sherlock Holmes Goes West". Brian has been narrating Belanger Books audio releases since April 2023.
www.belangerbooks.com and
www.redbubble.com/people/zhahadun and
zhahadun.wixsite.com/221b

Derrick Belanger, BSI ("The Board Schools"), PSI ("Albert, the Dove") is an award-winning author, publisher, and educator most noted for his books and lectures on Sherlock Holmes and Sir Arthur Conan Doyle. Derrick is co-owner of the publishing company Belanger Books, which published the first eBook editions of the original Solar Pons books by August Derleth. Derrick's work has been published in *The Baker Street Journal*, *The Sherlock Holmes Journal*, *The Strand Magazine*, and in *The Mysterious Bookshop Presents the Best Mystery Stories of the Year (2023)*. Derrick is a board member of Dr. Watson's Neglected Patients, the Denver-based Scion Society. In January 2020, Mr. Belanger was awarded the Susan Z. Diamond Award in recognition of outstanding efforts to introduce young people to Sherlock Holmes, and in 2024, he won the Arthur Conan Doyle Society Doylean award in fiction for his short story, "The Joyce-Armstrong Confession". Derrick currently resides in Broomfield, Colorado. Find him at:
www.belangerbooks.com

Mike Chinn's first ever Sherlock Holmes fiction was a steampunk mashup of *The Valley of Fear*, entitled *Vallis Timoris* (Fringeworks 2015). Since then he has written about Holmes' archenemy in *The Mammoth Book of the Adventures of Moriarty* (Robinson 2015), appeared in several volumes of *The MX Book of New Sherlock Holmes Stories*, and confronted the retired detective with cross-dimensional magic in the second volume of *Sherlock Holmes and the Occult Detectives* (Belanger Books 2020). He also had a non-Holmes story published in the Lovecraftian anthology *Sherlock & Friends: Eldritch Investigations* (Tule Fog Press, 2024).

Martin Daley was born in Carlisle, Cumbria in 1964. His thirty-year writing career has seen over twenty books and numerous short stories published. Inevitably, Holmes and Watson remain his favourite literary characters, and they continue to inspire his own detective writing. In 2010, Martin created Inspector Cornelius Armstrong, who carries out his police work against the backdrop of Edwardian Carlisle. With the publication of the first *Inspector Armstrong Casebook* (published by MX Publishing), Martin became a member of the Crime Writers' Association. Most recently, he published *The Selected Cases of Sherlock Holmes.* He lives with his wife Wendy, in Kirkcudbrightshire, in Southwest.

Sir Arthur Conan Doyle (1859-1930) *Holmes Chronicler Emeritus.* If not for him, this anthology would not exist. Author, physician, patriot, sportsman, spiritualist, husband and father, and advocate for the oppressed. He is remembered and honored for the purposes of this collection by being the man who introduced Sherlock Holmes to the world. Through fifty-six Holmes short stories, four novels, and additional Apocryphal entries, Doyle revolutionized mystery stories and also greatly influenced and improved police forensic methods and techniques for the betterment of all. *Steel True Blade Straight.*

Steve Emecz's main field is technology, in which he has been working for about thirty years. Steve is a regular speaker at trade shows, and his tech career has taken him to more than seventy countries. In 2008, MX published its first Sherlock Holmes book, and MX has gone on to become the largest specialist Holmes publisher in the world with over 600 books. MX is a social enterprise and supports three main causes. The first is Undershaw, Sir Arthur Conan Doyle's former home, which is a school for children with special educational needs (SEN) that MX has been partnered with for a dozen or so years and raised over $135,000 for. Steve has been a mentor and Advisory Council member for the World Food Programme's Innovation Accelerator (based in Munich) for several years, and was part of the Nobel Peace Prize winning team in 2020. The third is Happy Life, a children's rescue project in Nairobi, Kenya, where he and his wife, Sharon, spent every Christmas at the rescue centre in Kasarani for a decade. They have written two editions of a short book about the project, *The Happy Life Story.*

Mark A. Gagen BSI is co-founder of Wessex Press, sponsor of the popular *From Gillette to Brett* conferences, and publisher of *The Sherlock Holmes Reference Library* and many other fine Sherlockian titles. A life-long Holmes enthusiast, he is a member of *The Baker Street Irregulars* and *The Illustrious Clients of Indianapolis.* A graphic artist by profession, his work is often seen on the covers of *The Baker Street Journal* and various BSI books.

John Atkinson Grimshaw (1836-1893) was born in Leeds, England. His amazing paintings, usually featuring twilight or night scenes illuminated by gas-lamps or moonlight, are easily recognizable, and are often used on the covers of books about The Great Detective to set the mood, as shadowy figures move in the distance through misty mysterious settings and over rain-slicked streets.

Liz Hedgecock grew up in London, England (a train and a tube ride away from Baker Street), did an English degree, and then took forever to start writing. Now Liz travels between the nineteenth and twenty-first centuries, murdering people. To be fair, she does usually clean up after herself. Liz's reimaginings of Sherlock Holmes and her Victorian and contemporary mystery series are available in eBook and paperback. Liz lives in Cheshire with her husband and two sons, and when she's not writing you can usually find her reading, messing about on social media, or cooing over stuff in museums and art galleries. That's her story, anyway, and she's sticking to it.

Paul Hiscock is an author of crime, fantasy, horror, and science fiction tales. His short stories have appeared in a variety of anthologies, and include a seventeenth-century whodunnit, a science fiction western, a clockpunk fairytale, and numerous Sherlock Holmes pastiches. He lives with his family in Kent (England) and spends his days taking care of his two children. You can find out more about Paul's writing at: *www.detectivesanddragons.uk.*

In the year 1998 **Craig Janacek** took his degree of Doctor of Medicine at Vanderbilt University, and proceeded to Stanford to go through the training prescribed for pediatricians in practice. Having completed his studies there, he was duly attached to the University of California, San Francisco as a Professor. The author of over two-hundred medical monographs upon a variety of obscure lesions, his travel-worn and battered tin dispatch-box is crammed with papers, most of which are records of his fictional works. These include several collections of *The Further Adventures of Sherlock Holmes*: *Light in the Darkness, The Gathering Gloom, The Treasury of Sherlock Holmes, The Travels of Sherlock Holmes, The Chronicles of Sherlock Holmes, The Histories of Sherlock Holmes, The Acts of Sherlock Holmes,* and *The Assassination of Sherlock Holmes* – as well as two Dr. Watson novels (*The Isle of Devils* and *The Gate of Gold*), the complete and expanded *Adventures* and *Exploits of Brigadier Gerard* (*Set Europe Shaking* and *A Mighty Shadow*), and two non-Holmes novels (*The Oxford Deception* and *The Anger of Achilles Peterson*). His short stories have been published in several editions of *The MX Book of New Sherlock Holmes Stories, Part I: 1881-1889* (2015), *Part IV: 2016 Annual* (2016), *Part VI: 2017 Annual* (2017), *Part VIII: Eliminate the Impossible* (2017), *Part XI: Some Untold Cases* (2018), *Part XVIII: Whatever Remains Must be the Truth* (2019), *Part XXIII: Some More Untold Cases* (2020), *Part XXV: 2021 Annual* (2021), *Part XXXII: 2022 Annual* (2022), *Part XXXVI: However Improbable . . . .* (2022), and *Part XXXVIII: 2023 Annual* (2023). Other stories have appeared in *Holmes Away From Home: Tales of the Great Hiatus* (2016), *Tales from the Stranger's Room 3* (2017), *Sherlock Holmes: Adventures Beyond the Canon* (2018), *Sherlock Holmes, A Year of Mysteries – 1881* (2021), and *Sherlock Holmes: Stranger than Fiction* (2021). He lives near San Francisco, California with his wife and two children, where he is at work on his next story. Craig Janacek is a *nom-de-plume.*

Roger Johnson, BSI ("The Pall Mall Gazette"), ASH, PSI, etc, is a member of more Holmesian Societies than he can remember, thanks to his eighteen years as editor of *The Sherlock Holmes Journal* - a responsibility he has recently and gratefully passed over to Dr. Mark Jones. Roger founded and for thirty-two years edited *The Sherlock Holmes Society of London*'s newsletter, *The District Messenger*. For six years, it was edited by his wife Jean Upton, ASH, BSI, and is now in the safe hands of Holly Turner. At its 2025 Annual Dinner, Roger was awarded Honorary Membership of *The Sherlock Holmes Society of London.*

Steven Philip Jones has written fiction novels for adults and young adults, comic books, graphic novels, radio scripts, non-fiction, and advertising pieces. His Sherlock Holmes pastiches include the novel *The Adventure of the Coal-Tar Derivative* from MX Publishing and the radio dramas "The Adventure of the Petty Curses" and "A Case of Unfinished Business" for Jim French Productions' *Imagination Theatre*. He currently makes his home with his family in northern Utah.

Susan Knight's newest Mrs. Hudson novel is *Death in the Harem* (October 2024, MX publishing), in which Sherlock Holmes and Dr. Watson enlist their landlady's help in solving a series of murders at the court of the Sultan of Turkey. Susan has written four previous Mrs. Hudson books, starting with a collection of short stories, *Mrs. Hudson Investigates* (2019). This was followed by the novels, *Mrs. Hudson Goes to Ireland* (2020), *Mrs. Hudson Goes to Paris* (2022) and *Death in the Garden of England* (2023). She has also contributed to many recent MX anthologies of new Sherlock Holmes short stories and enjoys writing as Dr. Watson as much as Mrs. Hudson. Nine of these stories have been included in *The Strange Case of the Pale Boy and Other Mysteries* (MX, 2023), and another story, *The Case of the Reluctant Footman*, has been released on Kindle Unlimited as Volume 7 of its *Discoveries* series (2025). She is the author of two other non-Sherlockian story collections, as well as three novels, a book of non-fiction, and several plays, and has won several prizes for her writing. She lives in Dublin, Ireland.

Susan Knight *also has a story in Part LI*

Bonnie MacBird, BSI is the author of six critically acclaimed Sherlock Holmes novels for HarperCollins. They have been translated into fourteen languages and have been praised by *The London Times*, *Washington Post* , and *The Wall Street Journal*. MacBird read her first Sherlock Holmes story at age ten, and has been a fan since then. She's had a forty-year career in entertainment as a studio story editor, a screenwriter, a multiple Emmy winning documentary film producer, and a screenwriting teacher. She's also acted professionally and directs theatre. She lives in London with her husband, computer scientist Alan Kay, where she continues to write, as well as work in theatre.

David Marcum plays *The Game* with deadly seriousness. He first discovered Sherlock Holmes in 1975 at the age of ten, and since that time, he has collected, read, and chronologicized literally thousands of traditional Holmes pastiches in the form of novels, short stories, radio and television episodes, movies and scripts, comics, fan-fiction, and unpublished manuscripts. He is the author of over one-hundred-thirty Sherlockian pastiches, some published in anthologies and magazines such as *The Best Mystery Stories of the Year 2021* and *The Strand*, and others collected in his own books, *The Papers of Sherlock Holmes, Sherlock Holmes and A Quantity of Debt, Sherlock Holmes – Tangled Skeins, Sherlock Holmes and The Eye of Heka*, and *The Collected Papers of Sherlock Holmes* – seven volumes and more to come. He has won back-to-back first place fiction awards from *The Arthur Conan Doyle Society* (2023 and 2024) and from the Nero Wolfe *Wolfe Pack*. He has edited over 1,200 Holmes adventures and one-hundred books, including dozens of traditional Sherlockian anthologies, such as the ongoing series *The MX Book of New Sherlock Holmes Stories*, which he created in 2015 to promote traditional Canonical Holmes. This collection is now finishing at fifty-two volumes. He was responsible for bringing back August Derleth's Solar Pons for a new generation with his collections of authorized Pons stories, *The Papers of Solar Pons* and *The Further Papers of Solar Pons*. Pons's return was further assisted by his editing of the reissued authorized versions of the original Pons books, and then several volumes of new Pons adventures. He has done the same for the adventures of Dr. Thorndyke, and has plans for similar projects in the future. He has contributed numerous essays to various publications, and is a member of a number of Sherlockian groups and Scions, as well as *The Mystery Writers of America*. His irregular Sherlockian blog, *A Seventeen Step Program*, addresses various topics related to his favorite *Book Friends* (as his son used to call them when he was small), and can be found at *http://17stepprogram.blogspot.com/* He is a licensed Civil Engineer, living in

Tennessee with his wife and son. Since the age of nineteen, he has worn a deerstalker as his regular-and-only hat. In 2013, he and his deerstalker were finally able make his first trip-of-a-lifetime Holmes Pilgrimage to England, with return Pilgrimages in 2015, 2016, and 2024, where you may have spotted him. Another Pilgrimage is planned in mid-2025. If you ever run into him and his deerstalker out and about, feel free to say hello!

J. Lawrence Matthews has contributed fiction to *The New York Times* and *NPR*'s *All Things Considered* and is the author of *One Must Tell the Bees: Abraham Lincoln and the Final Education of Sherlock Holmes* (East Dean Press, 2021). The first novel to bring Sherlock Holmes together with Abraham Lincoln during the American Civil War, *One Must Tell the Bees* was called "*beautifully written and immediately engaging*" in the summer journal of *The Sherlock Holmes Society of London*. Matthews is at work on the sequel, which takes Sherlock Holmes to Tibet in 1891 for Holmes's encounter with the 13th Dalai Lama. He resides in Naples, FL, where his favorite breaks from writing are travel, book club meetings with his readers, visits from children and grandchildren, and, when the house gets a little too quiet, playing the drums.

John McNabb is a Welshman and an archaeologist, and a proud member of *The Sherlock Holmes Society of London*. He has published academic analysis of aspects of Conan Doyle's work, as well as its broader context. Mac also has a long-standing interest in Victorian and Edwardian scientific romances and the portrayal of human origins in early science fiction.

Adrian Middleton is a Staffordshire-born independent publisher. The son of a real-world detective, he is a former civil servant and policy adviser who now writes and edits science fiction, fantasy, and a popular series of steampunked Sherlock Holmes stories.

Sidney Paget (1860-1908), a few of whose illustrations are used within this anthology, was born in London, and like his two older brothers, became a famed illustrator and painter. He completed over three-hundred-and-fifty drawings for the Sherlock Holmes stories that were first published in *The Strand* magazine, defining Holmes's image forever after in the public mind.

Orlando Pearson is an accountant. He commutes into London by day and communes with the spirits of Baker Street by night. He was born a short rather than a long shot away from 221b. He is the creator of the series, *The Redacted Sherlock Holmes*, which runs to eight collections of short works, two novels, and a book of plays. A new collection of short works is appearing later this year and a Mycroftian novel will come out in 2026. These accounts of real events were redacted one-hundred or so years ago at the time The Canon was being published. The liberality of modern times means we can now read of Holmes's exposure of the rigging of the home-insurance market, his identification of an alternative claimant for the British throne, and his investigation into someone even better known than himself who rose from the dead. Orlando's profile can be found at:
https://www.amazon.co.uk/Orlando-Pearson/e/B07DWP857S/ref=dp_byline_cont_book_1

A professional author since 2007, **Josh Reynolds** has over thirty novels to his name, as well as numerous short stories, novellas, and audio scripts. Born and raised in South Carolina, he now resides in Sheffield with his wife and daughter, as well as a highly excitable dog and something he hopes is a cat. A complete list of his work can be found at *https://joshuamreynolds.co.uk/*

487

Roger Riccard's family history has Scottish roots, which trace his lineage back to Highland Scotland. This ancestry encouraged his interest in the writings of Sir Arthur Conan Doyle. He has authored the novels, *Sherlock Holmes & The Case of the Poisoned Lilly*, and *Sherlock Holmes & The Case of the Twain Papers,* which was featured at the Museum of London Sherlock Holmes Exhibit in 2015. In addition, he has produced dozens of short stories, and has now joined the Sherlock Holmes 60+ Club, having exceeded Sir Arthur Conan Doyle's number of original Sherlock Holmes stories. All of his books have been published by Baker Street Studios and can be found at his website: *www.sherlockriccard.com* He credits his success to the encouragement of his wife/editor/inspiration and Sherlock Holmes fan, Rosilyn. She passed in 2021, and it is in her memory that he continues to contribute to the legacy of the *"man who never lived and will never die"*.

Dan Rowley practiced law for over forty years in private practice and with a large international corporation. He is retired and lives in Erie, Pennsylvania, with his wife Judy, who puts her artistic eye to his transcription of Watson's manuscripts. He inherited his writing ability and creativity from his children, Jim and Katy, and his love of mysteries from his parents, Jim and Ruth.

Andrew Salmon has won several awards for his Sherlock Holmes stories and has been nominated for the Ellis, Pulp Ark, Pulp Factory and New Pulp Awards. He lives and writes in Vancouver, BC. His novels include: *Fight Card Sherlock Holmes: Work Capitol, Blood to the Bone,* and *A Congression of Pallbearers* (collected in the *Fight Card Sherlock Holmes Omnibus) The Dark Land, The Light Of Men,* and *Ghost Squad: Rise of the Black Legion* (with Ron Fortier) and his first children's book, *Wandering Webber.* His work has also appeared in numerous anthologies covering multiple genres. His tales from the award winning *Sherlock Holmes Consulting Detective* series were collected in *Sherlock Holmes Investigates. Ace of Devils*, the second novel in the Eby Stokes series featuring the female pugilist turned Special Branch agent, is out now and he's working on the third book, as well as a myriad of other projects. To learn more about his work check out: *amazon.com/Andrew-Salmon/e/B002NS5KR0*

Shane Simmons is the author of the occult detective novels *necropolis* and *Epitaph*, and the crime collection *Raw and Other Stories.* An award-winning screenwriter and graphic novelist, his work has appeared in international film festivals, museums, and lectures about design and structure. He was born in Lachine, a suburb of Montreal best known for being massacred in 1689 and having a joke name. Visit Shane's homepage at *eyestrainproductions.com* for more information.

Award winning poet and author **Joseph W. Svec III** enjoys writing, poetry, and stories, and creating new adventures for Holmes and Watson that take them into the worlds of famous literary authors and scientists. His *Missing Authors* trilogy introduced Holmes to Lewis Carroll, Jules Verne, H.G. Wells, and Alfred Lord Tennyson, as well as many of their characters. His transitional story *Sherlock Holmes and the Mystery of the First Unicorn* involved several historical figures, besides a Unicorn or two. He has also written the rhymed and metered Sherlock Holmes Christmas adventure, *The Night Before Christmas in 221b*, sure to be a delight for Sherlock Holmes enthusiasts of all ages. 2024 saw the publication of *Sherlock Holmes for Letter or Verse.* Joseph won the Amador Arts Council 2021 Original Poetry Contest, with his Rhymed and metered story poem, "The Homecoming". Joseph has presented a literary paper on Sherlock Holmes/Alice in

Wonderland crossover literature to the Lewis Carroll Society of North America, as well as given several presentations to the Amador County Holmes Hounds, Sherlockian Society. He is currently working on his first book in the Missing Scientist Trilogy, *Sherlock Holmes and the Adventure of the Demonstrative Dinosaur*, in which Sherlock meets Professor George Edward Challenger. Joseph has Masters Degrees in Systems Engineering and Human Organization Management, and has written numerous technical papers on Aerospace Testing. In addition to writing, Joseph enjoys creating miniature dioramas based on music, literature, and history from many different eras. His dioramas have been featured in magazine articles and many different blogs, including the North American Jules Verne society newsletter. He currently has fifty-seven dioramas set up in his display area, and has written a reference book on toy castles and knights from around the world. An avid tea enthusiast, his tea cabinet contains over five-hundred different varieties, and he delights in sharing afternoon tea with his childhood sweetheart and wonderful wife, who has inspired and coauthored several books with him.

Peter Coe Verbica lives in the redwoods of Northern California. He grew up on Rancho San Felipe, a cattle ranch, where he learned the value of a strong work ethic. He obtained a BA from Santa Clara University, a JD from Santa Clara University School of Law and an MS from the Massachusetts Institute of Technology. Readers can find ten of his short stories in *The MX Book of New Sherlock Holmes Stories* anthologies, edited by David Marcum. These include "The Disfigured Hand", "The Magic Bullet", "The Adventure of the Matched Set", "The Musician Who Spoke from the Grave", "The Dutch Imposters", "A Ghost in the Mirror", "The Deceased Priest", "The King of Spades", "The Hyde Park Blackmailer", and, most recently, "The Ambassador's Dilemma". An additional seven stories, including "The Lucky Strike", "The Mystery of the Five Keys", "The Man Who Didn't Smoke", "The Noble Heart", "The Curious Case of the Bald Prince", "The Lost Uncle", and "Death at Hampton Court" can be found in *The Missing Tales of Sherlock Holmes*. Mr. Verbica is the author of non-fiction articles as well, including "Rise of the Rothschilds: A Legacy of Lessons", featured in *Opportunity Now Silicon Valley*, "We are thinking about . . . Artificial intelligence and trading platforms" featured by Silicon Private Wealth, and "The Divine Leaven of Self-Sacrifice (written in honor of Lenah Sutcliff Higbee)" presented at the Mast Stepping Ceremony of *USS Lenah Sutcliff Higbee* (DDG-123). His free verse works, such as "Small Mound of Stones", "A Visit with Quentin", "Dreams of a Burning Man", "The Locusts", "Visitor 231", "A Thanksgiving Lesson", "Small Miracles", "Brazil", Gold", "Fear of Long Words", "Speak Easy", "Heaven", "The Home Which Dreams", and scores of other pieces appear in various anthologies and books across the globe. The author has also served as moderator and host of a popular speaker series, featuring the former CTO of the US Space Force; Deputy Director of the National Intelligence Agency on cybersecurity; the former US Ambassador to Ukraine on Eurasian security issues; the former US Ambassador to Thailand on US-China relations; a former USN Rear Admiral on the importance of civility in society; an expert on US tax law regarding proposed changes, and other speakers of merit, including the preeminent publisher of Sherlock Holmes-based fiction. Mr. Verbica currently serves as a Managing Director and Principal of Silicon Private Wealth, a Registered Investment Advisor where he helps "clients achieve their dreams through prudent and personalized investment planning." He won a top-two slot in the primary election for Board of Equalization in the State of California. He has served as President, Vice-President, and Chair for numerous non-profit local and statewide non-profit and political organizations' boards. For more information, please visit:
www.peterverbica.com

I.A. Watson has written over fifty Sherlock Holmes stories, and is always surprised that there are still new things for The Great Detective to do, which is a real testament to the genius behind Doyle's most famous creations. His most recent Holmes activities though were in providing extensive notes for a talk about the character in a New York public library, which was quite a different creative challenge. In addition to the novel *Holmes and Houdini*, the anthology *The Incunabulum of Sherlock Holmes*, and the forthcoming *The Paralipomena of Sherlock Holmes*, I.A. Watson has provided entries to all twenty of the *Sherlock Holmes Consulting Detective* books, to about the same number of MX volumes, and another dozen or more in other eccentric places. In his spare time he produces other novels such as *The Death of Persephone*, *The Labours of Hercules*, *The Legend of Robin Hood*, *Women of Myth*, *The Transdimensional Transport Company*, and *Vinnie de Soth, Jobbing Occultist*. It is perhaps not traditional to use an "About the Author" paragraph to offer thanks, but I.A. Watson would like to dedicate this "About the Author" piece to Mr. David Marcum for his astonishing accomplishment with the MX Holmes series, and his tireless enthusiasm as one of the stoutest Holmesians. A full list of I.A. Watson's publications is available at:

http://www.chillwater.org.uk/writing/iawatsonhome.htm

Emma West joined Undershaw in April 2021 as the Director of Education with a brief to ensure that qualifications formed the bedrock of our provision, whilst facilitating a positive balance between academia, pastoral care, and well-being. She quickly took on the role of Acting Headteacher from early summer 2021. Under her leadership, Undershaw has embraced its new name, new vision, and consequently we have seen an exponential increase in demand for places. There is a buzz in the air as we invite prospective students and families through the doors. Emma has overseen a strategic review, re-cemented relationships with Local Authorities, and positioned Undershaw at the helm of SEND education in Surrey and beyond. Undershaw has a wide appeal: Our students present to us with mild to moderate learning needs and therefore may have some very recent memories of poor experiences in their previous schools. Emma's background as a senior leader within the independent school sector has meant she is well-versed in brokering relationships between the key stakeholders, our many interdependences, local businesses, families, and staff, and all this while ensuring Undershaw remains relentlessly child-centric in its approach. Emma's energetic smile and boundless enthusiasm for Undershaw is inspiring.

Ian Ableson is an ecologist by training and a writer by choice. When not reading or writing, he can reliably be found scowling at a clipboard while ankle-deep in a marsh somewhere in Michigan. His love for the stories of Arthur Conan Doyle started when his grandfather gave him a copy of *The Original Illustrated Sherlock Holmes* when he was in high school, and he's proud to have been able to contribute to the continuation of the tales of Sherlock Holmes and Dr. Watson.

Mike Adamson holds a Doctoral degree from Flinders University of South Australia. After early aspirations in art and writing, Mike secured qualifications in both marine biology and

archaeology. Mike has been a university educator since 2006, has worked in the replication of convincing ancient fossils, is a passionate photographer, master-level hobbyist, and journalist for international magazines. Short fiction sales include to *Metastellar, Strand Magazine, Little Blue Marble, Abyss*, and *Apex, Daily Science Fiction, Compelling Science Fiction*, and *Nature Futures*. Mike has placed some two-hundred stories to date, totaling over a million words. Mike has completed his first Sherlock Holmes novel with Belanger Books, and will be appearing in translation in European magazines. You can catch up with his journey at his blog "The View From the Keyboard":
http://mike-adamson.blogspot.com

Tim Newton Anderson *also has a story in Part L*

Hugh Ashton was born in the U.K., and moved to Japan in 1988, where he remained until 2016, living with his wife Yoshiko in the historic city of Kamakura, a little to the south of Yokohama. He and Yoshiko have now moved to Lichfield, a small cathedral city in the Midlands of the U.K., the birthplace of Samuel Johnson, and one-time home of Erasmus Darwin. In the past, he has worked in the technology and financial services industries, which have provided him with material for some of his books set in the 21st century. He currently works as a writer: Novelist, freelance editor, and copywriter, (his work for large Japanese corporations has appeared in international business journals), and journalist, as well as producing industry reports on various aspects of the financial services industry. However, his lifelong interest in Sherlock Holmes has developed into an acclaimed series of adventures featuring the world's most famous detective, written in the style of the originals. In addition to these, he has also published historical and alternate historical novels, short stories, and thrillers. Together with artist Andy Boerger, he has produced the *Sherlock Ferret* series of stories for children, featuring the world's cutest detective.

Deanna Baran lives in a remote part of Texas where cowboys may still be seen in their natural habitat. A librarian and former museum curator, she writes in between cups of tea, playing *Go*, and trading postcards with people around the world.

Donald I. Baxter has practiced medicine for over forty years. He resides in Erie Pennsylvania with his wife and their dog. His family and his friends are for the most part lawyers who have given him the ability to make stuff up just as they do.

Alan Dimes was born in Northwest London and graduated from Sussex University with a BA in English Literature. He has spent most of his working life teaching English. Living in the Czech Republic since 2003, he is now semi-retired and divides his time between Prague and his country cottage. He has also written some fifty stories of horror and fantasy and thirty stories about his husband-and-wife detectives, Peter and Deirdre Creighton, set in the 1930's.

Stuart Douglas is an author, editor, and publisher, and the creator of the Lowe and Le Breton Mysteries. He has written four Sherlock Holmes novels for Titan Books, and contributed stories to the anthologies *Encounters of Sherlock Holmes, Further Associates of Sherlock Holmes*, and *The MX Book of New Sherlock Holmes Stories.* He runs Obverse Books and lives in Edinburgh with his wife, three children, a dog named after Dusty Springfield and cat named after David Bowie.
Follow him on Bluesky: *@stuartdouglas.bsky.social*
and on Instagram: *@stuartamdouglas*

Brett Fawcett is a humanities and Latin teacher at the Chesterton Academy of St. Isidore in Sherwood Park, Alberta. He lives with his wife and son in Edmonton, where he is a member of The Wisteria Lodgers (The Sherlock Holmes Society of Edmonton). He vividly remembers the first time he finished reading the Sherlock Holmes stories in Grade 6, and has been a student of Holmesian literature and scholarship since then. He is also a frequent author of columns and articles on topics like theology, education, and mental health, as well as the occasional mystery story.

Arianna Fox is a triple-published and bestselling author, keynote speaker, actress, professional voiceover talent, award winner, book editor, and public figure whose passion is to motivate, educate, and entertain others through her work. From stories that connect with a modern audience to classically inspired works of literature, one of Arianna's foremost passions has always been writing. An avid Sherlockian and lover of all things Victorian, Arianna disliked reading for years until she read the first few paragraphs of *The Return of Sherlock Holmes* in a bookstore and immediately fell in love with classic literature and the intricate themes woven into its messages. As a whole, Arianna's ultimate goal is to empower others to achieve maximum success and keep their brain-attics well stocked.

Mike Fox is a CEO, entrepreneur, multi-award-winning filmmaker, director, producer, writer, designer, actor, voiceover talent, and all-around versatile creative professional. His professional work is known across the U.S. and has received numerous accolades and awards. As a filmmaker and director, Mike has produced three full-feature films, with over twenty-five Film Festival Awards, including several shorts and many commercials. With a unique flair for suspenseful storytelling, he derives much inspiration from the Sherlock Holmes universe, both of The Canon and adaptations. He was named Alignable's "Business Person of the Year" four years in a row, and has been featured in several news and media outlets, along with a myriad of interviews on podcasts and more. Mike's goal is to impact, empower, and inspire through various forms of media. His professional work is known across the U.S., including having received numerous accolades and awards, including receiving the prestigious Delaware Press Association (DPA) several years in a row. He continues to speak, write, film, and direct to bring quality content to audiences.

Paul D. Gilbert was born in 1954 and has lived in and around London all of his life. His wife Jackie is a Holmes expert who keeps him on the straight and narrow! He has two sons, one of whom now lives in Spain. His interests include literature, ancient history, all religions, most sports, and movies. He is currently employed full-time as a funeral director. His books so far include *The Lost Files of Sherlock Holmes* (2007), *The Chronicles of Sherlock Holmes* (2008), *Sherlock Holmes and the Giant Rat of Sumatra* (2010), *The Annals of Sherlock Holmes* (2012), *Sherlock Holmes and the Unholy Trinity* (2015), *Sherlock Holmes: The Four Handed Game* (2017), *The Illumination of Sherlock Holmes* (2019), *The Treasure of the Poison King* (2021), and *Sherlock Holmes: Tales of Darkness* (2023).

Dick Gillman is an English writer and acrylic artist living in Brittany, France with his wife Alex, Truffle, their Black Labrador, and Jean-Claude, their Breton cat. During his retirement from teaching, he has written over twenty Sherlock Holmes short stories which are published as both e-books and paperbacks. His initial contribution to the superb MX Sherlock Holmes collection, published in October 2015, was entitled "The Man on Westminster Bridge" and had the privilege of being chosen as the anchor story in *The MX Book of New Sherlock Holmes Stories – Part II (1890-1895)*.

John Linwood Grant is a writer and editor who lives in Yorkshire with a pack of lurchers and a beard. He may also have a family. He focuses particularly on dark Victorian and Edwardian fiction, such as his recent novella *A Study in Grey*, which also features Holmes. Current projects include his *Tales of the Last Edwardian* series, about psychic and psychiatric mysteries, and curating a collection of new stories based on the darker side of the British Empire. He has been published in a number of anthologies and magazines, with stories range from madness in early Virginia to questions about the monsters we ourselves might be. He is also co-editor of *Occult Detective Quarterly*. His website *greydogtales.com* explores weird fiction, especially period ones, weird art, and even weirder lurchers.

Arthur Hall was born in Aston, Birmingham, UK, in 1944. He discovered his interest in writing during his schooldays, along with a love of fictional adventure and suspense. His first novel, *Sole Contact*, was an espionage story about an ultra-secret government department known as "Sector Three", and was followed, to date, by three sequels. Other works include seven Sherlock Holmes novels, *The Demon of the Dusk*, *The One Hundred Percent Society*, *The Secret Assassin*, *The Phantom Killer*, *In Pursuit of the Dead*, *The Justice Master*, and *The Experience Club* as well as three collections of Holmes *Further Little-Known Cases of Sherlock Holmes*, *Tales from the Annals of Sherlock* Holmes, *The Additional Investigations of Sherlock Holmes* and *The Hidden Enquiries of Sherlock Holmes.* He has also written other short stories and a modern detective novel. He lives in the West Midlands, United Kingdom.

Paula Hammond has written over sixty fiction and non-fiction books, as well as short stories, comics, poetry, and scripts for educational DVD's. When not glued to the keyboard, she can usually be found prowling round second-hand books shops or hunkered down in a hide, soaking up the joys of the natural world.

James R. Hawkins, BSI writes: "I discovered Sherlock Holmes on my fortieth birthday, in Norman, OK. In high school, in Texas, I mainly read Ernest Hemingway and true-life stories set in exotic locations, like Alaska. I was inordinately interested in Eskimos.
I was born in Jacksboro, Texas, in 1944, the only son of Leon and Ruth Hawkins, owners of Hawkins Funeral Home, and little brother to Linda (1939) and Jane Hawkins (1940). My Dad wanted me to take over the funeral home, but I chose a life in music education, which took me to Oklahoma Baptist University in Shawnee, OK, and to the Eastman School of Music in Rochester, NY. With my vocal chops, I landed a place in The US Army Chorus in Washington, DC, during the Vietnam war, (1969-1973). Married in 1966, my wife and I struck out for Los Angeles to work on a doctorate in music at the University of So. California. From there, we moved to Norman, OK, where I was the music director at 1st Baptist Church in Norman before becoming the Youth, Adult, and Senior Adult Music Consultant for the Southern Baptist Convention in Nashville, TN (1985-1992). In 2001, I switched from music to aviation and joined that highly successful company, Southwest Airlines, where I held various positions, settling into the Flight Attendant job, retiring some sixteen years later in 2017. Since then, my life has revolved around Sherlock Holmes and the men and women who are Sherlockians, devotees of the detective "*who never lived, and so, could never die*". In 2018, I wrote about the man who influenced the most in my Holmes and Watson journey, John Bennett Shaw. The website I built for him caught the attention of many of The Baker Street Irregulars, who honored me with membership in their august body and shared with me the same investiture given to Shaw back in 1965, *The Hans Sloane of My Age*."

Stephen Herczeg is an IT Geek, writer, actor, and film-maker based in Canberra Australia. He has been writing for over twenty years and has completed a couple of dodgy novels, sixteen feature-length screenplays, and numerous short stories and scripts. Stephen was very successful in 2017's International Horror Hotel screenplay competition, with his scripts *TITAN* winning the Sci-Fi category and *Dark are the Woods* placing second in the horror category. His collection, *The Curious Cases of Sherlock Holmes*, is now at four volumes. His work has featured in *Sproutlings – A Compendium of Little Fictions* from Hunter Anthologies, the *Hells Bells* Christmas horror anthology published by the Australasian Horror Writers Association, and the *Below the Stairs, Trickster's Treats, Shades of Santa, Behind the Mask*, and *Beyond the Infinite* anthologies from *OzHorror.Com, The Body Horror Book, Anemone Enemy*, and *Petrified Punks* from Oscillate Wildly Press, and *Sherlock Holmes In the Realms of H.G. Wells* and *Sherlock Holmes: Adventures Beyond the Canon* from Belanger Books.

Christopher James was born in 1975 in Paisley, Scotland. Educated at Newcastle and UEA, he was a winner of the UK's National Poetry Competition in 2008. He has written three full-length Sherlock Holmes novels, *The Adventure of the Ruby Elephant, The Jeweller of Florence*, and *The Adventure of the Beer Barons*, all published by MX.

Steven Philip Jones has written fiction novels for adults and young adults, comic books, graphic novels, radio scripts, non-fiction, and advertising pieces. His Sherlock Holmes pastiches include the novel *The Adventure of the Coal-Tar Derivative* from MX Publishing and the radio dramas "The Adventure of the Petty Curses" and "A Case of Unfinished Business" for Jim French Productions' *Imagination Theatre*. He currently makes his home with his family in northern Utah.

Naching T. Kassa is a wife, mother, and writer. She's created short stories, novellas, poems, and co-created three children. She resides in Eastern Washington State with her husband, Dan Kassa. Naching is a member of *The Horror Writers Association, Mystery Writers of America, The Sound of the Baskervilles, The ACD Society, The Crew of the Barque Lone Star*, and *The Sherlock Holmes Society of London*. She works in Talent Relations at Crystal Lake Publishing and was a recipient of the 2022 HWA Diversity Grant. You can find her work on Amazon.
https://www.amazon.com/Naching-T-Kassa/e/B005ZGHTI0

Susan Knight *also has a story in Part LI*

John Lawrence served for thirty-eight years on personal, committee, and leadership staffs in the U.S. House of Representatives. A visiting professor at the University of California's Washington Center since 2013, he is the author of *The Class of '74: Congress After Watergate and the Roots of Partisanship* (Johns-Hopkins, 2018) and *Arc of Power: Inside the Pelosi Speakership 2005-2010* (Kansas, 2022). His collected "history mystery" Sherlock Holmes pastiches have been published in *The Undiscovered Archives of Sherlock Holmes, The Further Undiscovered Archives of Sherlock Holmes*, in numerous volumes of *The MX Book of New Sherlock Holmes Stories*, and in Belanger Books' *After the East Wind Blows*. His novel, *Sherlock Holmes: The Affair at Mayerling Lodge* was published in 2023. He blogs at DOMEocracy (johnalawrence.wordpress.com). He is a graduate of Oberlin College and has a Ph.D. in history from the University of California (Berkeley).

Gordon Linzner is founder and former editor of *Space and Time Magazine*, and author of four published novels and dozens of short stories in *F&SF, Twilight Zone, Sherlock Holmes*

Mystery Magazine, and numerous other magazines and anthologies. He is a full member of the *Horror Writers Association* and a lifetime member of *Science Fiction and Fantasy Writers Association*.

Steve Lockley is responsible for around 100 short stories and 20 novels, though not all under his own name, including contributions to a couple of Doctor Who anthologies and a novel based on the TV series *Ghost Whisperer*. He has also written several Sherlock Holmes stories, including an appearance in *Encounters of Sherlock Holmes* (Titan Books), and another due to appear in a future issue of *Sherlock Holmes Mystery Magazine*. Steve's work as both writer and editor has been shortlisted several times for British Fantasy Awards. He lives in Swansea and hates writing about himself in the third person.

David MacGregor is a playwright, screenwriter, and novelist. His plays have been performed from New York to Tasmania, and his work has been published by Dramatic Publishing, Playscripts, and Theatrical Rights Worldwide (TRW). He adapted his dark comedy, *Vino Veritas*, into a feature film, and several of his short plays have also been adapted into films. He is the author of three Sherlock Holmes plays: *Sherlock Holmes and the Adventure of the Elusive Ear*, *Sherlock Holmes and the Adventure of the Fallen Soufflé*, and *Sherlock Holmes and the Adventure of the Ghost Machine*. He adapted all three plays into novels for Orange Pip Books, and the novels have also been translated into Italian by Mondadori Publishing. In addition, he wrote the two-volume nonfiction *Sherlock Holmes: The Hero with a Thousand Faces*, which traces the evolution of the character over three centuries. He teaches writing at Wayne State University in Detroit. His website is: *david-macgregor.com*

David Marcum *also has stories in Parts XLIX, L, and LI*

Paul Metcalfe has been a librarian for twenty-eight years, starting in public libraries, but is now the librarian at a technical college in rural Western Australia. He has been a lifelong Holmes fan since reading the original stories aged twelve, and now enjoys many of the later pastiches and Holmesian nonfiction as well. In 2005, he made the semifinals of the ABC television quiz show *The Einstein Factor* with the Sherlock Holmes stories by ACD as his special subject. He thinks Jeremy Brett is the television Holmes *nonpareil*, he collects old books and antiques, and is a strong advocate of the use of graphic novels to encourage reading. This is his first work of fiction.

Mark Mower is a long-standing member of the *Crime Writers' Association*, *The Sherlock Holmes Society of London*, and *The Solar Pons Society of London*. His pastiche collections include *Sherlock Holmes: The Baker Street Case-Files*, *Sherlock Holmes: The Baker Street Legacy*, *Sherlock Holmes: The Baker Street Epilogue*, and *Sherlock Holmes: The Baker Street Archive* (all with MX Publishing). His non-fiction works include the bestselling book *Zeppelin Over Suffolk: The Final Raid of the L48* (Pen & Sword Books). Alongside his writing, Mark maintains a sizeable collection of pastiches, and never tires of discovering new stories about Sherlock Holmes and Dr. Watson.

Will Murray is the author of some 75 novels, including some 20 posthumous Doc Savage collaborations with Lester Dent, and 40 books in the long-running Destroyer series. Other Murray novels star the Executioner, Tarzan of the Apes, The Spider, Pat Savage and the Mars Attacks characters. His book, *Nick Fury, Agent of S.H.I.E.L.D.: Empyre* (2000) foreshadowed the 9/11 terrorist attacks. Murray has penned nearly sixty Sherlock Holmes short stories. Murray's Holmes short stories have been collected as *The Wild Adventures* *of Sherlock Holmes*, Volumes 1 through 4. His novelette, "The Adventure of the Vengeful Viscount", in which Tarzan of the Apes, otherwise Lord Greystoke, hires Sherlock Holmes to solve a mystery, was approved by both the Estate of Sir Arthur Conan Doyle and Edgar Rice Burroughs, Inc. Murray is the author of the non-fiction book, *Master of Mystery: The Rise of The Shadow*, which is an exploration of the famous radio and magazine character, and a sequel, *Dark Avenger: The Strange Saga of The Shadow. The Wild Adventures of Cthulhu* Vols 1 & 2 collect Murray's Lovecraftian short stories. For Marvel Comics, Murray created the Unbeatable Squirrel Girl with legendary artist Steve Ditko. Website: *www.adventuresinbronze.com*

Paul W. Nash is a librarian, bibliographer, and printing historian. He has worked at the Royal Institute of British Architect's Library in London and the Bodleian Library in Oxford, and is currently editor of *The Journal of the Printing Historical Society*. He writes fiction and composes music as a relaxation.

Tracy J. Revels, BSI, a Sherlockian from the age of eleven, is a professor of history at Wofford College in Spartanburg, South Carolina. She is a member of *The Survivors of the Gloria Scott* and *The Studious Scarlets Society*, and is a past recipient of the Beacon Society Award. Almost every semester, she teaches a class that covers The Canon, either to college students or to senior citizens. She is also the author of three supernatural Sherlockian pastiches with MX (*Shadowfall, Shadowblood*, and *Shadowwraith*), and most recently, the three-volume pastiche set, *Tales of Light, Tales of Shadow*, and *Tales of Darkness*. She is a regular contributor to her scion's newsletter. She also has some notoriety as an author of very silly skits: For proof, see "The Adventure of the Adversarial Adventuress" and "Occupy Baker Street" on YouTube. When not studying Sherlock, she can be found researching the history of her native state, and has written books on Florida in the Civil War and on the development of Florida's tourism industry.

Roger Riccard *also has a story in Part XLIX*

Dan Rowley *also has a story in Part LI*

Jane Rubino is the author of *A Jersey Shore* mystery series, featuring a Jane Austen-loving amateur sleuth and a Sherlock Holmes-quoting detective, *Knight Errant, Lady Vernon and Her Daughter*, (a novel-length adaptation of Jane Austen's novella *Lady Susan*, co-authored with her daughter Caitlen Rubino-Bradway, *What Would Austen Do?*, also co-authored with her daughter, a short story in the anthology *Jane Austen Made Me Do It, The Rucastles' Pawn, The Copper Beeches from Violet Turner's POV*, and, of course, there's the Sherlockian novel *Hidden Fires*. Jane lives on a barrier island at the New Jersey shore.

Geri Schear is a novelist and short story writer. Her work has been published in literary journals in the U.S. and Ireland. Her first novel, *A Biased Judgement: The Diaries of Sherlock Holmes 1897* was released to critical acclaim in 2014. The sequel, *Sherlock Holmes and the Other Woman* was published in 2015, and *Return to Reichenbach* in 2016. *Great Warrior* was published in 2024. She lives in Kells, Ireland.

Brenda Seabrooke's stories have appeared in thirty-eight literary magazines, mystery anthologies, and magazines. Twenty books for young readers were published, and then two Sherlock's Dog books. She discovered that she liked writing about the world's greatest consulting detective and mysteries. Two collections of Sherlock Holmes stories were published by MX UK, and her stories have been included in "4 Best Mysteries of New

England" (Level Best Books). She has received a grant from the NEA, a fellowship from Emerson College, and is an MWA runner-up. She has twice judged and once chaired Edgar mystery categories. Brenda is the former president of the Children's Book Guild of DC, a member of AG. *Viva* Holmes and Watson!

Peter Shumway is a retired computer professional residing in Pennsylvania with his wife, Patty. They have been married forty-one years and have two daughters and four grandchildren. In the early 1970's, Peter performed magic with Bill Baker's World of Magic, John Bundy's Magic Concert, and traded secrets with David Copperfield when they were teenagers. Peter read the original Sherlock Holmes stories while in college in 1979, and has enjoyed rereading them many times since. He published his pastiche *Sherlock Holmes and The Kiss of Death in* 2005 and *Gullible's Journey* in 2023. When he was offered the opportunity to write a short story for the MX Series, he picked up his pen yet again.

Shane Simmons *also has a story in Part XLIX*

Robert V. Stapleton was born and brought up in Leeds, Yorkshire, England, and studied at Durham University. After working in various parts of the country as an Anglican parish priest, he is now retired and lives with his wife in North Yorkshire. As a member of his local writing group, he now has time to develop his other life as a writer of adventure stories. He has published a number of short stories, and he is hoping to have a couple of completed novels published at some time in the future.

Kevin Thornton has, by his own count - and remember he's a writer, not an arithmetician – been in seventeen of these volumes, including this one. That's not a bad record, neither near the top nor the bottom, metaphor for his life mayhap. A middling student of English in South Africa, he was taught by two Nobel Literature Laureates to little noticeable effect, and has since been a soldier in Africa, a military contractor in Afghanistan, a forklift driver in Ontario, a bartender everywhere, and a logistician in Northern Alberta, which is, naturally, why he now works as a Communications Consultant for an Indigenous Nation of Cree, Denesuline, and Metis people. It has evolved into a good life, improved immeasurably by a tolerant, beautiful, and loving wife, two sons who smarter than they let on, and a Belgian Malinois with all of the energy of that breed and none of the intelligence. He lives in Northern Alberta, not quite in the North Pole, Santa Claus neighbourhood, but near enough for it to be a local telephone call. He is content.

William Todd has been a Holmes fan his entire life, and credits *The Hound of the Baskervilles* as the impetus for his love of both reading and writing. He began to delve into fan fiction a few years ago when he decided to take a break from writing his usual Victorian/Gothic horror stories. He was surprised how well-received they were, and has tried to put out a couple of Holmes stories a year since then. When not writing, Mr. Todd is a pathology supervisor at a local hospital in Northwestern Pennsylvania. He is the husband of a terrific lady and father to two great kids, one with special needs, so the benefactor of these anthologies is close to his heart.

A Sherlock Holmes fan since reading *The Hound of the Baskervilles* at about age twelve, **Tom Turley** has been writing pastiches since 2006. Most have appeared in previous volumes of *The MX Book of New Sherlock Holmes Stories*. All except the latest three have been collected in two books available from MX Publishing and Amazon. *Sherlock Holmes and the Crowned Heads of Europe* (2021) is a collection of four historical novellas that involve Holmes and Watson in the events leading up to World War I. The four stories are also available individually on Audible. As its title indicates, *Watson's Wives and Other Tales of Sherlock Holmes* (2023) focuses primarily on the Doctor's marriages. It likewise will soon be available on Audible. Currently, Tom is at work on a Sherlockian novel. A retired historian and archivist, he resides with his wife Paula in Montgomery, Alabama.

DJ Tyrer is the person behind Atlantean Publishing and has had fiction featuring Sherlock Holmes published in volumes from MX Publishing and Belanger Books, and an issue of *Awesome Tales*, and has a forthcoming story in *Sherlock Holmes Mystery Magazine*. DJ's non-Sherlockian mysteries can be found in anthologies such as *Mardi Gras Mysteries* (Mystery and Horror LLC) and *The Trench Coat Chronicles* (Celestial Echo Press), and on *Mystery Tribune*.
DJ Tyrer's website is at *https://djtyrer.blogspot.co.uk/*
DJ's Facebook page is at *https://www.facebook.com/DJTyrerwriter/*

I.A. Watson *also has a story in Part L*

Ashley Williford writes: "This is my first Sherlockian publication. I am a devoted Sherlockian and Ravenclaw and a member of my local Sherlockian scion society. *The Giant Rats of Sumatra* in Memphis, Tennessee. I have a hilarious three-year-old boy, Williford "Will" Roney, as well as two goldendoodles, Albus Percival Wulfric Brian Dumbledoodle (eight) and Merlin Aberforth Dumbledoodle (six). I am an Adult-Gerontological Acute Care Nurse Practitioner with a Doctorate in Nursing Practice, and I specialize in critical care. My favorite of my many hobbies include writing Sherlock adventures, hand embroidery, puzzles, games, reading, starting flowers from seeds only to abandon them after sprouting, and listening to absolutely everything Steven Fry narrates."

Marcia Wilson is a freelance researcher and illustrator who likes to work in a style compatible for the color blind and visually impaired. She is Canon-centric, and has written many acclaimed stories about Sherlock Holmes and the Scotland Yard inspectors who knew and worked with him. Long unavailable, nine of these novels will be released by MX Publishing in Spring 2025, with more in preparation.

DeForeest Wright III has a day job as a baker for Ralphs grocery stores. It helps support his love for books. A long-time lover of literature, especially of the Sherlock Holmes tales, he spends his time away from the oven hunched over novels, poetry, anthologies, or any tome on philosophy, mathematics, science, or martial arts he can find, sipping an espresso if one is to hand. He writes prose and poetry in his off hours and currently hosts "The Sunless Sea Open-Mic: Spoken Word and Poetry Show" at the Unurban Coffee House in Santa Monica. He was glad to team up writing with his father.

Sean Wright, BSI makes his home in Santa Clarita, a charming city at the entrance of the high desert in Southern California. For sixteen years, features and articles under his byline appeared in *The Tidings* – now *The Angelus News*, publications of the Roman Catholic Archdiocese of Los Angeles. Continuing his education in 2007, Mr. Wright graduated from Grand Canyon University, attaining a Bachelor of Arts degree in Christian Studies with a *summa cum laude*. He then attained a Master of Arts degree, also in Christian Studies. Once active in the entertainment industry, and in an abortive attempt to revive dramatic radio in 1976 with his beloved mentor, the late Daws Butler, directing, Mr. Wright co-produced and wrote the syndicated *New Radio Adventures of Sherlock Holmes*, starring the late Edward Mulhare as the Great Detective. Mr. Wright has written for several television quiz shows and remains proud of his work for *The Quiz Kid's Challenge* and the popular TV quiz show *Jeopardy!* for which the Academy of Television Arts and Sciences honored him in 1985 with an Emmy nomination in the field of writing. Honored with membership in The Baker Street Irregulars as "The Manor House Case" after founding The Non-Canonical Calabashes, the Sherlock Holmes Society of Los Angeles in 1970, Mr. Wright has written for *The Baker Street Journal* and *Mystery Magazine*. Since 1971, he has conducted lectures on Sherlock Holmes's influence on literature and cinema for libraries, colleges, and private organizations, including MENSA. Mr. Wright's whimsical *Sherlock Holmes Cookbook* (Drake), created with John Farrell, BSI, was published in 1976, and a mystery novel, *Enter the Lion: a Posthumous Memoir of Mycroft Holmes* (Hawthorne), "edited" with Michael Hodel, BSI, followed in 1979. As director general of The Plot Thickens Mystery Company, Mr. Wright originated hosting "mystery parties" in homes, restaurants, and offices, as well as producing and directing the very first "Mystery Train" tours on Amtrak, beginning in 1982.

The MX Book of New Sherlock Holmes Stories

Edited by David Marcum

(MX Publishing, 2015-2025)

"This is the finest volume of Sherlockian fiction I have ever read, and I have read, literally, thousands." – Philip K. Jones

"Beyond Impressive . . . This is a splendid venture for a great cause!"
– Roger Johnson, Editor, *The Sherlock Holmes Journal*,
The Sherlock Holmes Society of London

Part I: 1881-1889; Part II: 1890-1895; Part III: 1896-1929

Part IV: 2016 Annual

Part V: Christmas Adventures

Part VI: 2017 Annual

Eliminate the Impossible
Part VII: (1880-1891); Part VIII: (1892-1905)

2018 Annual
Part IX: (1879-1895); Part X: (1896-1916)

Some Untold Cases
Part XI: (1880-1891); Part XII: (1894-1902)

2019 Annual
Part XIII: (1881-1890); Part XIV: (1891-1897); Part XV: (1898-1917)

Whatever Remains . . . Must be the Truth
Part XVI: (1881-1890); Part XVII: (1891-1898); Part XVIII: (1898-1925)

2020 Annual
Part XIX: (1882-1890); Part XX: (1891-1897); Part XXI: (1898-1923) ·

Some More Untold Cases
Part XXII: (1877-1887); Part XXIII: (1888-1894); Part XXIV: (1895-1903)

2021 Annual
Part XXV: (1881-1888); Part XXVI: (1889-1897); Part XXVII: (1898-1928)

More Christmas Adventures
Part XXVIII: (1869-1888); Part XXIX: (1889-1896); Part XXX: (1897-1928)

2022 Annual
Part XXXI: (1875-1887); Part XXXII: (1888-1895); Part XXXIII: (1896-1919)

"However Improbable . . . ."
Part XXXIV: (1878-1888); Part XXXV: (1889-1896); Part XXXVI: (1897-1919)

2023 Annual
Parts XXXVII (1875-1889), XXXVIII (1889-1896), and XXXIX (1897-1923)

Further Untold Cases
Part XL: (1879-1886), Part XLI: (1887-1892) and Part XLII: (1894-1922)

2024 Annual
Parts XLIII (1874-1888), XLIV (1889-1897), and XLV (1898-1917)

Occupants of the Canonical Realm
Parts XLVI (1861-1889), XLVII (1890-1898), and XLVIII (1899-1924)

The True Mr. Holmes: England's Greatest Hero
Parts XLIX and L (18XX-18XX) and (18XX-19XX)

The MX Book of New Sherlock Holmes Stories
Edited by David Marcum
(MX Publishing, 2015-2025)

Part VI: *The traditional pastiche is alive and well . . . .*

Part VII: *Sherlockians eager for faithful-to-the-canon plots and characters will be delighted.*

Part VIII: *The imagination of the contributors in coming up with variations on the volume's theme is matched by their ingenious resolutions.*

Part IX: *The 18 stories . . . will satisfy fans of Conan Doyle's originals. Sherlockians will rejoice that more volumes are on the way.*

Part X: *. . . new Sherlock Holmes adventures of consistently high quality.*

Part XI: *. . . an essential volume for Sherlock Holmes fans.*

Part XII: *. . . continues to amaze with the number of high-quality pastiches.*

Part XIII: *. . . Amazingly, Marcum has found 22 superb pastiches . . . his is more catnip for fans of stories faithful to Conan Doyle's original*

Part XIV: *. . . this standout anthology of 21 short stories written in the spirit of Conan Doyle's originals.*

Part XV: *Stories pitting Sherlock Holmes against seemingly supernatural phenomena highlight Marcum's 15th anthology of superior short pastiches.*

Part XVI: *Marcum has once again done fans of Conan Doyle's originals a service.*

Part XVII: *This is yet another impressive array of new but traditional Holmes stories.*

Part XVIII: *Sherlockians will again be grateful to Marcum and MX for high-quality new Holmes tales.*

Part XIX: *Inventive plots and intriguing explorations of aspects of Dr. Watson's life and beliefs lift the 24 pastiches in Marcum's impressive 19th Sherlock Holmes anthology*

Part XX: *Marcum's reserve of high-quality new Holmes exploits seems endless.*

Part XXI: *This is another must-have for Sherlockians.*

Part XXII: *Marcum's superlative 22nd Sherlock Holmes pastiche anthology features 21 short stories that successfully emulate the spirit of Conan Doyle's originals while expanding on the canon's tantalizing references to mysteries Dr. Watson never got around to chronicling.*

Part XXIII: *Marcum's well of talented authors able to mimic the feel of The Canon seems bottomless.*

Part XXIV: *Marcum's expertise at selecting high-quality pastiches remains impressive.*

Part XXVIII: *All entries adhere to the spirit, language, and characterizations of Conan Doyle's originals, evincing the deep pool of talent Marcum has access to. Against the odds, this series remains strong, hundreds of stories in.*

Part XXXI: *. . . yet another stellar anthology of 21 short pastiches that effectively mimic the originals . . . Marcum's diligent searches for high-quality stories has again paid off for Sherlockians.*

Part XXXIV: *Mind-bending puzzles are the highlight of Marcum's fully satisfying 34th anthology, which again demonstrates that multiple authors are capable of giving Sherlock Holmes and Watson innovative mysteries to tackle while staying in character. Marcum's inventory of canonical pastiches shows no signs of being exhausted any time soon.*

503

An Investees' Anthology
Edited by David Marcum
(MX Publishing, 2022)

Selected Contributions to
The MX Book of New Sherlock Holmes Stories
by Members of
The Baker Street Irregulars

*All royalties from this collection are being donated
for the benefit of the preservation of Undershaw,
a school for special needs students located at
one of the former homes of Sir Arthur Conan Doyle*

Stories, Forewords, and Poems in this volume
have previously appeared in Parts I – XXXVI of
The MX Book of New Sherlock Holmes Stories

Featuring Contributions by:

Mark Alberstat, Marino C. Alvarez, Peter Calamai, Catherine Cooke, Carla Coupe, David Stuart Davies, John Farrell, Lyndsay Faye, Sonia Fetherston, Jayantika Ganguly, Jeffrey Hatcher, Roger Johnson, Leslie S. Klinger, Ann Margaret Lewis, Bonnie MacBird, Stephen Mason, Julie McKuras Nicholas Meyer, Jacquelynn Morris, Otto Penzler, Christopher Redmond, Tracy J. Revels, Steven Rothman, Nancy Holder, Mark Levy (and Arlene Mantin Levy), Nicholas Utechin, and Sean M. Wright (and DeForeest B. Wright, III)

MX Publishing

MX Publishing is the world's largest specialist Sherlock Holmes publisher, with over six-hundred titles and over two-hundred authors creating the latest in Sherlock Holmes fiction and non-fiction

The catalogue includes several award winning books, and over four-hundred-and-fifty have been converted into audio.

MX Publishing also has one of the largest communities of Holmes fans on Facebook, with regular contributions from dozens of authors.

www.mxpublishing.com

@mxpublishing on Facebook, Twitter, and Instagram

www.ingramcontent.com/pod-product-compliance
Lightning Source LLC
Chambersburg PA
CBHW032255020726
47495CB00001B/110